Praise for *Fox on the Rhine* and *Fox at the Front*

"The authors' attention to military detail and maneuvers would satisfy any drill instructor, and they imbue even minor historical characters with authenticity and personality, demonstrating how an individual's actions and reactions shape history. This is a thoroughly plausible what-if scenario, and as such will please and titillate alternate-history fans, WWII buffs, war gamers and others."   —*Publishers Weekly* on *Fox at the Front*

"Outstanding . . . must-reading for imaginative WWII buffs."   —*Booklist* on *Fox at the Front*

"For people who love history, written by people who know it well."   —Larry Bond, *New York Times* bestselling author

"An intriguing what-if scenario, and one that could have happened . . . Not since *SS-GB*, by Len Deighton, have I seen a more credible conclusion to WWII . . . the book is a triumph!"
      —Walter J. Boyne, *New York Times* bestselling author

"A colossal epic of a World War II that might have been . . . A real page-turner!"
      —Frank Chadwick, *New York Times* bestselling author

MACARTHUR'S WAR

A NOVEL OF THE INVASION OF JAPAN

DOUGLAS NILES

AND

MICHAEL DOBSON

A TOM DOHERTY ASSOCIATES BOOK
NEW YORK

This is a work of fiction. All of the characters, organizations, and events portrayed in this novel are either products of the authors' imagination or are used fictitiously.

MACARTHUR'S WAR: A NOVEL OF THE INVASION OF JAPAN

Copyright © 2007 by Douglas Niles and Michael Dobson

All rights reserved.

A Forge Book
Published by Tom Doherty Associates, LLC
175 Fifth Avenue
New York, NY 10010

www.tor-forge.com

Forge® is a registered trademark of Tom Doherty Associates, LLC.

ISBN-13: 978-0-7653-5142-5
ISBN-10: 0-7653-5142-0

First Edition: May 2007
First Mass Market Edition: July 2008

Printed in the United States of America

0 9 8 7 6 5 4 3 2 1

MACARTHUR'S
WAR

PROLOGUE

The Atlantic Monthly   Vol. 251, No. 6, June 1964 issue

Would the United States Have Used the Atomic Bomb Against Japan?

If the "Manhattan Project" had succeeded, the United States would have been the first nation with the A-bomb. Would we have used it to end World War II instead of launching General MacArthur's massive invasion? Would it have worked? What would the consequences have been?

The threat of atomic war was eliminated officially when the Geneva Convention of 1963 outlawed all nuclear weapons. Although no A-bomb had ever been used in war, the threat of massive "city-busting" attacks against civilians was so unthinkable that negotiators from all the Great Powers, including the USSR, agreed to ban these weapons.

It was 1956 when the Soviet Union detonated the first atomic bomb in the Siberian wastes, but we have only recently learned that the Russians were significantly aided by secrets stolen by spies from the ill-fated American laboratory in Los Alamos, New Mexico. . . .

• TUESDAY, 9 JUNE 1942 •

HIROSHIMA, JAPAN, 1115 HOURS

Ogawa Michiyo was seventeen today, and her father had given her ten yen to spend in one of Hiroshima's thriving outdoor markets. She had come to her favorite place, the square before the magnificent Aioi Bridge over the River Ota, to wander among the stalls. It was a beautiful day, warm enough for summer but still as green and lush as new spring. She looked at flowers, thought about a bit of sushi and rice, watched a vendor carve up an octopus, and gazed longingly at some startlingly vivid bolts of silk. She would have loved one of the latter, but they were too expensive, and besides, she was having too much fun browsing to stop and spend her money.

She glanced at the newspaper—the *Asahi Shimbun* was the most popular news source in Japan—to see a large, screaming headline.

COMBINED FLEET SINKS THREE AMERICAN CARRIERS AT MIDWAY ISLAND

The story was full of announcements about a huge sea and air battle somewhere off near Hawaii, but Michiyo was more interested in the activity in this vibrant marketplace than she was in the story. For now she left the paper in its stand. Before she went back home she would buy one for Papa, who could never get enough news about the war, but first she intended to enjoy the sights, sounds, smells, and tastes of this lively center of commerce.

Even as she breezily wandered, though, she sensed that there was something different about the recent battle. Men were speaking about it in unusually loud tones, some talking nonsense about invasions of Hawaii and California, others singing the praises of the Emperor and Admiral Yamamoto. Michiyo wondered why a victory was such big news. After all, Japan had won *all* the battles in this war! She had heard of the great Yamamoto-san, of course: he was the genius who had masterminded the attack on Pearl Harbor half a year earlier, and led the Imperial Japanese Navy across the whole of the vast Pacific, but those were all details about places that were very far away.

The market, on the other hand, was right here! She stopped to smell some chrysanthemums, surprised as always by the sour smell of such a sweet-looking blossom. On impulse she bought one to wear in her long, black hair. She was right at the bank of the river now, and she contemplated the surging power of the Ota, the blue-gray waters spilling from the mountains, hurrying toward the sea. It had always been so, even before the mighty bridge had been built. The river, like the Japanese Empire itself, was eternal.

She came to a vegetable vendor who was lining up beautiful cucumbers, radishes, and yams on his tray. When a young soldier came up, she moved to the side, glancing up at him—and then staring with a start of recognition.

Naguro Yoshi! He was her brother Taiki's friend, some five years older than her, and she hadn't since him since before the start of the war. An instinctive shyness held her tongue as she tried not to stare. Yoshi was inspecting the cucumbers very seriously, but she sensed that he would soon walk away. Could she be bold enough to speak to him?

Perhaps he would have news of Taiki! That was reason enough to free her tongue.

"Yoshi?" she said softly.

He turned to look at her, and she was prepared to explain how she knew him when he gladdened her heart by recognizing her and crying in delight, "Michiyo! Ogawa Michiyo! How are you?"

"I am well," she replied, thinking that he looked very splendid in his uniform. "And how are you?"

His face fell. "The army is sending me to school," he said. "In Tokyo. By the time I get my commission, this war will be over—and I will have missed it!"

"I am sure you will have a chance to fight!" she declared, surprising herself—and Yoshi—with her vehemence.

"Thank you for your confidence," he said sincerely.

"Tell me—have you heard anything of Taiki?" she asked.

"Yes. He is being called a hero for his actions leading his platoon in Malaya. His men were among the first into Singapore! And he was promoted to captain, you probably know. He commands a company of veteran infantry. I saw him briefly in Manila, before they sent him to Rabaul." Yoshi smiled. "He will make your father proud, too—he carries your family sword with him everywhere, does Taiki."

"Yes, the cupboard in Papa's study looks so empty with it gone. I hope the war ends and he comes back soon—" She caught herself. "But not before you get to lead your own men in battle!" she amended.

"Thanks for the thought," Yoshi said, again wistful.

Michiyo was embarrassed, sure she had hurt his feelings. "It was nice to see you," she said, bowing her head politely, feeling immense sympathy for him.

"And you, too!" he said brightly. "*Very* nice. Please—give your father and mother my regards."

"I will do that," she said.

His words, his obvious happiness at their chance meeting, heightened her celebratory mood. As she made her way along the bank of the river, she seemed to float over the ground, moving as lightly, as naturally, as the waters of the Ota making their way to the sea.

1942

I Shall Return

Dugout Doug MacArthur lies a-shakin' on the Rock
Safe from all the bombers and from any sudden shock
Dugout Doug is eating of the best food on Bataan
And his troops go starving on . . .

Dugout Doug, come out from hiding
Dugout Doug, come out from hiding
Send to Franklin the glad tidings
That his troops go starving on!

    —Sung by American infantrymen on Bataan
       to the tune of "The Battle Hymn of the Republic"

ONE

Hawaii

HICKAM FIELD, PEARL HARBOR, HAWAII, 1310 HOURS

The four-engine Douglas C-54 Skymaster transport plane emerged from the blazing tropical air, and for a brief instant it looked to the spy as if the plane was towing the sun across the sky like Apollo's chariot. The spy, who was posing as a reporter, listened to his supposed peers.

One of the assembled photographers started to lift his camera but gave it up as hopeless. "That's gotta be Mac's plane," he said, shaking his head.

A reporter standing next to him gave a single dry cough of a laugh. They had all been standing on the hot tarmac for nearly an hour. "You know the difference between Douglas MacArthur and God?"

"Naw. What?"

The reporter took another drag on his cigarette. "God doesn't think he's Douglas MacArthur."

There wasn't much laughter. Most of the press had long since heard that one, or some variation, and there wasn't much energy left for laughing, anyway. The regular afternoon rain shower hadn't come yet, and the normal flower-scented Hawaiian breeze had been hijacked by avgas and asphalt.

The C-54 descended, flying in a great circle over the harbor. The reporters and photographers, casual and friendly for the long and boring wait, now jockeyed and pushed for position. Notebooks and pens came out. Cigarettes were hastily finished and butts ground underfoot.

The spy stubbed out his cigarette and took out a notepad, too. He, too, was curious, though for different reasons.

"It's showtime," said the reporter who had compared MacArthur and God.

General Douglas MacArthur—*the* General to the people who worked for him and who had known him longest— looked through the windblasted and scratched port of the C-54. His chief of staff, General Richard Kerens Sutherland, sat across the aisle. The remaining passengers, all members of the "Bataan Gang," as MacArthur's inner circle was known, sat farther back.

"There's the *Arizona*," the General said, pointing. He spoke slowly, pensively. Sutherland could barely get a glimpse of the twisted hull and shattered deck of the battleship still resting on the muddy bottom of Pearl Harbor.

"You know, Dick," MacArthur continued, "the men of Bataan were the only Americans who put up any sort of a decent fight against the Japanese, the only ones who slowed the Rising Sun during these terrible months. The men of Pearl Harbor were brave, perhaps *as* brave, but their battle lasted only an hour, and they had no success to show for their tragedy.

"The men of Bataan delayed the enemy's advance for five months—and their suffering has yet to reach its end. Every day they suffer, MacArthur suffers with them."

"I know, General." Dick Sutherland nodded consolingly. As the plane leveled out for the landing approach, he walked to the back of the plane where a hook was fastened to the bulkhead. It held a coat hanger with MacArthur's uniform jacket on it. Row after row of medals and ribbons were perfectly in place. Sutherland cradled the General's barracks cap, old, faded, limp, in his other hand and carried both up the aisle to the waiting MacArthur.

MacArthur's eyes scanned the rows of ribbons. "My Mexican Service Ribbon is missing. Where's my Mexican Service Ribbon?" he demanded. "Dammit, Dick, I can't go out in public with my Mexican Service Ribbon missing!"

Even on a nine-row ribbon bar, the gap made by the missing ribbon was obvious. Sutherland blanched. Normally the duty of fetching the General's jacket and making sure his ribbons were in order would have been performed by an aide-de-camp, but Sutherland rarely gave away a moment of face-to-face time with the boss. He was going to be the Indispensable Man at all times, no matter what it took. "General, I made personally sure all the decorations were here. Give me one minute, sir." Sutherland began looking wildly around.

"Dick, Douglas MacArthur must have his Mexican Service Ribbon, do you understand?"

"Yes, sir. Absolutely."

Sutherland looked around frantically, then started moving toward the rear of the Skymaster. "The General's jacket is missing his Mexican Service Ribbon," he announced.

Everyone stopped what he was doing to help in the search. It was Willoughby—it had to be Willoughby, Sutherland's rival—who found it. "I've found it, General!" he announced loudly to MacArthur, rather than giving it to Sutherland. Willoughby's accent was German.

"Good man, Sir Charles," came MacArthur's sonorous voice. "MacArthur is grateful."

Sutherland's eyes narrowed. *I bet the bastard stole it in the first place.*

With a smug grin, Willoughby gave the green, blue, and gold ribbon to Sutherland, who trotted it back to MacArthur and quickly slid the missing ribbon back onto the ribbon bar, ears burning all the while.

As the passengers belted themselves in for landing, MacArthur took one last look out of the scratched and milky window. Far below, the *Arizona* rested in her watery grave.

As the Skymaster touched down on the long bomber runway at Hickam Field, the reporters started jostling again. The photographers in the front rank crouched on one or both knees, some snapping telephoto shots of the nose art: the word *Bataan* painted in large letters. That wasn't the name of this particular Skymaster. It was the name of *any* aircraft carrying Douglas MacArthur.

The transport taxied past the roped press area and swung around again, slowing. The immense roar of the four Pratt & Whitney engines drowned out all other island sounds as the flight line captain waved the C-54 to its designated parking spot and signaled "Cut." The engine noise began to die down as other ground personnel chocked the wheels. The army honor guard and the band both lined up.

The honor guard snapped to attention as the Skymaster's main door swung open. Two corporals quickly wheeled a mobile staircase in front of the door.

There was a pause.

An impeccably uniformed figure appeared in the entrance, haloed in black, sunlight glistening from mirrored sunglasses, rows upon rows of ribbons, every surface polished, every crease in place in spite of the long air journey. Only one note jarred: his old, worn barracks cap, grommet removed, thick with gold braid sported by no other officer in the United States military.

In the shadows he looked a bit like an old man, but when he stepped into the sunlight he seemed much younger, as handsome as a movie star.

MacArthur accepted the salutes of the welcoming troops, and the military band struck up a march. The General gave a firm salute in return, captured by twenty cameras. He then stepped forward to shake the hands of the welcoming party, which was led by a three-star U.S. Army general, Delos C. Emmons. MacArthur didn't know him well, but he was important to the plan.

Lieutenant General Delos C. Emmons was military governor of Hawaii and commander, United States Army Forces, Central Pacific Area. Emmons didn't work for Douglas MacArthur. MacArthur was CINCSWPA, commander in chief, Southwest Pacific Area. Emmons worked for CINCPOA, commander in chief, Pacific Ocean Areas. CINCPOA was Admiral Chester Nimitz.

Hawaii belonged to Nimitz.

This was the split command in the Pacific: two top dogs and one ocean that looked like it wasn't big enough for the both of them.

There wasn't a uniformed naval officer or a marine in sight. As far as the navy was concerned, MacArthur, traveling unofficially and out of his area of authority, was not here.

But he was. And he was in the process of invading Hawaii.

A colonel stepped forward, saluted crisply, and made the introductions. General Emmons saluted.

MacArthur reciprocated, then reached out to shake his hand. "Thank you for this warm welcome. You do this honor not merely for General MacArthur but also for the brave men languishing in Japanese captivity."

"It is indeed an honor, sir. I have a car waiting, if you would care to ride."

"Splendid. Splendid," the General said with a nod, preceding Emmons past the row of hungry reporters.

"General MacArthur! General MacArthur! Is it true that the Japs are planning to invade Hawaii?"

"I'm sorry. The General doesn't have time to answer questions today." Sutherland, at his commander's elbow, spoke brusquely.

"Oh, I believe the General may have time for one or two, just possibly." MacArthur offered a magnanimous wave of his hand. Sutherland looked quite frustrated.

MacArthur pointed at the man who'd shouted the question. "You, sir. You ask if the Japanese are now readying an attack on the Hawaiian Islands?"

"Um, yes. Yes, General, that's right."

"Let us look carefully at the facts. You're with the *Star-Bulletin,* if I recall correctly?"

"Yes, sir," the man replied. The spy noticed how impressed the reporter was at being remembered. And it was impressive of MacArthur to remember that much detail—that is, unless this was some kind of MacArthur trick.

"May I ask what the headline of your newspaper said on the eighth of June?"

"Uh, I think it was 'Defeat at Midway.'"

"What did the other newspaper headlines say?" MacArthur prompted.

"Well, pretty much the same thing," the reporter admitted.

MacArthur smiled triumphantly. "Several American carriers sunk, with only one Japanese carrier joining them. Correct?"

"Uh, yes, sir," the reporter acknowledged.

"And would Admiral Yamamoto know this as well, even though he's not a subscriber to your fine newspaper?"

A voice rang out in the back of the crowd: "How do you know he isn't?" Everyone laughed, including MacArthur briefly, but the spy suspected that underneath the mirrored sunglasses MacArthur's eyes had not smiled at all.

When the laugh died down, MacArthur repeated, "Even if Admiral Yamamoto doesn't have the advantage, as do I, of the fine information with which you supply your readers, do you think he knows the outcome as well as you or I?"

"Yes, sir," the reporter said.

MacArthur swooped in for the kill. "If you were Admiral Yamamoto, and after the cruel assault of December seventh and our recent loss at Midway, you had the opportunity to land troops on one of these beautiful Hawaiian Islands, islands America has taken into its sacred trust, and take its bountiful riches for your own, what would you do? And if your thoughts run in the same vein as my own, what would you then recommend MacArthur do?"

The reporter had to take a second to parse the question. "Well, I guess I would—"

MacArthur smiled as his mirrored eyes scanned the assembly, then interrupted. "Exactly. I'm afraid it doesn't take someone with MacArthur's grasp of matters military to see the risk that exists here, or to see why immediate and direct action is necessary. For all that the Pacific has been divided administratively into areas for the purpose of offense, clearly when it comes to defense, and especially the defense of these islands so close to our heart and our mainland, our aim should be cooperation. Cooperation! MacArthur is here to put his sword at your service, Hawaii! Together we will repulse the threat from the East, and together we will triumph against adversity. Thank you."

His sonorous voice, rich with an old-fashioned type of elegance, left some reporters rapt and others shaking their heads in skeptical disbelief. All of them, however, were scribbling furiously. The General finally turned to leave.

"General MacArthur! General MacArthur! Will you meet with Admiral Nimitz?"

"I'm sorry. The General really must move along now," Sutherland interjected. MacArthur, having said what he wanted to say, allowed himself to be escorted toward the waiting car.

The remaining members of the Bataan Gang formed themselves into a flying phalanx, like Roman lictors ready to lead their emperor through hostile streets.

The questions were falling like flak as the party moved out, but MacArthur, moving with majesty, ignored them with smiling graciousness.

Until one reached its target. "General! General! What about the Philippines? What about your men?"

Sutherland turned, glowering. "The General really must . . ."

"I—" The General paused, turned back toward the reporters. The focus of his mirrored eyes could not be determined. Finally he spoke.

"I promised the people of the Philippines, 'I shall return,' and I, Douglas MacArthur, shall keep that promise, with the help of God and with the American fighting man at my side. And as for my brave fighting men captured on Bataan, I pray for them nightly, and will deliver them when"—he paused—"when I can."

He turned.

"Will you see Admiral Nimitz?"

"The General really must move along now."

"What about Admiral Nimitz?"

"Move along now."

"What do you think went wrong at Midway?"

"Move along."

The spy was Captain Frank Chadwick, United States Navy. He was wearing civilian clothes to pose as a reporter. He wasn't well enough known to worry about being found out. Everyone who knew him mostly knew him for his cherry-red 1932 MG Midget, the joy of his life. The fake reporter put away his notebook and lit a Chesterfield. He stared at the reporter who asked the last question. *What would an* army *officer know about Midway, anyway? But that wouldn't stop Mac from spouting off on the subject. He probably does think he's God.*

THURSDAY, 11 JUNE 1942

One component of leadership is fearlessness in the face of one's opponent. Not foolhardiness, but fearlessness. One must always see the danger, but one must not surrender to it.

Knock-knock.

It was the white-coated Filipino butler. "General MacArthur? You asked to be notified, sir, if any communication was received from CINCPAC. There is a gentleman at the door in civilian clothes who says he is Captain Frank Chadwick, personal aide to Admiral Nimitz. He wishes to speak with you privately, sir, on a matter of great importance, he says."

MacArthur stubbed out his cigar. "The parlor is set up as I asked?"

"Yes, sir."

"Coffee in three minutes."

"Piping hot, sir."

"Good man. Show him in. Dick, Sir Charles, follow me. The rest of you, stay here. Get a little fresh air. You're going to suffocate." He blew out one final breath of blue smoke and strode from the room.

Captain Frank Chadwick's military bearing was obvious in spite of his civilian clothing. "I'm Admiral Nimitz's personal aide," he said, accepting an offer of coffee. "The admiral asks you not to be offended that a mere captain comes as his representative instead of coming in person himself. But the conditions of this visit, the General understands, make normal protocol impossible."

MacArthur occupied his straight-backed chair like a throne. He nodded regally. "That's completely understandable, and I'm sure the admiral does the Southwest Pacific Area great honor by choosing a man as intelligent and subtle as you. That *was* you standing among the reporters yesterday at the airfield, was it not?"

Chadwick chuckled, impressed. "Why, yes, sir. I'm amazed you noticed, sir."

MacArthur smiled. "Admiral Nimitz, a man of wisdom and skill, could not possibly have failed to have his own eyes and ears on hand to witness the arrival of Douglas MacArthur in Hawaii. As wearing the uniform of another service would be unthinkable, it was necessary for Nimitz's agent to wear mufti. It was easy then to find the Reporter Who Was Not. In your case, he was not taking notes. And he looked askance, rather than with jealousy, at his comrades when they asked particularly inane questions."

Chadwick laughed. "Ouch! Sir," he added quickly. "I'm embarrassed to have been that obvious, sir."

MacArthur waved his hand nonchalantly. "I think you would have passed muster for most observers," he purred. "You *slouched* like a civilian."

This last made Chadwick straighten unconsciously. *He's trying to shake me up.* His next thought: *He's succeeding.*

"The admiral would like to know why you are in Hawaii, out of your assigned area, without notifying him privately of your intentions. He would like to know why you tipped off the press about your visit only days after blasting the navy's performance at Midway. He would like to know what you are trying to achieve with your current behavior." Chadwick delivered his message all in a lump, unable to think of a smooth way to slip it into the conversation, especially with this man controlling the initiative. He looked at MacArthur to see how he would take it.

MacArthur stared coldly at him, waited. "Sir," added Chadwick.

There was a long pause.

MacArthur's eyes never left Chadwick as he crooked a finger. At his signal, General Sutherland clicked open a briefcase, pulled out the first sheet of paper without looking at it, and slid it across the coffee table to Chadwick. "Here is a copy of the radiogram, CINCSWPA to CINCPOA, informing the admiral of General MacArthur's plans. If it was not received or delivered to the admiral, the problem does not lie with CINCSWPA," Sutherland announced in his gruff, argumentative voice.

Chadwick glanced down at it. It was a clean copy of a radiogram, code-numbered and in proper format. Without doing any investigation, he was sure the numbers would check. And he was equally sure after the way the radiogram was presented that it was a counterfeit, a fraud manufactured on MacArthur's orders.

MacArthur spoke again. "To your second point: 'tipping off' the press. We have done nothing of the sort. How reporters discover such things is a mystery. This being Hawaii, have you considered the possibility the information came from someone in your own organization?"

That Mac hadn't done it was also a lie. Oh, perhaps there were numerous cutouts and go-betweens, and perhaps the connection to MacArthur was ultimately unprovable, but he had done it.

"Point three: criticize the navy for its handling of Midway. To that, I plead guilty as charged. I must point out, however, that I do not detect nor am I aware of any navy regulations or policies forbidding criticism of MacArthur's military operations, whether such criticisms hew to the facts of the situation or if necessary falsify the record in order to attain their predetermined conclusions. We, at least, refrain from the latter tactic, though the ancient principle of 'an eye for an eye' would surely entitle us to do so. But lest you think we are dwelling on some petty need for revenge, I say no. Not for Douglas MacArthur. My sole, complete, and absolute interest in the matter is sharing the humble perspective of a fellow soldier, a tactical and strategic perspective that has seen some smal! amount of service lo these many years, for the shared purpose of keeping the nation we so proudly serve free and strong among the nations of the globe.

"But this recent . . . debacle! Is it true what the reporters are whispering, that all three of our aircraft carriers were lost at Midway?"

"No," the navy officer replied defensively. "Because of the heroic efforts of her crew, Admiral Spruance was able to bring the *Enterprise* away from the battle."

"But she is damaged, out of action for how long?"

"I don't know, General." *I don't like this man,* thought Chadwick. But he had been warned. He forged ahead. "I am here to ask you to finish your business at once and return to your assigned area of operations."

MacArthur nodded acknowledgment of the message. "MacArthur will gladly comply with the wishes of Admiral Nimitz. Please tell him so. The business for which MacArthur came will conclude by about 1300 hours tomorrow. *Bataan* can be back in the air before 1500 hours tomorrow at the latest. Will that be satisfactory to the admiral?"

The last thing Chadwick expected was for MacArthur to fold in the first round. "W-why, yes, I—the admiral will—"

"Don't you think the admiral might ask what business General MacArthur came here to transact? I believe that was the first of the admiral's requests, was it not?" interrupted General Sutherland, his voice harsh after MacArthur's mellifluous tones.

My God! I just walked over a booby trap and didn't notice it! Chadwick thought. *Fortunately, it's one they* want *me to find.* "General MacArthur, sir," Chadwick said, "may I ask on behalf of the admiral what the nature of your business in Hawaii might be?"

MacArthur smiled again, and this one was not pretty. It was more triumphal in flavor. "MacArthur will be meeting with three United States senators who will be flying into Hawaii tonight. After that meeting is concluded, MacArthur and his party will quit these islands."

Chadwick took a sip of his coffee. The next question, and its answer, were inevitable, but the ritual must be followed. "May I ask the purpose of that meeting, sir?"

"These United States senators will be leading a congressional investigation of the naval disaster that was Midway. They wish to obtain a military perspective that is not predisposed to whitewash the navy. That is why they wish to hear the opinions and recommendations of Douglas MacArthur."

"And those recommendations would be?"

"That Admiral Nimitz should be relieved of CINCPOA duties and the CINCPOA role be abolished as a result of the debacle at Midway and the looming threat to the Hawaiian Islands. He'll still be CINCPAC, of course. I'll need a CINCPAC."

Chadwick put down his coffee cup and looked MacArthur in the eyes. *Dogs and generals can smell fear.* "You can't do that, General," he said, with all the calm assertiveness he could muster.

"Don't you tell General MacArthur—" snarled Sutherland.

MacArthur raised a hand. "Let him talk, Sutherland. He isn't under my command, and his job is to be loyal to Admiral Nimitz." MacArthur turned back to Chadwick. "You used the word 'can't.' Did you mean it? Or was that a wish, or a hope, or perhaps a refusal to grant permission? The last would be 'may not,' not 'can't,' if you'll recall your grammar."

"I'm aware of the distinction, General," Chadwick snapped back, then immediately regretted it. He'd allowed MacArthur to bait him into a loss of temper. More calmly, he continued. "I mean, there will be consequences, General. If you try to get the admiral relieved and you fail, the consequences are likely to be severe. If you succeed, you will have made a great many new enemies, and you'll pay a price there, too. An angry, resentful navy will do its job, General, but it's not what you want. Sir."

MacArthur digested for a few seconds, then switched gears smoothly. "No doubt you're right. But the alternative is to live with this two-headed calf with which the United States expects to defeat the Imperial Japanese Army and Navy. I would, in all honesty, prefer Admiral Nimitz to win supreme command if the only other alternative were a shared command."

Another lie, thought Chadwick. *But this one he probably believes himself, as long as nobody actually asks him to give up his half of the shared command.* "Uh, General, there may be other options, sir. Admiral Nimitz said if something like this was what you were up to, that it would be worthwhile for you two to talk. Privately. With one condition."

"What condition?" It was Sutherland who took responsibility for inspecting the fine print.

"No press conferences, no individual conferences, no leaks, no nothing, complete blackout until after you finish meeting with the admiral."

"Afterward?" Sutherland scribbled a quick note.

"Conditions appropriate to whatever deal you agree to."

"If there's no deal?"

"Then there would be no conditions. You'd be free to say whatever you wanted to say."

Sutherland's eyes flashed back to meet MacArthur's. The senior man nodded, then spoke up. "When will we be able to meet with Admiral Nimitz?"

"May I use your phone?"

Five hours later, Douglas MacArthur—mirrored sunglasses, old and worn khaki uniform—walked side by side with Chester Nimitz—big cigar, equally old and worn khaki uniform—through the ground floor of Queen Emma's Summer Palace. Behind them trailed a larger group, three aides for each commander, walking ten feet behind like chaperones, valiantly pretending they weren't listening in and didn't even want to.

MacArthur leaned over toward Admiral Nimitz as they walked and said sotto voce, "I've always thought this is a nice enough old Victorian, but it's not a *palace,* is it? Not nearly up to Philippine standards. Living here would remind me of the old story—I think it's Mark Twain—of the man who took a ride in a sedan chair from which practical jokers had stolen the seat. 'What did you think?' asked his friends. 'If it hadn't been for the honor and the glory of the thing, it was mighty like walking,' he replied."

Nimitz laughed politely. Not quite the smooth office tactician or diplomat of his counterpart in the Southwest Pacific, Nimitz had the home field advantage but was battling an opponent of greater maneuverability and speed. It was clear that his bonhomie was somewhat forced, whereas MacArthur could easily keep it up all day long.

Once the two men were seated and another Filipino steward had poured coffee, it was predictably Nimitz who cut short the diplomatic niceties and got to business. "So you came to my island to recommend to a bunch of senators that I should be fired, right?"

MacArthur spread his hands wide in a gesture of peace. "The imminent danger to Hawaii requires—"

"Imminent danger to Hawaii, my ass! Goddamn it, MacArthur, cut the bullshit and let's talk turkey. You want to try to cut my goddamn balls off, go right ahead, but don't expect me to stand there with my legs spread waiting for you. I've been around this man's navy for a year or two, and I may or may not be able to beat you, but I can damn sure promise that by the time I finish with you, you'll know you've been in a fight. And the only goddamn reason I haven't already come out swinging is that we've got a common enemy, in case you've forgotten, the stinking goddamn Japs, and I'm not going to cause an unnecessary internal war unless it goddamn well becomes necessary. Am I making myself clear?"

MacArthur smiled his most ingratiating smile. "Clear as water, Admiral. There is no reason that MacArthur and Nimitz cannot find common ground on which to stand. After all, as you so wisely point out, we battle the same ultimate enemy, the Japanese, and we serve the same great nation, having sworn the same oath to preserve, protect, and defend its glorious Constitution."

"So what did you have in mind?"

"Pardon me?"

"What did you have in mind?"

"If I am not very much mistaken, it was Admiral Nimitz who asked for this meeting, was it not?" replied the four-star general.

The four-star admiral put a cigar between his teeth and lit it. "You'd never have agreed to the meeting unless you wanted it. You've got something to put on the table."

"And you don't, Admiral?"

"Let's see your hand. I call."

MacArthur looked with cool amusement at his navy counterpart. "Very well, Admiral. You understand, of course, that there is nothing personal in all this. It's strictly business."

Now it was Nimitz's turn to smile, and it was an expression as cold as anything MacArthur had produced. "I'm disappointed, MacArthur. If you believe that, you aren't nearly as smart as you think."

MacArthur pulled back. He was not used to having his ego punctured so casually, to having his intelligence questioned in such a cavalier manner.

Nimitz looked at him knowingly. "See? If you don't know by now that people take it personally no matter how you mean it, you aren't as smart as you think."

MacArthur could only smile ruefully. "Point taken, Admiral."

He lifted a finger, and Sutherland came forward to hand a manila file folder to MacArthur. "Shall we sit down?" MacArthur asked Nimitz. He gestured toward the dining room of the Summer Palace. The two men went inside and sat down. The others waited outside the room. Sutherland was standing just inside the door, not quite within earshot but with any other information MacArthur might need on short notice.

MacArthur opened his folder and began to talk. "Admiral, there can be only one supreme commander in the Pacific. Not two. It's you, or me, or a third person to replace both of us. The navy thinks it should be a navy theater, the army an army theater, and the marines and the Army Air Corps wish they could become independent of the both of us and claim they have a better right to the theater than either of the senior services. Right now, the navy has to explain two humiliating defeats in a row—Pearl Harbor and Midway. The only success—even marginal success—in the entire Pacific has been in the Philippines. Since America must return to Japan by way of the Philippines, for our solemn word has been pledged, these circumstances mean that the navy has lost its command credibility, and leadership of the Pacific Ocean should pass to the army Supreme Commander."

Nimitz's mouth worked, the only place where his emotions showed. But when he opened his mouth to speak, only calm words came out. "Well, General, I can understand how you'd reach that conclusion. But what were you expecting me to do? Roll over and play dead?"

"In a word, yes." MacArthur held up his hand to stave off the expected interruption. "The American public expects heads to roll over this. Not just yours, but those of Admirals Spruance and Fletcher at a minimum, and Halsey for falling sick at the wrong moment. Coming as it does so soon after Pearl Harbor, the Midway debacle is the worst possible situation that could have befallen the United States Navy. When MacArthur's voice is added, it will be as the last pebble that sets off the unstoppable avalanche. And who will be left to run the navy? You and I cannot sit idly by and let that happen."

Nimitz chuckled. "You're the one holding a knife at my throat. All you have to do is put it down and walk away."

"And then what?" MacArthur asked, waving his arm in a great melodramatic flourish. "Will Congress fail to investigate Midway merely because this one man fails to speak up? No, my brother-in-arms." He shook his head sadly. "No, Judgment Day is fast approaching. If MacArthur does nothing, the navy loses and there is still no unified command. If MacArthur acts, the navy suffers the same damage, but command in the Pacific is unified, some small benefit coming out of tragedy otherwise unalloyed. I am doing you no harm that would not befall you and your men regardless. I am merely making sure that the outcome is not a complete loss in our primary war against the ruthless Jap."

"Well, thank you so goddamn much," Nimitz replied. "I'm glad you have the navy's interests at heart. Otherwise I would have thought you were a cast-iron son of a bitch."

Sutherland's eyes narrowed with anger, making it clear he was within earshot.

MacArthur, on the other hand, seemed unfazed. "Oh, a certain amount of being a cast-iron son of a bitch comes with the territory when you pin on a star," he said. "I imagine the same is true of you."

"Goddamn right it is. But I still haven't heard anything but your extortion threat. You announce you're going to stab me in the back—"

"In the front, Admiral, if you please," interrupted MacArthur, still smiling graciously.

"—Back, front—stab me, and tell me it's for the good of the service. What do you want next? Am I supposed to kiss your four-star ass? I'm wearing four stars myself, in case you hadn't noticed."

"Admiral, you misunderstand MacArthur's intent completely. 'Extortion' is an ugly word. Not at all appropriate. This was simply an expression of one potential direction that could be followed. Instead, the important thing right now is to save the careers of the fine officers underneath you and to minimize the damage to your own career."

"And how the hell do you propose to do that?" growled Nimitz.

"It's all in how the tale is told," replied MacArthur. "One brave man assuming total responsibility, even though that responsibility clearly is not his, protecting others by his own sacrifice, and as a result finding himself not a man without a career but rather a man whose career can be brought to glorious life once again, especially with the myriad challenges and opportunities this terrible conflict presents to the superior military talent."

"Let me get this straight. You're suggesting I volunteer to play fall guy, take everything on my shoulders to protect my subordinates—"

"And superiors, I should add."

"You mean King? How the hell does King get blamed for Midway? It's my operation."

"Inadequate intelligence? Compromise of cryptographic capabilities? Promoting the dual command structure in the Pacific? Pushing too hard for a navy success after Pearl Harbor, a public relations strategy masquerading as a military one? Those are a few quick thoughts. I could come up with more without too much effort, I believe."

"So I take the fall, and then my reputation gets . . . rehabilitated? And how do you expect to accomplish that particular feat of legerdemain, General? I don't think you have that kind of clout with the navy."

"Not with the navy, true. But MacArthur is not without friends in the United States Senate, and even in the White House. All of MacArthur's influence and discretion can be exercised on your behalf, and on behalf of the navy. That is, if you vacate the field voluntarily."

Nimitz scratched his chin. It was too early for the firestorm to have hit, but the early signs were there. Newspaper articles condemning "navy failures," questioning the "American will to win," arguing for the replacement of "superannuated admirals not fit for modern commands."

"I'm going to have to think on this, MacArthur," he said, standing up. "For one thing, I'm not at all sure I can trust you. When are you meeting with your senators?"

"The airplane arrives tonight. We will meet tomorrow at 1000. If I have your answer by 0900 I will be able to have everything ready for the story we both want to give them."

"All right, MacArthur. I'll give you an answer by 0900. But I'll tell you right now, I'm tempted to tell you to shove your whole plan up your keister."

MacArthur bowed his head slightly in acknowledgment. "If such an ultimatum were to be presented to Douglas MacArthur, the volcanoes would erupt and the ground would shatter with the force of earthquakes. But in the end, what is necessary for the common good would win out."

"Well, the first part sounds about right. I have to think about this for a while before I decide whether you're right about the second part."

"I have complete and serene confidence that you will come to the correct decision. It's of vital national importance that MacArthur and Nimitz have met face-to-face," MacArthur said. "Our nation depends on tight, positive cooperation between army and navy. I am grateful for your time today."

Nimitz stood up, and MacArthur followed. The two men shook hands. "General MacArthur, I'm going to ask you and your party to wait here about half an hour, just to shake off any busybodies who might be lurking in the bushes. After that, your drivers will take you back to your house. And after your meeting, I do still expect you to get the hell off my island."

TWO

Philippines

• THURSDAY, 11 JUNE 1942 •

POW CAMP CABANATUAN #1, LUZON, PHILIPPINES,
2140 HOURS

Johnny Halverson couldn't sleep. The irregular bamboo slats dug into his bony frame. He twisted around to find a more comfortable position but accidentally kicked Andy Sarnuss, who shoved Johnny's leg away. Six men slept—or tried to sleep, in Johnny's case—on the floor of a cramped square room so small somebody's foot was always in your face. There weren't any bunks or mattresses. Only two of the men owned a blanket, which made them rich by camp standards.

All of them had dysentery. Almost every night someone didn't make it to the latrine in time.

Their straw hut prisoner barracks, called *behais,* had twenty rooms just like it in each tier, all crammed full of prisoners in similar shape. Others, rows of them, comprised Camp #1, and there were other camps over the horizon but not far away. As an officer—he was a captain—Johnny was treated marginally better than enlisted men were, but not by much.

Johnny's eyes were wide open, but he couldn't see a thing. Indoors on this moonless night, eyes were useless. His ears, however, had their sensitivity heightened by his inability to see. In the dark, he could hear the drone of the invading Mosquito Air Force seeking out tonight's targets. He heard the rumbling stomachs of his fellow dysentery sufferers. By now, he felt he could recognize each man by his borborygmi. In the distance he could hear voices, loud and somewhat drunk. The Japs were having a party. He hoped they wouldn't get the idea of coming into the camp. Bad things happened.

Taste didn't provide much value. What food they got was bland and tasteless. Occasionally someone would catch and cook a rat. Rat was tasty, if you were hungry enough.

Touch was just reporting pain. His body was a mass of sores, bruises, and small cuts. His gums were swollen and his teeth were loose from scurvy. His testicles had swollen to the size of baseballs, the result of beriberi.

The smell was almost exclusively of shit. Shit was omnipresent. During the day, the prisoners dug latrine trenches using the few tools the Japanese provided. They stopped digging at night, but use went on twenty-four hours a day. It was a losing battle.

Shit, Johnny had concluded, was the fundamental by-product of life. It might even be the fundamental purpose of life. Human beings were machines designed by God for the sole purpose of converting food to shit. Shit thou wert and shit thou will be. Shit without end, amen.

Johnny's own stomach made its intestinal rumble. It was time to head outside before he fouled their cozy little nest.

He sat up and slowly got to his feet. In the absolute darkness, he crept forward, hands feeling for the wall, then along the wall for the corridor opening. He shuffled his feet to avoid stepping on anyone, but he drew a few mumbles and moans as he bumped first one, then another.

A low whisper: "Latrine?" It was Andy.

"Yeah," Johnny whispered back.

Johnny heard movement sounds, and a probing hand found his shoulder.

"Better to go together," Andy whispered. "It can be a son of a bitch to find your way there and back in the dark."

That was definitely true. Men had died from getting their directions mixed up and wandering too close to the fence. "Sure," he whispered back.

Blind Johnny stepped into the dirt corridor. Blind Andy, hand on Johnny's shoulder, followed. Johnny kept his hand on the right wall and followed it to the entrance.

"All we have to do is follow our nose," Andy said, giggling at his own joke.

The smell outside was different. Shit predominated, but the air was also heavy with moisture. It felt as if a storm was approaching. Rain was good news. A storm was mixed news. A typhoon was bad.

There were a number of men—in the dark, Johnny couldn't tell how many—also making the midnight latrine run. There was the occasional cursing when one of the trench sides collapsed, dragging a foot into the muck. That was routine. Then he heard a squishing sound followed by louder cursing as someone else lost balance and fell unexpectedly. Neither Johnny nor Andy laughed. It had happened to both of them. "There's somebody who hopes it'll rain," Andy said.

As they started back, Andy said nervously, "Think it'll be a bad one?"

"Can't tell. Hope not. It's not like I can do anything about it, though."

Andy snorted. "Are you still down in the dumps? An attitude like that will kill you. You can get under cover. You can hide behind somebody else. There are a lot of things you can do. Watch me. I'm going to get through this. Do what I do. You'll be okay."

The atmosphere felt like it had a charge in it. Johnny felt a little better, better than he had in weeks. "You know, you're right, Andy. Maybe we can make it through this."

"Damn straight I'm right. You gotta believe we're going to get through this. The Japs won't beat us. We'll make it outta here."

"Maybe, but not unchanged," said Johnny. "Not unchanged."

Andy made a spitting sound. "Who the fuck cares, as long as I'm alive?"

"I guess you're right," said Johnny. "Might as well look on the bright side. This will scare the hell out of my grandchildren someday."

"Yeah? Grandchildren? Naa, I'm more the confirmed bachelor type." He leered, unconvincingly.

As they started to make their way back, the first crack of lightning briefly outlined the compound, but the afterimages shone so bright and so yellow they followed wherever he turned his head. He felt in front of him until he found a straw wall. A little more probing and he was pretty sure he knew where he was. Andy offered a running commentary and advice on their route back. "No, I think it's the next hut to the right. I really do." The sound of rain was heading their way.

"I've been counting since we left. One more straight ahead and we're there. Trust me on this. Wrong choice and we get soaked," said Johnny.

"Next hut to the right, damn it! I'm telling you, turn right!" Andy insisted.

It was the one straight ahead.

The storm opened with a torrent of water. Johnny gasped when the water hit him and then stopped when he realized he could feel the dirt and filth sliding off his body. The water was uncomfortable at first, then more bearable, then pleasant, the first pleasant body sensations he'd felt in weeks or even months.

"Okay, you were right. Let's go back," said Andy urgently.

"Doesn't it feel good to be clean? Stand here for another minute."

"Fucking Christ! I'm getting soaked! I don't want to get fucking pneumonia! Let's get inside, okay?"

Grudgingly, Johnny led again, and they made it to the entrance of their hut in a few minutes. The storm was getting worse.

"Ain't you coming in?" asked Andy.

"No. I'm going to stand here as long as I can."

"Your funeral." Andy put a hand on the corridor wall and started feeling his way back toward their sleeping bay.

There was another flash of lightning and quickly thereafter the thunder. The wind picked up and the fresh air was almost as satisfying as food. Johnny crouched in the hut opening to lessen the torrent, but water still leaked on him through the thatched roof. He avoided the leaks as best he could. He didn't own a blanket or a towel.

The wind shifted, and suddenly he could smell cooking odors from the Japanese camp kitchen. His mouth began to salivate at the burnt smell of overheated cooking oil. Then came a hint of spice. Ginger he recognized, and soy sauce too. There was that spice that smelled like licorice, and a couple he didn't recognize at all.

The smell was precious, a rare gift. He breathed deeply to get every bit of it. As he breathed out slowly, he closed his eyes. The smell allowed his mind to wander, to escape briefly from his captivity, to return home. In his mind, he saw himself standing next to the McCormick warehouse in Baltimore Harbor, his home, where the scent of spice ruled the air for at least twenty feet in every direction. . . .

Rain lashed his face with renewed force, the shock of the cool wetness bringing Johnny out of his reverie. He was soaked, but it was a good feeling. Still, this storm might turn into a typhoon after all, he thought. The wind was so strong the rain pelted him from the side, drenching him even with the roof over his head. He could feel the dirt underneath him turning to mud.

The smell of spice was long gone, but the water and wind were keeping the smell of shit down, and the water was clean and fresh. That was a good day at Cabanatuan.

His bowels seemed to have calmed down. Fresh air seemed like a fine idea. Maybe Andy's advice was right. Maybe he just needed to think differently.

It couldn't hurt.

He stared into the darkness and his mind drifted back to the beginning. . . .

• SATURDAY, 23 AUGUST 1941 •

MANILA, LUZON, PHILIPPINES, 1538 HOURS

The muggy heat, noise, stink, and bustle of the capital city of the Philippines created the most exotic mélange of smells Johnny Halverson's nose had ever encountered. There were spice scents that reminded him of the McCormick warehouse back in Baltimore, his hometown, but that was the only connection he could find to home. To him, this was a landscape as alien as anything Seaton or Crane had discovered in E. E. Smith's *Skylark* novels, which were, in his opinion, the finest science fiction books ever written. The people, the food, the architecture—nothing looked the way he was used to. For several weeks, he kept expecting to wake up in his own bed, or in the hospital after his appendectomy, and find out it had all really been a dream.

Oh, it was surreal enough to be a dream. Some of the Philippine Scouts were real regular army types, but there were other army FUBAR victims, just like Johnny. Johnny had been wired, he thought, for a job at Aberdeen Proving Grounds, where he'd worked as a co-op student during college. It was some horrible, confused mistake that got him sent here.

They had assigned him as an artillery officer. He had worked on artillery in his Aberdeen co-op jobs, but on the research side. They figured out pretty quickly he wasn't an actual artillery officer, and someone had the rare good sense

to transfer him. He ended up in supply, where being method-
ical and logical was useful. Johnny, a creative thinker but not
always oriented toward detail, got himself "kicked upstairs"
in short order to the planning staff. He went from a single
gold bar to a silver one, and was now a First Lieutenant.

A towering stone wall, more than 350 years old, surrounded
the Intramuros, the ancient inner city of Manila. Atop the wall,
at No. 1 Calle Victoria, stood a large eighteenth-century house
with large formal gardens: the House on the Wall, Douglas
MacArthur's military headquarters in Manila. The house was
wedding cake pink, with white decorations molded onto it.
The balcony railings were twists and coils of wrought iron,
painted white; the topiary was elaborately carved.

Johnny's desk was one of three World War I–issue metal
desks crammed into what appeared to have been a servant's
bedroom. The room was painted government green. There
were no windows and no other ventilation. It was hot, stuffy,
and after a while, it smelled. At least it was near the kitchen.

Johnny's big boss, Brigadier General Charles Drake, got a
servant's bedroom office all to himself. That demonstrated
the relative priority of the Quartermaster Corps in the US-
AFFE hierarchy.

His immediate boss was Captain Moore, a plump, genial,
balding man with a mustache. Johnny shared his feelings of
the futility of it all and was surprised at Moore's response. "A
few months ago, I would have agreed with you. While you
were in transit, though, the president and the secretary of war
decided to make defense of the Philippines a priority. We're
getting everything we want and need, if it just gets here on
time." General MacArthur's USAFFE—United States Army
Forces, Far East—and Philippine Scouts would soon total
120,000 men, a formidable fighting force. Johnny would be
one of the planners making sure that the incoming supplies
were allocated to the fighting units.

The cloud of anger and despair that had colored every
minute of Johnny's day suddenly lifted. There was hope. He
pitched himself into his work with total devotion.

Although he was in MacArthur's headquarters, he never saw the great man, though people talked about him all the time. Other generals were "General So-and-So," but he quickly learned that only MacArthur was "the General," said in the same hushed tones as "the Lord."

About three weeks after he started, a Filipino colonel stuck his head in to ask for directions. The House on the Wall could be a confusing place to navigate. Johnny gave him directions and then took note of his name. "You're Colonel Bluemel, right, sir? Forty-fifth Infantry?"

"That's right."

"I've just finished some allocations, and I was going to send you the copies. If you like, you can have them now."

The colonel picked them up and thumbed through them. "Enfields and ammunition." He looked at Johnny with a somewhat jaundiced expression. "It would be useful if the men had shoes, blankets, and entrenching tools as well, Lieutenant. I suppose translators, though, aren't in your department." He took the requisitions with resignation and walked out.

Johnny sat still for a moment, and then walked to a bank of army green file cabinets to pull out a folder of requisitions and orders. Guns, yes, uniforms all accounted for. The colonel's battalion had everything it needed—on paper.

On his next day off he scrounged a car and went for a drive. He had been dealing exclusively with paper—he hadn't seen the real situation at all. It didn't take him long to find units whose American officers spoke English, Philippine officers spoke Tagalog, and the enlisted men a hodgepodge of Bicolanian or Visayan dialects that were mutually incomprehensible. The uniforms were mostly World War I surplus and were falling apart.

He went to see Captain Moore. "What do you think I ought to do, Captain? If it's all bullshit and mirrors, I can get my work done real fast. But if there's something I'm missing here, I'd like to know so I don't screw it up."

Moore tamped his pipe down and took his time lighting it. "Johnny, the situation isn't good. The question is how long before the shooting starts. If the Japs invade tomorrow, we're fucked. If they wait a year, we may have a shot. Supplies and training will catch up to reality, and maybe that will be enough. But congratulations are in order, your little snooping action just won you admission to a secret club."

"What kind of club, Captain?"

"For now, it's the club of people who've figured out we have a problem and keep their mouths shut. Understand?"

"No, sir," Johnny replied.

"I don't expect you to. For now, I want you to do your job and I'll have a few additional assignments for you. Depending on how well you do them and how well you keep your mouth shut, we'll go from there. Do you understand that?"

"Well enough to do it, Captain," Johnny replied. "And keep my mouth shut."

Moore puffed on his pipe. "That's what I want to hear. Dismissed."

Johnny thought he'd heard the last of the matter and was waiting for his special assignments, whatever they turned out to be.

But evidently someone had noticed his snooping where he didn't belong. And the report went all the way up to General Sutherland, MacArthur's chief of staff, and suddenly Johnny found himself on the carpet in Sutherland's office.

"Who the *fuck* do you think you are, running your own goddamn unit inspections and sticking your nose into the General's war strategy?" Sutherland's face, red with anger, was an inch from Johnny's. He had a thin head and his eyes were mean. He was shouting and his breath was sour. "When the General wants the opinion of some fucking little pissant lieutenant, he'll send for you. Until then, do what you're told and keep your mouth shut."

Johnny wanted to defend himself, but it was obvious that Sutherland had no interest in listening. "Yes, sir," he said, keeping his eyes rigidly forward. He hoped he wasn't trembling.

Sutherland leaned forward. Johnny desperately wanted to back away but dared not. "Who else have you told about this?"

"No one, sir!" Johnny blurted.

"You're lying, you fucking little weasel!" snarled Sutherland. "I know your kind! I'll bet you've been spreading latrine rumors all over Manila. I'm going to court-martial your
ass for this, goddammit!"

"I've only spoken with you, sir," Johnny said desperately.
"Nobody else. I swear, sir!"

"Not your roommate? Not some cheap hooker? Not even
your own captain? Come on, Halberton," Johnny didn't dare
correct the mistake in his last name. The shouting began
again. *"Who else did you tell?"*

Sutherland's tirade lasted a good twenty minutes, but it felt
like days. Johnny had flop sweat stains under his arms and
was trembling when he finally got out of there, not knowing
whether Sutherland was going to court-martial him. He
headed straight for Captain Moore.

"Tore you a new asshole, did he?" the captain remarked.
"What did you tell him?"

"Nothing, sir."

"Nothing? Not even my name?"

"You said to keep my mouth shut, Captain."

"Yeah, but he knows damn well you talked to me. Don't
lie when you know you're going to be caught. Now he thinks
you're lying about everything."

Johnny was too wrung out to care about military discipline. "I kept my mouth shut. So tell me about the fucking
secret club."

Moore obliged. It seemed there was a small, informal task
force that was slowly stockpiling materiél on the Bataan
Peninsula across the bay from Manila, operating with General Drake's tacit approval. MacArthur had ordered that the
primary supply dumps be placed close to the landing beaches,
so that they would be available to the troops who would defend against the landing. The problem was, there were very
few troops available to fight on those beaches, which ranged
all around the huge island of Luzon. If the Japs landed and
broke through the beach defenses—the defenses that still existed mainly on paper—American and Filipino forces would

have to withdraw into Bataan under a long-standing plan. The terrain there was rugged, good for defense, and the troops could hold out along a defensive line at the base of the peninsula. But they would need food, fuel, and ammunition dumps on the peninsula if they were to have any hope of holding out. By dint of his curiosity, Johnny had become the newest member of this conspiracy.

December 7 came on a Sunday, the Feast of the Immaculate Conception. There were flowers everywhere, and everyone of consequence in Manila was dressed up and parading in the Intramuros. The air around the spice merchants in Manila's large open-air market smelled like the McCormick warehouse, only more intense. The spice mixture was different, but Johnny didn't know enough about spices to name them.

In the evening, he had a few beers with a friend he'd made, David Hansen, who'd been sent to the Philippines as a dive-bomber pilot with the 27th Bombardment Group (Light). A number of pilots from the 27th had arrived in November. The only problem was that their planes, A-24 dive-bombers, were still aboard ships somewhere in the middle of the Pacific.

He got back to the BOQ about midnight.

Seven time zones and one International Date Line away, six Japanese aircraft carriers under the command of Admiral Chuichi Nagumo were just starting to launch the first wave of 181 planes against the U.S. naval base at Pearl Harbor.

• MONDAY, 8 DECEMBER 1941 •

BACHELOR OFFICERS' QUARTERS, HQ USAFFE, MANILA, PHILIPPINES, 0500 HOURS

"Attention!" The sergeant's bellow penetrated doors and walls with ease. "All leaves are canceled. All officers are required to report immediately to their duty stations!" Sleepy voices began pestering the sergeant for details. The sergeant was not forthcoming, but it didn't take long for the latrine telegraph to pass the word. The Japs had attacked Pearl Harbor. Some men thought it was a joke—how could those near-sighted, comical little people carry out a sneak attack across the biggest ocean in the world?

Johnny, with a sick feeling in the pit of his stomach, knew that it was true.

The House on the Wall was a chaotic mess. Captain Moore was already there, gathering up files. "Your buddy Sutherland needs the current logistics status, pronto!" he ordered.

Johnny, still dazed, stomach in turmoil, started working. He wanted to ask whether Sutherland wanted the real data or the bullshit, but figured by now it didn't matter. It took him about forty-five minutes to put it together. He gathered up his files and trailed after Moore in the direction of Sutherland's office.

The narrow hallways, sized for a household, not a military staff, were crowded with people in frantic Brownian motion. A major bumped into Johnny and sent his papers flying, and kept moving without apology. "Johnny, watch what the hell you're doing," complained Moore. He didn't bother to help as Johnny went down on his hands and knees to gather the papers.

By the time Johnny managed to corral them all, there were footprints clearly showing on several pages. *At least Sutherland will kill me before the Japs can,* he thought.

A sergeant-clerk guarded the anteroom. There were sofas, but neither Moore nor Johnny sat on them.

There were loud voices coming from Sutherland's office, which controlled access to MacArthur's. One was Sutherland's. The other Johnny didn't recognize, but Moore did. "That's Brereton—he's the air commander," he whispered. Both men shamelessly eavesdropped, though with the level of shouting it would have been hard not to do so.

"We're not going to make the first overt act!" shouted Sutherland.

"What the hell do you call Pearl Harbor?" Brereton shouted

back. "A fucking church social? This is a goddamn war, in case you haven't noticed!"

"This is the way the General wants it. You are not to commit *any* overt act, do you understand? Do *nothing* until the General says so. I will call you with orders when and if the General sees fit to issue them."

"Goddamn it, I want to see the General and I want to see him now."

"*You* don't give orders in this office, *I* do. And I'm giving you an order right now. Go back to Clark Field and await orders. Get your planes ready for a mission, but do *not,* I repeat, do *not* take any further steps without hearing from this office."

"I'm not going to take this from *you*. I *demand* to see the General!"

"Take one more step toward that door, Brereton, and I'll have the MPs throw you out of this building on your ass!"

The door opened and an angry two-star with a slightly receding hairline and glasses strode out into the corridor where Johnny and Captain Moore were waiting. "For Chrissake, Sutherland, this is wrong and you know it," Brereton yelled.

"Wait for orders, goddamn it! I'll call you the second I know something," Sutherland retorted.

Brereton slammed the door shut. He didn't look at the men waiting outside.

The sergeant waited a moment and then buzzed. "General Drake's people with the logistics information, sir," he said through the intercom. The sergeant motioned to Moore to go in.

Moore knocked on the door and opened it. "General Drake asked us to bring the logistics documents to you, sir."

Sutherland, face red, eyes narrow, sweaty, looked up at Moore. "Bring them here." He opened the folder. Johnny thought he looked tired, even though the day had barely begun.

Sutherland looked at the first few sheets of paper with a dull expression. "That will be all," he said.

Gratefully, Johnny and the captain turned to go, but suddenly Sutherland spoke. "What the hell is this?" His voice was deceptively calm.

Johnny turned around. Sure enough, Sutherland was holding a page that contained a big footprint right in the middle of it.

"What do you mean bringing me a file with papers that have been stepped *on?"* Sutherland's voice grew in fury with every word. His eyes were locked on Johnny's like a snake on a rabbit.

Captain Moore interjected, "Ah, General, I'm afraid that was my decision. Lieutenant Halverson here got bumped in the hall, and I made the call that you'd rather have these papers right now and have us get you a clean set in a few minutes rather than wait until we can get you that clean set. We'll have a clean set ready for you in no time at all, General. No time at all."

Sutherland's eyes stayed fixed on Johnny. "So you 'dropped the papers in the hall,' did you?" he said. "That seems to be typical for your performance around here. Nosing where you don't belong, questioning the judgment of your superior officers, everything but *doing the job you're supposed to do! You little* chickenshit, *how* dare *you—*" He stopped.

The door to the inner office had opened and MacArthur himself was moving toward them. The General didn't look like the image in his pictures. He was old, much older than Johnny realized. His skin was ashen. His eyes were unfocused, his gait halting. He looked as if he'd gotten up from a sickbed.

Sutherland looked at the two junior officers. His eyes were suddenly wild—*panicked,* Johnny realized. "Wait here. Don't say a thing. I'll deal with you later," the chief of staff hissed.

Quickly he moved toward MacArthur. "How are you, General?" Sutherland asked in soft, soothing tones, like a man talking to a child.

"I . . . I'm tired, Richard. So very tired . . ."

"Why don't we just get you back to bed, sir?" Sutherland suggested.

MacArthur ignored his chief of staff, drifted close to the two junior officers. "You seem like a fine young man," he said, putting a friendly arm on Johnny's shoulder. "What's your name?"

"L-lieutenant John Halverson, sir."

MacArthur's eyes came into a little bit of focus and seemed to fasten onto the Quartermaster Regimental Eagle insignia on Johnny's collar. "Halverson. You work for General Drake, I see. You've made sure all our brave soldiers have ample supplies for the upcoming battles, have you?"

Halverson felt Sutherland's glare with the force of a heat ray. "I-I've done my best, sir," he hedged.

"Of course you have!" The General leaned closer, as if to whisper in Johnny's ear. "But you can't very well allocate what you don't have in the first place, can you?"

Sutherland's face was shading from red into purple. Johnny knew he'd better be very careful how he handled this. "I do my best, sir," he said again.

The General frowned. "Have you done your best? Have I? The Japanese are here too soon and my enemies—Marshall, King, Pershing, Roosevelt—have thwarted me. They all hate me, you know . . . and . . . and . . ." MacArthur looked upward with an anguished expression. "There were no good choices! None! MacArthur couldn't run away with his army and hide. MacArthur couldn't get the supplies he needed to win. What was the General to do?"

He grasped Johnny by the shoulders and looked into his eyes as if he might have the answer. "What do we do now?" he asked in a plaintive voice. "You know, Marshall called me last night to tell me about Pearl Harbor. He did that for spite, you know, because he hates me. He ordered me onto war alert, but I never had the tools! It's a trap—a trap to discredit me and all my years of service. Do you know what I did?"

"No, sir," Johnny replied.

He turned toward Moore. "Do *you* know what I did?"

"I'm afraid not, General MacArthur."

He turned his head to look at Sutherland. "You, Dick—you know, don't you? You came over when you got the news. You always come. But you don't always help."

"I'll help, General," Sutherland said soothingly. "Why don't we go back—"

"No!" said MacArthur. "The General wishes to speak." He turned back to Johnny. He lowered the tone of his voice again. "You must listen to MacArthur carefully, and you will learn what you must do if you are confronted with a terrible choice."

Johnny waited. He didn't think MacArthur was looking for an actual reply.

"I asked my wife Jean to bring me my Bible. Then I sat on the edge of my bed and read my Bible. I have put myself in the hands of a Higher Power." He looked at the three faces in turn and smiled. "I have prayed continuously throughout this long morning. Continuously. And so I put my trust in Almighty God that He will deliver us from evil. Let us pray together."

General Douglas MacArthur knelt on the rug in front of Sutherland's desk. Johnny waited until he saw Sutherland and then Moore begin to follow, and then he also knelt and bowed his head. He snuck a glimpse through half-lidded eyes. The others had heads bowed and hands folded reverently as well.

MacArthur began to pray. "Almighty God, Maker of all things, Heavenly Dispenser of justice, see the rightness of our cause and send Your terrible swift sword to fight on behalf of Your children who now beseech you most humbly for deliverance. Amen."

"Amen," the three men chorused.

All Johnny could think of was the old saying—he'd heard it attributed to Napoleon—"God fights on the side with the best artillery." If that were true, God had already abandoned them. He wanted to scream at the old, tired man, to shake him until he realized the truth of their hopelessness.

For a moment MacArthur seemed transformed, radiant, majestic. Then he sighed, and it was as if the air had suddenly been let out of a balloon. His shoulders slumped. His face, already ashen, went gray and bloodless. His lips were thin.

In a low voice, he said, "I have deceived myself. *I've put the supplies near the beaches.* But what else could I have done? There were no good choices."

He turned away from Johnny, suddenly animated as he grasped Sutherland's shoulder. "Tell me, Richard, what do I do now? What now?" Sutherland was silent.

MacArthur looked a hundred years old as he slowly shuffled back into his office and shut the door.

There was a long pause, and then Sutherland turned back to the junior officers and spoke in a furious, low voice. "He is a *great* man. He is worth a hundred of any of the rest of us. What you saw is *not* who he is, and so if either of you say one word about this little scene to anyone—at any time—on any day—for the rest of your fucking, miserable, and probably short lives, I won't court-martial you, I will simply hunt you down and cut your fucking tongues out of your mouths personally using a dull knife, *do I make myself clear*? Now get the hell out of my office before I change my mind and shoot you both on the spot."

With hurried "Yes, sirs," Moore and Johnny got the hell out of his office.

Safely behind closed doors back in the servants' quarters, Moore said, "He means it. He really will cut your tongue out."

"Sir, I didn't doubt it for a second."

Moore thought for a moment. "I'm going to see if I can get to General Drake. Be where I can get you at a moment's notice."

Johnny went back to his desk. Even in the midst of chaos, the interoffice mail system still functioned. There was a War Department letter on his desk. It had his name on it. He stared at it for a minute, then decided to satisfy his curiosity the traditional way. He opened the envelope and pulled out its contents.

It was his transfer to Aberdeen Proving Grounds. He was

authorized to travel by "any available military transport," though with a pathetically low priority.

Fucking hell.

He was still sitting at his desk staring at the letter when Moore came for him. "Let's go talk to the boss," Moore said.

Johnny's voice choked. "Guess what, Captain? My transfer came through. I'm heading stateside on the first available military transport. I'm going home." He handed Moore his letter.

Moore looked at it and then stared at Johnny with pitying eyes. "Oh, fucking hell. Damn. Shit, I'm sorry, Johnny." He looked at his hapless subordinate, and then he started to laugh. After a few seconds, Johnny joined in. There was nothing else to do.

Manila's air-raid sirens began to blare a few minutes before noon. Reports began to pour into headquarters, and the rumor mill quickly spread them through the building. Bombs were falling on Clark Field. The fleet was retreating out of range. Even the polo field at Stotsenberg had been hit—the colonel in charge reported that not a single horse had panicked. There were rumors that Japanese paratroopers had landed in force just outside the city, that the Japanese fleet was even now steaming into Manila Bay.

MacArthur began to issue orders by midmorning. The paralysis that had seized him in the predawn hours had obviously begun to ease. It was not until Friday morning that the Japanese army landed in force. The defenders on the beaches held out surprisingly well, and for a time in mid-December Johnny could even believe MacArthur's radio promise—made to the troops and Philippine citizenry—to "drive the enemy into the sea." Maybe all the secret backup work had been a waste of time. It was a great thought.

It didn't last.

General Drake called his team in on December 23, the day after MacArthur's radio address. His face was pale as he said, "The Japanese are breaking through at the beaches. Another landing force is on the way. The Lingayen defenses have collapsed." He paused. "The General has decided to revert to War Plan Five."

War Plan Five meant retreat to Bataan Peninsula and the island of Corregidor. The most crippling logistics problem in this complicated withdrawal was a lack of transportation. Fortunately, the secret team—Moore, Johnny, a lieutenant named Andy Sarnuss, a few others—had already done some of the work without waiting for orders. Drake had approved the quiet shipment of half a million C rations and a million gallons of gas. Most of the food and other supplies stockpiled in supply dumps near the beaches would have to be torched or abandoned.

By January, the retreat had been successfully completed, and officers who understood such things called it "brilliant," "beautifully executed." As for Johnny, the supply problem took up all his time.

He hardly noticed the combat.

Except for the day a Jap Zero on a strafing run killed Captain Moore.

• MONDAY, 26 JANUARY 1942 •

LATERAL 8, MALINTA TUNNEL, CORREGIDOR ISLAND, PHILIPPINES, 2146 HOURS

In the early 1920s, the American military had begun constructing a concrete tunnel system on the island of Corregidor, which guarded the entrance to Manila Bay. More than five thousand men, sixty-eight women, and a handful of children inside lived the lives of besieged moles.

Malinta Tunnel had not been designed for people. It had a constant graveyard smell about it, mildew and rot and urine and sweat with liberal amounts of diesel fumes thrown in for good measure. The regular booms of artillery shells and bombs hitting the Rock, as Corregidor had come to be known, formed part of the background of life in the tunnels. There was traffic day and night and every sound echoed.

Bluish lights shone twenty-four hours a day. Bare bulbs illuminated work areas, casting monstrous shadows on the walls.

Johnny slept in a lateral crammed with bunks, sharing one shower and one sink with twenty-seven others.

He couldn't sleep much, so he decided to work.

There was a lot to do. First, all the supply calculations had to be thrown out the window. They were told there'd be a little over forty thousand troops. Instead, there were a hundred thousand, including thirty thousand civilians. General Drake put everyone on half rations in the first few days of January. If it hadn't been for the secret team stockpiling in advance, rations would have had to be cut even more.

Work was the great blessing of Johnny's life. Work took the place of thought. Thought was dangerous. It led to anger, to depression, to endless speculation of what minor changes would have spared him this fate. He didn't particularly believe in a personal God, but he made bargains with Him anyway, all the exemplary ways he would live his life if only He would rescue him from the Rock. Even during an air raid, Johnny would work. Everyone had a strategy. MacArthur—the "Coward of Corregidor" to so many of his trapped soldiers—went to the surface and stood outside as the Japanese bombed the Rock.

Johnny knew he was lucky to draw Corregidor rather than Bataan. At least it was an island and a fortress as well. General Drake's office of the chief quartermaster had moved there immediately, starting with a headquarters aboveground but—harassed almost continually by Japanese air attacks—soon transferred into Lateral 8 of the Malinta Tunnel.

He'd made captain with Moore's death, but all the extra rank meant was extra headaches. Calculating the supply situation was one of the worst.

The numbers were bleak. They had maybe thirty days' rations. Sutherland first insisted that the hundred thousand number had to be a gross exaggeration made by people trying to scrounge extra supplies. Johnny helped develop a complicated ration credit system to make sure the supplies were shared as fairly as possible. Sutherland looked skeptically at

Johnny's work but didn't yell. *As long as I keep my mouth shut, I've got some leverage,* Johnny thought. He didn't dare hope it might lead to an escape.

"Guess what, Johnny?" It was Andy Sarnuss, who also worked for Drake and who'd been part of the secret team. He'd gotten to know Andy well only after they'd moved into Lateral 8. Andy's cynicism and bitterness translated into humor, and Johnny could always use a laugh.

"You couldn't sleep, either?"

"Who needs sleep?" replied Sarnuss. "All times are the same around here, and nothing has meaning. Might as well relax. But go ahead and guess."

"I don't have the faintest idea and it's so late my brain hurts. So tell me or let me do something I can get my mind around, okay?"

"Sure, sure. Guess what? It's MacDoogie's birthday!"

"No shit." Johnny just looked at him.

"You're not impressed? You're not motivated to wander down and sing 'Happy Birthday' really loud in front of his private room, where he, unlike the rest of us, enjoys the happy privilege of a fuckable roommate?" MacArthur's wife Jean and young son Arthur were both with him.

Johnny was shocked. Not that Jean MacArthur wasn't good-looking, but she was the *General's.* "I can't believe you said that," he said. "That's disgusting."

"Hey, I didn't say I wanted to fuck *her,* I said I wanted a fuckable roommate. You've got a dirty mind, Halverson. Fuck Mrs. MacArthur? *Brrrr.*"

"Well, if you're dreaming, put me down for a nice three-inch-thick steak, and why don't you throw in a couple dozen Maryland blue crabs, all steamed and ready to crack."

"Yeah, well, we're out of those requisition forms. As soon as I can get some, I'll fill them right out for you. Whatcha got there?" Andy looked over Johnny's shoulder.

"I'm trying to figure out an equitable way to handle our remaining rations," Johnny said.

Andy whistled as his eyes skimmed down the column. "That bad, huh."

"Yep. If I could figure out that loaves-and-fishes gimmick, we'd be okay, but so far, nothing."

"Have you asked Mac? He can walk on water, you know, so maybe he can do that loaves-and-fishes thing. Have you thought of that?" Andy said in mock seriousness.

"I'd prefer to see him part the Pacific Ocean so we could all march out of here, maybe walk down to Australia, or all the way back to the States."

"That's a good idea," Andy said. "Let's take it up with him in the morning."

"First thing," Johnny said. He took the papers and put them in his desk drawer. Now that he'd had a laugh, maybe he could sleep for a while.

• TUESDAY, 10 FEBRUARY 1942 •

MALINTA TUNNEL, CORREGIDOR, 1148 HOURS

Johnny never liked going up to Lateral 3, which contained USAFFE headquarters. MacArthur's office was there, and of course his chief of staff Sutherland was never far away. However, supply reports had to be sent up regularly, carried by an officer able to answer questions if there happened to be any. That used to be Captain Moore's job, so now it was Captain Halverson's.

As he came out of Lateral 8, he turned and followed the trolley track east. The island trolley once ran right through the Malinta Tunnel as part of its route around the island, but the first major Japanese shelling had destroyed too much of the track to make operation worthwhile. The moist, mildew smell was even worse here, and the echoing sounds of conversations, footsteps, and other noises blended into a random and unpleasant cacophony.

Normally, Johnny handed the report to the sergeant on duty, waited ten or so minutes to see if there were any questions, then walked back to his own lateral. There were almost never any questions. Today, the sergeant came back and said, "General Sutherland would like to see you."

Johnny's heart sank. It was like going to the principal's office. What had he done *this* time to incur Sutherland's wrath?

He stepped into the office, snapped to attention, saluted, and said, "Captain Halverson reporting to the chief of staff as ordered, sir!"

"Oh, at ease, at ease," said Sutherland, who acknowledged the salute, stood up, came out from behind his desk, and shook Johnny's hand. "Have a seat, Johnny. It is Johnny, right, Halliwell?"

"Yes, sir," Johnny replied, deciding again not to correct Sutherland on the matter of his last name.

"I understand your captain, Moore, got killed in Manila?" the chief of staff began, making a forced effort at comradeship.

"Yes, sir. Killed by a strafing fighter."

"Too bad, too bad. But I see you got the promotion to his job. Congratulations. I remember getting the papers for my signature."

MacArthur's G-1, Colonel Stivers, had actually signed Johnny's promotion paperwork, but for all Johnny knew, Sutherland may have approved it as chief of staff.

Sutherland's eyes narrowed as he studied Johnny. "It seems you've kept quiet . . . about that little incident, when the war was starting. You haven't spoken of it?"

"No sir, not to anyone." It was the truth.

"Good. Good man. You know this is very important to the General, you know that. It would unfairly damage him if it were spoken about. I appreciate the way you've handled yourself. So does the General. You know that some . . . ah . . . questions have been raised. Maybe you've heard songs being sung?"

Like everybody in Bataan or Corregidor, Johnny knew about "Dugout Doug" and the "Battling Bastards of Bataan," two ditties that had been making the rounds. But what to *say*? "I've . . . uh . . . been aware of them, yes, sir."

"There's a reporter, Hewitt, and some other people who've been making noises, and they're particularly interested in any dirt they can dig up. Some people might remember that you were in the office that morning and come to ask you questions about it."

"No one has yet, sir," Johnny said.

"Good. I'm glad. But there's still a chance. Now, if it happens, I still need you to keep your mouth shut, and I also need you to let me know about anybody who's getting curious. Can you do that for me?"

"Yes, sir." *I* can. *The real question is whether* I *will. Keeping my mouth shut is one thing, ratting out other people is something else.*

It was as if Sutherland could read his mind. "I know you've got orders to go home. As a way of thanking you, I'm going to do my best to try to see if I can get those orders implemented, and get you out of here before . . . before the end."

Johnny's heart leaped at that suggestion, but he tried to keep his face impassive. He was about to stammer out a reply when Sutherland spoke again. "If you can help me, I may be able to help you. Are we clear?"

"Yes, sir. Yes, *sir*!"

"All right. Dismissed."

• **WEDNESDAY, 11 MARCH 1942** •

SOUTH DOCK, CORREGIDOR, PHILIPPINES, 1900 HOURS

The wharf and its facilities, at the base of the Rock, had been utterly exposed to air attack for months, and the Japs had done a real job on South Dock. Not a single building remained standing. The earth itself was rent and broken, the seawall chiseled away by craters. The two dozen men who stood out here now cast frequent glances skyward, when they were not watching the dark, cavernous entrance at the base of the nearby cliff.

The salt air stank of fish, but that was better than the stench of sweaty humanity crowded into Malinta Tunnel, or the acrid smell of cordite and gunpowder, the parching clouds of dust that accompanied each artillery barrage. Johnny stood

on the concrete wharf and took a breath of the sticky air,
tried to focus on the smells of Manila Bay instead of the nervous tumble in his gut. In any event, there was nothing to do
but wait.

The lapping of waves against the ruined pier merged with
the bass rumble of the idling torpedo boat engine. There were
some insect sounds, a few murmuring human voices, and otherwise an unearthly and deep silence. The tropics were so removed from the Pennsylvania landscapes of his upbringing
that he might as well be on a different planet: Burroughs's Venus, perhaps, or Doc Smith's Green System.

But those stories were fantasy. This terrible place, from
jungled Bataan to rocky Corregidor, was all too real. It was a
prison, a death trap, a hell. It was the place where Americans
and Filipinos had come to die. Most, but not all. The four patrol torpedo boats in tonight's mission would see to that.

Of these boats, the most important was PT-41. While the
other three picked up their lucky passengers from other
docks on the small island, boat number 41 bobbed in the outgoing tide alongside the charred and blackened pylons of
timber that made up what remained of South Dock. The worn
engines, too much maintenance delayed for too long, chugged
roughly, spewing exhaust heavy with oily smoke.

Johnny wanted to get on board that PT boat so much he
could taste it. Even knowing the risks involved in getting out
from under Jap patrols in Manila Bay, he was ready to leap
aboard in an instant. He had spent all afternoon on the ruined dock preparing for the mission, arranging camouflaged
fuel barrels so that the boat could top off its tanks, collecting
a few precious provisions for the crew and passengers that
would squeeze into the tiny vessel. All along his eyes had
swept the placid, brackish waters, seeking the low silhouette
of potential deliverance.

Sutherland had promised. He had *promised*.

Johnny had done what Sutherland asked—keep his mouth
shut and tell him if anyone came snooping around. But nobody came. He let Sutherland know, and suddenly the chief

of staff became hard to reach. He got one message from
Sutherland: "I'll do my best. I haven't forgotten."

What did that *mean*? Was he getting off the Rock tonight,
or was he staying behind?

Although there really hadn't been that much to do, he'd
made a show of checking everything three or four times.
Though he felt vulnerable in the sunlight, he'd wanted to remain outside, with that view of the water. A flight of dive-
bombers or strafing fighters could have come screaming
down from the hazy sky, and he would have thought long
and hard about whether or not to take shelter in the tunnel.

Now night had fallen. His duties done, he was simply
standing at ease with other soldiers, sailors, and marines,
waiting. There was a stir in the rank as the party came out of
the tunnel, a dozen people moving quietly, each avoiding the
eyes of the men lined up at the wharf. *Me. Me. Take me with
you.*

Johnny's boss General Drake was running the show, although he wasn't going. He herded his charges onto the
dock—to the extent anybody could herd Douglas MacArthur.
The General stood majestically to one side, aloof and apart,
while enlisted rates loaded personal effects aboard the tiny,
unarmored PT boat. The passengers were entitled to thirty-
five pounds of luggage apiece. MacArthur used none of his
allowance. He was not even properly in uniform; his socks
had loud civilian checks.

MacArthur was taking his wife Jean and young son
Arthur with him—understandable—but also his Chinese
amah, Ah Cheu, Arthur's nanny. Johnny wished the old lady
no harm, but hers was a place that might have been filled by
someone else.

"We're being abandoned by God Almighty Himself tonight. That makes it official. This *is* hell." Andy's nasal voice
was pitched low so no one else could hear, but it was so clear
in Johnny's ears that he was certain the eyes of MacArthur
would soon fasten on the two young officers with the impact
of a heat ray.

"You needed *official* confirmation?" Johnny whispered

back, trying to keep his voice even lower. His whisper seemed to carry, however, because he drew a sharp look from General Drake.

Johnny looked at MacArthur. The commanding general looked old and worn and thin, and above all he looked deeply sad. Was he losing his mind again? Did he feel as if he had really become the "Coward of Corregidor" by leaving? There had always been something about MacArthur's bearing and manner that was reassuring, and now it was missing. He looked broken, lost.

MacArthur had visited the Bataan Peninsula only once since reaching the Rock. He was not afraid to face the Japanese, Johnny was certain. He was still ashamed of his failures on and before December 8.

The PT commander, Lieutenant Bulkeley, stepped onto the charred timbers of the dock and made his way over the uneven planks to the General. Bulkeley, with his beard and a uniform stained by too many tropical months, looked more like a pirate than a naval officer, but everyone knew that the General had great confidence in him. MacArthur removed the pipe from his mouth and nodded calmly as the lieutenant approached, offering a simple "Buck," in greeting.

The naval officer replied in a low tone, but Johnny was close enough to hear parts of the conversation. The phrase "room for two more" emerged like a clarion bell.

The General nodded again. Johnny felt himself stiffening, at ease gradually morphing into attention. MacArthur's gaze swept across the line of waiting men. "Captain Lunney, come here," MacArthur said. The young officer addressed stepped forward with a look of disbelief. The man's wife had just given birth to twins, Johnny knew. Meanwhile, MacArthur's gaze moved on, approaching Sarnuss and Halverson at the end of the line. Those piercing eyes came to rest on Johnny's face.

Sutherland promised! I already have the orders! He wanted to shout out his claim. Sutherland stepped up, whispered in MacArthur's ear, and MacArthur looked away from Johnny.

That bastard. He's double-crossed me. He's abandoned me to the Japanese, figuring I'll never make it.

Someone coughed, a gagging rip of sound that doubled the man over. It was Lieutenant Pat Murphy, whose asthma had made life in the tunnel even more hellish than it was for most.

"Lieutenant, you come too," MacArthur said.

You fucking bastards! You fucking murdering bastards!

And that was it. Johnny watched the line of passengers, including Lunney and Murphy, slowly clamber into PT-41, bound for Mindanao and freedom. Several slipped on the charred and broken planks, while little Arthur scampered with the carefree gait of a child, evading his frightened mother's attempts to hold his hand. They all made it safely aboard.

Johnny was sure that particular boat would survive, no matter what happened to the others. No Jap was ever going to lay a hand on MacArthur—it would be more than lèse-majesté, it would be virtually deicide.

The PT boat was ready to cast off, but MacArthur was still ashore. He looked around at the men on the dock, his face white, a twitch at the corner of his mouth. His eyes stopped briefly on Johnny and the General opened his mouth as if to say something, but then he closed it.

He raised his gold-braided barracks cap, the one with the stiffening grommet removed, in salute to all those he was leaving behind. Artillery batteries high up on the Rock opened diversionary fire, shelling the Jap positions not too many miles away on Bataan.

MacArthur stepped into PT-41 and spoke to its commander. The 4,050-horsepower Packard motors, idling up until now, growled a little deeper, roiling the brown waters beside the wharf. Chugging loudly, pushing only a gentle wake, the torpedo boat steered toward the turning buoy. In the fading light, the other three boats were visible a mile or so offshore, waiting to form up on their leader.

Above, the shattering explosions of firing artillery and blasts of red and yellow light punctured the darkness. It was full nightfall now, and the wind picked up, splashing waves against the pilings. Johnny ignored the water, the air, the guns.

Instead, he kept his eyes fixed on PT-41, his last, best hope for freedom, until it slipped out of his world altogether.

THREE

The Pacific; Washington, D.C.

• THURSDAY, 11 JUNE 1942 •

APPROACHING JAPANESE CARRIER HIRYU, *EAST OF* MIDWAY, *1421 HOURS*

"The *Hiryu*'s in sight, Admiral," the pilot shouted through the tube.

As the Nakajima B5N2 torpedo bomber dipped through the cloud layer into the gray, rainy weather, the passenger in the rear seat, Admiral Isoroku Yamamoto, commander in chief of the Combined Fleet, barely could make out the damaged First Mobile Force through the light drizzle. There were three carriers where there should have been four. The fire on the *Kaga* had spread to its magazine; the resultant explosion had torn it apart.

Of the three remaining, two were damaged. As the fleet grew closer, Yamamoto could see where bombs had ripped through the *Akagi*'s deck. The *Soryu*'s flight deck was out of commission as well. Only the *Hiryu* of the four great carriers in the First Mobile Force was still able to conduct flight operations.

Admiral Yamamoto stared impassively from the cockpit of the Nakajima as it approached the *Hiryu*. The Americans had taken a worse beating, with at least two of their three carriers sunk. The pilots had claimed to have sunk all three of them, but a submarine captain had spotted one, apparently the *Enterprise,* limping away from the battle. The Americans could rebuild their fleet. Japan's capacity had been stretched too far already. Yamamoto was not likely to see the *Kaga* replaced. And even if steel could be obtained, the trained and capable pilots lost in this operation were a loss of incalculable value.

The admiral reached up to rub his shaved head, forgetting for a moment he was wearing a flight helmet. *This should have been* strategic *victory,* he thought with annoyance. *The plan was right. What went wrong?*

The objective of this operation was not to capture a specific piece of real estate, though he would have welcomed Midway being occupied by his own forces. Yamamoto needed to eliminate existing American naval power in the Pacific. If they lost badly enough in the early phases, they might bargain for terms. That's why he'd split his forces, sending the Fifth Fleet north to the Aleutians as a distraction while the First Mobile Force and the Second Fleet invaded and captured Midway Island, and with luck, eliminated the remaining American fleet.

But the Americans had shown up too soon, and with too many ships. The carriers had dueled, and these damaged flight decks were the result. The American fleet had been driven off, but the IJN ships were left without sufficient air cover available. As a consequence, the invasion of the island had been called off, the amphibious fleet recalled to Saipan. Yamamoto knew, rationally, that the cancellation of the landing might prove to be a blessing, since Midway was really too far beyond the Japanese defensive perimeter to be a useful base. Even so, the decision had the stench of defeatism, all the more galling because the previous month another landing—at Port Moresby, on New Guinea—had also been canceled following an inconclusive battle with the American aircraft carriers.

Perhaps it was just bad luck. *Shikata ga nai,* he thought. It can't be helped. Or was there another reason? A spy, perhaps. Probably a spy of some sort.

"Admiral, we've been cleared to land," the pilot shouted.

No matter how many times he'd been flown onto a carrier, the sheer improbability of hitting the tiny, bobbing target caused him to rivet his attention forward. The torpedo bomber descended gradually, the pilot carefully following the movement of the carrier. When it seemed collision was unavoidable, the pilot pulled up slightly and gunned the engine as the tailhook caught a wire. Yamamoto was thrown forward in his harness as the plane's velocity was arrested in a very short space.

"Good landing, lieutenant commander," Yamamoto said into the tube as the plane turned from the active landing area into its designated parking spot. Outside the cockpit, the line of senior officers and the formation of sailors were waiting for him.

A warrant officer quickly scaled the steps onto the platform that had been wheeled up to the plane and unfastened the cockpit locks. Yamamoto's rear section was opened first, and the warrant officer saluted his admiral before offering a hand to help him from the cockpit. Yamamoto stood on the platform and removed his flying helmet. The formation snapped to rigid attention, and from somewhere behind them military music began to play.

A light drizzle began to fall, so no one had much enthusiasm for a prolonged ceremony. For his part, Yamamoto cut most of the speech he'd prepared. "It is a great blessing for our nation that such men as you have been able to lead our fine fighting men against the enemy. I salute you." He bowed to show his respect.

Nagumo, as senior officer, replied, "We would have been directionless and lost without the genius of your leadership and planning as our daily operation," and bowed more deeply in return.

Neither Yamamoto nor Nagumo were inconvenienced by the rain. A tarp covered the podium. It was big enough to cover all the admirals—four for First Mobile Force, who fought the carrier battle; six for Second Fleet, responsible for the transports and the invasion of Midway Island. Add

Yamamoto himself; the commander of the Aleutians Fleet, Vice Admiral Moshiro Hosogaya; and Rear Admiral Kysaka Ryunosuke, chief of staff of the First Air Fleet; and barely half the captains were able to come out of the rain. Seniority mattered a lot.

After the ceremony concluded, Yamamoto and the most senior admirals adjourned to Nagumo's new quarters. Vice Admiral Nagumo had transferred his flag to the *Hiryu,* as it was now the only carrier capable of fighting, displacing Rear Admiral Tamon Yamaguchi, now on the *Soryu* and responsible for getting her and the *Akagi* safely into port.

The admiral's suite consisted of bedroom, private bath, sitting room, and private office. The sitting room could accommodate six men, enough for a small meeting. Eyes turned instantly toward Yamamoto.

Yamamoto rubbed his shaved head with his three-fingered left hand, a souvenir of the Battle of Tsushima in the Russo-Japanese War. Everyone was cheering his brilliant achievements in naval strategy, first at Pearl Harbor and now at Midway. The thought gave him little pleasure. Midway was a transient success. "My congratulations to one and all," he said, bowing again.

Nagumo, normally gruff, conservative, and skeptical of air power, was elated by his successes. "With two American carriers sunk and the third damaged and possibly sunk, the enemy battleship fleet out of commission, and his loss of face and honor devastating, the United States will cease to be a military factor for three years or more to come!" he crowed.

He seemed to be trying to convince himself as much as Yamamoto. The loss of the *Kaga* had shamed him, and he had been fretting over the repairs to the *Akagi* and *Soryu,* both of which lost many men when the American dive-bombers had struck. In one respect, the old fool had been lucky: the flight groups from those stricken carriers had been attacking the American carriers when their own ships had been bombed. If the airplanes had been aboard the ships, possibly in the midst of fueling and arming, the damage could have been truly catastrophic.

"You present an interesting theory," said Yamamoto, using words that he intended to convey the meaning, *You've got it completely wrong. Before the war, I predicted that I could run wild for six months, and after that have no expectation of success. This* victory *changes nothing permanent.*

But Nagumo acted as if he heard the words literally rather than as carrying their intended meaning. He, like so many others, dismissed Yamamoto's concerns about the American sleeping giant awakening as spinsterish at best, paranoid at worst. Nagumo saw the Americans as representing only weakness, corruption, dishonor, and cowardice. Nagumo had never been to America, never seen it, never gotten to know the Americans.

Yamamoto had. He knew.

He also knew that this war was inevitable in one way, utterly unnecessary in another. And now that it was raging, its course was inevitable as well: a period of unstoppable Japanese advance, followed by a retrenchment against an awakened and aroused America. In the end, the United States' manufacturing, economy, and sheer size must lead to a hideous defeat for the Empire of Japan.

"Will you say again, Yamamoto-san, that with all this success, we are in more danger than we suppose?" Nagumo said.

"Have I become that predictable? My humble apologies. I'm sure that with all your successes to date, you will continue to perform miracles no matter what the odds," Yamamoto replied.

Nagumo laughed. "You worry too much about the gaijin. Of course, that's part of what makes you such a great admiral. Do you know what the other part is?"

Yamamoto grunted from the belly. He wasn't sure he was in the mood for one of Nagumo's jokes, which were as heavy-handed as his tactics. "Today, no. Please tell me."

"It is because you refuse to give in to thoughts of victory

and happiness. No matter how many enemy carriers I sink, to you it is not enough. If I sink them all, why are there battleships left? If there are no battleships left, then what about cruisers and destroyers? Why did I not capture Midway Island? If I had captured Midway, why have I not yet captured Hawaii? And if I capture Hawaii, why have I not occupied Los Angeles, California? Such a high standard motivates all around you to strive endlessly for higher reaches of excellence, demonstrating yet again your glories as an admiral."

Yamamoto chuckled. That wasn't bad, especially coming from him. "Nagumo-san, I am indeed pleased with results at Midway, which turned out to be a more complex and problematic operation than we had planned. Your performance was exemplary and exceeded my expectations. By launching your strike against the American carriers as soon as they were discovered, you inflicted critical damage—and probably saved your own fleet. As to the island itself, it is unimportant, useful to us as bait but not as a base. You have my undying gratitude and respect. If I am called a great admiral, it is only for my great fortune in having such superior tactical, strategic, and leadership abilities in my honored fleet commander. You have been covered in glory for this day's work."

"But you'd still like more."

"Who would dare ask for more when given so much? It is always true in war that more success is preferable, but it is also always true that success deserves recognition, and your success in this battle matters."

"But you'd still like more."

"Yes, Nagumo-san. Capture Los Angeles for me. Especially that part of Hollywood where the movie stars live. Specifically, Marlene Dietrich's house."

While everyone was laughing, Nagumo said, "One day we'll do it. We have a destiny."

It is a funny joke, thought Yamamoto, *but the old fool actually believes we might conquer Los Angeles.*

He has no idea.

My nation. What is going to happen to you?

• FRIDAY, 12 JUNE 1942 •

OFFICERS' CLUB, SCHOFIELD BARRACKS, OAHU, HAWAII,
2117 HOURS

The trade winds cooled the evening so that the temperature on the veranda of the club was perfect. The bar within was crowded, and Ellis Halverson drew a breath of fresh air, relieved to be outside, finally able to move his arms without bumping into some raucous young officer. He held his highball in his left hand, a cigarette in his right, and reflected that the amenities here in Hawaii beat hell out of the sandy dugout that had been his home on Midway Island.

People sometimes said Ellis looked like Buster Crabbe, who played Flash Gordon in the serials. Ellis played up the similarities as much as he could; he even wore his hair like Crabbe. It was his starring role in an accidental movie that brought him here today.

During the final defense of Midway against the approaching Japanese troop transports, his twin engine B-26 light bomber, the *Skylark of Space,* came under fire, so he went into a steep dive to get away from them. When he tried to pull out of the dive, he was too heavy. He dropped the bomb load to lighten the plane, and to his utter amazement, the bombs skipped across the water like stones and smashed into the hull of the Japanese troop transport approaching Midway. He had wondered if anyone would ever believe his story, but the gunner/camera operator happened to catch the miracle.

He was surprised to find out what he'd done had a name: skip bombing. Major General George Kenney's aide informed him that General Kenney had thought up the idea himself. No one had done it deliberately. That made his accidental discovery even more important. The orders for Hawaii showed up within a day, and tomorrow he'd meet with General Kenney in person. Tonight, he was planning to get stinking drunk and, with any luck, find himself a sweet, pliable companion to while away the rest of the evening. Midway had been hell on his social life.

A chorus of laughs came from the young pilots at the table Ellis had just left. His head was spinning a bit, from the mixture of whiskey and the realization of his sudden, albeit minor, celebrity status. He hadn't had to pay for a drink all night. He had, however, told his story over and over, to a rapt audience including captains and majors—once even to a full bird colonel, a veteran of the old Army Air Corps who had graciously bought a round for the exuberant pilots. It was heady stuff for a young man less than a year out of Baltimore, Maryland. Yep, a fellow could get used to living like this.

This sure beat hell out of whatever kind of mudhole prisoner-of-war camp Johnny was sitting in right now.

If he was still alive.

Here's to you, big brother. I'm coming for you in the Skylark *as fast as they'll let me.* He finished his highball and threw the glass at a large stone about five feet from the veranda, where it shattered with a very satisfactory sound. There was more broken glass around. He wasn't the first person to make a toast like that.

In disgust he stubbed out his cigarette in a nearby pail of sand, then moved to the edge of the porch, trading the smell of sweat and tobacco for the sweet fresh smells of the hibiscus bushes, the blooming frangipani, and the green lawn.

There was a grip on his shoulder. Ellis turned, expecting to shake off some other drunken airman, but stopped at the sight of navy whites. A captain. Navy officers at the army club were not uncommon but a definite minority. Then he recognized the face. "Frank?" he said, startled. Ellis had heard his brother-in-law was somewhere in the Pacific, but the Pacific was a big place.

Captain Frank Chadwick grinned. "Hiya, Ellis. Damn, it's good to see you." Frank had met the oldest Halverson daughter while he attended the Naval Academy. "Anything new about Johnny?" he said, concerned.

Ellis shook his head. "No. Nothing. I was going to ask you if you'd heard anything from back home."

"Not a thing," Frank replied. "Not a damned thing." He

paused, then changed the subject. "I hear you're the hero of Midway. Good shooting."

Ellis laughed. "Nope. It was a happy accident. But it's got the brass interested in finding out if it can be done deliberately. I'm supposed to meet with the commanding general of the Fifth Air Force in the morning."

"Fifth Air Force. That's in SWPA, right?" The Southwest Pacific was MacArthur's theater.

"I think so. Why? I thought it'd put me closer to Johnny."

Frank paused. "I wasn't looking at it from that angle, but since you put it that way, I guess you need to take the assignment if it's offered. Though I'm sure it will be offered," he amended.

"I don't think they were planning to leave the choice up to me, anyway," Ellis said. "The Army Air Corps is funny about things that way."

Frank laughed. "Listen, Ellis, I really did come here tonight to see if I could find you. As soon as I heard your name, I was pretty sure you'd be coming to Hawaii. Unfortunately, tonight's a busy night, and I can't stay. Are you in town for a bit?"

"I guess even if they send me to Australia it'll take a week or two to get me shipped out."

"With typical army efficiency, it could be years," Frank added with a grin. "Anyway, it looks like we'll have some time. I've got a place on the other side of the island."

They made a tentative agreement for Ellis to come out to Frank's apartment for the weekend, and the navy captain slipped away.

He turned back to stare into the darkness, and there was another grip on his shoulder. "Frank?" he said, thinking his brother-in-law might have returned, but as he looked over his shoulder he was irritated to recognize one of the pilots from his previous table. The drunken lieutenant shook him eagerly.

"Did you hear? He's coming—gonna be here any minute." The drunken lieutenant's voice was slurred, but still understandable.

"Who?"

"Mac! Came to Hawaii yesterday!"

Ellis had heard that bit of trivia, General MacArthur having arrived a day after Ellis himself, with considerably more fanfare. At the time, the information had been just another tug at his memories of Johnny.

Already officers were spilling out onto the veranda as the news shot through the crowd. Army wives in evening dress clutched the arms of their uniformed husbands, straining to see. The higher ranks pushed through toward the front, and Halverson was content to let them pass. He spotted the colonel who had earlier bought the round for the pilots and was surprised when the senior officer waved him over.

"Come along, Lieutenant. There's someone I want you to meet."

People, faces, voices swirled around in a rising frenzy. Ellis felt stone sober, experiencing everything through precise, even magnified, vision. A long staff car, four stars flying from the pennant, was drawing up to the club as he made his way to the colonel's side. "Just wait here, son," the colonel said.

The car came to a stop and a sergeant stepped forward, opened the rear door, and saluted. MacArthur got out and stood, noticeably tall, handsome, and dashing in his battered cap, a pipe held casually in his left hand. The crowd of army officers and wives grew still. The General was followed by several other men, all wearing one or two stars but clearly his inferiors in rank, bearing, prestige. As he strode up the steps, MacArthur returned the salutes of the men in front, graciously chatting as the brass closed in and whisked him into the club. It was only then that the colonel—Leemann—started forward, pulling Ellis along with him. He was making a beeline for one of the generals in MacArthur's retinue, an affable-looking fellow with the wings of the Army Air Force on his chest.

"General Kenney, sir!" called out the colonel.

"Ah, Ted!" the general replied, falling out of the entourage, shaking hands with Ellis's companion. "Good to see you! Got your bags packed?"

"Good to see you, too, sir. And yes I do. General, this is Ellis Halverson, the pilot who accidentally skip bombed that Jap transport that turned back the whole Midway invasion fleet."

Ellis saluted on cue.

"Good to meet you, Lieutenant," General Kenney replied. "We're set up for tomorrow morning, right?"

"That's right—I mean, yes, sir," Ellis said, his liquor making him a bit more flustered than he otherwise would have been.

Kenney grinned. "This lieutenant is already ahead of me, Ted. Lead on in the direction of the bar."

"Right this way, General." The colonel led the general and the lieutenant through the crowd.

Shortly, Ellis found himself once more recounting the accidental hit. He was in the senior officers' private lounge, the only lieutenant present—in fact, the only one lower than a major as far as he could see. "I was too low, sir, and way too slow—since my plane had been shot all to hell. But we got the bombs away, and they bounced across the water a couple of times—like a skipped stone, you know?—and punched right through the Jap's hull. They tell me the ship sank less than an hour later. I got lucky, that's all."

Kenney chuckled. "Luck is a good thing in a pilot. I'm interested in whether you could do it again, and then whether you could teach it to others. I've had this idea for some time, you know. I'd like to be able to do it in a B-17."

Ellis thought as hard as he could given the amount of alcohol he'd consumed. "A B-17? Sir, it was tough enough in my little hot rod. I'm not a heavy bomber man."

"So you aren't. But you're all I have. Want to fly something bigger than a Marauder?"

"Sir, I'm from Baltimore, and so a Baltimore Whore's good enough for me." He regretted the words as they slipped out of his mouth. The manufacturer, Martin, was located in Baltimore, and the "whore" referred to the plane's tiny wings—the bomber had no visible means of support.

Kenney had the grace to laugh, to Ellis's relief. It gave the lieutenant a chance to add, "But it would sure be fine to hit a Jap ship with what a B-17 could dish out."

"What do you think, General?" Colonel Leemann asked.

"That's a decent answer. Okay. You're coming with us, Halverson. Let's still talk tomorrow, but I'll have the orders cut to bring you over to the Fifth Air Force. Leemann, anybody else you think we ought to have," Kenney asked.

"Um . . . General?" Ellis interjected. "My brother . . . he was on Bataan. I haven't heard from him, but I'm hoping he's a POW. I want to be out there where I can hit back at those bastards."

Kenney nodded. "All right. We'll see that you can."

A balding general whom Ellis had previously noticed in MacArthur's wake reappeared. "Let's go, George," he said curtly. "The General wants to show you off."

Kenney nodded. "Dick, here's a young pilot who'll be coming with us. His brother was back on Bataan. Lieutenant Ellis Halverson. Lieutenant, this is General Sutherland, chief of staff to General Douglas MacArthur."

Sutherland paid no attention to the introduction or to the lieutenant until the word "Halverson," then his head jerked around. "What did you say?"

"General, this is Lieutenant Halverson. He's our new skip-bombing instructor. I'm going to introduce him to the General."

Ellis had the distinct sensation that Sutherland loathed him on sight, and he had no idea why. In an effort to build rapport, he repeated, "My brother was on Bataan."

"There were over seventy thousand soldiers on Bataan, Lieutenant," Sutherland snarled. "It's ridiculous to think I'd know your brother. It's more ridiculous to expect the General to know. Kenney, I wouldn't waste the General's time with this boy if I were you."

Ellis was taken aback by Sutherland's reaction. By the look on his face, Kenney was surprised, too.

Ellis stood quickly, surprised to realize that he was drunk again—as if all the alcohol he had suppressed during his conversation with Kenney had surged to the surface. He didn't like this staff general, not at all.

"I'm going to help myself, and the army, sir," he said, barely articulating. "As to General MacArthur, I'd like to ask why he left my brother behind when he came out of Bataan!" Ellis was swaying a little bit. "Why didn't he stay there with them?"

Sutherland's face flushed. "Listen, you miserable little son of a bitch. He was *ordered* out by the president because that great man is *needed* here! And if you can't get that fact through your thick skull, you oughta stand up for a court-martial—"

"Dick, we're not going to court-martial him!" snapped Kenney.

They all realized simultaneously that another person was looming over them, obviously hearing every word of the conversation. General MacArthur stood nearby, staring. Ellis tried to meet that stare, but he couldn't; instead, he took an involuntary step backward, made a fumbling salute.

"Lieutenant Halverson, sir!" he said, voice slightly slurred.

MacArthur stopped in his tracks. "Halverson?"

"Yes, sir."

"Your brother is Johnny Halverson?"

Sutherland looked slightly panicked. General MacArthur looked concerned and kind.

"Um . . . yes, sir, he is," Ellis replied.

"He was on the list to go," MacArthur said. "He was on the dock. But it was a long list. At the end, there was a space left. But there were two of them . . ." MacArthur's eyes were far away.

"General, we really need to go, sir," Sutherland said, doing his best to push MacArthur away from Ellis.

"I wanted to bring him out," MacArthur said. He turned and looked at Sutherland with a questioning look. Sutherland looked daggers at Ellis, then turned and stomped away. General Kenney followed, giving Ellis a reassuring clap on the shoulder. Sutherland looked back as the retinue of generals approached the staff car. His eyes met Ellis Halverson's, and Sutherland flashed a look of fury, menace, and something even darker.

• MONDAY, 15 JUNE 1942 •

WASHINGTON, DC, 0917 HOURS

The petty officer knocked, entered. "Secretary Knox is calling."

Admiral Ernest J. King, chief of naval operations, picked up the telephone and waved at the rear admiral (lower half) serving as one of his assistant chiefs of staff to sit down and wait while he talked to the secretary of the navy. "Frank, good morning," he said.

"Ernie, are you reading the headlines?"

"Of course, Frank." All weekend, an unrelieved parade of newspapers and magazines full of anti-Navy propaganda. All of it, as far as King was concerned, was originating from MacArthur's well-oiled public relations machine.

"Looks like you've got an extra little shooting war going on in the Pacific. I think fighting one enemy at a time is enough, don't you?"

"If that son of a bitch will agree to a cease-fire, I'll stop, too."

"Then set one up. What do you need, me to hold your hand?"

"Now wait just a goddamn minute!"

"No, Ernie. You wait. The President spoke to me. He said that as a former assistant secretary of the navy, it embarrassed him to see those stories. He would be very appreciative if I could get them stopped. I'd like to see those stories gone as well."

"I don't think *he'll* stop until he gets what he wants." King didn't feel he needed to name names.

"In that case, he might have to get it."

"Not a goddamn chance in hell!" King roared.

"Then find another answer, but find it fast. The President wants it, Henry wants it"—Henry was Henry Stimson, secretary of war—"and I want it. Get those stories off the front page and preferably out of the paper. No matter *what* it takes."

There was ultimately only one thing to say. "Yes, sir," replied King, his sense of duty overtaking his outraged sense of fitness.

But if the Coward of Corregidor thought he had the U.S. Navy over a barrel, he hadn't reckoned with Ernie King. As soon as he could hang up on Knox, King flipped the intercom switch. "Get me Vinson," he barked.

Congressman Carl Vinson of Georgia—known as "the Admiral" throughout Washington political society—was the powerful chairman of the House Naval Affairs and Armed Services Committee. Vinson, whose Georgia district was completely inland, was always proud to claim that there was not a single naval activity in his district, and thus he was completely without parochial interest in his duties on the committee. While Vinson's support for the navy was absolute, he and King did not always see eye to eye about what constituted the navy's best interests. On the matter of who would have supreme command in the Pacific, however, King knew he could count on Chairman Vinson.

General George C. Marshall, chief of staff of the United States Army, frequently butted heads with his predecessor and now subordinate. Douglas MacArthur's tour as army chief of staff in the 1930s had been turbulent, culminating in the cavalry attack against the Bonus Army on the national mall in Washington, DC. Like many of his colleagues, Marshall was glad enough to see MacArthur retire to the Philippines. But MacArthur was often brilliant—and always impossible to ignore. When war had loomed, he had come out of retirement at the request of Philippine President Manuel Quezon to handle the defense of the archipelago.

This latest escapade was a lot, even for MacArthur: exploiting the navy's bad luck at Midway to advance his own claim for supreme command. What was worse is that Marshall felt compelled to support him. MacArthur was army; that was one factor. He had the public's attention and support, a mixed blessing but undeniable. And the two-theater strategy was a compromise borne of desperation. It could be made to work; it might even be argued that it had advantages. A single command, though, would be better. And right now, Douglas MacArthur was the better choice.

Well, he had better get busy. He was sure Admiral King was already at work. He snapped the intercom switch. "Could you find out when Secretary Stimson would be able to spare me a few minutes?" he asked.

About an hour later he was entering the secretary of war's private office. "Thank you for taking the time to see me, Mr. Secretary," Marshall said.

"General, my time is yours," Stimson replied. "How may I be of service?"

"It's about the Hawaiian business, Mr. Secretary," the army chief of staff answered.

"I thought it might be. How do you think this situation should be handled? I am confident I know Admiral King's answer already."

"I'm afraid my answer is no less predictable, Mr. Secretary. At the same time, this interservice conflict is no benefit to anyone except the Japanese. If there's a peaceful solution, I'm in favor of it."

"Threatening to saw the baby in half seemed to work for Solomon, if I recall correctly," Stimson said.

"In this case, unfortunately, half a baby is better than no baby at all," replied Marshall. "I think we have to continue to divide the baby. If there is a small adjustment in the lines of demarcation, perhaps we can have peace among our own forces and focus our hostility on our real enemies."

"Do you think MacArthur will settle for a small adjustment? How about Admiral King?"

"Frankly, Mr. Secretary, General MacArthur is right about where the successes in the Pacific have been thus far. He is popular, more so than the navy right now. And as we both know, public perception is important to the war effort."

"So it is," Stimson acknowledged. "But General MacArthur recognizes his political advantage right now. Do you think he'll settle for less than full control?"

"He'll have to," Marshall replied. "I'll support him up to a point, but not to excess. He deserves to have active navy co-operation in his campaign, and needs more support in the Pacific than he's gotten before. That much is perfectly reasonable and should be supported."

"Very well, I'll support that much," the secretary of war replied. "So you think you'll rein in Douglas MacArthur's wild demands? How do you think he'll react?"

"Oh, I'm sure there will be some heated language, but in the end, he'll have to see reason."

"You're right, I imagine," replied Stimson. "But I wonder—"

"Wonder what, Mr. Secretary?"

"I wonder if this wasn't the outcome he was banking on all along."

• TUESDAY, 30 JUNE 1942 •

CINCPAC HEADQUARTERS, PEARL HARBOR, HAWAII,
0811 HOURS

Captain Frank Chadwick walked into Admiral Chester W. Nimitz's office. He did not salute because in the navy one does not salute indoors unless under arms. "Good morning, sir," he said.

"Morning, Frank," the admiral replied. Chadwick thought he looked annoyed this morning. Nimitz held up a message sheet. "Here. Interpret this."

Chadwick walked over to the admiral's desk and took the proffered sheet. Knowing Nimitz, he was fairly sure that whatever impression he would have on first reading was probably not the correct one. He skimmed over the message quickly, and said, "On first glance, it appears to be good news, sir. In spite of you officially taking the blame for Midway, you've been asked officially to remain as both CINCPAC and

CINCPOA. I've seen some of the press you've gotten. MacArthur was right. Taking the blame was the best thing to do."

He looked at it again. "There's still a Pacific Ocean Areas. In spite of General MacArthur's efforts, both the Pacific theaters still exist."

Nimitz grunted. "Keep looking."

"I see one change. The line of demarcation that separates Pacific Ocean Areas from Southwest Pacific has been moved back to 161 degrees east longitude from 160 degrees." He walked over to the large map that covered most of an office wall. It was decorated extensively with pushpins. Labels stuck out of them representing all the assets under CINCPAC and CINCPOA control. "Hmm. Down in the Solomons, it looks like that moves one island from POA to SWPA."

He peered more closely. "Oh. I see, sir. Guadalcanal. But in our theater we still have everything for the planned navy route to Japan: the Marshalls, the Carolines, the Marianas."

"You've found the booby trap. Mac got the Solomons. The whole chain." Nimitz's office had several large windows that looked out at some palm trees and didn't quite screen out the industrial parts of an active navy port. He stood up and walked over to the windows, his back to Chadwick. "Our General decided to get smart instead of greedy. He didn't fight for all the marbles with a chance of losing. He asked for only the key marble because he knew he could get it."

The Solomon Islands had been assigned to CINCPOA's area of operations. Nimitz had the ships and the troops—in the form of the 1st Division of the United States Marine Corps—to do the job. MacArthur's forces were already tied up in the battle for New Guinea, so the Joint Chiefs had shifted the line over one degree from the original 160°. Now MacArthur was able to move the line back, and he'd sure as hell take the 1st Marine Division and all naval assets he could lay his hands on. Those assets included Kelly Turner's fleet of amphibious assault vessels and whatever aircraft carriers the country could scrape up, including the newly arrived *Wasp* and *Saratoga,* and the soon-to-be repaired *Enterprise*.

"If MacArthur had tried to go for the knockout blow, there's a good chance he would have failed," Nimitz said. "Instead, he makes a grab that gives him a chance to show what he can do with navy assets, and if he does well, there's going to be a battle to get them back. Once Mac finishes climbing through the Solomons, he'll try to move on to New Guinea without a pause. It's going to take everything King and I have got to stop him. You see, next it'll be a push for more resources, and a bigger role for his plans, and maybe postponing the two-pronged approach and just go to Japan up through the Philippines—"

"So MacArthur isn't going to try to eliminate CINCPOA?" Chadwick asked.

"Why should he? If what he's trying works, as long as he gets all the territory and equipment he wants, he'll graciously let me keep everything he doesn't need, and let me have the extra privilege of ferrying all his supplies across. I won't 'report' to him, as long as I get done everything he wants."

"Do you think he's going to be able to do it?" asked Chadwick.

"Before Midway, I would have said there was a snowball's chance in hell an army general, even MacArthur—hell, *especially* MacArthur—could get control of navy assets in the Pacific. This is *our* theater, the way Europe naturally belongs to the army. But MacArthur is every bit as much a politician as he is a general, and he knows how to milk a situation like this for all it's worth. Anything, and I mean *anything,* the navy does that can be made to look bad, MacArthur is going to smear all over the press. That's how he means to beat us."

Nimitz turned to face the window. "We have to be perfect. The trouble is, there are some personnel changes I haven't been able to make yet. That's why I'm worried. We're vulnerable. I'm working on some of the personnel issues. In the meantime, I need you to look into something else for me. Torpedoes. My submariners are telling me they're getting a high percentage of duds. The Midway reports said the same thing. I need to know what the problem is, and I need to know quickly so it can be fixed before MacArthur gets wind of it. We can't be caught with our shorts down around our ankles again."

"Yes, sir," Chadwick said.

"Good man. Dismissed."

FOUR

Australia; Tokyo; Hawaii

• WEDNESDAY, 1 JULY 1942 •

HEADQUARTERS, 63RD SQUADRON, 43RD BOMB GROUP,
5TH AIR FORCE, MAREEBA, QUEENSLAND, AUSTRALIA,
1017 HOURS

"We got a plane, boys! We're a real live bomb group at last!" crowed Major Bill Benn. The ground echelon of the 43rd Bomb Group had been in Australia since March, because it took time to build a functioning air base. The first members of the air echelons began to arrive in the Australian fall, and now, in the middle of the Queensland winter—highs in the seventies, lows in the fifties—the 63rd Squadron was just receiving its first airplane: the B-17 *Chief of Seattle,* a gift of the city itself.

Lieutenant Ellis Halverson was a de facto test pilot and instructor because he was the only person who had skip bombed a Japanese transport, albeit accidentally during the Battle of Midway. He'd done it, though, in his B-26 *Skylark of Space.* He wasn't qualified in the B-17. That meant he was sometimes a teacher, more often the student.

As copilot or observer pilot he'd now flown dozens of missions against a hulk in the harbor. At this point, he had more experience with skip bombing than anyone else in the Pacific Theater. He hadn't done it against an enemy ship yet—deliberately, that is—though others had. The thought of doing so was nervous and exciting.

Long hours of practice and numerous cases of trial and error—one fatal—had given them the method. You did it at night, or just at sunup with the sun silhouetting the ship for you and screening you from the ship. You approached the enemy vessel low, only 2,000 feet above the water. Then you went lower, skimming the wavetops at 250 feet while staying above two hundred miles per hour. You hoped the gunners on the ship didn't see you, but soon enough they'd hear you. The giant ship hull approached closer and closer, looming black, now with spotlights hunting you. At a couple of hundred feet away from the target, you released the bombs. They were equipped with a four- to five-second delay fuse, just enough time to skip over the waves toward the ship and settle into the water next to the hull. With luck, you'd crippled the ship, but first you had to climb upward, the B-17 banking sharply up, close to stalling, over the deck of the ship itself. You could sometimes tell then if you'd caused a lot of damage. Other times the tail gunner was the only one who could see results.

If the Japs had a fighter screen up, you might sneak in, but you couldn't just sneak out. As soon as you pulled up, you were shark bait. Your gunners had to be damn good, and you had to be fast, because it was time to go home.

It was several months before he got a B-17 of his own. He didn't love the heavy, ungainly thing, not like he loved his B-26, the closest thing to a fighter you could get in a bomber. But he could appreciate the power and relative grace of her bigger brother.

First Lieutenant Ellis Halverson put the final touches on his bomber nose art, then backed down the ladder to examine the nose of his new B-17 with a critical eye. In a big blue circle he'd painted a spaceship with a babe in a skintight space suit riding it astraddle, done in an Earle K. Bergey style. The spaceship jutting up between her legs was done in an imitation of Frank R. Paul's Art Deco style, ultrastreamlined and reminiscent of a sleek new diesel locomotive. Underneath the circular design was the plane's name: *Skylark II*.

His new top turret gunner, Sergeant Clem McDonald, wolf-whistled at the Bergey babe. "Damn, Skipper, she's gorgeous!"

Halverson jumped off the ladder, backed away, and nodded appreciatively. "You know, Clem, you're right."

The crew chief, who had been inspecting the lubrication on the nose gear, came over to have a look. "That's the best damn piece of nose art anywhere in Australia," he acknowledged.

"You bet it is!" Halverson said with a grin. Ellis gave his artwork a last, careful look. The perspective in the girl's left leg was slightly off. He'd have to fix that soon. And he wanted to put in two more figures, or suggestions of figures, though he wasn't sure how. But dammit, Johnny and Pete should be part of *Skylark II,* symbolically if not literally.

The *Skylark II* was not named directly for the immense ship in E. E. "Doc" Smith's classic *The Skylark of Space* but rather in honor of the Skylark Science Fiction League, consisting of Ellis, his older brother Johnny, and Johnny's best friend Pete Rachwalski. Of course, the club was named in honor of Doc Smith's books—the adventures of the brilliant scientist Richard Seaton and dashing millionaire M. Reynolds Crane versus the evil Marc "Blackie" DuQuesne in his attempts to take control of Seaton's discovery of X, the special metal that made interstellar flight possible.

The second *Skylark* in Doc Smith's *Skylark of Space* novels was lots bigger than the first, just as the B-17 was bigger than the B-26—although that raised the question of what kind of bomber could serve as the stand-in for the planetoid-sized *Skylark of Valeron*.

Ellis's big brother Johnny first discovered science fiction in 1935. He and Pete started the club, complete with an official charter from *Wonder Stories* magazine. Johnny was the leader, even though Pete, at seventeen, was slightly older. Ellis, on the other hand, was only thirteen, a baby, so he didn't count. About a year after the Skylark Science Fiction League started, Johnny scrounged a hectograph, a cheap duplicator that would produce a small run of hard-to-read purple pages, and put out an amateur magazine—named, naturally, *Skylark*. Johnny wrote a story and Pete a science article for the isue. Ellis, who liked comic books better back then, drew a cover more or less copied from an issue of *Thrilling Wonder Stories*. Johnny and Pete were impressed, and so Ellis became the third and final Skylark.

By 1939, when they traveled to New York for the first World Science Fiction Convention, they were well-known in science fiction fandom. *Skylark* was now mimeographed. At the 1940 Worldcon, they met Doc Smith in person—he was dressed as the Gray Lensman—and gave him a copy of the all–E. E. Smith issue of *Skylark*, #18.

Ellis was the best looking of the Skylarks, athletic and blond and strong. He was charming and lucky and people liked him, including girls—a talent in which Johnny was completely lacking. Ellis had gotten himself an athletic scholarship to Gettysburg College, where he planned to study art. He talked about going into advertising and maybe moving to New York City.

The war changed everybody's plans.

• TUESDAY, 14 JULY 1942 •

SWPA HQ, BRISBANE, AUSTRALIA, 0958 HOURS

"You realize that I will need the First Marines for use in the Solomon Islands," MacArthur declared, gesturing with his pipe for emphasis. General Sutherland nodded sagely. General Willoughby, on the other hand, allowed himself the hint of a scowl.

"That means we'll need Kelly Turner's transports, probably Admiral Ghormley's whole fleet," the chief of intelligence cautioned. "Nimitz isn't going to like it."

The General didn't skip a beat. "Of course he won't. But it's no longer his concern—the new line of demarcation gives me clear authority to conduct operations in the Solomons. I've sent Sanderson over to New Caledonia to take charge of the base at Noumea. We don't have time to waste. We need to take the offensive immediately, to bring this war back to the enemy!"

"Which enemy?" Willoughby asked, chuckling.

MacArthur grinned. "I've won a temporary victory on that front, but no more. MacArthur will have to strike again, and soon. All of us must be on the lookout for any signs of navy bungling or failure. I am confident that they will shortly hand us another club with which to hit them."

"What did Admiral King have to say about your requisition?" asked Sutherland, gesturing to the recently arrived communiqué that the General had read, then casually tossed to the side of his desk.

MacArthur smiled thinly. "I'm sure what he really said was unprintable. MacArthur is not King's choice to command his precious naval assets. But he had no room for maneuver in this situation. Yielding to force majeure, King has granted us use of all fleet and marine assets for the upcoming operation. Only this operation, you understand, and no other. However, we will have operational control, with Admiral Turner commanding the transports and Admiral Fletcher the aircraft carriers. Admiral Ghormley is the overall naval commander, but he is to follow my instructions. King insists that the chain of command ultimately passes through Hawaii, but that's really a formality. The important decisions—really, the only decisions—will come from right here in Brisbane."

"What's the target, then?" asked Willoughby.

MacArthur beamed as a knock, right on cue, sounded at the door. "Come in, George!" he declared, like an actor booming a line from a Broadway stage.

General Kenney entered and carried a folder over to MacArthur's desk. He put it down and several eight-by-ten glossy photographs slipped out. Popping the stem of the pipe between his teeth, the General reached down and scrutinized one after another of these shots.

"Look at this, Sir Charles," he said, extending them to the intelligence officer. Willoughby studied each for several seconds. "What do you see?"

"Obviously they're clearing space for an airfield, General. A large one, judging from the scale of the trees. Where is it?"

"It down at the bottom end of the Solomons, and it's going to be the first thing we take back from the enemy—the first rung on the long ladder back to the Philippines!" The General paused for dramatic effect. "Guadalcanal.

"It's a big island, and the enemy is working on turning it into a major base. The Coastwatchers have given us some preliminary reports—the Japs landed there just a couple of weeks ago and started working on that wharf you see there. Now they've landed trucks and earthmovers and what all, with two large labor battalions working on clearing and smoothing the airfield."

"This strip will be ready for operations by mid-August, and gentlemen, I want it to launch airplanes from the United States of America!"

"But—that's only a month away!" Sutherland sputtered.

MacArthur swept majestically around the room as if he hadn't heard. "We'll need to get the support of such carriers as the navy has managed to keep afloat—George, you say this is too far away for our own bombers to do much?"

"Yes, sir, General. Our B-17s can get over there from Australia, but all our medium bombers—the Mitchells and the Marauders—would be out of range. And never mind any fighters. We've P-40s and P-39s based in New Guinea, but they have their hands full just battling the Japs up there. Not to mention that even with external tanks they don't have the range to get over to the Solomons."

"Then it will have to be a navy show—sailors and marines." Willoughby noted pointedly.

"Yes." The General's tone was almost triumphant. "But they will be *my* sailors and marines—and they will be fighting my battle, and winning my victory!"

• FRIDAY, 7 AUGUST 1942 •

IMPERIAL PALACE, TOKYO, JAPAN, 0715 HOURS

In this, the seventeenth year of Showa, the Era of Enlightened Peace, His Imperial Majesty the forty-two-year-old emperor of the Great Empire of Japan took his morning walk in the vast formal gardens of the Imperial Palace, his mind composed and serene. Today he was in a part of the gardens he seldom visited, a section with twisted, narrow footpaths, old trees, and small mossy ponds, all located in the shadow of the palace wall.

He walked slowly, noticing the smallest notes of nature's beauty: there, the way the filtered cool light through the trees refracts through the drop of water on the oddly shaped leaf. Nearby, the dark green moss filling the deep crevasses in the bark of that tree.

By focusing on the details, he could remove himself from contact with the rest of the world. He could feel as if he were really alone.

Of course, that was an illusion. No emperor was ever really alone. Behind artfully designed fencing and carefully positioned shrubbery there were guards and retainers and various functionaries of the imperial household watching and waiting.

But a man could become alone within the confines of his own mind.

The emperor had used many names and titles in his lifetime. As a child, he was known as Prince Michi. When his grandfather, the Meiji emperor, died, he was invested as Crown Prince Hirohito. When his father, the Taisho emperor, sickened, he became His Imperial Highness Prince Regent Hirohito and took on all the duties of his father's office. He ascended the Chrysanthemum Throne in the Western year of 1926, taking on the mantle of Dai Nihon Koku Tenno, Emperor of the Great Empire of Japan. In doing so, Hirohito ceased to use the name of his birth. He was simply "the emperor." After his death, he would be known as the Showa Emperor, or the Emperor of Enlightened Peace. He was the 124th to occupy the Chrysanthemum Throne, scion of the longest-reigning dynasty on Earth. His ancestry could be traced in an unbroken line through Jimmu the first emperor to the goddess Amaterasu Omikami, source of all peace. This made Enlightened Peace Emperor semidivine, the literal Son of Heaven.

The emperor who would be known as Enlightened Peace knelt before a carp pond to contemplate the carpet of wriggling fish. He was pleased to see a frog on the shore, which reminded him of the Basho haiku. "At the old pond/A frog leaps in/Water's sound." But when he recited the haiku, the frog did not oblige him by leaping in.

"Don't you know I'm emperor? You should have hopped in the water when I said so," he chided the frog, but the unimpressed frog sat there. Well, that was a frog for you. Frogs had no respect for authority. Carp were different. Carp always came up to goggle at you. Clearly they recognized the importance of His Imperial Majesty.

There is a haiku in this, thought the Showa Emperor. He was quite good at haiku. And, most important, having a haiku to work on would give him something to do with his mind during the endless ceremonies that would make up much of the imperial day.

He stood, said a Shinto prayer, turned his back on the little pond, and walked slowly back along the manicured path under the shadow of the Imperial Palace walls. He was hardly aware of the guards, retainers, and functionaries moving with him.

There was to be a morning meeting of the Supreme Council for the Direction of the War. Before the meeting, he would have a premeeting, where he would hear what he was to hear at the meeting. After the meeting, he would meet again with the key people from the meeting, where they would discuss what he had heard at the meeting.

There had previously been a meeting to determine the agenda for the meeting, which he had not attended, and another meeting to settle certain issues that would come before the meeting, and after the postmeeting, there would come various smaller meetings to resolve conflicts and issues that arose from today's meeting. Most of these would be conducted by members of the imperial household and the genro, a privy council of former prime ministers, imperial confidants, and close relatives.

The formal meeting of the Supreme Council was to be held in the presence of the Showa emperor, but that did not mean they expected him to speak. His presence signified imperial assent to the conclusions of the meeting and was thus essential. However, laws and customs restricted any direct participation on his part.

The meeting was held in a long, rectangular conference room. The metallic print wallpaper gleamed dull bronze in the light of two elaborate chandeliers. The emperor's dais sat at the open end of a long U-shaped table covered with a checkerboard tablecloth. His highest-ranking military officers and war ministers sat on the two sides of the U. No one sat along the closed end of the U, for then they would be facing the emperor directly, and it was forbidden for mere mortals to look directly at the emperor's face.

The emperor's dais consisted of a bare elevated riser with a screen behind it, on which rested a rather uncomfortable low-backed chair and various ceremonial objects. His duty was to sit in that chair for hours at a time, erect and still, hands resting on his thighs, his face composed in a neutral expression. Although he was not expected to speak, the emperor listened carefully, both to what was and what was not said.

It was most interesting to hear what Tojo Hideki, the prime minister, was not saying. Tojo, a former army lieutenant general known as "the Razor," also held the portfolios of minister of war, home minister, and foreign minister. At this meeting he was acting as war minister and had the floor. Tojo was a strong-featured man with a thick black mustache and tortoiseshell glasses, aggressive and domineering.

"Our victory off Savo Island in the Solomons chain has all the characteristics of the decisive battle," the war minister announced. He began to give details of the battle. The emperor noted that there was no mention of an American presence on that island that was to be used as an airfield to interdict American shipping moving toward Australia. Well, perhaps they were only a minor nuisance; still, pretending those Americans did not exist was . . . interesting.

Serenely confident in the status of events, Tojo presented the meeting's real agenda, the argument between army and navy on the next campaign. It wasn't introduced that way, of course. He gave the floor first to Army Chief of Staff Sugiyama Hajime, who presented a revised version of Operation 21, an invasion of British East India through Burma.

Sugiyama had long opposed an invasion of India, favored by Tojo. Improved intelligence and experience fighting the British had convinced him that the invasion through Burma was now practical. Netaji Subhash Chandra Bose's Indian National Army, though not much of a fighting force, would provide necessary pretext and the nucleus of a puppet government.

The emperor thought that it must be difficult to be army chief of staff when the war minister and prime minister was himself an army general of distinction. Sugiyama was less than he appeared, because Tojo carried the real power. Would that give Sugiyama the wisdom to appreciate the frog in the garden? Military men often had tunnel vision about power. They believed power had some necessary relationship to weaponry. That was foolish. A gun could not make the frog hop on command, but merely kill it.

The navy, represented by their chief of staff, Admiral Osami Nagano, spoke next. "India represents an attractive opportunity. Of that, there is no argument." He bowed toward Sugiyama and Tojo. "But to reach the subcontinent will require an almost total naval commitment, including the taking of the Andaman and Nicobar islands, an amphibious assault in Orissa state, and a feint against Ceylon. To do all this and at the same time continue the offensive against the Americans in the Solomons and New Guinea, I respectfully suggest, would put an unacceptable strain on our resources at the present time. India will be there when the Americans are finally defeated, and the British pose no serious threat. Let us supply Bose, by all means, and allow him to appear to be a threat. Perhaps let us engage in a feint in the direction of India. But there is a far more attractive opportunity available to us in the short run."

Admiral Nagano picked up his pointer and walked over to a map perched on an easel that was located against the wall on the navy side of the conference table. "Here." He tapped the map with his pointer. "The Samoas. With the American presence in the Solomons all but eliminated, occupying the Samoas would allow us to cut American access to Australia. Shortly, the American efforts in New Guinea would falter, and afterward, we could sweep the South Pacific clear of all opposition at minimal cost. From there, the empire will be secure." He smiled, bowed, and returned to his seat.

Here, too, what was not said was of greater interest than what was. Nagano was, on the surface, as dismissive of the American threat as both Sugiyama or Tojo, but his plan took them seriously, at least. The threat in the Solomons was "all but eliminated" rather than gone. The New Guinea campaign needed to be starved. American supply lines needed to be cut. Nagano would herd the frog, jabbing it with a sharp stick to make it jump first in this direction, then in that direction, until it did his bidding.

Tojo stood up to rebut. "With greatest respect for the navy's insightful and brilliant plan, the American efforts in New Guinea will falter in any event, and the South Pacific will shortly be clear of all opposition whether Samoa is taken or not. The Indian subcontinent, on the other hand, is a rich prize in its own right, a worthy addition to the Co-Prosperity Sphere, not merely a strategic bomber base and ship refueling station."

Tojo believed that his willpower alone was enough to control the frog. And if the frog wouldn't cooperate, why then, he would kill it. He would never understand that killing it meant that it had forever escaped his control. But then, Tojo had been the head of the *kempetai* in Manchuria. The secret police always believed that the ability to kill was the ability to control.

It pleased the emperor to think about this for the duration of the meeting. No decision was taken as to whether the next objective would be Samoa or India, nor was it expected that such a decision would be reached at this meeting. Decisions took time. As well they should, for a decision bound everyone, and so consensus was essential.

One of the genro had the title of *naidaijin,* lord privy seal, for he had custody of all the imperial seals. But that was the least important of the lord privy seal's duties. Most important was that the *naidaijin* served as the emperor's closest confidant, emissary, and minister without portfolio. Its current occupant was Kido Koichi, a member of the nobility holding the rank of *koshaku,* or marquis. He was also one of the few people the Showa emperor trusted unreservedly. It was because of Kido that the emperor knew the full story of what had happened at Guadalcanal. In his private audience with Tojo and the two chiefs of staff, he could express his displeasure more openly.

"It is true that a human being is smarter than an animal, but one cannot safely conclude that an animal is not dangerous, and one ignores the danger at one's peril," the emperor said. "We find it distressing that Our army and navy are arguing about new campaigns when your Guadalcanal Island commander conducted his offensive based on the faulty information that the Americans had only two thousand troops on the island. Are army and navy communicating with one another? Are we so confident in our own superiority that we are underestimating the brute force and number of our enemies? Finish one thing, then contemplate starting something new." He sat impassively, signaling that the audience was over. Tojo and his chiefs of staff, embarrassed, bowed and withdrew.

"That will make them think, Your Majesty," said Kido, smiling.

"Let us hope so. Thinking is a habit worth encouraging in Our ministers," replied the emperor. "Oh—We thought of a new haiku today." He paused, recited. "Old frog sits by pond/No splash. Orders float in air/Curious carp laugh."

Kido nodded. "Excellent. A Basho Matsuo reference?"

"Yes," replied the emperor. "We saw a frog this morning."

"Somehow I don't think the prime minister would appreciate the sentiment," commented Kido, chuckling.

"We agree. It is a failing in his character. And, unfortunately, also a danger to the empire. Ah, but it's all fate, isn't it, Kido?"

"Yes, Your Majesty. But we mortals still struggle the best we can."

"We pray for Our people," replied the emperor.

"May the Gods grant the prayers of the Son of Heaven," replied Kido.

• MONDAY, 10 AUGUST 1942 •

SWPA GHQ, BRISBANE, AUSTRALIA, 1349 HOURS

"Ghormley steamed away?" An incredulous MacArthur stopped his pacing and struck a dramatic pose in front of the wainscoting. "He abandoned the marines without supplies on the beaches of Guadalcanal?" He gestured with the end of his unlit pipe at the small file folder of papers neatly centered and squared on his formal wooden desk. "Unbelievable! A disgrace to the traditions of the United States Navy!"

Admiral William Frederick Halsey Jr.—only the press ever referred to him as "Bull"—tried to interject a word of his own. He was sitting in one of the two leather chairs that flanked MacArthur's desk. He had just discovered that the comfortable chairs were a MacArthur trap; he had settled so deeply into the chair that he was having trouble sitting forward.

MacArthur's chief of staff, General Richard K. Sutherland, raised his hand to cover the involuntary grin on his face at Halsey's discomfort. He loved to see people try to argue with the General.

Finally Halsey managed to squeeze a few words of his own into MacArthur's monologue. "Ghormley had no choice. He was about to get caught flat-footed by the Imperial Japanese

Fleet. The transports would have gone right to the bottom, and with all respect, that wouldn't have fed or supplied the marines, either."

MacArthur was in no mood to brook opposing opinion. He fixed Halsey with a dramatic stare, the unlit pipe taking station under his chin like a mortar, and began to orate. "Has the navy never heard of fighting and winning against daunting odds? If the odds are too daunting for direct combat, has the navy no tradition of running convoys past the enemy at night? And at the very least, has the navy no tradition of making a vow of support to brave men in harm's way? Where was Admiral Ghormley's promise to the men of Guadalcanal that he would find a way to get them their supplies no matter what? Where was his push to unload at least one more transport before withdrawing, if withdraw he must, to show he shared the risk? Tell me, Admiral Halsey, does the navy have no traditions of leadership, risk, or inspiration?" He did not pause for Halsey to reply, though the admiral tried to interrupt, to defend navy honor. "Of *course* it is false, of *course* it is a calumny, of *course* the navy has such traditions. MacArthur can easily see the challenges in Ghormley's situation. Where MacArthur and Ghormley differ is that Ghormley gives up and runs away, and MacArthur never surrenders."

Sutherland could see Halsey's face reddening. "Halsey never surrenders either, sir," the admiral interrupted.

"Good *God,* man, of course you don't," MacArthur replied with an expression of shock that appeared nearly genuine. "I didn't mean to imply . . . No, no, Halsey, you're a fighter. My kind of fighter. I have the deepest respect for you, and for the navy as a whole, a few bad apples notwithstanding. That's why this Ghormley fellow outrages us both so much. He betrays what you and I both hold dearest. I'm so glad to see you agree with me. In fact, you've convinced me that I must do what I must do regardless of the consequences."

The General pressed a button on his desk and within seconds the double doors of his office opened, and a pool secretary—MacArthur did not use a personal one—entered, sat down, and flipped open her steno pad. Striking a new pose, this one in three-quarter profile, the General pronounced sentence.

"Immediate for Ghormley, COMSOPAC. You are relieved of command effective immediately. Report to MacArthur in Brisbane at earliest possible moment for review of your recent actions." The steno efficiently transcribed the words in neat Gregg shorthand. She waited until MacArthur nodded his head, then she stood and walked crisply out of the room.

Halsey, Sutherland noticed, was horrified that he had been boobytrapped into endorsing MacArthur's dismissal of Ghormley. Sutherland was a bit horrified himself. The General didn't always reckon on all the consequences of his actions. He'd have to say something once the two men were in private. But making it seem as if Halsey supported him was a clever move.

But MacArthur was already onto his next topic. "Bill, I'm appointing you as COMSOPAC, as soon as you can get out to the fleet. Your first order is to find a way to supply Guadalcanal. If you have to take some risks and if it costs some ships, that's the way it has to be. The United States of America is officially out of the business of leaving unsupplied troops to fend for themselves against the Japanese. I'm counting on you to figure out a way to get the job done."

Sutherland found Halsey's face particularly easy to read. He disliked Ghormley being criticized by MacArthur, an outsider, but at the same time he agreed with most of MacArthur's comments. And to be commander, South Pacific Area and South Pacific Forces, was *the* job in the Pacific right now. He'd do it as well as or better than anybody else alive.

Halsey was won over. One more person under the General's spell. That was MacArthur's genius. While any number of people hated his guts, just as many people worshipped the ground on which he walked.

Once Halsey had left and the door had clicked shut behind him, Sutherland spoke up. "The navy won't like your removal of Ghormley, General."

MacArthur raised one eyebrow. "And why should the navy's dislike trouble MacArthur, my dear Sutherland?"

Sutherland knew better than to argue. He waited for MacArthur to continue.

"In fact," General MacArthur continued, with a smug smile betraying his delight at his own Machiavellian cleverness, "the navy's dislike is high among the reasons for sacking Ghormley. Remember, MacArthur abjured all of you to find instances of navy failure or incompetence. And here, we see a magnificent example laid bare for all the world. Does MacArthur *fear* the navy's dislike? MacArthur *solicits* the navy's dislike! Imagine they take the trouble to overrule me officially. What will the newspapers think of them, excusing the man who left unsupplied marines stranded on the beaches of Guadalcanal because of cowardice? MacArthur wins. And if they accept my removal of Ghormley, MacArthur wins. Whatever the navy does or doesn't do works to MacArthur's benefit. This, you see, is what is better known as checkmate."

He paused and smiled, giving his sole listener a moment to absorb the General's wisdom and insight. Then a new idea crossed his mind. "Which reminds me. It is imperative that I go to Guadalcanal. The General must be with his troops in the heat of battle, to inspire and lead and show our forces and the world how an American commander *should* behave."

"But General . . ." Sutherland's objections came out as reflex. "It's too unsettled, too risky. In a few weeks, I'm sure we can arrange it, but right now . . ."

But even as he talked, he could see the lines around MacArthur's mouth harden. The General had made his decision.

• THURSDAY, 13 AUGUST 1942 •

PEARL HARBOR, HAWAII, 1300 HOURS

The long overwater flight from Australia on a C-54 Skymaster just made Captain Frank Chadwick's curiosity that much greater. He'd heard about MacArthur's firing of Admiral

Ghormley as COMSOPAC right before he boarded, and he could only imagine Fleet Admiral Chester W. Nimitz's reaction to the news. The MacArthur–navy war, far from being over, looked like it was heading toward greater conflagration.

He grabbed his bag, politely shrugged off a seaman's attempt to help him, and walked across the field to the parking lot where his baby waited for him: a cherry-red 1932 MG Midget started up immediately, despite having been sitting alone for several weeks, and he headed off base and windward. When he had first been stationed here, he had rented a second-story apartment on Kuuhali Street in Kailua Beach, not far from the water. When he could, he got in some surfing. In fact, it looked like a fine day for surfing, but duty called. He took a quick shower, changed uniforms, and was back in his MG in less than forty minutes. At least he could enjoy the fresh air as he drove, he thought as he turned onto Likelike Highway and shifted into third.

He showed his pass at the gate. The marine guard saluted, then added, "Nice car, sir."

"Thanks," Chadwick said, smiling.

A few minutes more and he was pulling up in front of CINCPAC headquarters. He got out, grabbed his portfolio filled with torpedo-related material, and went inside.

"How's the car, Captain?" the senior chief said by way of greeting.

"Beautiful. Thanks for taking care of her for me."

"It's a pleasure, Captain. I took my girlfriend up Ewa to Sunset Beach in her. That car is pure *magic,* Captain!"

Chadwick laughed. "And it's fun to drive, too. Is he available?"

"Let me check, sir." He picked up the telephone. "Yes, sir. Captain Chadwick reporting in, sir. Yes, sir." He looked at Frank. "You can go right in, Captain."

"Welcome back, Frank," Admiral Nimitz said as Chadwick walked into the office. "I got the torpedo study you sent back from Australia. Good job. Problem identified and documented. Now we just have to light a fire under the BuOrd people, and maybe we can start getting workable torpedoes out here in six months or so." He shook his head. "It would serve us right if MacArthur found out and crucified us over this. I'd court-martial the BuOrd people who've been dragging their heels, but only because we can't keelhaul them anymore."

"By the time Admiral King gets through with them, maybe they'll wish they'd been keelhauled instead," Captain Chadwick replied.

Nimitz chuckled briefly. "Now. Next item. Frank, you've done a hell of a job as my aide this past year, but it's time to see you move on. Given any thought to what you'd like to do next?"

"Well, sir, I want what all us brown-shoe types want: a carrier command at sea. But until the stream of new carriers gets going, you need your most experienced carrier skippers on the job, and that lets me out. The closest I've come to a carrier command was as skipper of the *Langley* for six months in 1939. And that was after she converted from carrier to seaplane tender." The *Langley*, a former collier, had been the navy's first aircraft carrier. "Command at sea is what I need most, sir, and I'd be happy with any opportunity that's out there. On the other hand, there's a war on, and I'll go wherever I can serve the navy best."

"Even if it's going to Washington and fixing the torpedo problem?" Nimitz asked.

"It's got to be fixed, Admiral."

Nimitz drummed his fingers on his desk for a minute. "Frank, you may end up in Washington at least for a while."

Frank's heart sank. "Of course, sir."

"But not just yet. Before it's time to shove an outsider into that mess, we've got to let the Washington hands work with it a little bit. Maybe you won't need to go, but don't count on it."

"In the meantime?"

"In the meantime, Admiral Halsey has got to get SOPAC up to speed, and quickly. Admiral Fletcher is out."

"Admiral Fletcher, too?"

"He and Ghormley are being kicked upstairs. Damn MacArthur! He had no right to can a navy officer in the performance of his duty." Nimitz grimaced, his teeth clenched. Frank sensed that the admiral was conflicted, even before he continued. "Still, Halsey is the best man for the job, no doubt about it. All those marines on that godforsaken island . . . if the Japs keep control of the seas around Guadalcanal, I don't like their chances very much."

"I don't think Admiral Halsey will let that happen, sir. He's not about to let the navy take it on the chin over this."

"He's a fighter, that's for sure. And that's what we need. There are some less senior officers who need to go as well. SOPAC has some top-notch people like McCain and Turner, and some deadwood. I'm sending Halsey the best I've got, and that includes you."

SOPAC was where all the action in the Pacific Theater was going to be concentrated for the time being. An assignment there was the best possible opportunity.

"Do you know what I'll be doing, sir, or will Admiral Halsey decide after I get there?"

"Yes and yes. How does captain of the *Portland* sound?"

Frank was elated. The USS *Portland,* CA-33, was a heavy cruiser, the first of her class. With just under 850 officers and enlisted men, nine eight-inch guns, and a displacement of nearly ten thousand tons, she was faster than a battleship, more powerful than a destroyer, and able to stand up against almost anything.

"Thank you. Thank you very much."

"Congratulations. It's well earned. You'll be meeting her in Noumea, which is now SOPAC headquarters. We've stopped worrying about the delicate sensibilities of the Free French on New Caledonia. Now, I don't know exactly how long you'll have the *Portland,* but with Bill Halsey in charge, there's a good chance it'll be long enough to see some fighting."

"Thank you, Admiral. It's been an honor serving you."

"You're a good man, Frank. I expect to pin stars on you before this war is over." Nimitz stood, followed by Frank, and the two men shook hands. Chadwick was suddenly in a hurry to leave.

He had a fighting ship to command.

FIVE

Guadalcanal

• MONDAY, 14 SEPTEMBER 1942 •

APPROACHING HENDERSON FIELD, GUADALCANAL ISLAND, SOLOMON ISLANDS, 1012 HOURS

They'd be touching down at Henderson Field in about forty minutes. Despite Kenney's assurances about the runway, Ellis had heard that the Japs were shelling it regularly, and it was primarily set up for single-engine aircraft, not medium bombers. The marine defenders were expanding the runways as fast as they could, of course, but the lack of supplies and the constant attacks made it tough. The plan was for the B-26s and the P-38 escort fighters to land, and for the B-17s to continue with their diversionary raid. After three or four hours on the island—enough time for MacArthur's whirlwind inspection and, hopefully, Halverson's evaluation of the field's suitability as a bomber base—they'd take off again for the long flight back to Australia.

It was good to be back in a Marauder. For all the virtues of the B-17, the B-26 was still a hell of a lot more fun to fly. The assignment was temporary, though. There was some question about whether a B-17 could land at Henderson Field, so the General hadn't taken the *Bataan,* his personal

B-17. General Kenney had recommended Ellis, remembering the connection he'd had with MacArthur, to serve as his pilot on this trip. General Sutherland had predictably bitched and moaned, but Kenney had convinced him that this was the safest way if the General insisted on visiting Guadalcanal in person.

When he got his Marauder, he quickly painted *Skylark III* on its side, even though the third *Skylark* in Doc Smith's novels was quite a bit larger than even *Skylark II*. The paint wasn't quite dry, though, when the word came down from Brisbane: this plane, like all others transporting General Douglas MacArthur, was to be named *Bataan*. Ellis was momentarily peeved, then inspired. *Bataan* was on the nose, sure enough, along with a quick painting of Johnny behind barbed wire.

When MacArthur saw the art, he stood very still for a minute, then turned to Ellis and asked, "Did you paint that?"

"Yes, sir," Ellis replied.

MacArthur continued to look at the painting for a moment, then climbed inside the plane. Ellis noticed General Sutherland looking daggers at him. Ellis wondered, not for the first time, what relationship Sutherland and MacArthur had with his brother, but he knew there was no way to ask. For the hours it took to fly to Guadalcanal silence reigned in the cockpit.

Guadalcanal came into detailed focus as they flew in from the southwest. The island was ninety miles long and up to thirty-four miles wide, and shaped sort of like a W with the final bar broken off, or like a one-humped caterpillar. Henderson Field was located just past the first dip in the W, about a third of the way down the island in the direction of their travel. A series of green, steep-sided ridges looked every bit as rugged as New Guinea terrain, even if the mountains weren't as high. The ridges rippled and twisted across the entire island.

The Japanese controlled all Guadalcanal except for the marine perimeter around the airfield, so the bombers didn't dawdle as they crossed the island and approached Lunga

Point, the Marine landing area, which was near the airfield. A few miles away, in the waters called Ironbottom Sound—because of the great number of ships that had sunk down there in the furious naval battles often waged within sight of the marines on shore—a freighter was anchored just off the shore as several smaller craft shuttled up to the beaches. *Bataan* was in the lead as the planes flew out over the sound and turned, separating into a file as they prepared for landing.

Ellis noticed waving and gesturing coming from the aircraft nearest his, a B-17 named *Grable's Gams,* piloted by a good buddy of his, Lieutenant Richard Vail. Following Rich's pointing finger, Halverson spotted the fast-moving specks diving toward them from the north.

There were Japs on their tail.

"General, we've got company," the pilot shouted. "I think we can outrun them if we head for home." He pushed the Marauder into a shallow dive, applying full throttle to both engines.

"Nonsense!" MacArthur replied from the copilot's seat, shaking his head. "We've come this far—we'll land as soon as they clear out."

"Yes, sir," Ellis replied.

Speed was still the best option. He trimmed the propellers to a faster angle and increased his airspeed, nosing his Marauder downward. "Japs on our tail," he announced on the crew intercom. "We're going to dive out of the way and hope some of those marine fighters put in an appearance. Gramps, Dale, we're going to run rather than fight if we can, but heat up those guns just in case."

The answering "Rogers" had barely died out before Ellis spotted the marines, flying Grumman F4F Wildcats, formed up in a combat air patrol at maybe eighteen thousand feet and heading in his direction. As they grew near he continued his dive, looking up so that he could watch the stubby little fighters fly past overhead.

A sudden loud hailstorm of metal against metal petrified him. It was the sound of fifty-caliber machine gun bullets puncturing his fuselage. And they were coming from in *front* of him.

"Goddamn it, the fuckers think we're Japs!" he yelled. The bullets were shattering glass now—the nose, dammit! "Gramps! Gramps! You okay?"

No answer. He banked his Marauder hard, always risky with a B-26, but he had no choice if they were going to live. The G-force wrenched him to the side, then reversed as he pulled through a tight S curve. He managed to recover without going into a spin, then nosed down more steeply while flipping on the radio with one hand—dammit, he needed a copilot right now, not a four-star deadhead who was going to get them all killed, and what was happening to Gramps, was he bleeding to death or already dead?

"Mayday, Mayday! This is Red Rover One. Red Rover One. Hold your fire! Hold your fire!" he shouted. "We're Americans—can't you see the fucking star on the wing!"

"Here, let me take that," said MacArthur calmly. "I can handle a radio. You just fly the plane. The faster we get down, the quicker someone can look at your nose gunner." The General began the Mayday chant but pulled rank. "Mayday. This is General Douglas MacArthur in the B-26. Mayday. Hold your fire. I say, hold your fire. This is General Douglas MacArthur. I'm coming in."

The Wildcats were past now, and whether they had recognized their mistake or simply preferred to tackle the enemy fighters, the marines were swarmed among the Zeros, scattering the outnumbered Japanese fighters in a snarling dogfight. The other Marauders still followed the *Bataan* in the dive toward the field.

Ellis did a damage control check. He could see the holes in the nose, but the engines and flight controls seemed to be functioning normally. He worried about the nosewheel, but when he dropped the landing gear all three struts came down and locked into place. He came in full flaps, descending at a very steep angle and maintaining his airspeed at about 150 miles per hour. Finally he leveled out at about thirty feet above the ground and came in nice and smooth, touching tail down with the nosewheel hitting with a hard thump a moment later.

The *Bataan* rumbled past a landscape of shattered palm trees and blasted, cratered ground. The runway had been patched in dozens of places, but it was smooth enough. Braking to a stop as quickly as possible, Halverson jumped out of his seat, cutting ahead of his four-star passenger. He hopped down from the flight deck, dropped to his hands and knees, and crawled underneath, dropped down out of the nosewheel well onto the ground, then jumped up to see into the bombardier area in the nose.

Gramps—he was slightly over thirty years old, making him an official old man—was one of the four survivors from the *Skylark of Space,* which had to make a water landing following the accidental skip bombing of the Japanese transport.

With blood everywhere and Gramps not moving, Ellis first thought he was dead. *Damn.* The bombardier had a wife and two kids back in Oklahoma.

It was the second time Ellis Halverson had lost crewmen.

It was the first time he felt tears stinging his eyes.

A hand clasped his shoulder. "I'm sorry, son. Another brave man lost to this war. This was a terrible accident, but it was just that: an accident, one of the many inhumane and deeply unfortunate parts of this tragic business in which we are all engaged. We mourn our dead between battles. During battles we press onward, ever onward." General MacArthur's deep, sonorous voice carried surprising warmth and sincerity.

Then: "Take cover!" It was a marine ground crewman, running toward them, waving his arms to direct them to a nearby trench.

The other members of the *Bataan* crew were already diving into sandbag bunkers on the edge of the runway. MacArthur, however, stood and watched the sky as a lone Zero flew the length of the field, spitting bullets and shells. Several zinged very near to the B-26, but the General took no notice of the flying slugs. Despite his grief—and rising anger—Ellis couldn't bring himself to leave MacArthur's side.

There was a moan. Gramps was alive! "Medic!" Ellis screamed. "I've got a wounded man here!"

Two men, one wearing a red cross armband, sprinted toward him. The one with the red cross quickly checked Gramps's pulse. "He might make it," the medic said, "but we've got to get him out of here fast."

As the strafing fighter passed, now with a pair of Grummans on its tail, the pilot looked up and watched the dogfight. The Japs had apparently already done some bombing—smoke was rising from burning gasoline drums not far away—and now the enemy fighters had stayed behind to mix it up with the angry swarm of marine F4Fs. MacArthur was still peering upward, shading his eyes with his hand even though he wore aviator sunglasses.

Another plane swooped in to strafe, and Ellis suddenly felt a burning urgency to run, to dive for the trenches. But there was Gramps to consider. He, the medic, and the third marine carefully lifted the unconscious body out of the shattered nose under the medic's direction. Once Gramps was free, they marched double time in the direction of a hospital tent, marked with the same red cross.

Ellis wished he were anywhere else as the Jap fighter flew low overhead. A C-47 transport plane took a direct hit and blew up. *What if they hit the* Bataan*?* he thought with sudden icy fear. They'd be stuck here.

A Wildcat began trailing smoke. It was badly hit and going down. Ellis had a momentary and fierce reaction—*maybe he's the son of a bitch who shot Gramps*—but a quick surge of shame quelled his anger. Dammit, it *had* been an accident, and they were all here to fight the Japs. There! The strafing Zero caught fire, and then there was what looked to him like a fuel line explosion. Suddenly the fighter had only one wing and was spinning like a Miss America fire baton.

Two more medics were running toward them. One relieved Ellis, another the third marine. "Nothing more you can do," the first medic said. "Pray, maybe." He watched numbly as they took Gramps into the hospital tent. Ellis turned back toward MacArthur, looking heavenward, one hand still shading his eyes.

A balding marine officer was striding over the churned sand in their direction, paying no more attention to the danger than did MacArthur. As the marine officer got closer, Ellis could make out two stars. That identified him as Major General Alexander Vandegrift, commander of 1st Marine Division and top dog on the island.

Top dog until now, anyway.

Vandegrift had a bloodhound face, somewhat jowly, with sad blue eyes. He was sweaty and his uniform sleeves were rolled up. Ellis came to attention and saluted. Vandegrift ignored him and saluted MacArthur. "Welcome to the Canal, General. As you can see, we put on a little show for you today. We have to make our own entertainment out here, as you know."

MacArthur returned the salute and gravely shook Vandegrift's hand. "I am delighted to meet you, sir, absolutely delighted. You and your brave marines have upheld the finest traditions of the United States military on these jungle shores."

"That's what we do, General," Vandegrift replied. "No matter how little we have to work with."

"I'm sure you could whip the Japanese with a handful of toothpicks if you had to, General Vandegrift, but you must know that MacArthur will do everything in his power to see that you are properly supplied, with all the resources at his command."

"It's good to hear you say that, General," replied Vandegrift. "I suspect you know more than most people how good those words can sound." Ellis had to think for a moment before he realized Vandegrift was talking about the Philippines.

"Yes, I do," MacArthur replied solemnly. He struck a pose of stoic self-pity. "I do indeed."

"Now that you've seen the show, General MacArthur," Vandegrift said, "can I invite you into a shelter? I have a hunch this young man's neck is on the line if something happens to you, and with that promise of resupply I've got a pretty strong interest in keeping you in one piece myself."

"Oh, don't worry about me. The bullet or bomb with my name on it hasn't been made yet. I'm perfectly safe."

"I believe you, sir," said Vandegrift. "But the show's about over, anyway. The Japs can't stay over Henderson Field very long. They'll need to haul ass for home in a few minutes."

"Very well, General," said MacArthur. "Lead on."

The General walked in a deliberate, steady pace, which drove Ellis crazy. He was ready to start running. He kept looking upward at the waning dogfight, hoping he could spot anything coming his way quickly enough to jump. True to Vandegrift's words, the remaining Zeros were winging toward the north, pursued by buzzing Wildcats. At least six planes that Ellis saw, most of them Japs, had gone down during the brief, violent contest.

"Watch your step, sir!" the third marine warned, just in time to bring Ellis up short. With his eyes studying the sky, Ellis had wandered a little distance away from the two generals—and another step would have dumped him into a slit trench at the edge of the runway.

Embarrassed, he looked at the third marine, seeing him clearly for the first time. "Thank—" he started and then halted in shock. The man was staring up at him with a similar expression. "Pete?"

"Ellis? Damn! I didn't recognize you with everything else going on!"

The marine sprang out of the trench, and they were hugging each other, clapping backs, shaking hands.

It was Pete Rachwalski, the third Skylark to come to the Pacific to make war.

1ST MARINE DIVISION HQ, GUADALCANAL, 1650 HOURS

"Ellis, my God! What the hell are you doing here? I mean—" Pete suddenly noticed the captain's bars and let go of the bear hug as if he'd been shocked. The other enlisted men in the trench were looking at him curiously, and a first sergeant he didn't know was giving him the evil eye. "Lance Corporal Peter Rachwalski, sir!" he said, coming to attention and saluting.

"Hell, Pete," Ellis said, "it's just me—the pesky kid brother. No need to . . ." Pete jerked his head slightly in the direction of the first sergeant while holding the salute, and he could see Ellis figuring it out. An officer too friendly with an enlisted man would get some informal private counseling. An enlisted man who got friendly with officers got worse.

Ellis's voice dropped an octave. He saluted, somewhat more casually than had Pete. "As you were, Lance Corporal," he said. "It's great to see you, though."

"Sir, yes, sir! It's a pleasure to see you again, too, sir!" Pete took the risk of glancing over at the first sergeant.

The all clear signal came, and the marines in the trench got on their feet, brushing off dirt. The first sergeant came over to them. "Captain, may I help you, sir?" he asked.

"Thank you, First Sergeant. I was General MacArthur's pilot. While I was following the General, I didn't watch where I was putting my feet, and would have fallen into the trench if it weren't for Corporal Rachwalski here. We knew each other Stateside, as I'm sure you could tell."

The first sergeant thought for a second. "I see you're with the Parachute Battalion, Corporal. They're up on the ridge. Why are you here?"

"I'm waiting for some maps from Colonel Buckley, First Sergeant. They should be ready in an hour or so, then I'll be heading back." Buckley commanded the marines G-2 section, responsible for intelligence.

"All right. In the meantime, why don't you give this army captain a tour of our jungle paradise?"

"Yes, First Sergeant." There was no official way for Pete to say thanks, but the sergeant had provided a way for Pete and Ellis to catch up informally given the realities of the military caste system.

"The nickel tour sounds like a great idea," Ellis said.

Pete first met Johnny Halverson when Johnny was sixteen

and Pete barely seventeen. The Halversons had moved to Dundalk, Maryland, an industrial town that had been virtually swallowed by next-door Baltimore, when their Lancaster County farm had failed during the Depression. Pete had been born there. Johnny's dad and Pete's dad both got jobs with the Glenn L. Martin Company when war production began to heat up.

Pete and Johnny were both outsiders, Johnny because he was from the country and Pete—Piotr on his birth certificate—because he was Polish. Their personalities were complementary; Pete was friendly and decent and open and an all-around nice kind of guy, but he didn't have Johnny's urgency or passion. Pete was smart, handy, mechanically inclined where Johnny was utterly hopeless, and he could do just about anything he turned his mind to. He wasn't brilliant at anything, but he was good at about everything.

Johnny and Pete weren't necessarily the kinds of guys you'd expect to become best friends, but it was like each supplied something the other lacked. Pete was content while Johnny could never sit still. Pete could make friends while Johnny was more often irritating. Johnny pushed Pete into uncharted territory, and Pete made sure Johnny was properly tethered.

Pete pointed out the highlights as they walked, though he really wanted to catch up on news from home. "Do you know anything about Johnny? And have you heard from home? We don't get much mail out here. I haven't heard from Sarah in months. John Ellis is eighteen months old, and I haven't seen him since February." Pete got married when he was nineteen to a girl named Sarah he'd met in his senior year. She got pregnant the next year and they had a boy, John Ellis, born in March 1941. He had a job in the printing plant of the *Baltimore Sun,* working his way up to become a typesetter and at the same time going to the University of Baltimore at night to get a teaching degree. That, too, was on hold until the war was over.

"I got a letter from my mom just a couple of weeks ago. She says she went by Sarah's parents' house, saw Sarah and

John Ellis, and they're both fine. John Ellis is walking and saying a few words." He paused. "As for Johnny—still nothing. You know, his birthday was two days ago."

"Damn. I hope he's all right. That's the hardest part of all this," said Pete. "Not knowing. Not being there. Maybe never being there. Maybe letting my boy grow up without his dad . . ." He could feel hot tears welling up in his eyes. He turned his head away, blinked, and quickly changed the subject. "This sure is a hell of a place—and I mean that literally," he said.

Henderson Field consisted of two runways joined to make an arrowhead shape, one runway a bit shorter than the other. A circular taxiway using the shorter runway as its diagonal was about a quarter completed. Crushed coral covered the finished runways. A line of SBD Dauntless bombers with Marine Corps insignia lined the finished portion of the circle. Toward the end of the line was an airplane graveyard, where planes too wrecked to repair were used as a supply of spare parts.

Most of the marine facilities—repair shops, quarters, mess hall—were inside the partially completed circle. A small control tower stood at the juncture of the two runways. On top of a small hill to the left of where the runway arrowhead pointed there was a shack with a Japanese-style roof. "We call that the Pagoda," Pete said. "That's where the pilots get briefed. There's a cave underneath they use for radio transmissions."

"So, what's it been like?" asked Ellis.

"Scary. Boring. Hot. That about sums it up," Pete said. Ellis looked so clean and freshly pressed that he obviously had no idea what the real war was like. But that was Ellis for you—the kind of guy who could fall into a pile of shit and not get dirty.

"Let me go check on my plane," Ellis said. "I've got to find out whether I'm going to be able to fly the General out of here."

Pete was amused to see the *Bataan* name and logo as they approached the B-26.

"It was *Skylark III* before MacArthur saw it," Ellis said.

"What happened to the first two *Skylarks*?" Pete asked.

"The first was a Marauder like that one. It had its tail blown off at Midway and we went into the drink. I lost three men," Ellis replied, and suddenly he looked older and more mature than Pete had ever seen. "I nearly lost one more today," Ellis added, walking around to the nose. "One of your Cactus Air Force hotshots thought we were a Jap bomber."

Pete noticed the shattered nose turret and the brownish stains of dried blood. "I'm sorry."

"There's a chance he'll make it, the medic said. He has two kids. One's six, the other eight."

Pete put his hand on Ellis's shoulder. "Damn. The second?"

"I'm in the big bomber business now. It's a B-17 and doesn't have a scratch on it. Too big to land on this field. I just flew this Marauder today to be Mac's chauffeur."

The crew chief came over, wiping his hands on a cloth. He was a big man, dirty and sweaty, and talked slowly. "Captain, my supply of Marauder parts in this here repair shop is kind of on the low side, if you get my drift," he said. "You're going to need a new magneto in that left engine of yours, and after that I reckon you ought to be able to get this here bird back up in the air. I have already took the liberty, sir, of radioing for that missing magneto back to Australia. Once I mentioned General MacArthur's name they purely like to fall all over themselves saying they would have it out here pronto. Once I have it, I'll just fit it in and tighten up a few screws, and you and the General can get about your business."

Ellis nodded. "Thank you, chief. I'll let the General know." He turned to Pete. "I guess the General will be with Vandegrift. But I'd like to check on Gramps first."

"Follow me," Pete said.

Gramps was still in serious condition, but the doc seemed fairly confident he'd pull through, and doctors were notorious pessimists. He wouldn't be flying back on the *Bataan,* though. His next stop would be a field hospital,

MACARTHUR'S WAR   103

and the way things looked, his war was over. At least he was
alive.

"You don't know what a relief that is," said Ellis to Pete.
"I can't imagine anything worse than losing men I'm responsible for. Thank God he isn't dead." He stood silently
for a minute. "Let's find the General, okay?"

"Which one?" asked Pete.

"In the southwest Pacific, there's only one who doesn't
need a name," replied Ellis with a grin.

Pete thought it was funny thinking of little Ellis flying
General MacArthur around the Pacific.

MacArthur and Vandegrift were in the command center
near the Pagoda, a sandbag-walled dugout with a low roof of
palm logs. Pete followed Ellis inside, saluted, and tried to be
invisible.

"Ah, Ellis," greeted the General, his pipe stem clenched in
his teeth. "Sounds like we'll be here at least until the morrow."

"Yes, sir. A new magneto is on its way, and according to
the crew chief, that should do it."

"He knows what he's doing," Vandegrift interjected.
"He's worked miracles keeping these Cactus Air Force
planes flying."

"No doubt, no doubt," MacArthur said breezily. "In the
meantime, MacArthur plans to visit the marines holding the
perimeter against the Japanese. Care to come along?"

Vandegrift looked exasperated. "General, as I've said,
that's an active trouble zone. I don't want to divert men to
protect you that I need to protect all of us against the Japanese."

"My dear Vandegrift, MacArthur has seen the elephant on
more than one occasion. You will find he is no stranger in a
combat zone, nor will you need to delegate troops for his
protection."

"Under protest, General."

"So noted, Vandegrift. Now, who can point me in the direction of the front?"

"Well, Lance Corporal . . . uh . . ."

"Rachwalski, sir."

". . . yes, that's right, he's with the 1st Parachute Battalion, and they're up at the ridge where we expect Japanese to come whenever they come. Now, refresh my memory as to why you've come here, Lance Corporal."

Vandegrift clearly didn't have the faintest idea who Pete was, but that was more than okay. "Sir, Major Miller sent me to pick up some maps from Colonel Buckley."

"And are those maps ready?"

"I was told to come back in two hours. It's about ten minutes shy of that, sir. I can check right now if the General wishes."

"Do that. In the meantime, I think I'll reinforce the position by a couple of platoons. You won't mind some company on the walk, will you, General?"

"I would feel more than safe under the protection of this corporal, General, but if you feel you want to reinforce the position in any event, we might as well all march together." It was clear to Pete that MacArthur was humoring Vandegrift. Vandegrift, by the expression on his face, realized it too.

After they left the tent, Pete winced and lowered his voice. "Ellis, the ridge isn't the place for someone acting like a goddamn tourist. We're expecting a Japanese attack. That ridge is the easiest terrain to traverse, so it's most likely the Japs will come through there. It could get nasty."

"Shit. That means I'd better ask if I can go along, too."

"Ellis, it's dangerous. I've been living here for a month. You haven't. Stay behind."

"If the General's going, then I think I have to," Ellis said. "If I go back carrying his body, they'll have my balls for breakfast."

It was clear General Vandegrift didn't want to take chances with his VIP. He sent a reinforced platoon as MacArthur's escort, with Pete as guide, and Ellis as a supernumerary.

Pete looked Ellis over. "Want a rifle?"

"I've got a .45 on board the *Bataan*. I don't normally need to carry it, but I'll fetch it. I'm qualified with the pistol. I'm not with a rifle."

"Get the .45, then, and draw a couple of extra clips from the armorer.

Pete took the point as the platoon set off for the trek up the ridge. By now, they were following what had become a well-worn trail. They climbed out of the shattered coconut plantation onto a hill that was barren of trees, covered instead with tall, sharp-edged grass. Ellis looked winded; MacArthur showed no sign of fatigue.

"Here's the forward headquarters, sir," Pete said, stopping as they neared the crest. He pointed into a nearby ravine. "Colonel Edson of the Raiders and Major Miller of the Parachute Battalion ran the battle from there last night. Should I take you down there?"

"No, that won't be necessary," MacArthur said. "It appears they are coming to us."

A marine officer was climbing up. He saluted as he got close. "Colonel Edson, First Raider Battalion, sir." Introductions having been made, Edson took over the tour.

The General wore his sunglasses even in the late afternoon, and now he seemed to turn his gaze southward, toward the far end of the grassy elevation. "That's where they attacked last night?"

"Yes, sir. Came out of the jungle like howling animals after we took some pretty heavy shelling. We beat them off okay, but we expect them back again tonight."

"Then that's where I wish to be," MacArthur said firmly. "Lead on, Colonel."

"Begging the General's pardon, but that's where the enemy is *most* likely to attack."

"Then, Colonel, that is where MacArthur *most* wishes to be."

There was a look on Edson's face that made Pete think he was going to start an argument, but he merely said, "As the General wishes," and led MacArthur where he wanted to go. Ellis followed suit.

The platoon plus Pete stood there until MacArthur, Ellis, and Colonel Edson were out of earshot, and then the platoon sergeant said, "My instructions were to follow the General and *keep him safe*. If I've got to write a report on how he died in *my* area, I will write it in *your* blood. Am I clear?"

"Yes, Sergeant," they chorused.

He looked in the direction of the three officers, shook his head, and said, "Son of a *bitch*."

The men of the platoon hunched over and moved quickly, almost jogging, as they traversed the long, exposed crest of the ridge. Colonel Edson had led MacArthur and Ellis to a company headquarters, which consisted of a dugout with a radio set, a map table, and one very surprised company captain.

The captain was awestruck and stuttering, but MacArthur asked him questions about his work. He removed his sunglasses and smiled, and Pete was startled to realize just how charming the General could be.

"Ellis—uh, Captain—we're in the Marine Raider area, and I'm with the 1st Parachute Battalion," Pete whispered. "Nothing's going to happen for a few hours, so I'm going to slip over, deliver these maps, let my platoon leader know where I am and why, and come right back."

The whisper wasn't quiet enough for MacArthur, who turned and said, "That's a fine idea. Halverson, why don't you go with him, then come back. Looks like sunset in about an hour, and I agree with the corporal. Nothing will happen until full darkness."

As the General turned his attention to the company captain's maps, Pete led his old friend toward his platoon's positions slightly down from the crest of the hill. Ten minutes later the two were hunkered below the level of the ground in Pete's own small foxhole, a hundred yards forward of the company command post. The platoon's lieutenant had trouble crediting Pete's story—"General *MacArthur*?"

The platoon's sergeant added, "Even if that was so, I wouldn't believe it."

Ellis helped convince them that it was all on the up-and-up, although Pete knew his sergeant would check the story out personally. Afterward, Pete delivered the maps to the battalion commander.

The commander, Major Charles Miller, upon finding out that Ellis was in the company of MacArthur, insisted on giving him a briefing. "We're exposed as all hell up here—I hope the Japs don't know it, but our flanks are hanging out in the air on both sides. Fortunately, that jungle is a real bitch to move through—that itself is our best protection. But they came up onto the ridge in a real shit storm last night and took pretty heavy losses. I wouldn't be surprised to get another attack tonight. You see that jungle down there to the south?"

"Well, I see jungle just about everywhere but on this hilltop," the pilot replied.

"There." Miller pointed. "We've been taking fire from there for two days. *Lots* of fire. That's because this is by far the best and easiest route to the airfield."

As Pete and Ellis walked back, Pete asked, "Sorry you came?"

"Well, I have my .45," Ellis said, trying to sound brave.

"You might have to use it," Pete replied. "But, hell—it is good to see you, pal. Kinda crazy for two Dundalk boys to wind up on a hilltop in the South Pacific, isn't it?"

"Crazy doesn't begin to describe it," the pilot replied.

"Looks like Tarzan would be right at home down there, doesn't it?" Pete remarked as they poked their heads up and studied the impressive face of the forest, with stout limbs spreading from some of the larger trees, tangling nests of vines, creepers, and a few vivid blossoms trailing down from the branches. It was eerily silent but alive and vibrant nonetheless, suggesting a whole universe of secrets masked from the prying eyes of any outside observer.

"Speaking of Tarzan, that reminds me. I got a copy of the August '41 *Amazing* from a navy petty officer in Brisbane, with a new John Carter story. "The Yellow Men of Mars." I've got it aboard the *Bataan*. You can have it." Ellis said.

"No kidding!" said Pete. "A real magazine, with words and pictures?"

"Yep."

"Are you sure?"

"I read it already, about fifty times."

"Man, you don't know what that means to me."

They talked for hours, exchanging notes on marine versus army boot camp, passing along news from home, talking about friends and their amateur magazines, and inevitably about Johnny. "He's either dead or captured by the Japs. But if this war takes me to the Philippines, I'll damn sure find out," pledged the pilot.

Night fell unnoticed by the two men, and it was fully dark when they heard a solitary plane flying overhead. "Sounds like Louie the Louse," Pete explained. "The bastard flies around, dropping flares or bombs, and just generally keeps us awake all night." It was after midnight that the sound of big guns started up, the crump of explosions several miles away carrying clearly through the still night.

"Artillery?" wondered Ellis.

"Most likely Jap ships out in the sound. Louie the Louse drops a flare over the airfield, and they sit out there on Iron-bottom Sound, lobbing shells for as long as they want. And there's not a damned thing our navy can do about it."

Pete could feel his heart pounding.

The very worst moment had been his first amphibious assault with the First Parachute Battalion against Gavutu. For most of the men, it was their first taste of combat, and it had been a shocker. Pete had lost control of his bowels in the middle of the fight and was deeply humiliated, until he found out he wasn't nearly alone.

By now, he was beginning to feel like a veteran.

Any further reflection was interrupted by a sudden, shocking wash of light. Immediately Pete was up, his rifle in his hands, as he peered over the lip of the foxhole. "Bastards are trying to get a look at us, now," he muttered.

Ellis cautiously looked over his shoulder, blinking in the unexpected illumination. The night beyond the circle of flare light looked even darker than before. "See anything?" he asked.

"Shit. Here they come," said the marine after a long silence. "That's a flare to light us up nice and bright."

By now Pete could see manlike shapes moving in the darkness at the base of the hill, still mostly concealed by shadows. "Look. Down there."

Ellis had gotten quiet. He had his .45 out.

He heard a fresh, closer eruption of artillery and then blinked as shells began to flash and burst among the enemy troops who were still emerging from the jungle. They erupted with terrific violence, flashes of light searing his corneas. The ground churned and buckled, smoke and fire obscuring their view of the tree line. Thunderous claps of noise assaulting his ears. It was a scene out of hell, and that hell was creeping closer as the next rounds of artillery burst even higher on the long slope.

"At least our 105s have the range," Pete observed approvingly, shouting to be heard over the lingering echoes of the latest blasts. "We have a couple of batteries supporting us." As he spoke, Pete pulled his bayonet off his belt and swiftly, smoothly attached it to the muzzle of his gun.

"Do you really think the Japanese are going to get that close?" Ellis said.

"Sorry you came?" Pete asked.

Ellis looked over at him. "I may be the kid, but I can do it."

Pete laughed. "You always used to say that."

"I was right, too."

Pete cocked a glance at Ellis, then looked down at the pilot's .45. "You know how to use that thing?"

"Well, sure," came the none-too-steady reply.

Pete looked around, wondering where MacArthur had taken shelter, and was stunned to see the General standing in the field next to the command post. His pipe was in his mouth, and his hands were in his back pants pockets as he stared into the flare-lit night.

"Damn, he's going to get himself killed!" Ellis snapped.

"Well, that's not my problem—or yours," Pete declared,

as if he expected his old friend to go racing to the General's rescue.

"You got that right—I'm staying right here," the pilot replied, hunkering low as another series of artillery shells pummeled the hillside. He jacked a shell into the chamber of his .45 and popped his head up again, ready to fire.

Pete couldn't resist another glance backward. Amazingly, MacArthur was striding toward the front line of foxholes, making no move toward cover—and showing absolutely no sign of fear.

Shaking his head in disbelief, Pete turned to look down the ridge. The enemy soldiers that had swarmed out of the jungle now advanced at a run, apparently unfazed by the explosions ripping through their ranks. One shell burst between two men and in the flash of light they simply disappeared. Others dropped to the ground as if they had been swatted by a huge, invisible fist. More than one Jap body could be seen tumbling lazily through the air, tossed like a child's toy.

But every time a man fell, it seemed like a whole platoon rushed forward into the gap. Machine guns opened up from the Marine position, tracers whipping through the night, blazing streaks of red just like ray guns. There was a lot of fire, and Pete knew just how thinly this hilltop was held. The marines battled from their little foxholes and strong points, isolated islands in the sea of grass, while the enemy infantry came on like a surging tidal wave.

More explosions rocked the night, this time erupting right on the hilltop, and the pilot ducked his head instinctively as a rain of dirt came down on them. His ears were ringing, and more crumping explosions rocked the night to all sides.

"Bastards are using mortars," Pete yelled, wincing as another violent blast shook the ground less than thirty feet away. "Get down!"

Ellis dropped low in the foxhole and clapped his hands over his ears—though he still clutched the .45 tightly.

The marine machine guns continued to stutter and roar.

Pete had no idea how many Japs had been killed, but the lethal fire so far had done nothing to slow down the attack. Instead, the enemy soldiers came on with shrill cries, a yodeling keen that was the eeriest noise the pilot had ever heard. He was reminded of supernatural banshees, otherworldly demons, even wild animals—all seemed more likely than human beings as sources of the hellish sound.

Pete stole a frantic glance back at MacArthur, certain that the mortar bombardment must have killed him, or driven him to shelter, but the General was standing only a dozen steps away. His face was locked into some kind of leer, almost like a grin, and his head turned this way and that as his eyes scanned the battlefield. He caught a glimpse of Pete—their eyes met for just a moment—and MacArthur nodded coolly, a gesture of approval.

Then the marines in a nearby foxhole opened up, and Pete did the same. The sharp cracks of the rifles seemed like a pathetic underscore to the booming of the artillery, the explosive mortar rounds, the ripping bursts of the heavy machine guns. But Pete could see more Jap soldiers falling, including a few he was sure he'd gotten personally.

Raising himself up, Ellis extended the pistol over the rim of the foxhole and fired wildly, the recoil jarring his arm. Pete glanced at him sharply. "Save that for the close-in work," he said. "I'd be obliged if you make sure none of them tries to hop into our hole from the side."

Many Japanese were actually passing between the marine positions, shooting at the defenders from both flanks, trying to infiltrate behind. They were shouting. "Banzai!" was the most common. They ran with fierce purposefulness. The enemy infantry carried rifles that seemed ridiculously long, with wicked-looking bayonets reflecting eerily the light of the flares, the burst of explosions and tracers. He could see individual faces now, and like the voices they were strange and alien, contorted by hatred or perhaps some kind of battle ecstasy.

Ellis took a shot at one with his pistol at the same time as a mortar round detonated; the Jap went down. There was MacArthur again, standing off to one side, observing as calmly as if this was a maneuver put on for his own benefit.

"Look out!" Pete swiveled to see a Japanese soldier abruptly looming beside the foxhole, his rifle held high, bayonet angled down toward Pete. Ellis frantically lifted his pistol and fired two shots—the second hit the attacker with enough force to slam him onto his back. Pete fired another shot into the man as he struggled to rise.

"Thanks," he said before turning back to the front.

It seemed that Japanese infantrymen charged everywhere, before them and to either side. Pete shot at more of them, unsure if he scored any hits. Ellis, he noticed with approval, was still firing. When his magazine was empty, he fumbled with a spare clip; it seemed to take forever, but he got the gun reloaded.

A marine runner came by, shouting. "Fall back—to the top of the hill! Get moving!"

He scrambled along behind Pete as the marines from the front line, those who survived, climbed out of their foxholes and started across the grassy incline, running toward the top of the hill. MacArthur was striding along before them, turning occasionally to look back at the pursuing enemy. He didn't seem to be in any big hurry. Pete cursed, spun around, and took a few shots with the bolt-action Springfield at enemy soldiers illuminated in the stark flashes of light.

A trio of Japanese charged toward them. Ellis took a shooter's stance, bracing his right wrist with his left hand. He shot carefully, the heavy slug knocking one of the enemy soldiers flat on his back. The other rushed close, his rifle held high—that hideous bayonet slicing closer—but Pete lunged and drove his own bayonet into the man's side.

The third man lunged past, ignoring Pete and Ellis. He was an officer, apparently—he carried a long, slightly curved sword. The hilt was clutched in both of his hands, and his face was distorted by a look of pure frenzy as he raised the weapon over his head and started to sweep it downward—

Straight toward General Douglas MacArthur.

• TUESDAY, 15 SEPTEMBER 1942 •

"BLOODY RIDGE," GUADALCANAL, 0120 HOURS

The approach into attack position had been a nightmare—it took Captain Ogawa Taiki more than six hours to get his company into place and to coordinate with the other captains so that they could make a battalion strength attack. Though the men covered only five hundred yards of front, it was impossible to see more than a small fraction of the position at any one time. Still, as they had filed into place, the exhausted, hungry men began to display some of their old fire. As the prospect of battle loomed, the wearying lethargy of the weeks-long march evaporated. The soldiers had joked and wrestled and challenged each other boisterously as night fell.

With darkness, they had fallen silent, preparing their weapons, and themselves, for battle. When the flare popped over the ridge to signal the start of the attack, Ogawa took only a moment to drink a solemn dram of sake from the tiny flask he had carried with him all the way from Taivu, just in readiness for this moment. The fire in his throat was pleasing; the fire in his heart was a compelling joy.

His father had given him the family sword, for their line had once been samurai. His baby sister Michiyo had calligraphed Chinese characters for bravery and good luck on the scabbard. The ink had mostly rubbed off, but he could still see hints of them.

Raising the sword of his father, the sword of all his ancestors, he had shouted the single word:

"Banzai!"

Ogawa charged from the jungle, shaking free of the tendrils and branches. He held his katana aloft and heard the echoing cries of many hundreds of men. Together they rushed toward the top of the grass-covered ridge. Impelled by the frenzied shouts, the colonel felt as if he were floating over the ground. The incline was unnoticeable, as were the blasts caused by the American heavy artillery. The night was magnificently beautiful, reminding him of the aurora borealis he had seen in the sky during a childhood visit to Hokkaido, northernmost of the Home Islands.

A wave of force slammed him from behind and he was smashed onto his face, but even as he fell he extended the sword to the side, preventing the blade from cutting him or— far more important—snapping in two under an awkward tumble. His face hit the ground hard enough to break his nose, but the katana was intact! It took him agonizing seconds to push himself up to his hands and knees, nearly a full minute to standing. He swayed unsteadily, blood streamed from his nostrils, but the pain of the injury slipped away to nothingness.

"Banzai!" he cried again, spitting blood, raising the sword in one hand, lurching unsteadily for a few steps, then breaking into a sprinter's run. Leaping over the torn body of a Japanese soldier, he dodged the smoking craters left by the American shells, moving steadily toward the top of the hill. Ogawa saw the red tails of tracers spouting from the enemy machine guns and he knew beyond any doubt that those bullets were not meant for him.

He spotted a pair of privates who had fallen to the ground, clutching their Arisaka rifles and staring toward the marine position. The captain cursed one and kicked the other; immediately their instincts and training took over and they rallied, bouncing upward to follow Ogawa to the attack.

Soon they were among the enemy foxholes, and now American and Japanese soldiers were locked in a true dance of death. Hand grenades exploded on the ground, fragments tearing into flesh of enemy and friend alike. Increasingly, the marines were falling back, coming out of their ratholes and racing away. A furious sense of glee filled Ogawa, and he chased one of them down, hacking his hamstring with the katana.

The man whirled about as he fell, his eyes locking upon the captain's. Ogawa was surprised to observe not fear but a grim and chilling sense of purpose. The marine's face was contorted by a consuming hatred that made the American look bestial, almost apelike. He was trying to bring his rifle around, to defend himself with the bayonet, but once again Ogawa's lethal sword slashed. He left the bloody corpse in his wake and surged on with the two privates still racing at his flanks.

The battle raged in front of them and behind, across the hilltop to both sides. The determined and courageous shouts of the Japanese mingled with the animallike howls and roars of the Americans. Rippling explosions overwhelmed the vocalizations for seconds at a time. Always there was that steady crackle of gunfire, rifles, pistols, and machine guns popping like firecrackers.

A man, an American officer, stood calmly amid the chaos. He was watching Ogawa charge closer and making no move to get out of the way. Such passive impudence infuriated the Japanese captain, and he veered directly for the officer. A blast brightened the night, and Ogawa *knew* the man was looking at him, must see that lethal and bloody sword. Other Americans were scrambling to protect this impassive fellow—a pistol shot whistled past Ogawa, felling one of the privates. A marine knelt nearby but worked his bolt in frustration—clearly he was out of ammunition.

Now the American officer closed his eyes and tilted his head back, as if he saw death and welcomed it. Ogawa cocked his arm, running in silence, aiming a slash that would cut the man from collarbone to waist.

But it was Ogawa's body that was torn suddenly, as a fiery pain ripped through his thigh. He fell, thrashing his katana in futility as his right leg utterly refused to obey the commands of his mind. The captain wriggled around and saw the marine with the empty rifle. With a gagging sense of dishonor he realized that he had been stabbed by that pathetic little bayonet—somehow the American had lunged across ten feet of ground to stop Ogawa's charge.

Blood was running from his leg, from high up near his groin. Ogawa felt cold terror for the first time—he was certain that the American bayonet had gored his manhood.

And then the blackness swallowed him.

"Come on—sir!" demanded Pete, taking the General by the arm, roughly pulling him toward the rear.

"Yes—of course. Thank you," MacArthur replied, seemingly distracted. He was looking down at the officer Pete had bayoneted.

The man thrashed frantically, waving that lethal sword. Ellis swung his pistol and fired one point-blank shot; the wounded officer instantly ceased his movements.

"Let's *go*—" Pete yelled.

Ellis took MacArthur by the other arm and the pair hauled him along, stumbling through the battlefield. Flashes of light illuminated the General's face—he was looking around with a kind of detached interest—and revealed that the retreating marines were entering the reserve positions that had been excavated behind the initial line.

Artillery came in right behind them as the gunners tried their best to hold the attackers at bay. Pete, Ellis, and their four-star charge found shelter in a shallow trench right at the hillcrest. MacArthur watched the battle from within the hole, at least. Pete collected a dozen new clips of ammunition, and here they popped away at the attackers who were still revealed by the sporadic bursts of light. They were emerging from the darkness to both sides, as well as in front of them.

"It's like Little Big Horn, isn't it?" Ellis shouted.

"Yeah, except the Indians aren't going to win this time," Pete yelled back.

But he couldn't shake the image of Custer's men surrounded on a similar grassy hilltop, or the knowledge of how that one had ended. Nevertheless, he settled down and took careful shots at the swarming enemy. Ellis, he was pleased to note, kept up his own fire. And MacArthur, recovering his focus, had pulled out his own .45 and was shooting away.

Of course, George Armstrong Custer hadn't had a battery of marine howitzers. Although they made a deafening racket, Pete wanted to cheer every time they fired. Slowly, the tide turned as those big guns pounded, while other brave men brought ammunition to the forward foxholes, and heroic spotters directed fire against every enemy concentration. Pete turned and looked at MacArthur again, saw the frown crease his brow. It was not fear, not even worry about possibly losing the battle . . . it was more like an ineffable sadness.

Pete remembered the look on MacArthur's face when the Japanese officer with the sword was charging him. It was as if he wanted it, as if he welcomed it.

He wanted to die out here. The thought came to Pete with a certainty overwhelming any doubt. *He's got a death wish.*

But the Japanese were coming again, and there was neither time nor reason to wonder about the General's purposes. Pete Rachwalski was too busy trying to stay alive.

Over the hours he lost count, though he would later be told—and believe—that the Japanese attackers hurled themselves at the marines twelve times over the course of that lethal night. Every time they were defeated, the survivors tracked down and exterminated, the frenzy of the battle fading only with the arrival of the sticky dawn and the rising of the blood-red sun.

And the marines still occupied their foxholes on the crest of Bloody Ridge.

SIX

New Caledonia; Solomons

• FRIDAY, 18 SEPTEMBER 1942 •

SOPAC HQ, NOUMÉA, NEW CALEDONIA, 0845 HOURS

A month into his new job as skipper of the *Portland,* Captain Frank Chadwick had acquired several collateral responsibilities. Initially, he was assigned to COMPHIBFORSOPAC—commander, Amphibious Forces, South Pacific Area and South Pacific Fleet—under the brilliant, impatient, and notoriously short-tempered Rear Admiral R. Kelly Turner.

Turner, stuck in Nouméa while his ships traveled regularly to the Solomons, worked hard all day, drank into the evening, then came back to work late into the night. No one could keep up with him. Wise men just tried to stay out of his way. As soon as Frank had completed his first cruise in the *Portland,* Turner assigned him command of a screening group, responsible for four destroyers in addition to his own cruiser.

Organizing a major command like SOPAC while dealing with immediate threats from a determined enemy and at the same time starting with major deficiencies in ships, men, and materiél would tax any man. Admiral Bill Halsey did superhuman work under difficult conditions.

COMAIRSOPAC—commander, Land-Based Aircraft, South Pacific Area and South Pacific Fleet—had a new boss, Admiral Aubrey Fitch. In addition to shortages, Fitch had to contend with army-navy rivalries, differences in supply, maintenance, training, and doctrine, a lack of forward air bases, all while fighting with what he had.

The army units in the South Pacific reported to the navy, rather than to MacArthur's South*west* Pacific command. That resulted in COMGENSOPAC—commanding general, South Pacific Area—Major General Millard Harmon, not having direct authority over the troops he technically commanded, causing enormous difficulties in the chain of command. Admiral Halsey kept a second role for himself, that of commander of the Air Support Force, the main carrier force. All in all, it was a situation that would take a top-notch leader months or even years to unsnarl. Halsey needed to get it done yesterday and was coming closer than anyone could have imagined. As it happened, by the middle of September he was ready to leave his desk in Nouméa and put to sea with his flag aboard the repaired *Enterprise.*

The admiral's first mission briefing was straightforward. "Our first responsibility is to make sure our marines are able to hold on at Guadalcanal. Admiral Nagumo's first responsibility is to make sure they don't. Our intelligence tells us that Nagumo's carrier force, who've roughed us up twice so far, at Pearl and at Midway, are going for three. Three on a match is unlucky, and I'd like that bad luck to rub off on him this time."

His eyes searched the room. "Once we've achieve our first goal—and make no mistake, gentlemen, we *will* achieve that goal—we will extend it by achieving absolute air superiority over the Solomons. Third, we'll evict the Japs from the rest of the Solomons. We will plan smart, fight hard, and play dirty. The road to Tokyo leads through Guadalcanal, gentlemen. We are on our way!"

They were good words, and they had an electric effect on the staff and the ship captains who attended the briefing. The situation on the water, however, was nowhere near as good as the admiral's words. More than a month after the debacle at Savo Island, the enemy still retained complete control of the waters around the island during the night. The enemy's skill at night fighting, especially its advanced optics for surface gunnery and fast, lethal Long Lance torpedoes, completely overmatched the U.S. Navy after dark.

During the day, however, the planes of the Cactus Air Force, as the Guadalcanal-based marine fighters and bombers were now known, were able to reverse the balance of power, forcing the Japanese to resupply and reinforce after dark. The dive-bombers based on the island took a deadly toll of any ships caught within range during the hours of daylight. The Americans, meanwhile, would race supplies in ashore in dribs and drabs during the day, but the ships would have to pull away from the island long before sunset or risk an encounter with Japanese surface ships after dark.

But the presence of Nagumo's powerful fleet, known to number at least four and possibly five carriers, could alter that delicate equilibrium. The Japs were making the Tokyo Express run just about every night, bringing reinforcements and supplies down to the island. Without air superiority, the marines—and Henderson Field—were doomed.

Despite the losses of Midway and Savo Island, Halsey's fleet was the most formidable armada that the United States

Navy had sent against the Japanese. With the return of the newly repaired *Enterprise,* as well as the arrival of the *Wasp* and the *Saratoga* from the Atlantic and West Coast areas, the admiral had three fleet carriers with air groups well rested and at full strength along with their full complement of screening and support ships. Veteran pilots who had survived the sinkings of the *Hornet, Lexington,* and *Yorktown* had been seeded through these groups. Promising new tactics and constant training allowed fighter pilots to maximize the advantages of their stubby Grumman fighters—four heavy machine guns and the capacity to absorb a lot of damage and still remain in the air—while minimizing the Zero's superiority in speed, altitude, and maneuverability. The flyboys were itching for a fight.

In addition, two new fast battleships—the *Washington* and the *South Dakota*—now gave Halsey a gunnery punch that had hitherto been lacking. Another modern battleship, the *North Carolina,* was currently escorting the transport fleet bringing a major reinforcement for the First Marine Division to the embattled island of Guadalcanal. A day earlier, the *Wasp* had been assigned to that same escort, but Halsey's first order had been to bring her back to join the other two carriers so that he could concentrate the punch of his air power.

The admiral announced his intention to cruise with his three carrier groups south of Guadalcanal, where the ships could benefit from the additional protection offered by the Cactus Air Force. The carrier air groups would still provide an umbrella as the transports made their run for Lunga Point and the airfield. The biggest threat down there came from enemy subs. The navy was doing everything it could with aggressive patrolling in the air and on the surface, as well as using every available destroyer to screen the precious flattops.

The day was filled with planning meetings involving task forces, boards, working groups, and committees of all sorts. Chadwick was in a meeting on improving fire support for transport groups en route to Guadalcanal when an officer brought in a freshly decoded communiqué from the transport fleet. Turner spat a curse as he read it, then gestured to the officer. "Tell the staff," he ordered.

"We got a flash in from the *North Carolina*—she took a hit from a Jap submarine," reported the lieutenant. "She's down to half speed and is going to try to limp back to New Caledonia. The task force commander reports that he intends to proceed with the rest of the fleet and the reinforcements."

"I wouldn't have expected any less—he's got to keep bulling through with his transports," Turner said. "Vandegrift needs those fresh marines, and the air units need more gasoline. In the meantime, let's get some combat air patrol over the *North Carolina* until she gets away." Two members of their working group left immediately.

Reports on the retreating *North Carolina* came in through the night. Her destroyer escort had attacked the offending submarine with no indication of success, but at least they had held the enemy boat at bay until the wounded battleship could steam out of the danger zone. By dawn it was clear that the ship's heavy belt armor—specifically intended for protection against torpedoes—would save her so that she could fight again.

Chadwick thought about Halsey's first order when he took command the previous day: determined to concentrate his carriers in one fleet, he had ordered the *Wasp* to come south. Up until that time, the *Wasp* had been assigned to the same task force as the *North Carolina*. Chadwick guessed that if the enemy sub commander had spotted a carrier going past, the flattop would have been a goner.

Still later, another communiqué arrived, hot from the decoding room. "Message from General MacArthur, sir," reported the courier.

Turner read excerpts. "Best wishes and godspeed to the gallant crew of the *North Carolina* . . . the transports continue bravely on to Guadalcanal . . . highest traditions of the United States Navy . . ." He looked up and smiled. "The General says he is sending bomber reinforcements to Henderson Field."

• WEDNESDAY, 30 SEPTEMBER 1942 •

ABOVE IRONBOTTOM SOUND, 130 MILES NW
OF GUADALCANAL, 0455 HOURS

It was the third mission in four days for Ellis Halverson's Lucky Dicers, the 65th Bombardment Squadron of the 43rd Bomb Group. Yesterday, rain had soaked the field so much that they couldn't even get a plane off the ground. But now, as he led his formation of B-17s across the Solomon Sea, Ellis believed that today's attack seemed to offer the best prospects yet. His stomach rumbled with hunger—hunger was a way of life for everyone living on the Canal—but the discomfort only heightened his determination as he flew toward the Japanese ships.

They had been briefed at 0230 and learned that the Japs had sent a run of the Tokyo Express—high-speed Japanese destroyers outfitted as transports—down the Slot, as the middle of the Solomons was known. The destroyer-transports were even then unloading their reinforcements and cargo on the shore of Guadalcanal. By dawn the ships would be headed for home. If the bombers were too late to interdict the supplies, they would at least see that those ships didn't survive to make another run.

Each of the Flying Fortresses was armed with a full complement of thousand-pound armor-piercing bombs set with five-second-delay fuses, ideal for skip bombing.

These were borderline conditions for skip bombing. The evolving manual on the practice gave the four conditions in which skip bombing was known to be successful: first, at the first light of the dawn with the approach made from west to east with just enough light to silhouette the vessel; second, on clear nights with the moon below forty degrees elevation, the attack being made into the moon; third, directly out of a very low setting sun; fourth, from very low clouds or poor weather where an element of surprise was completely possible.

The Lucky Dicers would hit past the first light of dawn.

Dawn broke into a clear day, good visibility among the patches of clouds that were never completely gone from this part of the world. The marines in the Pagoda—the Japanese-built mission hut—and in the cave below it on Guadalcanal kept the flight of army bombers posted on the retreating transports, even as the dive-bombers of the Cactus Air Force knocked out a couple of the enemy ships right after daylight. By the time the B-17s neared the target, the Japanese ships—six surviving destroyer-transports escorted by a couple of unmodified Japanese destroyers—were steaming north by northwest, passing the Russell Islands and making good speed into the New Georgia Sound portion of the Slot.

Coming in from the west, Ellis spotted his target and led his planes down to just over two hundred feet of altitude. The transports were outlined against the sun, as pretty a row of targets as you could ask for. If Halverson had anything to say about it, they had just completed their last task for the glory of the emperor.

Ellis toggled his microphone. "We're going in line abreast. Everybody choose your targets. Remember, you don't want to drop until you're within three hundred feet of the target. Good hunting, men."

Ellis guided the *Skylark II* with a skilled hand as they zoomed toward the second transport in the file. Looking to either side, he saw the squadron's big bombers all in formation, low and fast and streaking toward the target. A few antiaircraft bursts popped into view as the screening destroyers blasted away, but the shots were too infrequent even to draw much attention. The transports were turning, trying to present narrow bow targets to the bombers, but the B-17s were coming in too fast for the evasion to be successful.

They slowed and pulled up just a few hundred feet short of the target. Ellis released his bombs and quickly jammed the throttle to full speed, pulling into a climb. Something rocked the plane as one of the ack-ack shells blasted a little close to home, but then they were past the ships, all the bombers climbing and circling back.

"Hot damn, skipper!" It was Grisham, crowing from the copilot's seat. "We got a ton of hits! Look at those bastards burn!"

The aircraft of the 65th flew above their targets, and Ellis took the time to make a careful assessment while the bombardier shot up a whole roll of film snapping pictures. Of the six transports, four of them were burning furiously, falling out of formation. The two survivors streamed northward with one destroyer, while the other tin can circled around its stricken charges like an aggrieved border collie trying to protect a flock of wounded sheep.

"None of those guys will make it back to Rabaul," Grisham predicted. "Not if the marines can get a few SBDs up here to finish them off."

"Send out the position and bomb damage assessment," Ellis said. "Time for us to get back to Henderson." No planes lost. It was a good day in the Solomons for the Lucky Dicers.

• FRIDAY, 2 OCTOBER 1942 •

AKAGI, *200 MILES EAST OF RABAUL, 1845 HOURS*

Admiral Nagumo's stomach was roiling again. He should be confident, he knew—he should be sublimely certain that the *Kido Butai* would prevail when it inevitably matched strength and skill against the three American carriers known to be in the South Pacific.

After all, for the first time since before Midway, Nagumo had five splendid carriers under his command. The *Akagi* and the *Soryu* had been repaired and restored, their air groups replenished to full strength. The *Hiryu, Shokaku,* and *Zuikako* filled out the complement of carriers, as mighty a force of naval aviation as currently sailed the seven seas.

But there were too many variables, too many things he didn't know.

How many flattops were in the enemy fleet, and where were the American carriers? How aggressive would the new American admiral be? What about the planes based on Guadalcanal? They had been savaging the daily rat runs, as the Japanese called the replacement and reinforcement convoys running down the Slot.

How much of a threat would they be against Nagumo's precious carriers? If they found him before he found them, they could come screaming down from the clouds and shatter his beautiful ships in a matter of minutes. He had seen proof of that at Midway, and he was determined not to let it happen again.

Yet the only way to stay safe was to stay far away from the Americans, and that was a pointless course of action. Whatever the enemy tactics and deployments, the admiral knew that he had to strike. And he had a powerful force with which to make that attack.

Even more frightening, perhaps, than the enemy aircraft was the knowledge of Admiral Yamamoto, back at Kure now but still looming dark and forbidding over Nagumo's shoulder. The great man had been less than thrilled with Nagumo's victory at Midway! There was no pleasing him, and yet Nagumo was willing to risk his ships, and his life, in the attempt.

With that memory, his decision was made.

"Mark a course of one eight zero," he told his plotters. They would move closer to the Americans, let the enemy get a whiff of this mighty task force. Perhaps they could be drawn into a rash attack. Perhaps they could be smashed, and destroyed. If only the *Kido Butai* could close the distance without being discovered, he had a chance to win a great victory, perhaps even to change the course of the war!

But still, he was afraid.

• MONDAY, 5 OCTOBER 1942 •

PORTLAND, *80 MILES EAST OF GUADALCANAL, 1845 HOURS*

A patrolling American submarine spotted Nagumo's fleet, the Japanese First Mobile Strike Force, as it moved south from Rabaul and passed around the large Solomon Island known as Bougainville. Admiral Halsey's three carriers remained near the protective cover of Henderson Field and awaited the enemy's approach. Now, at last, they had an accurate position for their target. The coded radio broadcast included confirmation of at least two enemy aircraft carriers—everyone on the staff took it for granted that there were several more, as yet unobserved.

The cat-and-mouse game was on.

Frank Chadwick, commanding his fire support group, began plotting Nagumo's whereabouts to satisfy his own curiosity and to try and get a handle on Admiral Halsey's intentions. It was Halsey's job to engage and destroy the enemy when he could. It was Frank's job to see that transports made it to the Canal with their precious cargos intact and to keep them safe until they were unloaded.

He could imagine the frantic bustle aboard Halsey's flagship as staff scattered like dry leaves whirled in a cyclone. Captains and flight crews received their commands and readied their planes for launch. Crews slung bombs and torpedoes beneath the planes and topped off their fuel tanks. Screening vessels took up defensive positions around the big carriers, and every gunner's eye was trained toward the sky.

Within ten minutes of the submarine's report, bombers were rumbling down the three flight decks. The big-bellied TBF torpedo planes, having the longest range of the American types, launched first. They formed up in their lumbering squadrons as the SBD dive-bombers took to the air behind them. The Grumman Wildcat fighters were still launching as the bomber squadrons started toward the place where Nagumo's carriers had been spotted.

"Transport group commander calling, Captain."

Chadwick dropped quickly down to the radio room. *"Portland,"* he said.

"How long have we got?" the transport group commander asked.

"No news yet. We should have some definitive word on any air activity coming our way shortly. I recommend you keep working. Henderson Field is launching now, so we'll have air cover."

His task completed, Chadwick stepped out to the external bridge and watched the Cactus Air Force fighters roar past overhead, wishing for a moment he were among them. But he would have had to move away from flying no matter what, and command of a cruiser made a pretty good second prize.

AKAGI, 220 MILES NORTHEAST OF GUADALCANAL, 1850 HOURS

When the newest runner from the radio room entered the admiral's bridge, Vice Admiral Chuichi Nagumo, commander, First Carrier Strike Force *Kido Butai,* felt his stomach acid rise again. He burped, and a burning sensation shot halfway up his chest. He took another gulp of milk from the glass that rested on a silver tray next to his private chair. He never sat in his chair. He was too nervous for that. He tried to bite his right index fingernail, but it had already been bitten down to the quick.

The runner saluted. "Message from the *Akagi*'s captain, sir," he said. "He is coming to speak to you directly."

"All right. Give me the bad news," said Nagumo as soon as Captain Aoki Tajiro hurried into the admiral's command center.

"The Americans have observed us," the captain informed Nagumo. "A submarine has broadcast a message from only ten miles away. We must assume they have spotted at least one of our carriers."

Nagumo still didn't know where the American carriers were. It would be careless to the point of recklessness for *Kido Butai* to maintain its current bearing when an enemy air attack was virtually inevitable. Unlike Midway, he lacked a corresponding target of his own.

"Turn around! Make a course bearing three six zero!" the admiral ordered. "Flank speed to the north!"

Nagumo paced back and forth as the splashes from the

depth-charging destroyers were still crumping off to the east where the American submarine had been lurking. The boat had sent its radio report from very close to the Japanese fleet—a sign of true urgency—and Nagumo knew the captain had been right: his carriers had been located by the Americans.

As it was, there was nothing for it but to make a temporary withdrawal. This was not the time, nor the circumstance, for the Decisive Battle.

• SATURDAY, 10 OCTOBER 1942 •

HENDERSON FIELD, GUADALCANAL, 1905 HOURS

Ellis Halverson watched the last B-17 touch down, and he could only hope that the Japs didn't send a battleship down to bombard the field tonight. The revetments and taxi strips around the field were so crowded that a single randomly lobbed twelve-inch shell could hardly fail to disable a dozen aircraft. Those raids, not nightly but not infrequent either, were the greatest threat to air operations from Guadalcanal.

Some thirty-five of the Cactus Air Force planes were now bombers of the United States Army Air Force—three nearly full-strength squadrons, both heavy and medium. Combined with the fifty marine dive-bombers, they gave Henderson Field a punch that any surface ships of the IJN would do well to notice.

And notice they had.

Over the last few weeks, the Cactus Air Force had laid undisputed claim to the daytime airspace over the southern Solomon Islands. The convoys of the Tokyo Express had been suffering losses in the neighborhood of 50 percent on each mission, and as a result they were at least temporarily out of business. One ass-kicking air raid or naval bombardment of Henderson Field, however, might be enough to change all that.

Still, for weeks the Cactus Air Force had kept the pressure on—until the last few days when, by Halsey's orders, they had suspended the raids against the transports and stood by for a potential attack against the enemy carrier force. Bombs and fuel were preloaded, and the pilots and crewmen never strayed far from their planes. But for the last five days they had been cooling their heels, waiting for a target that never seemed to appear.

Halverson's stomach growled as he turned toward the mess tent. The pilots, like the ground crewmen, the marines, and the engineers, were routinely hungry on Guadalcanal. Many suffered from malaria, and the pilot thanked his lucky stars that, so far, he hadn't been one of them. As it was, he found it hard enough to fly, to maintain his concentration and reflexes at a level that didn't endanger his crew and himself. It seemed like ages since he'd had a good night's sleep.

He was still a hundred yards away from the mess tent—and the hot food he so desperately needed—when the thundering boom of big naval guns reverberated from out on the sound. A siren began to wail, and men scrambled for the slit trenches that crisscrossed the ground around the airfield. A few seconds later the first blasts shook the ground with a tremor that Ellis could feel through the soles of his feet. They were big guns, but not the earth-crushing shells from a battleship. Probably a cruiser with eight-inch batteries, he guessed—still capable of doing a lot of damage to human flesh and to delicate airplanes.

After one longing glance at the mess tent, he turned and jogged toward the nearest trench. It was shaping up to be another long, hungry night.

• SUNDAY, 11 OCTOBER 1942 •

SOPAC HQ, NOUMÉA, NEW CALEDONIA, 0621 HOURS

The *Portland* was in port for the first time in weeks when Frank Chadwick got word that there were new orders waiting for him. Wanting to stretch his legs, he took a boat to the dock and went right into the headquarters building. Five minutes later he was knocking on Admiral Turner's door.

"Come!" came the curt reply.

"Good morning, sir. You wanted to see me?"

Turner looked up. He was sweating and at the same time had the shivers. Malaria. But if he refused to go to bed or report to sick bay, there wasn't anything a mere captain could do to compel him. "Yes. The *Portland*'s been reassigned. You're now attached to the Air Support Force."

Chadwick raised his eyebrows slighly. "Not my idea, Chadwick. But it's not my decision."

"Just the *Portland,* sir, or my fire support group?"

"Right now, just the *Portland.* See Halsey for the rest. Dismissed." Turner went back to his paperwork without a moment's pause.

Chadwick went to Halsey's office, knowing that the admiral was at sea but still hoping he could get his orders clarified. He found the chief of staff, Admiral Carney, running the show ashore.

"Chadwick . . . oh, yes. The *Portland.* You're a carrier escort, part of the *Enterprise* group." Cruisers, destroyers, and other ships formed a screen around a vulnerable carrier to make a carrier group. Cruiser command would be in the *Minneapolis,* so Frank would be responsible only for his own ship. Halsey's flag would stay aboard the *Enterprise.*

Halsey made his intentions clear in the first meeting. "I'm fed up with this hide-and-seek bullshit! I've decided to give Nagumo a challenge he's not going to be able to ignore. We're going to make a run north, right into the Solomon Sea."

Frank Chadwick had memorized the geography of this part of the ocean weeks earlier. When he, along with every other man at the table, turned his attention to the large map on the bulkhead, he knew exactly what he would see. Until now, the fleet's position between the Santa Cruz Islands and the Coral Sea had given them lots of maneuver room and kept them a good distance from any land-based Jap aircraft.

They would lose both of those advantages in the Solomon Sea. The chain of islands with the same name formed a staggered but significant barrier to the right, bordering the sea to the east and northeast. Except for Guadalcanal, at the very southern end of the chain, those islands were under enemy control, and several of them contained forward air bases. The farther north Halsey steamed, the less support he could get from Henderson Field—they would move beyond fighter range within the first day of northward steaming. To the west and southwest of the Solomon Sea, embattled New Guinea provided a solid barrier against maneuver. New Guinea was also the site of significant Japanese bases at Buna and other places. Then, to the northwest, forming a barred gate across egress from the Solomon Sea, the island of New Britain stretched like a breastwork, anchored by the most powerful enemy base in the area: Rabaul.

But they all knew that Halsey's intention was to provoke a fight. *This should do it,* Chadwick thought with a mixture of apprehension and anticipation.

Indeed, there was something dramatic and dashing about the run into the Solomon Sea. The daring maneuver would bring Halsey under risk of attack, but it might just force Nagumo to expose his own carriers to battle. Chadwick admired the admiral's courage, even as he sweated out a thousand small details and concerns.

"Now, we're promised some land-based air cover from Milne Bay, for what that's worth," Halsey noted. His tone was contemptuous, and Chadwick shared the sentiment. It was widely known among naval aviation officers that the Army's P-39 and P-40 fighters—both based in eastern New Guinea—were even more outclassed by the Zeros than were the Grumman Wildcats. At least the F4F Wildcat pilots had come up with some innovative tactics for dealing with the more nimble enemy aircraft. Most recently, the Thach weave—named after its inventor, a pilot from the *Yorktown*—allowed two Grummans to protect each other and even pick off the occasional unwary Zero.

But now the fleet, with the task forces running together and each carrier surrounded by a ring of screening vessels, plowed through the tropical seas. It would face challenges lurking literally on every side.

What if the Japanese spotted them? The Cactus Air Force had shot down a lot of enemy planes over Guadalcanal. But how many bombers did the Japs have left on Rabaul? Could the Americans possibly find themselves under attack by both land- and carrier-based aircraft? Was there a Jap submarine out there right now, waiting to lance a torpedo into the bowels of the *Enterprise*—or the *Portland*?

And where were Nagumo's goddamned aircraft carriers?

SEVEN

Pacific Ocean; Solomon Sea

• MONDAY, 12 OCTOBER 1942 •

PBY BLUE LADY, *100 MILES NORTH OF SANTA ISABEL* *ISLAND, SOLOMONS, 1701 HOURS*

"Skipper, the weather is starting to close in. Whattya say we pack it in for the day before we run into a typhoon or something?" Lieutenant (j.g.) Willy Peters made the suggestion casually, but Derek "Duke" Whitman, sitting in the pilot's seat, could feel the intensity of his copilot's gaze,

"Dammit, Willy, those aren't more than a few thunderheads. I want to give it another fifty miles before we head back to Espirito."

"Yeah. Still bucking for admiral, aren't you?" Willy snorted, shaking his head. His tone was somewhere between teasing and disgust, but enough toward the latter that Duke was getting ready to lose his temper. Sometimes Willy just didn't take things seriously enough.

Duke was readying his rebuke when his copilot stole his thunder by straightening in his seat, craning toward the side window. "Holy shit!" he gasped. "There's a fleet down there!"

Duke altered course toward the north immediately, bringing the nose of the big seaplane around so that he, too, could see the sun-speckled swath of sea. There were too many ships to count on that calm surface, a massive armada steaming resolutely toward the southeast, running parallel to the chain of the Solomon Islands some seventy miles away. The clouds parted for them like the curtain opening on a Broadway stage, and they had a perfect view from one horizon to the other.

"Do you see what I see?" asked Willy, reaching for the radio.

The pilot only nodded mutely, listening as his partner radioed in the truth of what they could plainly observe: there, in the middle of that massive fleet, were no fewer than five aircraft carriers of the Imperial Japanese Navy.

PORTLAND, *1712 HOURS*

Chadwick could imagine Halsey's reaction when he first heard the PBY's report.

"Don't tell me it's too late to launch a strike!" Admiral Halsey would snarl. "I've been hunting that son of a bitch Nagumo for a month, and for the last thirty-six hours we've stuck our head right into his hornets' nest. Now that we've found him, we're going to hit him with every damn thing we have."

The admiral probably stopped to draw a breath, but it would not be an invitation to respond. "Get word to Cactus—we'll send a strike from Henderson as well. This time, he's not getting away!"

Thus, Frank was not surprised when his signalman reported the message on the flags flying from the *Enterprise*'s masts: "Prepare to launch aircraft." As he thought about the target, and the operation, Chadwick could think of a whole host of risks. The Japanese carriers were on the other side of the Solomon chain, more than 150 miles away—and that was close enough to maximum range that it didn't leave a lot of room for error. The planes of Halsey's three carriers would have to fly right over enemy territory and might even get jumped before they reached the target. Certainly their approach would be spotted and reported. And if they made it there and back, it would be past sunset and very nearly dark by the time they returned to their carriers.

Chadwick had cut his teeth in naval aviation, flying the old Grumman biplanes in the thirties, and he knew that landing a plane on a carrier was one of the greatest challenges any pilot could face. Doing so on a dark night was damned near impossible; yet those men, when they returned to the fleet, would be flying on nearly empty gas tanks, and their planes would be coming down one way or another.

The latter was the key issue in Chadwick's mind. No one was going to talk Admiral Halsey out of the attack. And every minute they spent arguing about it meant another minute later before those pilots would be bringing their thirsty planes back to their carriers. But how could they get the planes back safely?

Frank went out on deck with his binoculars. The fleet, trying to remain undetected for as long as possible, was sailing under radio silence, so signal flags did the communicating. While the *Portland*'s signal floozies would read the flag hoists and put the same flags up in reply, Frank liked to watch the signals. From the *Portland,* he had to look in two directions, toward the *Enterprise* and toward the *Minneapolis.*

The first hoist went up from the *Enterprise.* The flags read, "Turning into the wind. Aircraft standing by." His own hoist went up with identical flags, confirming the message was received and understood accurately.

"Prepare to turn into the wind," Frank shouted at the helmsman. He saw immediately that his ship would be on the outside of the turn. "And call down to the engine room—we're going to need flank speed to keep up."

"Prepare to turn into the wind, aye, Captain," the helsman answered, while a lieutenant (j.g.) rang the engine room to pass along the order for maximum steam.

As the *Enterprise* began its turn, Frank yelled, "Bring her around, and go to flank speed!"

"Turning into the wind, aye, Captain," came the answer. He felt the welcome surge of power as the big, fast ship fairly leaped forward, churning through the azure sea as she raced to resume her proper station off the carrier's port beam.

More flags from the *Enterprise:* "Launching aircraft." The *Portland,* back in position, kept pace with the great vessel and stayed in formation a thousand yards astern of the *Minneapolis.*

His glasses pressed to his eyes, the cruiser's captain watched the great flattop as, one by one, the torpedo bombers, the dive-bombers, and the fighters took off. Given the long distance to the target, he was not surprised to see each squadron setting forth independently—but he worried for the bomber pilots, who would not have fighter cover close at hand.

Chadwick stood on the bridge of the *Portland,* watching them fly away and praying to God that most of them would make it back home.

MUNDA, NEW GEORGIA, SOLOMON ISLANDS, 1820 HOURS

Lieutenant Takagawa Junichi was used to the sounds of aircraft passing over his island. Ever since the Americans had landed on Guadalcanal in August, Japanese bombers and fighters from the great base at Rabaul, northwest of Munda, had flown either directly over this island or very close to it on their missions against the tenuous but stubbornly held position of the U.S. Marines around Henderson Field, directly southeast of him. Takagawa would dutifully take his binoculars and observe the flights, privately wishing the pilots good luck on their dangerous missions. He would often see them return late in the day, and even from his casual observation point had noticed that, typically, far fewer planes flew back to Rabaul at night than had flown out in the morning.

The flyovers had actually become the high point in his rather mundane existence here. Like all of the Solomons, Munda was a malaria-infested, rotting jungle of a place. It was a big island, and Takagawa knew that there were Australian Coastwatchers hidden in the interior forests. Drawn from the ranks of the planters and missionaries who had lived here before the war, they lurked in the jungle, spying, making radio transmissions that were too brief for accurate homing. Takagawa himself had led several infantry patrols in search of the Coastwatchers, but they were almost impossible to find. And they, too, watched the airplanes and reported their numbers and bearing to their masters in Australia who, presumably, alerted the Americans on Guadalcanal.

But now as the lieutenant stared through his binoculars from the top of his spindly watchtower, awed at the streams of aircraft over his island, he also felt a cold chill of alarm. This was a larger flight than he had ever seen before, and these planes were making their way from the southwest toward the northeast, flying from the Solomon Sea toward some target on the other side of the chain of islands. He didn't know where they came from, or where they were going, but in the sun-drenched late afternoon Takagawa had no difficulty making out the white stars on the wings of the planes. Obviously this was a strike launched from American carriers. How far away were those ships? Takagawa had no way of knowing.

But at least he could report what he was seeing right now.

"Broadcast a message!" he barked to the private who was his radio operator. "An American air attack is under way. Bearing zero six zero. I count at least three squadrons of torpedo bombers—and there, those are dive-bombers as well . . ."

AKAGI, *200 MILES EAST OF RABAUL, 1830 HOURS*

"The enemy carriers must be in the Solomon Sea," reported Admiral Taguchi, Nagumo's operations officer. "Their course is leading them on a bearing directly toward us."

"Order a reciprocal attack immediately!" Nagumo's voice almost cracked, but with a glower at his attendant staff officers he brought his external emotions under control. "Plot the American fleet's position based on the course of these attacking squadrons."

His commands were precise, and—after his initial tautness—his voice was admirably controlled. He knew that he was doing the right thing, really the only thing he could do. But inside, hidden from all others, he was wracked by the most profound terror he had ever experienced.

All he had was a bearing to the American fleet—the direction from which the enemy planes were coming. The wind blew from the northeast, so at least he could turn his tail to the attackers as he launched his own planes.

Yet already he had lost so much precious time. The attack would arrive in less than an hour.

And the minutes ticked past with agonizing slowness as the Aichi Type 99 dive-bombers, with their elegant fixed landing gear, roared into the sky. They were followed by the Nakajima B5N torpedo bombers, each armed with one of those weapons that had proved so deadly against American ships. Finally came the Mitsubishi A6M Zero-sens, many winging off to escort the bombers, while others remained behind, circling over the fleet in the combat air patrol.

He had made his choice, taken his gamble. There was nothing else the admiral could do but wait until the dice stopped rolling.

THE PAGODA, HENDERSON FIELD, GUADALCANAL, 1831 HOURS

"We got a good position report from a PBY patrolling north of Santa Isabel," announced Colonel Thaddeus, commander of the 22nd Bomb Group. "The Jap carriers are too far away from here for the marine dive-bombers, so it will be up to the Forts. The marines will stand by and launch if it turns out that Nagumo is continuing to steam south."

"Fat chance of that," someone muttered to a round of dry chuckles. The Japanese admiral's reputation for caution had become something of a joke among the flyers on Guadalcanal.

This was the second time in the last five days that they had been ordered to scramble; and the first mission had proved to be a wild-goose chase.

"Even if he turns tail and runs like hell, your bombers will be able to catch up to him," Thaddeus continued. "Halsey launched a strike in late afternoon, and they should be working the bastards over pretty soon. It will be up to you fellows to pick off any targets the navy overlooks. First and foremost, that includes the enemy carriers."

"How many does he have, sir?" Ellis asked.

"The observers counted five, which is what intelligence has been reporting for the last few weeks. So it looks like they've concentrated their fleet all in one nice big bull's eye. We have Pathfinders going ahead of you—their instructions are to drop a couple of dozen flares over the fleet and keep them burning, so you should be able to see your targets."

He didn't add the corollary—that the targets would be able to see the planes, as well—but the knowledge was present in every pilot's mind.

"This will be a skip bomb attack—the first time we've tried it against warships instead of transports. I know the risks as well as you men do. But keep in mind that this is the big prize: if we sink those flattops, everything about this war changes in our favor.

"Major Willis will get you information on course to target as you head out to your planes. All three squadrons have been armed and fueled; I want you in the air as soon as you can take off. Good luck, and good hunting!"

There was little talking as the pilots filed past Willis and collected the mimeographed sheets detailing their bearing, formation, and altitude instructions. The men had become used to skip bombing, and all three squadrons had racked up impressive scores against the transports, and even the destroyers, of the Tokyo Express. But they'd never gone after anything as big and well armed as a carrier before.

"First time for everything, I guess," Grisham remarked as he and Ellis ran through the preflight check on the flight deck. A few minutes later they rumbled down the newly extended

Henderson runway and were climbing through the evening sky over the still waters of Ironbottom Sound.

Thirty Flying Fortresses, every one that could fly, formed up in their three squadrons. Ellis thought of the four seven-second-delay fuse bombs in the *Skylark II*'s bay. Would they find a worthwhile target? And would they survive the furious antiaircraft? His gut rumbled, and he realized he hadn't taken time to grab a bite of supper.

He didn't mind dying as much as he hated the idea of dying on an empty stomach.

AKAGI, 200 MILES EAST OF RABAUL, 1835 HOURS

The last of the bombers of Nagumo's airstrike were still climbing to cruising elevation when the Zeros of the combat air patrol pounced on the incoming Americans. Soon the gunners on the screening vessels were popping away with antiaircraft, puffs of black smoke appearing in the sky. American and Japanese fighters mixed it up in a snarling dogfight, and in the first two minutes at least a dozen planes, spewing flames and smoke, spiraled down to crash onto the flat surface of the sea.

Still the tenacious Americans came on. The *Akagi* twisted and turned. Zeros plunged through their own antiaircraft to press home the attack. More enemy planes fell from the sky, even as additional numbers of Nagumo's defending Zeros were also shot down. The Japanese fighters pressed home their attacks with fearlessness, exacting a high cost from both the enemy dive and torpedo bombers. An aide pointed out the most immediate threat, and the admiral watched the torpedo bombers zoom along above the surface of the ocean. He was pleased when most of the planes were shot down. Those that launched their torpedoes failed to score a hit on the frantically maneuvering carrier.

An aide approached him. "Another American attack inbound, Admiral. Dive-bombers, almost directly overhead."

He felt a qualm at the news. Dive-bombers were dangerous opponents, capable of plunging an armor-piercing bomb onto even a small, nimble target. They had struck three of his ships at Midway, sinking the venerable *Kaga*. Even so, he reminded himself, his fleet had defenses against this kind of attack. *Kido Butai* could be expected to decimate these squadrons as it had every other during this long and violent war.

"Thank you," replied Nagumo. "I think I'll watch from outside." He stepped through the hatch. Two aides followed.

He focused his binoculars to get a good look at the battle. There were a dozen or more dive-bombers over the *Akagi*, and another, somewhat larger squadron, in the direction of the *Shokaku*.

"These American pilots seem to know what they're doing," Nagumo said, surprising himself with his own equanimity. "They've selected their targets in two waves, some toward the *Shokaku*, others toward us in the *Akagi*." He felt a little more concern. "They are starting their dives—where are the Zeros?"

"Unfortunately, Admiral," one of his aides explained, "the fighters of the combat air patrol are scattered. The American fighters have attacked tenaciously, and our losses have been surprisingly high."

"Ah, yes. Of course." It was a truth of war: the longer you fought against a foe, the better that foe became at countering your tactics. Still, the carrier group was not without defenses. Already, puffs of black smoke erupted in the air as the full antiaircraft weaponry of the *Akagi* and her escorts blasted skyward. One American dive-bomber, an SBD Dauntless, fell out of the formation, plummeting seaward as it trailed a plume of smoke.

"The guns will have to get them, then—look, one is hit!" Even as he pointed out the kill in triumph, Nagumo was acutely aware that very many—most—of the enemy dive-bombers were plunging resolutely toward their target. He trained his binoculars on the approaching Dauntlesses and watched the unusual perforated flaps of the air brakes open along the wings of the attacking planes. They looked like lacy women's underwear, he thought irrelevantly.

Nagumo's eyes fastened upon one of the bombs, horrible and black, hanging from the pale belly of an American plane. The SBD continued its dive, through a cloud of AA that did nothing to throw it off course. Just when it seemed as though the American intended to fly straight down into the Japanese carrier, the plane dropped its load and pulled up. Nagumo's binoculars remained fixed upon the bomb that looked as if it had been aimed at him personally.

"Admiral, perhaps you should go inside," suggested an aide.

He could feel doubts and anxieties rushing back in.

Nagumo was frozen in place, unable to move as the bomb continued straight toward him. He dropped the binoculars, saw the weapon with his naked eye. Other bombs plunged in the direction of the *Akagi* as well, but only the one loomed so large in his vision.

It struck the empty flight deck near the bow and its explosion rocked the ship. Nagumo almost fell and braced himself with both hands on the armored rail. Flame and smoke shot high into the air, billowing from the hole in the flight deck. Planks and sections of metal, and the bodies of crewmen, tumbled lazily through the air, tossed by the powerful blast. The admiral could feel the heat from the blast against his face, an uncomfortable, burning presence.

Several bombs splashed to the sides—misses—but two more plunged through the flight deck aft. The explosions sent the ship lurching like she had been punched, convulsing so hard the concussion threw him off his feet. He scrambled to stand again, looked across the deck. His first thought was that fires were raging everywhere, but already damage control parties were scrambling toward the crater left by the first hit, playing powerful streams of water into the smoking hole.

Alarms sounded throughout the ship as crewmen raced to put out the myriad fires. Nagumo allowed his aides to help him back inside. He touched his forehead and saw blood on his fingers, not surprised that he cut himself there when he fell. Still, he shrugged off the arms of concerned staff officers who sought to assist him.

"Reports! What is the situation here, and in the rest of the fleet?"

News trickled in, from the *Akagi* first. The grand old dame of IJN aircraft carriers had taken four hits through the flight deck. She could not land or launch planes, but already the fires were being brought under control. In short order came word that the carriers *Shokaku* and *Soryu* had also taken hits from the American dive-bombers. The damaged *Soryu* was able to make way, though her flight deck—like the *Akagi*—was too badly damaged for aircraft operations. The *Shokaku* was on fire, and the blazes were reported to be growing. She had also taken at least one hit from a torpedo and was dead in the water.

And still more of these deadly aircraft survived, and they came in a wave. Now came word that the *Hiryu* was hit by bombs. Then her sister ship the *Soryu* took a bomb through her recently repaired flight deck. As a final insult, the *Hiryu* took a torpedo near the bow—it seemed that even those flawed American weapons exploded occasionally—and was forced to slow to half speed.

At last the American attack was over, and Nagumo allowed himself a measure of content. That was the worst the enemy could offer, he knew, and he still had one intact carrier—the *Zuikaku*—and real hopes that all the other ships could be saved. His air groups, as they had at Midway, were attacking the enemy ships even as their own fleet was bombed. And unlike at Midway, here they had bases in the Solomons—on Bougainville, Buka, and Munda—where the aircraft could safely land before they ran out of fuel.

All told, things could have been much worse.

PORTLAND, *SOLOMON SEA*, 2001 HOURS

"Captain! We're getting a lot of bogies on the screen!"

Frank Chadwick looked over his radar operator's shoulder, watching the green blip on the gray screen as it morphed into a large disturbance to the northeast. Like most U.S. Navy officers, he had become quite confident in the new technology, developed and employed by the British to such good effect during the Battle of Britain.

Now it was suggesting a very large group of aircraft coming from the northwest. He checked his watch; it was still too early for the American air groups to be returning to their carriers.

"Sound general quarters," he ordered tersely. As the klaxon rang throughout the ship and men went running to the gun stations or damage control parties, he raised his binoculars and looked at the flags running up the mast of the *Enterprise*.

He was not surprised to decipher the admiral's orders as, "Stand by to defend against air attack."

ABOVE ENTERPRISE, *SOLOMON SEA, 2019 HOURS*

A crackle of static sounded in Lefty Wayner's ears, broken by snatches of speech: "There, to the left—spotted one—I hit him!—Look at those flames!"

Lefty listened to those radio reports as he patrolled his lazy circle over the carrier that had been his home for the whole course of this war. He wished he was with the attacking formations, but he had drawn guard duty today, as he had at Midway. So he was once again circling the carrier, flying the routine of combat air patrol. Of course, knowing that the Jap carriers were out there meant that he was keeping his eyes open, craning his neck with extra vigilance. One reason was the real and practical need for alertness.

The other reason was that every time he closed his eyes he saw that little Jap biplane diving away from him, hiding in the clouds, and reporting back to the enemy fleet. It was Lefty's secret, and it tore at his heart: *I lost the Battle of Midway.* If he had just shot down that little scout before it had reported the location of the American fleet, the whole battle might have gone differently.

No one had ever criticized his effort at Midway—hell, he had even gotten a commendation when he'd shot down two Jap bombers during the battle—but Lefty Wayner couldn't help blaming himself. When he had tried to tell people, they dismissed his fears. "No one could have hit that scout. It wasn't your fault."

He didn't believe them.

If I'd seen that son of a bitch sooner . . . if my first burst had been aimed better. . . . The questions were never far from the surface of his consciousness. *The Japanese attack would not have materialized until much later. . . . The* Enterprise *would not have been damaged. The* Hornet *and the* Yorktown *might still be afloat and in action.*

In the months following the Battle of Midway, Lefty had been promoted to full lieutenant, had seen the *Big E* restored to serviceability, and had shot down two more enemy planes in action around the Solomons. But no number of victories, he knew, would ever be able to make up for the one that got away.

Now, the American strike had hit paydirt, and the bastards know we're here, Lefty reflected. No doubt some kind of return favor was on the way. In the fading light he scanned the skies to the east, watching; when his radio crackled with a warning from the ship—a report that radar had detected a large flight of bogies some fifty miles out—he wasn't surprised. The Wildcats of the combat air patrol climbed a little higher, dispersed into the path of the enemy formation; the pilots charged their guns and kept their unblinking eyes on the sky.

And then there was no more time for reflection. The Japanese bombers, about two hundred of them, were in sight.

Japanese aircraft designations were such a confusing mess that Air Technical Intelligence Unit in Australia had developed a set of code names for them. Whoever it was who ran the unit liked hillbilly names, because there were Zekes and Jakes and Rufes and Hanks and Slims.

The Aichi Type 99 dive-bombers with the characteristic fixed landing gear dangling like the talons of a hawk were now called Vals. They were on top, approaching in a wide V formation, with perhaps a dozen planes leading the way. Other flights of similar dive-bombers came beyond, all flying straight and level. Just as the radar operators on the *Enterprise* had reported, the enemy attacked in strength, on a direct course toward Halsey's fleet.

Lefty tilted the stubby nose of his fighter toward the enemy planes. His fingers tightened on the stick as he pushed his little fighter over, ready to exact vengeance for that little bastard scout plane at Midway. The Wildcat picked up speed, wind and engine noise blending into an eardrum-rattling roar.

The line of Vals continued on without wavering, the aircraft resembling a line of elegant storks. The diving Grumman zoomed closer, and Wayner selected his target. His thumb tightened on the trigger and four .50 caliber machine guns—two on each wing—stuttered. The navy pilot watched his tracers converge, guided them across one of the enemy dive-bombers, and was rewarded as the enemy plane exploded in a blinding flash of flaming gas and detonating bomb. A second later he was through the Japanese formation, banking around hard to make another attack. Half a dozen American fighters buzzed along with him, speeding from their long dives, now lurching and growling as they pitched upward and started to turn.

Lefty caught sight of the enemy fighters before he completed the maneuver. Sparkling in the rays of the setting sun, they swept downward and leveled out, mingling with the Wildcats, coming on very fast. One of the vaunted Zeros sped past, aiming at Wayner's wingman, and Lefty pulled his stick, kicked his rudder around. The target seemed huge just to the port of his gun sights, the enemy fighter settling into level flight, the pilot concentrating on his shot. But the Zero was too fast—it was gone before Lefty could line up his guns.

So he went for another dive-bomber, snarling down the now staggered line of Vals, pumping shots into several before another began to burn furiously. Lefty grinned, a fierce expression of glee, as the Jap plunged out of the formation, spiraling toward the ocean below. He saw a chute open. *You're not getting away that easily, you fucking Nip bastard,* he thought and fired a burst down through the parachute.

Another Zero went past, fastened like glue to the tail of a Grumman, and the American pilot curved to port in the Thach weave, as they had been practicing all summer. Lefty dropped his flaps to slow down, and this brought the Jap right across his nose. With a single burst he sent a fusillade of slugs into the nimble fighter and shouted aloud as he saw the port wing crumple and break away.

"Down on the deck—we've got Kates coming in from all sides!" The alarmed voice crackled in his earphones, a fighter director calling for help from the carrier. Six Wildcats, Lefty leading the way, screamed in a power dive toward the dappled images of the deadly Nakajima B5N "Kate" torpedo bombers converging on the *Enterprise* from both the port and starboard bows. Whichever way the great ship turned, she would present a broadside target toward one of the flights.

There was no time to make a choice—Lefty simply dived toward the nearest of the low, flat torpedo bombers. Wind rattled the canopy and shook the little fighter as he plunged through ten, eight, six thousand feet of altitude, starting to level out only as he screamed almost down to sea level. He roared in from the flank of the attacking formation and rattled off shots as soon as the targets were in range.

There were about ten of them, and they droned toward the broad beam of the *Enterprise,* flying less than a hundred feet above the water. Knowing that his carrier's survival was at stake—a torpedo was far and away the deadliest threat to his great ship—he aimed with care. A strange sense of calm pervaded him as he slashed into the Kates. His tracers converged on one of the bombers, flaming it immediately; the next one flipped over and crashed when his bullets shattered the cockpit glass and killed the pilot. The Wildcat blazed through the line and he drew a bead on the last plane in view, pouring slugs into the nose until his ammo ran out. As he flew past, he watched the torpedo bomber sink lower and lower until it splashed into the sea, immediately touching off a huge blast as the torpedo exploded.

He glanced back and saw that other Wildcats were scoring

against the Japs as well. One Kate survived long enough to launch its fish, but Lefty could see that the weapon's trajectory would take it safely past the *Big E*'s stern—though the torpedo was heading instead for one of the screening cruisers. At this distance he couldn't tell if it was the *Minneapolis* or the *Portland*. Either way, the explosion hit aft. Nearby, the *Wasp* too maneuvered frantically but had thus far avoided getting hit.

To the north, however, the picture was dire. The greatest number of enemy attackers had converged there, and even from ten miles away Lefty could see that the *Saratoga* had been hit, hard. A plume of black smoke already rose some two miles into the air, and as he watched, another explosion, and then still more blasts, rocked the very guts of the grand old ship.

PORTLAND, *SOLOMON SEA, 2101 HOURS*

Frank Chadwick watched the last of the Japanese torpedo bombers splash, and he cheered along with every other man on the flag bridge. They stood in the open air, watching the frenzy of the aerial battle, and remained there, limp and exhausted, as the last of the Japanese planes turned for home. The *Minneapolis* was damaged and could barely make way, so command of the screening group passed to Frank in the *Portland*.

Only when the battle was over, when damage control reports started to come in—the *Saratoga* had taken three torpedo hits and twice as many from bombs; her captain had already ordered "abandon ship"—did Chadwick's thoughts turn back to the American pilots winging their way back to their carriers.

It was already sunset; by the time they returned it would be fully dark. There was only one way to get those fliers back onto the carriers. It was dangerous, it was risky, but there was really not much choice. Whatever planes could be diverted to Henderson Field would go there; for the rest, the ships would have to turn on their lights. This would make them sitting ducks for any lurking submarines. There were submarine pickets all around, of course, and antisubmarine planes circling the fleet. The risk could be reduced—but it could not be eliminated.

Within an hour the signal flags from the *Enterprise* ordered every searchlight and running light in the fleet illuminated as the planes came straggling back from their attack. With the loss of the *Saratoga,* all the returning aircraft had to land on two carriers, but so many of the planes had been lost in the battle that there was enough deck space to handle the load.

And there was almost enough time. The last returning F4F stuttered and lurched as it approached the carrier. Chadwick, still watching from the bridge, willed it to find another sniff of gasoline in those empty tanks—but instead the stubby little fighter dropped like a stone as the engine quit entirely. It fell into the sea a hundred yards to the stern of the *Enterprise*. A destroyer steamed over to attempt a rescue, but it looked to Frank like the pilot never made it out of the plane.

OVER THE JAPANESE FLEET, 2242 HOURS

It looked to Ellis Halverson like the ocean had turned to flame. Fire exploded from Japanese ships on all sides— some because they had been gutted by bombs and torpedoes, others because they were blazing away at the attacking B-17s with every gun on deck.

The Pathfinders had done their work well: overhead, a series of flares lit up the night with searing brilliance, outlining the ships even as the enemy gunners blasted at the approaching bombers. Ellis could see two carriers that looked to be burning from stem to stern, but spotted another one—apparently undamaged—just a few miles away. He led his flight of B-17s directly toward it.

The *Skylark II* roared through the escort ring around the Japanese flattops, all guns blazing. The B-17 was pretty fast—better than three hundred miles per hour—but it wasn't fast enough to outrun high-velocity antiaircraft shells. That would take, simply, a very large amount of luck.

In the thunderstorm of antiaircraft coming at the *Skylark,* any bit of maneuverability or speed Ellis lost was a potential killer. He needed all of the nearly four thousand eight hundred horsepower in the four Wright Cyclone engines as he powered the heavily laden bomber toward the Jap carriers. Tracers whipped past the glass windshield. As Halverson watched the course of the streaking rounds, he saw bullet holes appearing in his starboard wing, walking outward toward the number two engine. He pulled on the stick and the bomber lurched to the side, out of the path of bullets. The Zero roared past, so close that he could see the fighter pilot's face, outlined in the garish light of the drifting flares, through the bubble canopy.

"Two more of the bastards at six o'clock!" Corporal Chuck Delaney, tail turret gunner/radioman, barked the news into the intercom.

Jesus Christ! There were so damned many of them! Everywhere he looked he saw wheeling, shooting, and diving fighters. The Zeros were faster and more nimble than the bombers gravid with their heavy loads—so much so that Halverson felt like a duck in a shooting gallery. The Jap fleet was spread across the whole horizon, an impossibly daunting target. What seemed like hundreds of huge ships twisted and turned slowly across the sea to avoid air attack, all bringing their guns to bear against the Americans.

Halverson, in the lead Fortress, wrenched so violently to the right that the plane stood almost on its wing as a pair of Zeros zipped past. Righting his plane for a moment, the veteran commander lurched the other way and once more came back to a level bearing. The numbers two through ten bombers of the squadron were strung out line abreast, each one maneuvering frantically. They were flying low, a necessity in order to skip bomb, but this only added to the sensation of having a large bull's-eye painted on the airplane.

Adding to the chaos were the antiaircraft bursts, black puffs of smoke appearing to all sides, occasionally sending

ripples of shrapnel against and through the *Skylark II*'s skin.
A huge flash, followed by a stunning concussion, knocked
the Fortress to the side. Halverson grimaced and swore. The
number three plane had been hit and its bombs had exploded.
As Ellis flashed past the cloud of wreckage, he noticed one
engine, the propeller still attached, tumble down toward the
ocean. No chutes. *Damn.*

They were through the ring of destroyers now, and it
seemed like every ship in the task force was blasting away
at Ellis Halverson personally. Ahead loomed the tall,
pagoda-shaped superstructures of enemy heavy cruisers
and battleships, every ship clearly outlined in fire and flare
light—despite the fact that it was fully after dark. The battlewagons even fired their big guns, explosive shells sending
up fountains of water in an attempt to knock the low-flying
bombers out of the sky. Halverson veered to the side, and the
surviving bombers of his small formation followed. A quick
glance showed him only six planes off his wing—had the
other three all splashed?

Doctrine called for them to split up, to coordinate an approach from two directions so that the Jap carrier would
have to expose a flank to one if it turned to present the narrow bow to the other. *Fuck doctrine,* Halverson thought—if
he could get close enough to drop his bombs, and then somehow get out of here alive, he'd call himself a Horatio Alger
hero.

He saw smoke trailing from both starboard engines of the
number two bomber and clenched his teeth, urging the pilot
to pull up, to stay in the air even over the force of gravity,
watching until the nose dropped and the B-17 hit the ocean
in a massive splash. *Four down. Shit.*

And then it was there, right in front of him: a Japanese aircraft carrier, stretched out like it was a half-mile long. He
saw the island superstructure, the command tower that was
tiny by American standards, jutting above the huge flight
deck. The ship was turning, and the Lucky Dicers had a shot
only at the starboard quarter. Still, that seemed big enough.
He took his plane down until he was practically skimming

the wave tops. The rest of the squadron followed, each pilot trying to see through a windshield that was now grimy with soot and oil and the mist that lingered from the spewing explosions in the water.

The pilots did the best they could to ignore the hailstorm of antiaircraft. A great flash and concussion ignited just to port, and Halverson grimaced as Dick Vail's *Grable's Gams* vanished. Pieces of metal pinged against the *Skylark II*, and he felt alarming shudders and thumps as explosions roared to all sides.

But there was the target, even bigger than life. The *Skylark II* was flying low, and Ellis had to slow down now, making the bomber a perfect target. But luck continued to fly along with him. He held his course almost to the point of madness until, a few hundred feet from the target, Halverson pulled the lever to let his bombs go, hurling them across the surface of the water as precisely as he could. There came an immediate and very welcome lurch as the B-17 freed of the cumbersome weight, popped upward.

Immediately he pressed the throttles forward, propelling the bomber right down to the deck, roaring past the big aircraft carrier's stern.

The five surviving Fortresses finally started to climb, turning away from the carrier. Now the bombers were speedy aircraft again, capable of pulling away from the enemy fighters. Halverson couldn't see the target anymore, but he listened to Delaney's excited description.

"Hot damn!" The tail gunner screamed into the microphone. "Captain, we blew that son of a bitch right out of the water!"

AKAGI, *200 MILES EAST OF RABAUL*, 2245 HOURS

Admiral Nagumo looked around at the night that had become his own personal hell. Where had these bombers come from? They were brave, coming in so slowly—it seemed that half of them had been shot down.

But the other half . . . they had completed their deadly

work. First the army bombers had blasted the *Shokaku* and the already damaged *Hiryu*. Then the final insult: a volley of bombs had skipped into the side of the *Akagi,* puncturing the venerable ship's bowels, blowing up deep within her guts. The flares still burning overhead cast their white brilliance like searing searchlights. All of his carriers were burning. . . . The *Kido Butai* fleet had been devastated beyond recovery by the two consecutive attacks.

Staff officers were pleading with him, even tugging at him, trying to get him to leave. But his feet would not move, his mouth could not articulate a sound. Didn't they *know*? Couldn't they *see*? His heart was broken in his chest. There was no purpose to anything, not anymore.

There was one essential strategic difference between the American fleet and the Japanese fleet. When a Japanese carrier sank, it was essentially irreplaceable. Japanese heavy industry was experiencing an increasing shortage of vital war materiél; in particular, there was simply not enough steel to build any more large warships. But the Americans, so far away in a land rich with natural resources, when they lost a carrier, simply built another, or two, or perhaps six. That was what Yamamoto had known and had warned about.

And finally, Nagumo understood.

The explosion that rocked the bridge did not even register on his numbed senses. The fire that swirled around him was a cleansing joy, the last joy he would ever know. And death, when finally it claimed him, brought the only possible relief from his disgrace and his shame.

IMPERIAL JAPANESE NAVY SUBMARINE I-19, SOLOMON SEA, 2246 HOURS

"I have a bearing on two carriers."

Captain Asagi held his eyes to the periscope, slowly swiveled the tiny viewer that projected above the surface of the sea. He had been stalking this fleet for hours, moving very slowly under the water, surfacing infrequently to consult his scope. The surface ships moved much faster than a submerged submarine, but here Asagi had been lucky: he had simply lurked and waited, and the enemy fleet was now steaming right above him!

His boat was submerged and undiscovered, literally in the middle of the American fleet. And there were two flattops visible in the scope. These were the prize targets of naval warfare—in this war, anyway—and both of them were within range of his lethal Long Lance torpedoes.

"Stand by to fire all the bow tubes," he ordered. "Then alter course by thirty degrees to starboard, and fire the rear."

Asagi's crew scrambled to prepare the shots, while the captain went back to viewing. Two carriers, in a stealth night attack. It would be an unprecedented feat of seamanship, and they might be able to do it! Never before had such a shot been attempted.

But then never before, to be sure, had he seen two targets so thoroughly illuminated by their own searchlights.

ENTERPRISE, *SOLOMON SEA, 2257 HOURS*

Lefty Wayner had never been so glad to feel the deck under his feet. Since they had a little more gas in their tanks, the CAP—combat air patrol—fighters landed after the strike aircraft. Even so, it was touch-and-go, and it wasn't until his tailhook snagged the wire that Lefty convinced himself he was really going to make it back to his cabin without getting wet.

"How many, Lefty?" his crew chief, Mike Sanders, asked as he popped the canopy and helped the pilot out of the tiny cockpit and onto the wing.

Lefty had spent the last hour circling in the darkness, going over the fight in his mind, and he was ready with an answer. "I got six—count 'em, six—of the bastards!" he crowed as he hopped down to the flight deck. "Two dive-bombers, a fighter, and three of them torpeckers."

"Hot damn—with the four from before, that makes you a double ace!" Mike clapped him on the back.

"You know, I guess it does. Not a bad outcome for a few hours' hard work," Lefty allowed.

He was turning toward the island, looking forward to a cup of hot coffee in the pilots' wardroom, when suddenly the pilot was airborne again—this time without benefit of an airplane. The deck jolted upward beneath him, tossing the chief and Lefty into the air. The Grumman, not yet strapped down, lurched and wobbled on its narrow landing gear as the two men tumbled down beside it. The right strut collapsed and the starboard wing smashed downward, pinning the crew chief to the deck, smashing his chest.

Only then did Lefty hear the explosion. A great roar erupted from the bowels of the ship, and a column of flame shot high into the sky, blasting the aft elevator right out of its frame. He felt the searing blast of the heat against his skin, and as he stumbled to his feet he stared down at Sanders, motionless with his mouth gaping and tongue protruding under the weight of the aircraft's wing.

Men screamed and shouted. Some kept their heads enough to issue orders: "Damage control over here! Get those hoses spraying! Corpsman! Corpsman!"

A klaxon sounded, not that anyone needed the clarification that the ship was in trouble. The terrible sounds of fire and explosion roared up through the elevator hatch and thundered through the hull.

Lefty didn't need a program to know what had happened: the *Big E* had taken a torpedo right in her guts. A Jap submarine was lurking out there somewhere, and as he knelt beside Mike Sanders he felt a rush of hatred for those sneaky bastards that went far beyond any emotion he had felt during his lethal dueling in the air.

"Help!" he cried to a pair of running seamen. "We've got to get him out of here!" The sailors continued to run and Lefty tried to lift the wing on his own. Mike was motionless, his eyes open and his chest crushed, but the pilot wasn't thinking rationally as he tried to pull the airplane off of the dead crew chief. He wept in frustration and fought the men who took his arms and pulled him away, back from the rapidly spreading fire.

They left the pilot with many other wounded men on the

forward part of the flight deck. It wasn't until Lefty tried to
get up and head back to help fight the fire that he realized
that his face and hands were blistered from the heat. His
throat was parched, and his legs refused to support him. A
corpsman gave him cool water from a canteen, and he
slumped back onto the flight deck, looking up at the pillars
of fire rising from the stern of his great ship.

Damage control parties were directing the spray of massive hoses onto the conflagration, but it was like trying to
put out a bonfire with a squirt gun. More blasts wracked the
ship as bombs in the magazine exploded; the noise was
louder than a violent thunderstorm, and even more relentless.

At first, the pain of his burns was maddening, but the
corpsman returned and gave him a shot of morphine. The
drug eased through his veins, bringing a dulling fatigue, so
much so that he didn't even care when he finally heard the
order pass through the ranks of the wounded:

"Abandon ship."

PORTLAND, *SOLOMON SEA, 2301 HOURS*

"Holy shit—the *Enterprise* just blew up!" The announce-
ment, by a seaman observer in a cracking voice, was not
strictly necessary. Chadwick could see the other carrier, less
than a mile away, erupt with a gout of flame shooting high
into the sky from the afterdeck.

The first torpedo struck astern of the carrier's island,
heaving the elevator upward and spewing that spectacular
column of fire. A few seconds later the pressure wave from
the explosion sent Chadwick—and hundreds of other men
aboard the *Portland*—staggering and sometimes falling,
rocking the heavy cruiser in the water like a toy boat in a
bathtub.

Moments later a second explosion ripped through the
stern of the *Enterprise*. Frank could see that the great ship
was savagely hit, burning furiously in the stern, with her hull
punctured in at least two places.

"There's a Jap sub out there!" Chadwick realized immediately. "Submarine! Lights out!" he yelled.

"Submarine, lights out, aye, captain," came the answering chorus.

He was not the only one to understand—already the lights on the fleet were blinking out, even though the last of the combat air patrol planes were still coming in to land.

"See if you can raise the *Enterprise*," he ordered.

His radioman got to work with the set, shaking his head in frustration. Frank stayed on the exterior bridge, hands clenching the metal rim of the rail, counting off the seconds, wondering if the *Wasp*, too, had been made a target.

The answer came with stunning violence. Another fireball blossomed amid the now darkened fleet, followed by the dull boom of explosions thundering over the sea. The other carrier was three miles away, but the men aboard the *Portland* still felt the concussion through the water and across the gulf of space.

The *Minneapolis* had serious engine room damage and was likely going to need a tow back to Nouméa. With the *Enterprise* down, that left the *Portland* as the lead ship, at least until Admiral Halsey could transfer his flag or establish communication from the *Big E*.

It didn't look like the latter eventuality was going to happen anytime soon, if ever again. Fire engulfed the whole stern of the ship, and the flames made steady progress, creeping through the midsection of the carrier, surrounding the island, encroaching toward the bow. Already she was settling by the stern as water gushed in through the two massive holes in her hull.

"We're going to be ready if the *Enterprise* needs evacuation," Frank ordered. "Send half the screening destroyers after the sub—even though he probably turned tail and ran after he fired all his tubes. As for the rest of us, we're not going to worry about it. Let's move in as close as we can. Order the rest of the DDs in as well. Put all the boats in the water, and let's get the survivors on board."

As the *Portland* closed on the *Enterprise*, Frank could see the great ship settling more dramatically by the stern. In addition, she was listing to starboard, so much so that the men on the cruise could soon see the carrier's flight deck as it leaned toward them. Fires from the engine room and magazine were spreading, slowly getting beyond human control. Through his binoculars, Frank saw men running in every direction, and amid them he saw motionless forms, bodies crumpled awkwardly, broken and shattered.

The crew of the *Big E* would fight to save the ship, but from here, her fate looked certain. Long rows of wounded men had been laid out near the bow while ropes were secured to the catwalks just below the flight deck. These lines trailed down to the water, and almost immediately men began to descend toward the sea.

There was still no communication with the stricken carrier, but it was clear that she was being abandoned. Already the ocean teemed with bobbing, swimming men. Oil spreading from the stern of the ship was burning, and the slick was growing dangerously.

"Closer—take us in closer!" Chadwick demanded. "There are men dying in that water!"

Ignoring the danger to his own ship, the captain took his heavy cruiser right up to the edge of the burning oil slick. Destroyers dodged in and out, while small boats were lowered, and many oil-soaked men—a good number of them wounded—were pulled from the water.

Meanwhile, other destroyers chased the elusive submarine. Depth charges boomed through the night, the sounds growing farther and farther away. Though the little ships couldn't claim a kill with any certainty, they at least drove the enemy sub deep enough so that it couldn't shoot again.

Through the long night, Frank directed the rescue operations. Out of two thousand two hundred men on board the *Enterprise,* his ships recovered only nine hundred, many hurt, some critically. Last to leave was the carrier's captain, when the fate of his ship was finally beyond any doubt. He brought along another man, badly burned and carried in a canvas stretcher. When that motionless figure was raised up to the *Portland*'s deck, Frank was standing there to assist. He looked down at the stern, weather-lined face, now relaxed as if asleep. It was hard to believe that snapping voice had been stilled, the indomitable spirit quenched.

But the ghastly wound in the chest and the peaceful visage made clear:

Admiral Bill Halsey was dead.

EIGHT

The White House

• MONDAY, 19 OCTOBER 1942 •

THE WHITE HOUSE, WASHINGTON, DC, 1700 HOURS

The movement of the President's wheelchair was the signal for the traveling road show in the Oval Office to meander upstairs to the Oval Study on the residence level. Although five o'clock signaled the end of the regular workday, it meant only a change of venue for the office of the President of the United States.

The President traveled through private study and then by private elevator, of course, accompanied by valet and personal physician. Various aides—assistants to the President and deputy undersecretaries and senior advisers and people so important they had no recognizable title whatsoever—milled haphazardly down from the West Wing into the residence, and from there up the wide staircase to the Oval Study. Some aides peeled off from the pack to go about their mysterious business until only three remained.

Captain Frank Chadwick, still disoriented from his rapid transit from the Solomons, and from the still smoldering work of disaster recovery management, let himself be drawn along with the mob. He was surprised no one was telling him to get lost, that he had no business in the company of these people.

In addition to the people he already knew—Navy Secretary Frank Knox and Chief of Naval Operations Admiral Ernest King—Frank also recognized Treasury Secretary Morgenthau. He was pretty sure the guy with the briefcase handcuffed to his wrist was OSS. The White House staffers who remained with the party included two old enough to be pretty senior and one young enough that he had to be acting as somebody's ADC, or whatever the civilian equivalent was called. The young guy, Frank was sure, would be writing down any action items and reminding his boss about them in the morning.

Because this was Frank Chadwick's first visit to the White House, they'd briefed him on what to expect, but he hadn't believed half of what he'd been told about the chaos surrounding the President. Although it certainly looked chaotic, in Frank's opinion the appearance was deceiving. President Franklin Delano Roosevelt was much more in control than it appeared.

Everybody wanted to be the first to tell Frank about the wheelchair, of course. He pretended polite surprise for admirals, "old news" familiarity for anyone of lower rank. The fact of the President's disability wasn't that well kept a secret.

What nobody had briefed him about was how *shabby* the presidential mansion looked. The paint was old and peeling in places, the carpet threadbare, the furniture cast off from various federal agencies. Generations of tobacco smoke, cooking odors, and human sweat merged in the humid Washington autumn to crowd out any hint of oxygen. The Solomons smelled almost pleasant by comparison. The President didn't seem to mind: the ashtray built into the arm of his wheelchair was already overflowing with ashes from the day's second pack of Camels by the time the navy men had arrived at four o'clock sharp, the original appointment time.

Chadwick trailed behind his two bosses. Frank W. Knox was an FDR man brought in to get the navy department under control. Ernie King, running the navy from his offices in the temporary buildings down on Constitution Avenue, figured Knox would just leak any real information to his press buddies and so seldom bothered to give him any.

The civilians wore linen or seersucker, mandatory in the humid Washington summer. Knox was a linen man. Chadwick and King, the only military officers present, wore navy dress blues. Knox, a natural politician, was at home in the give-and-take of Roosevelt's informal office. Admiral King's sour apple expression was slowly darkening, like mercury rising in a thermometer, as the men continued to wait their turn.

King had predicted this when he briefed Frank during the car ride down Constitution Avenue. "That son of a bitch will have people from his last three appointments still hanging around the Oval Office yammering away, and we'll walk in and cool our heels for God only knows how long until we have a chance to get our business done." Chadwick wasn't too surprised to hear King call FDR an SOB. For the CNO and COMINCHFLT—chief of naval operations and commander in chief, United States Fleet—that was mild language.

It was certainly true that Roosevelt had a unique management style, not at all what Frank had imagined from years of listening to fireside chats and reading the newspaper. He grinned as realized he'd half expected the President to be about the size of the statue in the Lincoln Memorial, but the wheelchair with built-in ashtray, the haze of smoke and sweat, and the chaos of six simultaneous conversations swirling around the President brought him down into the mortal plane. If anything, the mortal President impressed Frank more than the memorial-sized version.

The staircase opened up onto a wide corridor that ran the length of the residence level. It, too, had seen better days, but the carpet showed less wear. A white-jacketed Negro valet opened the double doors to the Oval Study, directly opposite the staircase, and the party flowed in. Frank noticed two discreet but obviously serious Secret Service agents, one blocking each way down the corridor in the event of any unauthorized tourism.

The Oval Study was, if anything, in much worse shape than the rest of the White House. Crowded full of sofas, card tables, bookcases, and knickknacks FDR had picked up over a lifetime, there was barely enough room for the eleven people who had packed themselves in.

FDR himself was already stationed behind the makeshift bar, ready to perform his self-appointed daily duty as mix master. After handing a rather wet martini to the secretary of navy, the President of the United States put the finishing touches on an old-fashioned for himself and made the first toast.

"Gentlemen," the President said. "To victory."

A ragged chorus of "To victory" came in reply, and those without drinks nodded or lifted an empty hand in salute.

"Now, where were we?" This was the general signal for conversations to start back up again. The evening work session at the Roosevelt White House was officially under way.

The President continued to serve his more senior guests before turning over bartending responsibilities to his valet. Either FDR remembered what everybody drank or nobody wanted to complain, because he continued to mix drinks without interrupting the flow of conversation.

FDR poured King a scotch, neat, of a brand Chadwick had never seen. "It's another single malt Winston sent over, Ernie. There's an extra bottle for you, too. I had it delivered to your office."

With the current emotional temperature reading on King's face, Frank expected the admiral to say something grumpy or worse—so, by the expression on his face, did Knox—but instead King gestured toward Chadwick. "Mr. President, I hope you won't mind pouring one more of those."

"And who might this young man be?" the President asked, reaching out one hand with the scotch and another to shake.

King made the introduction. "Mr. President, this is Captain

Frank Chadwick, recently of the Northern Solomons. Frank, I have the honor to introduce the President of the United States."

"It's a great honor indeed, Mr. President," Chadwick said, saluting.

"Nonsense, m'boy, nonsense!" the President replied in the mellifluous tones so well-known to every American with a radio. "The honor and pleasure is mine." He leaned forward in his wheelchair and stuck out his hand. FDR's handshake was surprisingly strong. While the polio might have crippled his lower half, his upper body had grown powerful muscles to compensate.

"A heroic battle, Frank, heroic!" He gestured for Chadwick to sit on the couch. Knox and King sat on either side. "As I recall, you oversaw the evacuation of the *Enterprise,* after poor Bill Halsey was killed. That's a sad blow to the navy—but you showed gallantry under fire moving your cruiser in with the possibility that more Japanese submarines might be lurking."

"Thank you, Mr. President. I'm flattered, but there was nothing I did that any other navy captain would not have done in the same circumstances—"

"Frank is up for the Navy Cross," King interjected. "By risking his own safety and that of his ship, he saved nearly nine hundred men."

"That's the same story I heard," Roosevelt said.

Chadwick was a little embarrassed by the amount of presidential attention he was getting. When FDR looked at him, it was as if he was caught in the beam of a searchlight.

The furniture might be shabby, but the White House liquor service was first rate. Chadwick sipped his scotch slowly and with appreciation. He had been traveling for nearly two days by military and civilian aircraft. His body still ached from being in confined spaces and his ears still rang from the roaring of aircraft engines. The cacophony of conversations was almost too much for him to handle.

As Knox prodded Chadwick to tell the President the story of the battle, Treasury Secretary Morgenthau was trying to get the President to pay attention to an elaborate discussion of movements in the long-bond market. Meanwhile, two White House staffers discussed the 1942 midterm elections, raising their voices in hopes that their specific worries would reach the Presidential ear. The third aide, the junior one, was trying to listen to every conversation at once so he could jot down any "to-do" items that came up.

A man with a briefcase, who Frank assumed was with the Office of Strategic Services—at a minimum he had some sort of involvement in the shadowy world of intelligence—made cryptic remarks about a recent Churchill cable that concerned a matter so secret even its code name was classified. There was one word—"Bletchley"—but Frank had no idea what it meant and knew enough not to be curious. The maybe-OSS man's eyes darted side to side as if one of the other guests might be a deep-cover Nazi spy. He looked as if he wished everybody else would go away nearly as much as Admiral King did.

Roosevelt bobbed and weaved through the various conversations, his famous cigarette holder serving as a conductor's baton. After a few minutes, Frank got the rhythm, telling a little piece of the story as FDR's attention landed briefly on deck and took off again. He spent the intervening time trying to edit what he would say next, to pack a lot of information into a few words so Roosevelt could listen.

King, impatient as always, walked around the room looking at the various ship models, looking back at Roosevelt and Knox from time to time for a heads-up that it was time for King's own audience. King was in the White House for his own business, not primarily to pin a medal on some captain.

There was a method beneath Roosevelt's madness. The President seemed able to keep track of three or four conversations simultaneously, letting debate—sometimes even open argument—continue for a while, then cutting in with a decision or a directive artfully disguised as a suggestion. Morgenthau got his answer about the long bond and left, the two quarreling aides got FDR's ideas for the 1942 midterms, and the OSS spook—if that's what he was—got a cryptic reply that seemed to satisfy him.

Unfortunately for Admiral King's growing apoplexy, as people left, others arrived. Now the group included a deputy undersecretary of state for some function Frank missed, two more White House aides without portfolio, and a fat army one-star wearing the Corps of Engineers castle. FDR seemed endlessly cheerful and energetic, and King continued to move along the spectrum toward purple.

The next arrival made Frank sit up and take notice. Both King and Knox looked surprised as well. It was "the Admiral": Congressman Carl Vinson of Georgia, chairman of the House Naval Affairs and Armed Services Committee.

This time, loud children's voices interrupted Frank's story. Four of FDR's thirteen grandchildren burst into the room. They were continuing a very active game of tag over, around, and under the overstuffed furniture in a room that suddenly felt reduced to half its former cramped size.

Chadwick felt a tug on his jacket and looked down at a solemn-faced boy of about eight. "I haven't seen you before," the boy said. "Are you new?"

Chadwick knelt down to be eye to eye with the boy. "I'm just visiting," he replied, reaching out his hand.

The boy shook hands solemnly. "You're a captain, aren't you? I'm going to join the navy and go to the academy," he said. "I want to captain a ship at sea."

"That's a fine ambition," replied Chadwick. "The navy can always use brave captains. Maybe we'll serve together someday."

"Fighting the Japs?"

"Well, I hope not. I'm sorry to say it probably will be over before you can get into it. But there's a lot to do in the navy even when you're not in a battle."

The boy thought about it for a minute. "Can you fire the guns anyway?"

Chadwick leaned forward, looked left and right to ensure privacy (and in so doing drew a quick stare from the maybe-

OSS man, who was whispering with Roosevelt), and whispered, "When you're the captain, you get to fire the guns
anytime you want. It's the best part of the job."

The boy's face lit up and he ran over to his grandfather,
tugged on his sleeve, and shouted, "Guess what, guess
what?"

The President held up a hand to ask the maybe-OSS man
to wait. "What?"

"If you're the captain of a ship, you get to fire the guns
anytime you want!"

There was a pause. King gave Chadwick a look that felt
like a volley from six-inch guns.

FDR looked up at Chadwick and grinned. "Well, now, that
means being captain of a ship must be the best job in the
world. Even better than being President. Ernie, what do you
think about that?"

King snorted and polished off his scotch. "As long as
you're firing those guns at the enemy, you can fire them all
you want, Captain."

There was only one reply Frank could make: "Aye aye,
sir."

Roosevelt laughed. One of the granddaughters ran past,
touched the boy on the shoulder, shouted, "Tag! You're it!"
and kept running. The boy shouted, "I am not! I was talking!
Time out!"

"You didn't call 'Time out'!" the girl yelled back.

Forgetting the conversation, the boy started chasing after
the girl, yelling, "Cheater! I'm going to get you!" as Chadwick straightened up. He noticed that both Roosevelt and
King were watching him, the President with a slight grin,
King with an air of disgust. Chadwick finished his own
scotch. Well, maybe a second drink wouldn't hurt.

Throughout, Frank Knox was completely in his element.
King's face, on the other hand, continued to redden slowly,
like mercury rising in a thermometer. Any other audience
would be witnessing one of King's famous outbursts by now.

Of course, Chadwick could have told him that his attitude

was guaranteeing that FDR would make him wait until last, but King wasn't looking for advice from a mere captain. As a former assistant secretary of the navy himself, FDR could be expected to show sympathy for the navy position in the Pacific, but not with King's contempt radiating in his face. This was no way to win the war against MacArthur, much less against the Japanese.

Throughout, Roosevelt continued to extract from Chadwick details of the Battle of the Solomon Sea. Frank started out thinking of the President as a civilian but soon realized his command of the details of the battle and of naval operations in general was formidable. Chadwick didn't think Knox would have quite the same command of the details.

FDR reached over and patted Chadwick on the knee. "And you've been traveling ever since, I understand," he said with apparently genuine sympathy. "What you need is a real pick-me-up." He signaled to his valet. "This fine young man could use one of your famous Irish coffees."

"Right away, Mr. President," the valet replied. "Nothing's too good for our men in the navy."

"George's son is a navy man. He's with the Pacific Fleet Service Forces," Roosevelt added.

"That's right, Mr. President," George replied as he worked. "He's a hard worker, doing well. Had a letter from him just last week. From New Guinea, it was." He handed Chadwick a cup and saucer branded with the presidential seal. "Careful, sir. It's a mite hot."

It was not only hot but also very strong. Frank resolved to keep his wits at battle stations, especially with King sailing on stormy waters.

Throughout, Roosevelt continued to handle simultaneous conversations. The deputy undersecretary of state got a decision on recognizing a government in exile. The fat army general got a presidential handshake. *I bet his job assignment is going to be a real son of a bitch,* thought Chadwick.

Congressman Vinson had his own agenda, and it became increasingly clear his presence tonight was no coincidence. "Admiral King," he intoned in a deeply Southern accent, one ham-shaped hand reaching out in greeting, the other wrapped around a highball glass that was nearly empty. "Such a pleasure to see you again, Admiral, and in circumstances more conducive to pleasant conversation than a hot and stuffy hearing room." The congressman wiggled his glass in the direction of George, who quickly and silently refilled it and returned it to the congressman's outstretched hand.

King grudgingly shook the outstretched hand. "Mr. Chairman," he growled.

The congressman pulled out a somewhat stained handkerchief to blot the sweat from his forehead. "I venture to suggest that hot and sweaty is the common condition of Washington, and not merely our hearing rooms, isn't that right, Admiral?" He laughed heartily at his own joke.

King did not.

The congressman paused, waiting for King to speak, then decided to fill the silence himself. "I have to say, Admiral, that I am puzzled. I am curious and I am puzzled. I am curious and I am puzzled as to why you have elected, with all the brave men in the history of the United States Navy, to nominate Admiral Halsey for the Congressional Medal of Honor. After all, and correct me if I am mistaken in any of the particulars, but did he not get our fleet sunk?" He turned, hands clenched to suspenders as if they were lifelines, to gather in the reactions of the audience, to assure himself that the public was on his side.

King looked ready to tear him open and eat his liver raw.

But it was FDR who spoke. "Oh, I'm completely in favor of Admiral Halsey's brilliant queen sacrifice being recognized, Carl. I think it was one of the greatest feats of strategic and tactical brilliance as well as personal bravery in the annals of sea warfare. It will go into the history books— right up there with Nelson at Trafalgar!" He puffed lazily on his cigarette holder and smiled, the audience in his palm. Even King was interested.

"Go on, Mr. President," Vinson said, a lazy grin appearing on his face. "But if I recollect my history books, didn't

Nelson's fleet survive the battle?" Chadwick interpreted this as the appreciation of one bullshit artist for another.

FDR smiled in return, his cigarette holder between his teeth. "The Japanese, simply put, cannot continue a ship-building program with the resources they have. When one of their carriers is lost, it is lost forever. The United States, on the other hand, is producing a new aircraft carrier each month. It is, perhaps, a Pyrrhic victory to lose our carriers in destroying the Japanese fleet, but it is in fact a strategic victory. Within a year, certainly within two, our fleet will be far larger than it was before the Battle of the Solomon Sea. But the Japanese fleet will be even smaller than it is today. All of this is thanks to Admiral William Halsey's strategic genius and courage. We owe him a debt we can never repay."

The congressman looked at Roosevelt with hard eyes. *That aw, shucks act is just so people will let their guard down,* Frank thought. *Vinson is smart as a whip.* After a moment, Vinson's face opened back up to the guileless expression he presented to the world. "And that will be the reason for giving him the medal?" he asked.

"That's right," replied FDR.

"Well, then, Admiral," the congressman said, shaking the reluctant King's hand with both of his own, "let me be the first to congratulate the navy on its wonderful victory against the Japanese. We mourn the loss of your brave sailors. And I'm certain we'll honor the courageous leadership that shows the world why our navy is the very finest afloat! Except for the submarines, of course," he added. He waited for the laugh. It didn't come.

King seemed somewhat mollified by the President's vigorous defense of the navy. "Queen's sacrifice," Chadwick heard him mutter, trying the idea on for size.

Finally, though, the CNO and COMINCHFLT could wait no longer. "Mr. President, I wonder if I might have a word with you in private," King asked.

Frank Knox stood up nervously and put a restraining hand on King's arm. "It's late. We should really continue this tomorrow when everyone's had a good night's sleep . . ."

King shrugged off Knox's hand. The President's mild expression had not changed, but his eyes were focused on King's. "Very well, Admiral," the President said. "In the next room, if you please." It was the first time that night Chadwick had heard FDR address anyone by anything other than first name.

Roosevelt began to roll his wheelchair forward. King followed. The valet left his station at the bar and opened the door set into the right side of the oval room. The President rolled forward into the darkness, followed by the stiff and formal King, and the valet closed the door behind them.

Knox, still standing, looked down at Chadwick and grinned weakly. "I wouldn't want you to get the idea that this is a normal meeting at the White House. King drives me crazy sometimes, but I hope to hell I still have a COMINCHFLT and CNO when that door opens again."

Chadwick didn't know what to think. Several stiff drinks and prolonged sleep deprivation had taken their toll, making him confess what he would otherwise have kept private. "I wonder what's going on in there," he said.

"You and me both, Captain," Knox replied.

The President's bedroom was adjacent to the Oval Study. The room was dominated by a large mahogany four-poster with a set of rails at one end to allow the President to lift himself in or out of bed unassisted. The covers had been turned down.

Only a single bedside table light was shining. Most of the room was draped in shadow. Underneath the lamp was a stack of books with random torn slips of paper stuck in them as bookmarks. One read TOP SECRET.

Roosevelt wheeled himself in front of his bed with the light behind him. There was no obvious place for King to sit, so the admiral remained at attention.

"What may I do for you, Admiral King?" said the President in a formal voice.

King replied with equal formality. "Mr. President, I came here to offer you my resignation. The war with MacArthur has gotten serious enough to damage the navy."

Roosevelt, expressionless, waited. King stood with equal stoicism. Finally, Roosevelt spoke. "Ernie."

King stopped. "Yes, Mr. President?"

After a pause, Roosevelt continued, "You know I could never accept your resignation." His voice sounded tired.

"Then you've got to rein in MacArthur. Interservice rivalry is all well and good. On one level it can be helpful. It keeps everyone on his toes. But when it starts to cause real damage, it has to be stopped. We've reached that level. Mac won the war to control the Pacific. I don't like it—God knows I don't like it—but it's the truth. But he's got to stop shooting at the navy now and let us take care of our own. I'm glad to see you're signing the recommendation for Bill Halsey. I really would have had to resign if you hadn't."

"I've always supported you, Ernie. I've made it clear that MacArthur's views were not the views of the White House or of me personally."

"In the form of a press release. Not in a personal statement, and not with any rebuke to MacArthur. It leaves the impression that you're on his side but just can't bite the bullet. It undercuts me, which may not matter, but it also undercuts the navy, and that's not acceptable. And you should know, he's not after my job. He's after yours. He's going to run against you in '44."

Roosevelt smiled. "Do you think so? Oh, I know about the letters he's been writing to Senator Vandenberg, but what our friend Douglas wants is for the Republicans to draft him, and the Grand Old Party isn't suicidal. They won't draft him, not in '44 anyway. Not unless he wins the war before their convention, and if he does that, he deserves the presidency, don't you think? Not that he'd enjoy it. Nor would you, Ernie. I imagine it's crossed your mind a time or two."

"I'm not political, Mr. President."

"Nonsense, Ernie. Of course you are. You're just used to having actual authority in your job. You'd hate this one, where all you get to do is horse-trade and make suggestions to people and occasionally twist an arm or two. Douglas will come in here and give commands and nothing will happen.

It will be quite frustrating for him. Too bad I won't be here to see it. No, Douglas's year is 1948, I think. Possibly 1952. And that depends on the extent of his victory in the Pacific."

"So you're choosing MacArthur."

"No, Ernie. I'm not choosing Douglas. I can't afford to lose either one of you. The country needs you. Your commander in chief needs you. I understand the problem, but you must find some other solution, some solution short of your resignation. Perhaps if Douglas apologized and withdrew his antinavy rhetoric?"

"Publicly."

"Publicly recanted. Would honor be satisfied enough to let me keep both of you?"

King paused, jaw clenched. "He's spending more time fighting the navy than fighting the Japs."

"Douglas has been waging a one-man war against the world ever since I've known him," Roosevelt said. "Anything or anyone standing in his way is the enemy, and he's deeply convinced there's a clique of people out to get him. By now, there is, but I think he helped create it. But he's captured the public's imagination and he's winning against the Japs. Right now, there's nothing more important to me in that part of the world, as much as I love the navy."

"He can't destroy the navy to win the war," growled King.

"And so he can't," replied FDR. "On the other hand, Ernie, there has been legitimacy in some of what our Douglas has been saying. Midway was unfair; that was bad luck. Ghormley, on the other hand . . ." Roosevelt let that sentence trail off.

"You've made your point, Mr. President," King replied gruffly.

"Have I? I'm not sure I have, Ernie. My point is that if Douglas has attacked you with some legitimacy, you must show that you can attack him with equal legitimacy."

"With what?" King said angrily. "The 'Coward of Corregidor' story? You and I know what a piss-poor performance Mac delivered in the Philippines, but he became a national hero over it."

"Ernie, Ernie," Roosevelt said soothingly. "Of course you don't attack him there. Not only would it be ineffective, it would also hurt the war effort. If I wanted to destroy Douglas MacArthur, or shut him up, I'd tell him I knew about the half million dollars."

"Half million dollars? Mr. President, I don't—"

"Ernie, I'm about to do you a big favor and give you one of the big guns I've been keeping around in case I needed it where Douglas is concerned. I *don't* want this in the press because I *don't* want him destroyed. But he'll shut up once he knows you have it."

"What is it?" King asked eagerly.

"Ernie, do you accept tips?"

"Tips?"

"Yes. Gratuities. Tips. Five dollars to the maître d' for a good table. Twenty-five cents to the bellhop."

"I—tips? No, of course not."

"So if some foreign government official offered you five hundred thousand dollars as recognition for your services, you wouldn't take it?"

King whistled. "MacArthur took a half-million-dollar bribe?"

"No, Ernie. Not a bribe. He didn't do anything extra for it. It was more on the order of a tip. A bonus. An award for services in the past."

"And MacArthur *accepted* it?"

"Yes, Ernie. He accepted it. He had won himself a waiver to the rule that forbade officers to accept payment from nations they advised. The Philippine president—Quezon—had promised the money to MacArthur. His staff got money too. Ike was offered sixty thousand dollars, but he turned it down."

"My God," breathed King.

"It's a rather dicey business. I don't want anyone to know—"anyone" specifically meaning Douglas—that I gave you this information. That means you have to find out some other way. Then you let Douglas know that you know, and afterward you both have reasons to keep your mouths shut about each other."

King looked at Roosevelt. "Do you have material like this on everybody?"

"Only the sinners, Ernie. Only the sinners. You do understand how you have to play this, don't you?"

"Yes, Mr. President. It'll work. I'm tempted to use it to take back the Pacific, but then I'd be guilty of what he's been doing."

"You're a good man, Ernie. I knew I could count on you. Now let's get back out there before poor Frank Knox has a coronary."

Eli, Eli, Lama Sabachthani

We're the battling bastards of Bataan,
No mama, no papa, no Uncle Sam.
No aunts, no uncles, no nephews, no nieces,
No pills, no planes, no artillery pieces.
And nobody gives a damn.

—Frank Hewlett, American war correspondent, 1942

And about the ninth hour Jesus cried with a loud voice, saying, "Eli, Eli, lama sabachthani?" that is to say, "My God, my God, why hast thou forsaken me?"

—Matthew 27:46

NINE

Arkansas; Philippines; Japan

• SUNDAY, 21 MARCH 1943 •

MCGEHEE, ARKANSAS, 1147 HOURS

Gregory Yamada, newly minted captain, United States Army, picked up his duffel and stepped down off the train. The last leg of his trip had been the worst. From Chicago, the *City of New Orleans* had taken him in comfort all the way to Jackson, Mississippi, where he'd gotten on the Missouri Pacific milk run to Little Rock, stopping at every two-bit hamlet on the way. He was the only passenger disembarking at McGehee. One person boarded.

As the train pulled out of the station, Yamada looked around.

McGehee, Arkansas, had a small redbrick passenger station located, logically enough, on South Railroad Street. The building was only big enough to handle about thirty people, but it was still separated into two parts, WHITE and COLORED. Drinking fountains and restrooms were similarly labeled.

As a Nisei, a second-generation Japanese American, he was never sure which one he was supposed to use, especially in the South, where these matters were taken seriously. He'd used the restroom on the train right before disembarking.

In Minnesota, where he'd been, March was still winter. Here in Arkansas, it was spring, the day bright and sunny. The air, now that the train was gone, smelled sweet.

He went up to the ticket window. "Excuse me, sir."

The clerk looked up and did a double take. Well, it was unusual to see a Nisei in McGehee, Arkansas, wearing an army uniform with captain's bars. "Why ain't you out in Camp

Rohwer with the others?" the clerk demanded. "That's where you're supposed to be, ain't it?"

"That's where I'm going, sir. Is there a taxi service, a bus, or some way to get there?"

The clerk laughed, showing yellow teeth. "Some way to get there? You're standing on 'em, boy. It's only about five miles right up State Road One. Won't take you more than an hour or two."

Shouldn't be surprised, Yamada thought. "Thank you, sir," he said, and turned to go.

"Hey, wait a minute! You didn't answer my question, boy."

"I'm sorry, what question?"

"How come a Jap like you ain't in the camp already? And how come you are wearing an army uniform?"

"I guess the answer is the same to both questions. I'm in the army, which is why I'm not in the camp and why I'm wearing this uniform."

"Don't get smart with me, boy," the clerk said with annoyance. "When I ask you a question, you just answer it, okay?"

Yamada waited, painting a pleasant expression on his face.

"How come a Jap like you is in the army?" the clerk asked.

"Well, sir, I speak Japanese. The army needs translators to interrogate prisoners and interpret radio signals, things like that."

The clerk digested the information for a moment. "I guess," he replied. "So that's why you ain't in no camp?"

"Yes, sir."

"Then what brings you to McGehee?" the clerk asked.

"My family. They're here. I thought I'd pay them a visit."

The clerk thought again. "I guess," he replied. "Listen here, boy. You may be telling the truth or you may not, but I reckon Sheriff Hudson will want to see you. You just wait for a spell, and then you can go see your family if Sheriff Hudson says it's okay."

"All right," Yamada said. It wasn't all right, but fighting might make it worse, and might cost him those captain's bars he'd so recently pinned on. But now he faced the dilemma he'd avoided previously: white or colored?

Colored seemed the safe choice. That waiting room was dingy, with walls that hadn't been painted in years, a floor that hadn't been swept in weeks, and two wooden benches on the verge of collapse. An old, stooped black man with shock-white hair sat on a worn wooden bench. He looked up with curiosity when Yamada walked into the room, then the curiosity died out and he began staring at the floor as if in a trance.

Two minutes later the clerk came bustling in. "What are you doing in here?" he demanded.

"Sitting," Yamada replied. "That's what you said."

"Not *here*. This is the nigger waiting room. You're not a nigger."

"I'm not exactly white either," Yamada pointed out.

The clerk held up his hand, then went around the corner and came back. "It's okay. Nobody's in there. So you go sit over in the other room and wait for Sheriff Hudson." The white waiting room had been painted within the last three years and the benches were clean. The room actually contained a spitoon, something Yamada had read about but never seen. He sat patiently for almost an hour until the sheriff arrived.

The sheriff was dangerously overweight. His eyes were small and piggy, and he chewed tobacco. "You're the Jap who says he's in the army," the sheriff announced.

"That's right, Sheriff. Would you like to see some identification?"

The sheriff chewed furiously, then spat. It rang like a bell when it hit the metal of the spitoon. "Yep."

Yamada handed over his military identification card. The sheriff inspected it minutely.

"Says you're a captain."

"That's right, Sheriff."

"We got Jap officers in the army?" Sheriff Hudson looked as if the foundations of his reality were about to tumble down.

"Somebody's got to speak the language. There are prisoners to question, radio transmissions to decipher, that sort of thing," he repeated patiently.

Watching the sheriff's mouth work the plug of chewing tobacco was fascinating and horrifying. "So you speak Jap."

"That's right."

"Say something in Jap."

"Anything particular you want me to say, sheriff?"

"Nope."

"You are an ignorant bumpkin with no manners and belong with the burakumin, you dung-eating mouth breather," Yamada said.

"What's that mean in real words?"

"I am happy to be visiting your fine community and appreciate your kind hospitality," Yamada lied, smiling.

The sheriff looked suspiciously at him and spat again. "All right. Donny says you're going to the camp to see your family."

"That's right."

"Going to visit long?"

"I'm on a thirty-day pass, then I'm bound for the South Pacific. I'm going to be part of General MacArthur's G-2 section. Army Intelligence. My branch."

"General MacArthur." The sheriff spat again. "Well, I guess it's all right. The camp is about five miles up State Route One. Won't take you more than a couple of hours."

"No taxicabs or buses?" Yamada asked.

"For whites," the sheriff said. "Not for colored. Which reminds me. Army uniform or no army uniform, you don't sit in a white waiting room again. You ain't white, so don't put on any airs, or you and I will have a little talk and you won't like it very much."

Yamada thought about protesting that the clerk had made him move but decided there was no percentage in that. "All right, Sheriff. Which way to State Route One?"

"Go one block up to Second Street, turn right, go about ten blocks to West Ash, and turn right. Then keep walking until you see the signs."

"Thank you, Sheriff."

He spat again, turned, and walked away without reply.

• **MONDAY, 17 MAY 1943** •

POW CAMP CABANATUAN #1, LUZON, PHILIPPINES,
0715 HOURS

Today the prisoners had been ordered to watch executions before turning out for work details, so they remained lined up outside the huts after roll call. Johnny Halverson's gut was cramping so badly that he could barely hold himself erect, but he managed a semblance of attention before the nearby Jap sergeant—the one he called "Fu" because of his long mustache—looked his way.

There were some five hundred men gathered in ranks at the edge of the broad field that served as the camp's parade ground. All told, at least twenty times that many Americans were held in the whole sprawling compounds of the Cabanatuan POW camps. There were almost as many more who had surrendered but never made it this far, killed or left for dead on the long, bloody march north from Bataan.

Halverson's last day of freedom, May 6, 1942, was more than a year ago now. Already the memories seemed to belong to some other person's life. His existence now was based on hunger and a terrifying sense that his life could end at any moment. All he knew, all he could allow himself to know, had become this camp, these prisoners, and—most important of all, for survival's sake—these guards.

The captain, Ogawa Taiki, was strutting to the front of the formation, limping his way up the three steps to the low platform from which he addressed his charges. The Americans had often assured themselves that the squat officer needed the elevation simply to look his prisoners in the eye, but no one made any remarks. Now Ogawa stood with his legs apart, fists planted on his hips as he glared across the faces of the assemblage with unconcealed contempt.

"Four men were captured before dawn, today," he said in

the clipped English that never failed to surprise Johnny. (Rumor had it that Ogawa had studied in San Francisco in the prewar years.) "They were attempting to reenter the camp, after paying a visit to the filthy Filipinos. Black marketers. Perhaps even saboteurs or spies," he added with a sneer.

Johnny knew the truth. The men had indeed slipped out of the camp after dark, passing through the concentric lines of guards on a perilous quest to reach one of the local barrios. They had taken a wristwatch and a few other miscellaneous treasures that the prisoners had managed to keep from the guards during the Death March and subsequent captivity, and they had bartered those possessions for food. The proceeds of that outing might have kept two score men alive for another month.

Except they never made it back to the barracks. Now two of them, as skinny and disheveled as all the rest of the prisoners, were prodded from the prison hut at bayonet point. They were each a mass of bruises and blood and one nursed an obviously broken arm; the Japanese frequently tortured their prisoners before killing them. Sergeant Fu grinned, or perhaps he was just squinting, as four guards wielded the ridiculously long, and very deadly, Jap rifles.

The pair of captives shuffled, heads down, knowing they were being pushed to their doom. One couldn't even make it to the far side of the field. He tripped and fell on his face, lacking even the energy to use his hands to break his fall. The guard right behind him shouted a hoarse, guttural word and lunged, driving his long bayonet through the small of the prone prisoner's back. Even then the American barely twitched, lying silently as the steel blade sliced down again and again.

The captain barked a command and his guards hastened to bring another man from the hut. Johnny knew the man, a young private from the 194th, barely eighteen when he'd arrived in Manila. Max something . . . Max looked a lot older now, as they marched him past the bloody corpse. Ogawa called the rank of prisoners to attention as their two comrades were pushed to their knees. Two guards lifted their rifles, muzzles barely a foot behind the skulls of the condemned men. Johnny winced as he heard the nearly simultaneous shots. He blinked involuntarily. When he opened his eyes the two prisoners lay facedown, unmoving.

The rest of the prisoners shuffled down to the chow line, to be served what passed for food at Cabanatuan. Breakfast was a bowl of *lugow*, rice stew with precious little rice in it. Afterward, the men quickly began to fall out and formed their work details. The Japanese made no distinctions for rank in these camps. All the senior officers, major and above, had been taken elsewhere. Everyone else worked. Even though he was a captain, and thus one of the highest-ranking officers in the camp, Johnny Halverson was a farm boy again. He was one of hundreds of prisoners who regularly worked in the fields of the camp farm through the full length of the 115-degree summer day. Now he started toward the detail's gathering point, at the east gate, but stopped at the sound of Sergeant Fu's voice.

"You! You!" The guard singled out Johnny and another prisoner, Andy Sarnuss. Halverson felt a stab of fear that gurgled audibly in his bowels, and hoped he wouldn't have an attack of diarrhea in front of the guard. Nevertheless, he stepped forward with Sarnuss. They both bowed to the guard—all prisoners knew that the penalty for failure to make this show of respect was at the very least a beating—and returned to attention.

Fu gestured that the two prisoners should follow him and started across the assembly field toward the slain prisoners. Johnny forced himself to walk, letting numbness seep through his senses as they drew closer to the corpses. When he stopped to stand above the two dead men, he did so impassively.

The guard gestured at the corpses, pantomimed using a shovel to dig in the ground, and then pointed toward the vast burial ditch along the edge of the camp compound. "Guess we're the graves detail," Sarnuss said laconically.

Fu nodded enthusiastically. *"Isogu!"* he barked.

Halverson and Sarnuss rolled Max over and lifted the corpse. Johnny's hands supported the dead man's shoulders, and he felt no meat, no flesh between the skin and the bones. The two men started across the camp with their grisly burden while Fu, apparently satisfied with their effort, turned to business with the agricultural detail.

"Poor bastard," Andy muttered, shaking his head. "All this to come back with one stupid fucking packet of rice."

"That's all he got?" Johnny kept talking, trying to ignore the charnel stench as they drew near the ditch. It was full— the camp was losing more than a hundred men a week. "How do you know?"

Sarnuss looked away, evasive. "That's what I heard," he said, shrugging. "Let's pitch him in and go back for the other two."

"Wait. I want to get his dog tags."

They set Max's body in the shallow trench. You couldn't dig more than about two feet before hitting groundwater, which is what made this good rice-growing land. Johnny tried not to look at all the bodies, but he could hear the flies buzzing, and he shivered when they started to land on his head. "Hurry up, damn it!" snapped Sarnuss, swatting at the insects.

For some reason, though, Johnny had to take his time. He opened Max's shirt, held with only a single cracked button, and gently eased the chain up and over the gory skull, getting blood and brains on his fingers in the process. Holding the metal tags in his hand like the trophy of some private contest, he clenched his fist for a moment and then dropped them into his shirt pocket.

"Okay, let's cover him up," Andy said. They threw enough dirt over the body to cover it and hoped it would be enough. During a big rain, sometimes the dirt would wash away and expose the bodies.

Johnny looked down, reluctant to move, to go after the second corpse. "I wonder how much longer we've got?" he asked.

Andy looked at him from his five-foot-two-inch height. "I'm not going to think like that, goddammit. I'm going to fucking make it out of here, you got that? You want to hang up your gloves, go right ahead, but not Andy Sarnuss!" Andy turned and started for the second body.

Johnny paused for a moment before following him. *Maybe Andy is right. Maybe I'm giving up too easily.*

Another wave of dysentery sent a cramp through his body. He knew he'd never make the latrine trench in time.

• FRIDAY, 15 OCTOBER 1943 •

HIROSHIMA, JAPAN, 1730 HOURS

"Yoshi! Come in!"

Ogawa Michiyo recognized her older brother's friend immediately and almost gave him an impetuous hug. Yet he looked so serious and imposing, in his neat Imperial Japanese Army lieutenant's uniform, that the girl instead stepped back, holding the door open for him while she bowed demurely.

"Michiyo!" he said, bowing in return and entering. "You have grown into a woman in the last two years!"

She blushed, smiling shyly. "Father!" she called. "Look who's here! It's Taiki's friend, Naguro Yoshi! *Lieutenant* Naguro Yoshi," she amended proudly.

"Invite him in!" came the gruff response from the den, where her father spent almost all of his time. "Quickly, Michiyo! And fetch us some tea! No, make it sake!"

"Come this way," she invited, her eyes downcast. But she was acutely aware of Yoshi's eyes upon her. And he certainly looked dashing in that uniform!

"Come in, Yoshi!" said her father. Ogawa Takeo actually smiled as the young officer came into his study. Michiyo allowed herself a silent prayer to her ancestors: let this visitor bring father out of his shell, at least for a little while.

She hurried away to get the rice wine, and when she returned her father was talking with some animation, gesturing to the empty ceremonial cabinet behind his desk. "That is where the ancestral sword of our family was displayed, until Taiki took it off to war."

A cloud marred the older man's face, and Michiyo, carefully pouring two small glasses of sake, knew that he was missing his son and worrying about him. "Tell me, Yoshi," he said gruffly. "Did you see Taiki after he came back from that island, Guadalcanal? We . . . we have not heard from him. He chooses not to answer our letters."

"Yes, Ogawa-san. I saw Taiki in Rabaul, before I was recalled to Tokyo. And I had the honor of talking to some of the men who served with him. They told great stories of his heroism."

Michiyo listened surreptitiously. She tried to make herself as small as possible, hoping that her father would not notice her and send her out of the room. But all of Takeo's attention was directed at the visitor. "Please, can you share some of these stories?"

"Indeed, Ogawa-san. That is the reason that I came. One reason, anyway." He shot Michiyo a look but quickly proceeded to talk of the war. "Taiki is indeed a hero, though he is too modest to apply the term to himself, or to allow others to use it in his hearing."

"Yes. That sounds like Taiki," the father said approvingly. "Good."

The young officer continued. "He led his company on an attack against the American marines on a ridge near their airfield. They had to march through terrible jungle for days, just to get into position. But he was ready to attack when ordered." Yoshi indicated the empty cabinet. "He carried the very sword of your ancestors as he charged up a hill into terrible machine gun fire and artillery. Many men were killed, but Taiki made it far into the American ranks. It was a very close battle, and almost ended in a great victory.

"Unfortunately, the enemy had too many men, and too many guns. And, though it grieves me to say it, there were other Japanese companies that did not perform with the same valor. Taiki was to be part of a regimental-strength

attack, but instead only a battalion of soldiers was in the
proper place at the proper time. The Americans shattered
the attack in the end. Taiki would have perished, except that
he was knocked unconscious by the concussion of a shell."

Michiyo gasped and her father grunted. After a respectful
silence, Yoshi continued. "When he awakened, the battle
was over, and he escaped with a very few of his men. They
speak of his courage with awe, Ogawa-san. He slew many
Americans with the sword. Some of them were like giants,
but he never faltered, never showed fear."

"Ah, good," said the older man. He took a small sip of his
sweet wine, seemed to search for the right words. "We heard
that he was injured. His . . . wounds. Have they healed?"

Yoshi frowned slightly, shifting in his chair. "For the most
part, yes, Ogawa-san. His leg was badly injured by an enemy
bayonet, but now he walks very well, with just the slightest
limp."

"I wish he would write to us," Takeo said. "I should like to
hear from him."

"I will tell him, sir. I believe that I will be seeing him
soon. We are both being posted to Manila."

"So far from the front?" said Michiyo's father with a
frown. "But what about Rabaul? And the Solomon Islands?"

Yoshi cleared his throat. "Naturally, Ogawa-san, it is not
for a humble lieutenant to question such things. But the battles in the Solomons following the fall of Guadalcanal are
far from the zones of strategic importance to the empire. I
believe there is some concern in army headquarters that the
American general, MacArthur, is very determined to recon-
quer the Philippines. Of course, we will make sure this does
not happen."

"Of course. Thank you for coming to see us and bringing
us this news, Lieutenant."

"It was my honor, sir." Flashing Michiyo a thin smile, the
officer bowed to her father. "Ogawa-san, I would consider it
a great privilege if you would allow me to escort your daughter on a walk to the river. That is, if she would like to accompany me on a brief stroll?"

"Oh, yes!" Michiyo cried, then clapped a hand over her mouth at Takeo's look of disapproval. But after a second her father looked at her as if seeing her for the first time, and then scrutinized the polite and handsome young lieutenant.

"Very well," he said with a curt nod. "Please return before dark."

Yoshi made his farewells to the older man while Michiyo changed into her finest kimono. She combed her long black hair, using several pins to arrange it in a neat bun. After kissing her father on the cheek, she accompanied the soldier out the door.

The little lane on which the Ogawa house stood was near the city's main crossroads, almost in the shadow of the towering edifice of Hiroshima Castle and around the corner from the large, modern Fukuya Department Store. Michiyo walked along with Yoshi, past the store, simply taking in the sights in the bustling city. The war seemed far away. Even though there were fewer automobiles than there had been a few years before, bicycles crowded the roadways, especially now as workers made their way home from their jobs. They stopped at a stall and Yoshi purchased some sushi and rice balls, which they ate on the sidewalk.

They followed the sidewalk onto the grand Aioi Bridge over the River Ota, then paused in the middle of the span to look down at the deep but rapidly flowing water. Michiyo told the officer about little details of her life: her mother's youngest sister, Auntie Ui, had just married a navy flier; Michiyo herself had a part-time job as an aide at the Red Cross hospital, across the street from Hiroshima University, and she was thinking of becoming a nurse. He seemed impressed, and his praise made her glow.

After a few minutes, they moved on, following the bank of the great river, and finally came to the Asano Sentai Park, right on the water. Strolling beneath the tall pine trees, Michiyo found that she could almost forget about the war, the terrible things her brother had experienced, the deepening gloom that had been surrounding her father as Taiki continued to ignore their letters.

But she sensed that Yoshi was holding something inside. They came to a bench near the riverbank and sat, watching the sun as it began to set. She was wondering if he would ever speak his mind, when he looked at her seriously.

"What is it, Yoshi?" she prodded gently. "Do you have more to say?"

He nodded, staring at the ground for a moment before meeting her eyes. "Yes. I am worried about your brother. I did not speak of this to your father, but I think you should know."

"What is it? Are his wounds worse than you let on?"

"No . . . his physical injuries are as I described. But the battle on Guadalcanal did something to his spirit. I believe he wishes that he died there. He is angry and bitter, in a very sad way. He carried your father's sword into the battle but lost consciousness when he was wounded. When he awakened, the sword was gone—it is probably an American's souvenir, now—and he feels that shame as deeply as the shame of the failure of the attack. He does not want to talk, or even have my company—or anybody else's."

"That's why he doesn't write back to us, isn't it?" she asked.

"Yes. He feels that he has dishonored himself, and your family—all of your ancestors. I wish I could help him."

"I'm glad you told me," she said, daring to take one of his strong hands in both of hers.

"Me too," he agreed. "And I am glad that you could walk with me." He sighed and looked at the sky as it shaded toward twilight. "Now we had better go back, before your father starts to worry."

They made their way slowly to the little house, arriving just before the appointed hour of sunset. Yoshi promised that he would call again before he shipped out to the Philippines.

It would have been a perfect day, except for the miasma of worry that settled around Michiyo like a dark and ominous cloud.

TEN

Southern California; Hawaii

*THE PRESIDENTIAL TRAIN, APPROACHING SAN DIEGO,
CALIFORNIA, 0234 HOURS*

The civilian in the top berth was snoring again, drowning out
the *clickety-clack* and gentle swaying of the rolling train. The
loud cacophonous sound woke Frank Chadwick, trapped
directly underneath in the lower berth. Frank could also hear
the creaking of springs and had the feeling that the top of his
coffinlike sleeping compartment was in danger of giving way
under the weight of the fat man in the upper booth. The smell
of stale air and human sweat gave him the same claustropho-
bic feeling as being on a submarine—his least favorite navy
experience.

It had been years since Frank was forced to share a bunk
with anyone. Navy captains normally received private quarters when in transit, but not when traveling with the presidential party on the presidential train. Berths had been
assigned in the order of White House rank and status; that's
how a heavyset deputy assistant undersecretary ended up in
the upper berth.

The President had his own railcar; a lavishly decorated
Pullman named *Roald Amundsen*. It had been built in 1928,
when Hoover was still president, for a little over two hundred thousand dollars—the President's salary was seventy-
five thousand. Following the presidential car was a formal
dining car serving only the most important guests. Then
came a Pullman with six staterooms for the most senior of the
president's entourage and then Frank's car. Frank's Pullman

was configured with seats for twenty in the daytime and could be changed into a double row of ten bunks at night. A second, less luxurious dining car fed the staff, and then came cars identical to Frank's but for less exalted persons. The only indication of his rank was the car's proximity to FDR. Otherwise there was no difference between Frank's berth and that of, say, the radio operator who ensured the President was linked to the White House at all times.

Not that Frank was particular. He didn't mind the bunk at all, but he definitely minded the snorer. He was prepared to argue that the snoring was louder than the roar of a six-inch gun. It was certainly more irritating.

Giving up the futile attempt to go back to sleep, Frank pulled back the privacy curtain and slid himself out of the berth. If he was awake, he ought to tackle some more of the work he'd brought along with him. A few days away from easy telephone contact and some physical separation from Washington was a welcome luxury.

There was a thin line of light where the thick Pullman curtains joined. Frank pulled them aside and got out of bed. He blinked a few times in the comparatively bright light. The ubiquitous train smell, which had been kept at bay by the curtains, was particularly noticeable, coal and diesel fuel and creosote and the occasional reminder that lavatories emptied directly onto the tracks.

His clothes were in the closet at the dining car end of the Pullman, and there was a washroom in which he could wash his face, shave, and dress. As he started to move down the corridor, the black porter, immaculate in a white jacket buttoned up to his neck, got up from his chair at the end of the corridor and walked slowly toward Frank. "Is there anything I can do for you, Admiral, suh?" Frank had tried correcting him, but then he noticed the porter referred to anyone in the navy as "Admiral"—including ordinary seamen.

"Can you stuff a sock in his mouth, Willie?" Frank replied, jerking his finger in the direction of the upper bunk. The snoring was surprisingly muffled outside the thick curtain material.

Willie laughed. "I sure wish I could, Admiral. I sure wish I could. He's snorin' to beat the band. Snorin' something awful." He shook his head sadly.

"Well, looks like I'm up for good. At least there isn't going to be a line for the washroom at this time in the morning," Frank replied.

The porter laughed obligingly. "Can I fix you some coffee, Admiral, suh?" he asked. "I can make breakfast for you too, if you're ready for it."

The thought of food was not a pleasant one. "Let's stick with coffee for now, okay, Willie?"

"Coming right up, Admiral," Willie replied. "Coming right up."

It was probably unfair to blame the snorer exclusively for Frank's being awake. Some of the nagging problems and worries he'd brought with him weren't helping his sleep, either. The torpedo case, for example. He had a briefcase full of papers to boil down into a report that had to balance Frank's responsibilities to the President and Frank's responsibilities to the navy.

The magnetic detonators on the prewar torpedo designs simply hadn't been tested adequately. Earth's magnetic field distorted the detonators so that, in the South Pacific, they went off prematurely. About 80 percent of them were duds. Fierce turf protecting by the Bureau of Ordnance and congressmen from torpedo-producing states hugely complicated a task that would otherwise involve fairly straightforward engineering. That was what brought it to the presidential level. His orders from Admiral King were to "solve this damned problem before that bastard MacArthur gets hold of it. By the time the President finds out about this, I want to tell him that it's already taken care of."

Meetings with Secretary Knox, Congressman Vinson, and other Washington powers that initially intimidated him were now old hat. By making sure that blame was deflected from the guilty, Frank had been able to get things moving. The quality of torpedoes reaching the submarine fleet was much better. When the President asked, Frank would have the right answer, with a complete report ready for his desk—his current project.

Frank had not quite realized how much *work* went along with being naval aide to the President. He had three other projects as technically and politically difficult as the torpedo project. Only one concerned navy business: coordinating the distribution of intelligence gathered by navy code breakers. Frank was surprised, though pleased, to find out that the navy was reading Japanese codes routinely. That was an important secret. But White House status depended on how many important secrets you were in on, so Frank was the recipient of regular political pressure to put one more person on the distribution list. Learning to say no to people who seriously outranked him was a new skill; his training as a navy officer was about following orders, not rejecting them.

In addition, he had protocol responsibilities whenever the President's guests had navy connections. His formal dress uniform with the short unbuttoned jacket and white bow tie had seen more use in the past six months than in his entire navy career. He even contributed to the occasional speech when the topic fell in his areas of expertise.

POTUS—President of the United States—habitually called him "Frank" and loved to introduce him to others as "the hero of the Solomon Sea," which embarrassed him. He understood why POTUS wanted the association with a hero, and that it was in the navy's best interest for him to act the part, but there were a lot of other men who had been real heroes. Bill Halsey came to mind—his audacity during the Solomons battle, Frank felt pretty certain, would end up winning the war.

How exactly to go about winning that war was the question at the root of this current trip. Image counted. There were a number of ways FDR could have reached Hawaii. He chose a cross-country train trip and spent the time talking with the officials and heavy political hitters of the states through which he passed. He was already running for 1944.

Once in San Diego, he was taking delivery of the new *Hornet,* replacing the one sunk at Midway, and planned to present it personally to CINCPAC when he got to Pearl Harbor. The Secret Service was happy that the entire *Hornet* task group and a full complement of aircraft were going with the President.

A lot of time at the White House was spent reacting to events around the world. Whatever plans Frank made could be tossed out the window in a minute. As the immediate go-between for both the senior presidential staff and the senior navy brass, he was thrown at problems that were not quite important enough to involve POTUS, the navy secretary, and the CNO personally but still had far-reaching effects. The decisions had to hew pretty closely to those FDR, Frank Knox, and Admiral Ernest King would have made. Frank's nominal boss at the White House, Fleet Admiral William Leahy, a longtime friend of the President's, was another power center. On this trip, Leahy, who was chief of staff to the commander in chief, stayed at home. But his wishes still mattered.

Fleetingly, Frank wished he had one of those mind-reading rays from the sort of magazines his brothers-in-law Johnny and Ellis Halverson used to read all the time.

After washing his face and hands, rubbing Vitalis into his hair, and putting on his dress whites, he drank two cups of coffee—black, two sugars—and smoked his first Chesterfield of the day. He was beginning to feel halfway human. The train ride was gentle enough that he didn't worry about the coffee spilling: its speed was restricted to no more than thirty-five miles an hour for the sake of the President's constitution. He brushed his teeth and lit up another Chesterfield. Life was good—or at least tolerable.

The berth in which he traveled was no great hardship, but the lack of an office was. Over the six-and-a-half-day trip, Frank had gotten into the habit of commandeering a table in the dining room for workspace. He wasn't alone; the waiter had to shoo the poachers out at every mealtime. Breakfast was still a good three hours away; Frank would have time to get a lot of work done. A radio played behind the bar, and he found himself whistling to Tommy Dorsey's band playing "In the Blue of the Evening."

He sat down, pulled out his fountain pen, and took the first file folder in his satchel. It contained a thick report. He began reading and taking notes, boiling down the entire case to something small enough to command the President's brief attention.

The satchel was filled with file after file of mimeographed reports on various aspects of the torpedo problem. The technical issues fascinated Frank—he could understand how, at least initially, the effect of Earth's magnetic field on torpedo detonators could have been missed. Furthermore, the weapons had been designed with faulty impact detonators. But that was the nature of the development process. The inadequate testing was more of a problem; testing was meant to find mistakes like these before production began. The part that made Frank furious was the subsequent cover-up and concomitant refusal to correct the problem when real sailors were being endangered. The bureaucrats had merely claimed that sub commanders were too timid! If it were up to Frank, he'd have made everyone involved serve on submarines equipped with the faulty torpedoes.

Delivering justice, however, wasn't his job. Protecting the navy and the President was—which meant he collaborated in, even led, the cover-up he so despised. The big threat that concerned him didn't come from the Japanese but rather from General Douglas MacArthur. Through his shrewd exploitation of navy failures and shortcomings, the General drained Pacific Ocean Areas of ships and marines. His planned advances came off on schedule and worked, not least because he had the resources.

Mistakes gave MacArthur something to attack. Frank knew the cycle well. *MacArthur attacks the mistake and uses it to pry loose navy ships and men, then waits for his next opportunity. Because the navy has fewer ships and men, it conducts fewer operations with higher risks. Higher risks lead to more mistakes, and mistakes give MacArthur another opportunity to attack. Around and around we go. . . .* Keeping this mistake out of MacArthur's hands was critical, Frank knew.

Not that the army—MacArthur's army in particular—was

free of flaws or foul-ups. But somehow the navy had more trouble pinning the responsibility on MacArthur than vice versa.

Right now, MacArthur was winning the interservice war as well as the one with the Japanese. That made a showdown between MacArthur and the chief of naval operations inevitable. POTUS was traveling to Hawaii to preside over the fight for the heavyweight championship of the Pacific.

President Franklin Delano Roosevelt was showing signs of strain. The job was aging him, but his boundless will and his sharp intelligence made him as formidable as ever. A year from now—well, Frank was glad this conference hadn't been postponed for some unknown time in the future.

His fountain pen continued to scratch notes.

"Burning a little midnight oil, Frank?" It was Stephen Early, the press secretary. He was rocking back and forth with the gentle motion of the train.

Frank looked up with a start. It was nearly five o'clock in the morning. He'd been up two and a half hours. Suddenly his eyelids sagged. The *clackety-clack* of the train created an insidiously soothing rhythm. "Couldn't sleep." Frank yawned. "So I decided I'd better work."

"Good man," replied Early. "A better man than I am, Gunga Din. I'm up this early only because I've got to be ready by the time we pull into San Diego." He held up a stack of mimeographed sheets produced by a small and overtaxed secretarial office in the President's car. "Press releases."

Frank took a press release and skimmed it quickly. He chuckled. "Early, you've damn near written their story for them."

"I hope so, I devoutly hope so," said Early, rolling his eyes upward for effect. "It would save everyone a whole lot of trouble." He looked over Frank's shoulder. "So, what are you working on in the wee hours? Oh—the torpedo matter." He chuckled.

Frank was shocked. "You know about it? Does the President?" This could be very bad news indeed.

The press secretary noticed the expression on Frank's face, and laughed. "The President knows *everything*. Count on it. Relax. You're doing fine. Sometimes the President's right ear doesn't know what his left ear is hearing."

Early paused. "I don't think MacArthur will be dumb enough to attack the navy on the torpedo problem," he continued. "He doesn't need to. He's doing well enough on his own."

"What if he doesn't see it that way?" asked Frank.

"He'll make too many powerful enemies. Even for him. No, count on it. MacArthur will have something up his sleeve, but it's not the torpedo issue. You can get that situation squared away both technically and politically."

Frank nodded in agreement. Then he started thinking. *What could MacArthur have up his sleeve?*

• WEDNESDAY, 24 NOVEMBER 1943 •

B-17 BATAAN, EN ROUTE FROM BRISBANE, AUSTRALIA, TO HAWAII, 1741 HOURS

General Richard Sutherland, MacArthur's chief of staff, had abandoned his seat, the normal bombardier's position, for a bit of floor behind the copilot's seat. The B-17 was not well configured for transporting passengers. The seats were cramped, headroom was restricted, and clambering about the aircraft was dangerous as well as difficult. Crew and passengers mostly sat, the light chop bouncing the plane around enough to make it feel like riding a horse, with a similar soreness at the end of a long day. Sutherland found his ad hoc seat no more uncomfortable than the official one. At least it was a change of position.

He wished he were a bit higher, so he could get a view of the escorts. They were past fighter cover, but the Japanese were not a threat any longer, not in this part of the Pacific.

Two other B-17s flew escort, and a C-54 Skymaster cargo plane—the same aircraft type as the President's own *Sacred Cow*—carried everything else the General's party needed, including secretaries and code clerks. The General planned to remain firmly in command no matter where he personally happened to be. If only MacArthur had been willing to accept the more civilized comfort of the C-54 for this long flight! But no, the General desired the martial aura of this heavy bomber.

With a frown, Sutherland noticed that one of the escort bombers was named the *Skylark II*. That was flown by Johnny Halverson's brother, the arrogant pilot. Dammit, why did the Halverson matter keep coming up?

Sutherland was confident he hadn't done anything wrong. Protecting the General was his duty, and letting some pissant army captain go around spreading rumors that the great man had come unglued the day the Japanese invaded the Philippines was unacceptable. What made some junior supply officer think he could blackmail Sutherland into special privileges, taking him away from the Rock just so he could spread rumors and lies about the General? Men were going into Japanese captivity, thousands of them, most of them more valuable as soldiers than Johnny Halverson.

Neither Sutherland nor the General had ever brought up that morning when the Japanese invaded, but both men remembered, he was sure of it. The General felt a moment's weakness toward Halverson just because he happened to be in the room at the wrong time. That meant it was up to Sutherland to do what had to be done. Now the General was sentimental about the younger Halverson boy, especially because this Halverson was one of Kenney's favorites.

Now the General pretends that it's all my fault, all my doing, thought Sutherland with frustration and annoyance. *MacArthur acted as if everything was Sutherland's fault. Sutherland did that on his own initiative. Not me. Not the great General.*

Sutherland's predecessor as MacArthur's chief of staff, Colonel Dwight Eisenhower, decided he'd had enough when

MacArthur ordered an expensive parade of the Filipino army over Eisenhower's objections, then blamed Eisenhower for the mess when Philippine President Quezon complained. Eisenhower never forgave MacArthur. That made it easier for Sutherland to get rid of his rival and take over as chief of staff. *Some days I know just how Eisenhower felt,* Sutherland thought. *But I'll stay loyal to the end—no matter what it takes.*

Sutherland knew he should just ignore the Halverson brother, pay no attention to him. Ellis Halverson knew nothing. He couldn't possibly know anything. If Sutherland stayed hostile, he might provoke Halverson into sticking his nose where it didn't belong.

Even if Johnny Halverson survived Japanese captivity, Sutherland wasn't worried. He would be able to argue that the boy's mind had been affected, that he imagined the whole thing. No matter what happened, Sutherland had the situation well in hand. *The General is safe. That's all that matters.*

"How much longer?" MacArthur shouted over the roar of the large Wright Cyclone engines. He was sitting, as normal, in the copilot's seat and had the view.

General George Kenney, commanding general of the Fifth Air Force, piloting the *Bataan,* looked at his gauges. "If this tailwind keeps up, we should land around 0300 hours tomorrow," he shouted back.

"Not good. Not good at all," responded MacArthur. "I don't want to land in the darkness. I want good light. Do you hear me? MacArthur must be seen when he sets foot on Hawaiian soil."

Sutherland, crouched on the floor behind his boss, shouted, "What if we could get lights? Big spotlights?"

MacArthur thought for a moment. "No," he said definitely. "We'd still be waking up the press corps early in the morning. Hauling a reporter out of bed is no way to get good news coverage. Always pamper the press, Sutherland. Always pamper the press. That's the way to get good coverage."

"You're right, sir," Sutherland shouted back. "Then that means we need to land somewhere and wait a few hours."

MacArthur looked at Sutherland and an annoyed look crossed his face. "MacArthur was just about to suggest that a surprise inspection tour of our base in Samoa would be in order."

"We could make Samoa by 1800," shouted Kenney. "Depending on what time you want to arrive at Hickam, we could leave as late as 0400 and arrive in time for Thanksgiving dinner."

"Hmm. Too late for an inspection, but a rest and refueling stop wouldn't be out of order. I could shower and shave," MacArthur said.

"Shall I radio Samoa and arrange the stop?" Sutherland asked.

"Yes, do that, Sutherland. MacArthur does not intend to play into the hands of this 'Mister Big'—as if I don't know who is summoning me to Hawaii!"

MacArthur had railed about the command to go to Hawaii ever since he had received the coded message in Brisbane. He flat-out refused to come and reluctantly let himself be forced into the trip. But Sutherland was used to MacArthur's tirades. It was part of what the great man needed to get his work done. He listened as if he was hearing it now for the very first time.

"It is bad enough MacArthur has been forced to leave his command at this very critical moment," MacArthur went on. "But not to be told officially with whom I am to meet?" He shook his head. "Of course, it's the President. But Ernie King is behind this—you mark my words! One would think the navy would figure out that we are all on the same side, but this petty interservice rivalry is costing men's lives. If the shoe were on the other foot, MacArthur would gladly subordinate his needs for the good of the service."

"Of course you would, sir," replied Sutherland soothingly. "Of course you would."

"They don't appreciate me, Sutherland. They have never appreciated me. They will never appreciate me." MacArthur twisted around in the copilot's chair to face Sutherland directly. "It's not as if I have ever had ambitions for myself. I only serve my country, my comrades, and my conscience." He paused, savoring the phrase. "My country, my comrades, and my conscience.

"But no! The navy will not have it so. They insist on attempting to thwart MacArthur at every turn. They have even turned the President against me. He used to be assistant secretary of the navy, you know. He is prejudiced in their favor. Admiral King has his ear, and George Marshall, who should be my champion, is part of the Pershing clique that has persecuted me for my entire military career."

He paused and then turned back to stare into the depths of the blue Pacific below. Sutherland waited. After a minute, MacArthur turned back to him. "They think they'd be better off without me, that's what they think," he said, biting off each consonant in a low, taut voice. Then his eyes looked to the side, over the ocean, and he said more softly, "Maybe I should give them what they want. Roman generals and Japanese nobles took their lives as a way to protest ill treatment and disrespect. I would only be following tradition, you know. Then let them see how much they like being without me. But it would be too late." His jaw jutted strongly, defiantly. "Too late."

MacArthur occasionally threatened to take his own life when he felt he was not being given his due by the "powers in Washington." Sutherland was confident the General didn't mean it. He hoped the General didn't mean it.

"General, I think they're bringing you to Hawaii to recognize you as you deserve. You'll have a chance to present the case for how the war is progressing before a lot more of the stay-at-home press."

MacArthur smiled wanly. "The stay-at-home reporters have never liked me as well as do those reporters who travel into danger in the company of MacArthur."

"You'll win them over, sir. You've done it before."

"I have, I know. But I have so many more *important* things to do. There has been such progress—from the capture of the Solomons to our triumphant isolation and destruction of Rabaul as an effective enemy base."

Sutherland knew this well but listened carefully. The General was seldom off the mark in any detail about his battle triumphs and tended to rehearse out loud. Sutherland was one of the principal audiences for that purpose.

In addition, Sutherland and his staff had prepared extensive briefing materials—on board, taking up a full shipping trunk. Whatever the topic might be, the General would have charts, photographs, and documentation whenever he needed them. The actions had been numerous: the successful Guadalcanal resupply; the conquests of New Georgia, Munda, and other northern Solomon islands all the way to Bougainville, then on to New Britain and the major Japanese navy base at Rabaul. Lae and the rest of Eastern New Guinea were all firmly in Allied hands—*MacArthur's* hands.

The neutralization of Rabaul had been a stroke of MacArthur genius, Sutherland thought. The General understood that it was the fighting capacity of the Japanese base, not the soldiers and sailors themselves, that had to be destroyed. Airplanes and ships were the targets, and MacArthur was prepared to ignore the place now that Rabaul's offensive capabilities had been eliminated. "The Japs won't surrender," MacArthur said. "Killing them all will be a bloodbath for our boys as well. Now that they're helpless to do anything other than defend, they're unimportant. Let's move on." The Japanese navy, steadily eroding as one ship after another fell to skip bombs, unable to replace its losses from the Battle of the Northern Solomons, was no longer in shape to force passage to Rabaul.

"Our friends in the navy would have starved us of ships and aircraft so they could rush off into the Gilbert Island group. Tarawa! Bloody Tarawa!" MacArthur occasionally used Britishisms as a link to his World War I days in Europe. "What good would there be in invading Tarawa? It would have not brought us one step closer to the Philippines! No, Sutherland, the Gilbert Islands were an unnecessary and potentially expensive target. It is well that we never attacked there! Our sole aim, our compass point, must rest on Manila, and the liberation of our comrades-in-arms who have suffered so cruelly waiting for MacArthur to redeem his promise. I *shall* return, Sutherland. I *shall*."

He paused in silent reflection, turning his face toward heaven. Then he lowered his eyes to talk to Sutherland again. "This conference will make news because MacArthur is there. Therefore, MacArthur must make news first. I want a car, Sutherland, but not just *any* car . . ." The General thought for a minute. "Sutherland, take this down."

• THURSDAY, 25 NOVEMBER 1943 •

ARMY AIR FORCE OFFICERS' CLUB, HICKAM FIELD, HAWAII, 1412 HOURS

"A martini drinker, I see, Colonel Beckwith—ah, James, is it? Do you like James or Jim or Jimmy?" Franklin Delano Roosevelt said pleasantly to the commander of Hickam Air Force Base, cheerfully mixing the requested cocktail and proffering it to the colonel without pausing for an answer. "Thanksgiving in Hawaii—what a delightful change from Hyde Park or even Washington."

The colonel managed a "Yes, sir, Mr. President. Thank you, sir," as the President moved on to his next customer.

FDR was serving as mix master on the patio of the Hickam Officers' Club awaiting the call to Thanksgiving dinner. The bar had been thoughtfully set up at chest height for the President's convenience, with all necessary bar supplies in a semicircle before him. The Hawaiian air was sweetened by the scent of yellow and red heliconia, snowy white frangipani, and blue birds-of-paradise.

The President wore a frangipani lei, as did most of his guests, at least those who were out of uniform. Fleet Admiral Ernest J. King had arrived the day before, flying from Washington. It had been decided it would be impolitic to have him accompany the President. King, immaculate in dress whites, was one of those without a lei, though not without a glass of scotch in his hand. It wasn't his first. He was leaning over a rather pretty blonde, the wife of a commander. The commander was standing in a small conversational group, but he kept turning around to keep an eye on the situation—though it was hard to imagine what he could say or do about it.

Of Douglas MacArthur, there was no sign.

"Frank," the President called.

Frank Chadwick, who had stationed himself not far away, was at the President's side in a moment. "Yes, Mr. President?"

"Where is Douglas?" FDR said in a low voice.

"I don't know, Mr. President. The *Bataan* has landed, I'm sure of it." Frank lowered his own voice in turn.

"It's been two hours. It doesn't take a man that long to take a shower and put on a set of clean clothes," the President said in an annoyed tone. "Find out what Douglas is up to, Frank."

"Right away, Mr. President," Chadwick replied, as FDR turned to the next dignitary awaiting his drink, a wide smile on his face. Chadwick picked up a telephone sitting beside the President and dialed.

The question of Douglas MacArthur's whereabouts was settled before Frank Chadwick's call went through. First came the wailing of police sirens, which grew louder as two MPs on motorcycles drove up to the canopied entrance to the club. Every eye on the patio except for Admiral King—and the blonde's husband—turned to look at the display.

Behind the police sirens, the longest car anyone there had ever seen drove up, followed by two more motorcycles. All the sirens stopped simultaneously, and the driver of the car jumped out and hurried around the side to open the door for the General.

MacArthur stepped out of the car and struck a pose. The newsmen present, rushing like moths to a flame, had grabbed their cameras and headed for the Supreme Commander, Southwest Pacific Areas. Big blue bulbs flashed, then they were ejected onto the bricked walkway.

Everyone knew that this dinner with the President was a formal occasion. Every officer wore his finest uniform; civilians were in black tie. Douglas MacArthur, however, wore an old field uniform, pale and soft from frequent washings, and wore no insignia except the pentagon of stars showing his rank. Over it he wore a leather aviator's jacket, this one too showing the signs of age and hard use. He wore mirrored sunglasses against the glare and carried a corncob pipe in his right hand. MacArthur looked around, saw the people milling on the patio, and strode forward, stepping over a low wall to join the party.

Now that the car was empty, the four flanking motorcycles omitted their sirens but kept in formation with the car as all drove away. Two other cars, not quite as striking, pulled up behind the MP escort, and the core members of the MacArthur party came out. There was the chief of staff, Sutherland; and over there was Willoughby, intelligence; and Kenney, air force.

MacArthur shook hands with people as he passed them, first-naming some, clasping others on the shoulder, and responding to various greetings. The President of the United States sat behind his bar, completely ignored as the General made his way through the crowd. He reached the President, stopped, and saluted. "General Douglas MacArthur reporting as ordered, sir!" he said.

The President, though, had means of his own and was not easily upstaged. "Douglas, Douglas my boy, how good it is to see you again." He reached up to shake the General's hand. "Here, hold on a minute. Boys," he said to the photographers who had followed MacArthur into the reception, "here's the main act. Ernie, Ernie, over here, Ernie," he called.

Admiral King looked up from the blonde with annoyance and sulkily complied. He and MacArthur shook hands, King with visible distaste, but MacArthur looking warm and friendly.

"Here, on both sides of me. Help me up," Roosevelt said. The President placed one strong arm on the shoulder of each man and pulled himself up from his chair. "Fire away, boys, fire away." The three men stood under the onslaught of bulbs flashing, until finally the President waved them off. "It's going to be dinnertime shortly," he announced. "We'll have a little food brought out for you. Enjoy your Thanksgiving. We'll have a press conference tomorrow, if you don't mind. Today, I'd just like to be like all Americans and enjoy my turkey."

"Ernie King, what a pleasure to see you," MacArthur said with apparent sincerity.

King looked at his rival. "MacArthur," he said with a growl.

"That's my boys, always friendly," the President interjected. "It's Thanksgiving. Tomorrow we'll go aboard the *Hornet* and have a private little chat. For today, though, please oblige your President and get into the spirit of the festivities."

"Douglas MacArthur is delighted to honor your wish, Mr. President. In fact, I was already looking forward to a pleasant Thanksgiving dinner. Tomorrow will be soon enough for more casual discussions. As soon as I read the radiogram ordering me to report here for a meeting with 'Mr. Big,' I took for granted it was you. I was immediately delighted, even though as you know there is so much more to do in my area."

Frank Chadwick looked surprised. There was a young officer accompanying General Kenney, medium height, brown hair, handsome, fit, wearing gold oak leaves. Frank started working his way through the increasingly crowded patio, coming up behind the young officer. "Welcome to the big time, brother-in-law," he said to Ellis Halverson.

"Frank—uh, Captain!" Halverson's surprise was evident. Then he grinned. "Seems the last time I saw you was in a different officers' club. Do you do anything besides drink?"

"Listen, you young whippersnapper," Frank replied, "you have no idea how much hard work it takes to be this dissolute." Both men laughed

The initial insults out of the way, Frank and Ellis compared notes. Ellis had gotten home once. Frank, whose White House assignment enabled him to move his wife, Elllis's big sister, into an Arlington apartment, had been to Baltimore a few times to see her family. No one had any news of Johnny.

General Sutherland, who had been watching the conversation, came over to Ellis. "Major Halverson, would you introduce me to your navy friend?"

Ellis looked startled, and then did as he was asked.

"Chadwick—you look familiar," Sutherland said.

"Yes, General. We met before, on General MacArthur's previous trip to Hawaii. I was the aide to Admiral Nimitz at the time."

"Oh, of course," said Sutherland. His expression, sour to begin with, became sourer. "And how do you two happen to know each other?"

"He's my brother-in-law," Ellis said.

Sutherland looked as if he were going to make a reply but walked off instead.

"What was that about?" Frank asked.

"I don't know, Frank," Ellis replied.

Two navy officers were holding the shoulders of the commander with the blond wife, talking to him in urgent, low voices. Douglas MacArthur was holding court, sitting on a waist-height brick wall. The President of the United States turned to a photographer standing near him. "Psst!" the President said.

The photographer came over. FDR pointed across at MacArthur. "Look closely," he said. "Do you see what I see?"

The photographer stared intently and then stifled his own laughter. From the angle of the President, it was quite clear that MacArthur's fly was open. The photographer lifted his camera and began to focus—then MacArthur turned toward Roosevelt with a disdainful look on his face and crossed his legs.

"There goes your shot at the cover of *Life*," FDR said, laughing.

The reporter's face had a somewhat disgruntled expression. "I've been on the cover of *Life* already, Mr. President, but it would have been a great shot, even if I could never publish it. This photo is going to turn into a fish story, Mr. President. The one that got away." He shook his head ruefully.

MacArthur was ignoring both men ostentatiously. When he stood up, he angled himself away from the photographer's line of sight and vanished momentarily into the club.

A Filipino waiter stepped out onto the patio. "Thanksgiving dinner is served," he announced loudly and then walked backward through the open patio doors. By protocol, the President had to make the first move. He pushed himself firmly back from the bar and rolled his chair out, then led the way into the dining room. The most senior dignitaries went next: admirals and generals with four or more stars. As King and MacArthur started to the door simultaneously, MacArthur stopped and graciously ushered King before him. King looked for a moment as if he wanted to protest, then strode into the room, MacArthur following.

The seating chart had been carefully prepared, and there was some milling around as each person found his or her name tag. Ellis was with his boss Kenney; Frank was with the local dignitaries: the commanding admirals and generals of the various Oahu facilities as well as several mayors from smaller cities on the island. The mayor of Honolulu and the governor of the territory were both with the President. Frank's old boss, Admiral Chester Nimitz, was also at the President's table. Nimitz had arrived late, though not as late as MacArthur, and Frank had not yet had a chance to talk with him personally.

MacArthur had kept his word to Nimitz, more or less. Nimitz had taken full, public responsibility for the defeat at Midway and asked to be relieved of his role as CINCPAC. The President immediately cabled back that he had the fullest confidence in Admiral Nimitz and consented to an organizational change that seemed to remove Nimitz from power but in reality gave him better control.

After the destruction of the American fleet in the Battle of

the Northern Solomons and the death of Admiral Halsey,
Nimitz pushed through a major reorganization of the navy in
the Pacific. Recognizing that most of the naval role in the
Pacific was now in SWPA, MacArthur's area, he reconsti-
tuted the remaining Pacific navy forces into a single fleet,
keeping the Third Fleet name. Now responsible for the navy
in both Pacific theaters, Nimitz became Commander in
Chief, Third Fleet, a position technically lower than CINC-
PAC but practically more powerful. Admiral Frank Fletcher
was now CINCPAC, a smaller role than it had been but
enough to gain Fletcher his fifth star. It was an open secret
that Fletcher's chief of staff, Vice Admiral Raymond A.
Spruance, was running the place.

The new Third Fleet was much larger than the old one. A
single task force in the new Third Fleet had four flattops and
the full complement of support vessels, from cruisers to destroyers, oilers, cargo ships, and more. A new carrier a
month was joining Third Fleet. It was already the most powerful seagoing force in the history of the world, and its ex-
pansion and modernization were just getting started.

After dinner came dancing. Enough WACs and WAVEs had
been imported to provide partners for those who were there
stag. King renewed his attentions to the blond wife of the
commander, who sat at his table looking increasingly furious as his two friends continued to counsel him.

The commander suddenly stood up, fists balled. His
friends clung desperately to his arms. The commander
bumped the table, knocking several glasses to the floor and
spilling a bottle of wine at the same moment Douglas
MacArthur was passing by. The wine sloshed down the General's pants leg.

All eyes turned toward the three petrified officers as
General MacArthur calmly took a napkin from the table and
began to blot his leg.

"I-I'm so sorry, General," one of the two companions began to stutter.

MacArthur put up his hand. "Quite all right," he said with

a benedictory smile. "It's an old uniform, and worse things have spilled on it."

The three men visibly relaxed.

MacArthur smiled genially and patted the furious commander on the shoulder. "Happy Thanksgiving, son," he said. Then he walked onto the dance floor, took the hand of the blonde, asked, "May I have this dance?" and swirled her out from King's grasp.

The surprised fleet admiral looked at his rival with anger equal to the commander's, but he controlled it and headed for the bar. MacArthur danced one fox-trot with the wife, bowed, kissed her hand, and shooed her back in the direction of her husband.

As soon as dinner ended, Frank Chadwick moved to the President's table because he wanted a chance to talk with Admiral Nimitz, and to be within the President's earshot in case FDR needed him. He was there when the wine was spilled and watched MacArthur's actions. FDR leaned forward and said, "A masterful performance, don't you think? Our Douglas could give Lionel Barrymore a run for the money in Hollywood."

Nimitz and Chadwick both laughed.

• FRIDAY, 26 NOVEMBER 1943 •

USS HORNET, CRUISING OFF THE COAST OF OAHU, HAWAII, 1037 HOURS

The loud, penetrating hiss of the steam catapult and the roaring engines of the carrier aircraft taking off dominated the ship's deck, but the admiral's bridge—high above the carefully choreographed activity on the flight deck—had been designed to make conversation possible. The carrier was churning directly into the wind to launch aircraft, and the resulting cool sea breeze softened the tropical heat. The air was generally sweet, punctuated with the occasional whiff of aviation fuel.

Roosevelt sat in his wheelchair. Neither MacArthur nor

King used the two remaining chairs. There was a low table between the two chairs and the President. On each side of the deck was an easel, and below the easel was a small pile of posters on heavy board. One poster from each service—both of them maps—was displayed on each easel.

"I'm glad to be *warm,* you know?" remarked the President of the United States. "I find as I grow older that cold has become more painful." He looked out into the ocean. "I'm not looking forward to the Washington winter." Roosevelt shivered slightly. He had on a panama hat for sun protection, and dark glasses to protect his eyes. A light blanket was draped over his lap. He wore a seersucker suit and white shirt for the sessions with photographers, but when he was safely out of sight of land, he had changed his white shirt and bow tie for a Hawaiian shirt featuring purple hibiscus.

Douglas MacArthur laughed. "I remember Washington winters well. They were high on my list of reasons for returning to the Philippines." MacArthur still wore his plain working uniform and battered hat. His leather aviator's jacket was draped over a chair.

Admiral Ernest J. King, stiffly formal in dress whites, shook his head in mild disdain. "Doesn't bother me. I *like* Washington winters. Bracing."

"That's a navy man for you," said FDR approvingly. "Strong constitution. Knows how to resist the elements."

"Washington winters make me think of my sailors in the North Atlantic," King explained, wearing a look of offended dignity.

"As well you should," commented MacArthur. He was leaning against a bulkhead. He carried his unlit corncob pipe in his right hand and used it as a pointer. "The tropical heat and humidity here remind me of Bataan. My brave men there are never far from my thoughts."

King looked from the President to MacArthur and back again. "Can we get down to brass tacks?" he interjected roughly. "Let's not pretend we're here to enjoy one another's company. Now, we're here to—"

"Hold on just a moment," said MacArthur. "If you don't

mind, I'd like another cup of coffee. Either of you want anything?" He raised his hand to summon one of the Filipino waiters looking through the window, in sight but out of earshot. MacArthur asked for coffee in Tagalog, flustering the waiter, who responded in English.

Within a minute, the waiter emerged with the coffee. MacArthur waited patiently until the waiter was done, then turned to King. "I'm sorry for the interruption. You were saying?"

"I was saying that we have to put a stop to this war between you and the navy before you do serious damage to the war effort," King said, staring angrily into MacArthur's eyes.

"War? Damage? You must be joking." MacArthur dismissed King's statement with an airy wave of his corncob pipe. "That's exaggerated nonsense, Admiral. Interservice rivalry predates both of us. You know that. There's no 'war' between MacArthur and the United States Navy. The only war is the one we fight together. We're having a principled disagreement on the best military organizational structure for the Pacific. Why personalize the matter? It's just business. Believe me, if it is determined the best leader for the Pacific Theater is someone other than MacArthur, I shall gladly accept a lesser role. That would be far better than continuing with this absurd separation of a single theater into two."

"Then we're done," King growled. "You report to Nimitz, and then there will be only one theater."

MacArthur laughed and shifted his attention to Roosevelt. "But we haven't determined who is better to lead this theater, nor whether the navy or the army is better suited to furnish the supreme commander."

King argued back immediately. "The Pacific, Mr. President, belongs to the navy. Just look at the battlefield. It's ninety-nine percent water. The supreme commander of the Pacific Theater will be primarily directing ship operations, Marine Corps landings, and naval air operations. The Army Air Force is the only army force that will matter. We'll capture landing bases as we move forward on the shortest, most direct route to Japan. We'll extend the reach of American bombers until Tojo and his gang receive an American welcome card right through the ceiling."

"Au contraire, mon Admiral," replied MacArthur. He stood up and began orating as he paced. "Douglas MacArthur does not pretend to be an admiral. As for King's skill at being an army general—" He paused and smiled, shrugging his shoulders slightly. "But the good admiral is completely in error about the nature of the terrain. Yes, MacArthur needs ships in order to land troops, but every inch of enemy-held soil will have to be wrested from the Jap with the skills of the common infantryman. Ground must always be won the hard way, I'm afraid. A ship cannot take and hold land. Nor can a bomber. What difference does it make how much water is in the Pacific Ocean? No, Mr. President, I don't envy you this decision, but as much respect as I have for Admiral King, I still would argue to my last breath that the army's work in this theater is as great as that of the navy—nay, greater. For the navy man takes his cot and mess hall along into battle. The soldier carries only his weapon." MacArthur paused dramatically.

"Now wait just a goddamn minute, MacArthur!" sputtered King. "Don't you tell *me* that sailors don't take risks! Have you ever been on a ship that's been hit and is starting to sink? Have you? Well, if you haven't, then you don't know the first goddamn thing about who's got it tougher."

MacArthur drew himself up stiffly. "I had no intention whatsoever of disparaging the terrible risks sailors routinely encounter, any more than you were trying to disparage my brave comrades on Bataan and Corregidor." He paused and then added, "Or are you?"

King stared at MacArthur through narrowed eyes. Both men stood stonily for a long minute. Then King grudgingly said, "No, I wasn't."

"Now gentlemen—" said FDR, pushing his wheelchair in between the two men. "Let us turn our attention back to the real problem. Why don't we start by having each of you tell me what you would do as supreme commander?" He looked back and forth between the two men. "Well, would one of you prefer to go first?"

"I'm ready now," said King forcefully.

"Then if Douglas has no objection . . . ," said FDR.

"None whatsoever, Mr. President," said MacArthur. "Go ahead, Admiral. I'll be interested to hear what you have to say."

King looked angrily at MacArthur for a moment and then began to talk. "First, the objective is Japan. Not the Philippines."

"My dear King!" exploded MacArthur, hands flying out dramatically. "Of *course* the objective is Japan. The road to Japan, however, lies through the Philippines, for we must redeem this nation's honor."

"Mr. President!" King barked.

"You're right," said FDR. "Now, Douglas, you'll get your turn in a few minutes. For now, I want us both to listen carefully to what he says, and then we'll listen to you."

MacArthur wore an innocent expression. "I was simply helping to lay the groundwork for this discussion."

FDR looked sharply at MacArthur for a second, then he chuckled. "Go ahead, Ernie. I'll keep Douglas quiet."

"Silent as a mouse," agreed MacArthur, just as King opened his mouth again.

"As I was *saying,*" said King, "the objective is Japan. Now, what's the best way to get there and end this work? Air power. What does air power need? Bases." He walked to his easel, a map of the South Pacific.

"What we need are air bases. We'll take them away from the Japanese, island by island, using each captured base to stage the next attack. It's the direct route. We'll bypass the Gilberts but take the key Jap bases in the Marshalls. Then it's on to the Marianas, where we'll have bomber bases to strike the Home Islands. From there we're ready for Okinawa. We won't have entire countries to take, just small islands."

"How about the Southwest Pacific?" asked Roosevelt. "What would you do with Douglas and his forces?"

"We outgun their navy now, and get farther ahead every week. Soon, we'll have the resources to go in both directions at once, catching Japan in a squeeze play. Then we'll be able to transport MacArthur's army, defend it, and get it onto shore."

"Let me see if I understand," purred MacArthur. "I should send word to my brave, loyal soldiers in Bataan and elsewhere that they can sit and wait another year because the navy wants to take all the ships and attack Kwajalein and Saipan, for example, targets with minuscule military value. Is that right? Is that what you're suggesting?"

"No, you know damned well that's not what I'm suggesting. The road to the Philippines is through Tokyo. We'll rescue the Bataan survivors, MacArthur. But it'll be because the Japs have surrendered."

"So your proposal is to liberate Manila by conquering Kwajalein Island?" asked MacArthur. "I'm afraid I don't see how that—"

"You can't just dismiss this out of—"

"Dismiss it?" said MacArthur with a look of incredulity and innocence. "Dismiss it? No, Mr. President. My respect for the navy is boundless, truly boundless. In fact, Mr. President, let me say once again that MacArthur would sooner you give the supreme command to the navy rather than allow us to continue with this absurd split of forces. We need a unified campaign against Japan. Anything else is a waste. Admiral King recommends pushing through the Marshall Island chain at God only knows what costs, then on to the Marianas, simply to allow bombers to attack mainland Japan and its most closely held possessions. It's madness! Why go to all that terrible and tragic waste when a liberated Philippines can provide every air advantage and more!"

King rounded on his adversary. "The Philippines. Always the Philippines. Just because you want to repair your failure—"

"My *failure*?" MacArthur's face flushed. "My dear Admiral King. With the precious few resources I had available, and only a fraction of the supplies that were promised me, my brave men of Bataan and Corregidor held out against the

Jap invaders longer and better than any other force in the Pacific. If you want to talk about *failure,* shall we look at the navy record?" His smile was cold.

King charged back. "Those twisted rumors and accusations you keep spreading are reprehensible, MacArthur. You don't give a damn about American armed forces; you just want to satisfy your Philippine obsession. Got another a mistress stashed there?" King said with heavy sarcasm, referring to MacArthur's long-ago affair with "Dimples" Cooper.

MacArthur's eyes narrowed. "It is a good thing for you, Admiral, that the day of dueling is past. You have attacked my honor, sir."

Roosevelt looked from MacArthur to King and back. "Boys, boys," he pleaded. "Let's be civil. We have a problem to solve, and name-calling won't help." The men looked like two boxers being kept apart by the referee. Roosevelt tried again. "Ernie, you want to hop up this island chain, bomb the Japanese enough to soften them up, then gain Okinawa as a base for invading the main islands if they don't surrender. Is that about right?"

King nodded. "Essentially, Mr. President," he agreed.

"And Douglas, you want to liberate the Philippines and then use those islands as a staging area for bombing and an invasion. Right?"

MacArthur waved his hand airily. "In a nutshell," he said, "but there's so much more that needs to be said. We have already secured eastern New Guinea. In January we will launch a bold operation—an amphibious assault against Hollandia that will carry us four hundred miles to the west in one stroke."

"Are you forgetting about Wewak?" King challenged aggressively, jabbing. "There's a hundred thousand Japs there, and it's a helluva lot closer to you than Hollandia!"

"I am pleased to see that the admiral, like the General, has done his homework," MacArthur said with a twinkle in his eye. "You are right—there are a hundred thousand enemy troops at Wewak, and at Wewak they will stay. We will simply pass them by."

As King digested this bit of audacious planning, the General swept on. "From western New Guinea we are splendidly positioned to reclaim the Philippines—I believe, Mr. President, that my men can be in Manila sometime in the middle of 1944."

"Look at the size of those islands!" King protested. "New Guinea! Luzon! Think of all the ground that you have to take, compared to Saipan, or Guam."

"Spoken like a true admiral of the high seas," MacArthur noted. "But therein lies the advantage of my route to Japan. The very size of those islands means that the enemy cannot fortify every beach, every little village and sheltered cove. We will get our forces ashore with minimal losses and then win a battle of maneuver. On Saipan, on the other hand, our brave marines would have to charge ashore under a veritable storm of steel and cordite! The costs of those landings—"

"All right," interrupted FDR. "There are three choices I see. First, take Douglas's route, in which case it makes sense that he be supreme commander. Second, go with Ernie's route, and it would make sense for a navy man to be supreme commander. So far, so good, gentlemen?"

King nodded grudgingly. MacArthur opened his mouth, ready to argue again, but Roosevelt kept talking. "Or I can reaffirm the division of the Pacific and let each of you take your own route to Japan. Make it a race, so to speak, army against the navy."

FDR rolled his chair close to King's easel and looked at the map. "Ernie, as I see it, if we had started these approaches to Japan simultaneously, or if you'd started first, it would be absolutely clear that the approach should continue. But that didn't happen. The Solomons took priority, and Douglas is getting close to taking control of all of New Guinea. He's ahead of you."

"Because of his scurrilous attacks on the navy!" King said, his voice rising in volume.

"That's not entirely true. His troops have performed splendidly, you must admit. Besides, it doesn't matter why," replied Roosevelt. "Not anymore."

MacArthur spread his arms in a welcoming gesture. "I agree. Let's let bygones be bygones. But the President is right, Admiral. I am ahead. If you do some sort of abbreviated campaign, you can distract some of the Japanese navy, but the main action is the road through the Philippines and Okinawa into the underbelly of Japan."

"'Bygones,'" snarled King. "You sound like the boy who murdered his parents and then asked for mercy because he was an orphan."

MacArthur laughed. "That's pretty clever. I shall have to remember it."

Roosevelt chuckled as well. "That was said by my most distinguished predecessor, Abraham Lincoln." King grinned at MacArthur's discomfiture at not knowing the quote. FDR turned back toward King with a serious expression. "But Ernie, even if I agree that Douglas was a bad boy, that doesn't change the facts. He is ahead, and the other campaign is going to look like a sideshow."

"All right," growled King. "Let MacArthur plan his little battles, and I'll make sure the navy helps him—but under central command from here at Pearl. Nimitz is your man, in spite of MacArthur's attempts to ruin him."

"That's outrageous," MacArthur snapped. "I *rehabilitated* the man. To say I somehow—"

"Oh, shove it up your ass, MacArthur," replied King. "You make pretty speeches, but I can see exactly what you're trying to do. You want the entire Pacific, and you'll say or do anything, even at the cost of the war effort, to get what you want. Well, I'm on to you. It's not going to work this time."

The two standing men looked daggers at one another. The President looked back and forth between his two senior officers. Finally, he sighed.

"Ernie, I'd like to talk with you privately for a moment," the President said. "Douglas, do you mind?"

MacArthur had a look of suspicion on his face. "I think it would be better to say everything in this group."

"And I disagree, Douglas," said the President. "Ernie, come with me." Roosevelt began to wheel his chair away from MacArthur.

When the two men were out of MacArthur's earshot, FDR turned to his chief of naval operations. "Ernie, he's right. I know what he did to get it, and I wish there were something I could do to even the score. But he's right."

"That bastard is *not* getting my navy!" King growled forcefully. "I won't stand for it."

FDR shook his head sadly. "Ernie, it's galling to lose to that man, I know. But you are going to have to. Can you do it with good grace?

King stood mute.

The President looked at him. "Ernie, the last time you offered to resign, I talked you out of it. Now it's your turn to talk me out of asking for your resignation. If you can't do this, I have to get another chief of naval operations."

King, eyes narrowed, looked across the deck at his nemesis MacArthur. There was a long pause. Finally, he spoke. "I won't preside over destroying the navy's Pacific Fleet, Mr. President."

"I'm sorry to hear that, Ernie. Very well." FDR looked visibly older. "Would you like to be supreme commander of the Atlantic navy? You'd have to do what Ike wants, but you might find it easier to work with him. And you will have to run the navy's end of the invasion of the European continent next year."

"What I *want* is for that bastard to keep his hands off my navy. Hasn't he done enough already?

"He's done enough and more, Ernie," the President said. "But on this, he's right. He's made himself right." FDR paused. "Who would you recommend to succeed you?"

King spoke without hesitation. "Chester Nimitz," he said.

"Nimitz. That's a fine recommendation. I'll take it. And Ernie, believe me, I tried to keep this from happening."

"Very well, Mr. President," King said stiffly. "Do you need me here any longer?"

"No, Ernie," said FDR sadly. "You are dismissed."

The President of the United States began rolling his wheel-chair back toward the new supreme commander of FORPAC, the U.S. Forces Pacific Theater, leaving the demoted admiral standing still, his normally furious expression clouded by an aura of stunned disbelief.

MacArthur had been pacing back and forth. He stopped when the President came toward him.

"I've made my decision, Douglas," Roosevelt said.

MacArthur looked at the President warily, ready to argue. "Sir?"

FDR went on tiredly. "You won, Douglas. You get the Pacific. Ernie will take the Atlantic."

MacArthur paused, nonplussed. "I beg your pardon?"

"Chester Nimitz will become the new chief of naval operations. Ernie King will be commander in chief of the Atlantic Fleet."

"I—well, I'm sorry to hear that, but—"

"Douglas, be quiet," FDR said, his own voice soft. "For once, be quiet. Your little games have cost me enough."

"Games? Mr. President, I must—"

"I said be quiet. Douglas, you get what you want, this time. Your maneuvers have worked. But you did me a serious disservice. You have made me angry, and you may have weakened the war effort. Watch yourself, Douglas. This affair has cost you, too. Don't give me an excuse to get rid of you."

MacArthur put on his most gracious expression. "Mr. President, I'm very sorry that you perceive the situation in this manner. MacArthur only wants to be of service, and he serves at the President's pleasure. If recalling me is good for the nation, then—"

"It's not good for the nation, and you know it," interrupted FDR. "Cross me again, though, and you'll be through. I mean it, Douglas."

The man in the wheelchair looked calmly at his Pacific supreme commander, and the new CINCFORPAC looked back. After a few moments, MacArthur looked away. FDR turned his wheelchair around and rolled off the deck. King, still looking daggers, swiveled on his heel and followed the President.

MacArthur stood alone on the deck overlooking his Pacific Ocean.

ELEVEN

Philippines; New Mexico; Japan

• THURSDAY, 11 MAY 1944 •

BILIBID PRISON, MANILA, PHILIPPINES, 1320 HOURS

Carrying his battered tin cup carefully in both hands so as not to slosh any of his precious water over the rim, Johnny Halverson stepped out into the painfully bright sunlight. The dirt burned his bare feet. When he reached the shady area on the far side of the compound, he stepped gingerly around and over the sprawling bodies. No one offered to move. That took energy.

The prisoners had been moved to Bilibid, an ancient Spanish dungeon, some weeks earlier. The guards had been quiet as to the reason for the change, but the Filipinos had whispered the truth: MacArthur was coming! His armies had landed in the Philippines, and the liberation of the archipelago was well under way. For the prisoners of war, it was now a race: would liberation come first, or death?

Johnny reached the wall and squatted down in front of one of the men. "I brought you some water, Jerry," he said, handing him the tin cup. "It's even sort of clean."

Lieutenant Jerry Rocker had a coughing spasm, after which he spit out some blood. He took the cup with both of his shaking hands and slowly drank about half of the warm, brackish water. Then he leaned his head back against the concrete and closed his eyes, as if the effort had exhausted him. "What's the latest?" he asked in a voice not much above a whisper.

"There's a helluva battle on Leyte right now. The Jap navy is finished," Johnny said. "It can't be too long before Mac gets up here to Luzon. Hold on for another month or two, and you'll sleep in a real hospital bed with sheets and everything."

"Son of a bitch," Jerry said and went into a coughing spasm. "In a month I won't be here."

"Sure you will," Johnny replied in a soothing tone. He took a small piece of torn uniform cloth out of his pants pocket, dipped it in the remaining water, and patted it on Jerry's forehead. It made no discernible difference in his fever. "I wish you'd go to the hospital," he said.

Jerry shook his head weakly in response. "You know what they got in that goddamn place? Sick people. Germs. Worst place to be. You go there to die." He coughed again, face contorted with pain, and spit up more blood.

A buzzing sound became steadily louder: an aircraft engine. "One of ours," Jerry said.

"How do you know?"

"I don't. But the Japs are losing, so it's gotta be ours. I bet we own the skies now." More coughing, more blood. "Help me up. Help me move out in the sun. I want to see it."

Reluctantly, Johnny helped Jerry to his feet. He weighed next to nothing, but so did Johnny. The two men staggered out into the sunshine. Johnny shielded his eyes. Jerry stared straight up, waiting. The plane, a single-engine dive-bomber with U.S. Navy markings, swooped low over the prison courtyard and waggled its wings. The belly of the aircraft was pale, almost white, but a brief glimpse as the pilot half rolled showed the upper surfaces to be a beautiful deep blue. The white star on the wing seemed as big, and as bright, as the sun.

"They know we're here," Johnny whispered.

Although the plane was out of sight, Jerry was still staring in that direction. "Low-wing, radial engine—damn. I bet that's one sweet bird to fly. I bet my old A-24 is as obsolete as a P-26 these days." He coughed again, doubling over in pain. It was all Johnny could do to get him back into the shade and sitting on the ground. His place at the wall was taken.

They heard the roaring of distant aircraft, the sharp crump of exploding bombs, and knew that the navy dive-bombers attacked ships in Manila Bay.

"So he's really coming back—just like he said he would," Jerry mused.

"That's all the Filipinos talk about," Johnny agreed. "He said he would return, and he is! While we spend the whole goddamn war just waiting for it to happen."

"What a stupid war," Jerry said in a matter-of-fact voice. "I was going to be high above all this nasty ground-pounder stuff. But some jackass forgot to send me a plane. Me and the whole 27th Bombardment Group—they put us in foxholes and called us infantry!"

Johnny nodded. He had shipped with Jerry and another old friend, David Hansen, in the *President Hoover* an eternity ago, and the men had compared their stories so often it had become a ritual with them. He touched the worn pocket of his uniform shirt, where he kept Dave's dog tags—Dave hadn't made it out of Cabanatuan, back in the summer of 1942. Johnny had vowed to bring those tags out with him, with the others he had been collecting—so that, somehow, the families of those men who didn't make it would know that their loved ones hadn't been alone, or forgotten, at the end. He shuddered at the thought that Jerry Rocker's dog tags might be the next set to join his memorializing collection. Johnny shook the thought away—there were already too many of them.

"I was greased for Aberdeen Proving Grounds. Some personnel fuckup sent me here to Shangri-La instead." He imitated a travelogue narrator. " 'Enjoy wine, women, and song in the mysterious Far East.' "

Jerry cracked a small smile. "Well, Mac may not get here

soon enough for me, but he'll be here for you. You'll get the wine and women yet. Singing you can get anywhere. Even here."

"I've heard the singing, and a deep bass is no substitute for a soprano in a tight skirt and a low-cut blouse. Mac damn well better show up soon. I've got my orders for home, you know. And after you get better, maybe you'll get a hot bomber like the one we just saw."

Another bout of coughing was his only reply.

A day later, Jerry Rocker was gone. Johnny quietly slipped off his dog tags and added them to more than a dozen other sets.

You'll be remembered, he promised to himself.

• WEDNESDAY, 6 SEPTEMBER 1944 •

LOS ALAMOS, NEW MEXICO, 2311 HOURS

The starry sky spilled into the far limits of infinity, the vastness of space illuminated by the countless specks of distant suns. Here in the high desert, the view of those stars was unimpeded by smoke or haze or city lights. The nearest community of any size, Santa Fe, was miles away; closer by, the surroundings consisted of uninhabited desert. Even here in the great scientific complex on the mesa, surrounded by its concentric rings of barbed wire, the tall towers occupied by alert, steel-eyed guards, the gates that were locked and double-barred and protected by machine-gun-toting sentries, it was dark.

But that did not mean that Los Alamos was sleeping. Especially not in this place, at the very heart of the compound, where the Critical Assemblies group was conducting crucial tests.

This was G Division, centered in the drab-green two-story building that was shaped like a long rectangle, with clapboard sides and a shingled roof. It was surrounded by its own security fence, a perimeter within the perimeter, where only the most privileged were allowed to venture. A car, headlights dimmed, approached the building. The over-worked physicist at the wheel steered impatiently around a slow-moving army truck and parked his government green Studebaker at the south end of the structure. He brushed the dirt off his suit—a futile gesture; none of the Los Alamos roads were paved—and walked up to the guard post.

Even though Dr. Robert Oppenheimer was the director of Los Alamos, the guard still inspected his identification before passing him through the last barbed-wire fence surrounding the building. The main entrance was in the center of the long side of the rectangle.

Oppenheimer went through that door, wiping the perspiration from his forehead. It was noticeably hot inside, even though the blazing New Mexico sun had set hours earlier. The temperature in the building was modulated slightly by the fans in every open window. They kept the air circulating and made it bearable.

A staircase led upward directly in front of him, while a corridor extended to the left and right. Oppenheimer turned left. At the end of the corridor, about twenty yards away, another door. The corridor itself was lined with offices. With annoyance, Oppenheimer noticed papers lying around in full view, and in one case a file cabinet drawer left open. This would inevitably draw the attention of the security people and waste more time. There was no time left to waste. That damned flunky of MacArthur's—Sutherland—was increasing the pressure for results! Results! *Results!* He evidently thought the Manhattan Project was like the Sears catalog. Just put the item number on the order form and you'll get it COD.

Oppenheimer shook his head, disbelief mingling with frustration. After all, the project had made unbelievable progress in only a few short years. Starting with experiments in New York and Chicago, the greatest physicists in the world had answered the summons of the American government. Millions of dollars—an unprecedented investment in untried technology—had led to crude experiments in radiation, the assembly of materials to make a pile that would approach critical mass. Keen scientific minds had worked together, steadily advancing the understanding of physics, radiation, and the potential of atomic energy.

It had not been long before security considerations, not to mention the potential danger to large communities, had forced the relocation of the Manhattan Project to this barren Southwestern desert. Almost overnight this mesa had become a small city, with scientists and their families living here and a vast army security presence protecting the whole. Huge manufacturing facilities had been created at Oak Ridge, in Tennessee, and along the Columbia River at Hanford. These factory complexes were producing enriched uranium and plutonium—a totally new element, the first ever created by man. Progress was still astounding, but to the army—and especially to that bastard Sutherland—it could never be fast enough. Hence the need to work like this, toward midnight and beyond.

Tonight's experiment involved work on the Little Boy uranium bomb. The Oak Ridge facility had shipped enough pure U 235 to meet the theoretical needs of the bomb, but the theory still required testing. Oppenheimer was responsible for the Fat Man plutonium bomb as well. Much of the plutonium from the Queen Mary plant at Hanford had recently been delivered to Los Alamos, making the secret city in the New Mexico desert the repository of the largest collection of radioactive material in the world. Oppenheimer would not have a good night's sleep until it was all over, but the end was in sight. *And an end to all this stress,* he thought.

The far door led into a crowded two-story-high laboratory space that was about thirty yards long and twenty wide. A number of complicated mechanical structures filled the space. At the moment, two scientists were building stacks of uranium 235 bars within a framework of bricks of beryllium. Subcritical assemblies—called Lady Godivas because they were unshielded—involved building these piles of several dozen bars and measuring the increased neutron activity as the stacks approached critical mass.

Otto Frisch was one of the two men who stood in front of a ten-foot-tall iron frame nicknamed the Guillotine. Frisch had wiry black hair that he brushed back over his high forehead, a large and bulbous nose, and a tendency to slouch. He was also one of the world's top physicists, and this was his experiment.

The other man was a young graduate student from Princeton named Richard Feynman. Brilliant and blunt, he had once reviewed the work of a senior scientist on one experimental program and summed it up in two words: "It stinks." Feynman had compared this experimental program to tickling the tail of a sleeping dragon. Frisch, who liked a good joke even when he was the target, promptly named it the Dragon Experiment. It was extremely dangerous. They should have built it offsite, but under the most recent demands of MacArthur and Sutherland, there had been no time for such an extensive precaution. *Everyone's under too much stress,* he thought.

The G Division team had previously performed this experiment with uranium hydride—less radioactive than U 235—but today was the real thing. The idea was to assemble a subcritical mass of the small blocks of uranium, minus a big hole in the center to allow neutrons to escape. Then the remaining portion of uranium would be dropped from the top of the Guillotine to pass through the center hole. During the split second when the dropping mass was in line with the stationary uranium, there would exist a critical mass—that is, the fundamental condition needed for a self-sustaining nuclear reaction. That reaction would momentarily flare into reality until gravity pulled the uranium through the bottom of the hole and canceled the condition.

In proposing the experiment, Frisch had said, "It's as near as we can possibly go toward starting an atomic reaction without actually burning up." Now, as he watched the last-minute preparations, Oppenheimer felt all the tension and excitement implicit in Frisch's observation.

The early experiments had gone extremely well, producing the first controlled nuclear reaction that went supercritical with prompt neutrons alone.

This would be the real thing.

The central mass of U 235 had been pulled to the top of the

Guillotine by a chain. At Frisch's command, the mass would be released to drop freely through the hole in the center of the remaining U 235. Geiger counters stood by, clicking steadily, and a recorder and backups were ready to preserve the results of the test. An engineer stood beside the Guillotine, ready to process the data on a log-log decitrig slide rule.

Frisch started the count. "Five."

All other work in the laboratory had stopped. Everyone was watching the Guillotine.

"Four."

The Lady Godiva nearest to the Guillotine was barely subcritical. The scientist building it moved closer to the stack as Frisch continued to count.

"Three."

The hydrogen in that scientist's body began to reflect back neutrons.

"Two."

Almost instantly, the flickering monitoring lamps that detected neutron activity went to nearly solid red. The Geiger counters clattered so fast the noise became a buzz. The temperature of the Lady Godiva began to rise. Out of the corner of his eye, the scientist noticed the change. He turned, his arm swinging, to knock blocks away and make the stack subcritical again.

"One."

He hit the stack with too much force, knocking a cascade of uranium bars in the direction of the Guillotine. "Shit!"

"Drop—wait!"

The technician holding the chain turned to see the blocks falling in his direction, skidding across the floor. He let go of the chain.

The mass of U 235 dropped, but still chained, not free. The clatter of the chain made the technician turn back.

He grabbed the chain.

The core stopped in the center hole.

The lab technician released the load.

Warning lights turned red. Geiger counters hissed like demonic serpents.

The technician yanked on the chain with all his strength. The chain came off its pulley. The critical U 235 was stuck.

"Dammit!" Frisch jumped forward to dislodge the falling U 235 from the stationary mass.

The neutron count passed 10^{20}. The temperature of the critical mass was rising two degrees per millisecond. Frisch burst into flames.

Fires erupted all over the lab. Feynman, his lab coat burning, ran for the corridor door across the room from the Guillotine, which was now a molten mass. Oppenheimer was right behind him, feeling the searing heat against his back, seeing his own stark shadow in the terrifically brilliant light of the reacting uranium.

"Unnatural work produces too much stress," Oppenheimer said. Feynman, not a student of Hinduism, didn't recognize the passage from the Bhagavad Gita.

As the U 235 passed the ten thousand-degree mark, he didn't have time to ask.

• THURSDAY, 7 SEPTEMBER 1944 •

BILIBID PRISON, MANILA, PHILIPPINES, 0600 HOURS

"Me ga sameru!" The guard banged on the metal door of Johnny's cell, shared with four other prisoners, and shouted at them to wake up. Johnny opened his eyes slowly. He ached from the long night on the bare cell floor, from the constant hunger, from his swollen testicles. It was cold inside the cell at night, and dew had formed on the slimy walls. He still didn't own a blanket.

In the dim light from the single small rectangular slit window he could see his cell mates stirring as well. All five men rose slowly and awkwardly to their feet. They did not talk. There was nothing new to say.

They had all heard the rumors, of course, spread by the Filipinos who worked in and around the prison. MacArthur was on Luzon! His armies had landed at Lingayen Gulf, the same place the Japs had come ashore in '41. To the prisoners,

Lingayen Gulf was still a long way away from here, from Manila. And by all accounts there were hundreds of thousands of Japanese soldiers in between the two places.

Johnny pushed the heavy metal cell door open. The Japanese never bothered to lock them in.

Normally in Bilibid Prison the daily muster was pretty informal, but today the guards were making the companies line up in formation and at attention. This was never good news, if only because it delayed the meager rice soup they called breakfast.

The Japanese captain in charge of the prison walked into the courtyard after all the men had lined up. He was carrying a clipboard. Behind him marched his translator and two officers Johnny hadn't seen previously.

The guards had set up a small wooden box as a speaker's platform. The captain stepped up onto the box and looked coldly at the prisoners. They bowed in unison. There was a penalty for failing to bow. No one wanted to pay the penalty twice.

The captain began to speak in Japanese, pausing after each sentence for the translation. "Attention to orders. Companies One through Five will follow Lieutenant Sato. Companies Six through Ten will follow Lieutenant Watanabe. The others will remain in position until these ten companies have departed. That is all." The prisoners bowed again. The captain stepped off the box and strode out of the courtyard. The translator stayed behind to help the two lieutenants line up their companies.

Johnny stepped out in front along with Sergeant Owens. As captain, he gave orders only to Sergeant Owens, who in turn shouted them to the men. "Attention! At ease, march!" The "at ease, march" order meant the men didn't have to maintain cadence but did have to maintain proper interval and distance. The prisoners marched sloppily even by that loose standard. As they paraded past, Johnny noticed many of them had the hundred-yard stare, that glassy-eyed dead look of a man who had surrendered hope.

Johnny suspected his own eyes looked the same.

They marched out of the courtyard, through the long dimly lit corridor lined with cells, then into an outer perimeter courtyard. In front of them, the great trellis gate opened with the creaking sound of worn machinery, and Johnny passed out of Bilibid Prison.

The procession marched through the streets of Manila. Filipinos bowed respectfully, ostensibly to their Japanese masters, but angled so their bows aimed instead to the prisoners. The only thing the men of his company were leaving in Bilibid Prison was breakfast. Johnny could smell food—real food—cooking. His mouth salivated and his stomach rumbled. The thought of eating real food was so overwhelming that he had to resist the temptation to break ranks and follow the spicy scents of Philippine cooking, even if that meant his death. It was the first emotion he'd felt in days.

Lieutenant Sato gave directional commands to Company One's commander, and Johnny's Company Three simply followed. A Japanese sergeant supervised his company but did nothing except look menacing. It took about an hour of marching to reach Manila Harbor. The harbor was crowded with ships, but Johnny had no idea whether that was normal. All he sensed was the scent of sea air and the stink of rotting fish. Even rotting fish smelled appetizing.

Two ferries were tied up against a long pier. The companies marched onto the pier and stopped. With some shouting and pushing, the Japanese filled the ferries to the point of overcrowding with the first two companies. The remaining three companies stood on the pier and watched the ferries steam toward one of the larger ships. They could see the prisoners disembark, and within half an hour the ferries were on the way back.

Johnny had been at attention for a long time, and he was feeling faint. Several men had collapsed. The Japanese, unusual for them, didn't beat or kick the fallen men but simply let them alone. Johnny thought about feigning a faint just to get some rest but didn't do it. He was the captain.

The ferries returned, and it was time for Companies Three and Four to board. With gestures, the Japanese indicated the prisoners were to carry the collapsed men with them. Johnny's ferry was crowded with the two hundred men of his company. He made sure the seats went to the men who needed them most, and he stood.

Again the ferries returned to the large steamship in the harbor. Johnny could make out its name: *Noto Maru*. The ferry pulled up alongside a gangplank, and in response to more Japanese orders, the men marched aboard. The ship, a large cargo vessel, seemed spacious enough. But their destination, he soon learned, was the hold below. The first two companies were already inside. It was hot inside— suffocatingly hot.

Companies Three and Four made it a very tight fit. Company Five would make it unbearable.

The Japanese closed the hatch. Some light filtered through small openings in the hatch cover. After his eyes became adapted to the dark, he was able to get an idea of the space he was in. It was a large cargo hold, with the overhead deck about twenty feet above. The space was rectangular in shape. There was no bathroom; there was no water supply; there was nothing.

It was obvious they were being moved to secure facilities away from the Americans. Maybe Formosa, maybe Okinawa, Johnny thought. Or maybe Japan.

Johnny reached into the rag he called a shirt and pulled out the many sets of dog tags he was wearing. He looked at them. One set was his. One had belonged to Max Kellerman, a man he had never known. Johnny had carried those tags for more than a year. A third he had had since 1942. They were engraved with the identification of a man who had become his friend . . . the pilot who never had a plane. He could barely read the name on that one in the dim light: David Hansen.

David . . . I'm glad you missed this part, Johnny thought, looking at the dog tags.

The hatch clanged shut above him. The diesel engines churned, and the ship moved toward the open sea.

• FRIDAY, 17 NOVEMBER 1944 •

GINZA DISTRICT, TOKYO, JAPAN, 2120 HOURS

The taxi stopped, and a short man wearing civilian clothes and a white gauze mask got out. The white gauze mask was not unusual. Most often, such a mask indicated that the wearer had a cold—but this man was very healthy. The civilian clothes were more unusual, because his hair was military short. His eyes were expressive and warm. His posture was slightly stooped. The middle and index fingers of his left hand were missing.

In his right hand, he carried a rolled-up copy of *Asahi Shimbun*. The most important news story of the day was buried in a one-column story below the fold on the front page:

NAVAL DEFENSE FORCES LUZON JOIN GENERAL YAMASHITA IN BAGUIO CITY

One had to understand the situation to appreciate the beauty of that headline. The "Naval Defense Forces Luzon" was actually the Manila Naval Defense Force. For a month, they had fought savagely house-to-house in Manila against the Americans, killing huge numbers of Filipinos in the process. Their ragtag remnants, those who did not manage to die gloriously for the emperor, had finally withdrawn and joined Yamashita's army, also in retreat. It was bad news, even if only a few could understand just how bad.

The entrance to the Nakamura-ya *okiya,* or geisha house, was plain and unmarked. The man entered through the street door, walked down a short, dark corridor, and slid open a second door to find himself in a tasteful and elegant room. The floor was dark, polished wood, the walls were screens with images of cranes, a pagoda, and elegant, long-limbed trees.

A coiffed and elaborately dressed geisha bowed. She was an "older sister," a middle-aged woman whose waist had thickened and whose features were no longer as delicate as a china teacup, but her artistry was of the highest quality. This was her establishment, and she was an old and dear friend to the man in the gauze mask.

"Koben-wa," she said. Good evening. "Eighty-sen, how wonderful to see you! It has been such a very long time. Will you have time for a game of mah-jongg when your business is concluded?" It was an old tradition between the two. The man called Eighty-sen loved to gamble and spent many hours and many yen in geisha houses playing games of chance.

The man bowed courteously in return. "Ah, Toshiko, nothing would give me more pleasure. If only I could quit the navy and become a professional mah-jongg player, my life would be perfect. I would see you every day."

Toshiko laughed. It was a high-pitched, pretty sound. "And what would your Chiyoko say?"

"As long as it was only mah-jongg . . . ," replied Eighty-sen and laughed as well. "Has my guest arrived?"

"Yes. He is in a private room, and Umeryu is taking care of him. She was always the best—except for me, of course—until you stole her away. So tonight she is coming out of retirement, just for this. I'll walk you across as soon as you change."

Eighty-sen stepped into a small booth, pulled the privacy curtain shut, and removed his shoes, coat, shirt, and trousers. He left his white mask on. A kimono, plain in design but well made, clean white socks, and woven sandals had been laid out for him. All were in his size. He dressed quickly, then pulled the curtain back and emerged.

A small courtyard was all that separated the Nakamura-ya from the Umenojima, and that was deliberate. Kawai Chiyoko, whose geisha name was Umeryu, or Plum Dragon, established her own geisha house right behind the *okiya* where she had been working. And when Chiyoko retired, Furukawa Toshiko of Nakamura-ya acquired a second establishment. This could be particularly useful when private

meetings had to be arranged, because each party could take
a separate route and enter a separate way.

The courtyard was a Japanese garden, exquisitely laid out
and maintained. A *cha yo nu* house for performing the tea
ceremony, barely large enough for two people, overlooked a
small pond. A wooden bridge crossed the pond. Tonight, a
gibbous moon was reflected in the still water. In less hectic
times, the man called Eighty-sen had spent many happy
hours in that garden. He knew it well.

On the Umenojima side, four sliding doors made of paper
and wood faced the small courtyard garden. All were closed.
Toshiko stopped before the fourth and last of them. She
bowed again. *"Mata omeni kakaritai to omoi masu,"* she said.
I hope to see you again. She slid open the door and he walked
inside. The door eased silently shut behind him.

The private banquet room formed a rectangle about
twelve feet wide. The far wall, which was another sliding
door identical to the one that led to the garden, was about fifteen feet in front of him. Wainscoting of cherrywood covered the two sides to waist height. The upper portion of the
walls was painted white. A square wooden table in the center
was surrounded by cushions. A man in a similarly plain kimono sipped tea and ate salty edamame from a bowl. He was
not wearing a mask.

The geisha, Umeryu, was breathtakingly beautiful. It had
been a long time since she had taken on her professional
identity. It was the reason Eighty-sen had first fallen in love
with her.

Eighty-sen removed his mask. He was a handsome man.
His bones had an almost feminine delicacy about them. His
lips were full. His expression was slightly melancholy.

"Koben-wa, hachiju-sen-san," the geisha said, her melodious voice a delight. Her bow was low, languid, and highly
erotic.

"Koben-wa, Umeryu-chan," he said, bowing. He turned to
the other man and bowed more deeply. *"Koben-wa, Kido-
sama."*

"Good evening to you as well, Admiral," the Marquis Kido replied. "May I ask, how did you acquire the nickname Eighty-sen? It seems a little cheap for the admiral of the Combined Fleet."

Admiral Yamamoto Isoroku held up his three-fingered left hand and nodded at Umeryu. The geisha tittered, holding her fingers to her brightly painted mouth. "In the Shimbashi, the regular charge for a geisha manicure is one yen," she said in her melodious voice. "But that is for all ten fingers. The admiral gets a discount."

The emperor's lord privy seal roared with laughter. "He pays only eighty sen because he's missing two fingers!"

Yamamoto, laughing as well, joined in. It was a mark of honor and respect to be given a nickname by geisha. And it was also convenient to have a private identity so he could escape into the Floating World without the nuisance of prying eyes.

The two men exchanged pleasantries as Umeryu prepared skewers of yakitori on a small grill and kept both men's teacups full. This was a private business meeting, not an entertainment, and besides, Yamamoto didn't drink.

"I am honored," Kido said, "that you have entrusted me with your secret name. If this evening's meeting yields the need for further contact, may I use that name when I need to see you privately?"

"As my lord wishes," Yamamoto said. "I am at your service in all things, and you do me an undeserved honor by your presence."

"On the contrary," Kido replied. "It is I who am grateful for your masterful handling of events, your loyalty and service to the empire, and the burdens of work and danger you shoulder so ably. It is a privilege to be permitted to share this evening with you."

The warm, comfortable rhythm of compliments given and refused put both men at ease. This was how civilized men dealt with difficult and sensitive issues. It could be painful to deal with cultures that insisted every emotion be expressed in the rudest, bluntest, crudest way possible.

In the fullness of time, the conversation turned to the subject of the meeting. It was the marquis who opened. "His Imperial Majesty has asked me to obtain opinions as to the current strategic situation from more sources than just those that go into the official report. He would like to know, for example, more about those elements in the war that are not necessarily developing to His Majesty's advantage. When decisions are reached, they must be good decisions. I'm sure you would agree, Admiral."

Yamamoto scratched his nearly bald skull. His liquid brown eyes seemed softer and sadder than expected from the admiral who had conceived of the attack on Pearl Harbor, who had won the battle of Midway, who had done so much for his nation and his Emperor.

"So sorry, Lord Kido, but I do not entirely share your view. It is my observation that leaders exist for the primary purpose of making *bad* decisions."

Kido frowned. "Is that a joke, Admiral? I must confess I don't understand the humor. And I'm certain you did not mean to suggest that the Emperor's decisions might be in some way faulty."

Yamamoto smiled. "I'm quite serious. A good decision implies that for a problem, there exists a good choice. That is how my unworthy mind perceives it, at any rate. Good choices, in that sense, are easy. But what happens when all the choices are less than ideal? What if they are unpleasant, or inelegant, or contain high risk, or carry the certainty of secondary problems? Such decisions cannot be labeled 'good,' yet they are more difficult and more challenging to make. Thus, they are reserved for those of higher rank and position. The worse the problem, the higher is he who must decide."

Kido nodded. "I see. A novel outlook. If I understand correctly, you would argue that 'bad' decision making is a skill superior to 'good' decision making."

Yamamoto smiled. "My lord understands. The leader who believes he must always make a 'good' decision may fall into self-deception. He cannot accept the lack of a good choice, so he creates an illusion for himself. He makes a decision based upon the illusion. That cannot help. It will, in all likelihood, make the situation worse."

Kido nodded. "I can see that. The true leader must above all see clearly. For example, what might a true leader do if there were a need for a decision on continuing the struggle or . . . ah . . . pursuing the alternative. . . ."

Even in such a private setting, broaching the ticklish subject of a possible end to the war carried risks. Yamamoto appreciated the indirectness of the lord privy seal's approach. "An insightful example," Yamamoto replied. He paused to consider his wording carefully. "As elements of the conflict have not necessarily evolved in the manner preferred or intended in all cases, continuation carries a wide set of risks and problems. The alternative is, of course, unthinkable." He stopped, laid the copy of *Asahi Shimbun* on the low table, and quietly sipped his tea.

"The Americans are proving to be a very impressive foe," commented the marquis, looking at the paper and nodding. "Yamashita's men are still battling valiantly for the Philippines, and yet the enemy has the strength to strike close to our home."

"Ah, Okinawa," Yamamoto agreed with a solemn nod. "It has been home to Japanese people for a very long time. When MacArthur's armies landed there, I confess I felt it as a blow to my very soul. And now that he holds those great airfields, our Home Islands come into range of his fighters. The situation is grave."

"But the battle for Okinawa is not yet over, is it?" Kido queried. "I understand that our strongest defenses are in the mountainous south of the island. Surely many Americans will perish in the effort to take that ground?"

"*If* they try to take it," the admiral cautioned. "I am not sure that MacArthur will do that."

Umeryu rose gracefully to her feet and minced to the garden door. She slid it open, then came back to sit on her knees again. The two men turned to look at the exquisite small garden, and there was quiet for a while. Without turning away from the view, Kido asked, "In the practice of *zazen* meditation, are people not taught to 'think the unthinkable'? How is that done, Admiral?"

How beautifully indirect, Yamamoto thought. "I am ashamed to say that I have only the most passing of acquaintances with *zazen*. But thinking about the unthinkable is good practice for the military mind. Battle has a way of upsetting one's plans and expectations."

"I am curious, and would benefit greatly from your notable insight and genius. Can you elaborate on this process?"

"Me? Not a genius, surely, but merely a struggling warrior whose poor intellect, such as it is, is in the Emperor's service. I can't imagine my sparse knowledge will be of any special benefit, but if it is your pleasure . . ."

"I would be indebted to hear your insights," the lord privy seal said.

The proprieties having been satisfied, Yamamoto took another sip of tea. Both men having established their positions indirectly, they could now speak more directly to the issue at hand. "The first question is, 'Should the unthinkable be contemplated?' As reasonable alternatives have not yet been exhausted, the unthinkable is premature."

"Do you think *Ketsu-Go* is a 'reasonable alternative'?" asked Kido. "That is, if the Americans try to land on our Home Islands? You are a wise man. If, as contemplated, we sacrifice twenty million of the Emperor's subjects in *tokko* attacks, will it bring the Americans to the negotiating table?"

"The Americans would indeed come to the negotiating table. I know them that well." Yamamoto had lived in the United States for six years. "But it will not take twenty million to achieve this—as long as the Americans *believe* that we are willing to make this sacrifice."

Kido nodded. "That is so."

"But there is more to *Ketsu-Go* than that," Yamamoto continued. "If the Americans attack Kyushu and face unacceptable casualties, for example, the equation changes. That is why I believe the time for considering unthinkable options is not yet upon us."

Yamamoto took another sip of tea. "There is, of course, an alternative outcome, and that is that *Ketsu-Go* achieves an outcome less desirable than anticipated. Of course, this is highly unlikely. But if it should develop, it would be useful for those who would be burdened with such a terrible choice to have established a procedure among themselves for determining when or if the time has arrived."

"A procedure. Without, at this time, action to bring it about," Kido repeated. "I see. In doing so, we preserve our options and attempt to bring about the best outcome still possible."

" 'When it is not necessary to make a decision, it is necessary not to make a decision.' That is an English proverb but a very Japanese sentiment, I think. That is my humble opinion," said Yamamoto.

"Wise words."

Umeryu refilled Kido's tea. He drank and contemplated for a while. Then he continued. "As I was certain they would be. Your insights truly illuminate the most difficult of decisions."

"You are much too kind, Marquis Kido," Yamamoto replied. "You do me honor far above my poor and limited abilities."

"It was you, was it not, who suggested that the first major onslaught of aerial *tokko* be held back from the Okinawa defense and brought out in full when the Allies attack the Home Islands."

"That was my poor and unworthy suggestion," agreed Yamamoto. "To fight the decisive battle and achieve the *Ketsu-Go* objectives, the Allies must be lured into a major commitment of force against the Home Islands. If we are too successful in demonstrating our will to win, the Allies may not allow us to engage in the decisive battle at all. For example, MacArthur successfully resisted the temptation to take the whole of Okinawa. He merely took the half of the island with the airfields in order to use them against the Home Islands. The mountains in the south of Okinawa make strong defensive positions, but there is nothing to defend if the enemy does not attack. We hurl ourselves at MacArthur's fortified positions, but the enemy has the defender's advantage. If he had been unwise enough to attempt to take all of Okinawa, he might have been tempted to avoid a decisive battle altogether." He sipped his tea before continuing.

"If we make the battle appear too costly, they will not face us directly. Instead, they will blockade us, bomb us, and starve us. And we will eventually submit or we will die. We must, therefore, lure them into a fight and give *Ketsu-Go* its chance."

The two men settled into a comfortable, masculine silence and watched the gibbous moon's reflection move slowly across the wind-rippled surface of the garden's pond.

Yamamoto said, "This moon reminds me of my service with the naval attaché's office in Washington. I wrote a poem about it."

"May I hear it, Admiral?"

"It is a poor and clumsy construct, not worth your time."

"You are too modest, Admiral. I insist."

"Very well, but again you do me too much honor." Yamamoto bowed his head for a moment, and then recited from memory.

> "Tonight again
> The moonlight is pure
> And pellucid:
> It calls to mind
> My distant home."

Kido was silent as he contemplated the poem. Then he observed, "The same moon shines over the enemy's capital and ours, and reflects with equal beauty in the water."

"That is true, Kido-sama."

"Tell me, Admiral, have you considered returning to the political side, say, in a cabinet-level position?"

Yamamoto continued to look at the moon in the pond. "I could never be worthy of such an honor," he said quietly.

"It pains me to disagree with you, Admiral, but the Emperor

would benefit from your service in a higher role. He is known to have suggested that you would perform admirably as war minister."

"All my duty belongs to the Emperor," demurred Yamamoto.

"We will speak further," Kido said. He got to his feet.

Yamamoto stood as well. "As my lord wishes," replied the admiral, and the men bowed to one another.

As the lord privy seal departed, Umeryu slid the doors at either end of the room shut. Yamamoto sat down at the small table, thinking. Umeryu knelt behind the admiral. She began to massage his shoulders.

TWELVE

Okinawa; Japan

• SATURDAY, 30 DECEMBER 1944 •

OKINAWA, 1216 HOURS

The lead B-24 Liberator four-engine heavy bomber had a nose art design of interlocking rings with graduated marks around the circumference, over which was painted a skimpily clad woman wearing a colander-shaped helmet with wires dangling from it. Wavy lines of power and energy radiated from the helmet. Below the design was the name: *The Skylark of Valeron,* the fourth plane to bear the *Skylark* name. The *Valeron* was lead plane in the squadron formation, and Colonel Ellis Halverson was in command.

He activated his throat microphone. "Osnome One to Osnome Flight. We're getting in range now. Look alive, everybody." The Japanese forces on Okinawa had been contained but not wiped out. Every once in a while, a few Jap fighters would surprise a careless or unobservant American. Ellis wasn't about to let that happen to his men.

For hours, the flight had been cruising above the Ryukyu island chain, and now the largest of the Ryukyus, Okinawa, was in sight. Okinawa was about sixty miles long, with a narrow waist only about two miles wide. Most of the population lived in the southern portion of the island, where the two major cities, Naha and Shuri, were located. That part of Okinawa was still in Japanese hands, despite the pleas of the Tenth Army commander, General Simon Bolivar Buckner Jr., that he be allowed to root the enemy out of their trenches and blockhouses. "Let them rot," MacArthur was reputed to have said when he denied his aggressive army commander's request.

Tenth Army was now headquartered in the town of Hagushi, and it was toward nearby Yantan air base that Ellis was leading his flight. It was good to get back in the cockpit again. Over the past three years, Ellis had gone from being a pilot and aircraft commander to a teacher of skip-bombing tactics, then to squadron leader, group commander, deputy wing commander, and now as CO of what was currently VII Bomber Command, Okinawa.

Ellis called military air traffic control, arranged landing clearance, and led his flight down. A few feet away from wheels down, he pulled up the nose to level the plane and throttled down. The *Valeron* touched down on the main gear, the nosewheel settling so smoothly you could hardly feel the bump. He turned off the active taxiway and followed the flagman's signals. Beside him, the other planes lined up one by one.

As Ellis exited the plane, he saw a big sign painted on the hangar. It was a version of the Texaco star, and over it was written "337th Air Services Group/You Can Trust Your Crate to the Crew That's Always Great!" He chuckled.

There was a parked jeep right outside the fence. An officer got out of it and walked through the gate and toward Ellis. He was a medium-sized man with his sandy blond hair in a crew cut. "Colonel?" he said, coming to attention and saluting.

"I'm Captain Greer, VII Bomber Command Headquarters Squadron. I'm your adjutant."

Ellis returned the salute. "Glad to meet you, Greer. We're going to have a lot to do over the next month or so, and I'm looking forward to having you bring me up to speed. I've brought us another squadron, by the way. There'll be more."

"Thank you, sir. I've made an appointment for you to meet General Buckner—he's in charge of all of Tenth Army, which means just about everything on Okinawa—and of course General Mulcahy, who runs all of Tactical Air."

"I know General Mulcahy already, but it'll be good to see him again. Good staff work, Captain. I appreciate it."

"Thanks for noticing, sir. Oh—and I got you a driver and a jeep, courtesy of the marines. Right this way—one of the men will grab your luggage." Greer led Ellis through the gate to the waiting jeep. The driver—a marine gunnery sergeant—was slouched in the seat, cap pulled down over his eyes, apparently sleeping. Greer cleared his throat loudly.

The marine sat up and lifted the cap off his forehead. He grinned as he saluted. Instead of returning the salute, Ellis yelled, "Son of a *bitch*!" and gave the marine a hug.

It was his old friend Pete. "How the hell are you, Ellis—I mean, Colonel?" Rachwalski said.

"Great! Better now that I see you. How did you get this assignment? I mean, a marine gunny normally doesn't do driver duty."

"Thank your adjutant here. He did a little digging around, passed the word to see if anyone knew you, and I happened to be taking a little I & I. It all worked out." Rest and Recreation (R & R) was also known to the troops as Intoxication and Intercourse.

Ellis turned to Greer with a big smile. "Captain, this is one of the finest pieces of sucking up I have ever experienced in this man's army. I am seriously impressed. Write yourself up for a commendation and I'll sign it." First-rate dog robbers were hard to come by, and Ellis felt extremely fortunate to have one on his team.

"Why, thank you, Colonel. I hoped you'd appreciate it," Greer replied.

Although there was nothing Ellis wanted to do more than catch up with Pete, duty called. His jeep stopped in front of his new headquarters, a small warehouse that had been hastily converted to offices. Greer held the door for him as he walked in. "I got you the office with the window," he said.

Ellis said. "Remind me to promote you, Greer, as long as it's not to a rank that means you have to go somewhere else."

Ellis barely had time to hang up his flight jacket before Greer was pulling him along to his first meeting. The improvised conference room still smelled of slightly overripe vegetables. The single bare lightbulb hanging over the "conference table"—a sheet of plywood resting on cinder blocks—had an annoying tendency to sway back and forth every time a truck drove by, which was often.

"Colonel, these are your group commanders," Greer said. Five men stood.

"I feel like it's old home week," Ellis said. "I've flown alongside the 41st many times, and as for the 38th—well, I knew them back when they were still 7th Air Force. I flew with 69th Squadron off Midway Island. It was a damn shame about Captain Collins." His old commander had bought it during the Guadalcanal campaign.

The 41st and 38th Bomb Groups (Medium) both flew B-25 Mitchells. The 41st had always flown the B-25. They were the group that flew the Tokyo Raid in 1942 under the command of Jimmy Doolittle. Their current CO was Harry Durrance. The 38th had been a B-26 group originally. The B-26, sadly for Ellis, had been phased completely out of the Pacific Theater. Don Hall was in command.

"As for the 494th, I understand that Okinawa has been the first major action for 'Kelley's Kobras,' right?"

Larry Kelley nodded. "That's right. But not the last."

"And Russ"—Ellis shook the hand of Russell Waldron, commander of the 11th, "it's good to be part of the mighty Grey Geese again." The two heavy bomb groups, with a total of eight squadrons, flew B-24 Liberators. Ellis had commanded the 11th for about six months when it was just converting to Liberators from the older B-17s.

"But most important, of course, is this man," Ellis said, shaking the hand of the commander of the 13th Air Services Group, whom he hadn't met before. "Without him, we all stay on the ground."

"Damn right," said the group commander, grinning as he shook Ellis's hand. "And don't you ever forget it! The name's John Connelly, boss. This place is a nuthouse, but you get used to it."

With Greer running his headquarters squadron, his team was complete. Ellis was very pleased. It looked like he had top-notch people working for him, and it was a whole lot easier being in charge when you had good people you could trust. Ellis sat down, and his commanders followed suit.

"General Kenney sends his compliments, which will follow in writing shortly. Excellent work. You made 5th Air Force proud," Ellis said.

"Does that mean we get to go home now?" Connelly joked.

"I wish. But as they say, the way home runs right through downtown Tokyo, and the faster we get that over with, the faster we all get to go home. You've done a great job on the Okinawa mission, but it's mostly over. There may be some additional missions you'll be flying to support Tenth Army, but basically Operation Iceberg is over."

"We're just going to let the Japs sit at the south end of the island?" Russ, the commander of the 11th Bomb Group (Heavy) asked.

"Yep. Why not? We've let them sit on islands all over the Pacific. And the terrain in the southern half of this island is hell: rock ridges, valleys, miles of fortifications. Mac himself is the one who said we should just let them rot there. As long as they can't bother anybody too much, they might as well be dead for all the support they'll give Hirohito."

"Right," Connelly said. "I met an Aussie colonel yesterday who says that his division, and two more from down under, are going to sit on those lines until the Japs come out, or the war ends. He wasn't too happy about it, either—says his men have been getting the short end of the stick all over the Pacific, while Mac and 'his' marines get all the headlines."

"True enough," Ellis said with a shrug. "But either way, fewer of our boys get killed. Besides, what do we need this island for, when it comes down to it?"

"Airfields," said Bob.

"Airfields," agreed Ellis. "We've got them. And now we've got to start planning for the next phase, which is called Operation Olympic. We'll be flying tactical support for the invasion of Kyushu. Here's problem one: this is VII Bomber Command, but it's really a slightly overstrength bomber wing. We need at least three wings, so we're going to be bringing in a whole lot of people and planes and getting them to work together. And we don't have a lot of time.

"We've got three air forces in the Pacific Theater now. There's us, 5th Air Force. We're the tactical specialists. We're supporting the invasion, all phases. There's the new 20th Air Force. They're strategic, built around the new B-29s."

"Don't they have that new general from Europe?" asked Bob.

"That's right. Curtis LeMay is his name. Eats nails for breakfast, I understand."

"Is he under Kenney?"

"Nope," Ellis replied. "He's equal to General Kenney but subordinate to General MacArthur."

"How about 13th Air Force?" Russ asked.

"They're responsible for air transportation, convoys, and whatever minor missions are left over. We're stripping away a lot of their units for 5th Air Force."

"Which means they end up a vacation resort, just like 7th Air Force," the commander of the 38th chimed in. The 7th, reporting to Admiral Frank Fletcher in Hawaii, had nothing to do but escort and shipping duties. It was comparatively easy duty, and the other aviators tended to make semiresentful fun of them.

"Pretty much. So, problem two: the fastest way to get everybody together is going to be to swap some squadrons around, and maybe even some officers. I know that's not pleasant to contemplate—" A chorus of groans had already started. "But we have to do what we have to do." Ellis stood up and looked at his team. "I know you'll do what's necessary."

Halverson's meeting with General Buckner, commander of Tenth Army, was a quick courtesy call, consisting of a handshake, a welcome, and a dismissal. More substantive was his meeting with General Mulcahy. Mulcahy was a two-star marine general whom Ellis had met when Mulcahy commanded all marine aviation on Guadalcanal. He was a gruff man and often quite demanding, but Ellis felt he could get along well enough with him. Mulcahy, however, had been more concerned with the battle for Okinawa than for any preplanning for Kyushu, so Ellis ended up briefing him more than he got briefed in return.

When he finally felt he could take a breather, he got Pete to drive him first to the PX for some liquor, and then to his new quarters, which were in the only hotel in Hagushi. "Come in for a drink. I'd take you to the O Club if I could, but you know the rules."

"Yeah, I know," Pete replied. "No worries, mate. Uh, sorry. Been hanging out with Aussies too much." Ellis laughed.

The hotel was Japanese in style. Ellis got a room about ten feet square, with a futon on the floor, a small dresser for his stuff, and thin paper screens that afforded little privacy by American standards. The two men sat cross-legged on the floor. Ellis unwrapped the package of Dixie cups he'd bought at the PX, put out one for each of them, and poured them full of scotch. He lifted his paper cup. "To Johnny."

"To Johnny." They drank.

Ellis crumpled up his paper cup and threw it at the screen door. "God*dammit!*"

"What?"

"I just missed him. I *just* missed him."

"Johnny?"

"Yeah. In the Philippines. I was there when they liberated the first camps. I found out Johnny had been moved to Manila. When we got into Manila, I managed to get in with the first units and I was there when they broke into Bilibid Prison. There were men there, but Johnny had been taken away days before. *Days!*" His eyes were wet.

"Damn." Pete was quiet. "Damn. That means he got shipped to Japan, right?"

"Yeah. On a ship without Red Cross markings. Which means we might have torpedoed it."

"You don't know? Have you been able to find out anything?" Pete quietly took out another Dixie cup, filled it full of scotch again, and handed it to Ellis. Ellis downed it in a gulp. Pete poured a third but didn't hand it over immediately.

"Nothing. I haven't been able to find out a thing. The Japs don't care if they furnish the information or not. Every once in a while a list of names comes through, but it's so old you don't know whether those people are alive or not." Ellis put his face in his hands. He felt Pete's hand on his shoulder.

"It's too bad you're not flying the real *Skylark of Valeron*," Pete said. "You could simply go get him."

Ellis lifted his head. "Hell, with the real *Valeron*, I could whip Japan and be back before dawn." He grinned. His eyes were wet. "I think about him all the time."

"So do I," said Pete. "It isn't the same without him. I hope he makes it through so the Three Skylarks are still a team when the war's over."

Ellis shook his head. "You landed here."

"I did, but strangely enough, this turned out to be a cake-walk. It was two weeks before we blundered into any major Jap positions, and then instead of fighting, we decided to hell with it."

"Kyushu won't be like that. I presume you're scheduled."

"Yeah. And you're the boss, but I'll bet you'll be flying at least some of the missions."

"I have to. It's part of command."

"Well, considering the situation, there's *two* ways we could all reunite . . . ," Pete said.

Ellis raised his eyebrows. "Now *that's* a positive outlook on things."

Pete laughed. "Ah, hell. We can't do anything except our best. No, that sounds too sappy. Let's drink to Lady Luck, okay? And maybe to getting to Worldcon in '45?"

Ellis hoisted his cup. "To Lady Luck—and an end to this goddamn war!"

CAMP SHINJUKU, TOKYO, JAPAN, 0145 HOURS

The hold was packed solid with men and filth and vomit. Outside, explosions rocked the ship, each blast closer than the last. The concussions threw men against each other, crushing those closest to the wall. Prisoners screamed and wept in the utter darkness. They hammered on the unyielding hatch and begged the Japanese to unlock the hold and let them out. The bodies of the dead were trampled, and the sick and incapacitated were likewise trampled until they were dead.

As always, the Japanese had other concerns. The prisoners meant nothing to them. They'd proved that time and again.

Another explosion, much louder and closer than the others, shook the transport. Metal shrieked in protest and the ship slammed sideways like a child's toy smacked by a baseball bat. The vessel heeled over nearly ninety degrees, turning bulkhead into deck and deck into bulkhead. Men tumbled and fell into one another in the darkness, then tumbled once again as the ship righted itself. Cries of pain added to the cacophony. Airplanes, engines whining, roared past the stricken ship.

"Our own fucking planes are trying to sink us!" someone screamed.

It was too much for Andy Sarnuss. He joined in, screaming, "Stop it! Stop it! Stop it!" until the words stopped making sense to him. He was going to die. He knew he was going to die. He was helpless, trapped like a rat in a cage—it was a POW ship, but it was marked as any other Japanese freighter, and now it was a sitting duck for American planes. He looked desperately at the bolted hatch atop the metal ladder. There must be a hundred men in front of Andy, all massed together. It would take them forever to get through the hatch, even if it were somehow, miraculously, opened.

A second torpedo hit the transport and the ship seemed to groan in physical pain. This time the blast lifted the ship into the air, then dropped it roughly back into the sea. It slammed down and continued to sink.

Then came a new sound: rushing water. The sound came from behind Andy. The metal bulkhead creaked and buckled, admitted a gush of cold seawater with force like a fire hydrant unleashed. It surged around his feet, climbing to his ankles, chilling his calves.

"Don't let me die in the dark!" came another scream from a voice almost childlike. "Please don't let me die in the dark!"

Only vaguely did Andy realize that the sound was coming out of his own mouth.

The burst of water grew into a torrent, white froth churning angrily into the compartment, picking men up, tossing them out of its path. The bulkhead a few yards behind Andy continued to give way. Cold seawater gushed into the hold, now swirling around Andy's knees, icy fingers reaching higher and higher. The shriek of bending and breaking metal and the roar of rushing water drowned out the screams and cries. In the meantime, the deck angled downward, toward the breach, as the ship canted unevenly toward the depths. They were all going to drown.

The hatch to their watery tomb tore away, and blazing light cut into the darkness like jagged glass. It was a flickering, dancing light. Fire. The ship was on fire.

Although the ladder leading to the hatch was only ten yards away, it might have been a mile. Hundreds of desperate, screaming men blocked his way. They fought for places on the ladder, tore each other away from the rungs, they pushed and shoved and fought. The water continued to rush in from behind Andy, rising past his waist.

"Take turns! One at a time! It's faster that way!" Andy screamed. No one listened.

He was too far back. Others might get out in time, but not he. Andy felt the rising waters climb his gaunt body, now reaching his chest. He screamed, but his cry was drowned out by the panicked begging of hundreds of others.

The area around the hatch was on fire now, making further escape impossible, even if Andy could get through the mob. As the fire ate through the deck, the opening grew. Andy saw glimpses of the chaos above. Fires raged across the deck, silhouetting cranes and winches and on-deck cargo. Andy saw running, shouting Japanese seamen, some of them human torches, screaming their last as they plunged into the cold seawater to extinguish everything.

The water was rising. It was up to his neck. It was swallowing his head. He couldn't breathe. In a minute, he would open his mouth and the water would rush inside and . . .

Andy woke up.

Something was on his face—someone's hand covering his mouth! He couldn't breathe. He flailed around and more hands—several pairs of hands—grabbed his arms and legs and held them down.

It was still dark, as dark as it had been in the hold, but this was not a ship, it was . . .

It was Japan.

He remembered where he was: Barracks #6, Camp Shinjuku, on the outskirts of Tokyo. He was still a prisoner of the Japanese. *I didn't* drown in the hold of the *Arisan Maru. I survived.* His body sagged with relief. As it did, the hands released him, including the hand stifling his mouth.

"Another bad one, Andy?" That was Mark, with a voice graveled by too many cigarettes.

Andy's heart was pounding and he gulped in huge breaths of air. He was covered in sweat. "I was back in the hold . . . ," he managed to choke out.

Even in the darkness, he could sense reactions. People shifted position, they breathed differently. He wasn't the only one with nightmares of that hold.

"I had to put my hands over your mouth like that. You started screaming," Mark said apologetically. "Didn't want the Japs coming in to find out what the racket was all about." That would have resulted in beatings, or worse.

Andy nodded, dizzy from breathing hard. He didn't want the Japs in either. He was terrified of the Japs. He reached over and patted Mark's bony arm to signal his gratitude. It was another full minute before he was able to talk coherently.

"Same nightmare?" Mark asked.

"Same one," Andy replied. "But I'm all right now."

"You sure?" asked Mark.

"Yeah. Let's get some sleep. We all need it. Sorry to have woken everyone up."

"No problem."

"S'okay."

"Don't worry about it."

Voices in the dark.

Andy heard shuffling feet on the packed dirt floor feeling their way to nearby bunks, the rustle of rice husks in the burlap sacks used as mattresses as men climbed in. After a while, he heard steady breathing and the occasional snore. From outside the thin-walled barracks he could hear the wind.

After a while, he slept again. This time, the dreams were too deep to trouble his limbs, to provoke any audible outburst. He lay silent, still, panting.

And he was still in that hold.

Condition and Conquest

I knew that on every ship nervous men lined the rails or paced the decks, peering into the darkness and wondering what stood out there beyond the night waiting for the dawn to come. There is a universal sameness in the emotions of men, whether they be admiral or sailor, general or private, at such a time as this. On almost every ship one could count on seeing groups huddled around maps in the wardrooms, infantrymen nervously inspecting their rifles, the crew of their ships testing their gear, last-minute letters being written, men with special missions or objectives trying to visualize them again. . . . Late that evening I went back to my cabin and read again those [biblical] passages . . . from which I have always gained inspiration and hope. And I prayed that a merciful God would preserve each of those men on the morrow.

—General Douglas MacArthur

THIRTEEN

Okinawa; Tokyo; Hiroshima

CONFERENCE OF LANDING FORCE COMMANDERS,
FORWARD HEADQUARTERS, SOUTHWEST PACIFIC
AREAS (SWPA), OKINAWA, 1441 HOURS

Newly minted Rear Admiral (lower half) Frank Chadwick was impressed in spite of himself. Douglas MacArthur's forward headquarters—it was, naturally, named "Bataan House"—had a spectacular view of Haguchi Bay.

Bataan House had been the private estate of a Japanese moneyman. And as it was by far the best estate in or near Haguchi, Mac's dog robbers had grabbed it as soon as they found it, booting out the commander of Tenth Army, Lieutenant General Simon Bolivar Buckner Jr., in the process.

The conference room formed the upper level of a two-story Japanese-style building. Many interior walls had been removed to open the space into a very large room. The lower level retained the original partitions and was used as offices for the Bataan Gang: MacArthur, Sutherland, Willoughby, and the others. There were two staircases inside: General MacArthur's personal staircase, off-limits to everyone else, and one for the common man.

You could reach the conference level either through the offices or up an outside staircase. The outside stairs led to a peaceful and shady veranda that surrounded the conference room. Chairs of rattan and teak with thick, soft cushions lined the side that faced the bay.

The veranda was a great place to have a quiet smoke while sitting in a comfortable chair and looking out to sea. Whenever the planning for Operation Olympic—the upcoming invasion of Kyushu, one of the Home Islands of Japan itself—got to the point where tempers began to fray, it was a place to cool off. It was also a good place for a quiet negotiation afterward.

Chadwick had come out for the first reason. There was only so much MacArthur he could take.

This February day it was sunny and crisp, like early spring weather back home. The sliding Japanese-style doors were half open, sending a fresh sea breeze through the room. Older flag officers almost inevitably smoked cigars or pipes, and oxygen could get scarce in a long meeting.

From where he was standing, he could see the garden—also off-limits to mortals—that led to MacArthur's private quarters. He could only imagine the splendor. Everybody knew the Supremo of the Pacific lived like a monarch. His native servants even wore, rumor had it, kimonos of red, white, and blue.

"Nice view, eh?"

The voice surprised Chadwick, who thought he'd been alone on the veranda. He turned to see a stocky, dark-haired man with a cigar in his hand, wearing stars and Army Air Force insignia.

"General," he said. He decided that the roof over the porch rendered this an indoor space and so he didn't salute. He looked at the general's name tag: LeMay.

"Hello, Admiral . . . Chadwick," General LeMay said, looking at Frank's name tag in turn and gesturing with his stogie. "You probably came out here for the same reason I did."

"Fresh air, sir? It's the nectar of life."

"Sure." The Army Air Force general's eyes crinkled into the hint of a smile. Chadwick didn't know him, except by reputation, but that reputation was formidable. LeMay had commanded Eighth Air Force in England, where he had presided over the bombing campaign that had reduced Germany's cities to rubble. Now he came here to oversee the operations of those amazing B-29s Chadwick had seen. Huge and silver—as if camouflage coloring was worthy only of lesser aircraft—the Superforts had been assembling in the Philippines for the last six months. They operated out of a network of air bases centered around Clark Field and could fly all the way to Japan and back on their missions of bombardment. Recently, one of the air bases on Okinawa had been designated as an emergency strip so that B-29s in danger of splashing into the ocean could land there instead.

"All those plans—for an invasion that might not be necessary," LeMay remarked, exhaling a cloud of blue smoke. He shook his head sadly and looked as though he might have been talking to himself.

"Sir?" asked Chadwick, uncomfortable in the presence of virtual heresy.

General LeMay shook his head. "Never mind, Admiral. It's not like we're going to wait around for some secret weapon we can use to blow all the Japs to smithereens. Just make the most of this fresh air." Still carrying the smoldering cigar, the general returned to the planning room.

Frank Chadwick stubbed out his Chesterfield, threw the butt over the side, took one final deep breath of sea air, and returned to the planning session. The room was illuminated by bright electric lights, with knots of men gathered around each of the six large tables. The buzz of conversation was steady, measured, and masculine.

Planning, of course, had been going on for months. Individual commands had conducted practice beach assaults and various military maneuvers, and the individual planning documents, if put into a single volume, would put *War and Peace* to shame. Integration of such a mammoth operation was an additional challenge. At this conference, the individual landing force commanders were merging their plans, looking for and resolving conflicts, and bringing the final operation together into a whole. In spite of the years of experience, the enormous amount of staff preparation, and the extensive work that had already gone into this project, there was still a tremendous amount of work left. X-Day, as the invasion date was known, was only a month away. The planners were using

X-Day for OLYMPIC and Y-Day for CORONET because the traditional generic "D-Day" was so associated with Normandy that it couldn't be used for any other operation. *That must have annoyed Mac no end,* thought Frank with a smile.

Worse, continued intelligence updates made the planning environment very fluid. The Japanese weren't exactly going to sit still. Word of the Japanese buildup on Kyushu threatened to put many aspects of the operation in jeopardy. Chadwick was aware of many of the intelligence reports and knew that there were other sources of information that were classified far above his own Top Secret clearance. The data was so detailed and, during the course of the war, had proved so accurate that the young rear admiral had formed a hypothesis as to where it came from: American intelligence agents had obviously broken some very high-level Japanese codes and were, in effect, reading the enemy's mail. Even as his suspicion had evolved into certainty, however, Chadwick knew better than to ask anyone about this, or to mention his idea aloud.

The conference room had been set up with six large, rectangular planning tables, and no chairs—the chairs were all out on the veranda. Each table had a name tag. Five were types of cars: Station Wagon, Roadster, Town Car, Limousine, and Delivery Truck. The remaining table was Sixth Army.

Frank was part of Roadster. This particular landing area consisted of a line of beaches along the southwest coast of Kyushu, leading to the cities of Kagoshima and Sendai. Major General Harry Schmidt, known as "the Dutchman," commanding V Amphibious Corp, was the team leader. There were three other marine generals, the commanders of 3rd, 4th, and 5th Marine Divisions, and three admirals.

Vice Admiral Harry W. Hill commanded the Fifth Amphibious Force, with overall naval responsibility for the amphibious phase of the landing. Frank was commander of Amphibious Group Five, the fast-attack carrier force in support of the landing. He was responsible for preliminary bombardment and air operations. Rear Admiral (lower half)

Theodore White commanded Amphibious Group Four, responsible primarily for transportation and ship-to-shore movement.

All the tables were covered with maps, reports, and pads of paper with hundreds of scrawled notes. Two senior NCOs per table took continual notes during the working day and transcribed them onto mimeograph stencils during the night. By the start of each day, a mimeographed report was ready for each officer. The reports came in yellow clasp envelopes labeled OLYMPIC TOP SECRET. Every action, decision, and assignment was fully documented.

The Roadster table was conveniently next to the Sixth Army table, which made it easy to eavesdrop on the big brass. General Walter Krueger was technically leading that team, but with MacArthur there, the commander was a subordinate at his own table. Sutherland lurked like a dark cloud over the General's shoulder.

The four major corps commanders shuttled between the headquarters table and their own tables. Also at the headquarters table were the air bosses, General George Kelley for tactical, and the new man, General Curtis LeMay, for strategic. They both reported to Mac, with a dotted line to Sixth Army for the operation. Vice Admiral Kelly Turner, commander of amphibious operations; Admiral Frank Fletcher, the commander of Naval Forces Pacific; Admiral Raymond A. Spruance, his number two, also serving as commander of Fifth Fleet; Vice Admiral Thomas Kincaid for Seventh Fleet, and Vice Admiral Mark Mitchner for Third Fleet were there for the navy.

But all of them were under the command of Douglas MacArthur.

Now the General himself threw a red-bound report down on the table.

"I see no reason to give credence to these clearly inflated intelligence estimates. There aren't that many potential soldiers left in all of Japan, and they've virtually exhausted their oil stocks and most raw materials. The idea that we will face opposition of this magnitude on Kyushu is absurd on the face of it," MacArthur said stiffly. "Among the many reasons for doubt is the military performance of the Japanese both in the liberation of the Philippines and the island on which we now make our base. The MacArthur strategy of isolating and ignoring Japanese troop concentrations has kept casualties among our brave fighting men the lowest in any active theater of operations. Why, the Japanese don't even defend the beaches!"

Rear Admiral Frank Chadwick stole a quick glance at Spruance. The man everyone said was actually running the Pacific Fleet listened stoically, then interjected. "Not logical, General MacArthur. This is their homeland and precedents are not reliable. In my judgment, this buildup is real."

"My dear Admiral," MacArthur said, a wide smile on his face, "of course the Japanese are going to be *more* obstreperous than in the recent past. MacArthur is fully aware of *that*. But the numbers given here for reinforcements into Kyushu are so *clearly* inflated that one suspects those responsible for this so-called report have been sampling Chinese opium." He looked around, smiling as if he were looking for a round of applause.

"Not true, General," said Spruance calmly. Everyone else got quiet. One did not tell MacArthur he was wrong, especially before an audience. "I personally reviewed the data gathering and analysis, and designed several verification experiments. The probability is well over ninety percent that this information is accurate."

General Sutherland stepped forward, his jaw jutting pugnaciously. "Admiral, we've been dealing with these Nips out here for the last three and a half years. I suggest you give the General the benefit of that experience."

"Facts trump experience, General Sutherland," responded Spruance, his voice calm, monotone, logical. "Even if one assumes the potential error is larger than indicated, ordinary prudence argues for our planning to use the higher ranges for anticipated Japanese resistance. Any other strategy will result in far larger loss of life. Unnecessary loss of life."

"Are you accusing the General of callousness with the lives of his men?" demanded Sutherland, almost snarling. "That's outrageous!"

One of Spruance's eyebrows went up, but before he could reply MacArthur spoke again, this time turning his attention to Fletcher, not Spruance. "Surely even the most cursory review of the forces arrayed here would demonstrate conclusively that *regardless* of whatever undertrained, underequipped, undersupplied, and ill-motivated cadres the Japanese Imperial Army is still able to muster in the field against us, they shall all be as naught against the invincible might of your good naval arm, Admiral Fletcher! Or are you less confident in your brave sailors than is MacArthur himself?"

"The U.S. Navy can whip any power on Earth, General," replied Fletcher.

Spruance spoke up. "That is, however, an irrelevancy at the present time. It is the cost of victory, especially the human cost, that concerns me. These Japanese reinforcement figures translate directly into increased casualties unless this conference plans for the worst case. Hope, General MacArthur, does not constitute a strategy."

Frank could see Mac's eyes narrow. Work stopped at Frank's table as everyone else gave up the pretense that they weren't eavesdropping. *Score one for Spruance,* Frank thought.

Sutherland was not about to let the challenge pass. "The General's record on *that* score needs no defense, Admiral," he replied. He leaned forward, planting both fists on the table.

But the Supreme Commander waved him back with a big easy smile that dismissed the whole matter. "But neither do I believe that it is in the interests of the great nation we both serve that our brave prisoners wait one moment longer in cruel captivity than they must, that the nations held captive under Japan's brutal fist continue to suffer, or that the mothers of America continue to be separated from their sons. Due diligence is meet and proper. Excessive and unwarranted timidity is not."

The General smiled tightly, an expression without amusement. Sutherland, once again, took up the baton. "There is no time to waste, Admiral! Ultimate victory stands within our grasp, and these petty political arguments do no one any service."

Spruance ignored Sutherland and spoke directly to MacArthur. "It is, of course, the Supreme Commander's prerogative to select the battle plan of his choice. However, the current plan fails to take into account the Japanese buildup. It will, in all probability, result in casualties far in excess of forecast."

Sutherland was about to jump in again, but MacArthur injected himself smoothly into the middle. "Admiral, your objection is duly noted," said MacArthur. Sutherland visibly relaxed at the General's soothing tone. "We must, however, stay the course," he continued.

MacArthur's eyes fell upon Curtis LeMay, and once again they glinted with that hint of humor. "Or perhaps we should do as General LeMay urges. Simply discontinue land and sea operations, and wait for the enemy to decide that bombardment from the air has become too much of a nuisance to be endured."

LeMay flushed, clenched his jaw. But he didn't back down. "General MacArthur, sir. I have simply suggested that we change our bombardment tactics. German cities were made of stone and masonry, and we smashed them with high explosives. But Japanese cities are made of wood and, literally, paper! If we drop enough incendiaries on them, we'll burn each one to the ground! With respect, General, we can torch the whole damn country!"

Nobody said a word. Every eye was focused upon El Supremo. Chadwick found that he wasn't even breathing, until he saw MacArthur nod once, the emperor giving acknowledgment to a courtier's beseeching.

"You know, Curtis, I have been giving the matter some thought. This is not the place to discuss it, of course, but I think I will have you go ahead and try this new tactic of yours. I'll want details, of course, and I don't expect it will win the war. But it might be worth trying. Now . . ." His attention returned to the plotting table. "Where were we?"

Spruance was looking thoughtfully at the main map. He said, "We were discussing estimates of enemy strength."

"Not quite," replied MacArthur. "If I recall correctly, we had just *finished* discussing estimates of enemy strength and had decided to move on."

Fletcher looked at Spruance as if wishing he could make his subordinate shut up.

Spruance was not giving up. "Very well, General," Spruance replied. "Let me make a final observation. If the Japanese empire were poised to invade California, I would expect to prepare numerous surprises to make their attack more difficult and more expensive."

"Then it is a good thing, Admiral, that the Japanese don't have you on their side," said MacArthur with a gracious smile. "We are immeasurably greater for your talents."

Frank couldn't stand the sneaky SOB, but he had to admire his skill.

The veranda became the arena for a lot of minidebates during the next break. Overall sentiment was breaking MacArthur's way, though the navy was showing an attempt to be loyal to Spruance.

"It's their home, like Spruance said," an admiral from Task Force 71 argued. "We've got to go in prepared for the Japs to try things they've never tried before."

A general from XI Corps replied, "The Japs are like wasps. In Okinawa, if we'd gone south and tried to push the Japs out of the rest of the island, I bet we would have been in for a hell of a fight. But we didn't, because we didn't have to. The same thing's going to be true this time. We're not trying to take over Kyushu. All we want is enough territory for air bases and a defense perimeter. It's not like we're planning to go cave to cave and roust the yellow bastards out."

Spruance did carry the day on one point, and Frank had the idea it might have been what the admiral had been up to all along. The order of battle on the American side got beefed up even more.

MacArthur was right. In the Philippines and on Okinawa, the Japanese had not shown the stomach for a serious fight. Once their navy had been destroyed, a lot of the fight had gone out of them. That's what logic said.

But Frank looked at the intel reports on the Japanese buildup in Kyushu himself. They were up to *something*. This might be the occasion where the Japs surprised everybody. Maybe Spruance was right.

In any fight with MacArthur, he sure hoped so.

CAMP SHINJUKU, TOKYO, JAPAN, 0600 HOURS

"Kyo-o-o-o-tsu-ke!"

The camp commandant, Captain Ogawa Taiki, drew out the "o" sound clearly and sharply. In the chilly, dim light of early morning, the prisoners shuffled into formation and came to attention. None of them moved quickly. Many moved like old men—the "beriberi shuffle," it was called. Andy glanced right and left quickly, then stepped back about six inches. He didn't want to be caught out of line again. The penalty for that ranged from a public slapping to a personal encounter with "Jap vitamin sticks" wielded by some of the more brutal guards.

"Kyoshu naga!" Andy locked his eyes on the Japanese captain in unison with the other prisoners. The captain saluted and slowly pivoted on toe and heel while holding the salute until he had turned from the right flank all the way to the left flank. He kept perfect posture throughout. This was notable because the captain had a limp, brought on by his wound. The prisoners had agreed that was the reason why the captain was a camp commandant rather than in a combat unit. He had been one mean SOB at Cabanatuan, and the trip to Japan had done nothing to improve his temperament.

Andy heard a thud behind him followed by a choked-off moan. Someone in the second rank had been sloppy and earned a little love tap from one of the guards. Andy could feel the presence of the guards behind him and his skin crawled. He could almost feel a club hitting him in the kidneys and he had to stop himself from cringing reflexively. That would surely get him beaten.

"*Nori!*" Eyes front again.

"*Yasume!*" At ease.

"*Bango!*" Count off!

The prisoners began counting off in Japanese. "*Ichi! Ni! San! Shi! Go! Roku! Shichi!*" The prisoners called the drill "Bango" and had no idea what the Japanese called it. "*Yasume*" had become a generic term for resting or time off.

Andy needed a little *yasume*. Last night was bad again—nightmares. Nightmares came often now. He had many different nightmares related to the sinking of the *Arisan Maru*.

Last night, he had been trapped in the hold of the *Arisan Maru* again. He had a different nightmare for each of the moments when he might have died. For instance, right when he was sure he was going to drown, the burning deck collapsed into the hold below, freeing those who could not escape through the tiny hatch. Several prisoners died in the wreckage. A blazing deck plank had crushed the skull of a man not three feet away. The horrific image had imprinted itself like a photograph on Andy's mind. In his dreams he was often that victim. Sometimes, the victim came back as a monster, like in the movies, to stalk him.

Then there were nightmares about the inferno of the burning deck itself, the terrifying free-fall into the black, turbulent ocean, and the desperate hope he wouldn't land on some piece of flotsam in the dark waters below.

One of the worst was the moment when, clinging to a floating door, he saw a gray fin crest the water. Sharks. And there was the nightmare that he was really marooned in mid-ocean, rather than within a mile of the Formosa coast, as the wonderful dawn revealed.

Andy and the other officers cultivated a small vegetable garden to keep boredom at bay. They were exempt from the slave labor performed by the enlisted men. Most of what the officers grew was given to the guards, but a few leftover roots, leaves, and less appetizing specimens supplemented the meager prisoner diet. Andy didn't mind gardening, even though it sometimes brought back memories of the Farm, at Cabanatuan.

Today, however, one of the Jap guards was wandering around in the compound, smacking his billy club into his hand, over and over. Andy began to shake uncontrollably. The guards terrified him. They beat people sometimes for no reason. If they had a reason, the beating was more savage.

Now the Jap was standing right behind him. His shadow fell across the dirt Andy was laboriously breaking up with a stick. Andy's trembles worsened.

"Isogaseru!" The Japanese guard shouted at Andy to work harder. He emphasized his order with a kick to Andy's ribs.

"Ossu!" Yes, sir!

But he couldn't. His hands were lifeless around the stick. He stabbed futilely at the dirt, trying to break up a big clump, but nothing happened.

Another kick. *"Isogaseru!"*

"Ossu! Ossu!" He started to cry.

At that, the Japanese guard grabbed Andy's hair, pulled his head back to see the tears. Disgusted, he spat in Andy's face. *"Gesuonna,"* he said contemptuously. Andy had heard the term before. The guard was calling him a woman, and a useless, low woman at that. The guard kicked him a few more times for good measure, then strode away.

Andy lay facedown in the dirt, sobbing.

When Andy was adrift amid the wreckage of the *Arisan Maru,* he had killed a Japanese. He was terrified that somehow, some way, the Japs would find out, and they would torture him to death. Every time he saw a Jap look at him, he couldn't help trembling.

It had been surprisingly easy to kill the Jap. He had a broken arm and was clearly exhausted. He babbled words Andy couldn't understand, but his meaning was clear: *Help me onto your raft.* Andy looked around and saw a jagged piece of wood floating within an arm's reach. He picked it up and held it out toward the Jap, making an arm signal: *Swim closer. Grab the wood and I'll pull you in.*

When the Jap reached the edge of the floating door and grabbed on with his one functioning hand, Andy took the wood and clubbed the Jap in the broken arm. He screamed something in Japanese. Andy panicked. *What if someone heard?* He brought the wood down on the Jap's head over and over until he slipped beneath the waves.

Andy's constant fear was that the Jap had somehow survived and would somehow turn up here, recognize him, and turn him in. Every Jap face now made him cower.

He didn't dream about Mark, who did join him on the makeshift raft, and poor Steve, who did as well. Together, they made shore, only to run into a Japanese patrol. It was poor Steve who became the punishment target for the vengeful guards, who were angry so many of their own had died, while worthless *holio*—flower sniffers—survived.

Steve died under that beating.

Any moment, Andy expected the same thing to happen to him.

• TUESDAY, 27 FEBRUARY 1945 •

HIROSHIMA, 1549 HOURS

The knock at the door was not unexpected: Ogawa Michiyo and her mother had been receiving a regular stream of visitors for the past fifteen days. The ritual would continue for another twenty, and only then would the urn containing her father's ashes be interred in the nearby Buddhist cemetery. Mama was dozing on her futon, so Michiyo rose at the sound of the knock. She made sure that a fresh stick of incense was burning and went to greet the new visitor with her face composed, her movements and bearing serene and graceful.

When she recognized Naguro Yoshi, however, the dam of emotions broke and she burst into tears.

"I'm so sorry, Michiyo," he whispered into her hair, pulling her close, holding her in arms that felt very strong.

She hadn't seen the young officer in more than a year, but

she had cherished his many letters. Now he had come here when she so desperately needed him. Almost as soon as it had erupted her grief receded enough for Michiyo to regain her self-control. She lifted her face, sniffling embarrassedly, and stepped back from the soldier to bow demurely.

"Please, Yoshi-san, won't you come in?"

"Thank you." He bowed with equal formality and entered.

"Mama, here is Naguro Yoshi," Michiyo said as the older woman looked up questioningly.

"Oh, Taiki?" Mama said hopefully as she took in the sight of the dapper first lieutenant's uniform.

Yoshi blinked in surprise, but Michiyo replied for him. "No, Mama—it's Taiki's friend Yoshi. He's come to visit, to pay his respects to Papa."

"Yes, there he is," Mama said, waving vaguely to the simple urn.

Yoshi nodded and pulled a stick of incense from his pocket as he went to the urn on the mantel. Bowing his head, he touched a match to the fragrant twig and remained lost in his own thoughts as a smoky tendril drifted toward the ceiling, the woody, spicy scent intermingling with the cloud that would hover in the little house throughout the period of mourning.

Michiyo waited patiently as Yoshi completed his prayers. He seemed so serious and dignified. But there remained a youthful, even boyish, character to his appearance. Even before the war, Taiki had looked older than that, though the two men were almost the same age.

After he finished his prayers, Yoshi turned and knelt next to Michiyo's mother. "I am so sorry for your loss," he said quietly. "But I know Ogawa-san now does his ancestors— and you—credit."

"Yes . . . yes, I suppose he does," Mama said sadly.

Yoshi and Michiyo sat on the floor beside the low table. She was eager to hear his stories—she knew from his letters that he had returned from the Philippines to duty in the Home Islands and was commanding a company of soldiers now— but instead he looked at her so intently, so seriously that she felt like she was undergoing some kind of inspection.

"You look so thin!" he exclaimed softly. "Are you eating well?"

"As well as anyone," she replied with a shrug. "No one eats well, not in the winter."

"No, I suppose you're right," he said sadly. "But we used to." He shook his head, and it was as if a cloud of melancholy slipped away and he was bright and smiling once again. "Tell me, Michiyo—will you go for a walk with me?"

She had hoped he would ask. Throwing on a cloak— threadbare now, as she had been wearing it since before the war—the young woman joined the soldier in a quiet stroll along the mostly empty streets. Shortages of food, fuel, and raw materials had curtailed much of the city's bustle, but for now Michiyo felt warm and happy.

Yoshi told her that he had obtained several days' leave and had come to Hiroshima on the train. She told him about her work at the hospital, trying not to complain about the shortages in basic medicines, gauze, and other supplies. They did not mention the war. Instead, he offered her his arm, and she took it shyly, holding onto him for warmth and support when a February gust of wind swept past.

They made their way past the department store, toward the River Ota, and soon were crossing the Aioi Bridge—the span she had come to think of as *their* bridge, though this was only the second time they had walked across it. The winter afternoon was cool but not bitingly cold. Leaden clouds masked the sun, which was nearing the western horizon, broadening the chill. Looking down, Michiyo saw that the water, which surged so vibrantly in spring, was now a sluggish trickle.

"It looks like such a small river," she commented. "So sad and weak, now."

"It is a small river," Yoshi replied with startling vehemence. "Because it flows from such a small country. Japan is too small to have a Yangtze, or an Amazon, or a Mississippi, or a Nile."

"I never thought of that," Michiyo admitted. "But in spring, the Ota rages and roars!"

"But it doesn't last, does it?" the young officer replied

bitterly. He turned his face away, but she sensed that he was clenching his jaw.

"Yoshi!" Michiyo implored. "What's wrong?"

"I—I'm sorry," he said, shaking his head. "It's so sad, about your father. I remember seeing him the last time I visited. How strong he was!"

"Not for a while," she corrected gently. "He had been failing for more than a year. When Taiki came to Japan—but still would not come home to see him—I think maybe his heart broke."

"Taiki feels a lot of shame," Yoshi said with surprising bluntness. "I think he could not face your father." He smashed the bridge railing with his fist. "This damned war! It comes closer all the time, and yet I have never fired a shot at the enemy, never even commanded my company in combat! I have been a lieutenant for three years, but I might as well be a garbageman!"

"Don't talk like that!" she said, mustering a sternness of her own. "You will have a great part to play, I am certain."

He was looking south, toward the mouth of the Ota and the sea beyond. "The Americans have taken Okinawa away from us. Do you know how close that is?"

"I—I think so." In her mind she pictured the maps she had studied in school and for the first time saw the war as a thing that was approaching, like some vague but no longer distant menace. "Okinawa is not terribly far from Kyushu, is it?"

"No, it is not."

"Do you think the Americans will come to Kyushu next?" The idea burst on her like a clap of thunder; she had never considered it before.

"If they do, I hope I can fight them. But I am still posted far away from the battlefields!"

"Where is your company now?" she asked, secretly hoping he would say Hiroshima.

Instead, he replied, "The Kinai Plain, near Osaka," which was glad enough news: only a half-day train ride away from here! She was going to tell him that she was proud of him, but he went on. "If you can call it a company! Old men and farm boys, mostly. We have ten rifles and almost a hundred men. If the Americans come, we will probably throw spears at them!"

She didn't know what to say, so she just squeezed his arm again and, tentatively, laid her head upon his shoulder. For several minutes they remained silent, close together, warm in spite of the chill.

"Did Taiki come home for your father's funeral?" Yoshi asked abruptly.

"No. We still have not seen him since before he left for Rabaul and that other island—what did you call it?"

"Guadalcanal."

"Yes. Have you seen him since that time in Manila?"

"No. And I think I told you in my letter, even when I found him at the prisoner camp, he didn't want to talk to me. The war was close, but neither of us were fighting—and I think that deepened his shame. We both came back to Honshu on ships full of American prisoners. But I haven't seen him since."

"We hear that he is a camp commandant somewhere near Tokyo," she offered, feeling again the dull ache of her brother's absence.

"I hear that, too. In truth, there is a reason I'm glad that he is not here right now." He looked at her again, strangely serious and yet somehow imploring. "Your father has died, so I would speak to your brother if he were here. But he is not, so I hope you will forgive me speaking directly to you."

"About what?" Michiyo asked—and then, by that intent look in his eyes, she knew. Her heart fluttered, and she felt a light, anticipatory joy that seemed like it belonged only in memories.

He removed something from a small felt pouch he had been carrying. It was a jade figurine, a Buddha, suspended from a leather thong. "I offer you this gift of peace and beauty. I bought it for you when I was in Nanking, after we saw each other in the marketplace all those years ago. I have been thinking about you since that day."

"It's beautiful," Michiyo breathed. "I will treasure it always!"

"And now, now I must ask you: Ogawa Michiyo, would you do me the honor of becoming my wife? Will you marry me?"

She swayed, clutching the strong stone railing of the bridge for support against the sudden onset of dizziness. "Yes, Yoshi—a thousand times yes!" she cried, throwing her arms around him. His arms *were* strong, and his lips were surprisingly soft as they met hers in a sudden, impetuous kiss.

A moment later the jade figure was suspended around her neck. They were somewhere on the street, walking back to the house, but Michiyo didn't even remember leaving the bridge.

FOURTEEN

Kyushu

• MONDAY, 19 MARCH 1945 •

USS GEORGE CLYMER (APA-27), ROADSTER BEACH ZONE,
OFF THE WEST COAST OF KYUSHU, JAPAN, 0045 HOURS
(OPERATION OLYMPIC, X-DAY, N-HOUR – 0515)

Reveille sounded over the ship's loudspeakers, and more than a hundred enlisted men of Fox Company, 2nd Battalion, 3rd Marine Regiment stirred fitfully in their hammocks. The 3rd Marines was one of the three regimental combat teams, or RCTs, making up the 2rd Marine Division, V Amphibious Corps, United States Sixth Army. Fox Company and the rest of the RCT would be landing on Pontiac Beach. Every man present knew that, by tonight, some of them would have drawn their last breaths.

Pete Rachwalski, as the senior sergeant of Fox Company, had made a private deal with one of the petty officers to wake him up a half hour before anybody else, and he woke up the platoon sergeants. It was part of the image. "Rise and shine, boys!" he shouted in a cheerful voice. "The faster we eat breakfast, the faster we can go have fun today!"

The cavernous hold where they were billeted had the ambience of a jail cell, except it was painted white. Exposed pipes ran along the ceiling; rivets were everywhere. The air was damp and thick, the bulkheads slick with a mixture of oil and condensation. Bunks for the entire company, plus a few extras, were laid out four across, three high, and fifteen deep, crowded so close together that you had to move single file through the aisles. There was a hatch at one end, the only way out. It was no place for a claustrophobe.

He expected the grumbling as his men stumbled blearily to their feet and got in line for the head. It was the first of many lines they'd stand in today.

The second line was for breakfast. The mess hall could handle better than two hundred at a time, but the full battalion consisted of nearly a thousand men, and they were all aboard. So they ate in shifts, as quickly as possible.

The food was plentiful and good: eggs, steak, and potatoes. The steak was tough, but it was steak. It would be a while before any of them would see hot food again. For some—for too many—this would be a last meal.

Some men ate heartily and some not at all. There were risks with either strategy. Pete grabbed a tray and piled it high, even though he had no appetite. This was his fourth landing. It didn't get any easier. In fact, he was more frightened of today's landing than he'd been at Guadalcanal, Leyte, and Okinawa.

He sat with the senior NCOs, and that was a relief. He didn't know how well he could conceal his fear from the men. He could talk to other sergeants, though. Several of them looked as gray faced as he felt.

There wasn't a lot of conversation. There wasn't really a lot to say.

After breakfast, the men of Fox Company joined a third line—well, a series of lines, actually—for equipment and supplies they hadn't yet been issued. Walking from one station to another, each marine stopped and had something else piled on his outstretched arms. When finished, the typical marine was equipped with his Springfield 30.06 rifle, ammunition, a bayonet, a combat knife, a full canteen, a map case, a life belt, and a combat pack that contained a poncho, three changes of socks and underwear, a three days' supply of C rations, and three packs of cigarettes. A few were armed more exotically, with Thompson submachine guns or Browning automatic rifles. Others carried sections of mortars or machine guns, or ammo for those heavy weapons.

Bargaining started almost immediately. "I got Pall Malls here. Anybody got menthols?"

"Cigarettes for canned peaches over here!"

"I'll trade these fucking egg and bacon packs for damn near anything!"

"Pipe down! Do your trading up on deck!"

By the time they were fully outfitted and topside, each marine labored under more than fifty additional pounds. They needed the equipment, but the weight was dangerous. On deck, Pete announced, "Line your packs up by platoon. Then take a load off. The smoking lamp is out."

The night was still very dark, but the air was refreshingly cool after the stifling hold. The ship rolled gently, making very little headway, and Pete deduced that they were very nearly in position to launch the landing.

Fox Company was on the starboard side of the large central deck. The forward third contained the bridge, crew quarters, and other ship functions and was generally off-limits to passengers. The after third held officers' quarters, wardrooms, medical facilities, and the officers' mess. In between was a large open deck, with ship's boats and other cargo competing for room with the marines who would be embarking in the initial waves. The rest of the enlisted men and cargo rode below. The blackout was complete, and there was a background of quiet cursing as the men bumped each other, stepping on feet, stumbled over the piles of equipment.

Fox Company was in the second wave of 2nd Battalion but in the third wave of 3rd Marines. That was still uncomfortably close to being at the head of the line, but it could have been worse.

It was 0300 now.

Captain Rod Gilder, company CO, called the platoon leaders together. Gilder had been a shavetail back on Guadalcanal three years ago, although Pete hadn't been in his platoon. They both had moved from 2nd Marines to 3rd Marines when the latter regiment was being created. That was when Pete had first advanced from PFC to lance corporal. After three long years of combat, Gilder and Rachwalski had a lifetime's more experience than the vast majority of their peers.

That doesn't stop me from being scared shitless, Pete thought.

The battleships opened fire at 0330. Huge flames from the sixteen-inch guns rose into the air like the biggest fireworks anyone had ever seen, and the shells arced slowly toward the beach. Then there was a tremendous flash and a few seconds later the sound of a terrific explosion. The explosion made his bones shake. The flames outlined the dark, inhospitable landscape, rendering into a place more closely resembling hell than any place on planet Earth.

That initial salvo was the signal for the other ships to join in: cruisers firing their eight-inch and six-inch guns, destroyers adding to the racket with their five-inch guns, until the explosions started coming so close together it sounded like gods firing machine guns. The earth lit up with a white light that flickered on and off, making the landscape look like a slightly out-of-synch movie projector image.

The bombardment continued without pause. It was 0430. Half an hour to go.

Pete called the company together, and Captain Gilder gave the locker room talk. "Let me start by reminding all of you that we know the mission, we've rehearsed this many times, and every one of us is a marine. Do it like you did in practice and it'll be just another walk in the park. Second of the Third is going to clean out the southern section of Beach Pontiac. Fox Company is in the second wave, and the first wave has generously promised to leave us a few Japs to kill. After that, we'll unite with 1st Brigade, and then 3rd Marines will push south into the Japanese city of Kagoshima. That's the major port for Kyushu."

The overall command, V Amphibious Corps, with its three marine divisions, the 3rd, 4th, and 5th, was simultaneously invading a total of nine beaches in what was called the Roadster Beach Zone. Each battalion had to take about two thousand feet of beach and clear it so that the next wave of heavier equipment and fresh troops could come in.

And that was just Roadster. There were six other beach zones and twenty-six more beaches. Ten army divisions grouped in three corps would take them. Three more divisions had already taken some of the surrounding islands to use as air bases. Two divisions were feinting to Shikoku in hopes of drawing off some of the defenders. Two more divisions were ready for follow up, and another corps was in reserve afloat. That totaled more than four hundred thousand invading troops. In addition, over two thousand ships and three thousand aircraft—the largest armada ever assembled—supported the invasion.

The captain looked relaxed and in control, exactly the way a company commander should act. Pete, however, observed the fidgeting of the captain's hands. He couldn't keep them still.

We're all petrified.

Gilder continued. "We got some messages. Okay. Here's the first one." He unfolded a small sheet of paper. " 'From the Supreme Commander, Pacific: We are united this day in the single greatest military operation in the history of the world. We undertake this supreme challenge in the name of those who have suffered and died in service to this nation and at the hands of our enemy. We pledge ourselves that freedom shall prevail and justice shall triumph. With God and the right as our sword and shield, we go forth together. God Bless the

United States of America.' It's signed 'General of the Army Douglas MacArthur.'"

About a third of the men clapped and cheered, a third rallied halfheartedly, and the remainder rolled eyes, spat, and made groaning noises. Pete glared at one loudmouth, who shut up immediately—but not before attracting the attention of his platoon sergeant, who loomed in his face with an unamused expression.

Gilder looked around, officially oblivious to the dissenters. "Okay. Here's the next one. 'From Commander, United States Sixth Army: In the long months of planning and training, I have daily grown in respect for the soldiers, sailors, and marines I am honored to lead. I am confident that you will continue to demonstrate the exceptional performance that has been the hallmark of Sixth Army. God bless you all.' This one is signed 'General Walter Krueger.'" He looked around. Pete also looked. The dissenters, having expressed their opinion, were quiet now. His platoon sergeants were doing their job.

The captain continued, "I've got more notes. There's one from Commander, V Corps; one from Commander, 3rd Marine Division; and . . . well, they all say pretty much the same thing. Everybody thinks you'll do just fine. I do, too. Good luck, men."

He paused. "The General's cousin will now say a few words." Snickers and guffaws burst out.

"The General's cousin" meant Pete.

Pete was used to people who couldn't spell his name. He'd heard all the Polack jokes. But when people learned that the commander of Sixth Army, General Walter Krueger, was also a Pole, they started kidding him about his supposed connections in high places.

Only staff sergeants and above could get away with kidding him to his face. The captain, of course, could say whatever he damn well pleased. Considering the laugh he got, it was probably a good idea. Pete didn't mind taking a joke for the sake of morale. Especially not this morning.

He stepped up beside the captain. As a gunnery sergeant, his job was to give a different kind of speech. "My Uncle Walter says . . . excuse me, I mean General Krueger says . . ." He let the laugh get past the midpoint, then continued. "General Krueger says you're doing great. Everybody including the captain thinks you're great." He looked around at his marines. They were sprawled around the deck under several of the small ship's boats. "But as for me . . ."

He gave them his "sergeant look": eyes narrowed, shoulders forward, chin out. "I don't think you're doing all that great. I think you've been lazy. I think you've been half-assed. So you stumblebums better act like *real* marines out there, instead of a bunch of candy-assed sailors, or you won't have to worry about the goddamn Japanese because you'll have *me* on your ass. Got it?" He was actually fairly pleased with them, but there were rules to this game, and he had learned that sometimes you needed both a kiss and a kick to get the job done.

"Yes, Gunny."

"Yeah."

"Sailors? Are you kidding?"

"Got it, Gunny."

"Maybe if you tell the Japs who your uncle is, they'll all run away."

"Who said that?" A platoon sergeant.

But in the predawn stillness, the soldiers all looked alike.

"I gotta piss before I get in the boat."

"Why? You're gonna piss yourself as soon as you see a fucking Jap!"

"Yeah? Fuck you."

"Fuck you too."

"Fuck you twice."

"Pipe down, assholes, or I'll *give* you a reason to piss yourself right now."

Nervousness and tension increased. As a sergeant, he could pace; lower ranks had to stay seated except to go to the head. He couldn't read his watch and he was suddenly desperate to know the time. He wandered closer to one of the lights, skirting the edge of a ship's boat covered with a tarp.

His watch said 0442. The sweep second hand took *forever* to get around to 0443.

He waited a good ten minutes before checking again.

Now it read 0445.

He held the watch to his ear and shook it. It had to be broken. That couldn't be right.

The watch made a *tick tock* sound. It was working. Damn. *Screw it. Let's go to work.*

"Rise and shine, ladies," he announced. "It's off to work we go."

"Gunny, we've got another twelve minutes," came a plaintive cry.

"It'll take that long to get your packs on and get inspected."

"Inspected?"

"Damn right. I want each man checked head to toe. No mistakes."

Pete didn't care about the resultant grumbling. Men died for minor mistakes.

Ten minutes of strap tightening, load adjusting, and safety hooking later, it was time to go over the side.

Captain Gilder had a final word. "Stay together, keep an eye on each other, and remember the mission. Gunny?"

"Keep your heads down and your weapons up. Get scared all you like, but keep moving until you've got good cover. Fight like hell. *Fortes fortuna juvat!*"

The men shouted back. *"Fortes fortuna juvat!"* That was the 3rd Marines' motto: Fortune favors the brave.

Then I'm shit out of luck, he thought.

But he was committed.

"Let's go," he said.

At 0500, dawn had progressed enough to illuminate the dark water and the gray shapes of the neighboring transports. The first elements of the regiment began boarding the transports, climbing down a swaying cargo net in the dark to a Higgins boat that was itself bobbing up and down. This called for careful handling. A few men thought climbing down the net was worse than the actual invasion. It was important to be secure with each handhold. One slip and you were in the water. With fifty pounds of gear, it was straight to the bottom. There had already been a few casualties that way. It was a hell of a dumb way to die.

The Higgins boat, also known as the LCVP (landing craft, vehicles and personnel), was a shallow draft boat that could operate in as little as eighteen inches of water. It could run at high speed through vegetation, logs, and debris without fouling the propeller or damaging the hull. It could land a platoon of thirty-six men with equipment, turn around in the shallow water, and go back for more.

There were lots of other landing craft as well—LCTs for tanks, LCIs for infantry, LCSs for support—and landing ships, large enough to travel under their own power, that could carry huge numbers of tanks or soldiers. There was the LSD—landing ship, dock—that served as a floating base for the smaller LC-type craft. Thousands of them were in the process of being loaded all along the Kyushu coastline.

As Pete watched the loading, he noticed out of the corner of his eye that some new streaks of light were coming from the shore out to the fleet. "They're shooting back, Captain," he said.

Gilder looked where Pete was pointing. "I believe you're right. Looks like aircraft."

The sky continued to brighten, and now they could see the looming bulk of a mountain on shore, just north of their beach. Specks moved through the sky, approaching the fleet, and the snarling sound of aircraft engines reached the ears of the marines on deck. Tracers sparked through the air as navy fighters dove at the enemy planes; the men on the transports cheered as one, then another Jap plane exploded into a bright flash.

Instead of dogfighting with the Americans who tried to engage them, the Japanese fighters shrugged them off and kept flying. They were heading toward the transports. In fact, one was heading in the direction of the USS *Warren*, the next ship over. Pete waited for the tracers of machine gun fire from the Japanese plane and imagined the marines on the *Warren* diving for cover, but there were no tracers.

Then, to Pete's shock, the Japanese pilot flew right into the *Warren*'s bridge. The plane exploded, taking the super-structure with it. Wreckage and flames scattered over the ship's deck.

"He did that *deliberately*," Captain Gilder said in disbelief.

"Yes, sir," replied Pete. "That's what I saw, too."

"Well, I'll be a son of a bitch," Gilder said. "Damn! There goes another one!"

Pete watched with amazement as Japanese planes intentionally crashed into every transport they could hit. And more were coming.

The shore suddenly looked like it was a long distance away.

ABOVE ROADSTER BEACH ZONE, OFF THE WEST COAST OF KYUSHU, JAPAN, 0525 HOURS (X-DAY, N-HOUR –0035)

Lefty Wayner was comfortable in his role, flying high above the fleet, scanning the skies for enemy aircraft. This air war was a far cry from the desperate battles of 1942, at Midway and in the Solomon Sea, where the enemy planes came against the American carriers in waves, nimble Zeros flying circles around the clumsy Wildcats. Then it had been a fight for survival, a frantic effort to stay alive and to inflict damage upon an enemy with superior equipment, training, and experience.

Things were different now. The Grumman F6F Hellcat—Lefty's had nineteen little red meatballs painted just below the canopy—had replaced the Wildcat and rendered the air war into a whole new ball game. Whereas the F4F had been slower and clumsier than the Zero, the Hellcat was faster, more powerful, and capable of absorbing punishment that would knock three or four Zeros out of the sky.

Now commander of VMF 48, the fighter squadron aboard the new aircraft carrier *Missionary Ridge,* Lefty had been piloting an F6F since the end of 1943. In early 1944 he had been flying air protection for the invasion of the Philippines. When Admiral Spruance brought his newly replenished carrier fleet, now protected by the doughty Hellcats, within range of the enemy fighter bases, the Japs had unleashed every land-based plane they had. Flying from fields throughout the archipelago, and from as far away as Formosa, the Nipponese aircraft had swarmed toward the American carriers that were supporting Mac's landings on the island of Leyte. Lefty had personally shot down three fighters and six bombers in the air battle that had since come to be known as the Luzon Turkey Shoot. He and his fellow pilots, flying from more than a dozen carriers and light carriers, had virtually obliterated the enemy air forces in a bloody day and a half of battle.

From that time forward, the United States Naval Air Forces had ruled the skies over the Pacific Ocean. As Lefty looked at the hundreds of ships below—including four flattops that he could personally see right now, in addition to the two dozen more lying over the horizon—he had no reason to believe that today would be any different.

The sun was already up, and for once the clouds were few, almost nonexistent. Lefty's eyes scanned the horizon, especially toward the east, toward Kyushu. He could see the land over there, a brown swath of rugged terrain, still in the shadow of the newly risen sun. Any Jap planes coming from there would have to be picked up by radar—there was no way any pilot could see much against that brilliant backdrop.

Sure enough, his radio crackled. "Sheepdog One, we have numerous bogies overland, approaching Roadster from multiple bearings. Go to work."

"Sheepdog One, acknowledging. Tallyho," he replied.

"Good hunting," came the final sendoff from the flight director aboard the carrier below.

Lefty dipped his wings and headed toward Kyushu. The fifteen other fighters of his squadron formed up on him, in pairs, and they all leaned into a shallow dive. They had been

patrolling at twenty-two thousand feet so that they could ac-
celerate quickly toward any threat, and within seconds every
one of the Hellcats was flying at better than 300 mph, airspeed.

The squadron flew over the transports, hundreds of them,
arrayed in ranks several miles offshore. Scattered amid the
troop ships were battlewagons and cruisers, continuously firing broadsides at the smoke-shrouded beaches, spurts of
flame marking each new volley as it spewed forth. Around
the transports, little boats—the landing craft—scuttled about
or bobbed in the waves. A rank of these doughty craft was
already churning toward the beaches, a white wake trailing
behind each boat.

Lefty raised his eyes and immediately picked up the
specks of enemy airplanes. Some were sweeping along the
beach, coming down from the north. A stream of planes was
visible emerging from the interior of Kyushu, flying around
the shoulder of one of the great mountains rising just beyond
the landing beaches. The commander of VMF 48 led his
Hellcats toward this target, the two groups of airplanes converging at a combined speed of more than 500 mph.

The distance closed quickly, and Lefty could see that still
more enemy planes were coming into view. They were
small, flying low and steady at something under ten thousand feet. The Hellcats were still a few thousand feet higher,
diving and converging. The pilot could see that the enemy
before him included a surprisingly large number of Zeros
and other types of single-engine planes. They were fighters,
but they weren't climbing or otherwise trying to challenge
the Grummans for air superiority over the beaches.

The Hellcats continued their dives to intercept, and
Lefty's tracers converged on the nose of the leading Zero.
Curiously, even now the enemy pilot made little effort to
evade—instead, he put his nose down and tried to fly right
past. Lefty was too good a gunner to allow that, and the Jap
plane disintegrated in a ball of fire while the Hellcat was still
two hundred yards away.

At that distance, Lefty felt the *whump* of the blast shake

his heavy fighter like a child's toy. *What the hell was that?* It was a lot more than the fuel tank exploding, he knew. *As if the son of a bitch packed his fuselage with explosives before he took off!*

Hellcats roared through the enemy formation, shooting steadily. A dozen enemy planes flashed into nothingness, or fell out of formation, trailing smoke. Guns barked all across the squadron as the flight of Grummans dove through the stream of enemy aircraft and banked through tight, high-g turns. As the Hellcats came around, the surviving Japs still made no effort to engage. Instead, they simply plunged away from the fight, spreading out as they neared the unarmored, motionless transports below.

The Americans came after them at full throttle, but before they could close the gap, the first enemy plane flew right into a transport, vanishing in a ball of fire that seemed to engulf half the ship. Another Jap blew up in the air, hit by antiaircraft fire, but then the next one, and the next, plowed into the helpless ships with fierce eruptions of flame.

And still more of them were coming off the land.

USS GETTYSBURG (CV-44), ROADSTER BEACH ZONE,
OFF THE WEST COAST OF KYUSHU, JAPAN, 0550 HOURS
(X-DAY, N-HOUR −0010)

Frank Chadwick winced as he read the impersonal communiqué delivered to him on the flag bridge moments before.

0548 HOURS X-DAY
FROM: COMMANDER V CORPS
TO: ALL COMMANDS
SEVEN TRANSPORTS BURNING; TWO SUNK. LANDING
STRENGTH SERIOUSLY IMPAIRED. ENEMY EMPLOYING
SUICIDE PLANE ATTACKS ON MASSIVE SCALE. MANY
HITS FROM TORPEDOES. SUSPECT MANY OF THESE
SUICIDE CRAFT AS WELL.
    SECOND WAVE AWAY AT ESTIMATED FIFTY REPEAT
FIFTY PERCENT STRENGTH.

Rear Admiral Chadwick commanded Amphibious Group Five, part of the Fifth Amphibious Force, commanded by Vice Admiral Harry W. Hill. Fifth Amphibious Force, consisting of Amphibious Groups Four and Five—Four for transportation and landing, Five for naval gunfire and air support—was responsible for transporting and landing V Amphibious Corps. It was in turn part of the United States Fifth Fleet, under the overall command of Admiral Raymond Spruance. The Fifth Fleet was responsible for transporting and landing the entire invasion force. The Seventh Fleet, under Vice Admiral Thomas Kincaid, and the Third, under Vice Admiral Mark Mitchner, provided strategic support, both sea and air. And they reported to Commander, Naval Forces Olympic, Admiral Frank Fletcher. Admiral Nimitz, chief of naval operations, just "happened" to be in the area in case Fletcher couldn't handle things.

Chadwick also had "dotted line" accountability to the commander of the Fast Carrier Force for Fifth Fleet, Vice Admiral John McCain, who was his normal boss when he wasn't part of an operation.

Chadwick's command consisted of two new fleet carriers, the *Gettysburg* (CV-44) and the *Missionary Ridge* (CV-48); two light fleet carriers, the *Corregidor* (CVL-56) and the *Normandy* (CVL-57); two battleships; three light cruisers; one antiaircraft light cruiser; and seventeen destroyers. He was using the *Gettysburg* as his flagship.

Now, Chadwick passed the message around and waited for one of his staff to make some useful suggestion. God knows, *he* couldn't think of anything they could do to help.

"Admiral, the fighters over Roadster are starting to run low on fuel," reported the flight operations officer. "I recommend we bring them in and replace them with the combat air patrol standing by overhead."

"Right," Chadwick agreed. "Make it so."

He thought of the life-and-death struggles being waged twenty or thirty miles away, over and around the key beaches in the Roadster Zone. Dammit, they couldn't even *see* that battlefield from their position here, safely over the horizon!

It was that frustration that gave rise to a small idea, the only thing he could think of under the circumstances that might make the lives of the fighting men a little less deadly. "Let's take the fleet in closer. At least, we can make sure our fighters don't have to drive so far to come back and gas up."

"You mean, take the flattops in view of shore?" asked Commander Dickens, his chief of staff.

"I mean exactly that," Chadwick replied. "Get orders to the captains. I want to park my carriers as close this battle as we can get."

"Sir? Should we call Admiral Hill and request permission?" Dickens wondered aloud.

"Tell him that we're doing it. I'm staying within the parameters of the plan but bringing my flight decks a little closer to the action."

"Aye aye, sir," replied the commander. Already the staff was bustling, cutting new orders, plotting courses, opening communications to the many ships of Amphibious Group V.

As ever in the navy, the admiral's will be done.

ABOVE ROADSTER BEACH ZONE, OFF THE WEST COAST OF KYUSHU, JAPAN, 0730 HOURS (X-DAY, N-HOUR + 0130)

Kuroda Akida steered his *oka* (Cherry Blossom) toward the storm of fire and smoke that sprawled across so much of the sea. His hands were steady on the stick, and the roaring fire of the rocket engine propelled him through the air at blinding speed. He knew that he should feel a sense of deep honor since he had been chosen to die in one of the empire's most modern, and lethal, weapons.

Yet, surprisingly, he felt kind of numb.

The *oka* was like a flying torpedo. It had tiny wings and a very powerful rocket engine that currently propelled Kuroda at an unbelievable speed. That engine roared like a steady drum of thunder as it converted fuel to flame, leaving a trail of fire and smoke through the sky. A few moments ago, a pair of American fighters, land-based P-51s flying from Okinawa, had tried to give chase but had vanished to the rear as if they had been standing still.

The Cherry Blossom had been carried aloft beneath the belly of a twin-engine Mitsubishi bomber based upon Shokaku. Kuroda had already been aboard, strapped in to his small seat, ready for his mission. The pilots of the bomber had flown bravely out to sea, almost within sight of the American fleet. At the last minute, the *oka* had been dropped away and the rocket motor ignited.

From that moment on, Kuroda Akida was doomed. The suicide pilot flew what was in effect a flying bomb. He had a very limited supply of fuel and absolutely no way to land— the *oka* was not equipped with landing gear or amphibious flotation. His orders were to seek out an American transport and destroy it with his final act, a *tokko* flight for the glory of the Emperor and Japan.

Like many of the *tokko* pilots flying today and those preparing to fly in the weeks and months to come, Kuroda was a volunteer. Because of his willingness to fly the mission, and the aptitude he had demonstrated on his two training flights, he had been granted this special weapon. The Cherry Blossom had the speed to evade the enemy fighters, and a warhead explosive enough to devastate even the largest American warship. The aircraft was a marvel of technology, powered by rocket engines unlike anything developed in Japan before. Kuroda had heard rumors that German scientists had designed and perfected the engines, and that the plans had been carried halfway around the world, transported by U-boat, to enable his own countrymen to share the lethal technology. He didn't know if it was true or not, but he found himself believing the tales.

His Cherry Blossom, in fact, was far more deadly than most of the aircraft embarking upon their one-way missions. Many of them were obsolete types, such as the Mitsubishi Zero. At one time the state-of-the-art in fighter plane performance, the Zero had been outclassed years ago by the American Hellcats, Corsairs, and Mustangs. Now the slender, maneuverable Mitsubishis were only fit for carrying virtually untrained pilots on doomed flights against the American fleet. Inevitably, most of those suicide attackers would be shot down before they reached their targets.

Although he had only had two hours of flight training, Kuroda had little difficulty in handling his rocket plane. The engine controls were simple—the rockets were either on or off—and he was traveling at such speed that he wouldn't need to maneuver to avoid enemy fighters. He experimented slightly with the stick, lifting and then dropping the nose, veering a little bit to port, then back to starboard. He felt confident that he could control the *oka* well enough to fly it into an American ship.

Before dawn this morning, he had put his affairs in order. He wrote a letter to his mother and father, and then he composed his death haiku: "Divine winds roil the sea./Cherry blossoms bloom, then fade./Enlightened peace reigns." He and the other young suicide pilots at the base on Honshu, all of them former college students, had drunk a toast to the Emperor, and then to each other. In silence they had trooped into their cockpits, the Cherry Blossoms slung beneath the bombers that would carry them toward Kyushu. The sun was not yet over the horizon when they had taken off, but as the planes climbed they were soon brilliantly illuminated by the warm, bright rays.

Kuroda did not exactly want to die, but—like so many of his countrymen—he had come to realize that he had no choice. The war had already claimed so many Japanese. It seemed reasonable to expect that it would probably claim every one of his countrymen before it was over. It would claim him today. And if death was inevitable, why not make it count?

To that end, his orders vexed him. A transport was a dull ship, common and pedestrian. He was like a proud hunter who had been told to bag a cow in a dairyman's pasture. That order, even more than inevitable death, was galling. Kuroda desperately craved to die with a target worthy of his ancestry and his emperor.

. Approaching the landing fleet now, the pilot could not help but be impressed by the vast array of ships spread out below him. The little landing boats scuttled back and forth like ducklings, while the great transports sat like giant, motionless turtles. Already the *tokko* flights had done great damage—Kuroda spotted at least a half dozen transport ships that looked to be completely engulfed by flame. One had capsized, and another was sinking by the stern, still smoking as it slipped beneath the waves. Propelled by his hot-burning rocket, he flew above a flight of single-engine Japanese fighters, watched as they dove, one by one, toward the fleet sprawled below.

Which should he strike? It didn't seem to make much difference, he reflected in disappointment. All of these long gray ships looked the same. He might as well go for the closest one.

Wistfully, he raised his eyes, scanned the horizon for one last look at the world. When he glimpsed the flat, unmistakable shape on that horizon, perhaps ten miles away, his heart quickened. His hands, on the control stick, trembled like a young hunter's when he spots a trophy stag almost within range of his gun. Kuroda reacted instinctively, veering slightly, bringing the *oka* onto a bearing that carried him away from the transport fleet and out toward the open sea.

His original targets were already burning and mostly wrecked, he rationalized. Yet here, before him, was a target worthy of a Cherry Blossom! His flying bomb streaked through the sky, the sleek nose aimed directly for the deck of the American aircraft carrier that had, like a gift from the gods, appeared before him during his last moments on earth.

ABOVE ROADSTER BEACH ZONE, OFF THE WEST COAST OF KYUSHU, JAPAN, 0738 HOURS (X-DAY, N-HOUR + 0138)

Lefty Wayner was leading his squadron home with nearly empty fuel tanks. His hands were cramped and his ass was sore. A film of oil coated his goggles and the interior of the cockpit. But his mind was unaware of these mundane physical facts. Instead, he remained stunned by the scale of dying he had witnessed, the thousands of Americans immolated by the furious onslaught of suicide planes. The Hellcats of VMF Forty-eight had splashed some two dozen Japs, and the shipboard AA had claimed more. But all too many had gotten through. Now the Hellcats were heading back to fuel up. He hoped they could make the ship before anyone splashed on an empty tank.

Fortunately, the captain had brought the *Missionary Ridge* in closer to the action. As he approached, Lefty was surprised to see three more carriers—the whole of Admiral Chadwick's task group—also in view of the shore. It was a daring move but one for which the pilot could only be grateful.

He touched his microphone. "Sheepdog One to all Sheepdogs. If you're on your reserve tank already, go in first. Rest of you, line up and take turns like nice flyboys." Lefty, of course, held back as the Grummans of his squadron started into their landing patterns. As squadron commander, he would be the last to touch down.

A voice crackled in his earphones, the flight control officer from the *Missionary Ridge*. "Sheepdog One, we have a bogey, eight o'clock low, coming in fast. Can you intercept?"

Lefty looked over his right shoulder, banking the Hellcat so he could look down toward the surface of the sea. He spotted it almost instantly: a small plane, almost wingless, approaching quickly. It was hard to pick out the little aircraft itself, but it was clearly marked by the stream of smoke drifting along behind. It was bearing directly toward the *Missionary Ridge,* still three or four miles away, coming on with incredible speed.

Immediately the pilot put his F6F into a power dive, veering toward the mysterious enemy plane. It must be some kind of rocket, he reasoned, since he could see no sign of a piston engine, and nothing else easily explained that blazing velocity. The Hellcat dove steeply, almost straight down, in a frantic effort to intercept that approaching plane. Even from a mile overhead, Lefty could see that it would be close—he'd have only a split second to make a shot before the rocket blasted past him.

The enemy plane never veered, shooting straight toward the carrier like an arrow, or a bullet. It was two miles away, then one, and the ocean was coming up fast below the screaming Hellcat. Lefty would get one quick burst.

"Lead the target—lead it!" he barked to himself as he kicked the rudder slightly, aimed for a spot in front of the Jap rocket plane.

He touched the triggers and the six heavy machine guns chattered. The stream of bullets, marked by tracers, shot past the nose of the plane—and the Jap flew right into that stream.

The explosion slammed through the skies, shattering the glass of Lefty's cockpit, jamming his controls. Blinded by glass, debris, and the sheer force of the wind, he pulled back on the stick, bringing the Hellcat out of the power dive and into nearly level flight.

But he was still descending, slightly, and then the ocean was right there.

USS GETTYSBURG (CV-44), ROADSTER BEACH ZONE, OFF THE WEST COAST OF KYUSHU, JAPAN, 0740 HOURS (X-DAY, N-HOUR + 0140)

Chadwick watched as the suicide plane erupted into a cloud of debris. Like every other observer, he held his breath as the Hellcat that had made the kill struggled to pull up. He exhaled sharply, bitterly, as he saw the splash. A nearby destroyer immediately veered toward the site of the crash, but the admiral couldn't take the time to watch any longer.

"What the hell *was* that thing?" demanded one of the staff officers, a young lieutenant commander.

"Has to be a rocket," said the flight control officer. "Packed with explosives. Like a German V1, only with a pilot."

"Looks like our flyboy made it out," reported another man, a spotter with binoculars pressed to his eyes. "The DD is fishing him out of the drink."

"Thank God for that," Chadwick said fervently. "That pilot probably saved a thousand lives."

"But why was that rocket plane coming toward us?" asked Dickens. "They've been concentrating on transports all morning."

"I'll bet anything that SOB had orders to attack transports. But he can't resist an aircraft carrier, can he?" Chadwick said to his chief of staff.

"I guess not, sir."

The admiral strode to the outer flag bridge and looked across his fleet. He could see the other three carriers a few miles off. Toward shore, the island of Kyushu was completely screened by the thick clouds of smoke rising from the burning transports. It took only an instant for Chadwick to make up his mind.

"Get Admiral Hill on the horn. I want permission to take these flattops in closer. I want every goddamn Jap suicide pilot to see us here, and maybe we can draw 'em off the transports long enough to get the troops ashore."

"Aye aye, sir."

It was only a minute before Admiral Hill was back on the TBS radio. "You want to use the carriers as *decoys*?" he asked, getting right to the point.

"Yes, Admiral. At least until we get those transports unloaded. If we can take a little pressure off, we might be able to save a lot of lives."

"Hell, go for it," Hill replied. "Anything that gets more of my marines onto that beach, I like. I'll pass it upstairs for review, but in the meantime, good luck, Frank."

"Yes, Admiral. And thank you, sir."

The connection was broken, and by that time the big, gray hull of the *Gettysburg* was coming around, carrying the great flattop even closer to the enemy shore.

USS INDIANAPOLIS (CA-35), LIMOUSINE BEACH ZONE, OFF THE SOUTHWEST COAST OF KYUSHU, JAPAN, 0745 HOURS (X-DAY, N-HOUR + 0145)

Admiral Raymond Spruance paced back and forth on the flag deck as a steady stream of messages came to him—mostly concerning suicide attacks.

What a hellish battle this was. The relentlessly depressing dispatches had been pouring in all morning. This transport, then that transport, obliterated by enemy suicide planes. Five hundred men killed on this ship, a thousand perished with the next. And there seemed to be no end to the relentless stream of aircraft flown by these fanatical pilots.

Even so, he had been brought up short by Admiral Hill's message. Four carriers—and all their escorts—brought in practically on top of the landing fleet? Already the *Corregidor* had taken a hit on the flight deck, and the fighter pilots of all the ships were buzzing around like crazy, trying to protect the flattops from the numerous Japanese that suddenly turned toward these tempting targets.

But it had been twenty minutes since the last hit on a transport, and that was real breathing room, by God.

"Chadwick is logically correct," he agreed. "Let him stay where he is—and send out orders to the rest of the carriers. Bring them in close to all the beaches and have them stand ready to attract the attention of these suicide attackers."

USS GEORGE CLYMER (APA-27), ROADSTER BEACH ZONE, OFF THE WEST COAST OF KYUSHU, JAPAN, 0750 HOURS (X-DAY, N-HOUR + 0150)

Like an armada of spiders, marines in full fighting gear climbed down the huge rope net that hung down over the side of "Lucky George" and led to the waiting landing craft below. Some marines moved quickly. Pete took his time and made sure the men in his company took their time as well.

Fox Company consisted of three platoons, each commanded by a lieutenant with a sergeant as deputy. Each platoon had three squads of about a dozen men, each led by a corporal. The squads were further broken down into fire teams of four, with a lance corporal as team leader. Two were rifle platoons, one was a weapons platoon. The weapons platoon had mortars, machine guns, and flamethrowers.

That was the theory, anyway. Casualties, transfers, and the "needs of the service" often meant platoon and company strength was lower than it should be. Funny how that never seemed to alter the mission, though.

All around, black pillars of smoke rose into the air, each marking death and destruction on a transport of the V Amphibious Corps. The sky was thick with Japanese intent on suicide attacks. Pete was very anxious to make it into a landing craft before "Lucky George" got hit. He heard another nearby explosion, saw the blossom of crimson flame surge into the sky. Scratch one more transport, with a thousand men or more.

Then a particularly loud aircraft engine sound made him look up. It was a Zero, and it was coming straight at the deck. Black bursts of antiaircraft fire scattered around it, maddeningly close. But the Jap plane banked sharply and vanished from Pete's sight as it flew behind the bridge.

"Hold on, everybody!" he shouted.

The explosion shook the cargo net violently. Pete wrapped his arms tightly around the rope and held on for dear life, even when he was smashed face-first against the ship's hull. Two men in his company didn't make it. He heard their screams as they fell into the water. There was little or no hope of rescuing them.

Above, he could hear the crackle and roar of flames as "Lucky George" burned. Damage control parties were already on the way, according to the ship's loudspeaker. "Let's go, Fox Company!" he shouted. They moved more rapidly but still with great care.

Navy men were there to help them make that last difficult leap from the cargo net into the boat. It wasn't unusual to make it face-first. Anything beat landing in the water. Pete waited, directing the men of his company into the various boats and ensuring in each case there was an officer and a sergeant on board. Finally, he got on the last boat, following Captain Gilder.

The normal procedure was for someone from the deck to yell, "Shove off, Coxswain, you're loaded!" but they were busy.

"Let's go," Gilder ordered, and the captain of the boat gunned the engine and motored toward the rendezvous point.

Pete turned around. A plume of black smoke, shot through with streaks of angry flame, billowed upward from the transport's bow. The damage control parties were obviously getting things under control on "Lucky George," but there were waves of suicide planes still on the way. Another one was heading right at the transport. It looked like "Lucky George" was out of luck.

Suddenly, that plane banked to the right and sped off in a new direction. Pete swiveled to follow it and was shocked to see a huge ship cruising only a few miles away. *What the hell is that carrier doing out there?* The Jap was heading toward that ship, not another transport!

But the aircraft carriers were supposed to be farther away, where they could launch without being targets themselves. Why was it inviting attack? Was it here to lure the planes away from the transport?

If so, it was working. Pete could see three more planes turn toward the carrier like moths drawn to flame.

And then it was time to head for the beach.

FIFTEEN

Kyushu

*APPROACHING BEACH PONTIAC, ROADSTER BEACH ZONE,
KYUSHU, JAPAN, 0815 HOURS (OPERATION OLYMPIC,
X-DAY, N-HOUR + 0215)*

As the Higgins boat churned toward the beach, the chop increased into gray swells, lifting the little landing craft onto the crests and then dropping it precipitously into the troughs. The bow kept lifting up and slapping hard on the water. Already, nearly a third of the marines had puked, the vomit mixing with the sea spray and coating the bottom of the boat. Whether the vomiting was seasickness or nerves, Pete didn't know. From the sickly white looks of terror on a lot of faces—officers as well as enlisted—nerves certainly played a big part.

This was Pete's fourth beach landing. The first was Gavutu, part of Guadalcanal, which had been nasty. He'd just made lance corporal then. In the Philippines, where he went from corporal to staff sergeant, the opposition was pretty tough, but he was in a late wave. At Okinawa, the landing had been unopposed. Nothing from the enemy for about two weeks, then the shit hit the fan.

What else could he do? How else could he prepare his men for what they were about to experience?

"Everybody's scared shitless," he shouted over the roaring diesels. "Some get scared before, some during, and some after. Your best bet is to get scared after. Before is okay. During can get you killed." That was true enough. "I'm scared shitless the whole time, but I keep moving. I don't bunch up with other marines. I don't freeze. Those three things get a lot of men killed. Focus on your job. Afterward, you can get the shakes. But that's what booze is for."

Pete didn't know if a marine gunnery sergeant was supposed to admit he was terrified, but it was the truth. The biggest reason he hadn't died so far, though, is that he didn't let his fear freeze him. He kept moving. He hoped that advice would make the soldiers a little calmer. A few were listening in, and that was good. Calmness was increasingly in short supply as they got closer and closer to the beach.

As for Pete, he felt the odds were against him. He'd done this before. So many people had died around him, it was simple justice that it would be his turn this time.

Down in the boat, he couldn't see the action, but he could hear it. A barrage of explosions, swooping aircraft engines, and the occasional gush of water were about all that could make it over the diesels of the Higgins boat. Overhead, the dawn skies had turned brimstone black from the incredible barrage, as if marking a signpost: "You are now entering hell."

The boat churned onward, bouncing more violently as they neared the breakers. Closer to shore, the Japanese artillery opened up with a barrage so intense it felt like rain. Pete couldn't stand not seeing anymore, so he stuck his head up. His stripes kept the three-man crew from ordering him to keep his head down and the rest of him the hell out of their way, but he stayed carefully to the side anyway.

Plumes of water shot up as shells hit the water. Many rounds fell short, spuming ocean and sand up from the shallows. Other shells hit true. A burst of flames marked the funeral pyre of a nearby landing craft that didn't make it in—the boat was incinerated, a whole platoon killed, at the moment of impact. Another boat about twenty yards to the right took a direct hit. Pete could see bodies and body parts flying into the air. A minute later, there was an explosion right in front of them. As the boat hit the wave, it was lifted several feet into the air, canted to the right, and came crashing down, knocking men and equipment everywhere. One of his men fell out of the boat altogether. He couldn't tell who it was. The poor bastard was probably drowning, and there was nothing anyone could do. Maybe he'd get lucky and shed his equipment before he died. Maybe.

Pete could see the boat's coxswain struggling to keep on course. At least there wasn't too much danger from mines. Divers had been busy for several nights clearing safe lanes. Still, they might have missed a few.

There was a horrible skidding and scraping sound from underneath the boat as they reached shallow water. The front bow began to open.

"Weapons! Keep 'em high and dry! Move! Make sure you know where your feet are! Head for cover as soon as you get to shore!" All the platoon sergeants were hollering the same advice at their men. Everybody knew what to do, but when there was live ammo, people tended to forget the small stuff.

"Come on, men! Let's show those Japs what American marines can do!" shouted Captain Gilder, and the men piled out of the boat and into the water. The cold came as a shock. The water came up only to Pete's waist, but some marines were at chest depth. Holding their rifles overhead, the marines slogged forward into a hail of machine gun bullets. He could hear them whizzing by like angry bees. He could see them splash into the water. One hit the water directly in front of him only a foot away. He could feel the impact, but not much. Someone screamed, right in his ear, but he didn't stop to see who or why.

He was in a lottery of death. Skill and experience meant nothing. The bullets hit you or they didn't. You moved as quickly as you could in the water, but it was agonizingly slow. The water was another enemy, viscous and stubborn and resistant, dragging down his feet with its leaden weight. He pushed on, dragging his boondockers through the soft, shifting sands.

A bullet hit Private McKinlay in the face, spattering blood and pieces of skin and bone around him. He fell backward into the water, probably dead. Pete's only thought was relief.

It wasn't me. Thank God it wasn't me. McKinlay was from Ohio somewhere. That was all he could remember.

Corporal Lichtman, who was ten feet ahead of him, crumpled forward and landed facedown in the water. Pete didn't see what happened. Lichtman had been with the company since the Philippines. *It wasn't me. Thank God. It wasn't me.*

More angry bees buzzed by him. Then suddenly there was a sharp pain in his upper right shoulder. *Shit! Omigod omigod omigod I've been hit! Don't let me die don't let me die.* His heart pounded in his chest. He vomited the remainder of his breakfast. But he wasn't falling, wasn't dying . . . not yet.

There went one . . . two . . . five more of his men. Even those who were only wounded fell with loaded packs into the water. The only ones who stood up again had dropped pack and weapon.

The water was taking on a pink froth, the tinge visible in the curling breakers, the explosions of brine as the waves broke and crashed onto the sloping sand of the shore. The waves dumped more than water onto the beach—they cast limp bodies onto the land and rolled back out to collect more flesh. Some of those bodies lay motionless, soaked and lifeless, while others twitched and groped and clawed their way farther out of the sea.

Ahead of him was the beach, *right there.* It was only another ten yards or so. Each step he took was an agony of slow motion. He had the strange sensation that the strand of dry land was moving *away* from him, warping like a fun house mirror. Waves still carried the detritus of battle, the bodies of marines cast upon the land as the breakers crested, surged, and broke.

The beach itself looked like a Chesley Bonestell painting of the surface of Mercury, the side that always faced toward the sun. It was cratered and alien. A massive DUKW, an amphibious truck that had been torn in half by a direct hit, lay on its side and burned. The huge fire was painful to look at as the intense heat blistered the air for twenty or thirty feet.

The continual barrage made the surface roil in a constant tremor. Sand flew through the air in stinging blasts, mixed with spray, tainted with blood. Nothing felt steady.

The beach ahead was littered with corpses from the two earlier waves. Just a quick glance at the bodies told Pete it had to have been hell, worse than any fighting he'd ever seen. Some corpses were intact. Others had been blown apart, body parts strewn randomly and intermixed. Still others had been reduced to a smear of blood, flesh, and char. The air stank. It reeked of petroleum and cordite and gore and shit.

The early waves had put machinery on the beach. A flamethrowing amphibious tank, burned black, still had flames licking out of it. A crewman who had been caught halfway out gave off the smell of cooked meat. He was nearly unrecognizable as a human. Other amphibious tanks, armored amphibian tractors sporting 75mm howitzers, and various American and Japanese fighters had all been twisted into strange modern sculptures by the application of high explosives.

It was all cover, though. Even the corpses.

He felt warmth in the cold water and realized he'd pissed himself. At least no one would know. And he'd done worse. In the Leyte invasion he'd lost control of his bowels. He hadn't been the only one, though, not by a long shot.

An artillery shell landed at the water's edge about twenty feet away. The ground shook under him, a miniature earthquake, and sand spattered up in his face, blinding him temporarily. The spray drenched every part of his body that wasn't already soaked.

He kept slogging through the water, rifle over his head. Bullets buzzed angrily past him to slap against the water. Waves surged from behind him, pushing him. He'd been fighting the water all the way in, and now he hated that irresistible propulsion, impelling him in the direction he had been trying to go.

Another Marine in Fox Company fell. He saw the face, he

knew who it was, but for the life of him he couldn't think of the man's name. The body hit the surface of the water and began to sink slowly. *Who the hell was that? (It wasn't me it wasn't me it wasn't me . . .)*

The water receded below the level of Pete's knees. He could move faster now, pulling his feet free of the clutching surf. Finally he was on the beach. Twenty more feet and he'd be temporarily safe behind a metal nightmare that looked like it had its origins in a P-38. Other marines had already reached it. Another artillery shell burst a few feet away. The explosion knocked him sideways. He crawled behind a marine corpse for shelter.

Pete's ear hurt. He reached up with his good arm and touched it. When he looked at his hand there was blood. He noticed that all the battle sounds had become distant. The explosion had knocked out most of his hearing.

Pete took a look at the dead marine. His stomach had been torn open and the guts were spilled onto the beach. He glanced at the face. Private Palermo. Second Platoon. Good-looking. He'd done some professional crooning in nightclubs before the war and everybody kidded him about being the next Sinatra. It wasn't going to happen now.

Pete shouted through the din at Privates Carr and Sullivan, who had just escaped the deadly surf at the cost of their packs and rifles, "Take what you need from the bodies. Rifles and ammunition first."

Carr looked at him in shock, like he'd just proposed eating the dead. He said something Pete couldn't hear. "Dammit," Pete shouted, "take what you need! They don't have a use for it anymore!"

Then it all stopped mattering to Carr as red flowers appeared on his chest and he, too, crumpled forward. That motivated Sullivan to dive onto his belly and begin creeping forward to Pete's position.

"Stay the fuck away from me," Pete yelled. "Groups attract more fire. I don't want to be hit by the bullet with your name on it! We all meet up at the end of the beach."

"Fuck you, Gunny," Sullivan gasped. "I'm gonna take the rifle and supplies off—shit, it's Palermo."

Pete suddenly realized he could hear the words through a loud ringing in his ear. His hearing was coming back, though slowly. Pete patted Sullivan on the shoulder by way of an apology. The sudden sharp pain in his arm reminded him that he had a little scrape to take care of, but right now nothing was more important than moving forward. Pete looked around for his next bit of cover, and did a sprint.

Gasping for breath under the weight of pack and supplies, he dived for cover behind the wreckage of the P-38. He felt himself trembling all over. He was wet and cold, colder than he should be.

Fox Company was spread out along several hundred feet of Beach Pontiac. They needed to be pushed forward, when the temptation was to stay behind the first piece of decent cover you found. That was part of Pete's job.

Crouching low and dodging as best he could, Pete started to work his way across the line, getting his company reorganized, collecting stragglers, and helping men who'd been separated from their teams. Twice he hid behind corpses and felt bullets thud into the already-dead bodies. The spray of blood and other fluids stuck to his face.

In between the P-38 and the burning tank, Pete could see Captain Gilder. He was pointing toward a couple of wrecked tractors about twenty yards ahead of them. "Platoons! Move forward and take cover behind those tractors!" The lieutenants passed the word and the sergeants pushed their men forward—for those platoons that still had a lieutenant. Fox Company was already down two lieutenants, one a shavetail. Sergeants were running the show now.

Pete took a deep breath and started his run toward the tractors. He saw bullets ping off metal hulks and thud into the sand. He could hear them. He felt as if he was running in a dream, his limbs heavy and unresponsive. And then, suddenly, he was almost at the tractor and he dived once again and threw himself on the ground next to Captain Gilder.

The captain said something. Pete couldn't make it out.

"I stood too near an explosion, Captain. My ears . . . I can hear a little."

"How are we doing?" shouted the captain.

Pete panted for a minute and said, "It looks like we've lost about forty so far." He had been keeping rough track in his head, and the number was bad. That was a casualty rate of around 20 percent. They'd planned on no more than 10 percent, and they were only twenty yards away from the surf.

"I thought the Japanese weren't supposed to fight us at the beaches," the captain shouted. "That's what the briefing said."

"I guess the Japs missed the briefing," Pete replied.

"Guess so. Shit. What a complete fucking nightmare."

Pete looked back. At the water's edge, the Higgins boats were pulling away, heading back to the transports for another load. At a platoon per load, they would be ferrying troops for hours. As he watched, a Japanese artillery shell hit one of the outgoing boats, and the wooden craft exploded in a hail of splinters. *At least it was going out, not in,* he thought. Then he thought about the three men on board. Three more down.

Gilder's eyes were glassy, his skin pallid as he looked frantically around. The captain was a bit shell-shocked, Pete knew, realizing that he felt the same way himself. All around them, the carnage was terrific. The American advance was pressing forward slowly, but at a terrible cost. The Japanese defenders were evidently determined to make the Americans pay a high price for every foot of ground. Artillery shells continued to thunder around them while machine gun bullets fell like hail.

Gilder took a deep, shuddering breath. "Okay. We'll do it the way we rehearsed it. Our first objective is those machine gun emplacements. We're right in line for them, as planned." They had done this landing under simulated conditions four times and rehearsed it on paper a dozen more. While "no battle plan survives first contact with the enemy," as the saying went, at least having a plan was a definite improvement over trying to improvise one while people shot real bullets at you.

"Gunny," the captain said, "get me a real head count, okay?"

"Yes, sir." The platoon leaders, the captain, and Pete had walkie-talkies. Pete unhooked his. "Torpedo Two." Torpedo was a prewar Pontiac model. Pontiac had stopped making cars for the duration. "Check in."

"Torpedo Three," was the first platoon, the only one with an officer left. First Lieutenant Straw had seen the elephant at Okinawa and had done pretty well. "Eight down."

"Torpedo Four. Sergeant Schalles commanding. Fifteen down, including the lieutenant."

"Torpedo Five. Sergeant Townley. Nineteen down, ditto."

"Torpedo One." That was Captain Gilder.

Once the captain had a handle on his actual losses—the equivalent of a full platoon—he issued orders. Scouts went out right and left carrying two of the precious walkie-talkies. About ten minutes later, they reported in. The Japanese were holed up in a concrete pillbox on a small hill about forty feet away. There was little cover on the direct line between Fox Company's position and the Japs. A direct attack would be suicide.

"What do you advise?" asked the captain.

"Circle around and hit it from the rear, sir. More cover there."

"Roger. Stay in position and report on any changes."

"Yes, sir."

"Torpedo One out."

The captain thought for a moment. "Okay. Gunny, here's what I want. You take two rifle squads and keep firing. When you hear from me, really open up. I'm going to circle left with the rest of the rifles and our flamethrowers until I'm behind the pillbox, if I can get there. Meanwhile, I want the mortars to circle right, find a good spot, and wait for my signal to send them a little love note from Uncle Sam. Got it?"

"Suggestion, Captain."

"Go ahead."

"A rifle team with the mortars. In case there are some

loose Japs roaming around. And one mortar team here, if you can spare it."

"Yeah. Okay." Gilder took a quick swig of water from his canteen. "Go ahead."

Pete toggled his walkie-talkie. "Torpedo Two to Torpedo Six."

"Torpedo Six." That was the scout on the left.

"Mark a route and find a good staging area. You've got company for dinner."

"Torpedo Six. Mark route, find staging area, welcome dinner guests."

"Confirmed. Two out."

It took less than five minutes of coordination for Pete to put the teams together. The captain and the mortar team moved out to left and right respectively, keeping low and moving from one bit of cover to another. They now had the other two walkie-talkies, leaving Pete with the last one.

Pete called out, "Good hunting, Captain."

He had one sergeant, Townley, and a full corporal, Canfield. The mortar team had a lance corporal as team leader. "Let's spread out the line and fire widely to make them think it's a whole company back here," Pete told them. "The better job we do, the better chance the captain has of putting those machine gunners out of commission permanently." Townley knew weapons, so he could oversee the mortar teams.

Now that they had some cover and were shooting back, a little life was coming back into his men. Pete duck-walked down the line, staying low. He stopped beside one private. "What's the matter, son?" he asked, even though the private was maybe two years his junior. The private—the name badge read Sanvito—was aiming his rifle but not firing.

"I've—well, I've never shot at a human being before."

"I see. The Japs don't seem to have that trouble, though, do they?"

"No, Gunny. But—"

"I know. It may surprise you, Sanvito, but you're not the first marine to have this problem."

Sanvito, who was clearly expecting to be bawled out, court-martialed, or shot, looked at Pete. There were tears in his eyes. "I *can't*!"

"Okay." Pete kept his voice calm. If he screwed up, he could ruin a perfectly good potential marine. "Try this. Don't shoot at human beings. See that wrecked tank?"

"Uh—yeah, Gunny?"

"Shoot at that. It's not a human being."

"Okay," the private said, a slight question mark creeping in at the end. He shot.

"Now shoot at that pillbox. Not at the slit, just at the building."

"Okay." He shot again.

"This is suppressive fire, Marine. I don't care if you kill anybody or not. I want them to keep their heads down and not shoot at us. Can you do that?"

"Well, I—I guess—if you put it that way . . ."

"Good man," Pete said, patted him on the shoulder, and moved on. He was satisfied to hear a steady stream of rifle shots. It was hard to shoot at humans. A lot more soldiers—even marines—failed to shoot their rifles in combat than most people suspected. It was one of the many surprises he'd found when he first became a sergeant.

The second mortar team opened fire. Blasts of sand and smoke erupted from the crest of the dune, where the pillbox was located. The crump of explosions, so close in front of him, seemed more real than the distant artillery, the continuing thunder of the naval bombardment.

The Japanese pillbox was taking quite a pounding. Pete could imagine what they were going through. He'd been on the receiving end of a mortar himself.

The walkie-talkie crackled to life. "Torpedo One to Torpedo Two."

"Torpedo Two."

"Am passing to the attack. Stop suppressing fire."

"Roger. Torpedo Six, cease fire." That was the second mortar team. Then, off the walkie-talkie, he shouted, "Cease firing!"

Now the noise was coming from the hilltop as the captain and the rest of the company moved in. It was hard to tell the grenades from the flank attackers from the background artillery shelling that was still going on.

It was easy to tell when the constant machine gun fire stopped.

"Looks like the captain did it," Pete shouted and received cheers in return. "Move forward by squad." His two squads and the mortar team began to move forward toward the now-silent pillbox; the squad that wasn't on the move crackled off suppressive fire while the other marines crawled and scrambled onward.

The radio burst into noise. "Torpedo Five! Stop where you are! The fucking Japs have—"

The titanic explosion threw the pillbox nearly twenty feet into the air.

"Jesus fucking Christ!" said Corporal Canfield. "They mined the fucking thing and blew the shit out of it when they got breached."

"Yeah, and they took themselves with it," Sergeant Townley pointed out.

Pete stood there in shock, and then in horror as the torso of a dead soldier landed right in front of him, followed by a red spray that spattered everyone in his small command. He retched and gagged emptily; he couldn't help it. He went down on his knees, wracked by dry heaves. The smell of blood and offal mixed with the sulfurous odor of gunpowder kept him in spasms for a long minute, even though there was nothing left to come up.

"You okay, Gunny?" Townley asked.

"Yeah," said Pete weakly. He straightened up as best he could. *I must look like warmed-over shit,* he thought. Hardly a sight to inspire confidence in his men. "Townley, Canfield, each of you send three men to scout the perimeter for survivors. Don't go closer than about twenty feet. There may be more mines."

With Gilder and Lieutenant Straw dead, that left Pete in charge.

There were seventeen survivors. Added to his existing force, that gave him the equivalent of three squads.

One platoon.

That was all that remained of Fox Company.

BATTLESHIP USS OREGON (BB-65), KUSHIRI STRAIT, ROADSTER BEACH ZONE, KYUSHU, JAPAN, 1021 HOURS (X-DAY, N-HOUR + 0421)

"All hands brace for impact!" crackled the loudspeaker.

Rear Admiral (lower half) Theodore White couldn't see anything to hold onto, so he put his back up against the aft bulkhead of the flag deck as an antique Japanese Zero flew directly into a twelve-inch gun battery on the forward deck. The resulting explosion shook the entire ship, throwing the 3rd Marine Division commander, Major General Graves B. Erskine, to the floor. White had to catch his balance a few times as the ship lurched back and forth, but he managed to remain standing.

The petty officer maintaining the situation board had also managed to keep standing. He cursed under his breath. Some of the marker pieces on his table had slid out of position, even though they were magnetized. He moved ships and shore units back in position with nudges of what looked like a Vegas dice stick.

"Those bastards are beating the hell out of us," Erskine said, climbing to his feet. He wiped his hand across his nose, grimacing in disgust as he saw the blood on his fingers. "You've got to protect those transports better! We've got to get more armor to the beach, and we need it there *now*!"

White looked down at the deck. Damage crews were spraying hoses on the flames. He could see medics carrying sailors away on stretchers. The heavily armored turret had been ripped open like a tin can slashed by the blow of an ax.

As the petty officer received a transmission slip and pulled another transport off the board, Major General Harry Schmidt rubbed his cheek absentmindedly. The Dutchman was the commanding officer of V Amphibious Corps, and he was flying his flag aboard the *Oregon* until the situation permitted him to move his headquarters ashore.

Admiral White also flew his flag aboard the *Oregon*. He was commander of Amphibious Group Four, the amphibious operations task group responsible for transportation and landings for the nine beaches in the Roadster Beach Zone. He reported to Vice Admiral Hill, commander of the Fifth Amphibious Force, with "dotted line" responsibilities to the overall commander of amphibious operations for Olympic, the irascible but legendary Kelly Turner.

Turner was managing an invasion involving landings on seven times as many beaches as were involved in the entire Normandy invasion. This was by several orders of magnitude the largest such operation in world history.

And the suicide bombers were putting it all in jeopardy. From the flag bridge, White could see the funeral pyres of at least six ships. There were more, smoking and dying along the horizon. He couldn't be sure how many; the smoke obscured a lot. More black puffs appeared in the air as the fleet's antiaircraft guns spat desperately at the fanatical enemy fliers.

"General, these suicide attacks are devastating us," White replied. There was no way in hell that he was going to take all the shit here. The marines were having trouble, too. And Erskine knew it.

The rain of attacks on the transports had cost the lives of thousands of soldiers and marines just in his beach group alone. Worse, it looked like suicide attacks weren't limited to the air. The Japanese were sending out small boats and minisubmarines loaded with explosives. The subs were particularly dangerous, like intelligent torpedoes. Only a little while ago he'd seen a modern destroyer, steaming at flank speed, blow up from some unseen attack. The ship's back was broken, and the two halves had vanished into the sea, the whole ship disappearing only a couple of minutes after the attack.

But the reports from shore were just as grim as the carnage he witnessed at sea. The Japs were fighting like hell for every scrap of soil, and then blowing it—and often themselves—up in the process, taking a hell of a lot of fine soldiers with them. Casualties had passed the 25 percent mark and the landings weren't even five hours old. Worse, even the initial objectives of the campaign were already far behind schedule. Most of the landing platoons had yet to make it through the dunes and over the seawall.

Working from south to north along the west coast of Kyushu, General Erskine's 3rd Marine Division was responsible for Beaches Pontiac and Red, with ten thousand feet of beachfront property to claim. General Clifton B. Cates and his 4th Marine Division had Beaches Rolls-Royce, Saxon, and Star, with eight thousand feet. General Keller E. Rockey, commander of the 5th Marine Division, had Studebaker, Stutz, Winton, and Zephyr, another eight thousand feet, but considered particularly tough because of the challenging terrain.

White looked at the board and tried to think of a respectable option he hadn't already tried. "General, the navy's got every airplane they can get into the sky and I'm unloading the transports as fast as I can. They've even brought the goddamn carriers into sight!"

Erskine clenched his fist and pounded it into his other palm. The smoking wreck of an escort carrier was in view only a couple of miles away. Another flattop, this one a modern fleet carrier, had taken a suicide attack into the flight deck, but the wreckage had been cleaned up, the fires extinguished, and the ship—in plain sight to the west—continued to conduct flight operations. "I know, I know. But *everybody's* got to do better. We do, you do, the flyboys do. 'Good enough' just isn't good enough for this situation. Whatever the Japs throw at us, we've got to throw it back, and more besides."

The admiral wished he knew how his counterparts were faring on other beaches. Was he doing about as well as average? Below average? Even above average? It wasn't the sort of question one could ask.

White looked at the depressing landscape represented by

the board. Each ship counter represented a ship, but marine counters represented companies. That meant the marine situation was even worse than it looked, because some of those companies had been pretty badly chewed up.

"General, we'll move the reserve transports up and start filling them. Admiral Chadwick has still got to recover the planes. There's not much more he can do. I understand that more aircraft, including army bombers, are on the way from Okinawa." White opened his arms. "We're going to take casualties going in. That's a fact. I'm sorry as hell."

"Son of a fucking bitch," growled Erskine. "I hope it's enough. What asshole decided to plan on the theory that the fucking Japs weren't going to defend the beachheads?"

General Schmidt said, "Listen, Graves, I know goddamn well who made the decision about the beaches. It was wrong, okay? But nobody—I mean *nobody*—could have predicted this suicide shit."

White nodded. "They just aren't human," he said. "Not like you or me."

EAST OF SENDAI, KYUSHU, DELIVERY WAGON BEACH ZONE, 1243 HOURS (X-DAY, N-HOUR + 0643)

Ellis toggled his microphone. "DuQuesne Flight, this is DuQuesne One. Time to look alive, gentlemen. Target the airfield and let's put it out of commission." He nosed the *Skylark of Valeron* into a dive. This was low-altitude precision bombing, a really tough way to make a living. If they succeeded, there wouldn't be any more suicide planes taking off from this airstrip—at least, not for today.

Already VII Bomber Command had every available aircraft in flight. The original mission, laid on during the exhaustive planning sessions, had been the bombardment of enemy fortifications. Squadron after squadron of medium bombers had been designated for close support to the marines and soldiers as they fought and clawed their way ashore. The heavy bombers were taking out airfields and major fortifications.

But the suicide plane attacks had changed everything. Ellis had seen the shit storm at sea, as they flew past the shambles of the invasion fleet. Hundreds of ships were burning or sinking, and planes were taking off from all over Kyushu. Responding to the threat, swarms of army and navy scout planes had been assigned to photo recon flights for the last few hours, watching for takeoffs, and doing everything they could think of to find the originating fields. Put those strips out of commission, and—the theory went—you would slow or stop the attacks, at least long enough to get the forces on shore. Unfortunately, the airfields and hangars were underground, camouflaged, and ringed with antiaircraft guns.

He had one heavy bomb wing (the 5th) of three bomb groups and two medium bomb wings (the 57th and the 2nd). The 5th Bomb Wing, because of the longer range, was heading for the east side of Kyushu. The 57th had the east sector and the 2nd the center. Ellis was flying with the 5th. They couldn't wait for photo intel to reach Okinawa, so they took off without it, breaking all kinds of radio silence rules as the target info was relayed, in the clear, to planes already flying toward Japanese island.

Once they had the information, Ellis had broken his command into mission groups. It wasn't normal to do it in flight, but this wasn't a normal situation. All of the targets were small, well-camouflaged dirt strips, scattered about central and northern Kyushu, so he divided his aircraft into six plane sections, one section targeting each airstrip as the recon observers reported in. Before taking off, Ellis had ordered his pilots to fly low and slow, to really get a fix on the target before they plastered it with a mixture of incendiary and cratering bombs.

For his own section he flew toward a target in a central valley of the large, mountainous island. He led his group of six B-24 Liberators in on the beam sent by a photo-equipped P-38, making direct radio contact with the observer as the heavy bombers came around the shoulder of Mount Aso, one of the higher summits on Kyushu.

"DuQuesne Flight, this is Eyeball Ten; got y'all on visual,"

· came the laconic introduction from the spotter. He spoke in an improbably thick Alabama drawl and pronounced it "Doo-ques-nee" rather than "Doo-Kane."

"Eyeball, this is DuQuesne One," Ellis came back. "Whattya got for us?"

"Down yonder, where the two cricks come together, there's a lane along through that rice flat, there. They sent two Zekes up that sumbitch not fifteen minutes ago. On the far side of both cricks," Eyeball added helpfully.

Even then, Ellis couldn't immediately see the strip. He held the *Valeron* in a shallow dive, picking up speed even as he backed off on the throttles. Only as he scanned the rice paddies for the third time did he see it: a long, straight strip raised above the wet ground. As he zoomed closer, he spotted several barns and groves of trees where the Japs could have concealed any number of planes. A truck rumbled into view, rocking and lurching down the lane of dry ground, racing toward the far end off the strip.

He pressed the throat mike on the intercom, speaking to his crew. "Everybody in line back there?" he asked.

"Lined up like a Fourth of Joo-ly parade," replied Dick Sweeney, his tail gunner.

"On my lead," Ellis ordered, switching back to the radio. "We've got revetments and a strip. Use your guns to sweep up."

The *Valeron* picked up speed as he goosed the engines. To either side, he could see the flash of ack-ack guns, several of them popping off along the adjacent ridge crests. He felt a little pucker, and for a moment he wished he still had his little hot rod of a B-26.

But, hell, they hadn't spotted DuQuesne Flight too early, and the flak was bursting high. The airspeed indicator on the *Valeron* crept into the red zone and he backed off the throttle a little more. He pressed the trigger, firing the heavy machine guns aligned with the fuselage, while the twin turret guns erupted behind him. Sandy Barker, the gunner, was good; the racing truck abruptly exploded into flames and veered off the wide roadway to crash into the marsh.

Ellis kept up the fire from the nose guns, watching the tracers march along the runway as Japanese mechanics and pilots scurried for shelter. He released his bombs low. Two hits on the runway, and hot damn! An occupied revetment! It must have been a fully armed plane, too, because it went up with an explosion that shook his B-24 as he pulled up.

Behind him he could hear other drops. It took a lot of bombs to put a runway out of commission, especially a dirt strip, and it was too easy to get the runway back in shape.

As he gained altitude, he banked right sharply to turn in a full circle. Had everyone made it? Damn. He could see the blazing wreckage of one of his bombers in a stand of trees just past the runway.

"DuQuesne One! Check in!" he called.

"DuQuesne Three," drawled the North Carolina accent of Lieutenant Bob Widener.

"DuQuesne Five." Elliott Sewell, from Long Island.

One by one, the rest of his flight checked in.

The missing plane was DuQuesne Two, *Madam, I'm Adams*. Fred Adams was from Massachusetts and claimed to be a distant relative of the two former U.S. presidents. Ellis had done the nose art personally, a portrait of Adams bowing to a hooker in a low-cut dress.

Adams had been married a half year before, just before shipping out. He had been delighted by the news that he had a kid on the way.

One bomber for one runway. The Japs wouldn't put up any more suicide planes out of here, not today. He'd be back to see them again tomorrow.

But it still hurt to lose a plane.

BEACH PONTIAC, 2141 HOURS (X-DAY, N-HOUR + 1541)

Pete opened a can of peaches and poured them into his mouth, letting some of the juice run down his chin. When he finished the fruit, he held the can over his nose to mask the miasma of ashes mixed with death. Right now, the ashes were winning out. The death smell would shortly beat it, but by then, 2nd Battalion of the 3rd Marines—what was left of it—would have moved to another burning ash pile. The arm movement, the act of lifting the can, still hurt a bit. The bullet had put a pretty nice tear in the skin and everything was sore, but it was hardly the million-dollar wound.

The sun was low on the horizon. Fox Company needed to hole up for the night. This looked like a good place, smell or no smell. Most of the sandbags were still in place. The booby-trapped pillbox where Captain Gilder bought it was a good two hundred yards and a dozen dead marines, behind them.

Pete was sitting with his back against a piece of scrap metal that had once been much of a Japanese mortar emplacement. A small hill stood between this little clearing and the beaches. Nearby was some concrete rubble that originally served as either a barracks or ammo dump. They'd found a covered hole that served as a larder, but it was filled with weird as shit Jap food that nobody wanted to eat. He'd stationed guards behind the sandbags, but he wasn't counting on the barrier to provide much protection. It hadn't stopped *his* men.

The area about him was blackened from fire from the explosion: the Japanese had mined *all* their positions, as far as Pete could tell. Corpses—about fifty Japanese, about ten American—had been scattered about, but he'd made his men drag them to the edge of the position. He couldn't be sure of the exact numbers, because few of the corpses were whole. Many were burnt into shapes not quite recognizable as human. He thought about throwing the corpses over the sandbags and out of their makeshift camp, but he was afraid they'd draw animals and noise.

The rest of the men were sitting in a ragged circle, except for the guards. The sound of artillery fire was still constant, though more distant. The machine guns, for the time being, were silent.

Pete tried his walkie-talkie again to see if he could pick up anybody else. Nothing. His hearing, fortunately, had come back completely by the end of the day.

Fox Company had shrunk from one platoon to two squads in the process of getting off the beach and taking out three pillboxes and this mortar battery. Pete's marines had come across Baker Company when they were pinned down by a Japanese machine gunner and taken that gun out as well.

In terms of men, Baker Company had done a little better than Fox. It had nearly two platoons left. The combined Baker-Fox force had one mortar team and two flamethrowers, making five rifle squads and one weapons squad, more or less.

And Baker Company had an officer.

He was a second lieutenant, a platoon leader named Kinney. He found Pete while the gunnery sergeant was still enjoying the sweetness of the peach juice slicking his lips, coating his tongue. Kinney crouched down next to Pete, his eyes wide, looking back and forth through the darkness.

"Look at us! We've been chewed to bits! We've got to get the fuck out of here, or we're all going to die!" He was whispering, but his voice cracked at the end, almost rising to a scream.

Although the lieutenant was the ranking officer and technically in charge, the opinion of a gunnery sergeant counted for a lot. Sergeant Townley, who was behind the lieutenant, gave him a significant look. *Need some help with this jelly bean?*

Dammit, he couldn't afford this right now. Slowly, he stood up. "Lieutenant, let's talk over here," he suggested.

Kinney turned on him. "Gunny, dammit, I know what you're going to say, but it's over! We have to get out of here! We have to get reinforcements, and then we can come back later! Don't give me any of that 'we're marines' bullshit! We're not Japs, and suicide isn't how Americans fight! Understand? We're leaving, and that's an order! That's an order, understand? An order!" His eyes were getting a little wild and he put his hand on his service .45. Behind him, Townley was resting his hand casually on his rifle.

Pete repeated himself calmly. "May I speak with you in private, sir?"

There was a pause as the lieutenant looked at him, then

looked around at the men, then looked back at him, all while keeping his hand on his pistol. His eye movements were getting wilder and wilder. He was about to break. "All right, Gunny, but make it quick. We're getting out of here, understand? We're getting the fuck out of here!" He wheeled around, yelling at all the men. "We're getting the fuck out of here! All of us!"

Pete could see some hope among the privates. *Goddammit.* "Come with me, Lieutenant," he said firmly but calmly, and started walking. Kinney followed.

Pete heard Townley growling at the men behind him: "All right, you jarheads, look alive!" The gunnery sergeant led Kinney away from the remnant of the company.

The lieutenant was panting, almost like a thirsty dog. He glanced over his shoulder, but Pete kept walking and Kinney followed along, coming around the corner of the shattered, shell-torn building. Part of the cinder-block wall was still standing, after a fashion. It blocked them only to about waist height, but it was the best Pete could do. He crouched down, pulling the lieutenant with him.

"We've got to get the fuck out of here," Kinney said, fixing Pete with a wild-eyed stare. "Don't you see? I've got to get out of here!"

Checking to see that he was safely out of sight of the rest of the men, Pete backhanded Kinney across the face. "Goddammit, you fucking little shit rag, if you don't start acting like a marine, I am going to shoot your fucking ass right here and leave you to die. Do you understand me?"

"You assaulted a superior officer!" the lieutenant croaked. "I'll have you court-martialed!"

Pete slapped him again. The lieutenant reached for his pistol, but Pete grabbed his wrist and pushed him back against the wreckage. "I will fucking kill you right here," he growled, his face an inch away from the lieutenant's. "You are going to die one way or another unless you get yourself under control. *Now!*"

There was a pause, and then the lieutenant began to sob. "I'm sorry . . . I'm sorry . . . I'm sorry . . . ," he moaned.

Pete put his hands on Kinney's shoulders. "Look, it happens. You're not the first. And it's not too late. You need to go back, go. But go like a marine."

This took Kinney by surprise. "Go? I can go?" he said, looking up. The tears had traced lines through the dirt on his face.

"Yes, sir. Look, Lieutenant. We've still got a mission to finish, no matter how chewed up we are. But we've got wounded as well, and there are probably more wounded— marines we maybe thought were dead—all the way back to the beach. Right now, there's no help for them, no rescue, no nothing. But we're not going to leave them there. Marines don't abandon marines. That's part of the mission, too."

The lieutenant was intrigued. "You mean I should get the wounded back to safety?"

"That's right. Take our wounded, gather all the others you can, get them to safety, then come back and get some more. The situation isn't as bad down there, but it's still dangerous enough. You can handle it. Take care of your fellow marines, Lieutenant. That's your job. *Semper fidelis,* remember?"

"A-all right, Gunny. All right." Pete could feel him relax. The crisis was past. "Uh, Sergeant?"

"Yes, sir?"

"Uh—am I . . . uh—do you—"

Pete grinned. "Do I think a few minutes of stress make you a coward, sir? Is that what you're asking?" *Damn right I do. Hell, I'm just as scared as you. Maybe more. But I'm not running out on the job.*

"Uh—yeah."

"No, sir. Absolutely not," he lied. "First time under fire, right?"

"Yeah."

"It happens all the time. You take care of the wounded like I suggest, you keep doing your job, you'll be okay. You'll make a fine marine officer, sir. I know you will." *If a line of bullshit helps turn you around, I'm happy to crap it out.*

"T-thanks, Gunny."

"Don't mention it. Let's get back to the others."

The rest of the men had taken the opportunity to down a bit of food or smoke a cigarette. Two had managed to fall asleep. They all managed to avoid expressions of curiosity when Pete and the lieutenant returned. "The lieutenant has some orders for us," Pete said.

Kinney looked at Pete questioningly, then at the men. "Uh, I'm dividing us into two groups. Everybody who's wounded will follow me. We're going to retrace our steps, find other wounded, get them to safety, then come back and find some more. Marines don't abandon marines. It's our mission to get any of our people to safety we can find. Gunny and the rest of you will continue with the original plan to clear out Japanese emplacements and link up with the 1st Battalion. Understand?"

"Yes, *sir*," Pete said, saluting the lieutenant. He then walked along the line of men. Most of them had wounds of some sort—Pete himself had that scrape on his arm where a bullet had grazed him. He picked out the three men in worst shape. For good measure, he pointed to Corporal Canfield as well. He hated to lose him, but the shavetail needed an experienced marine to babysit him. "These are the wounded, sir," he said, turning to the lieutenant.

"Thank you, Gunny," Kinney replied.

He had the good grace to be ashamed. Maybe he'd turn out to be a decent officer after all. You could never tell.

"Finish your food and smokes, then we'll move out," the lieutenant added.

Not bad, thought Pete. *Now he's starting to get it.*

SIXTEEN

Kyushu

USS GETTYSBURG *(CV-44), ROADSTER BEACH ZONE,*
OFF THE WEST COAST OF KYUSHU, JAPAN, 2210 HOURS
(OPERATION OLYMPIC, X-DAY, N-HOUR + 1610)

Rear Admiral (lower half) Frank Chadwick braced himself on
the hatch frame and looked around the flag bridge, now
canted crazily to port as the *Gettysburg* continued to settle unevenly into the ocean. The gash in her hull was a fatal
wound—of that there was no longer any doubt. She had been
ripped by a terrific underwater explosion, a blast much greater
than that of the lethal Long Lance torpedoes that the Japs had
used so effectively throughout this war. Speculation—and
Chadwick was inclined to agree—had it that suicidal enemy
submariners had driven a midget sub up against the carrier's
hull and detonated it. In any event, water had flooded the engine rooms, and too many compartments were breached to
keep the ship afloat. Loss of life was heavy among the black
gang, the sailors who fueled, ran, and maintained the carrier's
big diesel engines.

The admiral's bridge was illuminated now by emergency
lights, abandoned except for the chief signalman standing
next to the coding machine and a few other sailors waiting
for orders to clear out. Commander Dickens leaned through
the hatchway, somehow looking unflappable even though
his uniform was torn and his face smudged with oil and
soot.

Chadwick drew a breath, shook his head. It was time.

"Cable to Admirals Hill and McCain," he told the signalman. "I am transferring my flag to *Pensacola,* then to *Missionary Ridge* as soon as possible."

The *Gettysburg* listed heavily in the calm waters. There was no hope of saving her, of dragging her to Ulithi, Manila, or Pearl Harbor for repairs. A half dozen destroyers and destroyer escorts circled the stricken flattop; they had already hoisted most of her crew from the water. A glance through the fading twilight showed the cruiser *Pensacola* approaching with a bone in her teeth, ready to take the admiral's party and a complement of surviving crewmen aboard.

And now it was time for the admiral to go. Captain Withers was still on the bridge—he would be waiting for the flag staff to depart before he abandonded ship—and there was no point in hanging around any longer. Chadwick followed Dickens as the chief of staff led him down the ladders, through the passages, out of flag country and the carrier's tall island. The admiral came along numbly, his mind a myriad of questions extending far beyond the shell of this stricken flagship.

Had the desperate diversion been worthwhile? Certainly, the carriers had drawn plenty of suicide planes, as well as the deadly submarine. Something like six hundred of the *Gettysburg*'s crew had died in the battle. The light carrier *Normandy,* too, had taken several hits but during the evening steamed away from the combat zone under her own power. The rest of the fleet had filled the sky with antiaircraft fire and tried to hang on for dear life. Several of Chadwick's escorting ships had been subjected to near misses, and one DE had taken a hit right in the bridge, killing the captain and dozens of men.

And maybe two or six or ten transports had been spared; and each of those transports might have put a thousand marines onto the beach.

All day long the Hellcats of the carrier's fighter squadrons had fought savagely to defend their carrier and the transports. Navy pilots risked barrages of antiaircraft in single-minded pursuit of enemy planes. The Grummans of Amphibious Group V—reinforced by fighters from some of the other carriers still over the horizon—shot down the incoming Japanese suicide planes in droves. The enemy pilots were either terribly inexperienced, or so fixed in their determination to crash into a ship that they disdained any opportunity for air combat. They plunged through the screen of fighters, right into the thick puffs of antiaircraft that, over the course of the day, had blackened the skies like an ominous thundercloud.

Chadwick's task group now had a new mission: recover four carriers' worth of planes with two carriers' worth of deck space. Some planes wouldn't come back, of course, but enough would that they'd have a problem. At least the *Gettysburg*'s sacrifice had drawn away those suicide planes: they'd been hit by three and succeeded in stopping dozens more. Most of the crew had evacuated successfully. Aboard the *Gettysburg* now there was only the captain, himself, and the skeleton crew of damage control parties and medical people.

They crossed to the edge of the flight deck and descended one more ladder, Dickens bringing Chadwick to the catwalk below the flight deck on the port side, the low side. They were still thirty feet above the water, which rolled gently against the gray hull, the ocean utterly black in the night, and very, very deep. Ropes dangled from the railing of the catwalk, hanging all the way to the water, and lots of small boats from nearby destroyers were busily picking up the sailors who had been evacuating for the last hour.

"A bosun's chair for the admiral?" asked a chief petty officer. His face was slicked with soot and blood, and sweat glistened on his arms and his chest where it was visible through his ripped tunic.

Not far away a few brave swabbies—good swimmers, the admiral heartily hoped—advanced one at a time to the railing of the catwalk to launch into the water with dives, cannonballs, and other antic plunges.

"Thanks, Chief. The rope will do fine," Chadwick replied,

joining the short file of men waiting to descend on the nearest line. A seaman first class stepped aside to let the admiral through.

"Thanks, son. But that's okay—I'll wait my turn," Frank said, touched.

The batteries on the nearby destroyers and the *Pensacola* suddenly erupted, blasting a fresh volley of metal and explosives into the night sky. Chadwick braced himself, listened to the fire wax and wane over the course of a minute. In the thickening dusk he couldn't see an enemy plane; when the guns ceased firing, he couldn't hear it either.

"False alarm?" the nearby swabbie said hopefully.

"Or they got the son of a bitch," the grizzled CPO replied, before gently prodding the young sailor to the edge of the catwalk. "Your turn, kid."

Even at night that AA fire, Chadwick observed as the sailor shimmied down the rope, had been a real shit storm in the sky. As the admiral stepped forward to take his own turn, his mind wandered, considering the implications for the future. Tactical doctrine had changed over the course of this war. Now ships, including the carrier and all of its escorts, were outfitted with a bristling array of three-inch cannon, Bofors guns, .50 caliber machine guns, all deployed to defend against enemy air attack. Each carrier had an AA cruiser among its escort, a vessel that had been designed and armed specifically as an antiaircraft ship.

But they needed more guns, faster firing, bigger calibers! What the hell were those Japs trying to do, anyway? What could drive them to mass suicide attacks? It's like they weren't even human, not in the sense of civilized people!

And then the admiral's turn came, and Chadwick sat on the edge of the catwalk, took the rope in his hands, and swiveled his butt off the edge. For a sickening moment, he swayed into space, but then started to slide down the line, using his legs instead of his hands to brace himself.

Fifteen seconds later, he was in the—shockingly cold— ocean, and a minute later a bosun's mate was hauling him into a whaleboat like a freshly landed catfish.

• TUESDAY, 20 MARCH 1945 •

*APPROACHING USS **MISSIONARY RIDGE** (CV-48), 0709*
HOURS (OPERATION OLYMPIC, X-DAY + 01)

Lefty was flying in a daze, guns empty and fuel tank nearly
the same, the tail end of a section of five fighters returning to
the carrier. It was his first flight on the second day of the
battle—and already his fifth sortie of Operation Olympic.
He had added eight planes to his kill total in that time—his
squadron had claimed more than fifty—but all those kills
were only a drop in the bucket.

Where the hell had the Japs been hiding all these planes?
And who in hell were they getting to fly them?

The second question was the more stunning to Lefty. It
had been churning in his mind for more than twenty-four
hours. He hadn't slept more than a few minutes the night before. Paperwork, debriefing, and planning had kept him up
until 0100; then he hit his bunk and spent the next few hours
tossing and turning, thinking about that question.

What kind of crazy fanatic would get into an airplane seat
knowing full well that he was going to die at the end of the
flight?

Were the pilots of Nippon braver than American pilots?
Lefty wouldn't concede that point, not while he could still
draw a breath. Were they cockier? He didn't think that was
true, either. From the flights he had seen, these were pilots
who had barely any training at all—they were lucky to get
the damned planes off the ground!

There had been some covering fighters, trying to interfere
with the Hellcats, flying cover for the suicide planes. Some
of these had been flown by veteran pilots, flying modern aircraft like the Oscar and Frank; Lefty had dueled one for
more than a half hour, the fight ending only when the enemy
plane's wings buckled as the pilot tried to pull out of a power
dive.

But that had been the exception. He'd seen suicide planes
try to juke their way out from under Hellcat guns only to
have the pilot lose control, augering in to the ground or the

ocean before the guy could pull out of the spin. Others flew straight and steady but couldn't quite hit the mark—vast numbers of suicide attacks had missed simply because the pilots lacked the skill to fly into a ship-sized target. Even so, they kept coming, waves and waves of them throughout X-day, and now it was looking like day two wasn't going to be any better.

He could see the belly of the *Gettysburg*—the big, new ship had turned turtle during the night—and the gaping hole where a suicide submarine had gashed her belly was an ugly wound. Not far away, the second wave of transports waited at anchor. They busily debarked more landing craft full of troops and supplies, and endured the enemy air attacks. Already this morning, two of them had been struck. They burned furiously, spewing pillars of black smoke into the sky between the *Missionary Ridge* and the beach.

Now the flight deck was in front of him. Lefty's F6F leveled out, lined up for the approach, and the pilot sighted "Paddles." He came in a little high, and the Hellcat bounced on the deck, dragging the tailhook far enough that it didn't catch until the third cable. *Damn,* he thought. *Haven't landed that rough since P'cola.*

He unfastened the canopy but was grateful when his crew chief scrambled up the ladder to push the glass enclosure back. Lefty pushed himself out of his seat, his mind on a cup of coffee and, if the coffee kicked in fast enough, a good crap.

"It's going to be at least three hours before she's ready to go up again, sir," the chief said. "We're going to replace the plugs and filters. Maybe you could catch a little sack time?"

"She was running okay," Lefty countered. "Belay the maintenance—I'll be ready to go in thirty."

"Um, sir. Commander Wiggins ordered me to do the work. Told me to tell you you could take a nap or help him fill out action reports. He led me to believe he didn't think you'd be much help to him with the reports, sir."

Commander Wiggins was the flight officer, commander of all flying operations on the *Missionary Ridge*. He was tough as nails but somehow managed to scare the shit out of you in an avuncular fashion.

"Thanks, Chief," Lefty said, relaxing a little. "I take the commander's point and will see you in three hours."

"Very good, sir."

As Lefty made his way to his bunk in his small cabin, he realized that he'd never been this tired in his whole life.

APPROACHING USS NEW GEORGIA (CVE-78), STATION WAGON BEACH ZONE, 1802 HOURS (X-DAY + 01)

The wreckage of the Japanese Zero was still burning within a nearby escort carrier. From the air, you could see that it had ripped a gaping hole in the flight deck and wrecked a great portion of the hangar deck immediately below. Damage control parties scrambled across the deck, and teams of sailors aimed the spray of powerful hoses into the smoking crater. The little CVEs were smaller, much less armored than the great fleet carriers, and this one would clearly be out of action for the foreseeable future.

Then that stricken ship fell behind, and the TBM-3 Avenger turned for its final approach to another escort carrier, the *New Georgia*. Gregory Yamada, sitting in the backseat, had time for one quick glance, and then every ounce of his being was devoted to prayer, because it looked for all the world as if the marine pilot was determined to plow right into the carrier's deck.

"How y'all holdin' on back there, Major?" the pilot shouted, nosing the Avenger down toward the water.

"Okay," Yamada lied as he watched the escort carrier bob up and down in the rough water. The view was making him seasick. He tightened his grip on the sides of his seat—he was holding on hard enough to leave marks, he suspected.

The pilot laughed while jinking up and down to stay in line with the randomly moving target. "Aircraft carrier's a big fucker until you try to land on one. Then the fuckin' boat's just a tiny little thing. Especially the fucking jeep carriers, y'know? Scared me shitless the first time I had to do it. Nearly joined the Order of the Wet Diaper."

Yamada thought he might join the Order of the Wet Diaper himself. He wanted to scream, "Pull up! Pull up!" because it was so abundantly clear that the Avenger pilot was going to crash. But the pilot was still talking as if nothing was wrong, so Yamada had to trust him—even though it seemed like a hell of a waste of a pilot, a major, and a perfectly good airplane.

The ride in was bumpy, and Yamada didn't like flying under the best of circumstances. He couldn't look anymore. He had been leaning forward in his seat to peer over the pilot's shoulder, but the view was just too disturbing. He leaned back, closed his eyes, and began to recite. "Hail Mary, full of grace. Our Lord is with thee. Blessed art thou among women, and blessed is . . ."

"Y'all prayin' back there?" shouted the pilot. "Put in a good word for me, if you don't mind. But don't worry about this landing. I've never yet had a fatal accident with an army major on board." He chortled at his own joke while wobbling from side to side. The wheels were going down, clunking into place with a jar that seemed likely to tear the wings loose, or something.

"Hang on!" the pilot shouted. "Here we go!"

Yamada tried to concentrate on his prayer. ". . . and blessed be the fruit of thy womb, Jesus. Hail Mary, full of grace . . ."

The pilot cut the throttle wide and the mighty engine suddenly fell silent at the same instant the arresting hook grabbed the wire. The stop was abrupt, throwing Yamada forward in his seat so hard he felt certain there would be a black-and-blue mark where his seat belt held him tight. Then and there was only the silence. Blissful silence. They were down.

"That wasn't so bad, now, was it, Major?" chuckled the pilot as he looked back over his shoulder at a sweating and pale Yamada.

"All in all, I'd rather be in Philadelphia," Yamada replied in a bad W. C. Fields voice, which drew another laugh.

"You're all right, Major. For an army puke, I mean. Sorry, pardon my French." The deck crew wheeled a ladder to the side of the plane.

"It's okay. For getting me safely onto this floating postage stamp, you can say anything you want." One crewman climbed up and began opening the cockpit.

Another laugh. "Floatin' postage stamp. That's a good one. Well, here you are, COD. Cargo on Deck. Thanks for flying Semper Fi Airways. Come again soon."

"Only when you start offering a liquor service, Lieutenant," he replied, which drew another laugh.

The hatch over Greg's head slid back and he took a few deep breaths of sea air. He'd avoided membership in the Order of the Wet Diaper and, with luck, would keep from throwing up until he was out of the Avenger.

Encumbered as he was in flight suit and helmet, he had to be helped out of his seat and down the ladder before he had enough working room to get rid of the extra garments. As usual, he observed the reactions of the people around him when they first saw he was Asian. One of the plane crew noticed first and punched the guy next to him in the shoulder. Both of them stared openly at him until the crew chief caught them and gave each a whack on the side of the head. The crew chief himself did a bit of a double take, shook his head in a way that said *goddamn army* more eloquently than any words, and ostentatiously turned away, the universal sign that none of this was any of his business.

The lieutenant commander who patiently waited for him wasn't surprised. Clearly, Yamada's name had to be written on that clipboard he was carrying. The navy officer was trying to keep his expression carefully bland, but he was clearly curious. Yamada wasn't yet sure whether the curiosity was about his mission, his ethnicity, or both. He'd assume both for now and see what developed. Yamada was going to need allies, and this young officer looked like he could be influenced pretty easily.

The navy officer stepped forward and saluted sharply, then started speaking with a pronounced Southern accent. "Welcome to the *New Georgia*, sir. I'm Lieutenant Commander Dan McPherson. If you can spare a moment, Captain Alexander would like to give you a personal welcome." McPherson was about medium height, stocky, with close-cut brown hair. His face was open and friendly. Yamada noticed a class ring. *Naval Academy. A ring knocker.*

"That's very gracious of him," Yamada said. "I know he's very busy, so I won't take much of his time. Will you be able to take me to see my prisoner afterward?"

"Of course," the lieutenant commander replied. "This way, sir." McPherson signaled to a seaman to take Yamada's luggage: a duffel and a briefcase. Greg let them take the duffel but kept the briefcase.

Most of the men clearly weren't expecting to see a Japanese man in a U.S. Army uniform. Some men were curious, some actively hostile. A few muttered under their breath as they passed. Yamada couldn't hear all the words, but he didn't need to. They were all some version of, "What's a fucking yellow Nip bastard doing here?"

What was more interesting was his escort's reaction. Most non-Asians never noticed, but as McPherson held open a door for him—*hatch*, Yamada silently corrected himself—the navy officer said, "I apologize for that, Major."

"No need, Commander. Army green just sets some of you navy boys off," Yamada said. He'd heard it all before. Better to turn it into a joke.

McPherson led Yamada up a gangway to the bridge. Captain Alexander was huddled with several officers around a tall metal table going over damage reports. He looked up as soon as Yamada entered the bridge. Like McPherson, Captain Alexander was not in the slightest surprised that Yamada was Japanese. He was angry, though. His eyes kept straying down to the papers—there must be bad news in them—and here Yamada was, complicating his work. There was something more, though. The way the corners of his mouth turned down spoke of revulsion. Yamada noticed the absence of an academy ring.

Seeing which officers were in the know was also important. Of five, three were carefully unsurprised: the captain, the XO, and a first lieutenant. The first lieutenant was a ring knocker like McPherson, the only one in the captain's inner circle. Maybe he could be of use, too. *I wonder if he's friends with McPherson. That would be useful.*

Two weren't in the know. One was a rather hapless-looking ensign, obviously the resident whipping boy. No ring. The other was a middle-aged, overweight commander who looked not at Yamada but at the XO and the lieutenant. The commander, probably of prewar career vintage, looked like he'd been passed over for captain a few times for being a mediocrity, and his two enemies were busily cutting him out of anything important aboard the carrier. *Both powerless,* Yamada thought. So far McPherson was his best bet.

McPherson made the introductions. "Captain, this is Major Gregory Yamada of Army Intelligence. Major Yamada, Captain James Alexander."

Alexander was a tall man, easily a foot taller than the five-foot-three Yamada, with brown eyes and close-cropped brown hair. He wore a thin mustache.

Yamada saluted first. He could feel Alexander's eyes boring in, narrowing as they contemplated his Asian features. The army intelligence officer put his briefcase on the tall table, snapped it open, and pulled out a sheet of paper. "My orders, Captain."

The captain took the orders and skimmed them. Then he read them again, this time more slowly. "You know some important people, Major," he said, the anger in his voice matched by the slight eyebrow movement when using Yamada's rank, showing suspicion of his legitimacy.

"No, sir. But Admiral Fletcher and General Krueger both believe my mission is important." Yamada didn't need a fight. Besides, lowballing his relationships was the strongest strategy.

Captain Alexander looked at him, his disapproval moderated slightly by the mention of his seniors. Then he read the orders through a third time, his mouth tightening progressively from first line to last.

"It says here that I am to keep the *New Georgia* completely out of harm's way until your business on board is concluded." Alexander said, omitting Yamada's rank altogether. "Right now, for your information, I'm flying close air support operations to cover the beachhead. In case you don't understand that, *Major,* my continued ability to fly in support of the brave *American* troops risking *their* lives while *others* warm chairs on shore rests on my ability to *stay—on—station*! I'll thank you to conclude this *business* as quickly as possible so this ship can return to its proper duty."

Okay, Yamada thought, *that's the game.* He snapped his briefcase shut. "Captain, may we speak in private?"

Alexander paused, obviously weighing his options, but without lessening his anger. If the captain thought he could win, he'd have it out in public. But if he thought he was going to lose, he'd want that in private. Yamada concentrated on looking calm and certain.

"Very well. In my ready room." Language curt and clipped. His junior officers traded glances. They knew he was probably going to lose. At least this way the captain would avoid witnesses.

Alexander waved Yamada ahead of him and closed the hatch behind them. The compartment had a small conference table and Yamada circled quickly to the table's head. Stake out your territory immediately and take the high ground where possible.

"I presume you're going to tell me just how quickly you can get the hell off my ship," Alexander said.

First came the obligatory peace gesture. Yamada put his hands out to his sides, palms forward. "I'm sorry to say, Captain, that the time varies. Your prisoner and what he may have in his skull is enormously valuable right now. I need you to move far enough away from shore so that you're out of reach of suicide planes, boats, submarines, or anything else that might harm that prisoner before I finish with him."

He didn't expect his rueful smile or his open-palm gesture to deflect much of what was coming his way, and he was right.

"If I had known that little son of a bitch was going to get my ship pulled out of the battle, I would have let him drown!" snapped the captain. "That's exactly what he was trying to accomplish, you know that, don't you?"

"Captain, when your men fished him out of the water, still alive, that fellow became the most important enemy in this whole ocean. He's the only one we've taken alive! Now, I need to get inside his head, find out what he knows, find out what the hell is going on!"

"And what about the brave *Americans* on shore? Or don't you care about them, now that you have a fellow countryman to protect?" The captain's voice was dripping with contempt and sarcasm.

An argument about racial versus national loyalty was an argument without a victory as far as Yamada was concerned. He ignored the attack altogether and went back to the facts. "Captain, you have your orders, as I have mine. You received your own set yesterday, and what I just gave you is identical." Yamada was bluffing, but from the angry reaction, he knew he'd hit paydirt.

"Goddammit! Who the hell . . ."

With the captain slightly off guard, it was time to attack directly. Putting both hands on the table and leaning forward, he said in a voice with more menace, "I don't know how they do it in the navy, but in the army, when we receive lawful orders, we don't have a fucking debating society about them. Getting the truth out of that boy you have locked up belowdecks matters more to the war effort right this minute than anything else you're doing. There will be another carrier here within six hours to pick up the slack. In the meantime, *Captain* Alexander, the *New Georgia* is to be moved well out of harm's way." He kept his eyes locked directly on the captain's and waited. It took about forty seconds for the conflict to resolve.

The captain did not acknowledge Yamada at all. He turned around, opened the door, and walked out, leaving Yamada to his own devices. Yamada followed after a discreet interval of about five seconds. Alexander strode through the bridge and said, "Plot a course for Take Shima. You have the conn."

"Aye aye, Captain," the XO replied, looking somewhat bewildered as Alexander swept by.

That went well, thought Yamada. Less than ten minutes and the captain was already pissed off. At least he was following orders. He turned to his escort. "Commander McPherson, may I see my prisoner now?"

Now that Yamada was officially on the captain's shit list, McPherson appeared to have cooled off considerably. "Yes, Major. Follow me." The use of his title rather than "sir" was a traditional way of expressing disapproval or dislike.

Yamada quickly lost track of where he was in the maze of passageways underneath the carrier deck. The ship certainly seemed much larger on board than it had looked when they were coming in on final.

Once out of earshot of the captain, McPherson's curiosity overwhelmed his official frostiness again. "Pardon me for asking, Major, but it's a bit . . . um . . . unusual to meet an officer who's . . ."

Yamada laughed. He wanted to encourage the young navy officer, and indulging his curiosity was a cheap way to build the relationship. "Nisei. That means second generation, or first generation born in the United States. My Japanese was good enough to get me selected for Military Intelligence School, so they sent me to Minnesota for advanced study in the language." That was a setup ending; the next question was always the same.

"Minnesota? You went to Minnesota to study Japanese?"

"The Military Intelligence Service Language School, Camp Savage, Minnesota." He chuckled. "There are more of us than you'd think. There's an entire Nisei regiment in the European Theater, the 442nd. But we can talk about that later, if you're curious."

McPherson grabbed the bait Yamada was dangling. "I'd like that, if you don't think I'm prying. I'm interested."

"Good. Maybe later." Yamada smiled.

The suicide pilot was in the infirmary, segregated in a

private room with a marine guard—a lance corporal— sitting on a chair beside the door. The marine came to attention when the two officers approached. He couldn't help one glance at Yamada made equally of hostility and fear before his face hardened into marine rigidity.

"This is the army interrogator, Major Yamada," McPherson said. "He's here to see the prisoner."

"Sir! Lieutenant Steffan must authorize access to the prisoner, sir!"

"Corporal, Major Yamada is now in charge of the prisoner, not Lieutenant Steffan. Step away from the door," said McPherson.

Yamada tried a different tack. "Corporal, I understand you have your orders, but I presume you can see the little leaf on my shoulder. Why don't you go find your lieutenant, tell him that an army major ran you off, and that the lieutenant can come talk to Commander McPherson here if he has a problem."

"Sir! Lieutenant Steffan must authorize access to the prisoner, sir!" The corporal's eyes were darting from side to side and his pupils were beginning to dilate. Caught between conflicting orders, he was starting to break. He wouldn't last long under interrogation, Yamada thought.

"Last chance, Corporal," Yamada said. "Go find your lieutenant. I'll count to three. One. Two."

The corporal was gone.

"Would you mind waiting for this Lieutenant Steffan, Commander McPherson? I'd hate to see that poor corporal take the fall for this. It's not right to put an enlisted man in the middle of this."

"I agree, Major Yamada. I'll have a word with the lieutenant when he gets here."

"If he gets here."

"If he doesn't, I'll go find him. Again, my apologies on behalf of the *New Georgia*. The prisoner is now yours, Major. If you need anything, please let me know."

"Thank you, Commander. I appreciate your help. A word of private advice, if I might?"

"Yes, sir?"

"Look a little reluctant. Maybe even resentful."

"Sir, I—"

"We're not going to change the world today. I'd prefer to see your career go well."

McPherson paused. "I—well, uh, yes, sir. I understand, I guess. I don't like it much."

"I'm not crazy about it myself. But right now, I have a job to do. Thanks for your help."

"I resented like hell having to do it," McPherson said with a grin. "Officially."

"Oh—tell Lieutenant Steffan to keep guards on the door. He can start with that corporal. He's a brave man." Yamada opened the hatch and went inside.

"Konichi-wa," he said to the young, bandage-swathed Japanese aviator in the hospital bed. *"Watakushi-wa Chui Yamada Kaito, desu."* Hello. My name is Major Gregory Yamada. Kaito was his adopted Japanese surname; there was no exact translation of Gregory, of course.

Silence. The prisoner turned his face away.

Yamada tried again. *"Onamae-wa?"* What is your name? Silence.

The prisoner was young, no more than nineteen, at a guess. His defiance was mostly bravado and shame at being in the enemy's hands. A child playing at being grown up, confused and scared and very much alone. Getting him to surrender the information the army needed wouldn't be too difficult. The problem was getting a dialogue started in the first place. Once he played the first piece of the puzzle, everything else should fall neatly into place.

Silence was a good strategy for the prisoner. But few people could resist silence in return. Yamada sat down and calmly waited.

The minutes ticked by with excruciating slowness. Yamada had long practice in the technique; the prisoner did not. The young suicide pilot could keep his face turned away only so long until the position began to ache, then he turned his head back to center, studiously avoiding eye contact with his interrogator. Yamada kept his attention on the man in the bed. He looked at the boy's forehead rather than into his eyes. It was much more relaxing that way, and almost no one could tell the difference, especially at a distance of four or five feet.

Yamada could keep this up for a long time, but he really wanted a cigarette. That was the worst part of the silent contest.

Now the boy's eyes were moving, looking at the ceiling, then at the featureless walls of the hospital room. There wasn't much to look at, except for the IV drips. His effort not to look at Yamada grew more strained, and finally he surrendered that battle. He looked directly at Yamada. He tried to put disdain on his face, but it failed. Yamada continued to wait.

Now there were signs that he wanted to talk, wanted to ask questions, wanted to express how he felt. At this point, Yamada could start asking questions, but it was better to wait, to get the boy to the place he *needed* to talk. Things were going quite well.

"Ishimaru Kawase." The first words after such a long silence sounded extremely loud, although in fact they were barely a croak from a voice hardly used since the crash.

"Arigato," Yamada said. Continuing in Japanese, he added, "Rest now. We'll talk more later." In the face of the boy's obvious confusion, he stood, bowed slightly, and left the room.

Fifteen minutes later, Yamada was sitting in the officers' mess, sipping a cup of coffee, smoking a Winston, and reading a week-old *Stars and Stripes* when the captain came in. He continued to sit and read until he saw the captain's shadow fall across his newspaper. Then he looked up.

"Well?"

Yamada stubbed out his cigarette. "The interrogation is proceeding nicely," he said.

Captain Alexander pulled out a chair and sat down opposite him. "What have you got so far?" he said sharply.

"His name."

"His *name*?"

"That's right."

"That's *all*? Just his goddamn *name*?" The captain's face was turning red.

Yamada leaned forward. "I'm afraid so."

"You pull my ship out of the goddamn war, you expose *real* soldiers to harm, and you sit there and tell me that you got his *name*? Is that what you interrogators call a full day's work?"

"Captain, that's a nineteen-year-old boy who's scared to death and who's trying to pretend to be a man."

"Other nineteen-year-old *boys* like that one have killed thousands of men in the last two days."

"You've got nineteen-year-old boys too, Captain Alexander. They've done some hard and heroic jobs, but they're still nineteen."

"Yeah? And what in the hell does that have to do with—"

"He's putting on this big hero face because he knows how his side treats prisoners. He's wondering when we're going to start. Instead, he's getting medical care and soft treatment. This is upsetting his entire view of the world. He tried the silent treatment with me, but he's desperate to talk. That's why as soon as I got him to tell me his name, I left the room. I'm going to give him another half an hour to stew in his own juices before I go back, and he's going to be so desperate to talk I'm going to have to write like hell to get it all down."

"And what makes you so sure—"

"The Japanese never signed the Geneva Convention. Their men don't expect to be captured; they expect to die. So when they decide to talk, they don't have any rules that tell them to keep their mouths shut. Our men will give name, rank, serial number, and stop talking. This Japanese POW, Captain Alexander, he'll talk. I've got a structured list of questions, and by the time I finish, I'll have everything he knows."

Alexander paused. Yamada knew he'd succeeded in upsetting the captain's worldview just as much as he had Ishimaru's. "You'd better be right," the captain growled.

"I've done this a couple of times before, Captain Alexander," Yamada said. He took a final swallow of coffee, pushed his chair back, and stood up.

Later, in the infirmary, he asked, "Where are you from, Ishimaru-san?"

The interrogation had begun.

• WEDNESDAY, 21 MARCH 1945 •

BEACH PONTIAC, 0546 HOURS (X-DAY + 02)

The huge LST—landing ship, tank—beached itself and the broad ramp of the bow started to come down with a rattle of winch and chain. The LST's 160-foot length dwarfed the Higgins boats that were continuing to shuttle troops a platoon at a time onto the beach. It was one of a dozen larger ships, flat bottomed and ramped, lined up along the beach.

The flat bow quickly dropped all the way to the sand, becoming a ramp, allowing egress from the long, cavernous interior of the hull. Two Sherman flamethrower tanks emerged, followed by three trucks of equipment and two jeeps. One of the jeeps flew a two-star flag. Rutted tracks crossed the sand in every direction, but a beachmaster waved the lead tank toward a route marked by temporary flags. The rest of the procession drove slowly behind the leader, rolling through soft sand, between the dunes, until they reached a small depression. Barbed wire and machine gun nests surrounded the location. A log platform supported by sandbags roofed over a dugout in the side of a sand dune.

Seeing the two-star flag, a major came rushing from the dugout. "General Erskine! Major Breault, sir! Welcome to Beach Pontiac, sir!"

The general, a look of annoyance on his face, stood and looked around the battlefield for a while. A large number of dead still littered the ground. The smell was beginning to be overpowering. "We need graves registration and some crews in here. These brave boys don't deserve to lie around on the beach."

The major's eyes widened and he pulled out a steno pad. "Yes, sir! Of course, sir. I'll prepare the necessary orders so we can get that taken care of immediately, sir." He scribbled rapidly.

"Hold on, son," the general growled. "First rule. Write down everything I tell you needs to be done. But don't run off and make it somebody's first priority without checking with me. I know damn well that there are more important problems right now than the already dead. But I don't want to make these brave boys lie around like that one minute longer than they have to, either. Use your judgment. If you aren't sure, wait until I look like I've got a free moment and ask. But there better not be too many issues you can't handle, not when you're wearing oak leaves. Do we understand one another?"

"Loud and clear, General. Yes, *sir.*"

The general had a skeptical look on his face. "Show me what I've got as a beach command post, Major. I'm not expecting the Taj Mahal. Make sure I can do my job before you make sure I'm comfortable."

"Yes, sir. I understand, sir."

We'll see, the general thought. But he was willing to be convinced.

The headquarters dugout was serviceable, meaning that it was the locus of a web of telephone wires coming from all over the beach, plugged into a switchboard manned by an alert marine corporal. Erskine was satisfied, as far as that went, but he needed to see more. He set his headquarters sergeant and clerks, who had ridden here in the two jeeps, to working getting a desk and map table set up, then stalked up and out of the dugout.

"Major Breault? I need a driver who knows his way around."

"Yes, General, right over here, sir." The major waved at a

marine private who was standing by the general's jeep. The boy, who looked barely seventeen, hopped behind the wheel and started the little vehicle, maneuvering nimbly through the soft, rutted sand as he drove over to the dugout.

"I'd like to have a look at the front," Erskine declared, climbing into the passenger seat. The major, without being invited, quickly scrambled into the back—an act that the general took as a good sign.

For an hour they drove through a landscape of hellish craters, blackened trees, and random rubble. There had been a few fishing villages and farms along here; now, not a single building remained standing. Bridges had been shattered, and Seabees had laid pontoon spans beside the wreckage. Everywhere Erskine spotted the bodies of his marines, lying where they had died. The carnage stood out as stark proof of the violence of this battle—never before in this war had U.S. marines fallen in such numbers that their comrades could only fight on without them.

The front itself was only a few hundred yards inland from the shore along the entire stretch of Beach Pontiac. Occasional bursts of enemy artillery exploded along the beach, but the naval guns—and ground attack aircraft—had been pretty effective against the Japanese big guns. It was the machine gun nests, the interlocking fields of fire, the concrete pillboxes, slit trenches, and burrows occupied by individual enemy soldiers that were delaying the advance, and killing so many of Erskine's marines.

The general spotted activity near the beach and directed the driver—his name was Smith, and he was a Dakota ranch kid who had learned to drive tractors in the Badlands—to pull up.

Three men, a lieutenant, a corporal, and a private, were dragging an improvised sledge with two more men on it. Only the lieutenant and the corporal weren't wounded, though they staggered with exhaustion as they approached the edge of the water. The corporal and private collapsed. The lieutenant, though unsteady on his feet, waved at an incoming Higgins boat, which changed course to beach close to his position. The bowman and the sternman came out to meet them. "Got a couple more for us, sir?"

"Yeah," said the lieutenant.

"We'll take them from here. We'll get them back safe and sound. Hey, Lieutenant, you ought to take a rest."

"No time. There are too many more."

The corporal gave the bowman a *Please-help-me* look, to which the bowman replied with an *I-tried* shrug.

"Come on," the lieutenant said, and the corporal followed.

Erskine got out of his jeep and approached the marines, who had apparently not noticed him nearby. "Lieutenant, I'm General Erskine. May I ask what you're doing?"

The lieutenant's face reacted with a combination of fear? Embarrassment? He stiffened to attention, and saluted. "Sir! Retrieving wounded, sir."

"Was that your original mission?"

"No, sir. But somebody had to."

"Where's your platoon?"

"Mostly dead, sir. The rest got folded in with another platoon. I was with Fox Company, 2nd Battalion of the 3rd."

The general nodded. "I see. So you became supernumerary."

"I guess, sir, if that means what I think it means."

"Surplus. Extra. Not needed."

"Oh. Yes. Yes, sir."

"So you gave yourself this job?"

"No, sir. The gunny gave it to me."

"The gunny? A sergeant gave you this order?"

"Not an order. Um, more like a suggestion."

The general paused. The lieutenant wavered on his feet. "So he suggested you do this job. And he gave you a corporal, too, I suppose?"

The corporal was trying hard to look invisible and wasn't succeeding. "Corporal, what do you know about all this?"

"It was just as the lieutenant said, sir," he said, coming to ramrod attention.

Erskine looked at both men suspiciously. Then he said, "All right. Carry on. But Lieutenant—"

"Yes, sir?"

"I want you to get a good night's sleep, and then report to me first thing in the morning. We'll get regular medics here to take over the job, and get you both back into action where marines belong. Corporal, make sure that happens. That's an order."

"Yes, sir!" the corporal said, without moving a muscle.

"And also, where in hell can I find Fox Company, and this gunny?"

The gunny looked like an elderly, grizzled veteran, which meant that he was older than twenty and had seen more than his share of this war. A tech sergeant had called out "Attention" as Erskine's jeep approached, and the gunny, with the rest of his weary men, pushed up to a standing position.

"As you were, marines," barked the general, even before his jeep came to a halt. He stepped out and approached the gunnery sergeant as the rest of the men settled back to their K rations, canteens, or interrupted naps. The company was deployed just behind a crest of dune, and the general was pleased to note sentries posted and machine guns placed for maximum effect. He was saddened to note that this force composed of the remnants of two companies numbered little more than a reinforced platoon.

"Is this Fox Company?" Erskine asked.

"Yes, General," the gunny replied. "What's left of it. Bravo, too, sir. Second of the Third."

The general, eyes narrowed, studied the sergeant. He was wiry, thin, unshaven. His uniform was filthy, though his weapon—a Thompson submachine gun—was immaculate. Erskine liked what he saw.

"Are you in command, here, Gunny?" he asked, trying to read the smudged name on his blouse. "Sergeant . . . ?"

"Gunnery Sergeant Rachwalski, sir. Yes, sir."

"Well, company command is no job for a gunny, wouldn't you say?"

"Sir, no sir," replied Rachwalski, without expression.

"So consider yourself a captain for the duration. I'll see

what we can do about making it official and have some bars
for your collar sent up here."

The gunny blinked, seemed confused for a moment. Then
he allowed himself the hint of a smile. "Sir, thank you, sir,"
he replied.

"No, son," General Erskine said. He put his hand on the
old/young man's shoulder. "Thank *you.*"

SEVENTEEN

Japan; Okinawa; Washington, D.C.

• WEDNESDAY, 21 MARCH 1945 •

CAMP SHINJUKU, TOKYO, JAPAN, 1820 HOURS

It was dark and the prisoners were in their barracks for the
evening. Captain Ogawa Taiki walked around the barbed
wire surrounding the prisoners' compound each evening to
ensure the guards were all on duty and alert. The walking
pulled at the torn muscle in his leg and caused him pain at
every step. That was good. It was a form of discipline, and
discipline was always good.

The guards and barbed wire, Ogawa thought, not for the
first time, were in fact unnecessary. Where would the prisoners go if they escaped? They couldn't blend in with the population. No one would give them shelter or food. And ten
compatriots would be killed as punishment for each man
who escaped. Still, forms must be preserved. The rules must
be followed. It was his duty.

The prison camp was the largest part of Camp Shinjuku.
A dirt road connected the camp's entry gate to the compound where the guards lived and worked, about fifty yards
from the camp proper. Just to the east and south stretched the

great valley of Tokyo, the hub of Nipponese history and might. The outskirts of that great city were less than ten miles away from here, but the intervening ridge prevented any direct view of the metropolis from the camp. Once, Ogawa had climbed to the crest of that ridge, but the sight had been singularly unimpressive: night had fallen during his hike, and by the time he reached the summit the blacked-out city was just another dark swath of countryside.

At the entry gate, Ogawa nodded to the guard sergeant, who in return saluted sharply. Ogawa returned the salute with grave formality, and with that, responsibility for the night rested with the sergeant. Ogawa's duty day had ended, or at least had ended as much as a commander's day ever did.

Ogawa allowed himself to favor his bad leg a bit more on the short walk to the compound. He passed three *dohyo,* circles made for sumo wrestling. The enlisted men frequently challenged one another to sumo matches, and competition was fierce.

Barracks, made of weathered wood similar to the ones inside the prisoner compound, made up the camp office and warehouse area. One barracks served as the camp office. Next to it was the mess hall. Then came the officers' barracks, and four more for the enlisted men. All the buildings formed a horseshoe around a circular road. A bare flagpole stood in the center of the circle. The flag had been taken down for the night.

Behind the buildings and parallel to the camp were several large sheds where equipment and supplies were stored. A sentry patrolled that area to guard against thieves. Shortages of just about everything made those sheds a tempting target.

There was some paperwork yet to be done, but it could wait. He needed a drink. Instead of going to his office, he walked to the officer's quarters two barracks to the right.

The officers—there were only four—shared a single barracks, in form not much different from the ones occupied by the prisoners. Each officer had his own small sleeping room, containing a futon on the floor, a simple chest, and a rack to hang his uniform. A shoji screen served as the only privacy wall. Ogawa's was otherwise bare.

Two officers had their quarters on each side of the main entrance. A small common room occupied the space in the middle. The room contained a low table and a few rolled pillows. A cast-iron stove gave off heat. There was a bare electric lightbulb hanging from the ceiling, but it was off. Light came from a candle stuck into an empty bottle that sat in the center of the small table.

All three of his lieutenants were waiting for him. Two were seated on the floor at the small table. Lieutenant Kawazoe Takumi had already placed a small pan of water on the cast-iron stove and was heating a bottle of sake. Lieutenant Kawazoe had a flat face and unusually big ears. He was a young man, one who would normally be serving at the front, but some administrative mixup had sent him to Shinjuku instead. Ogawa had endorsed his request for transfer several times, but nothing had happened yet.

"Konichi-wa, taii-san," Kawazoe said, standing and greeting his captain with a bow.

Ogawa grunted an acknowledgment as he unfastened his Sam Browne belt and removed his cap, placing them next to the door. He sat on the floor and pulled off his boots and placed them with his other equipment. He stood and put on a pair of slippers before joining the rest of them. He crossed his legs in a lotus position, which stretched his wound again, and took one of the small pillows and wedged it into the small of his back. Meanwhile, the lieutenant had taken the warm sake bottle from the simmering water and poured some into a flask. He sat down and poured sake into four small cups.

It was up to Ogawa to make the first traditional toast. He lifted his small sake cup and said, "Banzai!" The wish for ten thousand years was both for the emperor's prosperity and for long life and happiness for all the guests.

The three lieutenants dutifully repeated the toast and all four men downed the warmed rice wine. Ogawa shifted the small rolled pillow that supported the small of his back and

gestured at Kawazoe to pour a second round. That emptied
the flask, and Kawazoe filled it from the bottle on the stove.

"How have our flower sniffers behaved today?" Ogawa
asked, downing another cup of sake.

"The *holio* were shiftless, lazy, clumsy, and stupid. Which
is to say it was a normal day in all respects," Lieutenant
Saruwatari Taiki answered. Saruwatari was the tallest of the
four. Half his face was scar tissue, a souvenir of his encounter with an American flamethrower on Luzon. He had
been evacuated on one of the ships carrying prisoners—a
lucky ship, one that ran the gauntlet of American air and sea
power to make it all the way back to Japan.

Lieutenant Watanabe Kaito laughed. Kaito didn't speak
much. His shaved head was a mark of his practice of the
forty-eight vows of the Amida Buddha. He was much more
serious than the other lieutenants and spent much of his free
time chanting, meditating, or praying.

"Our *gesuonna* was in fine form today," Saruwatari continued. "I shouted at him and I thought he was going to piss
himself, he was shaking so hard." He laughed. "I gave him a
good slapping, but it didn't do any good. Some of the other
prisoners are almost like men, but this one—what a mewling
coward he is."

"There is one important thing to remember," Ogawa said,
his voice somewhat thickened by the sake. "Some of these
men surrendered and bear all the dishonor themselves. But
many did not surrender themselves. Their leaders surrendered,
and thus the leaders, not their troops, bear the dishonor. Some
of these men might have kept fighting and kept their honor."

"I would! I wouldn't dishonor myself, even if it were an
order!" Kawazoe, the youngster, blurted out.

"So sorry, but if it is a lawful order from those placed over
you, disobeying is a greater dishonor," Watanabe interjected.
His voice was calm. "Obeying is the highest virtue."

"But how could an order to surrender be lawful or correct?" argued Kawazoe. "Wouldn't such an order condemn
the man who gave it?" He looked at the other lieutenants for
support.

Watanabe shrugged. "I do not always know or understand the reasons behind each order I am given. Perhaps the order might appear wrong or useless based on my limited view. But my view is limited. Thus, I merely obey. That is my duty."

Ogawa put his fist down hard on the little table, causing the molten wax on the candle to splatter. "Correct! That is true wisdom, Lieutenant. We do not always know the reasons behind our orders. Therefore, we must obey."

Kawazoe wasn't ready to give up. "In what possible circumstance would an order to surrender make sense?"

Watanabe looked blank. Saruwatari shrugged. Ogawa leaned forward. "It is enough for you to know that such an order will not come unless there is reason. In the meantime, it's your duty to obey. Obey no matter what. *Wakarimasu*?" He growled the last word to signal that this discussion was over.

"Yes, I understand," Kawazoe replied. He knew he was pushing the limits of his captain. "Yes. Of course. Yes." He bowed several times.

It was time for Ogawa to change the subject. "As for tomorrow . . ." Ogawa started to speak, stopped as he heard a sound.

Air raid sirens.

"Shall we seek shelter?" Saruwatari asked.

"No," replied Ogawa. "I'll be damned if I hide from anything American."

Watanabe sat placidly, a meditative expression on his face. Saruwatari and Kawazoe looked at each other. Perhaps they would have preferred shelter. Let them worry, Ogawa thought with a silent sneer. It was not as if the Americans were coming to bomb a prison camp!

Another sound challenged the air raid sirens. It sounded first like angry bees, then grew louder. "Aircraft," Ogawa said. "Sounds like B-san engines." B-san was a Japanese nickname for the B-29. He got to his feet laboriously. "Let us go look," he said.

He led his four officers outside. A growing number of

enlisted men were gathering in the circle around the flag-pole, along with the civilian translator, Kazuma Inoue. The sound was growing still louder. "A large raid," observed one of the sergeants, Ishikawa Matsuo. He, like Ogawa, had fought at Guadalcanal and had been evacuated with serious wounds. "I don't think I've ever heard so many at one time."

The droning was constant, but distant, swelling in the south and veering to the southeast. Clearly, Tokyo was the target. Already searchlight beams came into view, playing upward from beyond the ridge, sweeping back and forth through the sky.

"They're coming in low," Ogawa observed. "Usually they are as high as the clouds—but look, you can see them flash silver in the spotlights!"

Indeed, this massive stream of bombers flew only a mile or two above the ground, instead of the five or six miles that had been the norm. Whereas the big, four-engined B-29s were usually just specks, visible only by daylight, these bombers stood out in clear relief whenever one of them was caught in the intense beam of light. Antiaircraft fire began to pop off, sounding like hundreds of distant firecrackers. One bomber burst into flames and plunged out of the formation; Ogawa nodded in silent satisfaction.

"Why do we not hear the bombs?" asked Kawazoe. They others listened for several moments, surprised. Tokyo had been the target of many air raids, but usually they could hear the thudding of the powerful explosives all the way to Camp Shinjuku. Now, there was only the sputter of the aircraft and the droning of that long river of silver bombers.

"Perhaps their target is farther away—Yokohama, maybe?" speculated Saruwatari.

"No. Why would they fly over all the guns of Tokyo on their way to a coastal base?" countered Ogawa. But he remained mystified—if the Americans were dropping high explosive bombs, they should at least sense the concussion here.

In the distance, a cherry glow, like an early hint of dawn, began to rise along the darkened horizon. The bombers continued to pass, and now they could even make out some of the planes in the eerie glimmer radiating up from the ground. Plumes of light like glowing flowers shot high into the air, fantastically beautiful as they swelled upward from the far side of the ridge before collapsing out of sight. Those plumes were the final proof to the captain.

"They are not dropping high explosives but incendiaries," Ogawa said. "They are burning the city."

All the men around him fell silent. Every Japanese dreaded fire. Fire was a terrible disaster in a crowded Japanese city, where the houses were built of wood, straw, bamboo, and paper. Tokyo had been the scene of many scourging deadly fires—sometimes whole neighborhoods would be destroyed. But this . . . this seemed like an eerie predecessor of the end of the world.

The deadly blooms continued to decorate the sky as B-san after B-san dropped its cargo of incendiaries on the paper city below. The air raid sirens and roar of bomber engines grew so loud that the sound enveloped them like a blanket. Slowly the red glow expanded to run the whole length of the horizon, like a magical dome of huge proportions. As the light grew brighter, the dome became merely part of a blood-red sky, an evil pseudodaylight. The captain could imagine the civilians running before the firestorm, burning, dying.

"How many of you have family in Tokyo?" Ogawa asked. Five hands went up. Four were enlisted men, including Sergeant Ishikawa. The fifth was Lieutenant Saruwatari, whose burn scar seemed to glow in the light of the fire. "Go and do what you can, but listen closely: your lives are not your own. They belong to the Emperor. If your families are in areas where the fire has not spread, or is just beginning, get them and bring them here. If your families are in areas where the fire has taken control, return here. Understand? This is a direct order."

"*Hai, taii-san*," the five men said in unison. They bowed and then began running for the row of bicycles parked outside the barracks. There was no fuel to spare for vehicles.

The air raid sirens stopped, either because they, too, were burning, or because they had become pointless in the face of the raging devastation. Then Ogawa heard another noise: cheers, shouts of delight and approval, even applause. The sounds came from the prisoner compound, raucous, loud, and obscene.

"The Americans," he snarled. "Cowards on the ground and cowards in the air. Why can't they face us like men?"

"Let's teach them a lesson!" said Kawazoe, grinning in anticipation. Several enlisted men began to grumble.

Ogawa thought for a minute, then decided. "Yes. Honor demands it. These prisoners are guest of the emperor, and their behavior shows an intolerable lack of manners. Punishment— severe punishment—is in order."

The mob around the flagpole—it had grown to about twenty, now, even with the departure of those with relatives in Tokyo—started moving in the direction of the prisoners' compound. Ogawa strode into the officer barracks, slid back the shoji screen, and took his katana from its stand on top of his chest. He had a momentary flash of shame for losing the sword of his ancestors on Guadalcanal. The honor of his family, generations of ancestors, had been invested in that shining steel blade. This katana was a fine sword even though it was not the ancestral blade of his fathers. *Let me start a new tradition by blooding this weapon*, he thought. He buckled it on, then hurried out to lead his troops.

The sergeant of the guard was arguing with the mob when Ogawa reached his men. "I *can't* let you in without orders, so sorry," he said, shrugging helplessly.

"That is correct, *gunso*," Ogawa said, pushing his way through the middle of the crowd. "But I issue the orders."

"*Hai, taii-san*," said the sergeant, bowing. The gates were two large wooden frames covered with barbed wire. When both were open, there was room to drive a truck into the compound. When the sergeant opened them, the mob flowed through.

Most of the prisoners were out of their barracks, still

cheering and yelling. Above their heads, a B-san waggled its wings, showing that it knew the location of these prisoners. It also showed how close the Americans were to the home-land, Ogawa thought. The fires of Tokyo were in the distance facing away from the gates, so the prisoners had their backs toward the angry guards. But when Ogawa shouted "Ban-zai!" and his men charged, the prisoners turned around in a hurry.

It felt so good to take revenge for the horrible, cruel, sadistic firebombing. Ogawa watched with approval as two guards clubbed and kicked a prisoner who had fallen. The prisoner lifted his arm weakly, then collapsed and lay un-moving under the continued blows. He was certainly uncon-scious, if not yet dead.

Ogawa wanted blood. He could taste blood. There was a prisoner running for the shelter of the barracks. Letting out a scream, Ogawa drew his katana and ran after him, getting in striking distance just a little bit before the man reached the entrance. His blade sliced into the prisoner's neck but struck bone. Ogawa had to step on him to pull the blade out. The dying prisoner flopped around like a fish for a minute, then stopped moving altogether as the blood pooled around him, jet-black in the red light.

He looked around for another target. There—there was an-other running prisoner. This time his blow struck true, and the prisoner's head separated neatly from his body. Blood spurted from the neck, spattering Ogawa's uniform.

A number of bodies—at least ten; Ogawa didn't take time to count—were lying on the ground. Targets were few. The prisoners who had stayed in their barracks and not cheered the fire were not fit targets for his sword.

But there, in the shadows, he saw a cowering man, desper-ately trying to hide. Ogawa approached him. It was the *gesuonna,* the woman-man, the disgusting weakling. Ogawa lifted his katana. "No," he said. "You're not worthy of this blade. You're not a man. You're beneath contempt." Two en-listed men, also out of targets, had come over and were standing behind Ogawa.

Then Ogawa had an inspiration. "Call the prisoners out of the barracks. Make them line up."

Shortly, two ranks of terrified prisoners stood at attention amid the carnage. Speaking through his translator, Kazuma, he said, "Your nation has committed a cowardly and desperate attack against the women and children of Japan. You are animals, not worthy of being part of the civilized world. Those of you who had the poor manners to applaud this uncivilized act have received proper punishment." He looked at the *gesuonna.* "With one exception."

Kazuma, speaking English, called out the name of the prisoner: "Andrew Sarnuss." Two guards grabbed the man and pulled him forward, then pushed him onto his knees in front of Ogawa.

The English words were strange and ugly. A fitting name for this contemptible thing. "Of all the *holio,* this man is the most cowardly. He is the most pathetic excuse for a man I have ever seen. He is so cowardly I think he would not have the courage to kill one of us if we were utterly helpless. And so I will not put him to death."

The prisoner began kowtowing with relief. Ogawa grinned. "But he is not a man. Therefore, he has no need for a man's equipment."

The *gesuonna* began to struggle, his eyes wide. Strange babbling noises—begging for mercy, Ogawa supposed, but he did not ask for a translation—came out of his mouth. The prisoner's pants were ragged as well as too large for his gaunt, bony form. The captain pulled them down easily and pulled out a small dagger.

He sliced. The *gesuonna*'s scream was quite satisfactory, as was the look of shocked horror on the faces of the assembled prisoners.

"Back to your barracks," Ogawa ordered. "And take this scum with you."

The two POW medical officers came forward. Ogawa thought for a moment about shoving them away, but it was a better lesson for this eunuch to remain alive. *Let them cheer again,* he thought with savage satisfaction.

But one prisoner, instead of shuffling back to the barracks meekly with the others, was scuffing his foot in the dirt. He was a tall man with a bushy black beard. What was he doing? Two guards headed toward the prisoner to make him join the others, but Ogawa ordered them to wait. He was curious.

Ah, the man was tracing a circle—a sumo ring. He was challenging Ogawa to a sumo match! How very clever, Ogawa thought. But it was beneath his dignity to wrestle with this man.

"Let me, Captain! Let me wrestle him!" said Lieutenant Kawazoe eagerly.

"Very well," replied Ogawa, smiling. "I'm glad to see there's a flicker of manhood left among these weaklings."

Kawazoe took off his gun belt, stripped off his shirt and boots, and strode over to the circle. Ogawa had seen Kawazoe in the intracamp matches. He was good. The American, from his stance, had little or no idea how sumo wrestling was supposed to work.

Ogawa didn't want to go back to fetch an actual *gunbai*, so he waited for both fighters to get into position and simply called, *"Gunbai wo kaesu!"* to start the match. Kawazoe and the bearded man charged at each other. Kawazoe's form was good, the bearded man's was terrible.

But instead of grappling as was proper in sumo, the bearded man brought his fist up and punched Kawazoe in the jaw, hard enough to rock him backward. The prisoner then kneed Kawazoe in the testicles before picking him up bodily and throwing him out of the ring. He turned to Ogawa and bowed insolently.

Ogawa was enraged at the prisoner's outrageous conduct. He put his hand on his sword, but before he could act, a shot rang out. Kawazoe had removed his pistol from the holster and shot his opponent in the chest. The prisoner kept his eyes on Ogawa for a few more seconds, then collapsed like a doll made of rags in the middle of the sumo ring. His blood flowed into the small trench that formed the circle's boundary.

"What have you done?" Ogawa shouted at the young lieutenant.

"He cheated! Did you see the way he behaved? I couldn't let him get away with that!" replied Kawazoe indignantly.

"You have disgraced us all with your shameful act," Ogawa said, with increasing anger. It was not proper for Kawazoe to take matters into his own hands like that. It smacked of poor sportsmanship. It was dishonorable. Instead, it was up to Ogawa as referee to take proper action.

The prisoner had stood up like a man. He deserved a man's death, not to be shot down by an angry opponent.

Kawazoe was still arguing. "But he cheated! You saw! He cheated!"

"Get out of my sight! Out! Out! Everyone out of the compound!" yelled Ogawa. Kawazoe's eyes were wide as he gathered his clothes in his arms and sprinted away.

Ogawa turned to Kazuma. "Tell the prisoners that as long as they are quiet, no further harm will befall them this evening." Not waiting for a reply, he spun sharply on his heel and marched out. The tall barbed-wire gates closed behind him.

• **THURSDAY, 22 MARCH 1945** •

BATAAN HOUSE, SWPA FORWARD HEADQUARTERS, OKI-
NAWA, 1030 HOURS (OPERATION OLYMPIC, X-DAY + 04)

The first thing Major Gregory Yamada noticed when he climbed the stairs to the second-floor conference room was the amazing view of Haguchi Bay, a blue expanse stretching out before him through the windows that made up the top half of the wall. He would have a hard time getting any work done with a view like that to distract him.

The second thing Yamada noticed was how much conflict was going on just beneath the surface.

Yamada unzipped the artist's portfolio he was carrying and took out the posters he would use for the briefing. The warrant officers who actually ran the establishment had provided an easel and a chalkboard. There was a podium as well, although Yamada would not use it—he never did. Yamada checked the order of the posters and reviewed his notes. He had the whole thing down to a little over ten minutes. He hoped that wouldn't be too long. With generals, you never could tell.

Yamada's nominal boss was Major General Charles Willoughby, MacArthur's G-2 (Intelligence). Willoughby was German by birth, a graduate of the University of Heidelberg, and spoke with a noticeable German accent.

Willoughby was first to arrive. He came over to shake Yamada's hand. "Good work out there. Very good work," he said. The word came out sounding a little like "verk."

"Thank you, sir."

"All is in order for today, then?"

"Yes, sir."

"My advice to you is brief the high points and give the rest in a report." Willoughby was the fourth person to tell him that so far today. Yamada resisted the urge to point out that he had briefed general officers before.

The other officers with "need to know" trickled in. The second to last to arrive was Major General Richard Kerens Sutherland, MacArthur's chief of staff, who glared at Willoughby. Willoughby, in turn, sat down placidly and waited for the briefing to begin. Yamada interpreted that as saying Willoughby's stock was on the rise and Sutherland's in decline. Sutherland had a thin, triangular face, thin lips, and a sharp manner.

"Attention!" the chief of staff said, and all rose for the entrance of Douglas MacArthur. This was the first time Yamada had seen the General in person. MacArthur looked both thinner and older than he'd imagined. He held his corncob pipe in one hand, but it was unlit. Without his famous cap, it was obvious the General's hair was thinning out rapidly.

MacArthur's eyes focused on Willoughby and he nodded toward his G-2. However, he kept his back toward Sutherland as much as possible and when he had to face him, his eyes never made contact. Yamada interpreted that as confirmation of his earlier observation.

When everyone was seated, MacArthur nodded at Yamada as his cue to begin.

"Thank you, General MacArthur, sirs. I am Major Gregory Yamada, Army Intelligence. I interrogated the first captured suicide pilot, and I'm here to brief you on what I learned." He stepped over to the posters, took off the blank to reveal the first one with information, and started to talk.

The first interruption came before he could even begin his briefing. "How did you get him to talk?" MacArthur asked in what was apparently genuine curiosity.

"Sir, the Japanese are nonsignatories to the Geneva Convention. They aren't bound by 'name, rank, and serial number.' As you know, they generally don't even think of surrendering. Most of our captives, like this pilot, have been taken while incapacitated by wounds or combat. This fellow, for example, was thrown from his cockpit when his plane hit the water. He was trying to swim under the water, drown himself, when the navy fished him out with a bosun's hook. After that, he was so ashamed that he simply collapsed."

"Until you arrived to talk to him?" the General pressed.

"It took some patience, sir. But he opened up, which is typical. Once the prisoner figures out that we aren't going to torture or kill him, he'll usually talk quite freely."

He stepped back into his presentation. "He told me that there are approximately five thousand aircraft hidden on Kyushu, minus those sent out in attacks to date, dedicated to destroying the American fleet." There. *That* got their attention.

He managed to get through the next two or three minutes without an interruption. Then he said, "The Special Attack Units, *tokubetsu kogekitai,* or just *tokko,* are going to be an integral part of Japanese strategy from here on out. The first aerial *tokko* unit was a navy fighter wing—"

"Sounds like something the navy would think up," Willoughby said.

This drew a sharp look from Sutherland. MacArthur merely

waved his unlit corncob pipe at Yamada as a sign the Army Intelligence officer was to continue.

"—called the Kamikaze Special Attack Corps."

"I have heard the word 'kamikaze' before," MacArthur interjected. "Something to do with the Mongols."

"That's correct, General MacArthur, though I must say there aren't a whole lot of Westerners I'd expect to know that." MacArthur looked like a man who welcomed all the praise he could get.

The Supreme Commander preened slightly. "MacArthur is one of the few in the West with a true understanding of the Oriental mind," he pronounced.

Yamada had no idea how to respond to that statement, so he ignored it. "Then for everyone else, I should say that *kamikaze* translates as 'divine wind,' referring specifically to the typhoons of 1274 and 1281 that stopped Kublai Khan's two attempts to conquer Japan. Each storm appeared in the right place, at the right time, to wipe out the whole invasion fleet. The Japanese now believe that the divine wind, the kamikaze, is in essence a god who, in response to the Emperor's prayer, protects Japan against invasion by outsiders.

"It's not working very well this time, is it?" Willoughby interjected, snorting at his own joke.

"Well enough," snapped Sutherland. "These damned kamikaze fliers are doing one hell of a lot of damage. And *look* at the casualty figures on the ground!"

Yamada knew he didn't want to get in the middle of *that* fight. "Besides the aerial *tokko,* the Special Attack Units include submersible and surface craft, air-to-air, and land attacks, such as human bombs attacking tanks. They have many thousands of small boats packed with explosives, and even battalions of volunteers who are prepared to carry charges in attacks against our tanks, blowing themselves up as they take out the armor. In this fashion, General, they plan to fight for every square inch of Kyushu, and inflict as much damage on our forces as possible."

Willoughby interjected, "Remember, their Operation *Ketsu-Go* plan envisions sacrificing twenty million Japanese if necessary to bring us to the negotiating table to offer 'honorable' terms."

Yamada controlled his surprise. Obviously, Willoughby was receiving direct intelligence from the Japanese from a very high level. *Probably reading their codes*, he thought.

"Twenty million." MacArthur put his unlit pipe in his mouth and then took it back out. "How did a fact like that escape our planning process? Charles?"

Sutherland pivoted on his chair to watch his colleague and rival get roasted.

Willoughby, on the hot seat, struck a match and lit a cigarette before replying. "I believe there was a debate about the accuracy of some of our intelligence gathering, and some planners—" MacArthur's eyes narrowed. Was Willoughby going to accuse the General himself of ignoring intelligence? Yamada noticed Willoughby's eyes looking up and to the left, which in his experience often corresponded with invention. "Admiral . . . uh . . . Spruance comes to mind— seemed to think that those estimates were overblown . . ."

"Spruance." MacArthur's voice was flat.

"General, I'm not entirely sure about that, but I do believe the skepticism was coming from our navy colleagues. . . ." The Prussian-American Willoughby's accent was getting thicker as his stress mounted. Sutherland seemed to have trouble controlling his glee.

"Are you sure the failure wasn't in *your* shop?" Sutherland couldn't resist sticking his own knife in. Bad tactics, thought Yamada. Not only was he violating the rule of "never interfere with your enemy in the process of destroying himself," but he was sticking his nose where it didn't belong while still on MacArthur's shit list.

"If the General requires assistance, he will inform you," MacArthur said frostily, confirming Yamada's analysis. Sutherland shut up, but the damage had been done.

"Suicide attacks or no suicide attacks, the United States had no choice but to invade," MacArthur intoned. "Therefore, the question of whether the intelligence estimates properly accounted for these . . . kamikaze . . . is in some sense moot. However, gentlemen, they are at present a concern and must be stopped. Overall, MacArthur is *not* satisfied with the progress of Operation Olympic. Some of this is unavoidable and no blame attaches to anyone. It is, after all, the largest amphibious assault in the history of the world, seven times as complex as D-day in Europe, and it would be too much to suppose that it would come off without a hitch. 'No battle plan,' gentlemen, 'survives first contact with the enemy.' And 'sufficient unto the day is the evil thereof.' "

MacArthur continued. "Now, even in the face of this tough nut, we must remember that we are dealing out incredible punishment to the Japanese. General LeMay's fire-bombing tactic, by all reports, is proving remarkably effective. We burned most of Tokyo to the ground with the first attack. And he is proceeding from city to city—I understand that ten have been essentially burned out as of this time."

General MacArthur smiled. "Let us therefore not seek after the guilty, nor inadvertently punish the innocent. If our naval friends misjudged certain intelligence estimates, it is hardly the first time in military history, nor are such mistakes limited to the gallant seaborne service that so ably delivers our troops to the decisive point, to fight the ultimate battle against tyranny and thus preserve the future of mankind."

The General paused, thinking, and Yamada knew better than to interrupt. MacArthur blinked, as if a thought had just occurred to him. "An unanticipated, successful enemy tactic requires a modification in our own tactics," he intoned.

"True, our initial objective was to occupy the south of the island of Kyushu in total, driving the enemy off of his home territory with a wave of force that would clearly establish our irresistible strength in the enemy's mind. However, to continue with that plan would entail a level of American casualties that will inevitably escalate to unacceptable levels. Now, what is it that we *really* need on Kyushu?"

Perhaps understanding the rhetorical nature of the question, none of the generals replied. Smiling tightly, MacArthur went on. "We need the airfields, the flat ground to the south of the island, so that we can cover the next stage of landings, on the large island of Honshu. Most of that ground is already in our possession—has been since the first days of the invasions—since the enemy is making his stand in the mountains. By attacking him there, we are playing into his hands. But if we change our tactics, they will need to change theirs in response."

The General sat back down, stroking his chin pensively.

Yamada, who had substantially more in his brief, could tell when his audience had finished listening. He stood patiently in the event he was mistaken, and when General MacArthur stood, he said, "Thank you, sir."

"No, thank *you*," said MacArthur, with a wave of his hand that could easily have passed for a papal blessing. "An excellent brief. I presume you have everything in writing as well?"

"Yes, sir."

"Leave our copy with General Willoughby," MacArthur said, then strode out of the room, his entourage following.

Yamada heard MacArthur mutter on the way out, "This complicates things."

And a moment later, "Spruance . . . *hmm*."

CAMP SHINJUKU, TOKYO, JAPAN, 1036 HOURS

A scared and contrite Lieutenant Kawazoe stood in front of Captain Ogawa Taiki's desk. "I have contemplated my conduct in the light of bushido, and I understand how I have brought dishonor on this command."

Ogawa tapped his fingers on his desk. "I'm glad you've figured it out, but it is a bit too late. I spent the early morning calling fellow officers, and I believe I have finally found you that fighting position you've been looking for."

"Really, sir? But after my disgrace . . . ." Kawazoe fell silent as Ogawa pushed a file folder across his desk at the flat-faced lieutenant. He picked up the folder and pulled out the single sheet of paper inside. "A *tokko* squadron. I see." He stood quietly for a minute, and then bowed to Ogawa. "Indeed, sir, you are much kinder to me than my poor behavior deserves. Thank you for this opportunity to redeem myself."

Ogawa smiled and stood up. "I knew you'd see it that way, Kawazoe. It is a great honor for you, and you have accepted it in the spirit it was offered. May the *kami* smile good fortune upon you."

Kawazoe saluted, spun on his heel, and marched out.

One problem down, one to go, thought Ogawa. He sent for his senior sergeant, Ishikawa, back from Tokyo. Ishikawa's family had been in the half of the city untouched by fire. Lieutenant Saruwatari had not been so fortunate. He was not able even to enter the section of the city where his family lived. It was not yet certain they were dead, but it was highly likely. He had given Saruwatari several extra days to search. Ogawa and Lieutenant Watanabe could run things by themselves.

"You know what happened last night," Ogawa began.

"Yes, Captain."

"The prisoners are to be treated like men as a sign of respect for the one true man among them. At least for a week or so. Make sure your guards know."

"Yes, Captain."

"Oh—and about the eunuch. I think it would be better for all concerned if he were transferred to a different camp. Not killed, not even hurt, but moved someplace else, *neh*? I think someplace up north would be good. Away from here."

"I'll take care of it, Captain."

"Very good, Ishikawa. This will wipe out the stain on our honor. In the meantime, I have good news."

"Yes, Captain?"

"I have my orders. I'm considered fit for line duty again. I must have passed the last physical."

"Congratulations, Captain. Any idea when?"

"As soon as I can arrange replacements. I'm thinking Saruwatari for camp commander. And I'm not sure I ever really needed two lieutenants, not with well-trained sergeants like yourself."

"Thank you, sir. I think either of the lieutenants would be quite suitable for advancement, sir."

The rhythmic sound of the train engine and the clacking of the track were the only evidence Andy Sarnuss had that he was actually moving. He was forbidden to lift the shades that blocked the window of his first-class compartment. He shared it with a single guard, a man with no English. They communicated in grunts and sign language as needed.

He was forbidden to lift the shades not so much to prevent him from seeing out but rather so his gaijin features wouldn't disgust the natives. The rocking train pulled at his stitches; he was still sore. On the other hand, it was a relief not to walk with the beriberi shuffle anymore. He was still in shock; he hardly thought about the nature or consequences of his injury except to wonder if this entitled him to a Purple Heart.

He could tell they were going north because every time the train stopped, a blast of colder air would rush through the car. It was a long journey, about ten hours. At its end, he was very happy to get off. He walked ahead of the guard, who directed him with pushes to the left or right shoulder as necessary. The town—he didn't know the name, it was all in Japanese— was small, and with fuel scarce, he and the guard walked the several miles to the camp. It was past dark when they arrived. The guard signed over his prisoner and Andy was pushed into the general prison population. He had missed dinner and hadn't eaten on the train. Although he was ravenously hungry, there would be no food until breakfast.

The senior POW was a British colonel. The colonel did a quick, brusque interview, and when he learned what had happened to Andy, he sent him to the hospital for inspection and treatment. Andy went gladly.

Word gets around a prison camp quickly, especially if there's something new. "There's someone here to see you," said one of the doctors. "Says he's an old buddy."

"Jeez, I hope I don't owe him money," Andy said. He couldn't imagine who might be visiting him at this hour.

In the dimly lit hospital ward, he saw the shadow of the approaching body before the face came into view.

It was Johnny Halverson.

• **WEDNESDAY, 11 APRIL 1945** •

BATAAN HOUSE, SWPA FORWARD HEADQUARTERS,
HAGUCHI, OKINAWA, 1859 HOURS (X-DAY + 23)

The General stood at his window, looking out across the deceptively peaceful bay. He was alone, but even so he posed, the cigarette held like a baton in his right hand, the elbow crooked to bring his forearm parallel to the floor. He frowned, watching the reds and oranges of a spectacular sunset.

The view was soothing but couldn't distract him from the painful truths writ across the pages of reports littering his normally tidy desk. The casualty reports were appalling, and they spread across the spectrum of the services. So far during Operation Olympic the navy had lost more than two hundred ships, many of them transports crowded with troops. The marine and army casualties on land had, in the first days of the battle, surpassed the estimates for the entire campaign. And the air forces . . . what did it matter that the USAAF and navy pilots ruled the skies, when the enemy planes were not trying to challenge that air superiority? When the enemy pilots, instead, gave up their lives willingly, even enthusiastically, in the cruelly effective kamikaze attacks?

There was a great map on the wall of the conference room, but the General didn't so much as glance at it—for he had it fully memorized, including the daily, and all too insignificant, advances since yesterday. The truth remained: only a small portion of Kyushu had been taken. In some of the coastal valleys the infantry had advanced far enough to secure some small airfields—only 30 percent of the runways planned for the eventual Kyushu base. That base was necessary for the next phase of the operation—but how could there be a next phase? If it was like this all over again . . .

All those troops, advancing at such cost, clawing their way for each square yard of ground—and paying for that real estate with irreplaceable blood! It was too much, and it could not continue. Everyone was second-guessing him: Marshall, the President, the Chiefs, even his normally dependable friends in the press.

He would not be pressured, but he could see the future better than the rest of them. There was only one thing to do: halt offensive operations on Kyushu. The army and marines would have to dig in where they were and hold on for dear life against the inevitable counterattacks. But at least it would bring an end to the litany of disaster, of loss, that had thus far been the story of the campaign.

The Battle of Kyushu would be declared a victory, of course—Sutherland could handle *that* task. But the losses could not be denied. And even armchair generals would be able to see that the advance, on any map, came up well short of logical objectives.

But he knew what he had to do, and he would do it. He pressed a buzzer on his desk, summoning a stenographer, and even before she came in he was drafting the simple statement of orders in his mind.

There will be a general consolidation along the current lines. Marine and army formations are not to advance, except in cases of clear tactical importance. Instead, they are to entrench and prepare to defend the ground already seized. . . .

• THURSDAY, 12 APRIL 1945 •

*THE WHITE HOUSE, WASHINGTON, DC, 0918 HOURS
(X-DAY + 24)*

For once, the President's office was not Grand Central Station, home to five simultaneous debates and four phone calls. The frail man in the wheelchair sat quietly, hands in his lap—his fingers had grown clubbed. There was a shawl around his shoulders and a blanket over his lap. On the sofa next to the

President's desk sat a vice admiral in dress whites; an oak-leaf insignia on his shoulder boards showed him to be in the Medical Corps.

Outside the Oval Office windows the sky was iron gray. Spring in Washington fought an uphill battle; this was a February day transplanted into April.

Grace Tully, the President's secretary, opened the door to the Oval Office. "Mr. President, it's Fleet Admiral Nimitz. He's a few minutes early."

FDR managed a weak smile and turned toward the vice admiral, the President's personal physician. "Ross, is it okay to let Chester visit, or do you want to tell him to go away until later?"

Vice Admiral Ross McIntire laughed. "Are you trying to get me court-martialed, Mr. President?"

Tully opened the door more fully, and Fleet Admiral Chester Nimitz, chief of naval operations, walked in. Admiral McIntire stood up.

"Good morning, Mr. President," Nimitz said.

"Good morning, Chester," replied Roosevelt. "You're here at the sufferance of Ross McIntire, you know. I wish you'd speak to him. He's determined to keep everyone out of my office. I had to argue with him before he'd let you in."

Nimitz smiled slightly. "He's following my orders, Mr. President. If he thinks it's best, he has the authority to throw me right out of here."

FDR started to chuckle and it ended in a cough. McIntire was at the President's side instantly, offering a glass of water. The President waved it away. "I'm all right," he said. "Never felt better in all my life. He can throw you out? That would be quite a sight. But not today. I'm glad to see you. What's the news?"

"I presume General Marshall has told you about General MacArthur's change of strategy."

"Yes, yes indeed," replied the President. "Douglas has surprisingly good sense about changing his own plans. What's your opinion?"

"I agree, sir. We have to focus on what we actually need to

accomplish, and sometimes that means we don't have to take every objective."

"Good. There are too many dead brave boys as it is, far too many. Every life we spare is a godsend. What about the next objective? When will that attack take place? Do you know?"

"All the plans are being reviewed in light of what we learned from Operation Olympic," Nimitz said. "That's quite unsurprising; plans normally change based on actual experience and new information. We believe the Japanese put every bit of their effort into Kyushu. That may mean Operation Coronet will be less expensive than planned. Alternatively, it may mean that the Japanese plan to fight till the last man, woman, and child. We'll win, but at a terrible price."

Roosevelt nodded his head. Then he turned to stare out the window. "We'll win, though. That's past the point of doubt."

"Yes, sir," replied Nimitz. "How long and how costly are the only remaining questions."

The President sighed. "That's good, Chester. That's good. I've been feeling an awfully lot like Moses lately, in sight of the Promised Land but not quite reaching it."

"It won't be long now, Mr. President. You'll see it through until the end."

"That's what Ross tells me—or at least he tells me that I will if I keep doing what he tells me to do. Confidentially, though, I think he's just blowing smoke, aren't you, Ross? You see, Chester, I mostly asked you to come by today so I could say good-bye. I'm leaving for Warm Springs today. I can't take another day of Washington springtime. I can't even tell it apart from Washington winter sometimes." He paused. "I don't expect to be back."

"That's nonsense, Mr. President!" remonstrated Nimitz. "Of course you'll be. You're tougher than the rest of us put together."

There was still a twinkle in the President's eye. "That's right. And only the good die young. If that were true, I'd live forever."

He paused and chuckled. "Along with Douglas MacArthur," he added.

• WEDNESDAY, 18 APRIL 1945 •

IMPERIAL JAPANESE ARMY HEADQUARTERS, TOKYO, JAPAN, 0630 HOURS (X-DAY + 17)

Two large pillars framed the entrance to the headquarters of the Imperial Japanese Army. Atop one pillar was an equestrian statue and atop the other was a lantern. Admiral Yamamoto Isoroku, newly appointed minister of war in the cabinet of Prince Konoe, admired the way the horse and rider seemed to float above the tree line from the perspective of his limousine window. He wondered briefly if that effect was intended by the designer of the monument or was merely a happy accident.

The purpose of his visit to army headquarters was more serious, however. General Anami, the minister of the army, was generally considered to be one of the most powerful men in Japan, as well as an inflexible obstacle to any peace proposals. The Supreme Council was split down the middle, and it was Yamamoto's job to bridge the gap between the parties.

The limousine came to a stop at the guardhouse. "The war minister to see the army minister," his driver announced.

The guard snapped to attention, saluted sharply, and waved them through. The limousine crawled carefully through the cobblestone streets, sized long ago for horses and men. The army minister's building was a two-story stone structure with a slate roof.

General Korechika Anami's aide was waiting for them at the entrance. Yamamoto's driver opened the door, and as the admiral emerged, the aide bowed deeply. "It is an honor to welcome the war minister," he said. "It is with the deepest regrets that I must inform you that the general is engaging in his morning *kyudo* practice and is not yet available." He bowed again, deeper than the first time. "The most profound apologies—"

"If there is fault, it is mine entirely. I am early," Yamamoto interrupted. "And the general is noted for his mastery of the art. With your kind permission, I will watch the general as he shoots."

"Of course, Minister." The aide bowed again. "It would be my honor to escort you there, if I might?"

"Please. I would be in your debt." Yamamoto followed the aide along a stone pathway that led between the army minister's building and another stone office building on the right. The morning chill was rapidly wearing off as the sun rose in the spring sky. It looked to be a glorious day.

"It's nothing, sir, nothing at all. I am delighted to have the opportunity to be of service. May I offer you tea?"

"I would be doubly in your debt. Thank you for your gracious hospitality."

"Think nothing of it, sir. Ah, there is the general."

Two men were standing in a small rectangular courtyard, deeper than it was wide. One man, wearing traditional garb, held a very long bow above his head, pulled back the string, and let the arrow fly at a small target nearly thirty yards away. Behind him, standing at ease, was an enlisted man, an orderly or a batman of some sort.

Stone buildings defined the four sides of the courtyard. A gravel walk rimmed a neatly manicured garden. A small pond off to the left had lily pads on its surface. There was an artistic absence of symmetry in the way a grove of bamboo anchored the far right and flowers the left. There was a large, intriguingly shaped stone. A path on the narrow end nearest Yamamoto led to a wooden bridge that crossed nothing.

There was a small target made of straw very close to the archer in addition to the target farther away. Arrows jutted from both targets, with some arrows stuck in the ground to either side of the farther target. The arrow just shot quivered in the center of the target.

As was proper when practicing *kyudo* archery, General Korechika Anami, Imperial Army minister, was dressed in a jacket that left one shoulder bare, *hakama* skirtlike pants, and the special *yukage* archer's glove on his right hand. His *yumi* bow was over six feet in length, significantly taller than the medium-height Anami himself. The army minister was slightly overweight. His hair was black except for a touch of gray at the temples. His hairline was receding, but he wore a wide mustache to compensate. His nose was wide and his ears were prominent.

Yamamoto did not call out make any other noise. Anami did not recognize Yamamoto's presence, either. He was giving himself completely over to the act of shooting itself.

Yamamoto was not an expert on *kyudo,* but he had some familiarity with the art and enjoyed watching a skilled practitioner of the discipline.

The nearby target, the *makiwara,* was used for warmup. The main target, the *mato,* was twelve *sun* in diameter. The *sun* was a traditional measurement that equaled a hair over one inch. The target was exactly twenty-eight yards away.

Anami breathed in a measured, very deliberate series of inhaling and exhaling. His posture was straight but not rigid. Smoothly and elegantly he performed the *hassetsu,* the eight stages of shooting. First, feet one arrow length apart, toes in line with the target. Then shoulders, hips, and feet parallel to the ground and straight to the target, bow resting on left knee. Bow up, arrow nocked. Then came *monomi,* or looking at the target with half-closed eyes. This sent the archer's spirit to the target. Anami would now neither blink nor move his eyes until after the shot.

He raised the bow over his head and drew until the string was well past his ear. A novice or clumsy *kyudo* archer could cause himself a great deal of pain if the string hit his ear or face upon release. Now he was at the moment of *kai,* in which the success or failure of the shot was determined. The release, *hanare* would merely confirm it.

In a way, Yamamoto thought, the idea of *kai* summarized how he felt about this war. The opening action had determined the inevitable result. Everything since had simply been *hanare*.

Anami held the bow at the moment of *kai* for a good slow count of six before moving to *hanare*. The arrow sped from the bow and the bow itself spun in Anami's hand, the string stopping in front of his forearm in a perfect *yugaeri*. Yamamoto was impressed.

His *haya* shot having been completed, Anami repeated the process with the *otoya* arrow in a fluid motion, then performed *yudaoshi,* the lowering of the bow. Neither of these shots, Yamamoto noticed, hit the target.

Anami stood silently for a minute in meditation, then handed his bow and the remaining arrows to the batman. He stripped off his glove and handed that over as well. Only then did he turn to Yamamoto.

"Good morning, Admiral." The army minister bowed, the slight inclination of a peer to a peer. Yamamoto returned the bow with equal precision. "I'm afraid the last two shots didn't go in."

"*Seisha seichu,* General Anami. 'Correct shooting is correct hitting,' and your form was admirable."

Anami smiled at the compliment. "You are too generous, Admiral. I am a poor amateur, a novice with little skill."

"Not at all. I thought your *hassetsu* was elegant and smooth in every respect. And not every *kyudo* artist can finish with a *yugaeri* the way you did."

"Luck, mere luck. You do me too much honor. And you must permit me to offer my congratulations on your elevation to the cabinet. The Emperor is fortunate to have such a devoted and talented officer in his innermost circle."

The pleasant game of giving and refusing compliments would have continued, except that Anami's aide returned, trailed by two enlisted men. One carried a lacquer tray on which a tea service rested. The other carried a small folding table. The aide bowed deeply to both men as the two enlisted men quickly and efficiently set up the tea service, including a small burner to keep the water hot.

"Shall we drink our tea in this lovely courtyard?" Yamamoto asked. "It seems a shame to be indoors on such a fine day, and I would be honored if you would drink tea with me."

Anami looked at Yamamoto appraisingly, almost as if he were practicing *monomi*. *Well, perhaps I am his target,* the admiral thought. *Or will be soon.*

"Yes, it is a pleasant day," the army minister replied. "But it is my honor to have the opportunity to drink tea with you. Let us walk, then, and I will show you this garden, small and limited though it is." The aide and his men kept the two ministers in sight, staying far enough to be out of conversational earshot and close enough to provide more tea at a simple gesture from either man.

Again, the two men engaged in the ritual of compliments offered and rejected. The garden really was quite nice, Yamamoto thought, especially considering its position. A peaceful place to walk or sit could be a great asset to a military leader. He would have to see about the Imperial Navy doing something similar.

They sat together on a wooden bench on the narrow end of the park nearest the formal *mato* target. Most of Anami's arrows were in the target. Only a few protruded from the ground. "Your *kyudo* is excellent, General," Yamamoto said.

"Oh, it's not very good at all," protested Anami, pleased.

"I understand you also fence?"

"I make a poor and clumsy attempt at kendo, yes. It's nothing. It distracts me from the cares of office, and that is a blessing."

"So it is. You're a wise man to think so deeply about how a man stays calm and centered no matter what the situation. I have much to learn from you."

"No, my dear Admiral, quite the contrary. While I stand out in the early morning plunking arrows at targets, you are popular among the best-known geishas in Tokyo. Now *that* is a distraction from the cares of office. Perhaps you'll teach me about that one day."

Yamamoto laughed, but underneath he was concerned. While it was no particular secret that he frequently spent his free time in geisha houses, to have the army minister rattle off the fact so casually suggested the army was watching Yamamoto.

"Speaking of the cares of office, you must forgive me, my dear Admiral, for interjecting a note of business into this most pleasant conversation. It is always a delight to see you, and you are welcome at any time, of course, but may I ask if there was something specific that brought you here to watch my poor archery skills so early in the morning?"

"Of course, General. I, too, would prefer this moment stay fixed in time, but we have similar responsibilities. Yes, I did come here this morning with news. The American president died in his sleep. Prince Konoe was notified first, of course, and he directed that I be awakened to convey the news to the other members of the Supreme Council for the Direction of the War while he went to see the Emperor."

There was no reaction. The general already had this news. However, he played his role in the appropriate way. "My heart is gladdened by the death of our enemy Roosevelt," Anami said. "If only it had come much earlier."

"Shikata ga nai," Yamamoto said. It can't be helped.

"You've lived in America, Admiral. Tell me, what does this mean? Is America stronger or weaker? Will it be divided while factions battle for control of the government? Is this good news for us?"

Yamamoto thought. "It's hard to say. Americans are a strange people. Their assistant president will assume the office, and there will be no direct challenge to his right to reign."

"So he's somewhat like the Emperor?" Anami asked.

"Forgive my poor abilities. It is very difficult to explain such an alien system, and I'm not sure I understand it all myself. The president is both head of state and head of government, but he's not elected by their diet, and they owe only a symbolic party loyalty to him. Governments don't fall, even when it's clear the legislature has turned against them, until the next four-year election."

Anami shook his head. "But this means someone who's lost the confidence of diet and people can remain for years as the head of the government! That's insane, Yamamoto-san. How can any system like that function?"

"I must admit I'm not exactly sure. While I lived in the United States for several years, there were parts I never did learn to understand. But it does seem to work, insane though it surely is. Personally, I think the idea of combining the role of head of state with that of head of government in a single person leads to no end of mischief. Because the head of state stays above politics, he can unify the nation. But the head of government must involve himself in the issues of the day, and thus divide the nation. But then, they're a young country. As they mature, perhaps their system of government will improve."

"I'd like to see it fall apart, quite frankly, and the sooner the better," Amani growled. "Any chance of that?"

"My guess is that it will not. The new president, who has an unpronounceable name, will at first be wholly subordinate to the men who surrounded Roosevelt, because it is through them he will have to work the levers of power. Because they are headless, they will not seek to change policy or direction in the immediate future, perhaps six months or so. But then the death of Roosevelt is not a big surprise. He has been failing for some time. American policy is now a cart moving on a well-rutted trail, stuck in its grooves."

Anami grunted in acknowledgment. "Thank you for these wise insights, Admiral. It is always difficult to understand the Americans, and your crystal-clear understanding is an asset to the Supreme Council."

"Oh, my insights about the Americans are nothing special, and I agree that they are a difficult people to understand."

There was a pause while both men sipped tea and contemplated the garden.

"Was this the only reason for your visit, Admiral?" Anami inquired gently. "I'm afraid I have little to add to what already transpired at yesterday's council meeting."

The meeting of the Supreme Council for the Direction of the War had been unusually confrontational. Premier Konoe, who led the council, also led the faction that was willing to consider a negotiated peace. On his side were the foreign minister, Shigenori Togo, and the navy minister, Mitsumasa Yonai. Yamamoto was also part of Konoe's alliance but was keeping careful neutrality in public to enable him to communicate with the other side.

Besides Anami, the war faction consisted of the army chief of staff, General Yoshijiro Umezu, a spit-and-polish career officer who would rather die than surrender no matter what the cost, and to Yamamoto's private annoyance, the navy chief of staff, Admiral Soemu Toyoda, who had been promoted to the position with the understanding that he would follow the lead of his naval superiors. Instead, he was in full support of Umezu, the most militant member of the council. Worse, he was a powerful, elegant speaker.

Yamamoto sat for a moment, collecting his thoughts.

Anami said, "This wouldn't, I'm sure, be a private attempt on your part to try to persuade me to accept the unacceptable."

"No, Anami-san." Yamamoto chuckled. "I know you too well for that." He thought for another few seconds. "Could you tell me more about the idea of *kai*? I have only a rough and clumsy outsider's understanding of the concept." He spoke while keeping his attention fixed on the interestingly shaped large rock. It had a number of variably sized faces, small, flat surfaces connected by smooth, rounded angles.

Yamamoto felt Anami's eyes on him, then he felt them looking forward, seeing the same garden view as he.

"Very well, Admiral," Anami began. "*Kai* is the essence of *kyudo*. One prepares to shoot by moving the body into exact position in a smooth and natural manner, while staying focused on the target. Once that is done, every part of the outcome is now established, whether good or bad. Releasing the arrow releases the tension of both bow and body, but it changes nothing. Whether the arrow will hit or miss the target has already been settled."

"Seeing the outcome is almost irrelevant, it would appear," Yamamoto summarized.

"That's correct. That part of the future has already happened."

"But what if there happened to be a great delay between the moment of *kai* and the outcome? Weeks, or perhaps even months."

Anami paused. Yamamoto could see that the general had figured out the trap.

"What, then, was your *kai* in this war?" Anami asked. *He counterattacks, of course, like the smart warrior he is.*

Yamamoto chuckled. "Your great intellect has found me out," he said. "Yes, I did have a moment of *kai*. It was early. It was at Pearl Harbor. You know my intent, of course."

"I'm not sure I do, Admiral. I know the broad outlines, of course. A brilliant and heroic action."

"It was a strategic strike, and I'm afraid it turned out to be a failure, though it took some time for that to become apparent."

"A failure? How could it possibly be considered a failure? No, Yamamoto, I must protest in the strongest possible terms. It was brilliant. Absolutely brilliant."

"To the extent that any praise attaches to the operation, it attaches to the fine officers and men under my command. Tactically, yes, it went off well enough. It is on the strategic level that Pearl Harbor failed. You see, the Americans had to be kept out of the Pacific until we had taken and consolidated the resource areas we required. Then, we would be defending, which is inherently stronger, and we would have better internal lines of supply, which would also dramatically change our situation." Technically, all Japanese were on limited rations, but there were exceptions both official and unofficial for those with rank. "To do that, we needed to destroy at least two out of the three major assets: the battleships, the carriers, or the oil tank farms and machine shops that made Pearl such a valuable American base. We got one of the three, the battleships. It wasn't enough. When I knew that, I knew my arrow had missed."

"You're too hard on yourself, Yamamoto. You've essentially given up when there is all reason to hope that the Americans will be forced to offer us terms far better than these 'unconditional surrender' insults."

"And Operation *Ketsu-Go* is working according to plan?" the war minister asked.

"Yes. That arrow—*my* arrow—has gone straight. We are in the middle of the Decisive Battle, and we are inflicting heavy casualties on the invaders. The pain will get too great for them to bear long before it becomes too great for us."

"How many divisions that were going to be held back to defend the inevitable second attack across the Tokyo plains have gone instead to *Ketsu-Go*?" asked Yamamoto mildly.

The army minister flushed. "I don't have that figure exactly," he said.

"It's not important," said Yamamoto. Both men knew that so far six divisions had been moved south through the Shimonoseki tunnel to Kyushu. That was six divisions—an army—fewer to defend against the final attack. "That tunnel is a great strategic asset to a country like ours, a country of multiple islands," the admiral noted. "We can hope the Americans remain unaware of its potential and do not realize that we can march troops from Honshu to Kyushu—or back, again."

"They will not be coming back, and indeed, we may reinforce them further. As you know," Anami went on, "the Decisive Battle is on Kyushu. One way or another, it will be settled there. Only that battle matters. We must inflict enough damage on the Americans to make them realize that they must provide honorable terms in order to end this war. We *must*." He turned to face Yamamoto. "Don't talk to me about peace. Peace without honor is just like death, only slower and more painful."

Yamamoto sighed. "No, I promise you, that is not the purpose of my visit."

"Then to what purpose are we talking, Yamamoto-san? Aside from the great pleasure of your company, of course. You are always welcome here."

"Thank you, dear friend," Yamamoto said. "You do me such great and undeserved honors. No, I came to ask you about the nature of war."

"The nature of war?" Anami looked incredulous. "What could I possibly teach the great Yamamoto about the nature of war? It is you who should teach me, if there is teaching to be done."

Yamamoto grunted ambiguously. "That German imitator of Sun Tzu, Clausewitz, tied warfare into state policy, saying that it was 'a continuation of politics with the addition of other means.'"

"Well, yes," Anami said. "But what does that—"

"A war is a result of conflict, but not just any conflict," Yamamoto interrupted. "Conflicts are negotiated away, or sometimes one side generously grants the wishes of the other. No, war occurs when the conflict becomes intolerable and is not amenable to any mutually satisfactory solution."

Anami looked impatient. "My friend, your wisdom on these matters is great, but—"

"Please, bear with me for another minute. My mind is clumsy and confused; I cannot speak as eloquently as I would wish."

"No, no, Yamamoto-san. You're doing brilliantly. Please go on. I shall pay careful attention."

"To summarize, such a conflict can, if the pressure builds enough, explode into war. But considering the origin and process, one thing must be true: both parties believe themselves to be right and justified."

"But one of them is in fact wrong."

"Sometimes. Sometimes, right and wrong are not at issue. But whatever the topic of the conflict, the war must be prosecuted in such a way as to support the political objective, even when that hampers certain military choices."

"What choices are you talking about?" Anami asked suspiciously.

"One last point. A war begins with an objective in mind, and decisions are made in accordance with that objective. But as men die and pain increases, the desire for revenge and retribution grows. The war can slip out of the control of its instigators and planners and take on a life of its own. The original objective then is overcome by the desire for revenge, with the result that both sides lose. Neither achieves its objective, even if one enjoys more military success than the other."

Anami thought for a minute. "I fail to see how any of this applies to the current military situation," he said.

Yamamoto put a look of mild surprise on his face. "Oh! I am so sorry, Anami-san. I misled you into believing I was discussing the military situation. Of course you would think that. How terribly clumsy of me. My deepest apologies. Please forgive me."

"Of course, of course," said Anami impatiently. "I misunderstood. The fault is all mine. Forgive me as well. If you weren't talking about the military situation, what war are you talking about? The Soviet Union?" Yamamoto noticed he was rushing through the obligatory blame ritual in his eagerness to find out what the admiral wanted. Good. The hook was truly sunk.

"I was referring to the Supreme Council for the Direction of the War, General Anami. We cannot afford a conflict in the council that escalates into war. Whatever the fate of Japan, let it not suffer because of the inability of the leaders to resolve their own conflicts and achieve harmonious concordance."

Anami looked at Yamamoto with some disdain. "In that case, I presume you've come to tell me the Peace Faction has decided to follow the honorable path and continue to fight while breath remains, thus resolving the conflict," he said.

Yamamoto smiled broadly. "In a way, Anami-san. In a way."

"What?"

"No one wants dishonor, Anami-san. And you don't want to see the Land of the Rising Sun wiped clean of Japanese, either. You want better surrender terms than the Americans are offering. I would like that as well."

"Then there is a proposal of some kind that should be considered?" Anami asked indirectly.

"If the army minister deigns to consider a suggestion?"

"Any suggestion coming from you, War Minister, deserves the best and most favorable consideration possible."

"I'm honored once again. Let me share it, then. The so-called Peace Faction would certainly prefer better surrender conditions than currently offered by the Americans. They are willing to support reasonable efforts to achieve such terms."

"And *they* define 'reasonable'? I'm deeply saddened, dear friend, but it would be very difficult for me to accept such a proposal. Very difficult indeed."

"I didn't intend for *them* to define 'reasonable.' I would ask you, instead."

"Me?"

"Yes. Who is better qualified?"

"You mean, define a specific point in which I'll give up and go along with them?"

" 'Give up' is, perhaps, stronger than intended. 'Work on a revision of our expectations and act accordingly' might better say it." Both sentences meant the same thing, Yamamoto knew. The second made it more palatable.

As Anami thought, Yamamoto tried one last attempt. "The *kai* of *Ketsu-Go* has passed, and we are awaiting the outcome. Militarily, it is performing beyond expectations. What is not yet clear is whether it will have the desired political impact. If it does, Anami-san, there will be one voice in the council and it will be yours."

Yamamoto paused to let the message sink in before continuing. "On the other hand, should it become clear that the arrow will miss the *mato*, it is the last arrow in the quiver, or close. This would require of the archer a rethinking and could lead to decisions heretofore not worthy of contemplation. You are only asked to choose a measurement in the unlikely event of *Ketsu-Go* failure. If you can find an acceptable place, the rift in leadership can be healed, and the Supreme Council can fulfill its mandate from the Emperor and its duty to the nation. We *must* find common ground,

General Anami. We must have a consensus, and everyone must be able to join."

He stood up, and Anami followed suit. Across the garden from Yamamoto, the aide and the two enlisted men started forward with the tea and tray, realized the conversation wasn't quite over, and scurried back to their previous spot.

"We can't afford a two-front war with the second front inside our own cabinet," Yamamoto said.

Anami chortled. "The second front inside our own cabinet! That's very funny, Yamamoto-san. Inside our own cabinet! Ha ha. I'm willing to try, because I agree with you that it's important for Emperor and nation. Unfortunately, I'm afraid I don't want to give up quickly. As long as we can field a fighting force capable of damaging the Americans enough to prod them toward the negotiating table, I believe we should do so."

"And the firebombing?"

"Those vicious monsters have done about all the damage they can. There's nothing much left to burn in most major cities. Let them drop all the fire they want on deserted mounds of ash. Savages! Those damned Americans are nothing but savages! Before the war they called us 'barbarous' and 'inhuman' for bombing civilians in China and now they do a hundred times worse themselves and excuse it by the bald-faced lie that they strike only at 'military and industrial targets.'" He looked at Yamamoto and growled. "My biggest regret in this war is that I didn't have a chance to burn a few of *their* cities."

"I share your indignation, my dear friend," Yamamoto said. "Can you find a point that is measurable, tied to potential American behavior, and reasonable enough to be accepted by all? If so, then we can cooperate to make this final act as expensive for the Americans as we possibly can."

"Yes, Yamamoto-san, I believe I can. And may I say," Anami answered, "your skills as an avoider of war are as formidable as your skills in prosecuting one."

"The general does me too much honor," demurred the war minister.

• THURSDAY, 19 APRIL 1945 •

FIRST HILL, 2 MILES INLAND OF BEACH PONTIAC, 0959 HOURS (X-DAY+19)

They called it First Hill because that's what it was. After three weeks of attacking, it remained First Hill, and the marines of the 3rd Marine Regimental Combat Team had finally reached the summit.

Captain Pete Rachwalski's company—still called Fox, though less than 10 percent of its marines had belonged to that company upon landing—had endured a good portion of that climb. They weren't on the very top of the hill, but Fox Company had fought its way to the crest of a long ridge leading down the south side of the elevation. After rooting out the few last Japs, by drenching their caves in flaming jelly called napalm, Pete's men were settling into place and catching their collective breath. The position overlooked a deep, wide ravine, and they weren't taking any fire from concealed positions on the opposite face of the gully, so it seemed like a good place to stop.

Pete decided they could risk a little campfire in the early morning hours. He had guards posted all along the ridge crest, with machine guns hidden in several key places. His mortars were zeroed in on the ravine floor and the far face. At least, for the first time in days, they could boil a little water and make some instant coffee.

General Erskine had been as good as his word, and his driver had brought up a set of a captain's bars for Pete the very next day. As he moved forward, and seemed to keep more of his men alive than most other company commanders, Pete had picked up more stragglers—the remnants of units that had been left leaderless. He had about 150 men now, and had organized them into ten squads of thirteen. The ten squads made up three platoons, with a weapons squad left over. They had scrounged enough mortars and flamethrowers to make a pretty good-looking fireworks show. This made up a company, and Pete, with the highest rank, was acting captain. He didn't have enough noncoms to go around, so he used the ones he had and breveted corporals and privates for the rest. There were plenty of candidates; marines grew up fast on Kyushu, or they didn't grow up at all.

They were sleeping in shifts, with each platoon taking its turn at guard duty. A couple of the men were snoring loudly enough to alert the Japs, if any happened to be around. He was tired, too. He could sleep another ten hours, easily. The dirt, crud, blood, and other shit from the battle on the beach had dried, but now his ass itched from lack of toilet paper. It was the little things that made combat such a pain.

"Hey, boss!" A loud stage whisper came from the ridge above.

"Yeah?"

"Patrol heading our way. Coming down the base of the ravine. Could be American, but I can't tell at this distance."

"Which direction?"

"Thataway." They had compasses. Since the maps had been with Captain Gilder when he blew up, there wasn't much use for them, so the sentry just pointed off to Pete's left.

Pete signaled to the active platoon, and he and the rest of his men moved as quietly as they could into positions along the rocky crest. The machine gunners took note and sighted their heavy, air-cooled barrels on the mostly hidden path below. Pete waved his hands so the platoon would spread out all along the line. If there were bad guys down in the gully, there were in for a surprise.

He said to the sentry, "Challenge them when they get close, but don't open fire until you're sure they aren't our guys."

"Uh—challenge them how?" the sentry asked.

"I don't know. Ask them something about baseball."

"Um, I really don't follow baseball, Gunny. I know that's not too normal, but I'm more the reading type."

Pete laughed. "Hell, so am I. What do you like? I like science fiction."

"Really? I like science fiction, too. But detective stories are my favorites. I want to be a detective when I get out. I mean, for real."

"Okay . . . then . . . ask them a—oh, I dunno—a radio question?"

"I got it! How about, 'Who knows what evil lurks in the heart of men?' "

Pete shrugged. "Try it. But don't shoot if they don't know. We'll try a couple if we have to. Shh. I hear them."

He waited until the rustle and stomping grew louder, then tapped the sentry on the shoulder.

"Halt!" the sentry cried. "Who goes there?"

"Marines! We're from 2nd of the 7th!"

"Wait! Uh . . . 'Who knows what evil lurks in the hearts of men?' "

"What?"

" 'Who knows what evil lurks in the hearts of men?' It's a question! To see if you know the answer!"

"How the hell should I know? Ask me something about Babe Ruth."

"I don't know any questions about Babe Ruth, okay? 'Who knows what evil lurks in the hearts of men?' "

"I already told you, I don't fucking know!"

Another voice cried out, "It's the fucking Shadow, okay? Don't you listen to the fucking radio?"

"I listen to fucking baseball, *okay?*" The man from 2/7 was growing irritable. "I don't know who the fucking Shadow is, *okay?*"

"You're definitely marines," Pete said, laughing. "Welcome to 2nd of the 3rd."

The patrol passed through the guard perimeter and into camp.

When they were seated around the campfire, Pete said, "You guys are pretty far forward. I didn't think you were going to get up here yet."

The patrol leader, a first lieutenant, shook his head. "We've been thrown in early because the fucking Japs have been so hard to root out. They won't surrender and they won't run away, and they think it's a victory if they take out one or two of you at the cost of their own lives. They're fucking nuts, the whole damn race, if you ask me. We fought our way around the back side of First Hill, and—well, you know how that was."

"Well, we got one goddamn hill. That's something, at least."

"Yeah?" the lieutenant countered. "You take a look over the top of this thing?"

"Our view is pretty much blocked by the other side of that ravine," Pete admitted. "What's it look like to you?"

"About a hundred more fucking hills. Each one bigger, higher, and meaner than the one where we've been living for the past three weeks."

"Jesus Christ," Pete said. His heart sank. There was no possible way he and his men would survive another hill or two, much less a hundred.

Pete's despair was obvious. The lieutenant added, "But don't worry, Captain. We don't have to take them—well, all of them. New orders have come down all the way from Mac himself. We've already got Kagoshima, more or less, and that means enough airfields. We don't need the rest of this shithole—pardon my French."

Pete chuckled. "Shithole is right. So what do we have to do if we aren't going to clean out the Japs?"

"Defense," the lieutenant said with a grin. "We're supposed to straighten out our line and then dig in and let them come to us."

Pete thought for a moment. "Yeah, that makes good sense. But answer me this, lieutenant. How the hell are we going to get the Japs to surrender if they don't mind dying?"

"I don't know," the lieutenant said. "I guess the brass know. I hope they do, anyway. Oh—I forgot. You haven't had any news up here for a while."

"No news and not much in the way of supplies, either," Pete said. "Does this mean we'll get supplied? We need food and ammo and damn near everything else."

"Not my area, Captain, sorry. Did you hear about the President?"

Pete shook his head. "No—is FDR okay?"

The lieutenant paused, then said, "He died. About a week ago, in his sleep."

Pete was stunned beyond belief. Roosevelt was the only president he'd ever known. He felt as if a family member had died. He was silent for a moment, and said, "So it's President Wallace now?" He could barely picture Henry Wallace; it had been a long time since he'd even seen a picture of the Vice President.

"No, don't you remember? FDR fired Wallace for being a commie." Vice President Wallace had been endorsed for re-election in 1944 by the American Communist Party.

"Oh, yeah," Pete said. "So it's President . . ." He looked expectantly at the lieutenant.

"Truman," the lieutenant said. "Harry S. Truman."

"Truman," repeated Pete. "I don't know a fucking thing about him."

The lieutenant laughed. "I don't think anybody else does, either. I guess we'll see."

"Roosevelt dead," Pete mused. He looked at the ravine and the exhausted faces of his own men. Suddenly, shockingly, he sat down on the rocky ground and started to cry.

• FRIDAY, 20 APRIL 1945 •

BATAAN HOUSE, SWPA FORWARD HEADQUARTERS, HAGUCHI, OKINAWA, 1859 HOURS (X-DAY + 24)

The General stood at his window, looking out across the deceptively peaceful bay. He was alone, but even so he posed with his cigarette held like a baton in his right hand, his elbow crooked to bring his forearm parallel to the floor. He frowned, watching the reds and oranges of a spectacular sunset.

The view was soothing but couldn't distract him from the painful truths writ across the pages of reports littering his normally tidy desk. The casualty reports were appalling, and they spread across the spectrum of the services. So far during Operation Olympic the navy had lost more than two hundred ships, many of them transports crowded with troops. The marine and army casualties on land had, in the first days of the battle, surpassed the estimates for the entire campaign. And the air forces . . . what did it matter that the USAAF and navy pilots ruled the skies, when the enemy planes were not trying to challenge that air superiority? When the enemy pilots, instead, gave up their lives willingly, even enthusiastically, in the cruelly effective kamikaze attacks?

There was a great map on the wall of the conference, but the General didn't so much as glance at it—for he had it fully memorized, including the daily, and all too insignificant, advances since yesterday. The truth remained: only a small portion of Kyushu had been taken. In some of the coastal valleys the infantry had advanced far enough to secure some small airfields—only thirty percent of the runways planned for the eventual Kyushu base. That base was necessary for the next phase of the operation—but how could there be a next phase? If it was like this all over again. . . .

All those troops, advancing at such cost, clawing their way for each square yard of ground—and paying for that real estate with irreplaceable blood! It was too much, and it could not continue. Everyone was second-guessing him: Marshall, the annoyingly blunt new President, the Chiefs, even his normally dependable friends in the press.

He would not be pressured, but he could see the future better than the rest of them. There was only one thing to do: halt offensive operations on Kyushu. The army and marines would have to dig in where they were, and hold on for dear life against the inevitable counterattacks. But at least it would bring an end to the litany of disaster, of loss, that had thus far been the story of the campaign.

The Battle of Kyushu would be declared a victory, of course—Sutherland could handle *that* task. But the losses could not be denied. And even armchair generals would be able to see that the advance, on any map, came up well short of logical objectives.

But he knew what he had to do, and he would do it. He pressed a buzzer on his desk, summoning a stenographer, and even before she came in he was drafting the simple statement of orders in his mind.

There will be a general consolidation along the current lines. Marine and army formations are not to advance, except in cases of clear tactical importance. Instead, they are to entrench and prepare to defend the ground already seized. . . .

• SATURDAY, 21 APRIL 1945 •

HIROSHIMA, 2030 HOURS

My dear Taiki-san,

How wonderful it was to get your telegram and hear that you are here, on Honshu! Even if you are all the way up in the Kanto, it still seems to me that you are close to home. I know you must wish to command troops, to lead men in battle, but Mother and I take comfort in knowing that you are guarding prisoners in a camp near Tokyo, rather than facing death on Okinawa or in the Philippines.

We received your telegram right after Father's funeral. It was kind of you to send it—we know how busy you are. I think you would have been pleased by the funeral. Uncle Fuji made a nice speech, and we dropped Father's ashes from the Aioi Bridge into the River Ota. They are in the ocean by now, mixed with the memories of all our ancestors.

But O! Taiki-san, how we miss you. Mother's health continues to fail—she is stronger than Father was, but grows weaker by the day. Of course, you know that she would never complain. She needs food, but she insists she is full, passing a little extra of her portion to me or—surprise!—the baby.

Hah! I can see your eyebrows rising in consternation, dear brother. But the baby is cousin Otomi. He is staying with us this winter. Auntie Ui is working in a factory, and so Mother and I are taking care of Otomi. He is a happy baby, a real giggle-bunny, and brightens both of our lives. I know you will be pleased and proud when you can finally come home and meet him.

　　Until that day, I pray for your safety and good health!

Your sister,
Michiyo

EIGHTEEN

Western Pacific

• **FRIDAY, 27 APRIL 1945** •

NAKAMURA-YA OKIYA AND UMENOJIMA OKIYA, GINZA DISTRICT, TOKYO, JAPAN, 2100 HOURS (OPERATION OLYMPIC, X-DAY + 39)

Under her thick, formal makeup and carefully styled expression, it was hard to tell what a geisha was thinking, but War Minister Isokoru Yamamoto knew this geisha very well. Toshiko, elder sister at the Nakamura-ya *okiya,* held her bow for just a little too long, averted her eyes with an almost furtive glance to the side. She was clearly disturbed about something.

"*Koben-wa,* Toshiko-chan," he said, his voice muffled under his white gauze mask.

"Eighty-sen!" she replied, with every outward sign of pleasure. "What a joy it is to have you grace our house with your presence once again. Shall we play a game of mahjongg, just you and I?"

The man known sometimes as Eighty-sen had pressing business, but if Toshiko wanted to talk with him privately, he suspected it was important enough for him to alter his plans slightly. "Any game with you, dear Toshiko, is always a treat," he said. "Though it will be a shame to take your hard-earned money away from you yet again."

She laughed, a beautiful high-pitched titter, and brought her hand to her mouth. "Such a wicked man you are, Eighty-sen," she teased. "Don't be so sure whose money will end up where."

She took his arm and led him around a shoji screen, then through a small hallway to a set of sliding doors. Inside was her office, efficient but not nearly so beautiful as the rest of the geisha house. "Please, Eighty-sen," she said, "sit down. May I serve you some tea?"

"Thank you, Toshiko-chan," Yamamoto said, taking off his mask and resting himself on a floor cushion. "And how may this humble client be of service to the most beautiful and most talented of all geisha?"

Toshiko simpered. "Such a flatterer you are. But don't stop. It's part of your charm. Along with your mediocre mah-jongg playing, that is."

Yamamoto grinned. There were not many people left in the world who felt free to tease him like that. "What can I do, Toshiko-chan?"

"My girls . . . hear things, you know? And of course anything said to a geisha is always kept in strictest confidence. But"—her eyes turned toward the thin paper of the sliding door and her voice lowered—"some of the officers who come here, the younger ones especially, are talking about . . . things. Terrible things."

Yamamoto leaned forward. "Dear Toshiko, take your time. I know this is difficult, and there is much you cannot say. But please tell me what you can."

She shot him a look of gratitude. "They're talking with contempt about great men. Claiming these men might seek a dishonorable peace, saying that they are showing weakness rather than strength at the enemy's challenge."

"And what do they propose to do about such dishonorable leaders as those?" Yamamoto asked.

"Assassination," whispered Toshiko.

"And has my name been mentioned?"

"Y-yes. Some people are saying you're playing both ends against the middle."

Yamamoto nodded. "Accurate enough, I suppose."

"Are you in favor of surrender?" Toshiko asked.

"I am in favor of Japan," he replied. "I am in favor of the Emperor."

They sat for a few minutes in silence, sipping their tea. "We're going to lose, aren't we?"

"That's not at all certain," Yamamoto said. He held up his three-fingered hand. "Several options still remain to us. We can lose . . ." He folded one finger down. "We can lose . . ." He folded down the second finger. "Or we can lose." He folded down the remaining finger. After a minute, he lifted his fingers up again. "We can lose our lives." Again, he folded down a finger. "We can lose our honor." The second. "We can lose our nation." The third went down, and he lowered his hand. "These are important options, *neh*?"

Toshiko kept staring at the space where Yamamoto's raised hand had been. "We've been incredibly lucky the fire-bombing didn't burn us out of business. But I lost three of my geisha in that first awful raid."

"I'm sorry."

"Others have suffered far worse. And those three are now beyond suffering, at least until they are reincarnated. Karma." She looked at Yamamoto directly. "Save our people, Eighty-sen. I will pray every night for your safety. And I'll have the girls gather all the information on what the young officers are plotting."

Yamamoto stood and bowed, then tied his gauze mask back on. "In that case, Toshiko-chan, it may be *you* who saves the empire."

After changing into a kimono, he slipped across the garden courtyard that separated the Nakamura-ya from the Umeno-jima. His mistress, the beautiful retired geisha Umeryu, whose real name was Chiyoko, was the only one he trusted for these clandestine meetings, and again she had everything in readiness.

He greeted his guest.

"*Konichi-wa*, Eighty-sen," General Korechika Anami, the army minister, said. "I have to say that if nothing else comes of this, I have finally been honored by this beautiful geisha with a gift that all men desire."

Yamamoto cocked an eyebrow.

Anami laughed. "A geisha nickname! Ever since you told me yours, I have been deeply, terribly envious. I confessed this envy to Umeryu, and after some thought, she gave me a name."

"He is now Otoya," Umeryu said. She bowed from her kneeling position. "Because he spins in the opposite direction." When she raised her head, both men could see her charming smile. After all these years, Yamamoto still found her breathtakingly erotic.

Yamamoto laughed. *"Konichi-wa,* Otoya-san,*"* he said, bowing as if to someone he'd just met. "Let us hope our opposite directions can be harmonized." He sat down at the small wooden table and took a proffered cup of sake. "To the Emperor," he toasted.

"To the Emperor."

Later:

"You're a wise man, Eighty-sen," the army minister said, tossing back another cup of sake.

Yamamoto matched him. It was a matter of pride, navy versus army. "No, Otoya-san, you do me an undeserved honor."

"In your great wisdom, I wonder if you can solve a dilemma that has been puzzling me of late."

"Whatever my poor sake-soaked brain can do, it will do, but I'm afraid its capacity is even more limited than usual."

Anami waved the remark off. "We venerate our ancestors and our history, do we not?"

"Yes, Otoya-san, we do. My intellect can stretch at least that far. I hope that was the question, but I'm afraid it was not."

"If we venerate the wisdom of our ancestors, then *how did we let these* children *get us into this mess*?" His voice roared. His fist wrapped around his empty sake cup as he slammed it on the table.

Yamamoto instantly sobered. The conversation had finally, naturally, turned to substance. He nodded. "Ever since the Manchurian incident, the captains and the majors have driven this war, rather than the generals, admirals, and ministers." The Manchurian incident of September 1931, an act of sabotage carried out by Japanese army officers and blamed on the Chinese, had provided a pretext for the annexation of Mukden. The first volley of what would become World War II, and intended to salve the Japanese military with easy victory over China, it was an act that had led directly and unequivocally to the current situation, fourteen years later.

"I have heard," Anami said, his voice muting, "they stand ready to assassinate anyone who doesn't choose to join them in their glorious self-immolation. It's the damned Buddhists. They're at the root, you know." The practice of Zen Buddhism in Japan had long been associated with the military classes.

Yamamoto merely grunted. "I want to thank you, Otoya-san, for your statement of conditions."

Anami laughed and held out his empty cup for a refill. "You're a sneaky one, Eighty-sen. If someone else had come up with a standard, I could have argued against it to my heart's content. Because I was 'privileged' to draw it up myself, I had to think through all aspects of the campaign to determine the right answer. It was not an easy chore."

"But a chore only you could have done, my dear friend. And the burden you felt would have been felt only by a man of honor."

It was Anami's turn to grunt. "The damned thing is likely to be my death warrant. *Both* our death warrants. The *children* will cry when the father cannot produce the moon on command, and lash out. We are under their control. The rules of a well-ordered world have been turned upside down."

"But what we have is better than youth, my opposite friend. We have wisdom. We have a unified Supreme Council," Yamamoto said.

"And we both have geisha nicknames," snorted Anami. "That, surely, must count for something." All three laughed.

"Perhaps it does, at that," Yamamoto said. "Opposite and cheap together. That sounds like a fortune-telling result, doesn't it?"

"Does it tell our fortune, Eighty-sen?"

"Perhaps. You are aware, for example, that the Americans have dramatically reduced their military activities on Kyushu?"

"Of course. They are soft people, and *Ketsu-Go* has caused them a great deal of pain. Now they have ceased marching into our guns, however, and so it is harder to kill them."

"Perhaps, for the first time since 1942, the initiative has returned to us? Maybe our combined fortune suggests that if we are to allow the idea of an endpoint to take hold, we should simultaneously increase our military efforts, thereby convincing the young ones that our intention is to continue at all costs."

"How does it say that, Mister Cheap Manicure?"

"In their hurry to strike at the Home Islands, the Americans have bypassed several significant positions. General Yamashita on Luzon, for example, commands a sizable force."

"Yes—he has been resisting in the northern mountains."

"As has General Yokoyama Isamu's Sixteenth Area Army on Kyushu. Perhaps the time has come for both of them to turn to the attack? And the same with our substantial forces on the south end of Okinawa. I understand that there are hundreds of Special Attack Force aircraft still concealed there—the aerial *tokko* the gaijin are now calling kamikaze. I think an attack on a new objective would prove destabilizing to the Emperor's enemies on both fronts."

Anami nodded, his head wobbling a little unsteadily. "I think you're absolutely right, and I will order it immediately, War Minister Eighty-sen." He moved to stand up but slipped back down immediately. "Tell me, Eighty-sen, why it is that you consistently offer brilliant advice that solves my problems and yet I don't really trust you?"

Yamamoto scratched his bald head with his three-fingered hand. "I think it's because you know that the other faction feels exactly the same way. The man who tries to bridge the gap between these opposing sides is always looked at with suspicion. Who is he? What does he want? What game is he *really* playing?"

"And what game, He-Who-Gambles-With-Geisha, are you *really* playing?"

"Know my objective the same way I know yours, Arrow-That-Spins-Counterclockwise. You are doing what you think is best, based on your experience, judgment, wisdom, and love for the Emperor. So am I. Nothing is concealed. Everything is available for your inspection."

Anami's brow wrinkled as he tried to think about Yamamoto's words. "I will solve this another time, Eighty-sen. I think your advice is probably good, I think you're probably right, but there's something about you I still don't trust."

Yamamoto smiled. "As I said, all the others feel the same way."

• **TUESDAY, 1 MAY 1945** •

KIYAMA-GUSUKU RIDGE, SOUTHERN OKINAWA,
0617 HOURS (X-DAY + 42)

Ensign Fujioka Tadao bowed with great dignity and accepted the small bowl of sake offered by his mechanic. He raised the vessel, his silk flying scarf draped like a mantle over his slim shoulders.

"Blessings, Fujioka-san!" declared young Ayoke, his eyes shining with unshed tears. "May your *tokko* flight end in a blaze of glory for the empire!" The mechanic stood at rigid attention in his grease-stained coveralls, staring at someplace over the pilot's head.

"Thank you, Ayoke," Fujioka replied, taking the cup. He knew that it was the last sake, probably the last anything, he would drink in his life. It was a little sour, and that saddened him. He bowed his head slightly so the young mechanic could cut off a lock of his hair. "Here. If you get a chance . . ." Fujioka handed the young mechanic several letters. Both knew how unlikely it was that the letters would reach their destination.

His eyes went to the aircraft that filled the space in the small cave, gleaming and dust free in the light of two gas lanterns. The Mitsubishi A4M Zero had been parked in here, out of sight of the sky—or American observers—for the past six months. Ayoke had lovingly tended it for the moment when it would be used, and now, in the terse order delivered by a messenger less than twenty-four hours ago, it would fly one last time. A hundred-kilogram bomb was strapped to the belly of the Zero. There was no release for those straps; the bomb would simply hit whatever target was struck by the plane itself.

"Three privates from the 24th Division are standing by to clear the brush from in front of the cave. They begged to have the honor of offering you their good wishes when they have completed their task."

The pilot was touched. "I will be happy to meet them." He glanced at his watch. "It is time to move." After a moment, he unstrapped the timepiece from his wrist and extended it to the mechanic. "Here," he said. "Keep it as a token of our time waiting together."

Ayoke wept then, unashamed as dawn's first light crept through the thinning screen of brush as the soldiers quickly pulled the camouflage away. Fresh air swirled into the suddenly opened cave. The three soldiers entered and bowed, watching somberly as Fujioka climbed into his seat. He strapped himself in but left the canopy open, the better to breathe the air and to see the sunrise.

The soldiers helped the mechanic wheel the plane down the slightly inclined cave entrance as the pilot ran through his control, checking the rudder and flaps for response. A minute later, he had the engine running, and the four men saluted as he rolled down the narrow dirt lane that would serve as his airstrip for this single takeoff. On his knee was a piece of paper, a map that had been issued to him with the attack orders. The map displayed the southern portion of the island of Okinawa and marked his target—which was only

twelve miles away. Circled in red was the city of Hagushi,
on the western shore of the island.

Home to the enemy headquarters.

BATAAN HOUSE, SWPA FORWARD HEADQUARTERS,
HAGUCHI, OKINAWA, 0712 HOURS (X-DAY + 42)

This was the fourth day in a row that General MacArthur
had avoided talking with his chief of staff, and General
Richard K. Sutherland was alternately angry and depressed.
*After all I've done for the ungrateful bastard . . . I lifted him
to greatness . . . sustained and protected him . . . a whole
war of loyal service . . .*

It was General Richard Kerens Sutherland who had put
himself on the line when General MacArthur didn't want to
believe the intelligence reports of the Japanese buildup on
Kyushu. It was Sutherland who went to Washington and
New Mexico when the General had learned about the Manhattan Project and put pressure on them to speed it up—at all
costs. If those physicists had been more capable, this whole
invasion might not have been necessary!

It was always Sutherland to whom Douglas MacArthur
turned whenever there was something the General didn't
want to take personal responsibility for. Sutherland was by
turns confidant, palace guard, hatchetman, press agent. It
was Sutherland who ensured that all stories coming out of
SWPA featured the General's name.

And when things went bad, it was Richard Kerens Sutherland who got hung out to dry. Somehow, the General seemed
to be blaming him for the whole Kyushu disaster. It was
Sutherland's fault that the intelligence MacArthur had ignored turned out to be correct. It was *Sutherland's* fault that
the damned scientists got in too much of a hurry and burned
up a big section of the New Mexico desert.

MacArthur was avoiding him, talking directly to others,
leaving him out of the loop, making his displeasure all too
clear. In other words, it was Sutherland's turn in the barrel.

Being the "staff SOB" was an important job, one that

required special skills, and Richard Sutherland possessed those skills in full measure. No one understood how much he suffered, how lonely he was, or what sacrifices he made to be so close to the seat of power.

He could feel the rest of the Bataan Gang gloating whenever he left his office. They could see his power slipping away. His misery was their joy. What was that word Willoughby used? Oh, yes: schadenfreude. Trust the Krauts to have a word for taking pleasure in someone else's frustration.

He could sense the lines of power shifting. There were meetings to which he was not invited. There were lunches and dinners and even bridge games where issues were settled, only to be ratified in a pro forma meeting later on.

Even the spectacular view from Bataan House couldn't dispel the grayness in his soul. *How could this happen to me? ME?* he thought. Sutherland knew he was the master of the inside game. He'd successfully put the skids under Colonel Eisenhower when Ike was Mac's chief of staff, way back before the war, taking the growing wedge between the two men and strengthening it.

That, too, MacArthur sometimes blamed on Sutherland. Eisenhower's subsequent rise to command of SHAEF and his worldwide fame rankled MacArthur no end. MacArthur's standard line about Eisenhower—"He was the best company clerk I ever had"—didn't begin to cover the resentment the General felt. And when he heard Eisenhower's comment about MacArthur—"Do I know General MacArthur? Why, I studied dramatics under him for five years!"—the General sulked for over a week.

Only Sutherland knew his weaknesses and how to protect him. But protecting MacArthur was, in essence, a thankless job. Sutherland had covered up the General's temporary breakdown in the Philippines. He'd even gotten rid of the eyewitness, leaving him behind on the Corregidor dock. But did MacArthur recognize his services? No. Instead, the great man remained as capricious and temperamental as ever, prone to threats of suicide or periods of deep self-pity. At least the suicide threats seemed to have abated since the liberation of the Philippines.

It's because of December 8. It's because I know the secret that really would destroy him. Now he's got to get rid of me.

If MacArthur thought he could do without Sutherland, or just toss him away, he was sadly mistaken. Sutherland knew where all the bodies were buried and in most cases had the documentation. If anything happened to Sutherland, MacArthur would go down with him.

Sutherland was jarred by the ringing of the telephone this early in the day. It was the HQ switchboard calling, and after a second the chief of staff picked it up. "Sutherland here."

The operator, a normally unflappable sergeant, spoke with a hint of agitation. "General, we have reports coming from the Aussies down on the line—lots of activity on the southern part of the island. The Japs have been launching planes, and it looks like lots of those planes are heading north."

"North?" Sutherland's eyes went out the window, to the view of Haguchi Bay. At least a dozen freighters, as well as a couple of destroyers, were anchored there. "Sound the air raid alarm!" he barked, before slamming down the phone.

He got up from his desk, slid back the door, and stepped out onto the lower balcony. Almost immediately he heard the drone of engines, the sound coming from the south—away from the major American bases on Okinawa. A loud snarl sounded overhead, and he saw a couple of P-51s—fighters assigned to permanent combat air patrol over SWPA HQ—dive out of their listless circling, angling toward an as yet unseen enemy.

The angry buzzing sound persisted, soft at first, then steadily louder. Sutherland scanned the horizon. Planes, small ones. Fighters. And lots of them, all coming from the south. Despite the numbers, the planes were not in a great, cohesive formation. Instead, they flew in pairs and triplets, little groups scattered all across the sky.

He was on the verge of crying out an alarm when someone beat him to it. The air raid siren began to wail. Quickly, he stepped back into his office, grabbed the important papers off his desk, and stuffed them into a metal safe. He spun the combination lock, then went back out on the balcony. Most of the other officers were there, including MacArthur, deep in conversation with Willoughby. The General held his pipe and glared at the incoming aircraft, his chin jutting.

"General! Take shelter, sir!" It was a sergeant of the HQ company, emerging onto the balcony to bravely address the Supreme Commander. "We have the bomb shelter ready across the street!" Several staff officers, responding to the NCO's urgent waves, started through the conference room.

MacArthur didn't move, only smiled thoughtfully. "Yes, good, good. Get everyone down there, at once—this could get dicey."

"But, sir—you have to come too!" demanded the sergeant in exasperation.

"Oh, no, of course not. Can't see anything from down there. I'll keep an eye on things from up here."

Sutherland's heart sank. It was a totally predictable response but so damned unnecessary. He turned to watch the first group of planes, three of them, come in low over the city, toward the waterfront. One of them wavered, perhaps hit by small arms fire, or maybe just flown by an inexperienced pilot. With a sudden dip it vanished behind a hotel; a second later a billow of fire surged into the sky, spewing black smoke and followed, almost instantly, by the sound of the tremendous explosion.

Sutherland watched the other two planes and MacArthur at the same time, saw the Japs skim low over a warehouse and then plunge into one of the two freighters tied up at the Haguchi wharf. In an instant the Liberty ship became an inferno from stem to stern. Huge explosions wracked the hull—it was still loaded with ammunition and other supplies.

"Kamikaze!" someone shouted. "Coming this way!"

They were coming from every which way, more accurately. A dozen fires blossomed along the waterfront and in the bay. Sirens wailed across the whole city, while antiaircraft guns—all too few of them—banged away. A few more American fighters entered the fray, shooting at the kamikazes, which didn't bother to shoot back. Instead, the suicide planes dived in all over Haguchi. The din of explosions became a constant roar, mixed with the angry snarling of wildly revving aircraft engines.

Another ship in the harbor was struck, a destroyer exploding in a massive fireball. Other planes hit the shore, blowing up warehouses and cranes and other facilities. Several crashed into a large school building that the army had been using as a replacement barracks; Sutherland knew the place was crowded with hundreds of men, barely out of their bunks for the day. In the back of his mind he thought, *These bastards are attacking on the basis of some good intelligence.*

And still others were veering past those facilities, past the port and the motor pools and barracks. Bataan House was wracked by a fierce explosion, and a far wing of the building erupted into flames. MacArthur—damn him!—still stood on the balcony, taking it all in, as if he was immune to burning gasoline and flying slivers of steel.

Immune, or perhaps he was as suicidal as the damned kamikazes.

One small fighter crashed into the street right in front of the headquarters building, exploding so close that Sutherland felt the blistering heat on his face, threw up his hands to block the debris from the blast.

The next one came in a little higher, and though Sutherland kept his hands in front of his face, those hands did little to divert the ton of engine, propeller, and explosive that smashed right through the chief of staff and into the conference room behind him.

Context and Circumstance

Across the sea,
Corpses in the water;
Across the mountain,
Corpses heaped upon the field;
I shall die only for the Emperor,
I shall never look back.

—*"Umi Yukuba,"* Japanese war song

Civilians, including vast numbers of women and children, are being ruthlessly murdered with bombs from the air. . . . A bishop wrote me the other day: "It seems to me that something greatly needs to be said in behalf of ordinary humanity against the present practice of carrying the horrors of war to helpless civilians, especially women and children." . . . War is a contagion, whether it be declared or undeclared. It can engulf states and peoples remote from the original scene of hostilities.

—President Franklin D. Roosevelt,
"Quarantine" speech, October 5, 1937

NINETEEN

Philippines; Hiroshima, Japan

• FRIDAY, 8 JUNE 1945 •

CLARK FIELD, LUZON, PHILIPPINES, 2102 HOURS

"So General Kenney wants you to see how we operate," growled General Curtis LeMay to Colonel Ellis Halverson. They were in LeMay's office, meeting a few minutes before the mission briefing that would be held in the nearby auditorium. "Well, fly along on tomorrow morning's raid, and you'll see it in full color."

"Thank you, General. I believe I will," replied Ellis. "I appreciate—as does General Kenney—the chance to see your operations up close and personal."

LeMay waved his hand in a think-nothing-of-it gesture, then nodded pensively. He was at ease here, in the center of his great headquarters building, a structure that looked like it might have been a secondary school before the war. Now, there were hundreds—probably more than a thousand, Ellis guessed—people working here, controlling the extensive operations of XXI Bomber Command. It was the nerve center for the strategic bombing of Japan.

LeMay rose from his chair and strode to a large map of the Japanese Home Islands displayed prominently on one wall.

"This target has seven rivers running across it, but if we plant our bombs right, the whole place oughta go up like a Roman candle," the general expounded. "One more city where the Japs won't be feeling any too enthusiastic about their emperor's war."

"Yes, sir," Ellis agreed. "I understand the firebombing has

been quite effective. To tell you the truth, I've never been on a strategic bombing raid before, only tactical runs."

"It isn't as exciting as skip bombing, but it's powerful and it'll end the war faster and cheaper than any other method," said LeMay with assurance. "You'll be flying right-hand seat with Captain Wagner—good man, goes about his business like a pro. I assured him you could hold the controls for a while if he needs to use the piss bottle."

Ellis chuckled and nodded. "I'm checked out in four engines, General. Never flew a 29, of course. But it can't be that much different from a 17, can it?"

LeMay took a long pull at his cigar. "You'd be surprised. But not to worry—Wagner's copilot will be riding in the flight engineer's seat. He'll be available to take the controls, if it comes up."

"I'm sure it won't, sir. Your men seem to have this bombing campaign down to a science."

The general nodded, pleased. "We're going to take out almost every major metropolitan area in the Empire of Nippon," he boasted. "In another two months, we'll have burned them all and be going back to torch the fringes—like we've done with Tokyo twice, since we changed tactics back in March."

"And you've left the Imperial Palace intact, I understand?" Ellis noted.

"Yup. The whole district around there, the palace and that Ginza area, we've spared—more or less intentionally. Kyoto too, on orders from Washington—lotta temples there, and other cultural shit." Warming to his topic, LeMay turned from the map and paced behind his desk.

"Air power is the secret to American success, Colonel, both here and in Europe. Take the war to them, and pretty soon they'll cry uncle. Frankly, my only real worry is running out of napalm, and that's only a temporary problem. We can make more."

"I understand, sir. Even so, seven rivers seems like they would make it pretty hard to burn a place."

LeMay shrugged and turned to the map behind him. "It's

all a matter of wind direction and a bomb pattern that's going to start lots of little fires. We already have the meteorology report—low humidity and a good strong breeze coming down the valley off the mainland." He stabbed his blunt finger at a city on the southeast coast of Japan.

"We'll come at them from over the mainland—we'll have fighter escort from the Ryukus and from a couple of newly operational bases on Kyushu. So we won't have to worry about the Jap interceptors, even though we'll be flying at less than ten thousand feet." He traced the route on the map with his finger. "Coming down this valley with the wind at our backs, we'll drop here, on the inland suburbs. We'll have drop zones all across this wide arc here, to allow for fluctuations in wind directions. With any luck at all, that wind will push the fires all the way to the waterfront.

"That's the target, sir?" Ellis asked.

"Yes. It's got the headquarters for the whole goddamn Jap Second Army, you know. Plus a port, Ujina Harbor, from which they've embarked probably better than half of the troops and materiél they've shipped over to China. It's been a major center of their war effort, but—as of tomorrow morning—that's all done. It's a delta, that's why there're these rivers running through it. But that means it's flat and spread out all over the place. Should burn damned well."

Ellis looked closer at the map, at the city name beside the port and the delta and the rivers. He had never heard of it.

"Hiroshima," he said, almost to himself.

"Clark Field" was an anachronistic term for the vast complex of air bases sprawling around the central Luzon plain. The great installations of General LeMay's XXI Bomber Command covered a huge area, better then twenty times the size of the prewar air base that had been the center of the American air power in the Philippines—until the planes were caught on the ground at lunchtime on December 8, 1941. Now there were airstrips, hangars, barracks, and supply depots sprawling across hundreds of square miles, making this area the largest aviation establishment in the world.

Ellis had met Captain Wagner at the start of the briefing, which had been a more detailed breakdown of the plan LeMay had outlined to him in his office. Afterward, the B-29 officers who had attended dispersed by bus, truck, car, and jeep to their wide network of airstrips. Wagner gave Ellis a lift, and it was a forty-five-minute jeep ride—over a good, paved highway—to the 415th Bombardment Squadron area. Though it was after 2200, the roads were crowded with military traffic. But the moon was bright, too, and Ellis enjoyed the ride through the warm tropical night.

"The Japs came down out of those mountains there," the captain explained, pointing to a ridge in the northern distance, outlined in the moonlit night. "The army chewed the shit out of them."

"Yeah, I was on Okinawa when they did the same thing. The Australians in the trenches took a hell of a pounding for a few days there. Plus the Japs kamikaze'd the hell out of El Supremo's HQ, among other things."

"Crazy bastards," Wagner said, shaking his head. "Sure, we took some hits, but it sounds like twenty, thirty of them bought it for every one of our guys."

"Hell of a way to fight a war," Ellis agreed.

Eventually they passed through a final checkpoint and rolled toward an area illuminated by bright electric lights. Soon Wagner was pulling up to the flight line where twelve sleek, gleaming bombers reflected the beams of the floodlights shining on the planes.

The B-29 Superfortress looked to Ellis's prejudiced eye more like a spaceship than a military bomber. First of all, there was that silver color. Other, lesser planes might need a coat of army olive drab for camouflage or uniformity, but not these looming monsters. They practically screamed, "Look at me! Here I am!" Their lines were almost surrealistically sleek, smooth, and modern. The nose was a simple aerodynamic dome, glass panels braced in a webbing of stainless steel. The tail loomed as high as a three- or four-story building. Instead of the glass bubble turrets common on the previous generation of bombers, the B-29s had solid metal domes lying almost flat against the fuselage. Each dome was equipped with a pair of heavy machine guns, but these too looked sleek and futuristic. Ellis knew they were controlled by a gunner at a remote control station inside the aircraft.

"Well," the captain said, indicating the forward landing gear. Ellis could just make out a narrow ladder there. "Best get ourselves aboard and strap in. We've got a city to burn. Catch a nap if you like. It'll be Saturday morning before we get there."

• SATURDAY, 9 JUNE 1945 •

HIROSHIMA, JAPAN, 0532 HOURS

Ogawa Michiyo fought back tears of despair, ashamed of the impulse that urged her to shake the squalling infant hard enough to finally quiet the piercing cries. She drew a breath and closed her eyes, trying unsuccessfully to meditate on something—*anything*—besides the baby's relentless wails.

Of *course* little Otomi was crying. He was hungry.

Michiyo was also hungry, and her mother, and everybody else in Hiroshima, and everyone across all of Japan. Her tears flooded out, wetting her cheeks just for a moment, but she blinked them away and roughly wiped the back of her hand across her face. They were all hungry, and there was no food. That was the truth, the way it was.

She didn't know what she had done to bring this fate upon herself, but that was the nature of life. Her offenses might have even occurred in a previous lifetime, before her incarnation as this young Japanese woman. Life, including all of its travails and suffering, was something to be faced, and endured, with strength and equanimity.

Sometimes she wondered, what had her mother done to deserve her fate? Her neighbors? All the rest? How could the whole country's karma be so terrible? Her brother Taiki, who had led men in battle and now guarded enemy prisoners, what had *he* done to deserve his fate?

It was the war's fault, of course. Everything came back to

this terrible and relentless war. Fishermen were afraid to venture out to sea because so many of them had been killed—or had their boats sunk—by American submarines and aircraft. There was no fuel to run tractors or trucks, so the farms produced little, and what there was could not be shipped into the city.

Michiyo was ashamed to remember that she had actually been reduced to eating paste that she purchased from a neighbor. Tasteless and thick, it contained at least a few minimal nutrients. The thick adhesive had been intended to glue together fiber sheets to form balloons. These balloons were sent aloft affixed with bombs, whereupon—Michiyo's neighbor had explained seriously—they were expected to drift across the North Pacific. Eventually they would land in the great forests of the American Northwest, where it was hoped they would ignite vast conflagrations. There had even been reports in the *Asahi Shimbun* about such fires. Michiyo alternated between pity for the people, especially the children, who would get burned, and hope that the attacks would help to bring the great United States of America to its knees.

Actually, the whole idea of burning forests by bombs carried by balloon over the biggest ocean in the world sounded absurd. Perhaps she told herself that to assuage the guilt she felt over her selfish use of precious war materiél. In any event, she hadn't argued with the price: a small pearl from her mother's oldest necklace in exchange for a container of paste nutritious enough to support her, her mother, and little Otomi for the better part of a week. The stuff had been bland and tasteless, but provided enough protein to dull their hunger pangs for that whole time.

She'd even had the strength to join the community labor parties, where she had worked long summer days clearing firebreaks through the crowded neighborhoods of Hiroshima. Mostly this meant widening streets and clearing burnable materials back from the rivers and canals, but in places they'd even had to knock down houses to make wide, bare paths. One old woman had refused to leave, and Michiyo and the other young women of her crew had watched sadly as apologetic fire marshals had gone into the house and carried the keening woman away. Immediately boys and old men bearing axes set to work demolishing the house, so that Michiyo's crew could carry the debris away. It was heartbreaking work, but it might mean the difference between fire contained and fire running wild. Still, at night she found herself remembering, very vividly, the hopelessness of the old woman's cries as she had watched her house come down.

She was expected to report back to the crew today, but how could she do that? Otomi hadn't slept, which meant that Michiyo hadn't slept. For a moment she allowed her resentment of Auntie Ui to bubble to the surface: Ui should be here, caring for her baby! In another instant her resentment was quelled by guilt—no, she, Michiyo, owed this to her mother's young sister, so that both of them could make a contribution to the waging of this terrible war.

She shook her head, surprised by something, and then realized that it was sudden silence. For reasons only he knew, Otomi had stopped crying. Michiyo gratefully picked him up and cradled him against her shoulder, swaying gently as she moved about the tiny room. The baby took a breath and gurgled. She relished the quiet after the eternity of piercing wails. Dawn had broken, and sunlight spilled through the small eastern window in almost horizontal beams. It was quiet in the city, too early for many people to be up and about.

But there was a strange undertone of noise to the stillness, she realized. It was like the droning of a great cloud of wasps or mosquitoes, a sound at the edge of her consciousness. It was steady, very faint, but unwavering. Not until the piercing shriek of an air raid siren began to cycle did she realize that the distant noise was caused by airplane engines.

"The B-sans!" she gasped.

She ran outside without hesitation, still clutching the now-gurgling Otomi. The pale blue of an early morning sky yawned overhead. She looked to the east and north, up the valley of the Ota, and she could see them in the distance, sparkling in the sunlight like droplets of silver. There were dozens, no, hundreds of them, distant and tiny and arrayed across half the sky. At first they seemed to be standing still, but as she watched them, openmouthed, over the course of a minute she realized that they were very gradually coming closer.

And still the siren wailed.

B-29 DRAGON LANCER, *APPROACHING JAPAN, 0615 HOURS*

Captain Wagner had been relaxed during the long flight— better than nine hours—from Luzon in the Philippines to Honshu, the largest island of the archipelago making up the Empire of Japan. Mostly they flew through the last half of the night, over a world of unrelieved blackness. The crew took turns napping, even the pilot. Ellis kept an eye on the controls, though he knew that the automatic pilot was actually flying the plane.

Ellis took the opportunity to examine the cockpit, which was filled with an array of dials and gauges that made the Mitchell or the Maurauder or even the Liberator seem positively primitive by comparison. The huge Wright Cyclone radial engines were contained in nacelles the size of a large garage. Two superchargers mounted on each engine pumped additional air into the pistons, dramatically increasing the horsepower output. Wagner had confirmed some of the stories Ellis had heard: the engines had been terribly unreliable for the first year and a half of the B-29s' service life, with problems up to and including fires igniting on the magnesium components. Such a fire, it was not hard to imagine, could bring a plane down in a hurry.

"We've got *most* of the bugs worked out," the captain had said with a wink. "Odds are better than even that we'll get home with our airplane intact."

Ellis knew that some problems remained, but had to acknowledge that no other plane in the world could have performed the missions the B-29s were called upon to do. They carried massive bomb loads over incredible distance, and they had been doing it again and again for months.

They were flying this mission at eight thousand feet, so they didn't need oxygen, but it was amazing to realize that this entire four-engine bomber with a crew of eleven men could be pressurized. There were those gun turrets, two of them each on the dorsal and ventral sides of the fuselage, but it was still astonishing to Ellis that no gunners sat in those turrets. He could see the tail gunner position on other planes, and that looked more normal—a bubble canopy with a pair of guns jutting out. But, unlike any other bomber in service, even the tail turret of a B-29 was pressurized.

Ellis looked over his left shoulder into the compartment directly behind the pilots' seats. The place was like a spacious office suite, at least when compared to every other aircraft interior space he had seen. The engineer sat at an elaborate instrument panel, while the navigator had a large plotting table. There were seats for the radio operator, the front gunner, and the bombardier—who would move to the very nose of the plane and run the controls during the bomb run. Beyond that compartment was a long tunnel, like a culvert, that passed through the two bomb bays and connected to the rear crew area, where four more men rode in comparative luxury. Ellis had been told they had a toilet and bunks back there, and he had no trouble believing it. The tunnel looked narrow and long enough, however, that he hadn't been motivated to crawl into the rear of the plane to see for himself.

The bomb bays were not pressurized, and they contained the reason for the B-29s' existence and the purpose of this great raid. There were twenty thousand pounds—ten goddamn *tons*—of bombs racked in there, each one filled with jellied petroleum designed to start fires that wouldn't go out for a very long time.

He was awestruck at the aerial power represented by this mighty air fleet. Silver bombers were arrayed to the right and left of the *Lancer,* a formation that stretched as far as he could see in either direction. Some two dozen miles ahead of them was another vast line of bombers, the ships of the initial attack wave. That flight numbered every bit as many planes as Ellis's group.

Immediately to starboard flew the *Pacesetter*. Behind, and a little below, droned the *Mayfair*. Other bombers trailed into the distance to the left and right, altitude slightly staggered among the three-plane Vs that were the building blocks of the great formation of B-29s, nearly four hundred strong. And those were only the bombers, he reminded himself. A glance upward showed two squadrons of land-based P-51 Mustangs flying overhead cover.

Wagner woke with the first glimmerings of light and immediately switched off the autopilot and settled back at the controls.

"Kyushu's off to the left, there," he said to Ellis, speaking through the plane's intercom mike. "And this is Shikoku, another one of the Home Islands, coming up."

Ellis saw the landmass before them, a brownish, wrinkled stretch of ground that rose steeply up from the sea. It reminded him vaguely of Southern California. He remained alert for antiaircraft or enemy interceptors, but they might have been on a peacetime training mission for all the signs of resistance he could spot around and below them.

After just fifteen or twenty minutes over land, they were again approaching open water on the far side of the island of Shikoku. "That'll be the Inland Sea," Wagner said. "And Honshu is just beyond."

They droned over the placid blue water, the protected sea nestled between the two islands. Ellis didn't see any boats or ships on the sea and took that as more evidence of American air supremacy. Soon they approached land again, and then the main island of the Japanese empire was below them. The landscape was rugged, with ridges of mountains to all sides. None of the heights rose up to anywhere near their altitude, which remained at a steady eight thousand feet.

Ellis watched as the bombers of the first wave executed a precise wheel to the left, the aircraft on the outer edge accelerating while those nearer the pivot point backed off on the throttle. As the formation flew over a high, rugged ridge, the planes started to descend very slightly. Soon the second wave of bombers duplicated the maneuver. Ellis watched as Wagner brought *Dragon Lancer* down to the bomb run height of seven thousand five hundred feet. They were following a river valley. From the briefing, Ellis figured it was the Ota.

They had yet to see an enemy fighter. The 415th Bombardment Squadron flew at the leading edge of the second wave of the attack. They were to act on initiative, seeking parts of the city that weren't already engulfed by fire. There was a third wave too, some twenty miles behind them, charged with mopping up.

Already the bombers of the first wave were turning onto the long, straight trajectory of the bomb run. They were flying southwest so that they could approach the city generally down the broad valley.

Ellis used binoculars to watch. He could see the Superfort bomb bay doors open on the first wave aircraft. He saw puffs of antiaircraft explosions erupt among the silver bombers and felt the inevitable pucker as he pictured red-hot bits of shrapnel tearing through the air, and the aircraft, and his body. He always hated getting shot at, but he felt more vulnerable than ever in his huge aircraft at its relatively low altitude. *Christ, how can the bastards miss us?*

As if to confirm his fears as fully grounded, a B-29 some fifteen miles ahead of him abruptly blew up, a massive fireball lingering in the sky while bits of miscellaneous junk, trailing smoke, tumbled out of the blast radius and plummeted earthward. The AA fire seemed to thicken, and he watched another bomber start to wobble, trailing smoke from both starboard engines. It banked into a dive of increasing steepness. A few parachutes popped into view, visible even to his naked eye as the planes of the 415th BS droned on.

"Poor bastards," Wagner said, his lips compressed into a tight line.

"What?" Ellis asked, before realizing that the pilot was staring at the white parachutes gently drifting down in the wake of the crashing bomber.

"*I* wouldn't want to be captured by Japs—would you?" Wagner asked, shaking his head.

"My brother was on Corregidor," Ellis said.

"Son of a bitch. I hope he makes it."

Ellis put the binoculars down for a minute. "Me, too," he said, the memories of Johnny welling up again, as they did with increasing frequency these days.

Ellis took a deep breath and put the binoculars to his eyes, watching the first wave as it droned over the city. He couldn't quite make out the individual bombs falling. Somewhat to his surprise, nearly all of the B-29s in that formation made it through the bomb run intact—he counted only the two, plus one more, knocked down by the enemy ack-ack.

The *Lancer*'s bombardier came forward, passing between Ellis and Wagner, sliding down through a hatch in the forward armor to settle himself in the wide-open glass canopy of the airplane's nose. He leaned forward to get a good look through the Norden bombsight.

Ellis looked down toward the sprawling city, and the effect of the first wave's bombs immediately flared into view. The explosions were silent to him—the only sounds were the droning of the massive engines and the crackle of radio static in his earphones—but the effects were dramatic. Puffs of smoke erupted only to be immediately shot through with orange fireballs. They popped up all over, hundreds of them appearing at the same time, turning whole neighborhoods to smoke. The long lines of the river and its attendant canals stood out like bright dividers between the brown sprawl of the city. The bombs seemed to be scattering everywhere, each salvo giving life to new, surging fires.

And that was just the beginning. Those blazes immediately spread, springing from building to building with a life of their own. The strong breeze was an asset, pushing the flames along. Smoke thickened into a pall over much of the city, but even through that murk they could see many flashes of bright red flame. Tongues of fire flickered upward here and there in a mockery of a triumphant dance, surging ecstatically as if to celebrate the discovery of some delightfully incendiary source of fuel.

By the time the second wave approached, Ellis could pick

out four main and dozens of smaller fires burning across Hiroshima. The main blazes burned in four of the city's five main districts, those regions separated by the channels of the delta. The AA fire buffeted them, but—for once—Ellis didn't notice the shots coming up from the ground. His whole attention was absorbed by that spectacle, the conflagration attempting to consume an entire city.

"Joe, you've got the plane," Wagner said into the intercom.

"Aye aye, Skipper," the bombardier replied. "Looks like we'll be able to drop this load right on the dime."

HIROSHIMA, JAPAN, 0645 HOURS

"Mama! Mama-san! Wake up!"

Michiyo tried to keep her voice even, but it cracked from the urgency. Her mother's watery eyes blinked open, and for a second the girl was certain that the wailing of the sirens, the droning of the bombers that was already beginning to shake the walls, the very foundation, of the little house must surely have roused her.

"Wake up, Mama! We have to run—to the shelter!" Michiyo was shouting now, trying to get through the haze of confusion that since her father's death had seemed to close in around her mother's mind.

"Oh, that's too much trouble. You go, take Otomi," her mother said. "I'm going back to sleep." With that, she rolled to her side on the thin futon, turning her back and shutting her eyes.

"No! You have to come, too!" screamed the young woman, raising her voice to a parent for the first time in her life.

Mama-san rolled back and looked at her with something like shock on her face. Abruptly, after a long, ragged intake of breath, she began to cry.

"I'm sorry, Mama. But you have to get up, to come away from here. We need to go to the shelter or to the river!" Michiyo dared to reach out with the hand that wasn't holding the baby, tugging on her mother's arm. Slowly, groggily, the older woman sat up, and then—with continued assistance from her daughter—rose to stand shakily.

"Your kimono—get it—put it on!"

As if she was sleepwalking, Michiyo's mother stumbled to her little wardrobe and pulled it open, eyeing her few precious garments as if she was trying to decide what to wear to a ceremonial event. Otomi started to fuss, and Michiyo held the baby to her shoulder, cooing and swaying until he quieted again.

For long, seemingly endless minutes, she fidgeted, holding the baby, hopping from one foot to the other in her agitation as Mama-san very deliberately draped a bright green kimono over her slight form. After she was dressed, the older woman turned slowly around, looking about her in confusion. "My combs," she said plaintively. "How will I hold my hair?"

"There's no *time*, Mama—we have to go now!" Michiyo fought back the urge to cry. She was stunned to realize how old her mother looked, how heavily the months had worn on her since her husband's death. It was as if she had aged twenty years in only the past two seasons. Now an old woman, she looked around in confusion and despair. Michiyo was reminded in a piercing and painful moment of the old woman whose house had been destroyed to help create the firebreak. Against the fear she felt now, the work of clearing the city seemed like a pitiful and useless waste of time.

With that realization, Michiyo ran out the door, calling for her mother to follow. Sirens were wailing in every direction, and the droning of the B-sans was a growl that she could feel in the pit of her stomach. She looked up, could not help thinking that the great silver bombers were strangely beautiful, flying in long lines from the mainland toward the city and the harbor beyond. They did not look dangerous, but the fear they inspired was audible in the great crying and shouting of humanity in the street.

She turned and saw Mama stumbling after her, one hand clutching the fold of her kimono, another patting helplessly at the tangle of her hair. Michiyo ran back and took her hand, tugging her forward while holding the baby, stepping off the little sidewalk to join the throng in the street.

They were mostly running to the right, toward the bomb shelter near the Fukuya Department Store. Michiyo joined the crowd, dragging her mother along. The baby again became restive, uttering a few curt squalls. Her mother stumbled but managed to keep up with the pace of the crowd. Somewhere several children were crying, and adults whispered tensely to each other, but there was no great outcry of panic.

Still, the pushing and prodding of the mass of people became rougher. Michiyo was swept along, as the pace of the crowd increased. Desperately she clung to the baby and to her mother's hand.

"Where are we going?" Mama-san said sharply. Her eyes were clear and serious, now, as if she was beginning to understand the circumstances.

Michiyo thought about the shelter in the large, stone department store and knew that it would be packed long before she got there. But the large Aioi Bridge, and the main channel of the Ota, lay just a few blocks beyond, and she made up her mind to go there.

"We're going to the river, Mama. That will be the safest place." She could only hope that was the truth.

It was then that she smelled smoke. In the narrow lane she could see nothing of the rest of the city, and the sky overhead was deceptively blue—though still speckled with the silver bombers and the black puffs of the exploding shells the antiaircraft gunners were shooting upward.

A few more steps carried them into an intersection, and here Michiyo could see down an avenue running parallel to the river, extending toward the northwest. She gasped when she saw that the sky there was black, a veritable wall of smoke spewing upward. Here and there she could see flames licking upward from the city underneath that smoke. The cloud was drifting in her direction, and the wind against her face was hot, dry, and smelled of soot—and darker things.

The crowd surged around, people streaming along the avenue away from the flames, toward the square bulk of the large store. In the swell and motion, Michiyo lost her grip on her mother's hand and was carried along with the flow of humanity.

"Mama! Where are you?" she cried and suddenly realized that lots of people were shouting, screaming, calling for loved ones.

Otomi cried lustily, and Michiyo almost stumbled as she spun to look for her mother. With a stab of fear she realized that if she fell, she—and the baby—would be trampled. Resolutely she pulled him close, tucked her elbows into her sides, put her head down, and concentrated on keeping her footing as she moved with the crowd. They came to another side street, and the crowd seethed and slowed as people were backed up at the doors of the Fukuya Department Store. Michiyo made up her mind and darted to the side, pushing against a few people who were trying to crowd into the street, finally breaking free to run a short distance up the narrow way.

She looked back helplessly and could see no sign of her mother in the tangle of terrified humanity. A building across the street burst into flames as if by magic, and she screamed as she saw burning debris—including large support timbers—topple onto the crowd. Now the screams were a keening wail, and people fled the newest fire, many of them running right toward Michiyo.

Turning her back on the sight, she sprinted along, holding the baby who—as if understanding the stakes—had fallen silent and simply looked at her with his big, dark eyes. The river was a block away, and all she could think of was reaching that water, immersing herself and the baby in cool liquid.

There was fire right beside her in a sudden burst, so close that she could feel painful heat against her cheek and hands. And then, like a ravenous and very cruel beast, the fire somehow sprang across the narrow street, so that the buildings on both sides were burning. An abandoned cart at the side of the road burst into flames, and Michiyo stared in horror at the wall of fire.

Otomi started to wail with all the force of his lungs, and she was horrified to see blisters forming on his face as the searing heat closed around them. Sobbing now, she lowered her head and charged toward the river.

The baby was on fire! Otomi's worn silk blanket burned fiercely, and Michiyo cried out in pain as the flames seared her fingers and her face. He shrieked and then stiffened, became terribly still. Michiyo's lungs burned even as she took a very shallow breath, stumbling through the curtain of fire.

And then the stone railing at the bank, with the dark waters beyond, was there in front of her. She half jumped, half stumbled over the barrier and stopped screaming only when the warm waters of the Ota closed over her head.

B-29 DRAGON LANCER, *OVER EAST CHINA SEA, 0751 HOURS*

The bombardier grinned up at Ellis from his position at the Norden bombsight. "We're giving them a hell of a pasting, Colonel. Want a look?"

"No, I can see enough from here," he replied. It took an effort to speak, and he realized that his hands were clutching the edge of his seat with a white-knuckled grip.

Climbing up out of the nose, the bombardier moved aft and then stopped to kneel between the two pilots' seats. "Feeling queasy, sir?" he asked.

"Just a bit," Ellis acknowledged. "Those are civilians down there, not soldiers."

The bombardier shook his head. "With respect, sir, that's not the way to think about it. No." His voice had a Midwestern nasal quality to it. "No such thing with the fucking Nips. Every one of them is a combatant. The kids are all gonna grow up to be soldiers and the women breed. Kill every last fucking one of them, that's what I say. You know the only thing I don't like about the bombing campaign?"

"What's that?" asked Ellis.

"It ain't enough. This 'unconditional surrender' bullshit, even if the Japs decide to take it, lets them live. Me, after we finish burning them out of their cities, what I'd do is I'd round all the survivors up, put them in one great big camp out in the middle of nowhere, and then you know what I'd do?"

Ellis didn't ask. The bombardier was sure to answer anyway, and within a second he continued.

"Then I'd send a bomber flight right over and fry every last Jap bastard. Give 'em a taste of hell before they spend eternity enjoying the real thing. Maybe keep a couple alive in a zoo or something. In this cage is *Homo Jap,* a degenerate human form, extinct in the wild, and about damn time, too."

The radio operator, who spoke with a pronounced Southern accent, added, "They're worse than niggers. Niggers is mostly just stupid and shiftless. I don't have anything against niggers. Hell, I kind of like them. I got niggers I call friends. But Japs are more like copperheads. They're not smart, but they got animal cunning. They're sneaky little bastards. And the only thing to do with copperheads is kill them. Kill every last one of them and smash their eggs and tear up the nest while you're at it."

The bombardier nodded enthusiastically. "Mark my words. If we don't kill every last Jap man, woman, and child, we're just leaving the problem for our grandchildren, because they'll just breed more slant-eyed bastards and we'll have to come back and fight all over again. Let's do the job and finish it this time, that's what I say."

"Amen, brother," the radio operator said.

Ellis hated the Japs as much as anybody, but the sight of flames rushing up from the burning city frustrated and upset him in ways he wasn't sure he understood. It was a tough and brutal war with no quarter asked or given. He had more than once turned his bomber in a circle so his gunners could shoot an enemy pilot dangling helplessly from his parachute. But that was revenge for what the Japs did to their prisoners . . . prisoners like Johnny. Besides, the Japs started it.

But he still felt queasy.

Behind him, the city of Hiroshima was invisible, entirely masked by the churning cloud of smoke that rose into the otherwise peaceful morning.

TWENTY

Washington, DC; Southwest Pacific

• WEDNESDAY, 13 JUNE 1945 •

THE WHITE HOUSE, WASHINGTON, DC, 0800 HOURS
(OPERATION OLYMPIC, X-DAY + 86)

Harry S. Truman, President of the United States of America, was poking the ceiling of the Oval Office with a broom handle when General George C. Marshall, the chief of staff of the United States Army, walked in for his regularly scheduled morning meeting.

Almost every day, the President had some fresh horror story to tell about the appalling condition of the White House. "Look here, General Marshall," Harry Truman said in his raspy Midwestern voice. "See? This damn broom goes right into the plaster. It's rotten clean through." He withdrew the broom handle and a cascade of plaster fell onto the worn rug below. "Hell. If I had a dustpan, I'd clean this up, but they won't let me touch a thing in this Great White Jail. Got to be waited on hand and foot. Know what I mean?" He looked at Marshall, then back up at the fresh hole in the ceiling. "This place is falling apart. We're about one good sneeze away from catastrophe."

Today, it was the roof plaster. Yesterday, mouse pellets. Last week, mildew. Always, the upholstery.

Marshall smiled. The new President was different in many

ways from the Oval Office's previous occupant. FDR had been patrician, sophisticated, and complicated; he never let his left hand know what his right hand was doing. Harry Truman was solidly middle-class, of comparatively narrow experience, and blunt. There were similarities, too. Both embodied enormous willpower and drive, decisiveness, and moral courage.

Truman tore his eyes away from the hole in the ceiling with one final disappointed shake of his head and turned his attention to the general. "Where are my manners? Good morning, General Marshall. Have you had breakfast yet? Hate to have a man start the day without a good breakfast. It's the foundation for everything else, you know. Always eat well first thing in the morning."

They went through this every morning. "Thank you, Mr. President. I've already had breakfast," Marshall lied. He had only grabbed a cup of coffee. Now that the President mentioned it, he did have an appetite, but if he admitted it, he'd be stuck with the President's idea of a good breakfast every day for the rest of the Truman administration.

"All right, all right, I'll stop nagging. Coffee?"

"Yes, sir, Mr. President. I could do with another cup of coffee."

"Milk, two sugars?"

"You've got it, sir."

"Have a seat, General. Make yourself comfortable." Truman walked over to a percolator that was set up on a folding table on the far curve of the room. He poured the general's coffee and brought it over to the conversation area.

In addition to the President's formal desk, which was normally kept spotless and paperless—another change from the Roosevelt years—there was a conversation grouping of two worn and tired sofas flanking a coffee table, capped with an armchair at each end. They sat on opposing sofas.

Marshall put his briefcase on the coffee table, snapped it open, took out his briefing materials, then closed the briefcase and put it down by his feet. He didn't expect to use the briefing materials. Truman would read every word of them later.

The President looked Marshall in the eyes. "Tell me how the war's going, General. How's that mess on Kyushu"—he pronounced it "Koo-Shoo"—"coming along? I'll read the book later. You know I like to hear it straight from the horse's mouth."

"Well, it's still a mess, Mr. President, but we're moving forward. Inch by inch, maybe, but forward."

"Hell." Truman shook his head. "Reminds me of the Great War. Meat grinder battles just eating up men and spitting out corpses. I missed the worst of it, being in field artillery, but I remember what it was like, being there. I hate like holy hell sending more American boys into early graves. Too bad the Great War didn't live up to its billing as 'the War to End All Wars.'"

"Amen, Mr. President. But it's hard to whip an enemy who doesn't care about the casualties they take."

Truman stood up and walked around to the back of his sofa, facing Marshall. "Now, you've told me this before. I still think it's the craziest damn thing I ever heard in my life. The Japs think that if they get enough of their men *killed,* we'll have to give them better surrender terms?"

"Yes, sir."

"And tell me again why the hell killing Japs is a *bad* thing?"

"First, sir, they're going to take a lot of our boys with them. That's what the kamikaze attacks do. If a soldier—more often a woman or a child—wraps up in explosives and dives under a tank, we're down one tank. There are lots of ways to kill the enemy if you don't care if you die in the process. Our boys are brave, but we aren't going to go for mass suicide."

Truman shook his head, then started to pace. "Damned right we're not. That is the goddamnedest idea I have ever heard. It's positively inhuman. What the hell makes them act like that? They're human beings, aren't they? Or are they?"

"They are, but they're still different. For one thing, their main religions, Shinto and Buddhism, believe in reincarnation. Death isn't permanent." Marshall stood as well. "Their Emperor Meiji, Hirohito's grandfather, said, 'Death is lighter than a feather; duty, heavy as a mountain.' That's part of their military creed. And they know we don't see it that way. In their eyes, that makes us weak and sentimental."

"Weak and sentimental. Okay. I've got it. Go on." Truman took a swig of coffee.

"The second reason they think their strategy might work is world public opinion. If we kill enough of them, we'll look like the bully."

"Maybe." Truman looked skeptical. "Go on."

"The third is that death is better, at least for the real fanatics, than the disgrace of surrender."

"So what are you telling me? Are you recommending that I change 'unconditional surrender' to something else?" Truman's fingers went *tap-tap* on the sofa's arm.

Marshall looked at his President. "No, sir. I just wanted to lay out the Japanese side first."

Truman looked back at Marshall. "All right. That makes sense. So, what do you folks propose to do about it?"

"First, we're going to stop trying to wipe them all out. One strategy that General MacArthur has followed with great success up till now is just going around large concentrations of enemy soldiers and leaving them to wither on the vine. They don't have the transportation to be able to move, so they're out of the war. No casualties—on *either* side. When it comes down to it, all we need on Kyushu is an air base large enough to let General Kenney's fighters do their jobs. The Japanese can have the rest of the island; we don't need it. We have medium bomber bases on Okinawa and the rest of the Ryukus and plenty of space on Luzon for LeMay's B-29s."

"Won't the Japs just come after you?" asked Truman. He started walking over to the doors that led from the Oval Office to the garden.

"Probably. But it's easier and safer to fortify a position than it would be to go clean out a thousand caves one at a time when those caves are filled with soldiers who are determined to take at least one of our boys with them," said Marshall, following him. "The Japanese counterattack on Okinawa caused some three thousand Aussie casualties, but the enemy lost more than ten times that many men KIA."

"Makes sense, I guess. But if I understand what you're saying, the *fewer* Japs we kill, the better?" Truman started pacing.

"There's an Oriental writer on war named Sun Tzu. He says, 'What is of supreme importance in war is to attack the enemy's strategy.' If it's what *they* want, then *we* don't want them to have it."

" 'Attack the enemy's strategy.' " Truman laughed. "Hell, that sounds like a Mark Twain joke. You know, I think everyone in this town must be using a corkscrew as a straightedge, the way things get twisted up. But I guess that's what it's like in the big leagues."

"I understand what you mean, sir. I feel the same way myself sometimes. Well, this plan is MacArthur's recommendation, and I basically agree with it, Mr. President.

"MacArthur's Johnny-on-the-spot, and I guess I'd better respect that. But General—tell me, just between us, what do you think about MacArthur? I get the impression that half the military thinks he's the greatest soldier since Joshua fit the battle of Jericho, and the other half think he's the most overrated, puffed-up SOB that ever walked the Earth. Now, I remember General MacArthur from my days with the 129th in France. Somebody was always talking about MacArthur. He was with the Rainbow Division, right? Chief of staff, wasn't he? How many silver stars did he win?"

"Six, sir."

"And I remember that damned scarf of his. It was in every picture."

Marshall laughed. "It was his trademark, the way that hat and pipe are for him now."

Truman walked over to the windows that looked out onto the South Lawn. He looked at the threadbare material and a place where part of the frame had broken off.

The President pointed to the broken frame. "Look at this, General. Just look at it. Rotten all the way through."

"I can see that, Mr. President. That's terrible."

Truman turned to look directly at Marshall. "Go on, go on. I just spend all my day sitting still, and that's not natural."

"Yes, sir," replied the chief of staff.

Truman let the curtains fall back into place and walked back toward the sofas, with Marshall following again. The President stopped suddenly in the middle of the office and turned around. "But if he's such a big hero, why did his troops start calling him the 'Coward of Corregidor'? Never understood that one."

"It's because he visited his men on Bataan only once during the entire siege. I don't think it was because he was a coward—well, a physical coward, anyway. I don't think he could face them after the mistakes he'd made."

"What mistakes were those? All I ever read made it seem like there was nothing MacArthur could have done." Truman sat down in the armchair nearest his desk.

The army chief of staff sat on the sofa to Truman's right. "There was no way to win. But there were lots of ways to lose. MacArthur can't bear losing, so he persuaded himself he could beat the Japanese at the beaches, and that they were going to wait another six months for him to get ready. When they arrived, he woke up and realized he'd left the food and ammunition where it was vulnerable. He led a brilliant retreat. It'll be taught as a textbook lesson someday. But he lost the food and ammunition he was supposed to have stored up on Bataan."

"Hell, no wonder he couldn't face them. They probably would have shot him."

"Douglas MacArthur is in many ways the finest military man the United States of America has ever produced. He's a visionary, a leader of men, and a genius at the art of war. On the other hand, he's got an ego that gets him into trouble over and over again." Marshall picked up his coffee cup and drank.

"I sort of figured out the ego problem all by my lonesome. I've known a few people like that myself," Truman said. "More than one of them since I came to Washington, if you want to know the truth."

"You know, Mr. President, I don't know how much you remember about Roman history, but he reminds me of Pompey
the Great."

"Pompey. About all I remember, to tell the truth, is *Gallia
est omnis divisa in partes tres* from Latin class. Oh, and
amo, amas, amat. Wasn't my best subject. By the way, what
made Pompey so great, anyway? Never met anybody who
could answer that."

"It was a nickname. Pompey made his own nickname up
and insisted people use it."

"He *named* himself 'the Great'?"

"Yes, sir. That's why MacArthur reminds me of him."

Truman chuckled. "Got it. When they were passing out
ego, Mac went around a second time."

"Or maybe a third. It gets him into trouble. Nobody can
praise him because he's already vacuumed up all the credit."

"Should we keep him? Has he made a big mistake in this
Kyushu mess?"

"Some overconfidence, I suppose. But whoever took us
into Kyushu would have run into the same problem. I think
MacArthur's recommendations are sound, and I endorse
them." Marshall finished his coffee and set the cup down on
its saucer.

"If you do, I do. Okay. Let's change the subject. Well, sort
of change the subject. Looks like George Patton is in trouble
again."

"I'm afraid so, Mr. President."

"What is it with these generals? You think it's something
in the water?"

Marshall laughed. "No, sir. But there *is* something about
senior command that attracts people with outsized egos . . .
and mouths. If we're in a war, there's no one I'd sooner have
leading my tanks than George Patton. But in peacetime,
well, a man like Patton has a bit of trouble fitting in. Ike is
moving him over to command the Fifteenth Army, which is
responsible for documenting the history of the war."

"You're going to turn Patton into a *historian*?"

"He's done it before, and he's surprisingly good at it."

"Now wait a minute, wait a minute." Truman stood up again and started pacing back and forth. "Didn't you tell me you were sending General Hodges over to command MacArthur's armored corps when he invades the main island of Japan?"

"Yes, sir."

"Is he as good as Patton?"

"He's a very competent officer."

Truman looked at him sharply. "I guess I'll take that as no. Why not send Patton over instead? That'll get him out of Europe altogether. Kill two birds with the same stone that way."

"Well, the major difficulty with that idea, Mr. President, is that MacArthur doesn't like subordinate officers who get as much press coverage as he does."

"In that case, General, I *definitely* want you to send Patton to Japan. Maybe he can get things moving over there. If that upsets MacArthur, then you just tell him you're following the orders of your commander in chief. I do get to make decisions like this, don't I?"

"When you want to, yes, sir."

"Good. It's settled." Truman stopped pacing. "Anything else we need to take care of this morning?"

"No, sir, Mr. President. Thank you for your time." Marshall stood up to shake hands.

"Always glad to see you, General Marshall. Tomorrow morning, same time?"

"Yes, sir."

"You send Patton over there, all right? Unless you think of a very good reason not to, in which case we'll talk about it tomorrow."

"I'll think about it, Mr. President, but I don't see a problem," Marshall said. *Those two—Mac and Patton—deserve each other,* he thought.

As the army chief of staff left, he looked back to see the President of the United States pick up the broom handle again.

• MONDAY, 9 JULY 1945 •

HALSEY FIELD, SWPA FORWARD HEADQUARTERS, OKI-NAWA, 0947 HOURS (OPERATION OLYMPIC, X-DAY + 112)

General George S. Patton, fourth star still new on his shoulder—a booby prize for being kicked upstairs, he thought bitterly—asked specifically for no honors upon his arrival in Okinawa. Presidential order or no presidential order, he couldn't afford to take MacArthur for granted.

Nevertheless, when the final propeller on the four-engine C-54 stopped spinning and as the aircrew ran the mobile stairs up to the front hatch, he looked out to see a brigadier general waiting for him along with a small honor guard. Well, he couldn't blame the one-star. Generals had been known to request "no honors" and throw a goddamn shit fit when their orders weren't disobeyed.

The hatch opened and the general's aide-de-camp, a lieutenant colonel, bounded up the stairs. "Welcome to Okinawa, General Patton!" he said in a voice just a little too loud, in case any of the other passengers had missed the fact that they were traveling with Old Blood and Guts himself. This was particularly useless because the entire passenger list consisted of members of Patton's headquarters organization, ranging from his chief of staff General Hobart Gay to his personal driver Sergeant John Mims.

"If you'd be so kind, General . . . ," he said, then waved his hand in a gracious arc to the open hatch.

Patton got up, back and hips aching from the long flight, and stretched. "Give me a moment, son," he said. The sergeant serving as flight attendant handed him his helmet and helped him on with his jacket, and then he preceded the ADC out of the plane.

He did a cursory inspection of the troops, paid a small compliment to the one-star, who was the base commander, and accepted a ride to his temporary quarters. He had just enough time to shower, shave, and change before his lunch meeting with MacArthur. Mims would have just enough time to press his pinks and greens. He planned to wear a normal barracks cap—it would look too obviously like sucking up to make it grommetless like Mac's—and leave his ivory-handled revolvers behind.

It had been a very long time since he'd been this nervous.

Patton could see the scars of the kamikaze attacks throughout Bataan House as he entered. One whole wing had been demolished, and even now carpenters were at work, framing in stud walls for the new construction. Within the existing building, the teak paneling was patched in places with plywood, and sections of the remaining paneling were charred. A balcony facing the bay was closed off with a big DANGER sign. He sniffed. The smell of smoke persisted everywhere—smoke smell was damned hard to get rid of.

MacArthur's secretarial pool was located in the open center of the floor, with offices around the perimeter. The warrant officer who spotted him shouted, "Atten-SHUN!" There was a brief sound of chairs scraping wood, as everyone simultaneously stood.

"As you were," Patton said mildly.

"General MacArthur's compliments, General Patton," the warrant officer said. "Coffee, sir?"

Patton nodded. "Black."

It was obvious to him which office was MacArthur's. It was the best corner office. It faced the bay on one side and a garden on the other.

The door of the office immediately to MacArthur's right and around the corner opened, and a one-star came out. "General Patton? Richard Marshall. I'm acting chief of staff."

"I heard about Sutherland," Patton replied. He didn't bother to add, "What a shame."

The warrant officer was bringing coffee as Marshall said, "General Patton, I'm sorry, but General MacArthur has been unavoidably detained and will be a little late for lunch. He hoped you'd feel free to use his office as a resting place in the meantime. You've come a long way from Europe."

"That will be just fine. From what I see it's a shame I can't sit out on that balcony."

"I wish you could, sir, but the structural engineers are still telling us it's not yet safe." Marshall opened the door to MacArthur's office and ushered Patton inside.

MacArthur's desk was to the left, angled into the room but placed so both views were always available. There were two leather chairs in front of the desk, both on the over-stuffed side, and there was a little conversation area with a sofa and two more chairs, all covered in a light brown fabric. A single bookcase mostly had pictures of MacArthur's young son Arthur MacArthur IV, with a few actual books for decoration. There were a few pictures of MacArthur himself with various dignitaries and receiving various honors.

Patton knew MacArthur was planning to play cat-and-mouse with him.

Five-star generals who command entire theaters of operation got to pick their own senior subordinates, for the most part. Even though the army chief of staff theoretically was in charge, in the real world, individual skills, alliances, track record, and office politics had a lot more impact on personal power than hierarchical position. Patton knew—Ike had told him—that he owed his current situation to a presidential order. Even so, he didn't discount Mac's political skills. If he didn't kiss Mac's five-star asshole in just the right way, he'd be out, president or no president.

Mac made him wait for a good twenty minutes before deigning to show up, then finally breezed in with the most clearly insincere apology Patton had ever heard. "How are you, George? Welcome to the final chapter of the war," MacArthur said, shaking hands with every appearance of friendliness. "Sit down. Make yourself comfortable."

Whenever Mac wasn't being a pompous, puffed-up ass-hole, he turned on what he evidently thought was "charm." As far as Patton was concerned, that overly familiar fake warmth just made him a patronizing asshole instead of a puffed-up one.

"Great to see you again," Patton said, wearing the most sincere-looking smile he could fake.

As MacArthur sat down behind his desk, Patton sat down in one of the leather chairs and only too late realized the trap: he was sinking so far into the chair he couldn't easily maneuver. For an armor officer, that was worse than anything.

MacArthur picked up a folder, obviously Patton's service jacket, and opened it up, all with the appearance of a man who'd never looked at it before. He turned the pages one at a time, his face deepening into somewhat of a frown, until he finally put the file down. He leaned forward, steepled his fingers, and said, "A lot of the work's already been done for this operation, and a lot was done with Courtney Hodges in mind." General Courtney Hodges had commanded the First Army in Europe.

"I've worked with Courtney, as you know. I can work with his plans." *They'll fit me like a straitjacket.*

MacArthur continued to look at Patton over his steepled fingers. "As you must have expected, George, the Operation Coronet plans have been changed substantially based on our Kyushu experience during Olympic."

"Of course. I'd expect to work with that." *I'll crawl over ground glass if I have to. I want this command. I want it so bad I can taste it.*

Again MacArthur paused, his eyes not leaving Patton, the rest of him still. "George, you were kicked out of Europe."

Not technically, he thought, but it was essentially true. "Yep."

"Because you can't keep your mouth shut."

"I've learned my lesson this time." *Don't think you're the only one in this room who thinks about strategy, Mac. You think you've got me pinned. Wait.*

MacArthur shook his head sadly. "George, George. That's not good enough. That's not good enough at all. Tell me a single reason the Commanding General should believe that."

"I want as close to a total news blackout as possible. No press, no press conferences, no photos, no nothing. I'll find an antipublic relations officer." *You really want to make sure I don't get any credit. Okay. If that's what it takes for me to command.*

MacArthur leaned back in his chair. *He's considering it,* Patton thought.

"The Pacific isn't Europe, George. We don't go for grandstanding here. From the lowliest recruit to the most senior flag officer, individual names and identities mean nothing. We're the United States Army Forces, Far East, and we're a team. We do it together and everybody shares equally."

MacArthur actually looked sincere, Patton thought. *He probably believes it, too.*

"That suits me fine. It really does. What you said when I came in, 'Welcome to the end of the war'—"

"—'*final chapter* of the war,'" MacArthur corrected.

"—'final chapter of the war.' You're right. This is it. It may be it for the rest of my life. I've got to be in it. Believe me, I've seen my name in the newspapers enough to be sick and tired of it."

At that, MacArthur smiled slightly. Then he leaned forward again. "I was talking about changes in the Operation Coronet plans earlier. Now that you're here, I think you may be just the man for the job."

"I'm all ears." *Did I win this easily? Hell no, the son of a bitch has something else up his sleeve.*

"I want another FUSAG diversion."

In the run-up to D-day, George Patton, having been relieved of command of Seventh Army after the infamous soldier-slapping incidents, was given responsibility for the largest deception of the war. He commanded an imaginary First United States Army Group in planning an imaginary invasion of Calais, a deception good enough to trick eighteen German divisions into waiting for that invasion for nearly two months after D-day in Normandy.

He had relished the assignment. He recruited set designers from the British movie industry to build inflatable rubber tanks, wooden landing craft, and giant empty fuel tanks. He arranged for His Majesty George V and Ike to tour his command. But at the end of the assignment, he'd gotten command of the U.S. Third Army and made history.

"I think a deception operation is a fine idea, and I'll be happy to take it on," Patton said with a heartiness he didn't feel. *But what about the invasion? Do I get a command?*

"The original plan involved a pincer around the two sides of Tokyo Bay. We've decided that's impractical. We're going to send your dummy force about sixty miles north, let you raise a ruckus, then land in the south as they move units up to deal with you."

"How big a dummy force?" Patton asked.

"The real part will be a corps—most of a corps, anyway. The fake—well, as big as you can make it. I hope you can make the enemy believe you are coming with a reinforced army."

"I can do that. Just how much of a corps are you talking about. Sir?" *The SOB wants me dead. Dead men can't steal credit.*

MacArthur frowned. "Well, we have two armored divisions that will land side by side—after a marine RCT goes in and takes the beach. Of course, if that's not a force worthy of—"

A marine regimental combat team was smaller than a division. The whole force was not even equivalent to a corps, Patton saw, but it was better than nothing. Much better.

"I'll take it."

MacArthur smiled triumphantly. "Good. Now that we've got that settled, how about joining me at the residence this evening for bridge? We can bore the youngsters to sleep telling them how much more heroic things were in the Big One."

"I'd be delighted." *I've got a command. A tiny fucking command, but a command. And it only cost me my dignity.*

"2000 hours?"

"2000 hours it is."

Now I have to lose to that fucker at bridge, Patton thought.

• WEDNESDAY, 1 AUGUST 1945 •

KASHIMA CANYON, EAST OF KAGOSHIMA, KYUSHU, JAPAN, 0700 HOURS (OPERATION OLYMPIC, X-DAY + 135)

Brevet Captain Pete Rachwalski, Charlie Company, 1st Brigade, 3rd Marine Regiment, 3rd Marine Division, V Amphibious Corps, United States Eighth Army, had just defeated Ming the Merciless and was about to make love to the beautiful Dale Arden (who looked disturbingly like Trisha Malone, his first love, the first girl he'd gotten to second base with) when he felt a tap on his shoulder.

He came instantly to a state of semiawareness and reflexively grabbed for his Thompson. It was never far from his side. In the slit trench he occupied with ten other men, there wasn't a lot of room to put it anywhere else.

"Cap'n?" a voice said softly.

It didn't sound like a combat emergency, so he relaxed his grip on his weapon and sank back into dreamland. Dale/Trisha had just taken the chewing gum out of her mouth and stuck it under the control panel of the spaceship and was letting him unhook the brass brassiere she was wearing. As their rocket took off, they sank to the floor in each other's arms, but the floor wasn't metal, but dirt and gravel, and his back hurt. He could feel every pebble by the indentation it had made.

"Cap'n? It's 0700."

They were back on the planet Mongo, which looked like a hillside in Dundalk, and he realized he had been trying to make it with her on a dirty, muddy, rocky canyon wall. She shook her head in disgust as she faded from view.

"Cap'n? You said to wake you at 0700."

Like it or not, he was awake. He was on the eastern side of Kashima Canyon, on the road to Kagoshima, one road picture he was sure Hope and Crosby would never make. The night had provided a little relief from the muggy heat, but even the little bit of light penetrating his closed eyelids let him know that today was going to be another steam bath.

"Yeah?" he replied groggily.

"You said to wake you at 0700. It's 0700."

"I must have been out of my fucking mind." Pete tried to open his eyes, but they were glued shut with sleep. He felt around for his canteen, poured a little water into his hands, and sloshed it on his face to melt the eye gunk. The world around him slowly started to come into focus. He looked at the person talking to figure out who it was.

"Brigade headquarters meeting starts at 0830." It was Private Schalles.

"Now I *know* I was out of my fucking mind." Pete removed his helmet to scratch his head. "Every goddamn bug on this island has decided to set up housekeeping under my helmet."

"Not *all* of them, Cap'n," Schalles said. "I got a little colony going myself. Bugs I never saw outside of one of those 'Quick, Henry, the Flit' ads."

Pete laughed. "I could use a little Flit myself." He slapped at a weird-looking beetle climbing up his arm. Flit, a popular bug spray, had turned "Quick, Henry, the Flit" into a national catchphrase with its ubiquitous ads. "Hey, you want to know something really strange? The guy who draws those Flit ads does Private Snafu, too."

"No shit," Schalles said. He didn't sound impressed.

Pete was desperate for coffee. He could dissolve some instant from his K rations into the tepid water from his canteen, which is what he did most mornings. The one good thing about the brigade meeting, though, was that they had hot water. That meant a cup of real coffee. In the meantime, he settled for a cigarette and eyed the bleak, rugged surroundings while he smoked.

Kashima Canyon had the virtue of being the only reasonably flat and more or less direct route from the landing beaches to the city of Kagoshima. It had the liability of being a genuine death trap for the marines who had been fighting their way, foot by bloody foot, along the canyon bed toward the city that was their objective. Pete's company was currently hunkered down among the jumbled rocks that had fallen from the canyon heights in previous eons. The rocks made good cover, and they had cleared the Japs out of every hidey-hole in the area. The canyon floor was swampy, impassable in many places even to men on foot. Across the swamp, at the base of the opposite wall, Bravo Company was similarly entrenched. Other marines held the high ground above them, on each rim of the canyon. As they advanced, they had used grenades and flamethrowers to clean out every cave, each shallow rifle pit or fortified machine gun nest they encountered.

It had been another long night. The Japs tended to attack under cover of darkness, as they'd done last night, a hit-and-run designed for maximum casualties. Last night they'd taken it on the chin—a raiding party of a dozen men knocked out with no marine casualties. The night before, Pete had lost two men killed and three wounded.

From time to time they succeeded in capturing an American. You could hear his screams as he was tortured, but you knew—from bitter experience—that any attempt to rescue him meant walking into a deadly trap. Most of the men had made death pacts, agreeing to shoot one another rather than let the Japs capture them alive. Pete always thought of Johnny when the subject came up. Johnny Halverson had been a Jap prisoner for three years and two months now . . . if he was still alive.

"Where's Sergeant Townley?" Pete asked.

"Two rocks over, Cap'n."

"Okay. Thanks, Schalles. Back to your post, and keep your eyes open. Townley's in charge till I get back. Pass the word."

"Got it, sir."

Pete's understrength Charlie Company consisted of two platoons instead of three, each with a lieutenant (one real, the other a brevet sergeant) and a sergeant (one real, the other a brevet corporal). One platoon only had two squads. Overall, he had fifty-six men—not quite half strength. Replacements had been trickling in, but it took a little while to learn how to survive under these conditions. Most of the replacements lasted a few days. If they survived two weeks, they were veterans. Charley Company had been in Kashima Canyon for two weeks, during which time they had advanced less than a half mile.

Pete put his helmet back on and crawled carefully out from behind his rock. He crawled twenty feet and slid into the hole behind the next large, square boulder.

"Hey! Watch where you put your fuckin'—oh, sorry, sir."

"Don't sweat it." Pete kept crawling, trying to wake up as few marines as possible. His boys needed their sleep.

Sergeant Townley, a tech sergeant now acting as gunnery sergeant, was the company's senior NCO. He was on his feet, looking carefully between two boulders, scrutinizing the ground in front of them. Although the lieutenants outranked Townley, Pete trusted the sergeant more than his young officers. "Townley, I'm going to brigade headquarters. Keep them safe until I get back."

The stolid and imperturbable Townley nodded. "The usual wish list, Cap'n. If you can bring anything back with you."

Pete knew it by heart: ammunition, fresh socks, grenades, rations, first aid supplies, and more ammunition—the normal needs of a company but damned difficult to get when you had to haul it by foot up this damned canyon. "I'll do my best. If I can't get it officially, I'll try to steal it. But you know what they're going to say."

"Yeah," said Townley. " 'Don't you know there's a war on?' "

Pete grinned. A momentary twitch at the edge of Townley's mouth might have been a smile. It was hard to tell.

Townley looked down the line of men in his trench. "Coad. Go with the captain." When Pete started to protest, Townley added, "You'll need somebody to help carry back all those supplies."

"Okay, Townley," Pete said, surrendering. "Coad, come on. They have hot coffee, you know."

"In that case," Townley said, "maybe I should go instead."

"Sorry," Pete grinned. "Somebody's got to mind the store."

Getting out of Kashima Canyon meant following a foot trail along the base of the wall. The path was mostly dry, but in several places you had to wade through calf-deep water. At least the Japs had been cleared out of the area—or so they said. The rear zone was only about a mile away, and it would have been an easy twenty-minute walk—except that they had to crawl for a half hour just to get around the first bend, where it was judged safe to stand upright. As much as men wanted a hot cup of real coffee, it wasn't worth dying on the way to the percolator.

Most of the vegetation in the canyon bed was fernlike, big, wide, flat, leafy plants with thick stalks instead of real trunks. The two marines, with Pete in the lead, passed a tall clump of these fronds and emerged onto a short, wide open stretch of trail.

"Shit!"

Pete heard Coad's curse a split second before he heard the sound of the rifle shot. Immediately he dropped to his belly and turned around to see the corporal lying on the path, grimacing in pain.

"Goddamn *fucking* shit, that hurts!" Coad groaned through tightly clenched teeth.

Pete scanned the heights, realizing that a goddamn Jap sniper had crawled back into position overhead—or maybe he had been laying low for the last week, ever since these cliffs and caves had been "secured." There was no sign of him and no second shot. Pete hoped the low brush along the trail was enough to give them cover, now that they were prone.

"Where are you hit?" he asked.

"Leg—high up, in the thigh," grunted Coad. "I'm bleeding like a stuck pig."

"Let me take a look," Pete said. Cradling his Thompson in his arms, he crawled back to the corporal, pulled out his K-bar, and slit Coad's trouser leg up to the thigh—and got a squirt of bright red blood in his face for his trouble. He couldn't remember how to tell if it was a vein or an artery, and he didn't care. He cut away the rest of the pant leg, took Coad's knife and sheath, and used the material to make a tourniquet almost as high as the man's crotch. The flow of blood eased, but crimson continued to soak through the rudimentary bandage.

"Can you crawl?" Pete asked.

The corporal nodded, sweat shining on his forehead. "Yeah, I can crawl. Don't leave me. Don't let the Japs get me, Cap'n," Coad whispered.

"Don't worry," Pete replied. "I'll get you to an aid station."

"How about the leg?" Coad asked. "Am I going to lose it?"

"I'm not a doc, but I don't think so. This may just be your million-dollar wound."

"Shit, I hope so. Damn! It hurts."

Using the low shrubbery as cover, they crawled slowly along the path. It seemed to take forever until they eventually moved around a jagged shoulder of rock. Pete decided to chance standing up.

"Damn, Captain. It's bleeding again."

"Shit." Pete knelt and cinched the tourniquet as tight as he could. He was no stranger to wounds, but it seemed that the young corporal was losing a lot of blood.

Pete knelt down. "I'm gonna carry you, okay? Put your arms around my shoulders. We'll do it just like we did in Boot. It's not too much farther."

Carrying Coad on his back was tricky. Mud and uneven terrain seemed to clutch at his boondockers, maliciously trying to trip him up. Pete could tell he was only one step away from overbalancing and falling on his face.

As the heat and humidity climbed, so did the strain on Pete. Each step sent fresh waves of pain through Coad. Every few minutes Pete checked the tourniquet, saw that the wound was continuing to soak through the bandage. Not good. Pete could also feel the blood coming through his uniform. His body felt extra sticky.

Finally he staggered up to the mouth of the canyon, where

armored bulldozers had made some semblance of a road. This was as far forward as the supply jeeps could come, and the captain was relieved to see one of the little green vehicles rumbling up to him, and he waved it over.

"Need a lift, sir?" the driver asked.

"Goddamn right. My corporal needs to get to the aid station, and I'm late for the brigade meeting."

"Emerson, McKinley, unload those crates and get that wounded boy into the jeep. You guys are gonna have to walk back; sorry," the driver said. "Captain, let's get your boy to the medic and you to the meeting."

Pete turned to the two privates. "There's a damned sniper up on the canyon wall, just around that last bend. Be careful."

"Aye aye, sir," one of them replied, looking up the canyon with a complete lack of enthusiasm.

Getting into the passenger seat of the jeep, Pete turned to the driver. "Thanks, Sergeant . . ."

"Couch."

Pete looked at him quizzically.

"Yeah, yeah, like in sofa. Get in, already, Captain . . ."

"Rachwalski." Pete grinned.

Couch laughed. "And you think *I* got a funny name? Hang on." He put the jeep in gear and gave it as much gas as he dared on the rutted road. Coad lay crossways on the small rear seat. Pete turned around to keep a hand on the tourniquet, pulling it as tight as possible. The corporal was looking fainter by the minute. "Hang on, Coad," Pete said. "Not much longer."

Ten minutes of heavy jolting brought them to the aid station. Couch honked the horn and two bored-looking orderlies meandered out. "Whatcha got?" one of them said.

"Advanced case of hangnails," Couch said. "Move it."

When the orderlies got a good look at Coad, they got a bit more serious about their work. As he was being moved inside, Coad said weakly, "See you around the campus, Captain."

"Say hello to America for me," Pete said.

Brigade Headquarters was inside what looked like a Japanese temple of some description. It had that distinctive witch's hat layered roof and the center was big and open, great for meetings. There was a dais at one end that now contained a lectern, and there were GI-issue folding chairs.

"—bogged down along this entire line. We've got to get to Kagoshima and get those airfields under our control in a matter of weeks, no matter what it takes," the brigade intelligence officer, Lieutenant Colonel John D. Berry, was saying as Pete tried to sneak in the back. Unfortunately, the colonel spotted him. "Ah, Captain Rachwalski. Good of you to find time in your busy schedule to join us this morning." Colonel Berry was a "squared-away marine." Everything about him was impeccable.

"Yes, sir. Sorry, sir," he said, moving to his seat.

"Wait a minute. I do understand the difficulty of keeping clean under field conditions, but you are rather abnormally filthy. What *is* that all over your uniform?"

Pete looked down. "Blood, sir."

"Whose? Yours?"

"No, sir. One of my privates."

The colonel paused. "Dead?"

"No, sir. Well . . . not when I left him at the aid station, sir. Sniper fire on the way out of Kashima Canyon."

"You carried him the rest of the way?"

"Yes, sir."

The colonel paused. "I don't think there are many excuses for an officer being late to a command meeting. But this is one. I'll see your man after the meeting."

"Yes, sir. Thank you, sir."

He turned back to his notes. "Gentlemen, we're all familiar with the problem in fighting an enemy who doesn't seem to care if he lives or dies. That's why our strategy changed from cleaning the Japanese out of every cave to defending the airfields and key positions leading into the city of Kagoshima. The airfields, not killing Japanese soldiers, are the mission. Killing Japanese is a means to an end and we must not confuse that with the end itself."

The way Pete felt, killing Japanese soldiers seemed like a perfectly fine objective. On the other hand, crawling into caves against suicidal armed Japanese wasn't exactly a pleasant alternative.

Betty continued, "However, the Japanese have had more success than we like at infiltrating our lines and making supposedly rear areas more dangerous than they should be." He paused. "A fact to which Captain Rachwalski can attest, as can many of the rest of you." There was a murmur of agreement. Pete was impressed the colonel could not only remember but also pronounce his name.

"Our situation will shortly be made more challenging. Some of you and many of your men will be transferred to the Coronet operation. Those who remain will have to work harder and under more dangerous conditions to keep the airfields operational. Therefore, before our forces begin to shrink, it's time to clear a wider swath around our lines. Gentlemen, I give you Operation Anthill."

" 'Quick, Henry, the Flit!' " some self-appointed wit shouted, to general laughter.

Pete didn't laugh. *Oh, shit,* Pete thought, *Crawling into caves again. I'm getting too old for this.*

• WEDNESDAY, 22 AUGUST 1945 •

NASU IMPERIAL VILLA, NASU, TOCHIGI PREFECTURE, JAPAN, 1900 HOURS (OPERATION OLYMPIC, X-DAY + 156)

Outside the Emperor's private cottage, wind lashed the windows and rain pelted the roof. The building was sturdy, but the fierce weather seemed determined to challenge the durability of this human construct. For this was not just any random storm: it was a typhoon. The big tropical cyclones regularly lashed the Empire of Nippon during the summer and early fall, and this one was gustier and wetter than most.

Inside, three men and a god drank tea as they listened to the rattle of rain on the roof and the whistle of the wind through the trees. Something clattered loudly, a tile pulled free to bounce down the roof and crash onto the stone-paved courtyard.

Yamamoto had driven up to the resort town of Nasu, a few hours northwest of Tokyo, where the emperors had long maintained a summer retreat. Unfortunately, War Minister Yamamoto was not here for a vacation. He was here for an inquisition.

The sky had darkened steadily, and the rain had begun by the time his car arrived at the Emperor's cottage, one of several buildings in the walled complex.

It was a "cottage" only by imperial standards, of course. The Taisho Emperor had rebuilt it in the 1920s. Yamamoto admired the clean and open lines of the anteroom and hallway. Rich brown planks of cherrywood framed panels of light bamboo in exquisite harmony.

The kimono-wearing imperial servant escorted him to a room containing one low square table made of teak. A small dish in the center of the table contained a single chrysanthemum, while a tea service and incense burner stood ready to the side. Sitting pillows were arrayed strategically and artfully around the small room.

The three men and the god sat at the table, legs folded underneath. The god, of course, was the Emperor. Yamamoto was one of the three mortal men. The other mortals were Prince Fujiwara Konoe, the prime minister; and Marquis Kido, the lord privy seal. The Emperor wore kimono. Kido and Konoe wore Western-style business suits. Kido's was old-fashioned, with a wing-tipped collar. Yamamoto wore dress blues.

The Emperor lit an incense stick and offered a Shinto prayer for the well-being of his servants, the success of this meeting, and the fate of the Empire. The mortal men chanted the appropriate responses and bowed.

"Tea, Yamamoto-san?" Prince Konoe inquired. He was a handsome man with a full head of hair, good bone structure, a thin mustache, and expressive eyes.

"*Arigato,* Konoe-sama," the war minister replied.

Konoe, as the senior mortal, served the others in reverse order of rank: Yamamoto, then Kido, and then the Emperor, all before serving himself.

Because they were in a private and informal setting, the Emperor was free to speak. "Yamamoto-san, We thank you for your services to Our Empire, and also for making this long trip so that we may all speak together freely."

Yamamoto bowed deeply from his kneeling position. "I am nothing but a poor, humble sailor who lives and dies at the Emperor's command. I exist to serve Your Imperial Majesty, and for no other purpose."

The Emperor acknowledged him with a small tilt of his head. "Then We know Our Empire is safe with servants such as you."

"You do this worthless servant too much honor, Your Majesty." The admiral bowed deeply again.

The three men and the god drank tea together and sat in communal silence for a time. The storm raged. There was a loud clap of thunder—then darkness.

Soft footsteps of sock-clad servants sounded from the corridors. The paper door to their room slid back and light appeared in the form of a servant carrying a candle. "Forgive this unwarranted intrusion by an unworthy servant," he said. "Would my lords wish candles?"

"Yes," the Emperor said, and within minutes the room was lit again with candles on the main table and lanterns on the floor.

It was Kido, not Konoe, who broke the silence. Kido was a highly distinguished-looking man, older than the others, with steel gray hair receding in the front, a strong black mustache and a rectangular face. He wore large round glasses with no frame around the lenses. "The storm is stronger than any enemy," Kido said.

The Emperor nodded. "That is how the god of the winds saved us twice from the depredations of Kublai Khan and his Mongols."

"My prayer is for another kamikaze, a divine wind that will destroy the American fleet as it moves toward Honshu," Kido said.

"We will also pray," the Emperor added. "Would such a wind make a decisive difference, War Minister?"

"It would change the military equation," Yamamoto answered, sipping his tea. "Whether it would alter the American position on 'unconditional surrender' is difficult to determine. They have now gained landing fields in Kagoshima, even though that struggle goes on."

"We see," the Emperor replied.

"The winds have always favored Japan," Konoe said. "As long as they do, we'll know the gods are on our side, and we'll eventually prevail."

Kido looked at Konoe. "So they have. But what if the winds changed direction?"

"Then the gods will have abandoned us," Konoe replied.

The servants began serving dinner in candlelight, but power came back on before the final course.

"I must say, Yamamoto-san, that I am impressed far beyond my expectations at your performance thus far as war minister," Kido said. "In such a delicate time, with such strong passions as our current situation naturally arouses in people, it takes unusual skills to lead. And may I say without offense that such skills are not necessarily always present in our finest military officers."

"My head is spinning with such undeserved praise, Kido-sama. Your good opinion is truly a prize to be valued above all earthly riches, but if anything has gone well in my time as war minister, it has been the work of all, not merely the work of one," Yamamoto replied.

"And so it has," replied Kido. "Yet it is the case that before your selection, the Supreme Council for the Direction of the War was being torn apart by dissension and conflict. After your selection, harmony."

Kido was being unusually blunt, cutting through the normal cycle of compliments given and refused. Without being unmannerly, Yamamoto had to match him.

"Perhaps, Lord Privy Seal, it is a coincidence," the war minister said. "But if I have made any slight contribution to the situation, it might lie in my feeble attempts to help those in opposition to each other find common ground on which to stand."

Kido nodded. "Indeed, the war minister speaks, as always, with commendable wisdom and insight. 'Helping those in opposition to each other find common ground.' *Hai.* It is an essential skill for someone in politics. Perhaps you missed your calling when you joined the Imperial Navy." Kido smiled.

"Forgive me, but I must argue with you. Such weak skills as I may possess in that area are also essential in the navy, Kido-sama," Yamamoto replied.

"Ah, you are a font of wisdom! Of course, of course, how stupid of me not to realize it! Yes, this skill would be essential to lead in the military, and indeed in any high leadership position, for at that level, *everything* becomes politics, *neh*? When this is over, my dear friend, I hope you will turn your hand to writing from your immense store of knowledge and experience to share with others. The Empire—the whole world, for that matter—would be enriched by it."

"I must protest, my lord. I am merely an imitator and student of those far wiser than I, doing my inadequate best to mimic what I have learned."

"It takes a wise man to learn from the wisdom of others," said Kido. "In the current situation, though, I have some questions, if the war minister will permit an inquiry from a mere citizen with no official status or role."

No official status or role other than being the Emperor's mouthpiece, that is, thought Yamamoto. "No question from you, Lord Privy Seal, could ever be unwelcome."

"The war minister is too gracious. Here, then, is my question. You have helped the army minister improve the success of Operation *Ketsu-Go,* setting the stage for further war. You have also gotten the army minister to establish a point at which he agrees that *Ketsu-Go* would have been shown not to work and thus withdraw his opposition to accepting Allied surrender terms."

"That is certainly the goal I had, Lord Privy Seal. General

Anami has established criteria to measure when—or if—his position on alternatives should change. By all of us agreeing to such a measured position, we can act in harmony."

It was Prince Konoe's turn. He leaned forward and said, "Whose side are you on Yamamoto-san? Peace, or more war?"

Yamamoto folded his mangled hand into the other, his two index fingers together and sticking up. Pensively he touched the fingers to his lips. "Your Highness, that is a question difficult to answer. Very difficult."

"Try, War Minister," Konoe said with shocking directness.

"As the prime minister commands," Yamamoto murmured. "I am on the side of the Emperor."

Now the Emperor joined in. "Yamamoto-san, We are honored by your support, but what side is that? What would your advice to Us be in this matter?"

"I am far too unworthy to offer advice to Your Imperial Majesty."

"Let Us be the judge of that, War Minister," the Emperor replied.

"As You command." Yamamoto bowed again. "The best of all strategies, says Sun Tzu, is to vanquish the enemy without fighting at all. Avoiding war and achieving the objective is to be preferred over all else.

"That having failed," Yamamoto continued, "the second best strategy is to win the war. In a war, each side has an objective that cannot be compromised or successfully negotiated. To win, one must break the enemy's moral will to resist so that you achieve your objective and force their acceptance or compliance.

"If one cannot achieve the victory objective, the third best strategy is to minimize the loss. Favorable and honorable surrender terms, a truce, status quo ante, whatever may be possible. One achieves this by making the enemy's price so high they are willing to settle for less than total victory."

He paused. "And if one cannot minimize the loss, the final strategy is to accept reality and move forward." Yamamoto bowed.

The Emperor nodded. "You would, We presume, place the Empire's present situation in the third and fourth categories?"

"With deepest regret, Your Majesty, yes. As long as there is some reasonable hope of the third outcome, it should be pursued. At the same time, we must know when such hope is no longer real and accept our fate. When the litany of cities burned and villages starved becomes unacceptable, then the unthinkable becomes necessary."

Konoe spoke again. "You're saying you aren't choosing sides between peace and war, then."

"Your Highness, I seek the virtue of potential harmony between the opposing sides, and in harmony lies the Empire's best chance, regardless of its eventual fate."

Konoe shook his head sadly. "What you have said is eloquently argued, deeply reasoned, and brilliantly executed. It pains me, therefore, that I cannot agree fully with your logic."

"The prime minister's wisdom is far better than my own, and my feeble mind may well have missed essential information. Please advise your servant."

Konoe nodded. "Yamamoto-san, I agree with you with but a single exception. And it is this: I wonder if the army will honor the bargain it has made with you. General Anami is an honorable man, but we have seen the consequences when senior officials fail to follow the will of our captains and majors."

Yamamoto bowed. "Ah, that is great wisdom indeed, Your Highness, and it is a matter of great and continuing concern. It is always a danger. That danger can be reduced, and I have taken whatever slight steps that lie within my power to do so, but I do not know any way it can be eliminated altogether."

"I hope you're right about reducing that danger, Yamamoto-san," Konoe said. "For all our sakes. But I'm afraid that a clever nuanced position like yours may turn out to be more dangerous than you suppose. There are people around who will not compromise, whatever the stakes."

Konoe looked directly at the war minister. "And at that moment, you'll have to decide which side you're truly on."

TWENTY-ONE

Western Pacific; Hiroshima

PACIFIC OCEAN, 200 MILES SOUTH OF CAROLINE ISLANDS, 0001 HOURS

There may have been a god in his palace in Tokyo and a god in his headquarters on Okinawa, but neither of them was aware of a third god—a god now taking tangible form in the southern latitudes of the Pacific Ocean.

It was gathering anew, but it was a god who had visited these waters, and these islands, many times through the centuries of history.

His name was Kami Kaze, and he was truly a Divine Wind. . . .

As always, he began to take shape above the warm waters of a tropical sea, as a swirling low-pressure weather system. Convection and increasing wind speeds pulled more and more moisture from the ocean, tossing the humidity upward with increasingly tumultuous force. In this September, the Kami Kaze gathered in the central Pacific. It began as a nondescript collection of wind and rain, united beneath a vast dome of gray clouds. It was not yet a deadly gale, or even yet a single intact weather system. But it was wet, the water below it was warm, and the broad center of low pressure reached out to summon wind and humidity from far away.

The Kami Kaze sprawled across the warm ocean current like an insatiable vacuum pump, sucking in more and more hot, moist air. This mass of cloud and rain spread across more than a thousand miles of the globe's surface. As the center of the system eased up to about twelve degrees north latitude, winds rose and spiraled into the spinning vortex. The pressure dropped still further, drawing great quantities of air—and the moisture carried by that air—with increasing force.

Turbulent air was further propelled into the growing Kami Kaze by high-pressure centers all around. Sweeping across the sea, the moving atmosphere accelerated, lashing the swells into whitecaps, then into waves that loomed over small boats and breakwaters. Storms and squalls arose, and their winds whipped the water even harder, pulling more and more moisture upward into the gathering core, the storm growing increasingly cohesive. Along the northern shore of New Guinea, the second largest island in the world, these storms manifested themselves in surging waves that pounded against the long coast. Rain soaked the perennially wet forests and wind whipped through the trees. People and animals scurried to shelter in whatever dry spaces they could find.

The upper heights of the storm ascended higher into the atmosphere, looming vast and dark over this great expanse of ocean. Winds, now swirling in the distinctive counter-clockwise pattern of a tropical depression in the northern hemisphere, picked up speed, lashing the surface of the sea even harder than before. The few small islands unfortunate enough to lie under the great stormy umbrella were inundated with tidal surges, heavy downpours, and sweeping gales. The swirling pattern became steadily more distinct, and the winds coursed up to fifty miles an hour. Humans piloting ships and aircraft steered to avoid the storm as much as possible, though no man yet grasped the full nature of the cataclysmic phenomenon that was coming into being.

Still the storm picked up strength as more and more moisture evaporated and was drawn into the swirling vortex. Instead of expanding, the storm seemed to draw in upon itself, but this was deceptive. Like a general marshaling his army—fully mindful of the maxim calling for concentration of force—the storm contracted and focused its might into a compact presence. The pressure in the center of the depression sank even lower. In its distinct eye, the skies were oddly placid. Around the eye the winds circled in that pronounced, counterclockwise swirl, picking up more speed, hitting gusts as fast as sixty-five miles per hour. Torrents of rain poured from the clouds in a blinding deluge.

And finally, like a living being gradually gaining sentience and will, the Kami Kaze began to move north and west. The damp and sweltering island of New Guinea fell behind, unscathed by the monster that had loomed so close offshore. Beyond, to the north and west of the vortex, the Pacific waited, unsuspecting, still as calm as the placid waters suggested by this vast ocean's name.

• TUESDAY, 11 SEPTEMBER 1945 •

OKINAWA, RYUKU ISLANDS, 1202 HOURS (OPERATION CORONET, Y-DAY -10)

The large fleet of landing ship, tanks, LSTs for short, lay at anchor, the vessels divided among the various Okinawan ports on the northern part of that long island. More than three hundred squat, reliable Sherman M4 tanks of XIII Corps had already rumbled over the wharfs and up the ramps to be strapped down in the cavernous holds. They represented the largest armored force that had ever been transported for a beach landing, and as a consequence were loaded for fast, aggressive debarkation once the initial wave of marines had seized the targeted beaches.

Dozens more standard troop transports swarmed with marines and soldiers, along with a variety of landing craft to carry those troops ashore. These ships lay alongside the LSTs, for all the amphibious vessels would sail together at the heart of this epic fleet. They would be accompanied by more naval gunnery and ship-based aircraft than had ever been assembled for one mission. Already hundreds of cruisers and destroyers, more than a dozen battleships, and some two score aircraft carriers and escort carriers had put to sea. They had made for Okinawa from bases as far away as Pearl Harbor and Australia. Now they circled patiently, waiting for the slower troopships to leave port and form into the task forces that would put these men ashore on Honshu, the main island of Japan.

These troopships and their escorts made up General George S. Patton's diversion force, the mostly mythical Third United States Army Group that was a reinforced corps in actual strength. It would approach Honshu ahead of the main amphibious force. Operation Coronet planners had decreed that Patton's XIII Corps would embark from Okinawa on September 11, ten days before the scheduled landing. While the number of transports was small when compared with the vast fleets assembled for Operation Olympic, the escorting fleet of warships was unprecedented.

The invasion planners devoutly hoped that when the enemy saw the level of bombardment and air cover swarming from these ships, he would be certain that this armada represented the main attack and redeploy the Japanese ground troops to meet the threat, while the main body—consisting of two very real armies, the First and the Eighth—approached the enemy homeland unseen and unsuspected.

Patton, brusque and profane, ordered his ships, troops, and tanks ready to go a full twenty-four hours ahead of schedule. Posing as the Third United States Army Group, or TUSAG, was the XIII Corps, consisting of the 13th and 20th Armored Divisions, a regimental combat team drawn from the 1st Marine Division (RCT-1), and the 32nd Infantry Division. Patton hoped to fool the Japanese into believing XIII Corps was actually two full armies. It was a dangerous mission, maybe even one step short of suicide, though Patton's unlimited self-confidence provided hope.

Patton had already improved the situation. Originally, the XIII Corps didn't even have the infantry division. The change had come about during advanced planning sessions, after the general had suggested, with unusual tactfulness, that he would need them to consolidate the landing zones.

He intended to put his tanks ashore as quickly as possible, so that his armor could strike out across the countryside. The 32nd Division was a fine unit, consisting of National Guard veterans of battles on New Guinea and in the Philippines. Their strength more than tripled the number of foot soldiers under Patton's command.

For all that MacArthur was trying to humiliate Patton by making a four-star general do the job of a corps commander, the diversion was still a good idea, and its success was in everyone's interest. In the end, the Supreme Commander had even agreed to designate one division of the floating reserve, the 104th Infantry, to reinforce Patton's beaches if necessary.

One way or another, Patton intended to fight the hell out of the Japanese with whatever he was given, and he was confident, he had told the men of his command, that "these cocksucking Nip fuckers will be piss-soaked and shitting in their pants after they've tangled with Georgie Patton's boys."

Everyone assured everyone else that there wasn't anything superstitious about the "13" in XIII Corps. However, men assigned to Patton began to refer to themselves as "Unlucky Forward," a play on the nickname of Patton's European headquarters.

It was pretty certain that the enemy counterattack would make things very hot for Patton's men. Compared to the reinforced army landed on Kyushu for Operation Olympic, and the two entire armies that would be under MacArthur's command for Operation Coronet, Patton's force was remarkably small.

Because it was intended as a diversion, not only was the XIII Corps landing before the rest of the Coronet forces, but it was landing much farther to the north. The beaches were in the vicinity of Iwaki, some 120 miles north of the capital. Tokyo, of course, was the stated objective for the whole operation. Thirty-six hours after the diversionary "army group" came ashore, the two armies under the Supreme Commander's direct control would land very close to the capital. The hope was that Patton's noisy and violent assault would distract the Japanese high command from the invasion's true objective.

As the ships were loaded and the last supplies hoisted aboard, the weather reports indicated a large storm brewing far to the south. But the sky over Okinawa was clear and blue, so the admirals and generals of Patton's force took little note of the distant storm. After all, they were sailing north.

So it was that XIII Corps departed from Okinawa upon smooth and balmy seas. Winds were noticeable but not dangerous. As the last of the transports cleared the breakwater on the harbor at Hagushi Bay, the commanding general stood upon the bridge of his flagship, the heavy cruiser *Indianapolis*. Patton held binoculars to his eyes and watched his fleet steam past.

When the captain ordered the *Indianapolis* to make flank speed, the general turned to his chief of staff, General Gay, and nodded in satisfaction. His mouth tightened in contemplation, then creased into a broad grin.

"All in all," he said, "the hand that MacArthur dealt me isn't nearly as rotten as he thinks it is. I've got this feeling that the gods of war are going to smile on me once again, Hobart." He grinned and slapped his chief of staff on the shoulder. "I guess the big question is whether you're riding with George Armstrong Custer at Little Big Horn or Leonidas at Thermopylae."

General Hobart Gay wisely did not point out that even at Thermopylae, Leonidas and all his men died.

On an otherwise nondescript troop transport, Captain Pete Rachwalski, commanding a new Charley Company—this one part of Marine Regimental Combat Team One—sat back with his copy of the February 1944 issue of *Astounding Science Fiction,* another present from Ellis, and started rereading the "Venus Equilateral" story for what must be the fiftieth time.

Only four weeks earlier, Pete had been rotated out of Kyushu, happy to have survived once again and to have brought at least a few of his men out of the campaign with their lives. On Okinawa the "fully recuperated" Corporal

Coad had rejoined the company. "That million-dollar wound, Captain?" he had remarked. "Turned out to be worth about a buck twenty-nine."

"Welcome back, Sergeant Coad," Pete replied, certain that the promotion would be approved.

Not two days later, he'd been pulled away from his unit. It seemed someone in the Marine Corps felt that a maverick who got a battlefield promotion from NCO to officer ought not to be around marines who knew him before. That part he didn't mind so much, but he found that his new unit had gotten swept up in this "diversion force" nonsense. Morale had plummeted, but these men were marines. They would do their duty—but not without a few choice comments.

As for Pete, he knew he was fucked. But he was an officer now, which meant he didn't get to bitch about it to the other men in his company. He leaned back against the bulkhead, closed his eyes, let the sun warm his face.

At least, he tried to console himself, the weather looked pretty good.

A baritone voice was singing. The tune was "The Battle Hymn of the Republic," but the words were different: ". . . and while possibly a rumor now/Someday 'twill be a fact/That the Lord will hear a deep voice say/'Move over, God, it's Mac.'/So bet your shoes/that all the news/that last great Judgment Day/Will go to press/In nothing less/Than Doug's communiqué."

The marines around the singer laughed. One observed, "Well, at least we've got our own god to match Hirohito. The Japs think Hirohito's god, don't they?"

"How about Jesus, you fucking moron?" an indignant believer shouted. "We've got *Him*!"

"It's a *joke,* asshole," protested the marine who'd made the reference.

If that little argument didn't quiet down quickly, Pete was going to have to go over and take official notice of it. Besides, they'd missed other gods. Mars, the god of war. Neptune, god of the sea.

The forces of nature were like gods, especially compared to men.

• THURSDAY, 13 SEPTEMBER 1945 •

PHILIPPINE SEA, 300 MILES EAST OF LUZON, 1522 HOURS

The Kami Kaze meandered across the vastness of the central Pacific. The path of the storm curved northwest, crossing over the Caroline Islands, gusts continuing to build in strength as more and more moisture was pulled into the spiraling low. Winds were now approaching eighty miles per hour, and rain fell by the bucketful.

Humans on the islands in the path of the storm fortified their homes, built dikes and drainage ditches, and finally took whatever shelter they could find from gusts that lashed trees, tore at roofs, and sent great waves crashing against the shore. There was nothing else for them to do beyond waiting out the looming storm. It would come, then it would soon pass away from them.

A few fishing boats and interisland ferries were caught at sea, where they were tossed like toys. Some, too slow to reach port, were lost. A freighter bearing supplies from Hawaii to Manila sank when her back was broken by a monstrous wave. A tanker bound for Luzon capsized two hundred miles east of Mindanao, spilling human beings and precious aviation gasoline into the uncaring sea.

A U.S. Navy PBY approached the storm from the west, flying into the windy, rain-lashed limbs of the great system. The pilot reported a shockingly low barometric pressure reading—barely a fraction above twenty-eight inches of mercury—and then declared his intention to fly farther into the weather system. That was the last transmission from the plane. No wreckage was ever found.

By now, the storm had taken on a life of its own. Winds reached out, howling and flailing, for hundreds of miles in every direction. Swirling with that imperious counterclockwise sweep, its gusts lashed the surface of the ocean, sending flood tides surging onto the low-lying islands of Melanesia. Water spewed from the heavy, moist clouds, pounding relentlessly over land, the accumulation building inch after deadly inch. Floods were common, and those people and animals that could not find some high ground on these low islands were in peril of death.

Moving north and west now at something like twenty miles an hour—the cruising speed of a warship—the storm swept past the Palaus, curving slightly, angling still more toward the north. The Philippines were the next barrier before it, but they were narrow islands around warm seas. They would not slow it down.

This Kami Kaze was a full-fledged tropical cyclone now. In the western Pacific, this kind of storm was called a typhoon.

• **FRIDAY, 14 SEPTEMBER 1945** •

MANILA BAY, LUZON, PHILIPPINES, 0800 HOURS
(OPERATION CORONET, Y-DAY -7)

The Supreme Commander had made it clear to everyone from army commanding generals and fleet admirals to the meanest buck privates and swabbies: delay, whether from weather or enemy action, would not be tolerated. It was perhaps a measure of his reputation or willpower that no one questioned his assertion. Instead, every man bent his back to the task of making sure that the great armada sailed from Manila on time.

Rain lashed the murky waters of the vast bay, and the wind—out of the northeast—continued to pick up power and speed. This was not yet the full brunt of the storm, for the center lay hundreds of miles to the east. Nevertheless, local gusts exceeded twenty-five miles an hour, and forecasts called for a steady increase in the strength of the storm, which now included winds approaching a hundred miles per hour surrounding the eye. If those meteorological predictions proved accurate, within a day and a half the seas would be dangerously rough for any ships attempting to leave the protected waters of Manila Bay.

Navy forecasters had already categorized the storm as a typhoon. They had even gone so far as to plot its course—a very new tactic in the field of meteorology—determining the heading to be north by northwest on a compass bearing of approximately 320 degrees. If it maintained that path, it would cross the Philippines directly over Leyte or Luzon and then make landfall on the mainland somewhere south of Formosa. There, it could be expected to dwindle and die as its source of moisture—the warm central Pacific—fell behind.

But when it reached Luzon, it would pound the Philippine archipelago for days. While the huge fleet would be relatively safe in the shelter of one of the finest natural anchorages in the world, the invasion would inevitably face delays if those ships had not already departed. The XIII Corps was already at sea and could be called back only with great difficulty. There was one glimmer of good news: additional information, again provided by those navy forecasters, suggested that the full brunt of the typhoon would not strike Luzon for some forty-eight hours.

The scheduled hour of departure was still twelve hours in the future when the latest weather reports came in to SWPA headquarters, now established on the bridge of the light cruiser *Nashville,* the fourth ship of that name. There was only one man who could make the decision, and so the General did.

MacArthur ordered the remaining loading to continue at double time and moved up the departure to 2000 hours September 14. As the work in the harbor proceeded at an increasing frenzy, the Supreme Commander ordered his admirals to alter the projected route of the invasion force, directing it to travel farther east than originally planned. The ships would make the course change as soon as they passed around the northern tip of Luzon. This would bring the great amphibious fleet to its landing beaches within the time frame required and carry the ships as quickly as possible out of the projected path of the typhoon.

Already the antisubmarine force had put to sea. Destroyers, destroyer escorts, and coast guard cutters patrolled the waters off Manila Bay and north past Formosa and beyond. Relentless hunters using the most modern sonar and antisubmarine warfare technology, they scoured the seas. Many Japanese submarines were found and destroyed, and the rest were driven so deep that they would not be able to observe the great armada as it sailed past.

Within the bay, many ships were already fully loaded, anchored in long columns, ready to sail. The transport ships of this huge amphibious fleet bore the troops of the First and Eighth armies, commanded by Generals Harmon and Eichelberger, respectively. Under MacArthur's overall direction on scene, they would land in the vicinity of Tokyo—First Army just to the south of Tokyo Bay, and Eighth on the Hanto Peninsula, due east of the capital—thirty-six hours after Patton's faux army group, the XIII Corps, had landed a hundred miles to the north.

The accompanying warships of the amphibious fleet's escort numbered fewer than the ships escorting the XIII Corps, especially in the area of fast carriers, since virtually all of the big flattops had sailed north with Patton. This was all part of the deception, however. In fact, the plan called for all of the fleet carriers to detach one day after the diversionary landing. At that time, they would head south and offer air support to the assault of MacArthur's main body.

In Manila, the approaching typhoon affected every aspect of the departure. Several barges and tenders overturned, and a dozen crewmen drowned. One transport suffered a ruptured hull when it was pitched against the stone quay by a sudden, surging wave. Because of the conditions, final loading operations were suspended at 1530 hours.

"If we don't have it aboard, we don't need it!" the Supreme Commander was heard to announce.

Naturally, everybody agreed. The fleet steamed forth from Manila Bay under the onslaught of thirty-mile-per-hour winds and the relentless drumming of the rain. The armada passed Corregidor and Bataan in file well before sunset.

These two positions, soaked in the history of this war, had been returned to American hands more than a year before. Now, none of the shipboard men could so much as see them through the rainy evening's murk.

Once the ships emerged from the bay, they turned to the north and steamed past the western shore of the large island of Luzon. The mass of land gave some protection from the wind, but the weather was sufficient to buffet the ships mightily. The gale came at them from the starboard bow, at an angle that rocked the flat-bottomed vessels with stomach-churning violence.

It was a rocky ride for the better than one hundred thousand men—most of them landlubbing soldiers—on the vessels of the invasion fleet as they rolled through the rough waters west of Luzon. For the long night, the weather only increased, and many men simply prayed for relief from seasickness or, failing that, a quick and merciful death. At dawn, the ships rounded Cape Bojeador on the northwestern tip of the island, and here the entire fleet altered course to the east. They followed the Bubayan Channel all the way past the northern coast of Luzon.

They were on the flank of the typhoon now, as the great body of the storm approached the Philippines to the south. The wind was stronger than ever. But here, at least, the ships drove directly into the teeth of the storm. The waves rose higher than they had farther south, but the ride was marginally better because the bows of the vessels met those surging seas head-on.

The center of the typhoon made landfall at Legaspi, the southernmost city on Luzon. A storm surge of more than a dozen feet flooded several barrios, and almost a hundred people perished. Winds exceeded 120 miles per hour, tearing the tops off buildings, flattening whole neighborhoods. The steeple of a church more than three hundred years old collapsed, destroying a row of shops.

The invasion fleet emerged from the Bubayan Channel during a rainy, windy dawn. The ships churned forward through waves that, while still rough, had grown measured and predictable. The rain ceased before 0900, and the winds died down throughout the rest of the day as the fleet sailed into the Philippine Sea.

True to the meteorologists' forecasts, the weather continued to ease. The rain and wind let up, and by Saturday evening, the troops—and the Supreme Commander—were treated to a beautiful sunset, brilliant reds and pinks and blues breaking through the clouds in the west.

• WEDNESDAY, 19 SEPTEMBER 1945 •

EAST CHINA SEA, 1419 HOURS

The Kami Kaze howled like a cruel and triumphant god. The rampaging deity was unstoppable, irresistible, a power beyond understanding. Dumping rain by the ton, with winds spiraling now at better than 140 miles per hour, the typhoon spread its limbs to embrace and to hammer the ocean and the land. It drove onward, purposeful, driven, determined—but capricious as well.

The Philippines lay behind it, whole mountainsides denuded of trees by flood and mudslide, villages carried away by storm-swollen streams. Coastal towns, especially along the eastern shore of Luzon, had been pounded by storm surge waves rising fifteen or twenty feet in the air. Where the shore was flat, those waves had swept inland for miles.

But Luzon had given the storm no pause. It was over the ocean again, and the South China Sea pumped still more water into the massive vortex. The willfulness of the great typhoon curled it onto a bearing of nearly straight north. It seemed to pull not just wind and water but also lives and property and everything it passed into the insatiable vacuum that lay at its core.

The typhoon came upon Formosa and drenched that hapless place thoroughly, driving Japanese occupiers and Chinese inhabitants alike into such shelter as they could find. A dam burst, inundating a village of better than a hundred people. Whole valleys full of rice nearing harvest were rendered into lakes, the nourishing crop lost to the relentless waters.

Fortunately for the few remaining Japanese fliers on Formosa, most of their airplanes were kept in sheltered caves— the few that sat in the open were picked up and casually tossed aside by the force of the typhoon. The troops, too, were well dug in and stayed in place except for a few that were forced to move to higher ground as the storm flooded their trenches. The people in the cities suffered more, as rivers swelled beyond their banks, and in the countryside the wind wreaked havoc on many small buildings.

Beyond Formosa lay the mainland of China and all the great continent of Asia. But for reasons unknown beyond the swirling scope of the great storm, the typhoon disdained a landfall there. Instead, it continued to the north, crawling across the surface of the East China Sea, lashing the coast as it swept steadily on, stubbornly refusing to turn inland.

Now Korea and the great warm swath of the Yellow Sea lay before the typhoon. The god-storm could go there, swell even more with fresh supplies of water and warmth, but there it would be trapped between the landmasses of China, Manchuria, and Korea itself. With nowhere to turn, it would of necessity spill onto the mainland and, slowly and with great lingering violence, dwindle away.

But the cyclone was lord of all weather, mighty and omnipotent, free of the constraints that bound lesser storms. It could reject the course laid before it for no reason other than its own will, could turn like a creature making the choice to follow a new path. No barrier could stand in its way. Its peak winds now approached 160 miles an hour. Its floods of rain could drown anything in its path.

The storm could go where it would, and so it did. Before it reached the tip of the Korean peninsula, the typhoon god veered onto a new course again, curving to the northeast, riding down the line of the Ryuku Islands. It was bearing upon the Home Islands of Nippon, roaring upward from the southwest.

East and southeast of Japan, thousands of ships and the full might of two great armies plus an armored corps continued to approach the long, storm-whipped coast. The men on the ships carrying the main body could see the great, dark mass to the west and could feel the freshening wind as the front edge of the typhoon came closer. At the same time, 150 miles north and east of that fleet, the diversion force of XIII Corps continued to sail forward under clear skies and only the most gentle of winds.

• FRIDAY, 21 SEPTEMBER 1945 •

*BANK OF THE RIVER OTA, HIROSHIMA, 0600 HOURS
(OPERATION CORONET, Y-DAY, N-HOUR + 0000)*

Ogawa Michiyo huddled under the lean-to, but she couldn't avoid the rivulets of water that streamed through the many cracks in her makeshift shelter. The whole wasted city was a landscape of water, and the rain pounded relentlessly. The young woman's shelter was crude, made from a few wooden walls, all of which were laced with cracks and pocked with holes. It had been her home for more than a month, the place she had slept ever since the B-sans had burned her home and her city.

Michiyo barely noticed her misery anymore. Even as she looked at the infected burn blisters on her arms, felt the gnawing of near starvation in her belly, the torment of her memory was worse. Baby Otomi was dead, incinerated by the fires that she had been unable to douse. She still had nightmares, remembering the horror of holding that tiny, lifeless body. Huddled in the waters beneath the Aioi Bridge, she had begged the baby to take a breath. But there had been no life in him.

Her mother was gone too, torn away from her in the midst of the panicked throng. The older woman was lost to the terror, certainly dead, together with the tens of thousands of others who had perished in the awful fire. Michiyo had searched for her mother anyway, hoping for a miracle, but met only other searchers.

Since that horrible morning, Michiyo had been hiding in the ruined city, dwelling in her small shelter near the banks of the Ota. She ate bits of garbage and flotsam to stay alive. Those whom she met she regarded warily, as they did her. She saw no one she knew. They were probably all dead. Perhaps her brother still lived, but he was a soldier. He would die before the dishonor of surrender, so it was as if he were dead already. Still, she wished she could see him one last time.

Most of those who had survived the attack had left the city, so she had little competition in her foraging. Always she kept near to the river, vividly remembering how the water had kept her alive when everyone and everything around her had burned. With all the buildings charred and blackened, the streets filled with wreckage—and in places still the bodies of the dead—the river was the one part of the city that was now mostly as it had been before. Though wreckage, soot, and even death floated past her, the river had once again become the heartbeat of Michiyo's city. Here, in those dark waters, Hiroshima was still alive.

But now, those waters took no note of her. As the rain pounded through the great watershed of the Ota, swelling the creeks and streams and tributaries and eventually the river itself, the water level rose and kept rising. She could not know that the Kami Kaze had chosen her delta as the place to make landfall. Tides surged in from the ocean, the force of the storm amplified by the narrow bay. Debris from the bombing, charred timbers and broken pieces of houses and trees, choked the channels, and the waters picked up the wreckage and carried it inland, bearing it like a battering ram straight up the Ota.

The full brunt of the storm came onto the broad, flat shore of Hiroshima. Water roared in from all directions. Michiyo's lean-to collapsed from the steady force of the rain, and the fragments of wood were picked up by the rising floodwaters.

The boards floated away. The waters rose around her scarred legs, the current pulling her, inviting her, welcoming her. She did not hesitate. She embraced the waters of the Ota and let them wash away her tears, her suffering, and her grief.

The dam of debris, borne by the furious storm, smashed into the support pillars of the Aioi Bridge. The concrete cracked and groaned, and finally the span collapsed, wrecked pavement tumbling into the channel, tossed about by the angry waves.

The flood rose above the riverbanks and swept across the rubble as the current pulled Ogawa Michiyo down into the depths. *Perhaps my burden will be less in the next life,* she thought, and opened her mouth to accept the water's intimate caress, as the Divine Wind scoured the charred delta that had once been Hiroshima, carrying its ruins away.

HONSHU, JAPAN, 0615 HOURS (OPERATION CORONET, Y-DAY, N-HOUR + 0015)

The Kami Kaze was in its full majesty as it boiled onto the great island of Honshu, making landfall at a bay, a long delta where once had been a great city. The whole place was black and stank of ashes and soot. Here there were signs of death, and memories of suffering, and evidence of war.

The storm god reached out a great tendril of wind and swept the site of the once-great city clean.

Then the Divine Wind swept from southwest to northeast, intent on scouring the entire nation of Japan. Waves and floods and storm surges assailed the coast. Rain and wind lashed the inland, driving people into their homes and sometimes even battering those homes into rubble. Rivers flooded, sweeping bridges away. The railroad system of the country, already heavily pounded by American air power, suffered additional damages as many tracks running through river valleys were washed away.

The soldiers of the Imperial Japanese Army, braced to defend their homeland against an anticipated invasion, suffered greatly from the onslaught of wind and rain. Lieutenant

Naguro Yoshi finally got to lead his men in battle, but it was a fight against a supernatural foe, not the Americans. On the airfields, all flight operations were suspended on central and southern Honshu—which was where almost all of the aircraft that had been saved for the last-ditch *tokko* missions had been placed. With the loss of bridges and the flooding effects on many other roads, movement overland was virtually impossible.

When preliminary bombardment began against the beaches around Iwaki, that part of the island had not yet felt the effect of the storm. Yet the reserves were south of there, gathered in the vicinity of Tokyo, and these troops were utterly incapable of movement toward the invasion zone. Electric power was disrupted throughout the capital and farther south and west, further impeding operations and even fundamental communications between army units.

This great typhoon had become one of the largest in history. The god of storms had come for his vengeance and showed no mercy. Instead, he swallowed up southern Honshu as if it were a tiny meal.

And still the storm was hungry for more.

PACIFIC OCEAN, 100 MILES SOUTH OF TOKYO, 0640 HOURS (OPERATION CORONET, Y-DAY, N-HOUR + 0040)

The weather reports came in to the Supreme Commander with irritating regularity. The navy meteorologists had tracked the mighty typhoon all the way northward from Luzon and now suggested that the storm was going to ravage much of the main island of Japan. The ships of his invasion fleet tossed and tumbled in the tumultuous seas, and the General was informed that the bearing of the storm was now certain.

Unless the fleet withdrew and sailed a hundred miles or more to the south, there was no telling how many of his ships and his men would be lost. Divisions and corps and even whole armies were at risk. Still he refused to give the order. He stood on the open bridge of his cruiser as if he himself were a god equal in strength to the Divine Wind, able to turn back the typhoon by the issuance of an order, or simply the steely glare of his determined eyes.

Initial reports had arrived a few minutes before, informing him that the diversionary force was landing on the beaches at Iwaki against surprisingly light resistance. Patton anticipated moving his armor ashore very quickly, possibly even before the morning was finished. The marines were moving inland quickly to consolidate the beachhead, and the infantry of the 32nd Division was already in landing craft, with orders to land and establish strong fortified lines to the right and left of the broad zone of beaches.

In the meantime, the surf pounded and lashed the shore of Japan's southeastern coast, extending up as far as Tokyo Bay and the Hanto Peninsula. Amphibious landings would be impossible in these conditions, certainly for at least the next three days and probably longer.

Finally, the Supreme Commander bowed to the inevitable. His hundreds of ships and thousands of men could do nothing for him now except wait in the deep ocean waters, men fighting seasickness, ships struggling to stay afloat. They were only a hundred miles away from their objective, but they could go no closer in the storm. Instead, they were compelled to withdraw.

"Send a message to General Patton," MacArthur ordered. "Phrase it, 'Suggest consolidation of current landing position. Main body delayed by weather. Good luck, and hold on.'"

Even as the message was broadcast, the vast armada turned to the south, fleeing the storm that was mightier even than a great army and a great navy. The fleet would sail beyond the full brunt of the storm and then circle somewhere to the west of Iwo Jima—a place of which most of the men had never heard. The officers would listen to the reports from XIII Corps, knowing that General Patton's small force would be in dire danger if the Japanese mounted a furious counterattack.

But only when the typhoon had passed could MacArthur's armies go ashore.

TWENTY-TWO

Honshu, Japan

• FRIDAY, 21 SEPTEMBER 1945 •

USS INDIANAPOLIS, *4 MILES EAST OF IWAKI PORT,*
FUKUSHIMA PREFECTURE, HONSHU, JAPAN, 0700 HOURS
(OPERATION CORONET, Y-DAY, N-HOUR + 0100)

When Admiral Spruance located George Patton, the general had his pants unzipped and was urinating over the side of the ship into the waters of the Pacific. The famed commander was watching the flotilla of landing craft heading back toward the transports, the troops moving out across the beach, and the pyres of smoke rising from the shelled and bombed positions beyond the landing zones.

Spruance cleared his throat loudly.

Patton turned his head nonchalantly and continued his business. "Morning, Admiral," he said cheerfully. "Fine day for an invasion, don't you think?" He finished, shook himself off, and buttoned his jodhpurs.

It was, indeed, a fine day. The air was crisp and clear, the seas calm. The surf was a steady roll of one- or two-foot waves.

"It's hard to believe there's a typhoon a couple of hundred miles away," Spruance agreed. "From the radio traffic, it sounds like Nimitz and Mac are taking a hell of a pounding."

The admiral went on. "General Patton, I trust you are aware that the *Indianapolis* is equipped with modern plumbing. Perhaps the nomenclature has caused confusion. In naval parlance, the toilet is known as the 'head.'"

Patton laughed. "Oh, this? You know how dogs mark their territory? That's what I was doing. I pissed in the Rhine, you know, when Third Army rolled across it. I'm just giving the same treatment to these Jap cocksuckers."

"That seems illogical. Perhaps it increases morale to witness the commanding general acting contemptuously toward the opposite side. May I suggest, however, that you verify the wind direction before attempting this again aboard ship? The consequences could be somewhat unpleasant."

Spruance spoke in such a serious tone that Patton couldn't tell if he was kidding or not. Before he could ask, the admiral continued.

"Our radio room has received a message to you from General MacArthur." He handed the paper to Patton.

Patton read it aloud: " 'Suggest consolidation of current landing position. Main body delayed by weather. Good luck, and hold on.' "

Patton looked at Spruance as he crumpled up the message. "Hold on? Well, he doesn't tell me exactly *what* I should hold on *to*," he noted. "I think I better make that as much of Honshu as I can possibly get my tanks on!" He chuckled, a high-pitched sound that was almost a giggle.

Spruance nodded. "It would be difficult, and certainly inadvisable, to suspend landing operations at this point. As the moment of your going ashore approaches, we are nearing the time where command of this operation switches from me to you. Is there anything you require that I can begin in anticipation of the command shift?"

The little ramped boats returning to the transports had landed the first wave of marines on shore just an hour earlier, but already a dozen LSTs were driving landward, bulling in between the smaller craft. Following reports that the marines had moved hundreds of yards inland under very light resistance, the flat-bottom ships drove right up onto the beach and immediately started to lower their bow ramps.

When the naval gunnery bombardment had eased, right as the first troops were wading up out of the surf, observers on the ships could see that the enemy had virtually no artillery in the area—or if he did, he was conserving it for later in the battle, since none of the big guns were firing at the vulnerable landing craft or newly landed troops. It was that piece of good news that had caused Patton, with Spruance's concurrence, to send in the tanks so soon after the first wave.

Patton looked back at his invasion force. Already jeeps and light tanks were rolling out of sight, advancing through the dunes and beyond the seawall. The skies overhead were full of American planes and the kamikaze attacks had been mercifully light. Most of the suicide planes had been shot down by the navy CAP—combat air patrol—before they could even approach their targets. And there was that dearth of enemy artillery—that's why they had ordered the LSTs to the beach, some six hours ahead of best-case schedule. All in all, it was a very auspicious start to an invasion that was less than an hour old.

"I guess you could have your radio room send a reply to Mac," Patton allowed.

"Certainly. What would you like to send?" Spruance gestured to a nearby clerk who came forward with a notepad and a pencil.

"How about, 'Advance Elements Third Army Group ashore and moving inland. Beachhead secure. Opposition light. Anticipate complete force ashore within forty-eight hours, commencing *now*!" He noted the exact time on his chronograph.

By forty-eight hours from now, Patton fully intended that MacArthur and the world would see exactly what a *diversion* could accomplish.

BEACH JACKSON, IWAKI, HONSHU, 0945 HOURS (OPERATION CORONET, Y-DAY, N-HOUR + 0345)

"Gunny, was it like this on Kyushu?"

Pete almost turned around when he heard the kid ask the question. He had to force himself to stop, reminding himself that he was a captain now, in charge of a company of marines. The young marine—Jones was his name, Pete recalled—was experiencing battle for the first time today and had directed his question at Gunnery Sergeant Rinehart, who lay in the sand just behind Pete's right shoulder. Rinehart had been a lance corporal six months ago but, like a lot of marines, had grown up fast on Kyushu.

"Kid," Rinehart said, pausing to spit a stream of tobacco over the crest of the dune. It hit the sand with an audible *splat*. "We come ashore here today wit' a hunnert and t'irty men in this company. Last I heard, we still got a hunnert and t'irty men. This landing was *nuthin* like Kyushu."

"That kamikaze scared the shit out of me," Jones admitted. From the top of the dune where Charley Company had paused to regroup, they could look back over their shoulders and clearly see the blazing transport with the wreckage of the Jap plane on the foredeck. Several escort ships had closed in and were spraying the fire with hoses directing powerful streams of water.

"It scared the shit out of me, too," the gunny went on. "But that's one ship burnin' out there. On Kyushu, there were a couple dozen before we even climbed down the ropes. Then bullets was flyin' as thick as flies on shit, and Jap artillery was dropping shells down on every side."

"Where are all the Japs?" Jones wondered.

"You know, kid. I think we'll find out soon enough. Keep your head down, do what your sergeants tell you, and you'll be okay."

"Thanks, Gunny," Jones said.

Yeah, thanks, Gunny, Pete thought.

He was lying at the crest of the sand dune, looking inland through binoculars. For a few minutes he had been scrutinizing a small cluster of houses that were just beyond the beach road. His veteran eye had picked out several good, concealed routes through a thin grove of ash trees that might be used for an approach. A couple of long, low factory buildings—the outskirts of Iwaki—were visible a little more than a mile beyond the houses. If the Japs had any prepared defensive positions between here and there, Pete had not been able to pick them out.

"Okay, Gunny," Pete said. "You know the drill. We advance by platoon. Those houses and that stretch of road are the first objective."

"Aye aye, sir," Rinehart replied. Pete slid backward down the dune to speak to his platoon commanders, while the gunny scooted off to the side to get the show on the road.

An hour later the farmhouses had been secured. They were shells of buildings, actually, having been pounded pretty hard during the prelanding bombardment. More important to the marines, they had been abandoned. Charley Company had yet to suffer so much as a stubbed toe.

Pete crouched inside one of the houses, using his binoculars again to peer through a gap in the back wall. He was eyeing the factories, noting that they could be reached only by going around the shores of what looked to be several large, rectangular ponds. The dikes dividing the ponds were topped with good roads, but he didn't relish at all the idea of sending his men out on those exposed causeways.

"I'll be damned, Captain," Gunnery Sergeant Rinehart noted laconically from the front of the roofless building. "Will you look at that?"

Pete came to the front door and shook his head in astonishment. A glance at his watch showed him that it was an hour short of noon, some five hours after the first wave of the invasion had come ashore. And yet, big-time help was already on the way. Rumbling along the narrow dirt road that passed just inland of the beach came a column of trucks and jeeps and—so help him God—at least two dozen big, beautiful Sherman tanks.

USS INDIANAPOLIS, *1640 HOURS (OPERATION CORONET,* Y-DAY, N-HOUR + 1040)

The fact that TUSAG was a gigantic diversion was something Major Gregory Yamada, newly assigned to TUSAG G-2, appreciated about his new assignment. Colonel Oscar Koch, Patton's longtime intelligence chief, a little man—as short as Yamada himself—with a pronounced nose, weak chin, and receding hairline, had asked him only one question in their first meeting: "How do you feel about not taking part in the 'real' war?"

Yamada laughed. "This *is* the real war, Colonel Koch. As far as I'm concerned, deception and bluff is the finest possible way to fight. I'm proud to have the chance to serve the world's only inflatable army."

"World's only inflatable army," Koch repeated. "That's a good one. I've got to share that with the boss. Good to have you on board, Yamada."

Yamada's section was responsible for translation, interrogation, and even part of civil affairs, given the language barrier, so he had a pretty full plate. Now he and his chief stood on the deck of the heavy cruiser, discussing the next phase of the deception.

"We need to make the Japs think there's already an army ashore and another one on the way. How about we get going on those initial broadcasts?" Koch said it like a suggestion, but Yamada knew an order when he heard one.

"Yes, sir!" he replied, ready with the details. "We've already got six radios—and twelve of our men—on Jackson, Beauregard, and Forrest beaches. I'll have them start chattering—anybody listening in will think those fellows are six whole divisions."

"I only hope someone is listening in," Koch remarked dryly. "I don't see a lot of evidence of the Japanese."

"Trust me," Yamada said, with utmost sincerity. "They're there."

USS NASHVILLE, *100 MILES SOUTH OF TOKYO, 1730 HOURS* (OPERATION CORONET, Y-DAY, N-HOUR + 1130)

The steel-gray sky slowly brightened with the rising sun. The winds had lessened and the whipping lash of the rain had muted to a steady downpour. Douglas MacArthur, wearing an oilcloth slicker, paced back and forth on the exterior bridge platform. His fleet, the mightiest transport force in the history of the world, nearly a thousand ships transporting the U.S. First and Eighth armies, consisting of three full corps with twenty-five divisions, was in disarray. The typhoon had scattered it over the water with the same abandon as a child kicking over a tower of blocks. Some ships had been lost in the storm, and merely pulling the fleet back into a semblance of order so the invasion could go forward would take two days at a minimum, Nimitz had said. MacArthur cursed and yelled, but the admiral held firm to his estimate.

In the meantime, after *ordering* that damned glory hound Patton to consolidate his landing and wait for the main body so the plan would go forward on schedule, Georgie had blithely radioed, in effect, "Too late." With his breezy assertions of "beachhead secure" and "opposition light," he was undoubtedly lying through his teeth.

Even so, there was already enough radio traffic coming off the beach at Iwaki to make it sound like there was half an army ashore, with a lot more on the way. How far would the damned fool stick his neck out with his two armored divisions? Those men were MacArthur's men, MacArthur's responsibility! How dare he risk them in some rash, vainglorious maneuvering?

Ostensibly, of course, the transmissions were being made to spook the Japanese, but American and British reporters were already listening in, and soon stories would be filed that said PATTON PATTON PATTON. Glory hound. Grandstander. "I want an anti-PR man. I don't want any publicity." Bullshit.

It was a plot. It had been another plot by the "Get MacArthur" crowd in Washington to take away what MacArthur so richly deserved. Someone had put Truman up to this. Marshall. It had to have been Marshall. Marshall had always been jealous of him. Always.

Three days—or more—before MacArthur could come ashore. Three days with Patton the only story.

But then it would be MacArthur's turn. Then Patton and his fake army would see what a *real* army could do.

• SATURDAY, 22 SEPTEMBER 1945 •

IMPERIAL PALACE, TOKYO, JAPAN, 1100 HOURS
(OPERATION CORONET, Y-DAY + 01)

The Emperor, resplendent in formal robes, entered the chamber, stepped up onto the dais, and sat down. The members of the Supreme Council on the Direction of the War stood as the Emperor intoned a Shinto prayer for the favorable outcome of today's meeting. This wording was slightly unusual, thought the army minister, General Korechika Anami.

Prince Konoe was once again prime minister, replacing Hideki Tojo. Yamamoto Isoroku, war minister, was also replacing Hideki Tojo, who had held both portfolios. Togo Shigenori, the foreign minister, had been fired in 1942 as a member of the peace faction but was now back in his old position. The important question was how everyone would vote. Would it be a dishonorable peace, or a hopeless but honorable struggle?

"War Minister, what is the current military situation?" Konoe asked.

Yamamoto stood, bowed to the Emperor, then to the prime minister, then to the assembled council. "Based on our most recent intelligence, less than an hour old, we are being invaded by a total of four armies. Patton's Third Army Group, consisting of the Tenth and Twelfth armies, is currently coming ashore at Onahama in Fukushima Prefecture. He has unloaded nearly a full corps so far. The total strength of Patton's command is estimated at five corps, consisting of twenty-two total divisions.

"Unfortunately, this powerful force has landed farther north than we anticipated. It has put them beyond the range of American land-based fighters on Kyushu, but they seem to have committed an unprecedented number of aircraft carriers to support the operation. Not to put too fine a point on it, but the enemy has complete mastery of the skies over the landing beaches.

"Our *tokko* aerial forces—and there are more than five thousand aircraft and pilots ready to serve in this role for

Your Excellency—are concentrated in the area of the capital. Because of the typhoon, most of these planes have been unable to take to the air. At this hour, the situation in Iwaki is fluid, though the Americans seem to have already taken most of the city. Judging from the size of the fleet offshore, we suspect that this total force is something like two armies.

"Farther south, our intelligence is sketchy. However, submarine reconnaissance had revealed another large American fleet. This is apparently a second invasion force, and it was proceeding on a course that would have brought it to the vicinity of Tokyo. Those ships have been tossed about by the typhoon, but have not, as we hoped, been destroyed like the Mongols were," Yamamoto continued.

"They are reforming as we speak, according to intercepted radio traffic. Best estimates are that they carry an additional twenty to thirty divisions, forming at least two additional armies. There are a number of good landing zones available to them in the vicinity of the capital. One estimate—and I find it very credible—suggests that one of these armies will land at Kujukuri Beach on the Boso Peninsula and the other at Sagami Bay, near Hiratsuka. Once on land, these two will move across the Kanto Plain to join together with the Third Army Group when all reach Tokyo.

"Storm damage to our own forces has been great. Defensive positions throughout the Kanto Plain have been flooded. Roads are muddy. Resupply is impossible. For the Allies, this storm has delayed them for a day, perhaps two. Most of our electric power must come from generators, and fuel for those generators is scarce. For us, the typhoon has wreaked havoc on our already limited ability to resist their invasion of the homeland." Yamamoto bowed toward the prime minister and the Emperor and sat down.

There was a buzz of whispered conversations at the news. Anami, who had contributed to the intelligence report, was unsurprised, yet he was affected far more than anticipated by the cold summary of the bad news.

"Army Minister," Yamamoto said, "would you describe our military resources and response at the present time?"

Anami took a deep breath. He knew this was coming. The army didn't have nearly the resources needed to repel the invasion, and Yamamoto wanted Anami to admit it before the council. "Certainly, War Minister. Sea and air *tokko* special attack units have been unable to function during the storm but are now able to oppose the U.S. First and Eighth Army landings. The Twelfth Area Army, commanded by General Tanaka, is responsible for the defense of the Kanto Plain and Tokyo. It consists of twelve full divisions and a number of mixed and special brigades, with a total of 560,000 men. This does not count army and navy air other than *tokko,* nor civilian resistance.

"And to counter this group of armies landing in the north, at Iwaki?" Yamamoto asked.

"We have additional forces, of course." *Don't ask me that. Don't humiliate me in front of the council.*

Yamamoto simply waited.

Finally, Anami answered. "The 113rd Mixed Brigade, a coastal defense unit, is in Iwaki. It will shortly be joined by the 72nd Division from Fukushima and the 332nd Division, another coastal defense unit, currently about six miles south of Sendai." *Two divisions and a brigade against twenty-two divisions. Even I think that sounds pitiful.*

The navy minister, Mitsumasa Yonai, picked up the attack. "May I ask, Army Minister, how many divisions originally scheduled for the defense of Honshu were moved to Kyushu?"

"Thank you, learned Navy Minister, for that most insightful question," Anami said. *At last, a straw to grasp.* "Because we determined that Kyushu would be the site of the Decisive Battle, it has taken first call on resources. Six divisions were moved from Twelfth Area Army to join that battle."

The army chief of staff, General Yoshijiro Umezu, joined in. "We have successfully tied up the *gaijin* invaders for months."

Prince Konoe interjected, "Do you have reason to believe the Americans are any closer to providing the honorable surrender terms we seek?"

Umezu puffed up his chest. "We will continue to fight until they do! Their will cannot be as strong as ours."

Yamamoto pressed in once more. "Army Chief of Staff, how many of the divisions both here and in Honshu have ammunition?" His voice was calm.

Umezu's face was turning purple. "The Japanese people will fight with swords, sticks, and stones before submitting to dishonor!"

"Army Chief of Staff, how many of the divisions both here and in Honshu have ammunition?" Yamamoto repeated.

"You can't measure the strength of an army using the tools of an accountant!" Umezu protested.

"Please answer the war minister's question, Army Chief of Staff," Anami said. There was no use in concealment any longer.

Umezu turned on Anami. "It's the wrong question! It tells us nothing!"

"I will answer, then," Anami said. He felt old and tired. "On paper we have a total of sixty-five divisions in the homeland. Many in Kyushu are already at half strength or worse. Even so, we can equip about forty and provide ammunition to only thirty. The rest must rely on their fighting spirit, their love for the Emperor, and their willingness to die."

Everyone knew the news was bad, but the bald numbers were still a shock.

"Have we, Army Minister, reached a point where further struggle is pointless according to the standard you yourself defined earlier?"

Yes. "Such a question requires thought and analysis, War Minister. It is possible that such a point has been reached. However, regretfully, I cannot fully confirm it at this time."

Umezu was ready to argue again but fell silent, as did everyone else.

The Emperor was standing.

The ministers and chiefs of staff bowed deeply.

In a high voice, using an ancient and hard to understand dialect, the Emperor spoke. "We have listened carefully to Our ministers and Our military chiefs. After much thought, and as much as it pains Us to say so, We have reached a decision.

"Twice, the Divine Winds saved these islands from the depredations of the Mongol hordes. This time, Our forces have been more damaged than those of our enemies. It is clear to Us that the Gods Themselves have turned Their faces away from Us in this cause.

"It is time to end it. Therefore, We have resolved to endure the unendurable and suffer what is insufferable," the Emperor said, and sat down.

CHARLEY COMPANY, IWAKI CITY, HONSHU, JAPAN, 1845 HOURS (OPERATION CORONET, Y-DAY + 01)

The factories Pete had seen from the beach were two miles behind them now. With the Sherman tanks leading the way, the marines had crossed the causeways of what had turned out to be a vast fish farm. Two thoroughly concealed enemy machine guns had been sited to cover that approach. Their crews had shown good fire discipline, allowing the tanks and accompanying marines to come three-quarters of the way along the exposed dike before they opened fire. Then, in a few short seconds of violence, they had both been knocked out by the tanks' main guns—though not, unfortunately, before Charley Company had taken its first three casualties.

Two wounded had been evacuated, but the loss of the KIA—a private from Ohio whom Pete had shared only a few words with—had affected the captain with almost gut-wrenching force. The first kid to die in the last battle of war—what a fucking rotten piece of luck.

He had turned his grief to anger, and in short order the company had cleaned out the defenders of the factory. These belonged to a civil defense battalion and consisted almost exclusively of old men and boys. Most of them had not even been armed with firearms and instead rushed to attack with swords, knives, and improvised bombs made from kerosene and glass bottles. Several marines had been wounded in the seventy-five or eighty minutes of furious fighting.

There were no prisoners.

Meanwhile, the tanks had circled the factories and over-run a trench and a few roadblocks on the streets leading into the city. When the factory buildings had been thoroughly cleared, Pete emerged to make the acquaintance of his army counterpart.

"Captain David Allen, late of Manhattan, Kansas," said the young reserve officer, who had been waiting in a jeep between a couple of the looming, hunchbacked Sherman tanks. "Company D, 117th Battalion, 20th Armored Division."

"Captain Pete Rachwalski, Charley Company, 2nd Battalion, 5th Marines, RCT-1. Looks like we could do some good work together, Captain."

"You know, Captain, I was thinking the very same thing," agreed Allen. "My orders are to advance to a crossroads where the main highway comes south out of town."

"I'm supposed to keep moving inland," Pete replied. "I don't see any contradiction there."

The two officers agreed to team up on an ad hoc basis, a mutually beneficial relationship—especially since the infantry component of Allen's company had been delayed in some snafu involving insufficient landing craft. As for the marines, they were more than happy to have some big armored vehicles to walk behind.

City fighting was the dirtiest kind of war, Pete knew. Yet for all of today they had advanced almost at will. They might have been passing through a ghost town—albeit one made lively by the occasional sniper, mortar round, or suicidal charging enemy. The tanks went first and blasted any obstacles with their main guns, their machine guns, or the flamethrowing cannon that equipped about every fourth tank. The marines, meanwhile, pushed through the rubble that was too rough for the vehicles, and on one occasion deployed to take out an antitank gun that had destroyed Allen's lead Sherman.

But the rest of the time, they were clearly moving against an enemy that had not been prepared for attack here, now. All day they had skirted the main heart of the metropolis, which was under attack by other marines and army troops, and by the end of the day found themselves on the south side of Iwaki, in undisputed possession of the intersection that had been the tank company's objective.

"This is the last crossroads south of town," Captain Allen remarked, as the two officers stood under a tall willow tree. The skies were cloudy, with the promise of rain—it seemed like the distant typhoon was at least going to baptize them before it withered and died.

"This is a good highway," Pete noted, gesturing to the smooth pavement extending into the farm country to the south. "Where did you say it goes again?"

Allen unfolded a map on the hood of his jeep. There was enough light to see the long, broad stripe extending from Iwaki, almost a straight as an arrow's flight, south and west.

The arrow came to rest in the target labeled "Tokyo."

IMPERIAL ARMY HEADQUARTERS, TOKYO, JAPAN, 2025 HOURS (OPERATION CORONET, Y-DAY + 01)

Anami stood quietly at the podium on the large auditorium's stage as his officers started shouting at each other and at him. "We'll carry this shame forever!" was one of the milder epithets.

Perhaps that was true, he thought. Nevertheless, the Emperor had spoken, and no matter what the army minister's personal feelings, the Emperor's will was more important.

As the room became more chaotic, other senior officers tried to bring order back to the proceedings. Anami, numb, walked to the edge of the stage and down the steps. With one last glance at the fractious rabble that he had once been proud to call his officer corps, he left the auditorium. He returned to his office, sat down at his desk, and called his aide. "Please inform me when the officers have chosen what they will do," he said, then folded his hands on his desk and sat quietly.

His *kyudo* bow was hung on the wall. He thought about the *hassetsu* of his own life and career. *Kai,* the completion of the draw, was the moment when *Ketsu-Go* began. The battle itself was the *hanare,* the release. His destiny and his nation's destiny had been set at the moment of *kai* and revealed only in the release.

Now he was completing the *zanshin* of his life, the sending forth of his spirit for victory. All that was left was *yu-daoshi,* the final lowering of the bow. He would wait upon the decision of his officers.

He did not have to wait long. Ten minutes after he closed the door there came a diffident knock. Anami's summons brought his aide into the room. The man looked serious, and a little shaken.

Minister," he said after an unusually deep bow, "could you come into the auditorium, please?"

Exactly nine minutes later, there was nothing left to be decided and only one thing left to say. The army minister stood ramrod straight at the podium. He allowed his glare to pass slowly across all the assembled officers in the large room. Very many met his stare sullenly or with visible anger. A few showed signs of weeping.

Anami drew a deep breath.

"If you have decided not to obey the Emperor's will, you are no longer soldiers of the Emperor, nor soldiers of mine," Anami declared. He turned his back on the rogue officers and walked back to his office. He touched the buzzer on his desk. "Will you ask my senior aide to enter, please?"

He opened a cabinet of black lacquered wood and took out a teak box with elaborate carvings on the top. Opening the box, he removed a paper-wrapped knife from it.

The aide entered. Anami bowed. "Will you do me the honor of being my second?" he asked. "My soldiers have shamed me by defying the Emperor's will, and my country is disgraced by my Emperor's decision. It is time for me to die."

The aide, a major, stared at him in shock, but he remained loyal. "Are you sure, Minister?"

"I'm sure. Take a sword from that cabinet." The cabinet

contained a fine collection of traditional weapons. The chief of staff took out a katana and tested its edge against a piece of paper.

"Will you reconsider?" the chief asked again as Anami knelt, knees folded underneath him.

"I cannot. Death will be a blessed release. Please do not strike unless you see I am about to lose control and shame myself."

"Very well." The chief of staff took up a position behind the army minister and swung the sharp sword backward and up over his shoulder. "I am ready."

Anami was quiet for a moment, composing a death haiku, then spoke.

"Arrows spin. Wind blows./Control? Illusion. Except/In *yudaoshi*."

The chief of staff thought for a moment, then nodded. "Very true, Minister. Beautifully phrased. Thank you for the privilege of seconding you."

Both men were still as statues, yet the tension grew until Anami suddenly drove the knife into his abdomen with all the strength his two hands could muster, then sliced right and up. He gasped as the blade penetrated, but the pain was less than he expected. *Shock, probably,* he thought.

The pain began and then rose faster and faster. As it threatened to overwhelm him, he said, *"Now,"* through gritted teeth.

The sword slashed.

Darkness.

Endure the Unendurable

If I become a prisoner of war, I will keep faith with my fellow prisoners. I will give no information nor take part in any action that might be harmful to my comrades. If I am senior, I will take command. If not, I will obey the lawful orders of those appointed over me and will back them up in every way.

—*Code of Conduct for American Prisoners of War*

The soldier, above all other people, prays for peace, for he must suffer and bear the deepest wounds and scars.

—General Douglas MacArthur

TWENTY-THREE

Honshu, Japan; Tokyo

*APPROACHING HITACHI, HONSHU, JAPAN, 1853 HOURS
(OPERATION CORONET, Y-DAY + 2)*

Pete Rachwalski glowered at the bridge and the two hills looming beyond the concrete span as if his disappointment would translate into a weapon of war. "This son of a bitch is going to be one tough nut to crack," he growled.

Then he ducked as another barrage of enemy artillery shells smashed onto the roadway ahead of him. A shower of dirt blasted upward, and he pressed his face into the wet ground as the debris rattled down, spattering across his back and rattling on his helmet.

He, both his gunnery sergeants, and Captain Allen of the 117th Armored lay in a muddy ditch in the drizzling rain, watching three of Allen's Sherman tanks burn. Most of the crew had made it out of the last one, but the first two had gone up within a few seconds of each other, victims of a well-positioned Japanese antitank battery. The tanks had started to burn like Roman candles, and the couple of men who made it out of one had been machine-gunned to death almost as soon as their feet had touched the ground.

"I shoulda known it was too good to be true," Allen declared, shaking his head in disgust. "A paved road all the way to Tokyo with nothing more than an occasional machine gun nest. Yep. Too good to be true."

"Well, we made it halfway before they slowed us up," Pete replied. "We just have to figure out a way around this position."

"Easier said than done," the army captain replied.

He was right, of course. Pete's men had deployed for a quarter mile on either side of the road and brought back enough information for the two officers to realize that they had come up against a very well-prepared position. It was structured around the good concrete bridge that carried this highway across a rain-swollen river and was backed up by the first significant heights they had encountered in twenty miles. The road threaded a nasty gauntlet between those two hills, and the enemy had patiently waited to strike.

When the American column had approached, the Japs let the first three tanks across the bridge. Then they opened up with at least two concealed antitank guns, hitting two of the Sherman M4s almost simultaneously. The third had been knocked out as it tried to back across the bridge to safety. The three wrecked tanks not only reduced the company's strength but also formed an impromptu roadblock, preventing easy egress even if they could advance across the bridge.

Then the Japanese artillery had come down, medium-caliber shells that had scattered perfectly among the marines and the rest of the tanks. The men took shelter in these muddy ditches, and the tanks pulled off the road. The Americans had wanted to return fire, but none of the enemy guns was visible. Making matters worse, a thin drizzle of rain had been falling, soaking through everything. It was shaping up to be a lousy day.

Pete turned to his sergeants. "Miller, find out if there's any chance of getting air support. Rinehart, I want to know if the bridge is mined." Both the sergeants and Pete were pretty sure the answers were no and yes, respectively, but Pete had to be sure.

The Japs had created a real hornets' nest for any attacking troops. They had plenty of high ground for spotting, guns positioned for indirect fire, and a number of well-entrenched machine gun nests. Even if Pete's men could get across the bridge and past the three tanks, there were no guarantees they would be able to accomplish anything more than getting killed.

Miller was first back, duck-walking up the trench. "As far

as air support goes, Captain, not only no, but hell, no. Not unless it clears up."

"About what I expected," Pete said.

A few minutes later, Sergeant Rinehart came crawling through the brush to the right of the road. He dashed over a clear space at the edge of the ditch and rolled down next to the two officers. His words did nothing to improve Pete's outlook. "They've got the bridge mined, Captain," he reported. "I can see the charges, but there's no way to get close without taking a lot of machine gun fire. We'll lose men if we even try to take them out."

"All right. Then we'll have to send patrols around to the left and right, looking for a way around." He turned to Sergeant Miller. "You two feel up to a moonlight stroll?"

"Shit, Captain Ski," said Rinehart. "Can't see no moon in this weather."

"Yeah," Miller agreed. "But I always was a sucker for a walk in the rain."

• MONDAY, 24 SEPTEMBER 1945 •

**NASHVILLE, *OFFSHORE AT HIRATSUKA, KANAGAWA
PREFECTURE, HONSHU, JAPAN, 1230 HOURS
(OPERATION CORONET, Y-DAY + 3)***

"I don't want to hear about the damned surf conditions!" the Supreme Commander snapped at the major. The G-2 of 1/41, First Brigade, 41st Division, had just been transported at some difficulty through the rough waters around the flagship to make his report in person. "I want to hear how quickly and efficiently the landing force is assembling and preparing to move out!"

"Begging the General's pardon." The major took a breath but didn't show any sign of backing down before the display of imperial temper. MacArthur was too distressed even to take note of the man's courage. "We have five LCVs that broached—that is, came in sideways—"

"I know what broached means!"

"Sorry, General. And we lost their trucks. If we try bringing any of the larger ships in to the beaches, the hulls will smash—they might be broken apart, General. We can get some men ashore." He didn't mention that those men were soaking wet and exhausted from fighting the surf, or that several had already drowned in the dangerous beach conditions. "But if you order them to push inland, their only option right now is to *walk* to Tokyo."

"Then, Major, I hope they brought some good, sturdy footwear!" snapped MacArthur.

"Of course, General." The major stood at parade rest, his expression implacable.

The Supreme Commander took a deep breath. The delays were not this major's fault, he knew, nor were they the fault of any human. The typhoon was a wild card, utterly unpredictable, and now incredibly frustrating. It tossed them about like playthings, wreaked havoc with schedules, plans, organization.

"What about the enemy's resistance?" he pressed. "We didn't have the ships to do as heavy a bombardment as I would have liked. Most of the big guns are up with Patton! Did the Japanese lay down a barrage when you came ashore?"

"No barrage, sir. That's a case—Jap resistance, I mean—where the typhoon might have actually helped us out. They had some really big waves on those beaches just a day ago, General. We've come upon a lot of prepared positions that were simply washed out—machine gun nests filled with sand, revetments knocked over or eroded away. We found a whole battery of 105s that look like they were tossed around like kids' toys—lying on their sides, barrels filled up with sand. No sign of the gun crews anywhere. The deepest entrenchments are all filled with water. As a result, our prelanding bombardment killed a lot more of the enemy because the high water drove them out into the open."

"That, I suppose, is something. But I need to get my men ashore! And my trucks and guns and equipment!"

"I understand, sir. We're taking risks, sir, in the interest of speed."

MacArthur's eyes narrowed. "Very well. Proceed with all possible haste. I will be coming ashore myself, in a matter of hours—perhaps that will give the men some added inspiration."

"Yes, sir. I'm sure that it will, General."

MacArthur inspected the major's face for any hint of sarcasm in his last comment. Seeing none, the Supreme Commander made a dismissal gesture with his pipe. After the major left, MacArthur looked through the rain-soaked porthole at the gray sea. Whitecaps were everywhere. He could well imagine the difficulties in maneuvering small boats through that kind of surf. But dammit, he *had* to get ashore!

This was the residue of that damned typhoon. It was as if the Almighty were personally mocking MacArthur. *Why now? Why here? Why not with Patton?* With all his "no publicity" prattle, MacArthur was aware of how many journalists wanted to be with that foul-mouthed show-off, and he was sure—absolutely sure—some of them had wangled their way into his entourage. *Probably with his knowledge and help,* MacArthur thought.

The great storm still lurked out there, though it had weakened steadily. The meteorologists were telling him that it had shifted back to a northwesterly course, that it would wander off toward Siberia and leave northern Honshu unscathed.

And as for Patton and his diversion? There had been no real word, only the puffed-up coded reports that provided some exaggerated idea of where the man's armored spearheads were. If he were to believe the reports, the vanguard of XIII Corps was halfway to Tokyo, having covered more than fifty miles! That broadcasting was for the enemy's benefit, of course. It was intended to distract and confuse.

But—goddamn it!—MacArthur *needed* to be ashore.

IMPERIAL ARMY HEADQUARTERS, TOKYO, JAPAN, 1314 HOURS

Captain Ogawa Taiki, with Lieutenant Watanabe at his side, marched into the office of General Umezu, the army chief of staff. He saluted stiffly, bowed, and came to attention. "Captain Ogawa reporting as ordered, sir. The general suggested I bring along a man I could trust. Lieutenant Watanabe is a fine young officer. We both served at Camp Shinjuku until it became clear that we were needed here."

"Yes, good men, both of you." Umezu waved at them with a distracted air, and they both relaxed enough to stand at ease.

Ogawa, scrutinizing the great general, was surprised by the change in the army chief of staff. Umezu had been angry, furious almost beyond the point of control, when they had listened to him in the auditorium the previous day. Now, that anger was gone, replaced with what looked like fatigue.

Or—and this was confirmed by a whiff of sweet fermentation, coming from the other side of the general's desk—he was drunk.

Probably he was exhausted *and* drunk, the captain decided. And with some good reason. The disgrace that had been ordered upon the Imperial Japanese Army was unprecedented, even beyond comprehension. *Surrender.* It was not a word that Ogawa had ever expected to hear, not when it was included in the phrasing of one of his own orders. Yet hear it he had.

Every unit of the Imperial Japanese Army that still maintained a communications link with Tokyo had received the order only a few short hours ago. The troops of Nippon were to capitulate, to lay down their weapons and to turn themselves over to the Americans. With that unspeakable order had come the news that General Anami had committed seppuku. The implication was that any officer whose honor required it was permitted, even encouraged, to take the same step.

"Captain Ogawa . . . and Lieutenant Yoshi," Umezu said, his words slow and slurred, "I am an old man and have played my role. If it has not turned out necessarily to my expectations, that is karma. Now I must complete my destiny, and my life can reach its close. You also have your own responsibilities—for there are acts for old men and acts for young men."

"Yes, General. We are unworthy to know your wishes but would be honored for any insights you would wish to share with us," Ogawa promised sincerely.

"You know about the shameful order issued to all units of the army, of course. But did you know, the same order—purportedly in the Emperor's own voice, his own words—is to be broadcast to the people over the radio?"

"Sir!" Ogawa declared, shocked. "The Emperor has never stooped to the indignity of speaking directly to his subjects!"

"Of course not. I believe, myself, that this is some cruel hoax. However that may be, the speech has already been recorded." Umezu looked at Ogawa sharply.

The captain lowered his head, ashamed. "My miserable intellect is unable to perceive the general's meaning," he admitted abjectly. "Recorded?"

"Yes. A record was made, with a recording machine," the chief of staff continued impatiently. "That record is now stored in the Imperial Palace. It is to be broadcast sometime tomorrow."

"Tomorrow?" Ogawa struggled to keep up, and in a flash he understood. "But that cannot be allowed to happen!" he protested strongly, only after a moment adding, "Sir!"

"No, it cannot," Umezu agreed. His eyes narrowed as he looked first at Captain Ogawa, then at Lieutenant Watanabe. The general nodded, correctly interpreting the grim determination he perceived in these young officers.

"It gladdens my heart to see that you understand me," the general said. "Now, leave me in peace." He gestured again, and this time he seemed to be very drunk, though he had imbibed nothing since Ogawa had entered the room. His eyes were dim, unfocused, as he slurred his final words. "May the gods be with you."

APPROACHING HITACHI, HONSHU, JAPAN, 1422 HOURS (OPERATION CORONET, Y-DAY + 3)

"They knew what they were doin', sir," reported Gunnery Sergeant Miller. He had just returned from an eighteen-hour reconnaissance, an attempt to find a way around the stubborn position that was blocking the road. "That hill over there is chock-full of caves, and each cave is chock-full of Japs. And beyond it is a ridge, and that ridge looks to be manned with the better part of a division. There's a couple of small bridges up the valley, but they got good fields of fire on all of 'em. And one'll get you ten that every one of the SOBs is mined."

Pete grimaced and nodded. Rinehart had reported back an hour earlier, with the news that the river before them grew larger and more rapid as it flowed toward the sea. His recon had taken him some ten miles, and he hadn't encountered another intact bridge. Ironically, a few spans had existed across that water not too long ago, but they had all been destroyed by American air attacks.

"Air power is still grounded," Captain Allen, returning from the radio jeep, reported. "If you can even call it 'grounded' when you can't take off from an aircraft carrier."

Pete met his eyes. "Well, looks like we do this the hard way, or we don't do it at all. Any word on the cavalry?"

"There's two more companies of tanks coming down the road. The first one is maybe twenty minutes out and the second one should be here in an hour. At least when they get here we'll give the Japs a few more targets."

"We'll have to try all the bridges at once," the marine captain reflected grimly. There was no other prospect before them. His men would try to disable the charges, of course, and some of them would get killed doing it. *And* they'd lose the bridge when the explosives went off. It was an ugly, painful prospect, and he wasn't sure he could bring himself to give the order.

"Hey, Cap'n. Take a look at this!" The normally unflappable Gunnery Sergeant Rinehart actually sounded excited, calling back from his observation post behind a Sherman tank.

"What is it, Gunny?" Pete asked, advancing to where the sergeant was peering into the murky afternoon. Two Japanese soldiers were on the other side of the river, advancing hesitantly toward the bridge. One of them held a stick high; a dirty white cloth was draped from the end of the makeshift pole.

"I ain't sure, Captain Ski. But it looks a hell of a lot like a white flag."

Pete snorted in contempt. "You mean, like they're surrendering? It's *gotta* be a trap."

"You want me to shoot the fuckers, Cap'n? I can take 'em both from here."

The urge to say yes was almost instinctive, but something held his tongue. Pete raised his binoculars and studied the two men. They looked like officers and were apparently unarmed. That didn't fool him—he'd seen more than one "unarmed" Jap suddenly pull out a grenade or a pistol. Still, this was strange.

"Keep your finger on that trigger, Gunny," he said finally. He stood up and stepped out from behind the tank. "I'll go see what this is all about."

OUTSIDE THE IMPERIAL PALACE, TOKYO, JAPAN, 1800 HOURS

Kojima Masahiro was stooped, bent, and old. But he still walked ten or twelve miles every day. Those miles kept him alive, for they gave him the means to explore the ruins of his burned, battered city. Those explorations invariably yielded him some tiny portion of food or some treasure that could be bartered for food.

Now he poked a stick through the piles of ashes, stirring them up in hopes of finding something metal, something he could sell for food. He was hungry and his feet hurt all the time. When the hunger became intolerable, he let himself focus on the constant excruciating pain in his swollen and misshapen feet, scarred and missing toes. When the feet became intolerable, he imagined a simple meal, a bowl of rice and maybe some sweet potatoes.

But there was nothing in the ruins of this house. On to the next he shambled, a wandering speck in the wilderness of ashes that had once been a vibrant community, hunting for metal, waiting eagerly for death to overtake him so that he might be reborn in happier times and might see his beloved Hayashi again. Here he poked through the ashes and made the effort to bend down so that he could see into the hollow space beneath a charred beam that had fallen but had not quite come to rest upon the ground.

A spot of whiteness caught his eye, and he reached in his hand to pull out—miracle of miracles!—a bone china teacup, somehow uncracked. This was a good omen, he knew, a treasure worth more than several days' worth of food. He cradled it to his chest, breathing hard from the exertion as he stood back up. Where to go—he had to enjoy this treasure, to take some time to reflect upon his wonderful good luck.

He knew just the place. The area around the Imperial Palace had not been burned, and several of the great gardens surrounding the Emperor's castle were verdant and peaceful, still beautiful even in the midst of war. Hobbling along with the teacup clutched to his chest, he made his way to the Higashi Gyoen, the East Garden. Passing beneath the willow and evergreen trees, he found a small bench beside a pool and sat down for a few minutes' quiet meditation.

But his wish for quiet was denied. He heard the rumble before he saw the column: war machines moving in single file along what once had been a street, a paved area between two empty lots of ash. They came into view quickly, moving unusually fast for vehicles in the city.

First came two Black Medal reconnaissance cars, followed by two Hokoku armored cars. Two machine guns bristled from the turret of each armored car. Masahiro knew his vehicles. He had been a factory worker and had helped build many cars and trucks. Like the column of old Nissan 97 four-by-two trucks, each filled with soldiers. Masahiro might even have built part of one of them. It was the right age.

He counted ten trucks, each carrying a platoon of twelve men plus sergeant and lieutenant. Then a staff car, an old

Nissan 70 he might have helped assemble as well. Bringing up the rear were four more armored cars and another Black Medal.

It was not unusual to see such a procession. It was unusual to see a procession heading in the direction of Chiyoda-ku, the central part of Tokyo. That wasn't in the direction of the enemy. Instead, they turned to drive right through the park and over a beautiful arched wooden bridge, traveling in the direction of the Imperial Palace.

APPROACHING HITACHI, HONSHU, JAPAN, 1842 HOURS (OPERATION CORONET, Y-DAY+3)

Major Greg Yamada had been a dozen miles south of Iwaki when he got the radio call—they needed a translator at the front, ASAP. He held on for dear life as his driver raced the jeep down the highway toward Tokyo. Less than twenty minutes later they came up behind a file of Sherman tanks parked alongside the road. A big marine gunnery sergeant with a Thompson submachine gun strapped from his shoulder stepped into the road and waved him down.

"Can I help you, sir?" he asked. Yamada, who was fully accustomed to the inevitable stares and frequent hostility from troops, and especially marines, wondered if the fellow had even noticed his features. The man's expression didn't change as the major climbed from the jeep as it rolled to a stop; this was both unusual and pleasant.

"Yes, Gunny," he said. "I heard you wanted a translator down here. That would be me."

"Right this way, sir. Captain Ski has a couple of Japs who turned themselves in. He thinks they're trying to tell us something."

"Prisoners? They turned themselves in?" Yamada was already intrigued.

"Yes, sir, it's weird. But here they are."

Five minutes later Yamada was on the radio with the biggest intelligence coup he'd ever had to report. He could hardly keep his hand from shaking as he held the mike, and pressed the "Speak" button.

SWPA FORWARD HQ, HIRATSUKA, KANAGAWA PREFECTURE, HONSHU, JAPAN, 1830 HOURS (OPERATION CORONET, Y-DAY + 3)

There were no photographers as General Douglas Mac-Arthur waded onto the shore of Honshu, and it was a good thing, too, because a monster wave knocked him on his ass as soon as he stepped off the landing craft. Frantic sailors and GIs pulled him dripping from the surf and up onto the beach, where he shook off the assisting hands and looked around.

"How soon until we can get trucks ashore?" he asked.

The same major who had reported to him on the *Nashville* was here with an updated status report. "General, we have secured a small port just a few miles south of here, a place called Togane. It's secure, and it has a concrete wharf and a working crane. We're pulling some of the freighters in there now and should be offloading transport within the hour."

Within the hour. Why did that seem like half a lifetime from now?

Because of George S. Patton, that's why. The Supreme Commander stood tall and let that information sink in. "Very good. Well done, Major."

"Thank you, sir!" sputtered the intelligence officer, obviously surprised by the praise.

The General turned to another officer, a one-star in charge of one of the 41st Division brigades. His men had been among the first ashore. "What is the situation vis-à-vis the enemy?"

"Sir, that's a little strange—but not bad news, at least so far as we can tell. They seem to have abandoned their positions along here, even the ones that weren't flooded by the storm. I don't know if they're trying to lure us into a trap, but we're following up as quickly as common sense will allow."

"Very good," the Supreme Commander repeated.

Indeed, it seemed that, at last, things were well in hand.

IMPERIAL PALACE, TOKYO, JAPAN, 1900 HOURS

The Emperor's valet was helping him into formal robes of state when the Marquis Kido found him.

"Emperor—" Kido began, but the Emperor raised a hand.

"Soldiers have crossed the Nijubashi Bridge. We know. Shortly they'll have control of the palace."

"It's not too late—"

"It is too late, my dear friend. By recording Our message of peace, We have earned the enmity of these soldiers. They will seek to impose their will on Us, to make Us change the proclamation and continue the war."

"That's why you have to get away," Kido said.

"That's why *you* have to get away. To Nikko," the Emperor said. "Our brother Prince Chichibu is next in line for the Chrysanthemum Throne, and as he has no male issue, Our son Akihito follows him."

"Of course, sire." The Emperor's young son Akihito, twelve years old, had been sent to the town of Nikko, where the first of the Tokugawa shoguns was buried, for his safety. "I will take Prince Chichibu and we will both head for Nikko. It is the army that is in rebellion; perhaps Yamamoto will find a naval escort for the heirs. But staying here, confronting those soldiers . . ." His voice trailed off and he looked at his Emperor and friend with a quizzical expression.

"We are still Emperor. We are still descended from Amaterasu Herself. They will not dare touch a hair on Our head, except"—he paused, a determined expression flitting across his face—"except by sheerest accident. But Our son could be used as a hostage against Us. Yes, Yamamoto is a good choice to protect the line of Imperial succession. He has been Our loyal subject. Let him help you discharge this responsibility."

There was another reason, a reason the Emperor left unspoken. Now that the Americans were here, in their anger they would seek revenge. As they were doing in Germany, they would identify "war criminals," convict them, no doubt hang some and imprison others.

The Son of Heaven cannot possibly become a "war criminal." That is not merely unendurable, it is unspeakable, thought Hirohito.

Ogawa felt almost blasphemous as he led his company into the Imperial Residence. Lieutenant Watanabe trailed immediately behind him. Both officers, with a hundred or so men accompanying them, advanced at a trot. The few remaining servants either scurried out of the way or bowed submissively. Those who bowed were taken by small detachments of soldiers and marched quickly to the holding area set up in the East Garden.

Four Imperial Guards stood sentry flanking the double sliding doors to the Emperor's private quarters. They wore the special Imperial Guard uniform: dark blue tunics with red breeches, red kepis, and the white chrysanthemum insignia of the Emperor. They stood at rigid attention; their rifles were at order arms.

"Please stand aside. We wish to see His Imperial Majesty," Ogawa said.

"We regret to inform the captain that His Imperial Majesty cannot at this time be disturbed," said the guard on the left.

"I am so sorry, but I must insist," Ogawa said.

"It is with deep sorrow that we are unable at this time to fulfill the captain's wishes in this matter."

The captain nodded. "Very well. Most honorable guards, it is regrettable that I must see the Emperor." He gestured toward Watanabe's men. "We will see Him. Will you move aside?"

"We regret that the captain's wishes cannot be fulfilled."

Ogawa turned to Watanabe. "We must see His Imperial Majesty. Please proceed through that door, even if regrettable actions should prove necessary."

"As you command, sir," Watanabe replied. He gestured to the first rank of six men to kneel. The kneeling men and the six or eight standing behind them aimed their rifles at the guards. Ogawa stepped back next to Watanabe, both men safely outside the line of fire. The Imperial Guards raised their rifles to port arms.

"Please withdraw and allow this meeting with His Majesty to take place," Ogawa asked once more.

"It is forbidden," replied the guard on the left.

Ogawa started to give the commands to his men. On "Take aim!" the Imperial Guards dropped to their knees, lifted their own rifles, and opened fire. Ogawa remained with his men, ordering them to "Fire!"

Several bullets of the first volley went high, tearing through the door behind the guards, and Ogawa's men had to fire a second time. In spite of repeated wounds, the guards continued to fight, and when the shooting stopped, six of the captain's own men were wounded, two critically.

"Sergeant Kawazoe, move the wounded to safety and remove the dead," Ogawa ordered. "Sergeant Akimoto, bring the first squad of the second platoon and follow me." Watanabe followed behind Ogawa's men.

Ogawa stepped forward, put his hands on the double sliding shoji doors, now rent with bullets, and pulled them open. *"He?"* What? Startled, he first questioned what he saw, and then, *"Kuso!"* Shit! "Lieutenant Watanabe! Hurry!"

The young officer pushed his way through the enlisted men. When he reached Ogawa's side and looked down, his eyes widened, and he whispered *"kuso!"* as well.

The Showa Emperor, in formal kimono, was bleeding from multiple bullet wounds, his life quickly draining away. He had been standing directly behind the shoji doors. He looked up at Ogawa and whispered, "Now We need not endure the unendurable any longer," and then closed his eyes.

The captain didn't have to take a pulse to know that the Showa Emperor was dead.

"We are disgraced," Ogawa whispered. His world seemed to tilt crazily as he struggled to stand at attention, to grapple with his disbelief over what he, and the men under his command, had just done.

Lieutenant Watanabe was pale with shock. With a moan, he sank to his knees and fell forward to brace himself upon his hands. He dropped his forehead to the ground near the Emperor's foot, his shoulders shaking with his sobs.

No other soldier moved.

TWENTY-FOUR

Coast of Honshu; Tokyo

• TUESDAY, 25 SEPTEMBER 1945 •

HIRATSUKA, KANAGAWA PREFECTURE, HONSHU, JAPAN, 0336 HOURS (OPERATION CORONET, Y-DAY + 4)

The dream stubbornly refused to fade. He was being attacked from every direction, and his hands were peculiarly useless—not bound, exactly, but limp at his sides. When he tried to move them, each limb seemed to weigh upward of a ton, and he could not fend off the relentless onslaughts.

Although his foes were legion, they were strangely lacking in shape and form. He wanted to protest, to demand an explanation, redress. But his mouth and tongue, when he tried to talk, could stammer only gibberish.

It was the harsh beam of the flashlight shining directly into his face that finally broke through his stubborn sleep. He swatted a suddenly responsive hand at it and the light obligingly moved away. Even then, it seemed to take a long time before Douglas MacArthur could calm his breathing, bring his rampaging emotions under control, and slowly force himself to wake up.

"What?" MacArthur demanded, when consciousness had finally returned. Another interval passed as he worked to lift his torso, to prop himself up on his elbows. And then it was like a switch had been turned on: his confusion was gone; he knew that he was in a roadside inn some eight miles inland from the coast. The place had been requisitioned as his overnight headquarters while his transport-strapped armies tried to close on the enemy capital. "Why did you wake me?"

"There's been a palace coup," Willoughby said, his German accent thickening with excitement. "We have intercepted a number of broadcasts over the last ninety minutes—many of them uncoded. It appears that Hirohito is dead, and the enemy government has been thrown into some confusion. The army is announcing that the surrender is a hoax and that all units are to fight to the end. The navy is announcing that all troops are to lay down their arms, by command of the Emperor—but the order was issued before Hirohito was killed. The prime minister, Prince Konoe, is announcing that Hirohito's brother Prince Chichibu is the new Emperor. Chichibu will also get custody of Hirohito's twelve-year-old son."

"Who's got the boy now?" MacArthur asked.

"The lord privy seal, Marquis Kido. He's a real power behind the throne."

"Yes, I know. I met him some years back with my father. He and Hirohito were very close. Where are they, or do we know?" MacArthur asked.

"Yamamoto, the war minister, claims they're safe. There's a recording made by Hirohito that everybody wants, and the radio station seems to be the *schwerpunkt,* the decisive point of this battle. There's going to be blood in the streets, I think—quite possibly even civil war."

MacArthur rose from the bed, energized, thinking. Willoughby obligingly held up a silk dressing gown. The Supreme Commander slipped his arms through the sleeves of the robe and absently pulled it closed around his chest as he paced across the room. Though it was the largest room in the hotel, it was still a small space. He could take only a few strides before he was forced to reverse course.

His mind worked through details, analyzing the new developments. The surrender news had reached him the previous afternoon, first in a broadcast from a very skeptical

George Patton. An hour later, advance units of the First Marine Division had reported that the enemy troops in front of their positions were laying down their arms and turning themselves in. Not long after that—and not far away from the initial surrenders—a column of the Seventh Infantry had been savagely mauled as it marched into a well-planned ambush on the road to Tokyo.

"The weather?" asked MacArthur.

"Still improving, General. But not fast enough."

"I know. I can see that." Looking out the window, over the small balcony, MacArthur could see clouds scudding across the sky, stars glimmering between them. But the speed of their movement indicated a powerful wind, and wind was the enemy of the troops still waiting to land on the storm-lashed coast.

The skies were continuing to clear as the typhoon moved off to the northwest. Even though both of the General's armies had seized several small ports, there had been so much storm damage at those installations that the offloading of heavy equipment was proceeding at only a snail's pace.

"Are we still awaiting the trucks and the rest of our transport?" the General demanded.

"Yes, sir. The surf has settled some, but it will be morning or midday before we can even begin to bring vehicles ashore on the beaches."

MacArthur sat down on the edge of the bed and propped his chin with his arm resting on one knee. He sighed. He knew the order he had to issue, though it was gall in his mouth.

"Radio Patton. Tell him that he must get to Tokyo with all possible speed. Support the new Emperor. Get that surrender message out. And order the First and Eighth armies to continue advancing on the double—on foot, until their trucks can catch up with them. Try to take surrenders whenever possible, but if the Japanese fight, then fight back. Awaken the headquarters staff, too—I want us to move out within the hour."

"Very well, General. Preparations for our departure are already under way. I will go now. Sorry to have awakened you, sir."

MacArthur waved him away. He was back on his feet, still

pacing, thinking, eager to be on the move, when his valet arrived thirty seconds later with his uniform, cap, and—strangely, in the predawn darkness—a new pair of sunglasses.

IMPERIAL PALACE, TOKYO, JAPAN, 0355 HOURS

Captain Ogawa Taiki stepped over the bodies of his men. More than three dozen corpses lay on the grounds of one of the palace gardens, neatly laid out in the rows where they had taken their lives. Only a few of the participants in the ill-omened raid were still alive. Some had elected to go home first, or perform some other necessary acts before dying. Perhaps there might be one or two dishonorable cowards who would simply run away to vanish into the growing chaos that was Japan.

Ogawa was the only surviving officer. Watanabe had blown his brains out almost as soon as he realized what had happened, and several hours earlier the captain had served as second for those among the junior ranks who wished to die immediately. It had been a hard task; without his sword, he had administered a killing shot to each man who committed traditional seppuku. For those without a knife, he stood by in case their bullet to the brain did not result in rapid death.

Afterward, he had wandered aimlessly through the halls, the gardens, and the courtyards of the great Imperial Palace. He knew that the place was not abandoned, but nobody interfered with his restless pacing or tried to accost him. His thigh wound, that almost forgotten stab from the ridge on Guadalcanal, had flared up with burning pain, but Ogawa had not allowed himself to limp. Instead, he endured the agony of each step as necessary, albeit only preliminary, punishment for his unspeakable crime.

He and his men had unwittingly slain a god, the Son of Heaven himself.

After an unknown time, he had returned to the scene of the tragic mistake to find that some people—servants, presumably—had quietly come to remove Hirohito's body. Ogawa was glad for that. He had been unwilling to touch the lifeless form—in truth, he was unworthy to commit such a blasphemous act—but he had not wanted the Emperor to lie where he had died. At least that minor detail had been attended to.

Now he was the last man standing. He would go without the help of a second, knowing he was unworthy of a traditional death. A bullet would suffice for him, as it had for so many of his men.

It was finally time. He lifted his Nambu service pistol to his head and looked one more time at the neat, still shapes that had been his men. He was ready to join them.

At the very last minute, a disturbing question occurred to him. Should he shoot himself in the mouth or underneath his chin? Perhaps in the temple? He couldn't be sure, but he suspected that a bullet in the mouth was the most likely to be fatal. Opening his jaws, he laid the barrel on his tongue, tasting the cold, slightly acidic metal.

He fired. A sharp sound, then darkness.

After a time there was light again, followed by excruciating pain. His lungs, as if in direct challenge of his intentions, strained to draw breath, and air somehow seeped through the blood and torn flesh that gurgled in his throat. The bullet had been too low, Ogawa could tell—it had emerged from the back of his neck without lodging in his brain.

Ogawa wept bitter tears. He had failed at even this task! Desperately he tried to grope for the pistol, to make a second shot.

It was then that he realized he could no longer move his arms or his legs.

**SOUTH OF HITACHI, HONSHU, JAPAN, 0622 HOURS
(OPERATION CORONET, Y-DAY + 4)**

The column of Sherman tanks, each M4 with five or six marines sitting on the hull, moved at a measured pace past Hitachi and proceeded down the road toward Tokyo. Major Greg Yamada sat on the lead tank next to the man they called Captain Ski, Captain Pete Rachwalski, USMC. The two officers

warily eyed the ridge on the inland side of the road and instinctively ducked at the sound of an engine backfire. Still,
there had been no shots since they had moved out at first daylight.

Yamada had thoroughly interrogated the Japanese lieutenant colonel who had commanded the defensive position
at the bridge. The man's troops had been inexperienced and
underarmed, but he had sited his two antitank guns and six
machine guns exactly at the right position to stop a column
moving down the road. When the marines had come back
from inspecting the positions, their faces had been gray.
They knew that many would have died if they had tried to
storm across the river.

The colonel had informed Yamada that he had received the
order to surrender over the Imperial Japanese Army channel
of communications. He and his men had been only too glad
to lay down their arms, and the nisei major from G-2 had
quickly understood why. They were mainly simple farmers
and laborers called up to serve in this civil defense battalion.
If they had followed their orders to fight and die here, they
would have inevitably called down destruction on the neighboring village, which is where most of them lived. For them,
as well as for the marines and the tankers, the war could not
have ended soon enough.

After the two companies—Rachwalski's marines riding
on Allen's tanks—had proceeded cautiously over the bridge
and through the defile, Yamada had concluded that the surrender was real, at least on the part of this one local unit. As
to whether or not the regular army troops would honor the
same orders, he readily admitted to both captains that he
could not be sure.

As a consequence, they advanced as if they were still on a
combat mission. Captain Allen rode in a jeep following just
behind the four lead tanks. The rest of the Shermans rumbled
along behind them, followed by the trucks and half-tracks
that constituted the rest of Company D. Each tank's commander rode high in the turret, the hatches open so that they
could get a good look around. Some of the tanks' main gun

barrels were trained down the road, while others were canted to the right or the left. Marines held their carbines and Tommy guns at the ready but displayed admirable fire discipline—there were no stray shots from jumpy fingers on the triggers.

"It's like the whole goddamn country is holding its breath," Rachwalski observed.

"Yeah," Yamada agreed. "Let's hope we can all exhale pretty soon, before anything else blows up."

"Captain! Captain Ski!" The shout, barely audible over the engines and road noise, came from behind them. They turned to see a sergeant on the next tank back waving and gesturing still farther behind on the road.

Yamada looked back past the column of Allen's armor and was startled to see that a lot more vehicles were back there than had been following them just a few minutes ago. Edging his way past the turret to the front deck of the tank, the major shouted at the company commander in the jeep directly ahead of him to get his attention.

"Captain!" he shouted, gestured to the road behind them. "We've got company!"

Whether or not Allen could hear what he was saying over the rumbling of the tank engines—it seemed unlikely—the captain understood what he was trying to communicate. Allen waved the company over to the side and stood up in his jeep to get a look behind as the M4s growled to a halt.

The overtaking column continued toward them quickly. It clearly consisted of more American tanks—the big, hump-backed Shermans were unmistakable—and as it drew closer they could see a jeep leading the way. The little vehicle was racing down the highway with almost reckless abandon, and when it got closer still, they saw a flag with four stars flying from the front fender. At least thirty or forty tanks rolled behind it, the whole group charging along at nearly top speed.

"Looks like your boss is coming," Captain Rachwalski shouted with a grin. He had come to the back of the tank after Yamada. The engine was idling now, so they could converse merely by raising their voices.

"Looks that way to me, too," the major admitted as the tank came to a halt. "Though, as I recall, you're working for him too, at the present."

"Aye aye, sir," said the marine, still smiling.

Yamada and Rachwalski hopped to the ground and joined Captain Allen in saluting smartly as General Patton's jeep rolled up and squeaked to a hasty stop. The CO of XIII Corps stood up in the passenger seat and was instantly recognizable—they had all seen dozens of pictures of him in *Stars and Stripes*—even before they saw the polished helmet and, the, twin, ivory-handled pistols, like a pair of Gene Autry's six-guns, hanging in holsters at Patton's belt.

"Hello, General," Allen barked. "Welcome to Company D of the 117th!"

"As you were," declared Patton, casually saluting but remaining standing in his jeep, his hands braced on the top of the windshield. His voice was surprisingly high-pitched. "Are you the men who took that surrender yesterday evening?"

"Yes, sir!"

"Nice bit of work—goddamn fine work!" declared the general, smiling broadly for a second. Then his craggy visage creased into a scowl. "But now, you're going too fucking slow!"

"Sir?" queried Captain Allen.

"We've got orders to get to Tokyo as fast as we can. You fellows were in the vanguard, but looks like you'll be following me for the rest of the way." Patton was smiling again, an expression of almost childish delight. "Tell me, are you ready to make some tracks?"

"Yes, sir, General!"

Patton's eyes wandered over to Yamada and narrowed. "You're the translator, right? From Colonel Koch's section? The one who reported back after talking to the prisoners?"

"Yes, General. That was me."

"Not bad work, boys. Almost good enough to have been Third Army," Patton said with a grin. All three officers took that for the high praise Patton intended. He waved toward the back of his jeep. "Hop in, Major . . . ah . . . Yamada. I might need to do a little parleying when we get down to the Imperial Palace."

"Very good, sir," the major replied, hastening to scramble over the rear fender of the jeep, wedging onto the small seat beside a captain who moved over just enough to give him room.

"You men pick up the pace," the general said, waving to Allen and Rachwalski. "We'll see you in Tokyo!"

"Yes, sir!" both captains replied, but their answers were lost in the roar of the engine and the rising cloud of dust as the command jeep accelerated down the road.

SOUTH OF MT. NIKKO, JAPAN, 0713 HOURS

A convoy of Nissan 70s filled with heavily armed Imperial Guards, with motorcycles taking point and rear, sped in the direction of Tokyo. The roads were of variable quality, and for stretches of miles the cars would bump and jostle their passengers unmercifully. During the early morning hours they had passed through small, sleepy towns like Kazo, Omiya, and—as dawn was coloring the sky—Kawaguchi. They had encountered no other vehicles throughout the seventy-mile drive, descending from the high country toward the Kanto Plain and the great capital city.

Lord Privy Seal Marquis Koichi Kido and the Emperor formerly known as Prince Chichibu rode together in a car indistinguishable from the rest. Kido understood the logic of the anonymous vehicle. It was important to keep their actual location a secret, because there were people—mainly young officers of the Imperial Japanese Army—who would not stop short of murder in order to see that this war continued. Young Akihito, Hirohito's son and the next in line of succession after the new Emperor, rode in a different car several spaces farther back in the convoy.

The marquis clutched the handle on the interior of the door as the convoy careened around a surprisingly sharp curve. Kido well understood the gravity of the situation. The Showa Emperor was dead. Before he had been killed, he had ordered a surrender of all the armed forces, and that order had been broadcast to all units of the Imperial Japanese Army and the Imperial Japanese Navy. Many units had laid down their arms. But some army officers were resisting.

And the people of Nippon had yet to hear their Emperor's final command.

The lord privy seal's hand closed around the envelope he had been gingerly cradling, ever since Yamamoto had brought it to him nearly ten hours before. It was a recording, the last official words—the last command—of the Showa Emperor.

After the attack on the palace, Yamamoto and Kido had escaped with the precious record, speeding into the country-side north of Tokyo, climbing the winding roads leading into the mountains, to the town of Nikko. This was where young Akihito had been sent earlier in the war for his own safety. Akihito's uncle, his father's younger brother Chichibu, lived there as well.

Yamamoto and his convoy had arrived at the royal residence before midnight, but it had taken several hours for the new Emperor and his nephew to recover from the shock of recent developments—the news of the Emperor's death had not reached them until the war minister's arrival—and to prepare themselves for the trip to the capital. Finally they had gotten onto the road, racing back to the city through the predawn hours.

With guards alert in every vehicle, the column now pulled into Tokyo. War Minister Yamamoto, in the lead Nissan 70, guided them to the Imperial Radio Complex. This official government installation was the central broadcast facility, backed up by a powerful transmitter and several tall antennas. By some stroke of fortune, it had escaped serious damage during the war.

They pulled up before the sprawling pagoda-shaped building. Yamamoto's people were in control. The whole installation was surrounded by armed men wearing the uniforms of the Special Naval Landing Forces—elite fighters who, like the United States Marines, functioned as soldiers under the command of the navy. These Imperial Japanese

Marines stood aside as Yamamoto, Kido, the Emperor, and young Akihito climbed the front steps of the building.

"Do you wish to come in with us, War Minister?" asked the lord privy seal. He still held the envelope containing the recording of the Emperor's first—and last—address to his people.

"I will stay here, with my troops," Yamamoto replied. "In case . . ."

"I understand," said Kido. "Good luck to you."

"And to you," the war minister replied. The two men bowed formally to each other.

Accompanied by a dozen bodyguards carrying light sub-machine guns, the lord privy seal turned and followed the royal party into the building.

Yamamoto had known that the army would come. First he heard the rumble of truck motors, and soon a convoy of vehicles raced around the corner and came to a halt before the unwavering line of SNLF troops. A light tank rumbled at the rear of the column, its tiny gun swiveling toward the building as more than a hundred soldiers spilled out of the trucks to form a menacing skirmish line facing Yamamoto and the radio building.

An officer got out of the cab of the lead truck and Yamamoto recognized General Umezu.

"Stand aside, War Minister!" demanded the army chief of staff. "I have business in this building."

"I am so sorry, Army Chief of Staff, but how can I permit the assassin of the Showa Emperor to enter the presence of the Son of Heaven?" asked Yamamoto calmly. He could see the looks of consternation on the soldiers accompanying Umezu. Apparently word of the previous night's events had not yet disseminated through the ranks. One young soldier, especially, grew pale and looked askance at the army chief of staff, and then at Yamamoto. Clearly he was wondering whom to believe.

"Those who led the Son of Heaven astray are the ones guilty of the Emperor's sad and unfortunate passing," retorted the general, taking a step forward, halting only as several of Yamamoto's marines loudly cocked their weapons.

"Is that so, General? Is the Emperor *baka,* then? You were there when he ordered the Supreme Council on the Direction of the War to accept the declaration of the Allied nations." More shocked reactions from soldiers and Japanese marines alike. Using the word "stupid" to describe the Emperor was an unheard-of blasphemy.

"Of *course* the Emperor isn't *baka!* He was misled!"

"Misled? And as a result, Army Chief of Staff, you sent armed troops into the Imperial Palace to assassinate the Son of Heaven. The gods look down on you in shame and disgust, Umezu. You are a nonperson. You are lower than *burakumin.*"

Umezu screamed, "Lies! I did not order his murder! It was an accident!"

The SNLF troops standing to each side of Yamamoto raised their machine pistols to firing position, training the weapons on the infuriated general. More soldiers gaped in disbelief at Umezu. Many of their guns wavered as they were reluctant to train them upon the highly esteemed admiral.

"Lay down your weapons," Yamamoto called out to the soldiers. "I speak in the Emperor's name, not for the Emperor's assassin."

"I am not the Emperor's assassin! It was an accident!" Umezu shrieked, his face contorted with fury.

"Accidents happen," Yamamoto agreed, still in that conversational tone. He gestured at the men of the Naval Landing Force and shrugged.

"But you should understand that if these men are forced to shoot, they will kill you very much on purpose."

Before the general could articulate a reply, static sputtered in the external speakers. The station was beginning to broadcast.

Twenty minutes later, it was all over.

The late Emperor had spoken from the grave. His voice, strange and high-pitched and in an ancient court dialect some of his people could barely understand, emerged with remarkable fidelity from the phonograph record. The radio signal was broadcast to the whole country and was played via loudspeakers mounted on the front of the radio installation. The army and navy troops alike stood at attention and listened.

"We, the people of Japan, have endured many terrible attacks and much overwhelming sadness," the Showa Emperor said. "Our cities have been burned, our soldiers and sailors slaughtered in their devotion to Our throne. Much has developed during this war that has not proceeded necessarily to our advantage. In these last days, even the Divine Wind has turned against us."

The voice of the Showa Emperor continued, declaring that the Japanese would accept the terms of the Allies' Potsdam Declaration.

Then the new Emperor, the former Prince Chichibu, came on live to say, "We endorse the policies and decisions of Our brother the Showa Emperor with respect to this message and request all citizens of Our empire, military and civilian alike, to follow these decisions likewise."

Then came the young Akihito, whose reign name, Heisei, had been chosen by his father long ago. He repeated what his uncle the Emperor had said in a confident tone that belied his years.

Even before the young heir had finished speaking, Umezu had climbed back into his truck and gone, accompanied by a few—a very small number—of his most loyal troops. As for the rest of the soldiers, hearing the voices of three gods had turned the day. They laid down their arms and told Yamamoto that they would obey the wishes of the Emperor.

TOKYO SUBURBS, JAPAN, 0902 HOURS (OPERATION CORONET, Y-DAY + 4)

The great column of olive-drab vehicles, with George Patton's jeep still in the lead, roared down the paved highway leading to the capital. Major Greg Yamada sat in the backseat, holding on for dear life. The other Americans in their tanks, jeeps, and half-tracks warily regarded the Japanese civilians who emerged from their towns and villages to watch the column pass.

The citizens came to stand beside the road, lining up like it was a parade route. Their expressions ranged from curious to apprehensive, but Yamada was surprised to see no evidence of resentment or hostility. The Japanese invariably bowed as the Americans rolled by. Nevertheless, that sign of respect—or submission—didn't keep the soldiers and marines from having fingers ready on their triggers. Once again the discipline held, however, and the conqueror's column rolled on with no shooting on either side.

As word of the surrender and of the American column's approach spread, more and more Japanese came out to watch the Americans driving toward Tokyo. By the time the column, with Patton's jeep still in the lead, entered the city proper the streets were so tightly lined with people on both sides that it was as if they were driving between walls of humanity.

There was no sign of resistance, no attempt made to obstruct them in any way. By all appearances, the opposition had vanished altogether. Here and there through the crowd Yamada noticed a soldier. At first he feared sniper attacks, then relaxed as he noticed that the soldiers were invariably unarmed. The military men, he noticed, bowed even more deeply than did many of the civilians.

The streets through the city had been cleared of debris, but the neighborhoods to either side were blackened ruins, charred beyond recognition. From his seat in the back of the general's jeep, the Nisei major looked across a landscape of almost unimaginable ruin. He saw chimneys standing with no houses around them, stilted frameworks of beams here and there, the occasional stone wall that had resisted the infernal heat of the firebombing raids. Yamada had heard about LeMay's tactic, knew it had been effective, even necessary, but the proof before his eyes was simply appalling.

We did this, he thought. *My God.*

"That's where we're going," Patton said, touching his driver on the shoulder and pointing.

The sun was well up by now, and they could see their destination looming like some medieval fantasy castle over the rest of the city. The Imperial Palace rose above the devastation, the ornate pagoda roofs gleaming in the morning sun, the wide parks around the place incongruously lush and green. Lofty walls circled the compound of spectacular buildings, and the sprawling grounds of ornate gardens and sculptured parks was almost heartbreakingly beautiful. Against the blackened ruin that was most of the city, it was a surreal image of timeless serenity.

Still racing, the column began to climb the gentle elevation leading to the palace. There were army troops here, but they were not carrying weapons, and they stood aside to let Patton's column pass. In moments the jeep was proceeding along a wide roadway, with the castle looming massively to their left. A rolling green landscape dotted with groves of trees and ceremonial gardens surrounded the palace like a vast, verdant skirt.

"There!" General Patton barked and pointed across the lawn toward the looming main gate. Immediately the driver turned off the road, bumping roughly over the curb, lurching onto the grass. Chunks of turf flew as the tires spun, then dug in with traction, propelling the little vehicle onward.

The general's jeep rolled right up toward the wall, cutting across the green lawn. The tanks deployed behind him, spreading out to both sides, main guns upraised while soldiers and marines dismounted to sprint toward the looming fortress wall and the open gate. They came over a low rise toward an elegant bridge spanning a moat. Abruptly, the driver hit the brakes, bringing the little vehicle to a skidding stop.

Yamada saw why: a man stood in the open gateway of the palace, atop the arching bridge. He was bald and bareheaded, wearing the dress white uniform of an admiral of the Imperial Japanese Navy. He wore a long sword at his belt, and one hand was missing two fingers. With a blink and a double take, the major recognized him as Admiral Isoroku Yamamoto.

Patton was already scrambling out of the jeep, standing upright to his full, impressive height. He gestured to Yamada, and the translator jumped out, straightening his dirty field jacket and following the general as his long strides carried him up to the Japanese admiral. Marines advanced to both sides, carbines and Tommy guns at the ready, but they stood down at a curt word from Patton.

The Japanese admiral saluted, then bowed deeply as the American general approached.

"Admiral Yamamoto," Patton said in his high, singsong voice, returning the salute as he stopped a few long strides from the war minister. "It is an honor to meet you, sir."

"The honor is mine, General Patton," said the Japanese commander in perfect English. "Your reputation as a warrior has preceded you around the world."

"From one warrior to another, I take that as the highest compliment," Patton replied with sincerity.

Yamamoto drew the sword—slowly, as they were all aware of the nervous marines and their array of ready firepower—and extended it, hilt forward, to the American general. A photographer had come from somewhere in the column and knelt in the rosebushes beside the bridge, snapping his shutter and deftly advancing his film, working his way through a series of shots.

"It is my grave duty as war minister to offer the surrender of the Empire of Japan and all of her armed forces," Yamamoto said solemnly. "I regret to inform you that the Emperor himself is dead."

"I am sorry to hear that," Patton replied solemnly. Looking every inch the very model of a modern battlefield commander, the general took the long, gracefully curved weapon, reversed it, and handed it back to the admiral.

"You are a man of honor, sir, and your word is enough," he declared. "I see no need for a symbolic transfer of your weapon."

Yamamoto blinked and bowed again—very deeply, for a

man of his rank. His face was composed, but Yamada could see the anguish lurking in the admiral's martial soul. Still, he was the picture of dignity and grace as he gestured toward the open gates behind him.

"Perhaps you will come inside, General?" he said. "There are many details we will need to discuss."

MACHIDA, TOKYO PREFECTURE, HONSHU, JAPAN, 1200 HOURS

"I'm sorry, General," explained a very unhappy colonel of engineers. "The flooding from the typhoon has caved in the whole side of the valley. The road is blocked by ten feet of mud and debris."

"How long until you can get it clear?" MacArthur asked, his face composed and almost devoid of emotion.

"We have a transporter bringing up a Cat, sir. It should be here in a little more than an hour."

"Is there another way to Tokyo?" the General asked. Willoughby, sitting beside him in the back of the staff car, looked up from the road map he had been frantically studying.

"Well, General," he said, pronouncing the phrase "Vell, Cheneral" in his exasperation. "We can go back a dozen miles and take this road, toward Yokohama and Kawasaki. "But it will probably take us two hours out of our way."

MacArthur was pondering the options, his face still implacable, when the sputtering growl of a motorcycle engine snarled through the sounds of the idling column of cars, trucks, and tanks. The General looked back to see a courier working his way along the side of the road, goggles and leather jacket spattered with enough mud to indicate a fairly reckless ride. The man pulled up next to MacArthur's car, shut off his engine, and saluted.

"General MacArthur, sir. An urgent cable from General Patton." He unzipped the jacket, reached into a weatherproof pouch, and pulled out a clean sheet of paper with a few lines typed upon it.

MacArthur merely glanced at the words:

ACCEPTED SURRENDER OF WAR MINISTER
YAMAMOTO AT IMPERIAL PALACE. RESISTANCE
NONEXISTENT. RECEIVING FULL COOPERATION AT
ALL LEVELS. AWAITING ORDERS. SIGNED: GEORGE
S. PATTON, GENERAL, UNITED STATES ARMY

"That's it, then," MacArthur said with a very small sigh. He let the piece of paper fall from his hand, and it quickly became saturated with muddy water. "It's all over, now."

TWENTY-FIVE

Northern Japan

• MONDAY, 24 SEPTEMBER 1945•

*CAMP NOMACHI (TOKYO CAMP 21-D), TOYAMA
PREFECTURE, JAPAN, 1019 HOURS*

Ellis nosed the *Skylark of Valeron* downward and lined up for his final approach. Even though the B-24 was loaded to the gills with medical supplies, it handled well—medical supplies weigh less than bombs.

The runway at Takaoka was short, but he'd landed on shorter. He aimed for the beginning of the smooth tarmac and hit the mark, easing down his main gear then back off the throttle so that the nose wheel touched down with nary a bump. Braking gradually, he slowed to an easy taxi and still had a hundred yards available when he turned right to get off the active runway.

He came to a stop in front of the lone hangar where a U.S. Army sergeant, a squarely built man with no neck, was waiting for him. Next to the sergeant was a rickety-looking Japanese prewar equivalent of a three-quarter-ton truck.

Beside the truck stood four Japanese workers in civilian clothes.

When Ellis disembarked, the sergeant saluted. "Welcome to Takaoka, Colonel."

"Glad to be here, Sergeant . . . Pickens," he said, taking a quick peek at the sergeant's name badge. "But I bet the medical supplies are more welcome than I am."

"Well, sir," the sergeant said, grinning, "let's say you're both welcome and leave it at that."

Ellis laughed. "Which way's the camp?"

"It's across the bay. We'll be taking the ferry."

"Well, Sergeant, I'm in a bit of a hurry, but if that's the only way, it's the only way. Let's get this plane unloaded."

Ellis wasn't too fond of letting strangers—especially recent enemies—inside his airplane, so they formed a line: Ellis and his copilot Grisham inside the *Valeron*, handing boxes to the sergeant, who in turn passed them down a line of three Japanese to the fourth man on the truck.

The job took about fifteen minutes. "It's been a while since I worked for a living," Ellis said as he dropped out through the bomb bay doors and mopped sweat off his forehead.

Ellis and Sergeant Pickens crowded into the cab with the Japanese driver. The others rode in back with the supplies. Grisham stayed with the plane. It took a couple of tries for the engine to crank. Finally, with a loud bang and a cloud of smelly black smoke, the antique truck rattled off toward the dock.

"The transportation system in this country's all fucked up, pardon my French, sir," Sergeant Pickens shouted over the truck's engine. "Of course, considering that we did most of the fucking, I guess that's okay, but right now we need all the capacity we can get. These POWs need food and medicine, and they need it fast!"

"Happy to help, Sergeant," Ellis said. "It was nice to carry something other than bombs for a change."

"You got that right, Colonel," the sergeant replied. "Fucking-A right. Pardon my French."

The ancient paddlewheel ferry had room for only ten cars and maybe fifty people. Theirs was the only vehicle, and the passenger load was light as well, ten people including them. As the ferry pulled away from the wooden dock, the industrial smell of the town gave way to cleaner air, polluted only somewhat by the smells from the chugging, smoking engines. Ellis watched Takaoka recede in the distance, forcing himself to be patient.

The end of the war had come so suddenly that everyone had been taken by surprise. Ellis, knee-deep in planning for new tactical raids, suddenly found all his work OBE—overtaken by events. He wasn't out of a job quite yet, though. There was paperwork involved in ending a war. The army being the army, a lot of paperwork.

That's why he had been so surprised to receive a call from the General's office asking him to report in person to MacArthur. The Supreme Commander was setting up his permanent headquarters in a downtown Tokyo insurance building that had somehow escaped the bombing damage. The place had been claimed as the temporary HQ by the XIII Corps after Patton's arrival, but the SWPA staff had begun moving in as soon as they arrived in the great capital city. It was already becoming known as the Dai Ichi, or Number One.

MacArthur, of course, was on the very top floor. His secretary checked and rechecked the appointment log, suspicious that a mere colonel could possibly have any business with the General. His name, however, had been duly recorded, so with a sniff of disapproval, he let him through.

The Supreme Commander's desk was uncharacteristically covered with paper. Apparently even the General was having some difficulty keeping up with the sudden end of the war. MacArthur looked at Ellis as if he couldn't remember who this visitor was or why he had come. Ellis, in turn, looked at MacArthur. The Supreme Commander was showing his age. His skin was pale, almost like parchment. There were brown spots showing on the backs of his hands. His hair was thinning.

The General's confusion was only momentary. The famous MacArthur smile spread itself over the General's face and all was right with the world. "Ellis, how good of you to come. I found something you might want. Now, where is it?" He flipped through one large pile of manila folders, selected one, and handed it to Ellis. The name on the tab read, JOHN HALVERSON, CPT, USA (RESERVE).

Inside, there was a copy of Johnny's service record and a series of dispatches and reports tracing Johnny's whereabouts during captivity. Ellis, his heart beating faster, scanned down to the bottom to find Johnny's current location. But then he wondered why the General would concern himself this much with a single prisoner. "I can't tell you how much I appreciate this, General, but why . . ."

MacArthur didn't let him finish the question. "Why do I have this? This was found as we were going through all the paper in General Sutherland's office after his . . . ah . . . tragic death."

That didn't make sense, either. "Why would General Sutherland be interested in my brother, sir?" Ellis asked.

"Oh . . ." MacArthur seemed flustered for a moment, then recovered. "Well, I think it's because . . . well, when we first met in Hawaii, I promised you . . . and so Sutherland decided on his own initiative, like a good staff officer should, to follow up and keep track of your brother."

"Thank you, sir. He's in this camp? Nomachi?"

"As best as we can tell, yes. Good luck, son."

Ellis had immediately returned to his own HQ and asked for compassionate leave, but his boss General Kenney suggested he fly some medical supplies up. "That way," Kenney had told him, "you'll have an empty plane coming back, in case you just happen to have some passengers or something."

The ferry docked on the other side of the bay, and the men loaded back into the old truck. It sputtered back to life after a few tries, and the driver maneuvered it carefully off the ferry.

It was about a two-mile drive from the ferry to the camp, but it took fifteen minutes for the truck to cover the distance on the rutted dirt road.

There was something about a military base that looked the same no matter where it was or what nationality ran it. A cheap utilitarian wood and wire fence with a few strands of barbed wire on top surrounded the installation. Identical barracks made of wood and tar paper were painted drab gray or not at all. Everything was built in the cheapest, most utilitarian manner possible. If it weren't for the Japanese faces on the guards, he could have been back in Colorado learning to fly B-26s at Atterbury Field.

The truck rattled into the camp and stopped in front of the hospital barracks inside the prisoners' compound. The gates to the camp were open, and Americans walked in and out as they pleased. There was a softball game going on, and both Americans and Japanese sat around watching.

When the truck stopped, Ellis got his first close-up look at some of the inmates. "My God," he breathed. The uniforms were just hanging off the men as if they were boys dressing up in their dads' outfits. The men weren't just skinny; they were walking skeletons.

"Yeah," said Sergeant Pickens. "Kinda hits you hard the first time you see these poor sons of bitches, don't it?"

Ellis nodded, speechless. He couldn't move for a minute, and then he realized he was staring and tore his eyes away from the awful sight. "Who do I talk to?" he asked.

"The senior POW is Lieutenant Sense. The head Jap is called the One-Armed Bandit. He's got a Jap name, but that's what the POWs call him. To find the lieutenant, just ask around."

Pickens jumped out of the truck and began waving to his Japanese workers to unload the supplies before Ellis could ask why a lieutenant was senior POW when there was a captain among the prisoners. There was one obvious reason, and he desperately hoped there was another explanation. Maybe Johnny had been transferred. Maybe he was sick. Maybe.

Ellis slid out and started looking around. The POWs all looked like old men. Hollow-eyed, they shuffled when they walked. Many had the thousand-yard stare that you'd see when crews came back from a particularly tough mission. Ellis started asking "Lieutenant Sense? Captain Halverson?" as he passed each walking skeleton.

After about five blank stares, he got an answer. "Check the camp commander's office."

The office was outside the prison compound, behind a flagpole flying the Stars and Stripes. Ellis looked more closely and realized it wasn't a real flag at all but a painted sheet.

"Hello? Anybody home?" Ellis called out as he entered the building.

"Come on in," drawled a voice from an office on the right. "Tell all your troubles to the lieutenant, 'cause we ain't got a chaplain."

The camp commander's office was sparsely furnished: a metal desk in government gray, a file cabinet, a chair behind the desk, two chairs in front. The lieutenant, as gaunt as the rest of the men, was leaning back in the chair with a cigar in his hand. His feet rested on the desk. When he saw the eagles on Ellis's shoulder, he scrambled to his feet to give a proper salute. Ellis waved him down. "As you were, Lieutenant. I'm not here to bust your balls or anything. In fact, I'm here unofficially. I'm looking for my brother—Captain Johnny Halverson."

The lieutenant put his feet on the floor and leaned forward. "Damn." He shook his head. "Colonel, I hate like hell to be the one to tell you this, but Johnny didn't make it. That's why I'm senior now."

Even though Ellis half expected that answer, he could feel the hot tears stinging his eyes. He sat down in one of the two visitor chairs. "You're sure?" he asked, even while thinking, *How could he not be sure?*

Sense linked his fingers together on the desktop. "Yeah. Sorry. I'm sure."

"Of course you are," Ellis replied. "I mean—"

"I know. Don't give up hope and all that. Been there myself."

Ellis felt ashamed. The thin and wasted lieutenant had obviously been through hell, yet he was offering comfort to a
well-fed colonel who'd slept in a bed with sheets just about
every single night of the goddamned war. Ellis tried to
clamp down his emotions. "When did he die?"

Sense looked away. "Two—maybe three—weeks ago,
about."

"Fuck." *Almost to the finish line, Johnny. So damned
close.*

"Yeah," agreed the lieutenant.

"What'd he die of?" Ellis asked.

"Here? Who knows? So many bugs get you that in the end
it's hard to say which one gets the final credit. Sometimes
it's an accident. And sometimes people give up."

Ellis put his face in his hands. "Did you know him?" he
asked.

"Johnny? Some. Not well. We bunked in different barracks. Each of us officers took responsibility for a different
group of men."

Ellis and the lieutenant sat silently for a moment, neither
knowing what to say next. Then the lieutenant spoke again.
"You know who knew him well? Andy Sarnuss. Andy took
care of him when he got sick. Hell, Andy was there when he
died, come to think of it. And those two had been together at
Cabanatuan. You want the story, you should talk to Andy.
He's your best bet."

"Andy. Where do I find him?"

"He works in the hospital. Assists the doctors. Empties
bedpans. Talks to the sick and dying. He's an officer and
ought to do more, but that's all he can do. He's not quite
there anymore, if you know what I mean."

"Thank you, Lieutenant," Ellis said, starting to get up.
"Oh—is there anything I can do for you and your men when
I get back to Tokyo?"

Lieutenant Sense looked up at the ceiling to think and
then looked back at Ellis. "Sure is, if you don't mind. I could

put together a shopping list. If you could get it in the proper hands, maybe say it was a colonel's priority instead of a lieutenant's . . ."

"Can do, Lieutenant." Ellis started to leave.

"Hey, wait a minute, Colonel," Sense said.

"Yeah?"

"Why don't I have someone go fetch Andy and bring him up here? You can have my office, or better yet, take the conference room."

The conference room had a single round table, four metal folding chairs, a single lightbulb dangling from a ceiling wire, and one dirty window that let gray light into the room. The ubiquitous Sergeant Pickens brought Andy in.

"Thanks, Sergeant," Ellis said. "Could you have someone bring us a couple of cups of coffee, if the mess can handle it, and maybe some—Andy, what would you like?"

Andy was one of those who had the thousand-yard stare. He was a short man. His untrimmed black hair was beginning to recede on top and his beard grew in clumps. He wore a Japanese uniform that hung off his skeletal frame as it did on the other prisoners. Except for the uniform, he could have passed for an ascetic in biblical times, or a mad monk in medieval times.

"Uh, coffee and . . . uh . . ." He paused and looked curiously at Ellis. "I don't know," he said.

"How about some soup?" suggested Pickens.

"How about it, Andy?" asked Ellis. "Soup sound good to you?"

"Soup." Andy thought for a moment. "What goes with soup? Crackers?" He gave a small, dry laugh. "I guess I've forgotten."

"Yep, soup and crackers. Good choice," the sergeant said in a voice normally reserved for children. "I'll have the mess hall take care of it. Same for you, Colonel? Or a sandwich instead?"

"Soup sounds good to me, too," Ellis said. "Have a seat, Andy."

Andy sat. He was looking in Ellis's direction but not at Ellis. His eyes looked into the distance.

"Cigarette?" Ellis asked.

Andy's eyes showed a glimmer of expression. "*Ossu.* Uh . . . yeah. I mean yes, sir. Please." His hands trembled a little as he took the cigarette, put it between his thin lips, and let Ellis light it. He took a long, slow drag and let it out just as slowly. He smiled. "Cigarettes. You don't know what it's like, going years with only the occasional butt and hard rolls of tobacco."

Ellis took out his pack of Lucky Strike Greens, shoved them across the table, and put his black Zippo on top of it. "Yours," he said.

"Colonel, I—" Andy paused. "You—you didn't have to do that." He looked as if Ellis had given him a thousand dollars.

"No problem. But if it makes you feel better, I'll bum one of them off you right now."

There was a brief flicker of resistance in Andy's eyes, and then he shoved the pack and lighter back. "For us POWs, this used to be money. And this would have been a fortune. But now—well . . . Help yourself, Colonel."

"Don't mind if I do," Ellis said. "Listen, Lieutenant Sense says you knew my brother Johnny. That you took care of him as he died."

Another brief flicker of emotion passed over Andy's face. Slowly, Andy nodded his head. "Yes. Johnny was my friend. He was a good friend. I knew him back before it started, and then when we were on the Rock."

"Corregidor?"

Andy nodded. "Yeah. Then we both became *mikado no kyaku.* That's one name the Japs called us. It means 'guests of the Emperor.' They called us other names, too."

He looked off into the distance again as he continued talking. "When we surrendered, we had to pick up the dead bodies on the Rock. Japanese first. Then Americans. Afterward, we rode the train to Cabanatuan together. At least we had a train—you heard about the poor bastards on Bataan?"

Ellis nodded. The story of the Death March was, at last, being reported in its grisly entirely.

"We lived in the same barracks, me and Johnny." Andy paused again. Then turned and looked into Ellis's eyes directly for the first time. "We got put on separate ships to Japan." His eyes squeezed shut tightly. "Separate ships . . ."

Then his eyes wandered away again and there was silence for a time.

"He talked about you," Andy said, abruptly changing the subject. "You and . . . Pete? Another brother?"

"No. Pete was his best friend in high school."

"He was like a brother, though. That's what it sounded like."

"Yes. All three of us were like brothers."

"What happened to Pete? Do you know?"

"Pete's a marine. He's alive, though God knows how. I saw him in Tokyo."

Andy nodded solemnly. "Pete made it. You made it. Johnny didn't make it." Another pause. "He told me about you. He talked about you a lot." Then a longer pause. "He told great stories. I loved to listen to them."

"I know," Ellis said. "I always thought he'd be a writer, and I'd illustrate his stories."

"That's what he wanted, too," Andy said. There was a strange affect to his voice—a lack of emotion, a lack of feeling. However, the words were starting to flow more easily, as if the hinges of thought were beginning to swing again after having been rusted for a very long time.

He's been to hell and back, Ellis thought. *Of course he seems distant and strange.*

"You said you were separated when you were put on ships for Japan," Ellis said. "Did you just end up at the same camp by coincidence?"

A strange half smile played around the edges of Andy's lips, which were thin and devoid of color. "I was at another camp first. Then I was moved. Yes, it's a coincidence that Johnny was here too. But I was very glad to see him. I was in bad shape." He stubbed out his cigarette and reached for another.

There was a knock on the conference room door. "Enter!" Ellis called out, although he was frustrated with the ill-timed interruption.

Nothing happened.

After a minute, Ellis got up and opened the door. An elderly Japanese woman carrying a large tray stood in the doorway. She bowed several times to both men, muttering, *"Dozo, dozo,"* under her breath.

Ellis knew just enough pidgin Japanese to know that the reply to "please" was *"Domo."* Thank you.

Andy waited for the woman to put bowls of soup and cups of coffee in front of both men. Then he stood up and bowed very deeply. *"Domo arigato gozaimashita,"* he said. That was the most polite form. You said it to your superiors, or if you had reason to be especially grateful.

The woman, flustered, bowed, and also said, *"Domo arigato gozaimashita."* Andy bowed again, and then she bowed again. Ellis finally shooed her out of the room.

Andy sat down and looked at Ellis. "I guess it's been slapped into me. Every Japanese, no matter how low, is higher than a *holio*—that's a flower sniffer. A prisoner. Someone not man enough to die in battle. If you aren't polite enough, you get a slapping." He must have seen Ellis's puzzlement, because he continued. "The Japanese are big slappers. If that doesn't work, they beat you with clubs. And worse." Andy shivered. "Much worse. You don't want to know.

"You know, we were sure the guards were going to kill us, rather than let us get liberated. But that day, when the war ended, they just cleared out of here. We woke up and they were all gone. We couldn't believe it—didn't know what to think. Then a couple of those big silver bombers flew over and dropped us food, and we really knew. It was over."

He stopped talking while he bent over his bowl of soup and blew on it. Then he took all his crackers and crumbled them into the broth until it all congealed. By then it was cool enough to eat.

Ellis had finished his entire bowl by the time Andy was ready to take his first bite.

"Can you tell me—" Ellis began and then stopped.

"How he died?" Andy asked. "Or how he lived?"

"Whatever you like. I want to know everything."

There was a strange look on Andy's face. "Everything?" he asked.

"Absolutely. As long as you've got strength to talk. We don't have to finish in one day, you know. I can stay here. Or I can take you with me to Tokyo and get you a room at the best hotel in town. It's the least I can do for a friend of . . . friend of Johnny's. . . ." The burning sensation in Ellis's eyes started up again and he had to choke back tears.

Andy looked on with the same colorless expression. "I can talk," he said. "If I get too tired, I'll tell you. Okay?"

"Okay."

Andy slowly spooned mouthful after mouthful of his soup as he began to talk in his curiously dead voice. Ellis listened with a combination of fascination and horror as Andy told the story of their captivity, the years in the Philippines, and the voyage to Japan. Johnny's ship had not been torpedoed like Andy's. However, the hold had been packed so tightly that there was no room for the men to sit down. For fourteen days and nights on the water they stood.

"No one on that hell ship was ever the same again," Andy said. "The same would have been true of my ship, but almost all of them died."

Then Andy explained how he came to Camp Nomachi. The lack of emotion in Andy's voice as he talked stood in stark contrast to the events he described. From time to time he would pause for anywhere up to a minute. His eyes would travel up and to the left, as if he were peering at an invisible movie screen and watching the action unfold, not as a participant but merely as a viewer. Ellis was fascinated and repulsed.

How do men survive this? Ellis thought. Looking at Andy, he knew part of the answer: they change.

Johnny, too, had changed. If he lived, he might be as distant, as broken inside, as Andy. *Dammit, Johnny,* Ellis thought, *why did this have to happen to you? And why couldn't you have held on another three weeks?*

Andy continued. ". . . The next morning, after they stitched me up, one of the guards came into the hospital to take me away. I was pretty sure he was going to kill me. Once we got to the train station, I decided he wasn't going to kill me. The train ride took pretty much all day. It kept getting colder, so I knew we were heading north. That worried me. I didn't have the clothes for it. Maybe they were going to work me until I froze. That would be a Jap thing to do. You know, 'waste not, want not.' "

Andy smiled thinly. He reached for one more cigarette. "Last one," he noted as he lit it. His ashtray was overflowing.

"You okay?" Ellis asked. "I can get more, probably."

"No. I haven't smoked in so long it's going straight to my head. I've probably had enough. In fact, I think I'll save this one for later." He put the pack in his breast pocket. He picked up the black lighter and began to pass it back and forth between his hands in a random and nervous fashion.

"Tell you what," said Ellis. "I've got a carton on the *Valeron.* I'll leave you some before I go. Or if you're coming with me, I'll make sure you have all you want." Ellis, who had smoked only two, took a sip of his long-forgotten coffee. It had gone stone-cold.

"Thanks," said Andy. "You don't have to do that. But thanks."

"Least I can do for my brother's friend."

Andy closed his eyes as if in pain. Then he continued talking. "Because the stitches were fresh and I was still in a lot of pain, I went to the hospital barracks. When the docs told the Japs what had happened to me, even they agreed I was entitled to a little *yasume.* I thought about killing myself, you know, and then I got kind of mad and decided I was going to beat these bastards at their own game and walk out of there on my own two feet. We knew the end was close. We could tell by the planes flying over how near to Japan the forward bases had to be. We didn't recognize the planes—all the new planes, they pretty much all came into service after we were captured. But first there were long-range bombers, then mediums. Then we saw navy planes, and finally those beautiful army fighters. They were coming off land bases—couldn't be too far away. They told us the end was coming pretty soon.

"We didn't expect to survive it. Most of us were sure the Japs would kill us all rather than let us go back and tell America what they'd done. If they were going to kill us anyway, we might as well go down with a fight. Some of us might make it.

"I was still pretty blue. Then the doc said there was someone to see me. I couldn't imagine who the hell even knew I was alive, but it was Johnny. Let me tell you, seeing an old friend at a time like that makes a hell of a difference.

"He came in every day and sat with me. We talked about before the war, and we even talked a little bit about after. But not much. It was bad luck to talk about after. So we didn't do it much. We talked about Dugout Doug a lot. And that fucker Sutherland.

"Really?" Ellis wanted to hear everything he could about Johnny. But this was interesting all by itself. "Johnny knew Sutherland? Directly, I mean."

"Yeah. Sutherland screwed him. Screwed him personally. Because he knew the secret."

Ellis leaned forward. "Secret?"

Andy's eyes defocused again. "MacArthur's secret. About the morning."

"What morning?"

"You know. When they came."

"Who? You mean, the Japanese? The Philippines?"

"That's right. He stayed in his office for a long time and nobody saw him. Except Johnny. Oh, and Sutherland, too, but he doesn't count."

"He. You're talking about MacArthur."

"Yeah. Dugout Doug. Johnny was there. Mac came out of

his office. He started talking about his enemies in the War Department and how he didn't have any good choices to make. That's why he pretended to himself that he could stop the Japanese at the beaches when he had to know he didn't have the supplies or trained men to do it. And because he thought that, he put all the food near the front lines. That's why we starved when we finally got to Bataan. That's why he didn't visit us. The bastard knew we knew. He couldn't face us."

A glimpse of hatred flickered in Andy's eyes. "And Johnny saw him.. Johnny saw him when he broke down. He made Johnny get down on his knees with him and pray. Like God was going to come smite the Japs. Hell, God *is* a fucking Jap."

"Johnny was the only eyewitness, I suppose," Ellis said.

"The others are dead. I heard even Sutherland got killed. You know, Sutherland promised Johnny a pass off the Rock for keeping his mouth shut but fucked him over. Claimed he didn't promise to do more than 'try.' Bastard. I think Mac knew about it, too." Andy had a satisfied look when he finished.

So that's why Sutherland was keeping that file. And why MacArthur has always been so odd where Johnny is concerned. Ellis drew a breath. *I have to investigate before jumping to conclusions.*

"Let me look into that a bit. If any of it's true . . ." Ellis said. If MacArthur turned out to have any role in Johnny's death, he'd find some way . . .

"Johnny always expected he'd make it through," Andy said. "Well, up to when we got separated. When we met again, he was different. Not that I wasn't different, too, but Johnny was really different. . . ."

"When he showed up in the prison hospital—which was just another underheated barracks except there were a couple of overworked docs and a whole lot of really sick or hurt men—he was *happy*.

"After a week, I was free to walk around. I didn't move

very fast, but I wasn't doing the beriberi shuffle anymore, either. I was angry and I complained too. On Luzon, Johnny used to be like that too. Pretty much everybody was, to tell the truth. But now Johnny was about the only one who was really *happy*.

"I thought maybe he'd seen God or Jesus, if either of them visited POW camps. But he didn't pray or tell other people about how he'd 'seen the light' or quote Bible verses or anything."

Andy paused again, and Ellis couldn't help prodding him. "So, what was it? Did you find out?"

"I think so, but I'm not sure I understand it. I asked him a couple of times and he sort of didn't answer at all, he just looked around and smiled a lot. Honestly, it sometimes sort of pissed me off a little because the rest of us were so fucking miserable most of the time."

"It's odd, though," Ellis said. "That kind of happiness never seemed to be Johnny's style. So, what did he say was the reason?"

"He leaned over one day, and he whispered in my ear. He said—I'll never forget it—'I'm not really here.'

"I said, 'Huh?' or something clever like that.

"He smiled again, and this is what he said. He said, 'I've mastered sixth-order thought.' Do you know what that means? I don't have a clue what that means."

Ellis's face went gray. "Oh, shit. I know what it means."

"What?"

"The Outlanders. It's from a book. He went to live in a book."

"I don't get it."

"There's this book—actually, it's three books. Science fiction."

"You mean like Buck Rogers? Ray guns and rocket belts?"

"Well, no—Buck Rogers is shit . . . but . . . oh, never mind. The *Skylark of Space*. That's what the book is called. The series, I mean. The heroes meet up with these creatures of pure mind. Johnny joined them."

"What?" Andy was completely confused. "Wait—are you saying there really *are* . . . "

"No, no, no. I mean, he went there in his *mind.* He didn't want to be in the camp anymore, so his mind went away. It went into the book."

Andy sat quietly for a minute, thinking. "Oh. Well, that sort of makes sense. Because he talked about a place called . . ."

"The Green System? And bad guys called the Fenachrone? Maybe Norlamin?"

"Yeah. Yeah. That's right. I couldn't keep all those weird words straight, except for the Green System. That sounded sort of normal. Yeah. He was . . . somewhere else." Andy shook his head. "I know it doesn't make much sense, but it's what happened."

Ellis looked up at the ceiling. "Jeez, Johnny . . . Well, at least you got to go." He turned his attention back to Andy. "So how did he die, exactly?"

"I guess his body sort of gave out. Maybe it's because his mind was kind of gone already. He got a cold, not too serious at first, but it got worse. He wouldn't eat, and then even when he did eat, it didn't seem to nourish him. He kind of wasted away, and then he died." Andy paused again. "I was there," he said flatly.

"I know he appreciated it, even if his mind was elsewhere," Ellis said, and Andy bowed his head.

"Thank you, Andy. Thank you very much," Ellis said. The single small window that had shed gray light into the room was now dark. A dangling electric bulb gave off sharp light and produced angular shadows. There were different dishes on the table because the efficient sergeant arranged dinner—and a pack of unfiltered Camels—to be brought from the mess hall. "Jeez, look at the time," Ellis said. "I guess I'd better turn in for the night. So, you want a lift to Tokyo? You've got from now to about 0900 tomorrow to let me know, if you want to think on it."

"I'll think about it a bit, if that's okay. The thought of a whole lot of people doesn't sound real good, though."

"Okay. But let me know what you need or want. I owe you."

"No, you don't," Andy said, waving him off.

Ellis left to arrange a bunk for tonight. Andy sat at the conference table, part of his dinner still untouched. He'd learned how little food he could eat before he threw up.

No, you don't owe me, Andy thought. *Because I didn't tell you what* really *happened when Johnny got sick.*

He wasn't taking care of himself anymore. That's why he got sick. We were all pretty tough, those of us who survived that long. But we were all running on empty. I tried to make him pay attention, but he was living someplace else.

I tried to take care of him, but he wouldn't do what the doctors said or anything else. He got sicker. Then he wouldn't eat all his food, as little as it was. I didn't give it back, like I should have. I ate it.

After a while, I stopped feeding him. I ate all his food when nobody was around. He was going to die anyway, and I thought the Japs would massacre us before we could be rescued.

He got weaker. The doctors kept trying to do something. I told them he was eating, so they brought him larger portions. I ate those, too. I watched him die.

His mind was gone by then. It was just his body that was dying.

Then he woke up one night. "Andy, you son of a bitch," he said. "Why are you killing me?"

He knew.

I tried to get away from him but he said, "If you're going to kill me, at least have the decency to keep me company."

I said, "I wouldn't have tried to kill you if I knew you were still there." But I wasn't sure that was true. I sat down. I kept him company. It was only for a few more hours. I offered to get him some food, but it was too late. He died the next morning.

I told myself I was doing this only because he was already gone. That it didn't make any difference. But I don't think that's true.

I wanted *to kill him.*
He was so fucking happy.

Andy sat in the conference room alone. The single bare bulb swayed slightly. Sharp, jagged shadows broke the room into random geometric shapes.

Much later, Andy got up and started searching the small, spare offices. Sergeant Pickens had a sidearm, but he usually didn't wear it. It was hanging from a coat rack in the office Pickens used.

He stared at the pistol. Then he put the barrel in his mouth. He closed his eyes.

The camp truck was coming in from the last ferry of the night. Ellis was walking from the mess hall to his barracks.

Ellis heard the loud bang.

He thought it was a truck backfire.

So he kept walking.

TWENTY-SIX

Tokyo

• **THURSDAY, 27 SEPTEMBER 1945** •

DAI ICHI BUILDING, TOKYO, JAPAN, 1819 HOURS

The newspaper lay on MacArthur's desk, the front page dominated by the dramatic black-and-white photo of War Minister Yamamoto handing his sword to General George S. Patton, U.S. Army. Much as he tried not to look, Douglas MacArthur's eyes were drawn to the picture, compelled to focus there by an urge he could not overcome.

The paper was one of several publications arrayed on the

desk, some from as far away as Manila and San Francisco,
but they all had one thing in common: that dramatic picture.

"That should have been me, Charlie," MacArthur said wistfully, gesturing with a glass that held only a small bit of the
whiskey the G-2 had poured into it a minute earlier. "By all
rights, it should be my picture on the front of that newspaper."

"Yes, sir, it should be. But the world knows the truth: you
are the conqueror of Japan! This great campaign is *your* victory, not Patton's. Remember, General, it is you who will accept the official surrender at the ceremony next week."

"Ah, yes. The ceremony. There is so much to plan, so
many details requiring my attention."

Because Generals Eichelberger and Harmon were still
commanding the forces of their two armies, which were
vigorously pursuing the occupation of Japan, MacArthur
was focused on planning the surrender ceremony, to take
place aboard a navy battleship in Tokyo Bay early in October. From the Dai Ichi, he made his plans and followed the
reports from the field.

The capitulation was now in evidence among Japanese
armed forces everywhere—even in places as far away as
Borneo, China, and Malaya. Patton had retired to a field
headquarters just north of the city, and MacArthur was in
no great hurry to invite the man who was already being
hailed as the "Conqueror of Japan" down to Dai Ichi for a
formal visit.

Tonight, Willoughby and the General were drinking.
MacArthur sat in a swivel chair behind his desk—it traveled
with him—leaning back with his feet up. Willoughby occupied one of the overstuffed leather chairs. He knew enough
to drag the seat near enough to the desk so that he could lean
forward and touch it.

Willoughby poured two more glasses of straight whiskey
from the General's private supply and shoved the General's
scotch across the desk.

"Here you are, General." The word came out "Cheneral" in
his German accent. Alcohol, like stress, seemed to bring the
trace of Willoughby's first language into his speech.

MacArthur leaned forward and picked it up. "Thank you, Charlie," He hoisted the glass. "To the last day of the last war." He emptied about half the glass.

MacArthur didn't get drunk often, but when he did, you could never tell what he would do. At one ball in Hawaii before the war, Willoughby had heard, the General had played leapfrog up a flight of stairs after finishing most of a bottle of champagne.

"Amen, sir," Willoughby said, taking a more moderate sip. He wanted to stay alert, just in case.

That paid off when a courier arrived with a freshly printed sheet of foolscap, an urgent message just in from XIII Headquarters. The G-2 read the note and whistled aloud.

"What is it?" MacArthur demanded, sitting up straight in his chair. He didn't reach for the paper, so Willoughby summarized.

"There has been an automobile accident. General Patton's jeep overturned. The general was thrown from his seat. It seems his neck is broken, General. I regret to inform you that he is not expected to live."

For a long minute MacArthur sat immobile, eyes closed, digesting the import of this news. Finally he spoke.

"Damn him to hell!" the General said with vehemence. "This will secure his place in history. Even dying, the man's a glory hound!"

"History will assign the credit where it is due. It was you. It was all you," the intelligence officer replied.

"History, as Henry Ford said, is bunk. They'll print the legend because it makes a better story." MacArthur snatched the dispatch from Willoughby's hand, read it, then crumpled it up and tossed it in the wastebasket.

"But MacArthur *is* a legend," argued Willoughby. "This magnificent campaign, this triumphant war, will assure your unchallenged place in history!"

"MacArthur *is* a legend. Is he legend *enough*?" the General asked rhetorically. "It's the dying that's such good showmanship, you know. If Georgie had lived to tell the tale, truth would necessarily have asserted itself. But when the angel of death adds her special touch to the proceedings, the ordinary becomes extraordinary, and the extraordinary becomes divine. Destiny intervenes where it will.

"General George Patton managed to die on the last day of the last battle of the war. Or close enough not to make any difference. That was the bastard's destiny." The Supreme Commander lifted his glass again. "To Georgie Patton, that lousy son of a bitch." He polished off that glass and hurled it against the wall, but it didn't break. Willoughby retrieved it.

"I think another is in order, Charlie," MacArthur said.

"If you're sure, General . . . ," Willoughby said, with a pause at the end in hopes MacArthur would reconsider.

"I'm sure. I'm even sure you're going to join me, Charlie."

"I suppose if you insist," Willoughby said, smiling to show he meant it as a witty remark. He took another sip of his current drink, a little larger this time.

"You're falling behind, Charlie," MacArthur said.

"Yes, sir."

"One more toast. Ready?" MacArthur stood, a trifle unsteadily, and Willoughby likewise hopped to his feet. "Banzai!" the Supreme Commander shouted.

Willoughby flinched at the volume of MacArthur's voice. "Sir?"

"Banzai! Ten thousand years to the Emperor! Drink with me!"

"Yes, sir. Banzai," he said without emphasis, and drank.

"You want to know why I'm toasting the Emperor of the enemies? Sure you do."

"I do, General. I'm consumed by curiosity."

"Okay. I'll tell you. It's because Hirohito had the good sense to get himself killed. It saves us no end of trouble. I mean, I might have had to put him on trial and, who knows, possibly hang him. I can't think of any better way to get the Japanese people permanently set against the United States of America. But he's dead. His brother will turn out to be implicated in something nasty, but he's not famous. We can get away with him on the throne. And the twelve-year-old obviously has to be innocent. That means I don't have to dismantle the Imperial household after all. I can use it to help run this country."

"In that case, General, let me toast again. Banzai!" Willoughby said, a little louder this time, and finished his own drink.

This time, when MacArthur hurled his glass against the wall, it shattered into a hundred pieces.

EPILOGUE

Today the guns are silent. A great tragedy has ended. A great victory has been won. The skies no longer rain death—the seas bear only commerce—men everywhere walk upright in the sunlight. The entire world is quietly at peace. And in reporting this to you, the people, I speak for the thousands of silent lips, forever stilled among the jungles and the beaches and in the deep waters of the Pacific which have marked the way.

—General Douglas MacArthur at the surrender ceremony

• SUNDAY, 30 SEPTEMBER 1945 •

HIROSHIMA, JAPAN, 1730 HOURS

Naguro Yoshi looked at the place where Michiyo's house had been. At least, he *thought* it was the place—it seemed the right distance from the looming brick shell that had once been the Fukuya Department Store. But the charring from the firebomb raid was so complete, so utterly devastating, that he couldn't be sure. He poked through the ashes, finding a few metal pots, the remnants of an iron cookstove that *might* mark the kitchen of the Ogawa house.

Of the people who had lived here, there was no sign.

Yoshi turned his back on the place, making his way along the ashen avenue, staying across the street from the looming, burned-out shell of the department store. He walked toward the riverbank, trying to get his bearings.

The water was sluggish and shallow, choked with debris, buzzing with flies. The magnificent Aioi Bridge, he saw, was simply *gone,* just a few piers standing in place to mark where the footings had been planted. He had heard that the typhoon had destroyed it, with a surge of floodwaters and debris roaring up from the ocean with such force that it swept the span right off of its footings. But still, it was hard to believe.

Yoshi was adrift, aimless and uprooted. His unit had disbanded upon word of the surrender. He had set out on his own, traveling by bicycle and, after breaking the frame, on foot for the last thirty miles. Hiroshima was his home, and it was the home of his beloved Michiyo.

But Hiroshima was no more. What the fire had spared, the typhoon had ravaged. The city was a wasteland, a moonscape. A few survivors huddled miserably in the rubble, but they bore all the signs of extreme shock. None of them knew anything of Michiyo, or of anyone of the Ogawa or Naguro clans. So the young lieutenant was left to wander on his own, trying not to visualize the many tragedies that had happened here.

He found two children poking through the ruins at the near end of the broken bridge. They scrambled over a slab of concrete and disappeared below it, near the water. When they again climbed into sight, one of them held a small green object, swinging from a leather strand, in a grubby hand.

It was a jade Buddha.

"Where did you get that?" Yoshi asked.

The boy pointed toward the shallow water, amid several massive concrete chunks where the bridge span had tumbled straight down. "The lady had it. She lived down there after the fire. Then the typhoon came, and she died," he said.

"I . . . I would like to buy it from you," Yoshi said.

The boy considered the trinket. Even though it was muddy, the purity of the jade, the precision of the carving, showed it to be an object of value. The boy shrugged.

"Here," he replied, handing it over. "You can have it."

The two children ambled off, searching for more treasures—or, more likely, food. Yoshi stood there alone for a long time, holding the jade Buddha, watching the river's nearly dead waters move past, working their way around the pieces of the ruined bridge. The current was mild, but even so the Ota managed to scour away some of the refuse around the foundation of that bridge. A piece of tattered silk, perhaps the sleeve of a kimono, drifted past.

Yoshi watched it float by. Then he raised his hand and hurled the Buddha as far as he could down the channel of brackish water. It landed with barely a sound, and just like that it was gone.

Aftermath

These proceedings are now closed.

> —Concluding words of the surrender ceremony

Now, where the hell are those airplanes?

> —MacArthur, immediately after the surrender ceremony,
> because the planned flyover was late

MACARTHUR LOSES!

Truman Reelected in Tight Race

(WASHINGTON) Harry S. Truman won the presidency at 3:13 this morning by a margin of less than 5 percent in yesterday's election. At 3:35, Republican candidate General Douglas MacArthur called the president-elect to concede. Afterward, before a cheering crowd outside the Waldorf-Astoria Hotel in New York City, General MacArthur echoed his famous quotation, shouting, "As I have returned before, so I shall return again!" while standing in front of the largest American flag ever made.

President-elect Truman won important battleground states including New York and Pennsylvania, while losing such states as California and Ohio to the Republicans. Illinois, which provided the president with certain victory in the electoral college, did not report until after two o'clock in the morning central standard time. The president-elect and the new vice president, General Dwight D. Eisenhower, claimed victory to riotous cheers before a crowded ballroom of supporters in Kansas City, Missouri.

Political observers in the USA had all but written off Truman. Indeed, most commentators had concluded that MacArthur would be the sure victor. However, last-minute

allegations raised disturbing questions about General Mac-
Arthur's conduct in the Philippines and in the invasion of
Japan. Despite Republican attempts to portray the accusers
as vengeful navy officers and the disgruntled relatives of
dead POWs, the questions stuck:

Did General MacArthur accept five hundred thousand
dollars in payments from Philippine officials? Was he incapacitated on the morning of the Japanese invasion and unable
to fight? Did MacArthur and his chief of staff conspire to ensure the captivity of at least one witness? The MacArthur
campaign has strongly disputed the nature and meaning of
evidence that has been released publicly.

The Philippine government has officially . . .

POINT OF HISTORICAL DEPARTURE

THE BATTLE OF MIDWAY
4–7 JUNE 1942

The Historical Battle

From June 4 to 7, 1942, the United States Navy and the Imperial Japanese Navy fought the Battle of Midway, the decisive naval engagement of World War II in the Pacific. The resulting American victory broke the back of the Japanese fleet only six months into the war. With her four best aircraft carriers (*Akagi, Kaga, Soryu,* and *Hiryu*) lost against the American loss of only one (*Yorktown*), the Land of the Rising Sun would never again go on the offensive in the Pacific. Indeed, it is fair to say that before Midway, the Japanese never lost an important battle, and after Midway they never won one.

The United States Navy, which had suffered a major black eye over Pearl Harbor, was redeemed by its performance at Midway. This enabled it to win another war, the conflict between General Douglas MacArthur, brave defender of Bataan and Corregidor in the Philippines, and Admiral Ernest J. King, chief of naval operations, over who was to command in the Pacific Theater. The Pacific had been divided into the Pacific Ocean Area and the Southwest Pacific Area, under Admiral Chester W. Nimitz and MacArthur respectively.

Admiral Nimitz, commander of the Pacific Fleet, had known from intelligence reports that the Japanese were planning a major offensive. The brilliant head of Admiral Nimitz's cryptology unit at Pearl Harbor, Commander Joseph J. Rochefort, successfully identified the Imperial Japanese Navy's main objective as Midway Atoll, barely a thousand miles away from Pearl Harbor. Armed with this foreknowledge, Nimitz planned his own ambush, and shortly a U.S.

carrier strike force consisting of two task forces was heading toward Midway. One was Task Force 16, commanded by Rear Admiral Raymond A. Spruance, consisting of the carriers *Enterprise* and *Hornet* as well as their cruiser group and destroyer screen. The other carrier strike force, Task Force 17, consisting of the carrier *Yorktown* and its associated ships, was commanded by Rear Admiral Frank J. Fletcher. Fletcher also commanded the overall strike force.

Admiral Isoroku Yamamoto, the architect of Pearl Harbor and overall commander of Japanese operation, planned to lure the American carriers to their destruction by threatening a base—Midway—that the U.S. could not afford to lose. He had immense superiority in ships, planes, men, and experience. If his plan had succeeded, the United States would have been unable to return in strength to the Pacific until late 1943 at the earliest, giving the Japanese time to establish their defensive perimeter almost as far east as Hawaii.

Yamamoto held two beliefs that influenced his planning—neither of which was correct. First, he believed the American fleet was down to two carriers, the *Enterprise* and the *Hornet*. He thought the third carrier, the *Yorktown,* had been sunk during the Battle of the Coral Sea the previous month. In fact, the carrier had been patched up in an amazing around-the-clock repair operation that was still under way as the *Yorktown* sortied from Pearl Harbor to participate in the Midway battle.

Second, he believed the Americans to be demoralized by their defeats in the previous months, and thus he needed an elaborate deception to lure the American fleet to its doom. As a result, the Midway plan involved widely separated Japanese formations in operations as far away as the Aleutians. These formations were unable to provide support to one another in case of surprises. This belief in Japanese infallibility, which later became known as the Victory Disease, led to overconfidence and what proved to be fatal assumptions about American plans and operations.

Vice Admiral Chuichi Nagumo, in command of the Midway striking force, launched his first attack wave before dawn on June 4. He firmly believed that the U.S. carriers were still at Pearl Harbor, but to be on the safe side he launched seven search aircraft to patrol the waters north of Midway Island—just in case. One of the scout planes launching from the Japanese cruiser *Tone* was delayed because of a catapult failure. This had serious consequences for the Japanese, because the delayed scout plane's course was the one that intersected the approaching American fleet.

The delayed scout plane from the *Tone* discovered the approaching American task force of the *Enterprise* and the *Hornet* too late. Task force commander Admiral Raymond A. Spruance had already launched his aircraft against the Japanese fleet.

Back at the Japanese fleet, Admiral Nagumo, torn between the need for a second strike against Midway and the need to attack the American fleet, elected to wait for his first strike force to land before launching his reserve forces. As a result, his carrier decks were filled with aircraft, ordnance, and fuel lines when American dive-bombers attacked. In five of the most crucial minutes in all military history, Nagumo went from having an intact fleet to having three of his four carriers rendered into blazing infernos, fatally stricken. Had Nagumo known of the American launch, he would surely have launched his reserve, and the Japanese carriers *Kaga, Akagi,* and *Hiryu* might have been only damaged, not sunk. Furthermore, Japanese planes from four carriers—instead of only from the one undamaged flattop, the *Hiryu*—would have participated in the attack against Spruance's and Fletcher's ships.

By the time Admiral Yamamoto ordered his shattered forces to retire, the Japanese had lost four carriers. On the American side, the badly damaged *Yorktown* survived two Japanese attacks but was sunk by a Japanese submarine on June 7. The Midway invasion force, aboard troop transports but now lacking air cover, withdrew with the remainder of the Japanese fleet.

With Americans and Japanese now having roughly equivalent forces, the Japanese were unable to continue expanding the frontiers of their empire. The myth of Japanese invincibility was shattered and American industrial capacity ensured that U.S. strength in ships, aircraft, and men would quickly outstrip the Japanese.

As a result, the strategic initiative passed to the Americans, who kept it for the rest of the war. Nimitz's navy campaign advanced through the Gilberts, Marshalls, and Marianas islands, eventually leading to Iwo Jima and Okinawa. MacArthur, much as described in this book, advanced down the length of New Guinea and up through the Philippines. The historical campaign, however, advanced on a slower timetable than we describe, because the carrier and amphibious assault fleets were in essence doing double duty, supporting navy landings on Pacific islands, then aiding army attacks on the larger landmasses.

Point of Departure

Chance played a significant, even decisive, role in the outcome at Midway. Even before the two fleets found each other, the launch of that particular scout plane from the Japanese cruiser *Tone* was delayed because of a catapult problem. That particular scout's course would have taken him right to Admiral Raymond A. Spruance's Task Force 16, built around two aircraft carriers, the *Enterprise* and the *Hornet.* Spruance, who had a better idea where his enemy was located, had launched his air attack before the Japanese discovered his fleet. If that scout plane had been on time, everything might have been different.

Fortune was capricious in other ways. The skies were partly cloudy throughout the battle, so at any time a wisp of vapor might have prevented a scout from making a critical observation, or the absence of a cloud might have meant crucial information reaching either admiral earlier than it did historically. The American dive-bombers that struck the key blow became lost when seeking the enemy carriers. In what was effectively a coin flip, Lieutenant Commander Wade

McCluskey of the *Enterprise* guessed right, and led his planes right to the target. They might just as easily have flown over empty ocean until low fuel forced them to return to the flattop or to Midway Island. In a courageous onslaught, the American torpedo bombers from all three carriers attacked without support, their low- and-slow flying squadrons virtually annihilated. The timing of this dramatic sacrifice was fortunate, in that the Japanese combat air patrol Zeros were all down near sea level shooting up the lumbering torpedo bombers as the American dive-bombers flew over the fleet. As a result, the latter were able to attack with virtually no fighter opposition.

In the actual fighting, Japanese superiority in aircraft quality and pilot skill was apparent, as a relatively small number of IJN aircraft inflicted lethal damage against an American carrier, scoring a much higher percentage of hits with bombs and torpedoes than did the U.S. Navy air forces. Some American aircraft types, such as the Brewster Buffalo flown by marine pilots in defense of Midway, were utterly obsolete—virtual deathtraps—while the doughty little Grumman F4F Wildcat, the U.S. front-line fighter, became a match for the Zero only later, when American pilots developed tactics to counter the speedy, nimble Mitsubishis.

The world of *MacArthur's War* begins aboard *Tone,* when a petty officer discovers and repairs the catapult. The scout plane is launched on time and the Japanese learn the whereabouts of the American fleet. Lefty, our navy pilot, sees the scout at the far edges of his range and fails to shoot it down. He blames himself, but the truth is that the shot was nearly impossible and depended completely on luck. The Battle of Midway turns from an American strategic victory to a Japanese marginal victory. The Japanese sink two of our carriers, damage the third, and lose only one of their own carriers in return. On the other hand, the accidental discovery of skip bombing by our fictional character Ellis Halverson scares away the landing force heading for Midway itself, so the Japanese invasion of the island is canceled. The withdrawal of the Japanese invasion fleet was strategically insignificant, because Midway was too far away from other imperial bases and too close to Hawaii to have been very useful to Japan.

We originally wrote a chapter on our alternate Battle of Midway, but decided it wasn't central to the story. For the curious, these and other deleted scenes can be found at http://www.dobsonbooks.com.

The first consequence of America losing at Midway is that the Japanese are stronger in the first year or so of the war.

The second consequence, we felt, of a navy defeat at Midway would be to alter the political balance of power between MacArthur and the army against the navy as to which service would be in overall command.

MacArthur, who surely wanted full and sole command, was a skilled office politician, though capable of enormous tone deafness, especially where his ego was concerned. It seems to us nearly certain that if MacArthur had been given an exploitable opportunity to wrest greater control over the Pacific from the navy he would have grabbed it with both hands.

The world evolves from this point and leads to the story you hold in your hands.

HISTORICAL NOTES

The behavior of Douglas MacArthur in planning for the defense of the Philippines and in reacting to the Japanese invasion on the morning of December 8, 1941, has been the subject of comment and speculation by numerous historians. The explanation of that behavior presented here is our own, though we subsequently have discovered that there is scholarly support for our theory. MacArthur's suicide threats and suicidal behavior following his escape from Corregidor have been documented by more than one of his biographers. General Sutherland's character and personality have been written about extensively in other books about MacArthur; his specific behavior in this book is a product of the authors' imaginations.

The *Skylark* books by E. E. "Doc" Smith are real. They aren't quite as good as Johnny and Ellis think they are, but they are classics of the field. The first novel in the series, *The Skylark of Space,* is the first story ever published in which mankind leaves the Solar System. As a chemist, Doc Smith is credited with developing the first process for sticking powdered sugar on doughnuts, one more example of the benefits science fiction has given our culture.

There are two real Frank Chadwicks in addition to our fictional character. One of them is our good friend, helpful critic, fellow game designer, author of the *Desert Shield Factbook* and of the finest yet-unpublished novel we've ever read. The other Frank Chadwick, a navy captain who in fact was an aide to Nimitz (though we were unable to establish exactly when), is someone we came across during our research. The name coincidence was too good to pass up, but our Frank Chadwick is completely fictional. Our character went to the Naval Academy; the historical Chadwick went to Brown. As for the game designer Frank, our fictional character is taller, for one thing.

Similarly, the sheriff of McGehee, Arkansas, is a fictional

character. There was in fact a Japanese internment camp near there, one of two in Arkansas. It is worth noting, however, that McGehee has a memorial to the men of Rohwer Camp who died fighting for the nation that imprisoned their families, and in 1992 hosted more than two hundred former internees and their families in a commemorative event.

For every detail presented about the Japanese treatment of American prisoners of war, we could have presented ten that were worse. Because it is not part of our alternate history, we don't treat the Rape of Nanking, Korean "comfort women," or other parts of the historical record in this book. The character David Hansen is real. He died shortly after enduring the Death March.

Ellis Halverson's accidental discovery of skip bombing during the Battle of Midway is fictional. General Kenney is credited with having thought up the idea, and the men of the 63rd Squadron, 43rd Bomb Group, Fifth Air Force did the hard and dangerous work of making it into a highly successful technique. Skip bombing was, as they say, a "hard way to make a living."

The typhoons of August 22, 1945, and September 21, 1945, are both real—including the irony that the September 21 typhoon, one of the worst on record, made landfall at Hiroshima. That sad city would certainly have been fire-bombed had it not been targeted for another weapon historically.

Our story of Operation Olympic is based on the actual battle plan and is as realistic as we could make, especially for the first days of that conflict. Our Operation Coronet, on the other hand, has been modified significantly from the historical plan. However, to think that Operation Coronet would have taken place without any modification based on the experience gained from Olympic, or that nothing whatsoever would have changed on the Japanese side as a result of *Ketsu-Go* in Kyushu, seems unlikely at best.

Historical maps reflect the original plans for both parts of Operation Downfall. You can see them in color by pointing your browser at en.wikipedia.org/wiki/Operation_Downfall.

Would the United States have had a million casualties, as is often claimed, had Operation Downfall proceeded as planned? Certainly the death toll for Operation Olympic would have been extremely and painfully high, whether the actual count turned out to be a million or not.

At the time that the invasion question became moot with the arrival of Fat Man and Little Boy, American planners were already leaning heavily toward canceling the proposed Operation Downfall. Intelligence about the Japanese *Ketsu-Go* buildup on Kyushu was causing a steady upward revision of estimated casualty figures. Instead, a policy of continued firebombing, blockading, targeting of railheads, and possibly an invasion in the north were considered as alternatives. These approaches would have resulted in far fewer American casualties than the Downfall estimates. It seems highly probable to us, however, that the number of Japanese casualties, civilian and military, would have far exceeded those resulting from the atomic bombing of Hiroshima and Nagasaki.

Yamamoto's explanation of "bad decision making," made to the Marquis Kido in the geisha house, reflects our beliefs. Going to war, firebombing cities, dropping the atomic bomb—these are terrible things. Such actions cannot be called "good." Yet the fact that they were "bad decisions" does not mean they were the worst decisions, or that the decision makers were wrong. Making the choice between bad and worse, in our opinion, still requires more judgment, more wisdom, and more moral courage than making the far simpler choice between bad and good.

There is no doubt that the right side won. Imagine the treatment of the United States by a victorious Japan compared to the treatment of a defeated Japan by the United States. The victims of war, however, are found among the victors and the vanquished, innocents and instigators, the blameless and the blameworthy.

ACKNOWLEDGMENTS

One of the great joys and privileges of this work has been the opportunity to hear firsthand so many true stories about the war.

Marshall Sumida, a volunteer at the National Japanese-American Historical Society, San Francisco, California (www.njahs.org), spent several hours telling Michael about life in the camps, in basic training, and in the Pacific with MacArthur's staff. Dr. David Walls-Kaufman told us the tragic story of the suicide of a Bataan Death March survivor that influenced the creation of Andy Sarnuss. Greg Hartley, retired Special Forces interrogator and coauthor of the book *How to Spot a Liar,* explained details of the interrogation process and obtained declassified World War II field manuals on the subject. Don Niles, Doug's father, proofread every draft of the book and made many helpful and insightful suggestions. Architect Grant Canfield told the story of his father at Pearl Harbor, as well as a hilarious, unprintable, but true story about "Butch" O'Hare, after whom the Chicago airport is named.

Michael Porter did a yeoman's job in pulling together extensive research information for us. Ralph Benko, Marcia Linebarger, and Rosana Linebarger provided a wonderful and kind favor that, alas, does not show up in the present volume but may in the future. Donna Hurley, reference librarian at the Nimitz Library, U.S. Naval Academy, dug deep into files to check details. We should also take the opportunity to thank the creators of Google, without whom this book truly would not have been possible.

Members of Michael's writers' group, the Vicious Circle, sharpened their knives and went to work on the manuscript. After turning each draft into a bloody corpse, they then offered advice, suggestions, and guidance that in every case improved story, characterization, setting, and impact. Our deepest thanks go to Ted White, Richard Moore, David Lee

Owens, Scott Andrews, and Paul McKinsey. Tim Brown and other members of the Alliterates writing society read various drafts and gave extensive and detailed comments.

Our long-suffering and patient editor, Brian Thomsen, gave us deadline extension after deadline extension. Tom Doherty, Forge publisher, did us the ultimate favor of rejecting the proposal we originally sent him and giving us our marching orders in the form of the idea for this book. Kristin Sevick conscientiously ushered the book through the production process at Tor/Forge. Our brilliant, eagle-eyed copyeditor, Cynthia Merman, caught numerous errors, especially when we moved scenes from one place in the story to another. Our agents, Elizabeth Pomada and Michael Larsen, continue to provide friendship, advice, direction, and support.

Josh and AnneLee Gilder, Humayun Mirza, Barbara Dobson, and many others spent uncounted hours talking about the evolving story. Internet friends Misha and Lee picked up dropped projects. Myra Strauss and Jack Knowles at Management Concepts gave Michael a year's extension on another book; other Management Concepts staff have been patient and supportive when the book has made Michael unavailable for his day job teaching project management classes.

For more, including deleted scenes and other information, see Michael's Web site at www.dobsonbooks.com and Doug's at www.alliterates.com.

As always, we value the support and love of our families, Chris, Allison, and David Niles and Deborah and Jamie Dobson, more than we can say.

—DOUGLAS NILES and MICHAEL DOBSON
November 2003–July 2006